Also by Brian Herbert and Kevin J. Anderson

Dune: House Atreides
Dune: House Harkonnen

DUNE
HOUSE CORRINO

Brian Herbert
and
Kevin J. Anderson

BANTAM BOOKS

NEW YORK   TORONTO   LONDON
SYDNEY   AUCKLAND

This edition contains the complete text
of the original hardcover edition.
NOT ONE WORD HAS BEEN OMITTED.

DUNE: HOUSE CORRINO

A Bantam Book

PUBLISHING HISTORY
Bantam hardcover edition published October 2001
Bantam export edition published February 2002
Bantam mass market edition / September 2002

ISBN 0-553-58033-7

Published simultaneously in the United States and Canada

Bantam Books are published by Bantam Books, a division of Random
House, Inc. Its trademark, consisting of the words "Bantam Books" and the
portrayal of a rooster, is Registered in U.S. Patent and Trademark Office
and in other countries. Marca Registrada. Bantam Books, 1540 Broadway,
New York, New York 10036.

PRINTED IN THE UNITED STATES OF AMERICA

OPM   10   9   8   7   6   5

To our wives,
JANET HERBERT
and
REBECCA MOESTA ANDERSON
for their support, excitement, patience,
and love during every step of this long
and complicated project

ACKNOWLEDGMENTS

Penny Merritt assists in managing the literary legacy of her father, Frank Herbert.

Our editors, Mike Shohl, Carolyn Caughey, Pat Lo-Brutto, and Anne Lesley Groell, offered detailed and invaluable suggestions through many drafts to fine-tune this story into its final version.

As always, Catherine Sidor at WordFire, Inc., worked tirelessly to transcribe dozens of microcassettes and type many hundreds of pages to keep up with our manic work pace. Her assistance in all steps of this project has helped to keep us sane, and she even fooled other people into thinking we're organized.

Diane E. Jones served as test reader and guinea pig, giving us her honest reactions and suggesting additional scenes that helped make this a stronger book.

Robert Gottlieb and Matt Bialer of the Trident Media Group and Mary Alice Kier and Anna Cottle of Cine/Lit Representation never wavered in their faith and dedication, seeing the potential of the entire project.

The Herbert Limited Partnership, including Ron Merritt, David Merritt, Byron Merritt, Julie Herbert, Robert Merritt, Kimberly Herbert, Margaux Herbert, and Theresa Shackelford, gave us their enthusiastic support, entrusting us with the care of Frank Herbert's magnificent vision.

Beverly Herbert gave almost four decades of support and devotion to her husband, Frank Herbert.

And, most of all, thanks to Frank Herbert, whose genius created such a wondrous universe for us to explore.

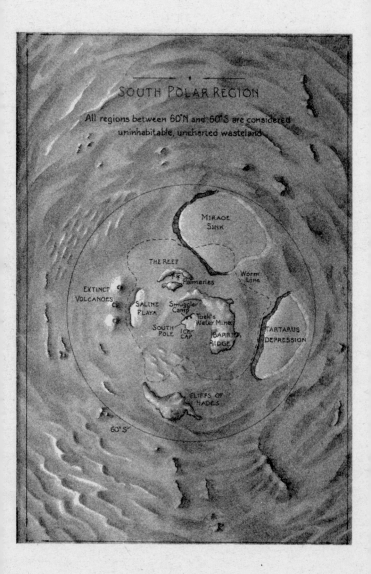

SOUTH POLAR REGION

All regions between 60°N and 60°S are considered
uninhabitable, uncharted wasteland

MIRAGE
SINK

THE REEF

Worm
Line

EXTINCT
VOLCANOES

Palmeries

SALINE
PLAYA

Smuggler
Camp

Teek's
Water Mine

SOUTH
POLE

ICE
CAP

BARRIER
RIDGE

TARTARUS
DEPRESSION

CLIFFS OF
HADES

60°S

CALADAN

GRASSY PLAINS =
FORESTS =
PUNDI RICE LOWLANDS =
SEAWEED =

WESTERN CONTINENT

River Gorge
Agamemnon Canyon
Cala City (Castle Caladan, Spaceport)
Chusuk Ball Fields
Paradan Melon Farms
Lake Argent
Hoxen
CORAL REEFS (Coral Gem Beds)
CORAL REEFS (Coral Gem Beds)
Underwater Park

EASTERN CONTINENT
Armada Bluff
Sisters in the Isolation
ELECRAN ISLANDS

SOUTHERN CONTINENT
Mine Region
Atreides Landing (Spaceport)
Cidrit Town
Paradan Melon Farms

SERENA'S NECKLACE
Wingboat Factories
Sea Creature Processing Islands

The axis of spin for the planet Arrakis is at right angles to the radius of its orbit. The world itself is not a globe, but more a spinning top somewhat fat at the equator and concave toward the poles. There is a sense that this may be artificial, the product of some ancient artifice.

—Report of the Third Imperial Commission on Arrakis

Under the light of two moons in a dusty sky, the Fremen raiders flitted across the desert rocks. They blended into the rugged surroundings as if cut from the same cloth, harsh men in a harsh environment.

Death to Harkonnens. All members of the armed razzia squad had sworn the same vow.

In the quiet hours before dawn, Stilgar, their tall and black-bearded leader, stalked catlike ahead of a score of his best fighters. *We must move as shadows in the night. Shadows with hidden knives.*

Lifting a hand, he commanded the silent squad to halt. Stilgar listened to the pulse of the desert, his ears probing the darkness. His blue-within-blue eyes scanned towering rock escarpments profiled against the sky like giant sentinels. As the pair of moons moved across the heavens, patches of darkness shifted moment by moment, living extensions of the mountain face.

The men picked their way up a rock buttress, using dark-adapted eyes to follow a steep, tool-hewn trail. The terrain seemed hauntingly familiar, though

Stilgar had never been here before. His father had described the way, the route their ancestors had taken into Hadith Sietch, once the greatest of all hidden settlements, abandoned long ago.

"*Hadith*"—a word taken from an old Fremen song about the patterns of survival in the desert. Like many living Fremen, he carried the story etched into his psyche . . . a tale of betrayal and civil conflict during the first generations of the wandering Zensunni here on Dune. Legend held that all meanings originated here, in this holy sietch.

Now, though, the Harkonnens have desecrated our ancient place.

Every man in Stilgar's commando squad felt revulsion at such sacrilege. Back in Red Wall Sietch, a flat stone held tally marks of all the enemies these Fremen had slain, and tonight more enemy blood would be shed.

The column followed Stilgar as he picked up the pace down the rocky trail. It would be dawn soon, and they still had much killing to do.

Here, far from prying Imperial eyes, Baron Harkonnen had been using the empty caves of Sietch Hadith to conceal one of his illegal spice hoards. The embezzled stockpile of valuable melange appeared on no inventory sheet ever submitted to the Emperor. Shaddam suspected nothing of the ruse. But the Harkonnens could not hide such activities from the eyes of the desert people.

In the squalid village of Bar Es Rashid at the base of the ridge, the Harkonnens had a listening post and guards up in the cliffs. Such minor defenses presented no obstacle to the Fremen, who long ago had built numerous shafts and entrances into the mountain grottoes. Secret ways . . .

Stilgar found a split in the trail and followed the faint path, searching for the hidden opening into Sietch Hadith. In low light he saw a patch of darkness beneath an overhang. Dropping to all fours, he reached into the darkness and located the expected opening, cool and moist, without a doorseal. *Wasteful.*

No bright light, no sign of guards. Crawling inside the hole, he stretched a leg down and located a rough ledge, where he rested his boot. With his other foot he found a second ledge, and below that another. Steps going down. Ahead, he discerned low yellow light where the tunnel sloped to the right. Stilgar backed up and raised a hand, summoning the others to follow.

On the floor at the base of the rough steps he noticed an old serving bowl. Tugging off his nose plugs, he smelled raw meat. Bait for small predators? An animal trap? He froze, looking for sensors. Had he already tripped a silent alarm? He heard footsteps ahead, and a drunken voice. "Got another one. Let's blow it to kulon-hell."

Stilgar and two Fremen darted into a side tunnel and drew their milky crysknives. Maula pistols would be far too noisy in these enclosed spaces. When a pair of Harkonnen guards blundered past them, reeking of spice beer, Stilgar and his comrade Turok leaped out and grabbed them from behind.

Before the hapless men could cry out, the Fremen slit their throats, then slapped spongepads over the wounds to absorb the precious blood. In an efficient blur of motion, Fremen removed hand weapons from the still-twitching guards. Stilgar seized a lasrifle for himself and passed one to Turok.

Dim military glowglobes floated in ceiling recesses, casting low light. The razzia band continued down the passageway, toward the heart of the ancient sietch. When the passage skirted a conveyor system used for the transportation of materials in and out of the secret chamber, he detected the cinnamon odor of melange, which grew stronger as the group went deeper. Here, the ceiling glowglobes were tuned to pale orange instead of yellow.

Stilgar's troop murmured at the sight of human skulls and rotting bodies, propped against the sides of the corridor, carelessly displayed trophies. Rage suffused him. These might have been Fremen prisoners or villagers, taken by the

Harkonnens for sport. At his side, Turok glanced around, searching for another enemy he might kill.

Cautiously, Stilgar led the way forward and began to hear voices and clanging noises. They came to an alcove rimmed with a low stone railing that overlooked an underground grotto. Stilgar imagined the thousands of desert people who must have thronged into this vast cavern long ago, before the Harkonnens, before the Emperor . . . before the spice melange had become the most valuable substance in the universe.

At the center of the grotto rose an octagonal structure, dark blue and silver, surrounded by ramps. Smaller matching structures were arranged around it. One was under construction; plasmetal parts lay strewn about, with seven laborers hard at work.

Slipping back into shadows, the raiders crept down shallow stairs to the grotto floor. Turok and the other Fremen, each man holding his confiscated weapons, took positions in different alcoves overlooking the grotto. Three raiders raced up the ramp that encircled the largest octagonal structure. At the top, the Fremen vanished from view, then reappeared and made rapid hand signals to Stilgar. Six guards had already been killed without making a sound, dispatched in deadly crysknife silence.

Now the time for stealth had ended. On the rock floor, a pair of commandos pointed their maula pistols at the surprised construction workers and ordered them up the stairs. The sunken-eyed laborers complied grudgingly, as if they didn't care which masters held them captive.

The Fremen searched connecting passageways and found an underground barracks with two dozen guards asleep among bottles of spice beer scattered on the floor. A strong odor of melange permeated the large common room.

Scoffing, the Fremen charged in, slashing with knives, kicking and punching, dealing out pain but no fatal wounds. The groggy Harkonnens were disarmed and herded to the central grotto.

His blood running hot, Stilgar scowled at the slouching, half-drunken men. *One always hopes for an honorable enemy. But we have found none tonight.* Even here, in the highly secure grotto, these men had been sampling the spice they were supposed to guard—probably without the Baron's knowledge.

"I want to torture them to death right now." Turok's eyes were dark under the ruddy glowglobe light. "*Slowly.* You saw what they did to their captives."

Stilgar stopped him. "Save that for later. Instead, we shall put them to work."

Stilgar paced back and forth in front of the Harkonnen captives, scratching his dark beard. The stink of their fear-sweat began to overpower the melange odor. In a low, measured tone, he used a threat their leader Liet-Kynes had suggested. "This spice stockpile is illegal, in explicit violation of Imperial orders. All melange on the premises will be confiscated and reported to Kaitain."

Liet, as the recently appointed Imperial Planetologist, had gone to Kaitain to request a meeting with the Padishah Emperor Shaddam IV. It was a long journey across the galaxy to the Imperial Palace, and a simple desert dweller like Stilgar could scarcely comprehend such distances.

"Says a Fremen?" sneered the half-drunk guard captain, a small man with quivering jowls and a high forehead.

"Says the *Emperor.* We take possession of it in his name." Stilgar's indigo eyes bored into him. The red-faced captain didn't even have enough sense to be frightened. Apparently, he had not heard what Fremen did to their captives. He would find out soon enough.

"Get to work unloading the silos!" Turok barked, standing with the rescued workers. Those prisoners who weren't too exhausted to notice seemed amused to see the Harkonnens jump. "We'll have our own 'thopters here soon to pick up the spice."

AS THE RISING sun blistered the desert, Stilgar hovered on the tense edge of anxiety. The Harkonnen captives worked, hour after hour. This raid was taking a long time, yet they had so much to gain.

While Turok and his companions kept their weapons ready, surly Harkonnen guards loaded packages of melange onto rattling conveyor belts that led to openings on the cliff faces near 'thopter landing pads. Outside, the Fremen raiders hauled away enough treasure to ransom a world.

What could the Baron possibly want with such wealth?

At noon, precisely on schedule, Stilgar heard explosions from the village of Bar Es Rashid at the base of the ridge— the second Fremen razzia squad attacking the Harkonnen guard post in a well-coordinated assault.

Four unmarked ornithopters circled the rock buttress gracefully, flapping their mechanical wings until Stilgar's men guided them onto the landing slabs. Freed construction workers and the Fremen commandos loaded the craft with the packaged, twice-stolen melange.

It was time for the operation to end.

Stilgar lined the Harkonnen guards along a sheer dropoff over the dusty huts of Bar Es Rashid far below. After hours of hard work and brewing fear, the jowly Harkonnen captain was fully sober now, his hair sweaty and eyes haunted. Standing before him, Stilgar studied the man with utter contempt.

Without a word, he drew his crysknife and slit the man up the middle, from pubic bone to sternum. The captain gasped in disbelief as his blood and entrails spilled out into the sun.

"Waste of moisture," Turok muttered beside him.

Several panicked Harkonnen prisoners tried to break away, but the Fremen fell upon them, hurling some over the cliff and stabbing others with sharp blades. Those who stood their ground were dispatched quickly and painlessly. The Fremen took much longer with the cowards.

The sunken-eyed construction workers were ordered to

load bodies into the ornithopters, even the decaying corpses found in the passageways. Back at Red Wall Sietch, Stilgar's people would render the bodies in a deathstill, extracting every drop of water for the benefit of the tribe. Desecrated Hadith would be left empty again, a ghost sietch.

A warning to the Baron.

One by one the loaded 'thopters rose like dark birds into the clear sky, while Stilgar's men trotted beneath the hot sun of afternoon, their mission complete.

As soon as Baron Harkonnen discovered the loss of his spice hoard and the murder of his guards, he would retaliate against Bar Es Rashid, even though those poor villagers had had nothing to do with the raid. His mouth set in a grim line, Stilgar decided to move the entire population to the safety of a distant sietch.

There, along with the captive construction workers, they would be turned into Fremen, or killed if they did not cooperate. Considering their squalid lives in Bar Es Rashid, Stilgar felt he was doing them a favor.

When Liet-Kynes returned from his meeting with the Emperor on Kaitain, he would be very pleased with what the Fremen had accomplished.

Mankind has only one science: the science of discontentment.

—PADISHAH EMPEROR SHADDAM IV,
Decree in Response to the Actions of House Moritani

P*lease grant forgiveness, Sire.*
    I crave a boon, Sire.
For the most part, Emperor Shaddam Corrino IV found his daily duties tedious. Sitting on the Golden Lion Throne had been a thrill at first, but now as he gazed across the Imperial Audience Chamber, it seemed to him that power lured sycophantic pests like sweet frosting lured roaches. The supplicants' voices slipped into the back of his mind as he went through the motions, granting or not granting favors.
    I demand justice, Sire.
    A moment of your time, Sire.
During his years as Crown Prince, he had schemed so hard to claim the throne. Now, with the snap of a finger, Shaddam had the power to elevate a worthy commoner to noble status, to destroy worlds, or to bring Great Houses crashing down.

But even the Emperor of the Known Universe could not rule solely as *he* saw fit. His decisions were beset on all sides by challenges from political string-pullers. The Spacing Guild had its own interests, as did Combine Honnete Ober Avancer Mercantiles, the trading conglomerate better known as CHOAM. It was a blessing to know that the noble families bickered with each other as much as they squabbled with him.

Please hear my case, Sire.

Have mercy, Sire.

The Bene Gesserit had helped him cement the early years of his reign. Yet now the witches—including his own wife—whispered behind his back, unraveling his Imperial tapestry, creating new patterns he could not discern.

Grant my request, I beg of you, Sire.

It is such a minor thing, Sire.

However, once his long-awaited Project Amal reached completion—the artificial spice secretly being developed on Ix—he would change the face of the Imperium. "Amal." Such a magical sound to the word. But names were one thing, and realities quite another.

The latest reports from Ix were heartening. At last, the damned Tleilaxu claimed success with their experiments, and he was awaiting the final proof, and samples. Spice . . . all of the puppet strings in the vast Imperium were made of spice. *Soon I shall have my own source, and Arrakis can rot, for all I care.*

Master Researcher Hidar Fen Ajidica would never dare to make baseless claims. Nonetheless, Shaddam's boyhood friend and philosophical foil, Count Hasimir Fenring, had been sent to Ix to check it out.

My fate is in your hands, Sire.

All hail the benevolent Emperor!

As he sat on the crystal throne, Shaddam allowed himself a mysterious smile, which made the supplicants flinch with uncertainty.

Behind him, two copper-skinned women dressed in garments of golden silkscales climbed the steps and lit the ion torches flanking his throne. The crackling flames were balls of harnessed lightning: blue and green, shot through with veins of light too bright to behold. The air carried a thunderstorm scent of ozone and the hiss of consuming flames.

After the customary pomp and ceremony, Shaddam had arrived in the throne room nearly an hour late—his small way of reminding these pitiful beggars how little importance he placed on their visits. By contrast, all supplicants were required to arrive precisely on time or have their appointments canceled.

Court Chamberlain Beely Ridondo had stepped before the throne and extended his sonic staff. When he struck it against the polished stone floor, the staff sent out a ringing tone that made the Palace foundations tremble. Bald and high-browed, Ridondo called out Shaddam's interminably long name and titles, proclaiming the court to be in session. He then glided backward up the dais steps without missing a beat.

Leaning forward, his narrow face wearing a stern expression, Shaddam had begun another day on the throne. . . .

The morning progressed exactly as he feared, an endless recital of petty matters. But Shaddam forced himself to appear compassionate, a great ruler. He had already commissioned several historians to ensure that the appropriate details of his life and reign were recorded and emphasized.

During a short recess, Chamberlain Ridondo paused to go over the long list of matters on the Imperial docket. Shaddam sipped from his cup of potent spice coffee, felt the electric rush of melange. For once, the cook had prepared it properly. The intricately decorated cup was carefully painted, one of a kind, so delicate it seemed to be made of eggshell. Each cup Shaddam used was destroyed after he drank from it, so that no one else could have the privilege of using the same china.

"Sire?" Ridondo stared at the Emperor with a disconcerting expression as he rattled off complex names without consulting notes. The Chamberlain, while not a Mentat, had a formidable natural memory, enabling him to keep track of the numerous details of the Imperial workday. "A newly arrived visitor has requested an immediate audience with you."

"They always say that. What House does he represent?"

"He is not from the Landsraad, Sire. Nor is he an official from CHOAM or the Guild."

Shaddam made a rude noise. "Then your decision is obvious, Chamberlain. I cannot waste my time with commoners."

"He is . . . not exactly a commoner, Sire. His name is Liet-Kynes, and he comes from Arrakis."

Shaddam was irritated at the audacity of any man who would assume that he could simply walk in and expect an audience with the Emperor of a Million Worlds. "If I wish to speak with one of the desert rabble, I will summon him."

"He is your Imperial Planetologist, Sire. Your father appointed his father to investigate spice on Arrakis. I believe numerous reports have been submitted."

The Emperor yawned. "All of them boring, as I recall." Now he remembered the eccentric Pardot Kynes, who had spent much of his life on Arrakis, shirking his duties and going native, preferring dust and heat to the splendor of Kaitain. "I have lost interest in deserts." *Especially now that amal is at hand.*

"I understand your reservations about him, Sire, but Kynes could go back and rile up the desert workers. Who knows what influence he has with them? They might decide to stage an immediate general strike, decreasing spice production and forcing Baron Harkonnen to crack down. The Baron would then request Sardaukar reinforcements, and from there—"

Shaddam raised his well-manicured hand. "Enough! I see your point." The Chamberlain always cycled through more consequences than an Emperor needed to hear. "Let him in. But clean the dirt off of him first."

LIET-KYNES FOUND the immense Imperial Palace impressive, but he was accustomed to a different sort of grandeur. Nothing could be more spectacular than the sheer vastness of Dune. He had stood face-to-face with monster Coriolis storms. He had ridden great sandworms. He had watched flickers of plant life thrive in the most inhospitable conditions.

A man sitting on a chair, however expensive, could not match any of that.

His skin felt oily from the lotion the attendants had smeared all over it. His hair smelled of flowery perfumes, and his body stank with unnatural deodorizers. According to Fremen wisdom, sand cleansed the body and the mind. Once he returned from Kaitain, Kynes intended to roll naked on a dune and stand out in the biting wind just to feel truly clean again.

Because he insisted on wearing his sophisticated stillsuit, the garment had been dismantled in a thorough search for concealed weapons and listening devices. The components had been scrubbed and lubricated, the carefully treated surfaces coated with strange chemicals, before the security men let him have it back. Kynes doubted the vital piece of desert equipment would ever function properly again, and he would have to discard it. Such a waste.

But since he was the son of the great prophet Pardot Kynes, Fremen would line up to the horizon for the honor of making a new garment for him. After all, they shared one goal: the welfare of Dune. But only Kynes could approach the Emperor and make the necessary demands.

These Imperial men understand so little.

Liet's mottled tan cape flowed behind him as he marched forward. On Kaitain it appeared to be no more than coarse cloth, but he wore it like a royal mantle.

The Chamberlain announced his name curtly, as if offended that the Planetologist did not carry sufficient noble or political titles. Kynes clomped across the floor in *temag* boots, not bothering to walk with grace. He came to a stop in front of the dais and spoke boldly, without bowing. "Emperor Shaddam, I must speak to you of spice and of Arrakis."

Courtiers gasped at his forthrightness. The Emperor stiffened, obviously offended. "You are bold, Planetologist. Foolishly so. Do you assume I know nothing of matters so vital to my Imperium?"

"I assume, Sire, that you have been given false information by the Harkonnens, propaganda to hide their true activities from you."

Shaddam raised a reddish eyebrow and leaned forward, his full attention now focused on the Planetologist.

Kynes continued, "The Harkonnens are wild dogs tearing at the desert. They exploit the native people. Casualty rates on spice crawlers are higher even than in the slave pits on Poritrin or Giedi Prime. I have sent you many reports detailing such atrocities, and my father before me did the same. I have also delivered a long-term plan detailing how plantings of grass and desert scrub brush could reclaim much of the surface area of Dune—Arrakis, I mean—for human habitation." He paused a beat. "I can only assume you have not read our reports, since we have received no response, and you have taken no action."

Shaddam grasped the arms of the Golden Lion Throne. Flanking him, the dazzling ion torches roared in what seemed to be a feeble imitation of the furnace inside the mouth of Shai-Hulud. "I have much to read, Planetologist, and many demands on my time." Sardaukar guards moved a little closer, attuned to their Emperor's darkening mood.

"And much of it is unimportant compared to the future of melange production, is it not?" Kynes's retort shocked Shaddam and the listeners in the court. The guards were on full alert now, blades at the ready.

Oblivious to his danger, Kynes went on. "I have requested new equipment and teams of botanists, meteorologists, and geologists. I have asked for experts in cultural studies to assist me in determining how the desert people are able to survive so well, when your Harkonnens suffer so many losses."

The Chamberlain had heard enough. "Planetologist, one does not make demands of the Emperor. Shaddam IV alone decides what is important and where to distribute resources through the benevolence of his Imperial hand."

Kynes was not cowed by Shaddam or his lackey. "And nothing is more important to the Imperium than the spice. I offer a way for history to remember the Emperor as a visionary, in the tradition of Crown Prince Raphael Corrino."

At this audacity, Shaddam rose to his feet—something he rarely did during Imperial audiences. "Enough!" He was tempted to summon an executioner, but reason prevailed. Barely. He might still need this man. Besides, once amal was in production it would be enjoyable to let Kynes see his beloved desert planet dwindle to nothing in the eyes of the Empire.

So, in the calmest of tones, he said, "My Imperial Spice Minister, Count Hasimir Fenring, is scheduled to arrive on Kaitain within a week. If your requests have merit, he is the one who will address them."

Sardaukar guards stepped forward quickly, took Kynes by the elbows, and escorted him out at a rapid clip. He did not struggle now that he had his answer. He saw that Emperor Shaddam was blind and self-centered, and now he had no respect for the man, no matter how many worlds he ruled.

Now Kynes knew that the Fremen would have to take care of Dune for themselves, and the Imperium be damned.

I n the banquet hall of Castle Caladan, well-
dressed servants maintained the appearance of
normalcy, though their Duke was only a shell of
his former self.

Women in bright dresses hurried down the
stone corridors. Nutmeg-scented candles illuminated every alcove. But even the best meals prepared by the cook, the finest china and flatware
service, and the gentlest music could not diminish
the gloom that had settled over House Atreides.
Every servant felt Leto's pain, and they could do
nothing to help him.

Lady Jessica occupied a chair of carved elacca
wood near one end of the table, her formal position
as the Duke's chosen concubine. At the head of the
table, her dark-haired lover, Leto Atreides, sat tall
and proud, distractedly polite to the green-liveried
servants as they brought forth various courses.

There were numerous empty seats in this hall—
far too many. To ease Leto's piercing grief, Jessica
had discreetly removed the little chair that had
been made for six-year-old Victor, the Duke's dead
son. Despite her years of Bene Gesserit training,
Jessica had been unable to break through Leto's

grief, and her heart ached for him. She had so much to say to him, if only he would listen.

On opposite sides of the long table sat the Mentat Thufir Hawat and the scarred smuggler Gurney Halleck. Gurney, who could usually liven up a gathering with a song and his baliset, remained preoccupied with preparations for a covert trip to Ix that he and Thufir would soon undertake, spying to discover any weaknesses in the Tleilaxu defenses there.

With a mind like a computer, Thufir would be able to make hundreds of plans and contingencies in an instant, which made him vital to the mission. Gurney was good at slipping into places where he didn't belong and escaping under the direst of circumstances. These two might be able to succeed where all others had failed. . . .

"I'll have some more of that Caladan white," said Swordmaster Duncan Idaho, raising his goblet. A servant rushed forward with a bottle of expensive local wine, and Duncan held his cup steady while rich golden liquid splashed out of the bottle. Raising his hand for the servant to wait, he gulped the wine, then gestured for more.

In the uncomfortable silence, Leto stared toward the wood-carved entrance doors . . . as if waiting, anticipating the arrival of one more person. His eyes were like chips of smoky ice.

The exploded skyclipper, the vessel in flames—

Rhombur mangled and burned, the boy Victor killed—

And then to learn it had all been caused by Leto's jealous concubine Kailea, Victor's own mother, who had thrown herself from a high tower of Castle Caladan in unspeakable shame and grief . . .

The cook emerged from the kitchen archway, proudly carrying a platter. "Our finest dish, my Lord Duke. Created in your honor."

It was a fat parafish wrapped in crisped aromatic leaves. Spiky sprigs of rosemary were tucked into folds of the pinkish meat; purple-blue juniper berries lay sprinkled about the platter like jewels. Even though she served Leto the choicest part of the fillet, he did not lift his fork. He continued to watch the main doorway. Waiting.

Finally, responding to the sound of plodding footsteps and humming motors, Leto rose to his feet, his face filled with concern and anticipation. Moving quickly on feather-light feet, the plain-featured Bene Gesserit Tessia entered the banquet hall. She scanned the room, noted the chairs, the stone floor where the carpet had been removed, and gave an approving nod. "He's progressing admirably, my Duke, but we must be patient."

"He is patient enough for all of us," Leto said, and his expression began to show the pale sunrise of hope.

With a calculated precision involving twitches of electrofluid muscle, the flexing of shigawire thread and microfiber nerves, Prince Rhombur Vernius lurched into the banquet hall. His scarred face, a blend of artificial and natural skin, reflected his intense concentration. Glistening pearls of perspiration stood out on his waxy forehead. He wore a short, loose robe; on the lapel glimmered a purple-and-copper helix, proud symbol of the fallen House Vernius.

Tessia hurried toward him, but Rhombur raised a finger of polished metal and polymers, signaling her to let him continue on his own.

The skyclipper explosion had blasted his body to a broken lump of flesh, burning away his limbs and half of his face, destroying most of his organs. Yet he had been kept alive, a fading ember of a once-bright flame. What remained now was little more than a passenger on a mechanical vehicle shaped like a man.

"I'm going as fast as I can, Leto."

"There is no hurry." The Duke's heart went out to his brave friend. The two of them had fished together, played games, caroused, and planned strategies for decades. "I'd be loath to have you fall and break anything—such as the table, I mean."

"Most funny, indeed."

Leto remembered how badly the vile Tleilaxu had wanted genetic samples from the Atreides and Vernius bloodlines, trying to blackmail the Duke in his hour of greatest grief. They had made an anguished Leto a diabolical offer, that in exchange for the mangled but still-living body of his best friend Rhombur, they would grow a ghola—a clone from dead cells—of the boy Victor.

Their hatred of House Atreides ran deep—and deeper still for House Vernius, whom they had overthrown on Ix. The Tleilaxu had wanted access to complete Atreides and Vernius DNA. With the bodies of Victor and Rhombur, they would be able to create any number of gholas, clones, assassins, duplicates.

But Leto had turned down their offer. Instead, he had engaged the services of the Suk doctor Wellington Yueh, an expert in the replacement of organic limbs.

"Thank you for holding this dinner in my honor, all of you." Rhombur looked at the serving platters and dishes arrayed on the table. "I'm sorry if the food has gotten cold."

Leto brought his hands together in a firm round of applause. Smiling warmly, Duncan and Jessica joined in. With her sharp observational skills, Jessica noticed a sheen of captive tears deep within the Duke's gaze.

The sallow-faced Dr. Yueh moved beside his patient, tracking readings, studying a dataplate in his hand that received impulses from Rhombur's cybernetic systems. The slender doctor pursed his purplish lips into an intent flower-bud shape. "Excellent. You are functioning as designed, although a few components still need fine-tuning." He circled Rhombur, moving like a ferret as the cyborg Prince took slow, self-conscious steps.

Tessia pulled out a chair for Rhombur. His synthetic legs were powerful and sturdy, but without grace. His hands looked like armored gloves; his arms hung like circuit-patterned oars at his sides.

Rhombur smiled at the big fish the cook had just served. "That smells wonderful." He turned his head, a slow rotational movement, as if on ball bearings. "Do you think I might eat some of it, Dr. Yueh?"

The Suk doctor stroked his long mustaches. "Just taste it. Your digestive system needs more work."

Rhombur swiveled his head toward Leto. "It appears I'm going to consume more power cells than desserts for a while." He lowered himself into his chair, and the others finally resumed their seats.

Leto raised his wineglass, trying to think of a toast. Then his face acquired an anguished expression, and he simply took a sip. "I am so sorry this has happened to you, Rhombur. These . . . mechanical replacements . . . were the best I could do."

Rhombur's scarred face lit up in a combination of gratitude and annoyance. "Vermilion hells, Leto, stop apologizing! Trying to find all the facets of blame would consume House Atreides for years, and we'd all go mad." He lifted a mechanical arm, rotated the hand at the wrist joint, and stared down at it. "This isn't so bad. In fact, it's marvelous. Dr. Yueh's a genius, you know. You should keep him around as long as you can." The Suk doctor fidgeted in an effort to keep from glowing at the compliment.

"Remember that I come from Ix, so I appreciate the marvels of technology," Rhombur said. "Now I'm a living example of it. If any person is better suited to adapt to this new situation, I'd like to meet him."

For years, the exiled Prince Rhombur had been biding his time, sending minimal support to the resistance movement on his devastated homeworld, including explosive wafers and military supplies provided by Duke Leto.

In recent months, as Rhombur grew stronger physically, he also grew stronger mentally. Though he was only a fraction of a man, every day he spoke of the need to recapture Ix, to the point where Duke Leto and even his concubine Tessia sometimes had to tell him to calm down.

Finally, Leto had agreed to risk sending the reconnaissance team of Gurney and Thufir, clutching at a goal of his own, a new determination to accomplish something good in the face of all the tragedies he had survived. It was not a matter of *if* they could mount an attack; it was a matter of *when* and *how*.

Tessia spoke without shifting her gaze. "Don't underestimate Rhombur's strength. You of all people know how one must adapt in order to survive."

Jessica couldn't help but notice the adoring look on the concubine's face. Tessia and Rhombur had spent years together on Caladan, during which time she had encouraged him to support the freedom fighters on Ix, so that he might regain his royal position. Tessia had stood by him through the worst times, even after the explosion. Upon returning to consciousness, Rhombur had said, "I am surprised you stayed."

"As long as you need me, I will remain."

Tessia was a whirlwind working on his behalf, supervising the modification of his Castle apartments and preparing devices to assist him. Much of Tessia's time was devoted to making him stronger. "Once Prince Rhombur is feeling better," she had announced, "he will lead the Ixian people to victory."

Jessica didn't know if the brown-haired woman followed her heart, or fulfilled an unknown set of instructions secretly given to her by the Sisterhood.

All through her own childhood, Jessica had listened to her teacher and mentor, Reverend Mother Gaius Helen Mohiam. She had followed her every draconian instruction, learning what the old woman had to teach her.

But now the Sisterhood wanted the Duke's genetics combined with hers. In no uncertain terms, Jessica had been ordered to seduce Leto and conceive an Atreides daughter. When she experienced unfamiliar and forbidden feelings of love for this dark and moody Duke, however, Jessica had developed a rebellious streak and delayed becoming pregnant. Then, in the wake of Victor's death and Leto's destructive depression, she had allowed herself to conceive a *son*, against the strictest of orders. Mohiam would feel betrayed and deeply disappointed. But Jessica could always bear a daughter later, couldn't she?

In his reinforced chair, Rhombur bent his left arm and cautiously thrust his stiff fingertips into a pocket of the short robe. He aimed carefully with his fingers, fished about in there. Finally, he grasped a piece of paper, which he painstakingly unfolded.

"Look at the fine motor control," Yueh said. "This is better than I had expected. You've been practicing, Rhombur?"

"Every second." The Prince held up the paper. "I keep remembering new things each day. This is the best sketch I've been able to make of a few obscure access tunnels on Ix. Gurney and Thufir will find them useful."

"The other paths have proven too dangerous," the Mentat said. Over the decades spies had tried to break through the Tleilaxu defenses. Several Atreides infiltrators had slipped in but never returned. Others had been unable to enter the underground world at all.

But Rhombur, the son of Earl Dominic Vernius, had dredged his memory for information about secret security systems and hidden entrances to the cavern cities. During his long and enforced convalescence, he had begun to recall obscure details he had believed long forgotten, details that might make the difference in penetrating the enemy stronghold.

Turning his attention to his meal, Rhombur lifted a large piece of parafish on his fork. Then, noting Dr. Yueh's disapproving gaze, he lowered the morsel to his plate and cut off a smaller portion instead.

Leto stared at his murky reflection in the hall's polished blue-obsidian wall. "Like wolves ready to prey upon any member who shows weakness, some noble families are just waiting for me to falter. The Harkonnens, for example." Since the skyclipper disaster, a hardened Duke Leto had grown unwilling to accept injustice in silence. He needed to make a difference on Ix as much as Rhombur did.

"We must let all the Imperium see that House Atreides is as strong as ever."

When we try to conceal our innermost drives, our entire being screams betrayal.

—Bene Gesserit Teaching

It pained Lady Snirul to see the Truthsayer Lobia dying on a woven mat in her austere apartment. *Ah, my friend, you deserve so much more than this.*

The ancient Sister had weakened in recent years but clung tenaciously to life. Rather than returning to the familiar halls of the Mother School on Wallach IX, as was her right, Lobia insisted upon continuing her duties for the Golden Lion Throne. Her marvelous mind—what she called her "most precious possession"—remained sharp. As the Imperial Truthsayer, Lobia faithfully ferreted out lies and deceit spoken in the presence of Shaddam IV, though the Emperor rarely showed any appreciation of her.

Now the fading woman looked up at Anirul, who stood haloed by the gentle light of glowglobes, her shadowed face concealing tears. This old Sister was her closest confidante in the immense Palace, not merely a fellow Bene Gesserit, but also a spry and fascinating person with whom she could share her thoughts and secrets. Now she was dying.

"You will be fine, Mother Lobia," Anirul said. The plastone walls of the sparse, unheated room retained a chill that penetrated to the bone. "I think you are getting stronger."

The old woman's answer was like crackling, dry leaves. "Never lie to a Truthsayer . . . especially not the Emperor's Truthsayer." It was an oft-repeated admonition. Lobia's rheumy eyes danced with self-deprecating mirth, even as her chest labored to maintain the rhythm of breathing. "Have you learned nothing from me?"

"I have learned that you are stubborn, my friend. You should allow me to call for the Medical Sisters. Yohsa can tend to your illness."

"The Sisterhood doesn't need me alive any longer, child, no matter how much you might wish it. Do I need to chide you for having feelings, or should I save us both the embarrassment?" Lobia coughed, then went through the calming regimen of Bindu Suspension, taking two deep breaths and completing the ritual. Her respiration became smooth, as if she were a young woman again, without the concerns of mortality. "We were not meant to live forever, though with the voices in Other Memory, it might seem so."

"I think you just enjoy challenging my preconceptions, Mother Lobia." They often swam together in the Palace's underground canals; they played intense strategy games, staring at each other for hours, winning through minute nuances. Anirul did not want to let go.

Though the ancient Truthsayer lived in the lavish Imperial Palace, there were no adornments on the walls of her quarters, no carpets on the hardwood floors. Lobia had removed the original opulent paintings, plush imported rugs, and prismatic-film window coverings. "Such creature comforts clutter the mind," she had told Anirul. "Personal objects are a waste of time and energy."

"And does the human mind not create these luxuries?" Anirul countered.

"Superior human minds create marvelous things, but thickheaded people lust after them for their own sake. I prefer not to be thickheaded."

How I will miss these discussions when she is gone. . . .

With monumental sadness, Anirul wondered if the Emperor had even noticed the old woman's absence. For decades, Lobia had been the finest of Truthsayers, able to note the tiniest sheen of perspiration on the skin, the tilt of a head, a curl of the lips, a tone of voice, and much more.

Without stirring on the hard mat, Lobia abruptly opened her eyes. "It is time."

Dread inflamed Anirul's heart like a hot coal. *I shall not fear. Fear is the mind-killer. Fear is the little death that brings total obliteration.* She whispered, "I understand, Mother Lobia. I am ready to help you." *I will face my fear. I will allow it to pass over me and through me.*

Fighting tears, forcing herself to maintain her Bene Gesserit composure, Anirul leaned forward and touched her forehead to the dry-skinned temple of the aged Truthsayer, as if bending over a prayer mat. One important task remained before Lobia allowed herself to pass on.

Anirul did not want to lose the old woman's conversation and friendship in this lonely Palace. But she need not relinquish the revered Truthsayer's companionship. Not entirely. "Share with me, Lobia. I have room inside for all your memories."

Deep in her consciousness, Anirul felt the excitement and clamor of the multitude there—Other Memory, the genetically recorded experiences of all her ancestors. As the Kwisatz Mother, Anirul's mind was particularly receptive to ancient thoughts and lives, dating back across the generations. Soon, Lobia would join them all.

Against her forehead, she felt the old woman's ebbing pulse. The heartbeat steadied, their minds opened . . . and the flow began, like a torrent through an open dam. Lobia poured her life into Anirul, transferring memories, aspects of personality, every bit of data contained in her long life.

One day, Anirul herself would pass the information to another, younger Sister. In this manner, the Sisterhood's collective memory was amassed and made potentially available to all Bene Gesserit.

Empty of life, Lobia sagged into an empty husk like a long-held sigh. Now the record book of the old woman lived within Anirul, among all the other voices. When the time was right, the Kwisatz Mother could call forth the memories of Lobia-within, and they would spend time together again. . . .

Hearing a soft voice, Anirul glanced to one side and immediately masked her emotions. She dared not let any other Sister see such weakness, even at a moment of great grief. At the doorway stood a pretty young Acolyte, motioning for her. "An important visitor, my Lady. Please follow me."

Anirul was surprised at how calmly the words came out of her mouth. "Sister Lobia is dead. We must inform Mother Superior that the Emperor will need a new Truthsayer." With a brief, longing look at the ancient woman lying cold and empty on the hard mat, Anirul departed with the merest whisper of footsteps.

The pretty Acolyte looked at her in astonishment, then accepted the news. She led Anirul to an elegant private parlor, where Reverend Mother Mohiam waited. A hollow-cheeked woman with graying hair, Mohiam wore a black aba robe, the traditional, conservative dress of the Sisterhood.

Before Mohiam could speak, Anirul crisply and emotionlessly told her about the death of Lobia. The other Reverend Mother did not seem surprised. "I, too, bring long-anticipated news, Lady Anirul. You will find it especially heartening on this day of passing." She spoke in an ancient, forgotten language that no eavesdropper could interpret. "At last, Jessica carries the child of Duke Leto Atreides."

"As she has been instructed to do." Anirul's expression lost its air of gloom, and she seized upon the bright prospect of new life.

After millennia of meticulous planning, the most important Bene Gesserit plans would soon come to fruition. The daughter now in Jessica's womb would become the mother of their long-awaited prize, the Kwisatz Haderach, a messiah under the control of the Sisterhood.

"Perhaps this is not such a dark day after all."

Human habitation of the planet Junction dated back before the founding of the Spacing Guild by the legendary patriot and commercial magnate Aurelius Venport. Centuries after the Butlerian Jihad, when the still-fledgling Guild had sought a homeworld that could accommodate their massive Heighliners, the sweeping plains and sparse population of Junction fit the requirements perfectly. Now the world was covered with Guild landing fields, repair facilities, immense maintenance yards, and high-security schools for the mysterious Navigators.

No longer entirely human, Steersman D'murr swam inside a sealed tank of spice gas and gazed out upon Junction with the eyes of his mind. The pungent cinnamon odor of pure melange permeated his skin, his lungs, his mind. Nothing could possibly smell sweeter.

His armored chamber was carried in the mechanical grasp of a podplane that soared silently above the skyline toward the new Heighliner to which he had been assigned. D'murr lived for making foldspace journeys across star systems in the blink of an eye. And that was only the smallest part of what he understood, now that he had evolved so far beyond his original form.

The bulbous podplane crossed a broad field of grounded Heighliners—kilometers and kilometers of monstrous ships, responsible for the commerce of the Imperium. Pride was a primitive human emotion, but D'murr could still take pleasure in knowing his place in the universe.

He gazed at the main yard and maintenance locks, where the vessels were serviced and upgraded with modular fittings. The hull of one immense craft was pitted from severe asteroid damage; an old Navigator had been severely injured aboard it. D'murr felt a flicker of sadness, another lingering shadow of the Ixian boy he had once been. One day, if he focused his expanded mind, even that remnant of his former self would be vanquished.

Ahead lay the neat white markers of Navigator's Field, which memorialized fallen Navigators. A pair of markers were bright and new, installed only recently, after the deaths of two Pilots who had been experimental subjects. The volunteers had been altered for a dangerous instantaneous-communications project called Guildlink, based on D'murr's own long-distance connection with his twin brother C'tair.

That project had failed, though. After only a few successful uses, the mentally coupled Navigators had collapsed into brain-dead torpidity. The Guild had scrapped further Guildlink research, despite the enormous potential profits: Navigators were too talented and too expensive to risk in such a way.

With a whir of jets and rushing air, the podplane set down at the perimeter of the memorial field, near the base of the Oracle of Infinity. The large, clearplaz globe contained swirls and streaks of gold, an ever-changing nebula of stars, moving and shifting. The activity increased as a uniformed Guildsman guided D'murr's tank out of the transport craft.

Prior to each tour of duty, it was customary for a Navigator to "commune" at the Oracle, to enhance and refine his prescient abilities. The experience, similar to the very act of traveling through the glories of foldspace, connected him with the mysterious origins of the Guild.

Closing his small eyes, D'murr felt the Oracle of Infinity fill his senses, wave after incoming wave opening his mind until all possibilities were apparent to him. He felt another presence watching over him, like the sentient mind of the Guild itself, and it gave him a sense of peace.

Guided by the ancient and powerful Oracle, D'murr's mind experienced the past and future of time and space, all that was beautiful in creation, all that was perfect. The spice gas in his tank seemed to stretch until it encompassed the mutated faces of thousands of Navigators. Images danced and shifted, from Navigator to human, back and forth. He saw a woman, her body changing and atrophying until she became little more than a naked, enormous brain. . . .

Inside the Oracle, the images faded, leaving him with an ominous, empty feeling. His eyes still closed, he saw only the swirling nebula within the clearplaz globe. As the claws of the podcraft grasped his tank and raised him again, flying toward the waiting Heighliner, D'murr was left in an unsettled quandary.

He saw many things through foldspace, but not all . . . not nearly enough. Powerful, unpredictable forces were at work across the cosmos, forces that even the Oracle of Infinity could not see. Mere humans, not even powerful leaders like Shaddam IV, could not understand what they might unleash.

And the universe was a dangerous place.

Melange is a many-handed monster. The spice gives with one hand and takes with all of its others.

—Confidential CHOAM memorandum, for the Emperor's eyes only

Within a complex of linked underground laboratory buildings, the white capsule-car sped along a tramway. Rattling over aging tracks, the car stuttered for an unsettling moment before continuing.

Through the clearplaz floor of the car, Master Researcher Hidar Fen Ajidica could see overpasses, conveyors, and technical systems functioning together for a vital mission. *All of it under my supervision.* Though the Emperor deluded himself that he directed all progress made here on Xuttuh, once called Ix, no man was as vital as Ajidica. Eventually, all the politicians and nobles, even the shortsighted representatives of his own Tleilaxu race, would begin to understand. By then it would be too late to prevent the Master Researcher's inevitable victory.

His capsule-car clattered toward the heavily guarded research pavilion. Before his people had conquered this planet, the advanced Ixian manufacturing facilities had produced vast wealth for House Vernius. Now, the laboratories and manufactories were put to even better use for the glory of God and the mastery of the chosen Tleilaxu race.

Today, though, he had different trials to face. Ajidica was not looking forward to another meeting with Count Fenring, the Imperial Spice Minister, but at last he had good news to report—enough to keep the Emperor's Sardaukar troops at bay.

In recent months, he had supervised a plethora of full-scale testing operations on the artificial spice—parallel analyses to compare the effects of melange and amal in the most minute detail. One difficult veil of secrecy, the ritualistic uses of melange by the Bene Gesserit Sisterhood, had been broken by a fortuitous occurrence, when one of the witches' spies had fallen unexpectedly into his lap. Now that captive woman, who had passed herself off under the name of Miral Alechem, served a higher purpose.

The whirring capsule-car came to a lurching stop at the pavilion, and Ajidica stepped out onto a spotless white platform. Fenring would already be there, and the man did not like to be kept waiting.

Ajidica hurried into a lift tube, which dropped him to the main level of the pavilion—but the round door did not dilate open. Annoyed, he pressed an emergency alarm and shouted into the comspeaker, "Get me out of here, and hurry up about it. I am a busy man!"

This lift tube was based upon an Ixian design, but now a simple door wouldn't open. What could be more basic? Too many things were beginning to fall apart in these supposedly wondrous research facilities. Could it be sabotage by those persistent faceless rebels? Or simply poor maintenance?

He heard men chattering outside and tools hammering against the jammed door. Ajidica disliked enclosed spaces, hated to live underground. Now the redolent air seemed to thicken around him. He whispered the catechism of the Great Belief and humbly asked God for a safe passage. Grabbing a vial from his pocket, he removed two foul-tasting lozenges and swallowed them.

Why is it taking them so long?

Struggling to calm himself, Ajidica reviewed a plan he had set in motion. Since the beginning of this project decades ago, he had been in contact with a small cadre of Tleilaxu who would serve him after he escaped with the sacred axlotl tanks. In the farthest reaches of the Imperium, protected by deadly Face Dancers, he would set up his own Tleilaxu regime for the true interpretation of the Great Belief.

Arrangements had already been made to conceal him, his Face Dancer entourage, and the secret of amal in a long-range frigate. After his escape, he would detonate a bomb that would destroy this entire laboratory complex; the massive explosion would take half of the surrounding underground city with it. Before the dust settled, he would be far, far away.

From his safe planet, Ajidica would take steps to solidify his power base and assemble a military force to protect himself from Imperial reprisals. He alone would control the vital and inexpensive supply of synthetic melange. *He who controls the spice controls the universe.* Ultimately, Ajidica might sit upon the Golden Lion Throne itself. If only he could get out of this malfunctioning lift.

Finally, with a great clatter and loud shouts, the lift-tube door squealed open, and two assistants peered in at him. "Are you well, Master?"

Behind them, wearing a bemused expression, stood Count Fenring. While not a tall man, he still towered over the Tleilaxu. "A bit of trouble, hmmm-ah?"

Straightening himself, Ajidica pushed out of the cramped tube, shouldering his sputtering subordinates out of the way. "Come with me, Count Fenring."

The Master Researcher led the Spice Minister to a familiar demonstration room, an enormous chamber with white smoothplaz walls, floors, and ceiling. The room contained scientific instruments and receptacles, and a red table topped by a translucent dome.

"Hmmm, you're going to show me one of the desert

worms again? Another small one, I hope, and not as sickly as the last?"

Ajidica brought forth a plaz vial containing an orangish ooze, which he held under Fenring's nostrils. "The latest batch of amal. Smells like melange, don't you agree?" Fenring's nose twitched as he inhaled. Without waiting for an answer, Ajidica pressed a button at the base of the dome. The foggy plaz cleared, revealing churned sand that half covered a meter-long sandworm.

"How long from Arrakis?" Fenring asked.

"We smuggled this one in eleven days ago. Worms always die away from their home, but it should live another month, maybe two."

Ajidica poured the orange liquid into a receptacle at the top of the dome. The receptacle dropped, embedded itself in the sand, and tilted toward the worm.

The snake-sized creature slithered toward the amal, its round mouth open to reveal tiny crystal teeth deep inside its throat. In a sudden violent motion, the creature lunged at the orange substance and devoured it, receptacle and all.

Meeting Fenring's inquisitive gaze, Ajidica said, "Just like real melange."

"The worms still die, though?" The Spice Minister clung to his skepticism.

"They die whether we give them amal or melange. It makes no difference. They simply cannot live away from their native desert."

"I see. I'd like to take a sample to the Emperor now. Have it prepared."

In a condescending tone, Ajidica answered, "Amal is a biological substance and is dangerous if not handled properly. The final product will be safe only after the addition of a stabilizing agent."

"Well add it, then, hmmm? I'll wait here while you do it."

The Master Researcher shook his head. "We are in the

process of testing a number of such agents now. Melange is an extremely complex substance, but success is imminent. Come back when I summon you."

"You do not *summon* me. I report only to the Emperor."

Looking through heavily lidded eyes, Ajidica responded in an arrogant tone, "Then report to him what I have told you. No person can tell the difference between amal and genuine melange."

Observing Fenring's frustrated reaction, he smiled to himself. The "stabilizing agent" was a sham. Neither the Emperor nor Ajidica's incompetent Tleilaxu superiors would ever receive true amal. Instead, the Master Researcher would escape and take everything with him, leaving no clues about the actual, extremely potent spice substitute, which he called "ajidamal." If the formulation could fool a sandworm of Arrakis, what more convincing test could there possibly be?

Fenring said, "Always remember that I convinced Elrood to begin this project in the first place, hmmm? Therefore, I feel a tremendous sense of responsibility." He paced the small room. "You have performed Spacing Guild tests, I presume? We must know if a Navigator can use your synthetic melange to envision safe paths through foldspace."

Ajidica struggled for a reply. He hadn't expected such a question.

"Apparently not? Mm-m-m-m. Did I strike a nerve?"

"Rest assured, a Navigator will notice no difference either." Ajidica touched the button to fog over the dome containing the worm.

Fenring pressed his advantage. "Nevertheless, the supreme test would be to place amal inside a Navigator's tank, hmmm? Only then can we be sure."

"But we cannot accomplish that, sir." Ajidica squirmed. "We cannot openly request Guild cooperation, since Project Amal must remain completely secret."

The Count's eyes glittered as schemes blossomed in his

mind. "But one of your Face Dancers might breach even the Guild's tight security. Yes, hmmm-ah. I will accompany your Face Dancer, to see that it's done properly."

Ajidica considered the suggestion. This Imperial functionary did have a point. Moreover, using a Face Dancer presented him with other possibilities . . . a way of getting rid of this meddlesome man.

Unknown to anyone except Ajidica himself, he had already disseminated hundreds of the tank-bred Face Dancers to strategic locations around the galaxy, transporting them in long-range exploration vessels to uncharted reaches. The shape-shifters had been developed centuries ago, but their possibilities had not been adequately explored. That was about to change.

"Yes, Count Fenring. I can arrange for a Face Dancer to accompany you."

⌘

WITH SO MANY distractions, Ajidica felt he would never finish his work.

An overeager group of politicians arrived from the sacred city of Bandalong on the Bene Tleilax homeworlds. Their leader, Master Zaaf, was a haughty man with rodent eyes and a perpetual upward curl of his tiny mouth. Ajidica couldn't decide whom he loathed more, Fenring or the inept Tleilaxu representatives.

Given the scientific abilities of the Bene Tleilax, he couldn't understand how Master Zaaf and other government leaders had bungled political affairs so badly. Forgetting the majesty of their place in the universe, they were content to be ground underfoot by *powindah* noble families.

"What did you say to the Imperial Spice Minister?" Zaaf demanded as he strutted into Ajidica's large office. "I must have a full report."

Ajidica drummed his fingers on the frostplaz desktop. He grew tired of explaining himself to outsiders. They always asked such inane questions. *One day I will no longer have to deal with idiots.*

After Ajidica had summarized the meeting, Zaaf announced in a pompous tone, "Now we wish to observe your amal tests ourselves. We have the right."

Though Zaaf was his superior, Ajidica feared nothing from the man, since no one could replace him on this project. "There are thousands of ongoing experiments. You wish to see all of them? How long is your life span, Master Zaaf?"

"Show us the most significant. Don't you agree, gentlemen?" Zaaf glanced at his companions. They nodded and grunted.

"Watch *this* test, then." With a confident smile, Ajidica took the vial of liquid ajidamal from his pocket and poured the rest of the contents into his own mouth. He tasted the substance on his tongue, inhaled the cinnamon essence into his sinuses, and swallowed.

This was the first time he'd actually consumed so much at once. Within seconds, a pleasantly warm feeling permeated his stomach and brain, matching any experience he'd ever enjoyed with genuine melange. He chuckled at the shocked expressions on his visitors' faces. "I've been doing this for weeks," he lied, "and there have been no ill effects." He was convinced God would not permit anything bad to happen to him. "There can be no doubt whatsoever."

The Tleilaxu politicians chattered excitedly, congratulating each other as if they'd had a hand in this success. Zaaf flashed small teeth and bent forward with a conspiratorial expression. "Excellent, Master Researcher. We shall see that you are properly rewarded. But first, we have an important matter to discuss."

Suffused in the warmth of ajidamal, Ajidica listened to Zaaf. The Bene Tleilax were still stinging from Duke Leto's rebuff of their calculated offer to make a ghola of his dead son Victor. Burning to avenge what they still believed to be an Atreides attack decades before, and angry at the continuing Ixian resistance here on Xuttuh that used Prince Rhombur Vernius as a figurehead, Zaaf wanted to seize Vernius and Atreides genetic lines for Bene Tleilax schemes.

With that vital DNA, they might tailor special diseases that could potentially wipe out House Atreides and House Vernius. If the Tleilaxu felt particularly vengeful, they could even clone simulacrums of Leto and Rhombur and publicly torture them to death—over and over again, if they wished! How much could the Atreides stand? Even fragmented genetic material from those bloodlines would be sufficient to perform many experiments.

But the Duke's refusal had crushed those plans.

To Ajidica's hyperfocused mind, Zaaf's words were distant and irrelevant. But he listened without comment, allowing Zaaf to plod through his plans to thwart House Atreides and House Vernius. He described a war memorial in the jungles of Beakkal, where almost a millennium ago Atreides and Vernius troops had fought side by side in a legendary last stand known as the Senasar Defense. Several of their heroic ancestors had been entombed there in a jungle shrine.

Ajidica fought off boredom as Zaaf continued, "We have arranged with the Beakkali government to exhume and take cellular 'samples' from any bodies we find there. Not an ideal situation, but it should provide enough genetic fragments for our purposes."

"And Leto Atreides can do nothing to prevent it," chimed in one of his companions. "Thus, we will get what we want—the perfect revenge."

The Tleilaxu never considered all the possibilities, though. Ajidica tried to keep the disgust from his expression. "The Duke will be furious when he discovers your intent. Do you not fear Atreides reprisals?"

"Leto is crippled with grief and has completely neglected his Landsraad duties." Master Zaaf looked far too smug. "We need fear nothing from him. Our retrieval operations are already under way, but we have encountered a small snag. The Prime Magistrate of Beakkal has demanded a huge payment from us. I . . . was hoping we could pay him with amal and allow him to think it is melange. Is your substitute good enough to fool them?"

Ajidica laughed, already envisioning new possibilities. "Absolutely." But he would use an early formula, similar enough to dupe them without wasting the precious ajidamal. The Beakkali used melange only in food and drink anyway, so they wouldn't notice the difference. It would be a simple matter. . . .

"I can produce as much as you require."

B eneath the tassled awning of an observation stand, Shaddam IV sat in pleasantly perfumed shade, watching the clockwork maneuvers of his troops. Of all the marvels on Kaitain, these Sardaukar were the most magnificent, as far as he was concerned. Could there be a more heartwarming sight than spotlessly uniformed men following his every order with cool precision?

How he wished all of his subjects responded to Imperial instructions as willingly.

A thin, elegant man with an aquiline nose, Shaddam wore a gray Sardaukar uniform, trimmed with silver and gold—he was their commander in chief, in addition to his other duties. Over his reddish hair he had settled a padded Burseg's helmet that bore the Imperial crest in gold.

At least he could watch the crisp parade in peace, since his wife Anirul had long ago grown tired of military exhibitions. Thankfully, she had chosen to tend to Bene Gesserit matters for the afternoon, doting on her daughters and raising them to be witches themselves. Or maybe dealing with funeral arrangements for the dead old crone

Lobia. He hoped the Bene Gesserit would provide him with a new Truthsayer soon. What else were the damnable Sisters good for?

On the open plaza below, the Sardaukar Corps paraded in flawless unison, boots echoing like gunfire across the swept flagstones. Supreme Bashar Zum Garon, a loyal old veteran from Salusa Secundus, guided his soldiers like a skilled puppeteer, performing spectacular maneuvers that demonstrated efficient battle formations. Perfect.

Unlike the Emperor's own family.

Normally, the Emperor loved to watch his troops practice, but at the moment his stomach was agitated. He hadn't eaten all day after swallowing some exceedingly bad news that was burning in his belly. Not even the best Suk doctor could treat this ailment.

Through his ever-diligent spy network, Shaddam had just learned that his father, Elrood IX, had sired a bastard son through one of his favorite concubines, a woman whose name had not yet been determined. Over forty years ago, old Elrood had taken steps to hide and protect the illegitimate son—who would now be a grown man, more than a decade younger than Shaddam. Did the bastard know his heritage? Did he watch with devious anticipation as Shaddam and Anirul failed to produce a male heir, child after child? Only daughters, daughters, and more daughters. Five of them, with baby Rugi the last. Did the bastard plan his moves even now, making preparations to usurp the Golden Lion Throne?

On the flagstone plaza, the soldiers split into two groups and rushed together in a mock battle, firing a webwork of simulated lasgun tracers so they could take possession of a sculpted, roaring lion fountain. High-powered military skimmers swept past in tight formation, ascending into the clear blue sky, where the fleeting clouds looked as if they had been painted by an artist.

With only moderate enthusiasm, a distracted Shaddam applauded the Sardaukar maneuvers, while quietly cursing his father's memory. *How many other secret children did the old vulture spawn?* It was a worrisome thought.

At least he knew the name of this one. *Tyros Reffa.* With connections to his adoptive House Taligari, Reffa had spent much of his life on Zanovar, a Taligari vacation world. Living a pampered life, the man must have little to do other than dream of seizing Imperial power.

Yes, Elrood's bastard could cause a great deal of trouble. But how to get to him and kill him? Shaddam sighed. These were the challenges of leadership. *Perhaps I should discuss this with Hasimir.*

But he exercised his mental muscles instead, stretching his mind, intent on proving that Hasimir Fenring was wrong about him . . . that he could rule without constant intervention and advice. *I make my own decisions!*

Shaddam had assigned Fenring to Arrakis as Imperial Spice Minister, as well as giving him the secret responsibility of overseeing the development of amal. Why was it taking Fenring so long to come back from Ix with his report?

The air was comfortably warm, with just enough breeze to make the parade banners flutter. Imperial Weather Control had laid out every aspect of the day in accordance with the Emperor's specifications.

Moving to a field of polygrass laid down across the plaza, the troops engaged in an elaborate demonstration of close shield fighting and flashing silver blades. Two teams attacked while mock enemy fire lit the square with flashes of purple and orange. In stadium boxes around the perimeter, an audience of minor nobles and court functionaries cheered politely.

The grizzled veteran Zum Garon stood impeccably attired, his expression critical, his standards high for every performance in front of his Emperor. Shaddam encouraged such public displays of military strength, especially now that several Houses of the Landsraad were starting to get unruly. He might need to use a little muscle, very soon. . . .

A fat brown spider dangled before him, suspended by a gossamer strand from the scarlet-and-gold awning. Irritated, he whispered, "Don't you realize who I am, little creature? I rule even the smallest living things in my realm."

More banners, more marching, more simulated fire in the background of his ruminations. A kaleidoscope of Sardaukar moved across the pageantry field. Pomp and glory. Overhead, 'thopters zoomed by in formation, performing daredevil aerial maneuvers. The audience applauded after each stunt, but Shaddam barely noticed, mulling over the problem of his bastard half brother.

He blew air across his lips and watched the intrusive spider swing in the sudden gust. The spider began to ascend its strand toward the awning.

You aren't safe from me up there, he thought. *Nothing escapes my wrath.*

But he knew he deluded himself. The Spacing Guild, the Bene Gesserit Sisterhood, the Landsraad, CHOAM—all of them had their own agendas and manipulations, tying his hands and blindfolding him, preventing him from ruling the Known Universe as an Emperor should.

Damn their control over me! How had his Corrino predecessors allowed such a sorry state of affairs to develop? It had been this way for centuries.

The Emperor reached up and squashed the spider before it could return and bite him.

The slithering leviathan rushed across the dunes with a scouring sound that reminded Liet-Kynes, incongruously, of a ribbon-thin cascade of fresh water. Kynes had seen the artificial waterfalls on Kaitain, constructed in pointless decadence.

Under the hot yellow sun, he and a group of loyal men rode atop one of the towering sandworms. Skilled Fremen sandriders had called the beast, mounted it, and pried open its ring segments with spreaders. High on the worm's sloped head, Liet held on to ropes to maintain his position.

The creature raced across the trackless sands toward Red Wall Sietch, where Liet's lovely wife Faroula would be waiting for him, and where the Fremen Council would be eager to hear his news. Disappointing news. Emperor Shaddam IV had been disappointing as a man, too, beyond even Liet's worst fears.

Stilgar had greeted Liet at the Carthag Spaceport. They had traveled out into the open desert, away from the Shield Wall, beyond the prying eyes of Harkonnens. There, met by a small band of Fremen, Stilgar had planted a thumper whose resonating heartbeat rhythm attracted a worm. Using techniques known to Fremen since ancient days, they had captured it.

Liet had scrambled up the ropes with familiar moves, planting stakes to secure himself. He remembered the day he had become a sandrider as a youth, proving himself an adult of the tribe. Old Naib Heinar had watched in judgment. Back then, Liet had been terrified, but he had completed the ordeal.

Now, though riding a sandworm was every bit as dangerous, and never to be done lightly, he saw the unruly beast as a mode of transportation, a swift means to get him home.

Tugging guide ropes and calling back to the riders, Stilgar stood stoically. The Fremen moved spreaders and planted additional maker hooks to direct the creature. Stilgar looked over at Liet, who remained preoccupied and clearly unhappy. He knew his friend's report from Kaitain was not good. However, unlike jabbering courtiers in the Palace, Fremen were not uneasy with silences. Liet would speak when he was ready, so Stilgar kept to himself beside his friend; they were together, each immersed in his own thoughts. Hours passed as they crossed the desert toward the reddish-black mountains near the horizon.

When he felt it was time, attuned to the young Planetologist's expressions and watching the reflection of troubled thoughts cross his face beneath the stillsuit mask, Stilgar spoke what Liet needed to hear. "You are the son of Umma Kynes. Now that your great father has died, you are the hope of all Fremen. And you have my life and loyalty, just as I promised it to your father." Stilgar did not treat the younger man in a paternal fashion, but as a genuine comrade.

They both knew the story; it had been told many times in sietch. Before he came to live among the Fremen, Pardot Kynes had fought six Harkonnen bravos who had cornered Stilgar, Turok, and Ommun—a brash trio of young Fremen. Stilgar was grievously injured and would have died if Kynes had not helped kill the Baron's men. Subsequently, when the Planetologist became a wild prophet of the Fremen, the three swore to help him achieve his dream. Even after Ommun had died with Pardot in a cave-in at Plaster Basin, Stilgar remembered the water debt he owed and paid it to the son, Liet.

Stilgar reached out to clasp the younger man's arm. Liet was every bit the man his father had been, and more. He had been raised as a Fremen.

Liet gave him a wan smile, his eyes deeply appreciative. "It is not your loyalty that concerns me, Stil, but the practicality of our cause. We will receive neither help nor sympathy from House Corrino."

Stilgar actually laughed at this. "The Emperor's sympathy is a weapon I'd rather not have. And we need no help killing Harkonnens." Now, as they rode the worm onward, he told his comrade about the raid on the desecrated Sietch Hadith. Liet looked pleased.

⌐

BACK IN THE warm confines of the isolated stronghold, Liet went eagerly to his quarters, dirty and exhausted. There, Faroula waited for her husband, and he would spend time with her first. After his sojourn on the Imperial planet, Liet needed a few moments of peace and calm, which his wife had always been able to provide. The desert people were anxious to hear his report and had already called a gathering for that evening, but by tradition no traveler was required to tell his tale until he could be refreshed, except in an emergency.

Faroula greeted him with a smile, flashing blue-within-blue eyes. Her welcoming kiss deepened as the privacy hanging fell across the door to their chamber. She had made him spice coffee and small honeyed melange cakes. He found the treats satisfying, but far less wonderful than simply seeing her again.

After another embrace, she brought out their young children, Liet-chih—her son by Liet's best friend Warrick, whose death had left Liet to take care of Faroula and the boy as his own—as well as their own daughter, Chani. He hugged the children, and they played and jabbered, until finally a nursemaid took them away, leaving him alone again with his wife.

Faroula smiled, her skin golden. She unfastened his now-worthless stillsuit, which had been taken apart and reassembled by the Emperor's security men. She applied thin salves to the bare skin of his feet.

Liet let out a long sigh. He had much to do, many matters to discuss with the Fremen, but he pushed them aside for now. Even a man who had stood before the Golden Lion Throne could find other things more important. As he looked into his wife's enigmatic eyes, Liet felt more at home than he had at any time since he'd stepped off the Guild shuttle in Carthag.

"Tell me about the wonders of Kaitain, my love," she said, her expression already filled with awe. "Such beautiful things you must have seen."

"I saw many things there, yes," he answered, "but believe me when I tell you this, Faroula." He stroked his fingers along her cheek. "I have found nothing in all the universe more beautiful than you."

The fate of the Known Universe hinges upon effective decisions, which can only be made with complete information.

— DOCENT GLAX OTHN of House Taligari,
A Child's Primer on Leadership, Suitable for Adults

One of the least opulent rooms in Castle Caladan, Leto's inner sanctum was a place where a leader would not feel overwhelmed by frivolous gaudiness when pondering the business interests of House Atreides.

The windowless stone walls featured no tapestries; the glowglobes were unadorned. A fire in the hearth gave off a sweet, resinous smell, driving back the dampness of cool salt air.

For hours, he sat at his battered teako desk. An ominous message cylinder lay like a time bomb in front of him. He had already read the report his spies had brought him.

Did the Tleilaxu actually think they could keep their crimes secret? Or were they simply hoping to complete their despicable desecration and be gone from the Senasar War Memorial before Leto could respond? The Prime Magistrate of Beakkal must have known that House Atreides would be deeply offended. Or had the Tleilaxu simply paid such a huge bribe that Beakkal could not refuse?

All the Imperium seemed to believe the recent tragedies had broken him, snuffed out his flame. He looked at the ducal signet ring on his finger.

Leto had never expected to assume the mantle of leadership at the age of fifteen. Now, after twenty-one years, he felt as if he had worn the heavy ring for centuries.

On the desktop stood a crystalplaz-encased butterfly, its wings bent at an awkward angle. A few years ago, distracted by a document he'd been studying, Leto had accidentally crushed the insect. Now he kept the preserved specimen where he could always be reminded of the consequences of his actions as Duke, and as a man.

Tleilaxu desecrations of war dead, committed with the blessing of the Prime Magistrate, could not be permitted . . . or forgotten.

Duncan Idaho, in full military regalia, knocked on the half-open wooden door. "You summoned me, Leto?" Tall and proud, the Swordmaster carried a slight air of superiority since his return from Ginaz. He had earned his right to be self-confident after enduring eight years of rigorous Swordmaster training.

"Duncan, I value your advice now more than ever." Leto rose to his feet. "I face a grim decision, and I must discuss strategy with you, now that Thufir and Gurney have gone to Ix."

The young man brightened, eager for the opportunity to prove his military worth. "Are we ready to plan our next move on Ix?"

"This is another matter." Leto held up the message cylinder, then sighed. "As Duke, I've found that there is always 'another matter.' "

Jessica stepped silently into the open doorway. Though she had the ability to eavesdrop unnoticed, she stood boldly beside the Swordmaster. "May I hear these concerns as well, my Duke?"

Normally, Leto would not have allowed a concubine to join in strategy sessions, but Jessica had extraordinary training, and he had come to value her perspective. She had given him her strength and her love during his darkest hour, and he would not dismiss her lightly.

Leto summarized how Tleilaxu excavation teams had set up a large encampment on Beakkal. Stone ziggurats, overgrown with vegetation, marked where Atreides troops had fought alongside their Vernius counterparts to rescue the planet from a pirate flotilla. The war dead included thousands of soldiers as well as the fallen patriarchs of both Houses.

Leto's voice became ominously hushed. "Tleilaxu exhumation teams are removing the bodies of our ancestors, claiming they wish to 'study them for historical genetics.' "

Duncan pounded his fist against the wall. "By the blood of Jool-Noret, we must prevent them."

Jessica bit her lower lip. "It is obvious what they want, my Duke. I don't understand the process completely, but it is possible that even with cadavers mummified for centuries, the Tleilaxu can grow gholas from dead cells. They may be able to reproduce a lost Atreides or Vernius genetic line."

Leto stared at the plaz-encased butterfly. "That's why they wanted Victor's body, and Rhombur's."

"Precisely."

"If I take the accepted approach, I must travel to Kaitain and lodge a formal protest in the Landsraad. Investigative committees may be formed, and eventually Beakkal and the Tleilaxu might receive some form of censure."

"By then it would be too late!" Duncan's alarm was apparent.

A log popped in the fireplace, startling them all.

"That is why I have decided to take more extreme action."

Jessica tried to insert the voice of reason. "Would it be possible to send our own troops to seize and remove the rest of the bodies before the Tleilaxu can exhume them?"

"Not good enough," Leto said. "If we overlook even one, our efforts will be in vain. No, we must eliminate the temptation, erase the problem, *and send a clear message.* Those who think Duke Leto Atreides has grown weak are about to learn otherwise."

Leto looked at the strewn documents that summarized his troop strength, the weapons in his armory, the available warcraft, even the family atomics. "Thufir is not here, so this will be your chance to prove yourself, Duncan. We must deliver a lesson that cannot be interpreted in any other way. No warning. No mercy. No ambiguity."

"I shall be glad to lead such a mission, my Duke."

In this universe there is no such thing as a safe place or a safe way. Danger lies along every path.

— Zensunni Aphorism

Over the nightside of Ix, a scheduled cargo shuttle dropped from the hold of an orbiting Heighliner. From the uninhabited wilderness, a hidden Sardaukar observation post watched the craft's orange plume as it descended into their detection grid. The shuttle headed toward the port-of-entry canyon, the guarded access point to the subterranean capital city.

Sardaukar observers did not notice a second, much smaller craft slipping into its wake. An Atreides combat pod. By virtue of a heavy bribe, the Heighliner was fitted with a camouflage-signal transmitter that tricked the ground-based trackers so that the black, unlit shape could move undetected, long enough for Gurney Halleck and Thufir Hawat to slip underground.

Gurney worked the controls of the tiny, wingless craft. Taking a different trajectory from the shuttle's plume, the black Atreides pod sped low across the rugged northern landscape. Lightless onboard instruments whispered data into his headset, telling him how to avoid the guarded landing cradles.

Gurney used daredevil skills he had learned from Dominic Vernius in a smugglers' band, streaking over boulder fields, skimming close to glaciers and high cirques. When he hauled contraband cargoes, he had known how to elude Corrino security patrols, and now he remained beneath the detection level of the Tleilaxu security net.

As the pod jostled through the atmosphere, Thufir sat placidly in Mentat mode, weighing possibilities. He had recorded all of the emergency exits and secret routes Rhombur had managed to remember. But human concerns kept breaking his concentration.

Although Leto had never criticized him for what might have been interpreted as security breaches—the death of Duke Paulus in the bullring, the skyclipper disaster—Thufir had redoubled his efforts, calling upon every skill in his personal arsenal, and adding more.

Now, he and Gurney had to infiltrate the besieged cities of Ix, ferret out weaknesses, and prepare for an outright military action. After the recent tragedies, Duke Leto was no longer afraid to bloody his hands. When Leto decided it was time, House Atreides would strike, and strike hard.

C'tair Pilru, a resistance fighter with whom they had long been in contact, had refused to abandon his efforts on Ix, despite crackdowns by the Tleilaxu invaders. Using stolen materials, he had fashioned effective bombs and other weapons, and for a time had even received secret assistance from Prince Rhombur—until all contact had been lost.

Thufir hoped they could find C'tair again this night, while there was still time. He and Gurney, acting on a few shreds of possibilities and a likely meeting place, had tried to send messages underground. Using an old Vernius military code that only C'tair would know, supplied by Rhombur, the warrior Mentat had proposed a possible rendezvous in the honeycomb of secret routes and hidden chambers. But the Atreides infiltrators had received no confirmation. . . . They were flying blind, led only by hope and determination.

Thufir gazed through the pod's small windows to get his

bearings, contemplating how they would go about finding the Ixian freedom fighters. Though it was not part of any Mentat analysis, he feared they would need to depend on . . . luck.

HUDDLING IN A musty storeroom in the upper crustal levels of what had once been the Grand Palais, C'tair Pilru harbored his own doubts. He had received the message, decoded it . . . and didn't believe it. His small-scale guerrilla war had continued for years and years, not always because of victories and hope, but because of sheer determination. Fighting the Tleilaxu comprised C'tair's entire life, and he did not know who he was or what he would be if the struggle ever ended.

He had survived this long by trusting no one in the once-beautiful underground city. He changed identities, moved from place to place, struck as hard as he could and then fled, leaving the invaders and their Sardaukar guard dogs in angry confusion.

As a favorite mental exercise, he pictured the original city in his mind, the gossamer connecting walkways and streets between stalactite buildings. He even envisioned the Ixian people as they used to be, filled with cheer and purpose, before the grim reality of the Tleilaxu invasion set in.

But now it all blurred in his memory. *It had been so long*.

A short while ago he had found the communication—a trick?—from representatives of Prince Rhombur Vernius. C'tair's entire life had been a risk, and now he had to take the chance. He knew that as long as Rhombur lived, the Prince would never abandon his people.

In the cold darkness of the storeroom, waiting, *waiting*, C'tair wondered if he was in fact losing his hold on reality . . . especially now that he knew the terrible fate of Miral Alechem, his lover and comrade, who might have become his wife under different circumstances. But the filthy invaders had captured her, used her body for their mysterious, awful experiments. He resisted visualizing Miral the way he had last seen her—an abomination, a brain-dead shape hooked up and converted into some hideous biological factory.

With every breath he took, he cursed the Tleilaxu for their cruelties. He squeezed his dark, haunted eyes shut, controlled his breathing, and remembered only Miral's large eyes, her narrow, attractive face, her raggedly cropped hair.

Rage, near-suicidal despondency, and survivor's guilt washed through him. He had set his mind on a fanatical course, but if Prince Rhombur had truly sent men to aid him, this nightmare might soon be over. . . .

A sudden loud whir of machinery made him scramble deeper into the shadows. He heard quiet scratchings, the skilled picking of a lock, then the hatch of a self-guided lift chamber opening to reveal two silhouetted figures. They hadn't seen him yet. He could still flee, or try to kill them. But they were too tall to be Tleilaxu and did not move like Sardaukar.

The older man looked tough as shigawire, with a sinewy face and the sapho-stained lips of a Mentat. His burly blond companion, a lumpy man with a prominent scar on his face, pocketed a small set of tools. The Mentat stepped out of the lift first, exuding wary confidence. "We come from Caladan."

C'tair didn't move or reveal himself. His heart raced. It might still be a trick, but he'd come this far. He had to find out for sure. His fingers touched the hilt of a hand-wrought dagger in his pocket. "I am here."

C'tair emerged from the shadows, and the two men looked toward him, eyes adjusting to the low illumination. "We are friends of your Prince. You are no longer alone," said the scarred man.

Moving cautiously, as if stepping on broken glass, the trio met in the center of the dusty storage room. They clasped hands in the half handshake of the Imperium, made awkward introductions. The new arrivals told him what had happened to Rhombur.

C'tair looked dazed, not certain anymore where reality and his fantasies separated. "There . . . was a girl. Kailea? Yes, Kailea Vernius."

Thufir and Gurney looked at each other, avoided the uncomfortable revelation for now. "We don't have much time," Gurney said. "We need to see and learn what we can."

C'tair faced the two Atreides representatives, trying to decide where to begin. Raw anger built inside, filling him with so much emotion that he could not bear to tell them what he had already seen, what he'd already endured here. "Stay, and I will show you what the Tleilaxu have done to Ix."

✺

UNOBTRUSIVELY, THE THREE men moved through crowds of oppressed workers, past facilities that had degenerated into decrepitude. They used C'tair's numerous stolen identification cards to enter and exit security zones. This lone rebel had learned how to pass unnoticed, and the downtrodden Ixians rarely looked at anything other than their own feet.

"We've known for some time that the Emperor is involved here," Thufir said. "But I cannot understand the necessity for two full legions of Sardaukar."

"I have seen . . . but I still don't know the answers." C'tair pointed out a sluggish monstrosity lumbering across a loading dock, a machine with a few human components strapped on . . . a battered head, part of a bruised and misshapen torso. "If Prince Rhombur is a cyborg, I pray it's nothing like what the Tleilaxu have created here."

Gurney was appalled. "What sort of demon is that?"

"*Bi-Ixians*, victims of torture and execution, reanimated

through machinery. They aren't alive, just mobile. The Tleilaxu call them 'examples'—they are toys for the amusement of demented minds."

Thufir stood dispassionately, mentally filing away every detail, while Gurney had trouble controlling the revulsion on his face.

C'tair managed a grim smile. "I saw one with a paint sprayer strapped to his back, but the thing's biomechanics broke down and stopped moving altogether. He had the sprayer full-on when he fell, and two Tleilaxu Masters got doused with pigment. They were furious, shouting gibberish at the machine-thing, as if it had done it intentionally."

"Maybe it did," Gurney said.

In the ensuing days the trio investigated and observed . . . and hated what they saw. Gurney wanted to fight right away, but Thufir advised caution. They needed to go back and report to House Atreides. Only then—with the Duke's permission—could they formulate a plan for an effective, coordinated assault.

"We'd like to take you back with us, C'tair," Gurney offered, compassion plain on his face. "We can get you out of here. You have already suffered enough."

C'tair was alarmed at the suggestion. "I'm not leaving. I . . . I wouldn't know what to do if I stopped fighting. My place is here, tormenting the invaders any way I can, letting my surviving countrymen know I haven't given up, and never will."

"Prince Rhombur thought you might say that," Thufir said. "We have brought many supplies for you in our combat pod: explosive wafers, weapons, even food stores. It is a start."

C'tair felt dizzy with the possibilities. "I knew my Prince hadn't given up on us. I have awaited his return for so long, hoping to fight side by side with him."

"We will take our report to Duke Leto Atreides and to

your Prince. Be patient." Thufir wanted to say more, to promise something tangible. But he did not have the authority to do so.

C'tair nodded, anxious to begin anew. At last, after so many years, powerful forces might aid him in his fight.

Compassion and revenge are two sides of the same coin. Necessity dictates which way that coin falls.

— DUKE PAULUS ATREIDES

Steam rose from the lush foliage of Beakkal as the yellow-orange primary sun lifted above the horizon. The bright, white secondary star already rode high in the sky. Dayflowers opened with a gush of perfume, calling to birds and insects. Bristly primates ran through the dense canopy, and predatory vines curled out to snag unsuspecting rodents.

Atop the overgrown Senasar plateau, gigantic marble ziggurats stood tall, their corners faceted with scooped mirrors that directed sun flares like spotlights in all directions.

On this plateau, besieged Atreides and Vernius men had once fought multitudes of raiders, slaying at least ten for every defender lost, before being overwhelmed by sheer numbers. They had sacrificed themselves to the last man, only an hour before the long-awaited reinforcement troops arrived and crushed the remaining pirates.

For centuries, the Beakkali people had revered those fallen heroes, but after House Vernius had gone renegade in shame, the Prime Magistrate had ceased tending the monuments, allowing the jungle foliage to smother them. The magnificent statues became nesting places for small animals and birds. The great stone blocks began to crack and weather. And no one on Beakkal cared.

In recent days, self-erecting tents had sprouted like geo-metric fungi around the fringes of the memorial. Teams of workers had cut down thick underbrush, removing decades of jungle debris, scraping down to the stones and un-earthing the sealed tombs. Thousands of dead soldiers lay buried in mass graves on the mesa; others were sealed in ar-mored crypts inside the ziggurats.

Beakkali supervisors had provided excavation equip-ment to disassemble the jagged ziggurats block by block. Small-statured Tleilaxu scientists set up modular laborato-ries, eager to test the cell scrapings from any exhumed bod-ies, dredging through the remnants of human tissue to find viable genetic material.

The jungle smelled of mist and flowers, pungent oils from dark green plants, herbs that grew as tall as trees. Smoke from the encampments and the thick exhaust of heavy machinery curled into the air. One of the gnomish excavators wiped sweat from his brow and flailed his hand to drive away clouds of blood-sucking gnats. He looked up to watch the flame-orange primary sun rise over the canopy like an angry eye.

Suddenly the sky lit up with purple lasgun beams.

Led by Duncan Idaho, Atreides ships descended from or-bit, targeting the isolated war memorial. He transmitted Duke Leto's message even as he opened fire. The recorded speech would be heard by the Prime Magistrate in the Beakkali capital city; a separate copy had been sent by Courier to the Landsraad Council on Kaitain, all accord-ing to the strictures of warfare laid down by the Great Convention.

Leto's iron-hard voice announced, "The Senasar War Memorial was established in honor of the service my ances-tors performed for Beakkal. Now, the Bene Tleilax and the Beakkali have desecrated this place. House Atreides has no recourse but to respond appropriately. We shall not allow our fallen heroes to be defiled by cowards. Therefore, we choose to erase this monument."

At the lead of a phalanx of warships, Duncan Idaho gave his troops permission to open fire. Lasgun beams sliced through the partially dismantled ziggurats, exposing long-sealed chambers. Tleilaxu scientists ran screaming from tents and laboratory shelters.

"In doing so, we have followed the forms precisely," Leto's recorded voice continued. "It is unfortunate that some casualties may be suffered, but we take solace in the knowledge that only those engaged in criminal activity will be harmed. There are no innocents in this matter."

The Atreides fleet circled and dropped thermal bombs, then shot purple blasts of light into the conflagration. In twenty standard minutes—faster than it took the Prime Magistrate to call a meeting of his advisors—the squadron had leveled the memorial, the Tleilaxu grave robbers, and their Beakkali collaborators. It also vaporized all the remaining Atreides and Vernius dead.

The plateau was left an uneven plain of melted glass, punctuated by lumps of smoking material. All along the fringes of the attack zone, fires grew brighter and hotter, spreading outward into the jungle. . . .

"House Atreides tolerates no insult," Duncan said into the comsystem, but there were no survivors to listen.

As he gave the order for his ships to return to orbit, he looked down at the devastation. After this, no one in the Imperium would ever question Duke Leto's resolve.

No warning. No mercy. No ambiguity.

The enemy to be feared most is one who wears the face of a friend.

— SWORDMASTER REBEC OF GINAZ

Underground on Kaitain, the Imperial necropolis covered as much area as the magnificent Palace itself. Generations of fallen Corrinos inhabited the city of the dead, those who had succumbed to treachery or accidents; a few had even died of natural causes.

When Count Hasimir Fenring returned from Ix, Shaddam immediately led his friend and advisor into the dank, poorly lit catacombs. "Is this how you celebrate the triumphant return of your Spice Minister? By dragging me down into musty old crypts, hmmm?"

Shaddam had dispensed with his usual retinue of bodyguards, and the two men were accompanied only by tethered orange glowglobes as they descended spiraling stairs. "We used to play down here as children, Hasimir. It gives me nostalgic feelings."

Fenring nodded his overlarge head. His wide eyes flicked from side to side like those of a nocturnal bird, searching for assassins and booby traps. "Perhaps this is where I developed my fascination for lurking in shadows?"

Shaddam's voice became harder, more Imperial. "It's also a place where we can speak without fear of being spied upon. You and I have important matters to discuss." Fenring grunted in approval.

Long ago, after moving the Imperial capital from ruined Salusa Secundus, Hassik Corrino III had been the first to be entombed beneath the megalithic building. Over the ensuing millennia, numerous Corrino emperors, concubines, and bastard children were also buried here. Some had been cremated and their ashes displayed in urns, while the bones of others were ground up to make porcelain funereal pieces. A few rulers were encased in transparent sarcophagi, sealed within nullentropy fields so that their bodies would never decay, even if their meager accomplishments were obscured by the fog of passing time.

As Fenring and Shaddam continued, they passed the sallow-faced old mummy of Mandias the Terrible, who lay in a chamber fronted by a fearsome, life-size statue of himself. According to the placard on his coffin, he was known as "the Emperor who made worlds tremble."

"I am not impressed." Shaddam looked at the withered husk. "Nobody even remembers him."

"Only because you refused to study Imperial history," Fenring countered with a thin smile. "Does a place such as this call to mind your own mortality, hmmm-ah?"

The Emperor scowled, surrounded by the rippling light of the mobile glowglobes. As they proceeded along the sloped rock floor, tiny creatures at the periphery skittered into shadows and cracks—spiders, rodents, modified scarabs that managed to survive by eating scraps of long-preserved flesh.

"What is this I hear about Elrood having a bastard son, hmmm? How could this have been hidden from us all these years?"

Shaddam whirled. "How do you know about that?"

Fenring answered with a condescending smile. "I have ears, Shaddam."

"They are too large."

"But used only in your service, Sire, hmmm?" He continued to speak, not waiting for the Emperor to make further excuses. "It does not appear that this Tyros Reffa has any desire for your throne, but in these times of growing unrest, he might be used as a figurehead by rebellious families, a rallying point."

"But I am the true Emperor!"

"Sire, while the Landsraad swears fealty to House Corrino, they show no loyalty to you *personally*. You have managed to, hmmm-ah, irritate many of the most powerful nobles."

"Hasimir, I am not required to worry about my subjects' bruised egos." Shaddam looked at the tomb of the ancient Mandias and muttered a curse against his old father Elrood for getting a child on one of his concubines. Surely an Emperor should have taken precautions?

As the need for burials continued century after century, the necropolis had been dug deeper, with more crypts hollowed out. In the lowest and most recent subterranean levels, Shaddam actually recognized some of the names of his ancestors.

Ahead lay the walled-up vault of Shaddam's grandfather, Fondil III, known as "the Hunter." The pitted iron door was flanked by the stuffed carcasses of two ferocious predators the man had killed: a spiny ecadroghe from the high plateaus of Ecaz and a tufted saber-bear from III Delta Kaising. Fondil, however, had taken his epithet from hunting *men*, ferreting out enemies and destroying them. His big-game adventures had been a mere diversion.

Shaddam and Fenring passed coffins and chambers for children and siblings, and finally an idealized statue of Elrood IX's first heir, Fafnir. Years ago, Fafnir's death (an "accident" arranged by young Fenring) had opened Shaddam's path to the throne. Complacent, Fafnir had never imagined that his little brother's friend could possibly be dangerous.

Only suspicious Elrood had imagined that Fenring and Shaddam might have been behind the murder. Though the boys never confessed, Elrood had cackled knowingly. "It shows initiative that you are able to make difficult decisions. But do not be so eager to take the responsibility of an

Emperor. I still have many years left in my reign, and you must observe my example. Watch, and learn."

And now Shaddam had to worry about the bastard Reffa, too.

He finally led Fenring to where the sealed ashes of El-rood IX waited in a relatively small alcove, adorned with shimmering diamondplaz, ornate scrollwork, and fine gems—a sufficient display of Shaddam's grief at the loss of his "beloved father."

The glowglobes came to a halt and shone down like bright embers. Disrespectfully, Shaddam leaned against the resting place of his father's ashes. The old man had been cremated to foil any Suk physician's attempts to determine the true cause of death.

"Twenty years, Hasimir. We've waited that long for the Tleilaxu to create synthetic spice." Shaddam's eyes were bright, his gaze intent. "What have you learned? Tell me when the Master Researcher is ready to go into full-scale production. I grow tired of waiting."

Fenring tapped his own lips. "Ajidica was most anxious to reassure us about the progress, Sire, but I am not convinced that the substance has been thoroughly tested. It must meet *our* specifications. The repercussions of amal will make the galaxy tremble. We dare not commit any tactical errors."

"What errors can there possibly be? He's had two decades to test it. The Master Researcher says it's ready."

Fenring regarded the Emperor in the dim light. "And you trust what a Tleilaxu says?" Around him he could smell death and preservatives, perfumes, dust . . . and Shaddam's nervous sweat. "I suggest we exercise caution, hmmm-ahh? I am arranging for a final test, one that will give us all the proof we need."

"Yes, yes, give me no more details about your dull tests. I have seen Ajidica's reports, and I do not understand half of what he says."

"Just another month, Shaddam, perhaps two."

Impatient and brooding, the lean-faced Emperor paced the crypt. Fenring tried to fathom the depth of his friend's mood. The glowglobes, keyed to follow Shaddam, tried in vain to keep pace as he moved back and forth in the confined area.

"Hasimir, I am sick unto death of caution. All my life I have been *waiting*—waiting for my brother to die, waiting for my father to die, waiting for a son! And now that I have the throne, I find myself waiting for amal so that I can finally have the power a Corrino Emperor deserves."

He stared at his clenched fist, as if he could see the visible lines of power trickling through his fingers. "I have a CHOAM Directorship, yet it carries no real ability to command. The Combine does whatever it wishes, because they can outvote me at any turn. The Spacing Guild is not required by law to follow my decrees, and if I don't tread carefully, they could impose sanctions, withdraw transportation privileges, and shut down the entire Imperium."

"I understand, Sire. But far more damaging, I believe, are the increasing examples of nobles defying and ignoring your commands. Look at Grumman and Ecaz—they continue their petty little war in violation of your peacekeeping efforts. Viscount Moritani practically spat in your face."

Shaddam tried to step on a glossy black beetle, which succeeded in scuttling to safety in a crack. "Perhaps it is time to remind everyone exactly who is in command! When I have amal at my disposal, they will all have to dance to my tune. Spice from Arrakis will be prohibitively expensive."

Fenring was contemplative, though. "Hmmm, many Great Houses have gathered their own melange stockpiles, though it is against an admittedly ancient and obscure law. For centuries, no one has bothered to enforce this edict."

Shaddam glowered. "What does that matter?"

Fenring's nose twitched. "It matters, Sire, because when the time comes to announce your monopoly on synthetic melange, such illegal stockpiles will allow the noble families to resist buying amal for some time."

"I see." Shaddam blinked as if he had not considered this. He brightened. "Then we must confiscate those hoards so that the other Houses have no cushion when I cut off the flow of melange."

"True, Sire, but if *you alone* crack down on hoarders, the Great Houses may rally against you. I suggest instead that you cement your alliances so you can deliver Imperial justice from a position of greater strength. Remember, honey can be a sticky trap as well as a sweet reward, mmm?"

Shaddam's impatience was clear. "What are you talking about?"

"Let the Guild and CHOAM locate the perpetrators and bring evidence of guilt to you. Your own Sardaukar can confiscate the stockpiles, after which you reward CHOAM and the Guild with a portion of the confiscated spice. The promise of such a prize should give them an incentive to uncover the most cleverly hidden hoards."

Fenring watched the wheels turning in the Emperor's mind. "In that way, Sire, you maintain the moral high ground, while keeping the full cooperation of the Guild and CHOAM. And you get rid of the Landsraad stockpiles."

Shaddam smiled. "I shall begin at once. I'll make a decree—"

Fenring cut him off. The wandering glowglobes paused as the Emperor did. "We will have to find some other way to deal with the spice on Arrakis itself. Perhaps we could install an overwhelming Imperial military force there to block access to the natural melange fields."

"The Guild would never transport the troops there, Hasimir. They won't cut their own throats. How else are we going to shut down operations on Arrakis?"

The tomb's idealized image of Elrood IX seemed to be watching these discussions with amusement. "Hmmm-ah, we might need a ruse, Sire. I'm sure we could come up with a justification to take control away from House Harkonnen. We could call it a change of fief. They're due for one in a decade or so anyway."

"Can you imagine the Guild's reaction when they find out, Hasimir, after they've helped me ferret out the illegal spice stockpiles?" Shaddam said, twitching with excitement. "I have always been irked at the power of the Guild, but melange is their Achilles—"

Then a slow smile crept across his face as an intriguing idea occurred to him. His look of delight made Fenring uneasy. "All right, Hasimir. We can score two victories with one blow."

The Count was puzzled. "Which two victories, Sire?"

"Tyros Reffa. We know the bastard has been coddled by House Taligari. I believe he has an estate on Zanovar, which I can easily verify." The Emperor's smile widened. "And if we were to find a convenient spice hoard on Zanovar, wouldn't that be a fine place to begin our crusade?"

"Hmmm-ah," Fenring said, with a grin of his own. "An excellent idea, Sire. Zanovar would indeed make a perfect place for a vigorous first strike, a lovely example. And if the bastard should accidentally be killed . . . all the better."

The two men left the deepest crypts and began to walk uphill toward the main section of the Palace. Fenring looked behind him to the end of the stone tunnel.

The Corrino necropolis might soon have need of another crypt.

A true gift is not just the object itself; it is a demonstration of understanding and caring, a reflection of both the individual who gives and the one who receives.

— DOCENT GLAX OTHN,
Excerpted Lectures for House Taligari

On the verdant fern path of his Zanovar estate, Tyros Reffa studied the scrollwork language on the laminated ticket in his hand, trying to interpret the obscure pictographs. He relished the challenge. Sunshine through the leafy canopy dappled the card. Puzzled, he looked up at his revered teacher and friend, Docent Glax Othn.

"If you cannot read the words, Tyros, you will never appreciate the gift itself." Though few members of the Taligari family remained alive, the Docent was one of a long line of teacher-lords who had inherited the fief from the last traditional nobleman and continued to operate it under the original name. He and Reffa shared a naming day, separated by a gulf of decades but bridged by an enduring friendship.

Hummingbirds and jeweled butterflies flitted around the waving fern fronds, chasing each other in fast, colorful aerial maneuvers. High in one of the scaly trees, an off-key songbird sounded like a dry, squeaky hinge.

"May the fates save me from an impatient teacher." Reffa was in his mid-forties, stout of build and athletic in his movements. His eyes held an unwavering intelligence. "I can translate something about the Taligarian Court here . . . performance . . . famous and mysterious . . ." He drew in a quick breath. "This is a ticket to the suspensor opera! Yes, I see the code now."

The Docent had given him only one ticket, knowing that Reffa would go alone, fascinated and voracious to learn, drinking in the experience. The old man himself no longer attended such off-world performances. With only a few years remaining in his life, he had laid out his time carefully and preferred to meditate and teach.

Reffa studied the ticket's scrollwork and deciphered every word. "This is a pass to go to the lighted tanks of Taligari Center, in fabled Artisia. I am invited to watch an illuminated dance presentation in subliminal languages, which describes the emotional overtones of the long and complex struggles of the Interregnum." He traced a finger over the strange runes, content in his abilities.

His gaunt mentor nodded with deep satisfaction. "It is said that only one in five hundred viewers can understand the nuances of the magnificent piece, and then only with extensive attention and training. Still, you will want to see the performance for its own sake."

Reffa embraced the Docent. "A wonderful gift, sir." They veered off the wide cobblestone path onto a smaller gravel lane that crunched beneath their slippered feet. Reffa loved every corner of his modest estate.

Several decades ago, Emperor Elrood had instructed the Docent to raise a bastard child in comfort and secrecy, without instilling in him any hope of his heritage, but keeping him worthy of his Corrino blood. The Docent had taught him to savor quality rather than extravagance.

Glax Othn gazed at the younger man's chisel-featured face. "There is also a matter of some concern, Tyros. Another reason it is perhaps a wise idea for you to go to Taligari for a while, leave your estate here . . . just for a month or two."

Reffa looked at the Docent, instantly alert. "Is this another puzzle?"

"Unfortunately, not one for mere amusement. In the past two weeks, several men have made rather rigorous inquiries into you and your property. You have noticed this, correct?"

Reffa hesitated, only slowly growing concerned. "It was perfectly innocuous, sir. One man was inquiring into prime real estate here on Zanovar, even hinting that he wanted to purchase my property. Another was a master gardener who wanted to study my conservatory. The third—"

"They were all Imperial spies," Othn said, cutting him off. Reffa was instantly speechless, and the teacher continued, "I was suspicious and decided to check them out. The identifications they gave you were false, and all three came from Kaitain. It has taken me a bit of effort, but I have proven that those men are secretly in Emperor Shaddam's employ."

Reffa pursed his lips, fighting his desire to blurt out questions. The Docent would want him to sift through the consequences. "So they were all lying. The Emperor is trying to check up on my home, and me. Why, after all this time?"

"Obviously, because he has just learned of your existence." The Docent took on a stern demeanor, and his voice became pedantic as he remembered the great speeches he had given inside echoing halls filled with students. "You could have had so much more, Tyros Reffa. And you deserve it precisely because *you do not want it*. It is something of an Imperial paradox. I think you could be in some danger."

The Docent understood why the young man must maintain his quiet life and not call attention to himself. This bastard son of Elrood IX had never posed any threat to Kaitain, had never shown any ambition—or interest—in Imperial politics or the schemings of the Golden Lion Throne.

Instead, Reffa preferred to make his mark by entertaining audiences, performing under a stage name with off-world acting companies. He had studied with the Mimbanco teachers of House Jongleur, the greatest entertainers in the Imperium, actors so talented they could manipulate the strongest emotions in an audience's heart. Young Reffa had loved those early years on Jongleur, and the Docent had been exceedingly proud of him.

Reffa stiffened. This went beyond the bounds of what they were permitted to mention, even in private conversations. "Do not speak openly of such things. Yes, I will leave this place and go to Taligari." Softening his tone, he added, "But you will diminish my pleasure in this wonderful gift. Come, see what I have gotten for *you* on this naming day." His face remained troubled, though.

Reffa clasped the ticket in his fingers, then turned to the old man and managed a smile. "You taught me, sir, that the act of giving is more effective by tenfold when it is reciprocated."

The Docent feigned surprise. "Right now we have greater concerns. I have no need of gifts."

Reffa took his mentor by the bony elbow and steered him through a hedge of feathertrees that opened into a central courtyard. "Neither do I. But neither of us ever makes time to treat ourselves to little pleasures unless we are forced into doing so. Don't deny the truth of what I say. I have arranged something for you, too. Look, there is Charence."

The dour-faced house master stood on the opposite side of the paved area, waiting for them by a scarlet pavilion. Charence looked to be a morose, ill-natured man—but he was highly efficient and had a bone-dry sense of humor that Reffa appreciated.

Abashed, Glax Othn followed the stocky young man to the pavilion, where he had placed a small wrapped box on a shaded table. Charence lifted the box and extended it to the Docent.

Othn took it in his hands. "What could I possibly want? Other than more time, and more knowledge, that is. And your safety." The old teacher tore open the foil wrapping with an expression of puzzled delight, followed by genuine confusion as he studied the shiny object. It was a crystal pass-chit, a one-day membership token. "An amusement park, with rides and displays and thrill-simulators?"

Seeing his reaction, dour Charence actually smiled.

"Zanovar's finest," Reffa said. "The children love it." He beamed. He had gone there himself, just to make certain it was not the sort of spot the overly serious Docent would ever have visited.

"But I have no children," he protested, "no family. This is not really for me, is it?"

"Have some fun. Be young at heart. You have always insisted that a true human being requires new experiences for sustenance."

The Docent flushed. "I say that to my students, but . . . Are you trying to prove me hypocritical?" His brown eyes twinkled.

Reffa closed his mentor's hand over the token. "Enjoy yourself, in payment for all you have done on my behalf." He clapped a palm on the Docent's shoulder. "And when I return, safe after a month or two on Taligari, we can compare our separate experiences—you on amusement-park rides and me at the suspensor opera."

The old teacher nodded thoughtfully. "I look forward to that, my friend."

The lone traveler in the desert is a dead man.
Only the worm lives alone out there.

—Fremen Saying

G iven enough training, any Mentat could become a capable killer, an efficient and imaginative assassin. Piter de Vries, though, suspected that his own dangerous nature had to do with the original *twisting* that enhanced his powers and made him what he was. His proclivity for cruelty, his sadistic enjoyment of the suffering of others, had been designed into his genetic blueprint by the Tleilaxu.

Thus, House Harkonnen was the perfect home for him.

Inside a high room of the Harkonnen Residency at Carthag, de Vries stood before a mirror framed with lacy swirls of oil-black titanium. Using a cloth dipped in fragrant soap, he scrubbed around his mouth, then leaned close to examine the permanent sapho stains. He powdered his pointed chin with makeup, but left the lips bright red. His ink-blue eyes and frizzy hair gave him the wild appearance of unpredictability.

I am too valuable to be used as a mere clerk! But the Baron didn't always see it that way. The fat fool often misused de Vries's talents, wasting his valuable time and energy. *I am not an accountant.* He slithered into his personal study, filled with antique furnishings, racks of shigawire spools and filmbooks. Filmledgers were scattered across his desk, covering the varnished blood-grain.

Any Mentat was overqualified to perform mere bookkeeping chores; de Vries had worked on ledgers before, but never enjoyed it. The tasks were too rudimentary, insultingly simple. But secrets must be kept, and the Baron trusted few people.

Infuriated by the Fremen raid on the Hadith melange hoard and several other hidden stockpiles, the Baron had instructed de Vries to check all Harkonnen financial ledgers to make certain they were in order, that they contained no evidence of the illegal spice stockpiles. All evidence must be expunged, to avoid the attentions of an inquisitive CHOAM auditor. If the stockpiles were discovered, House Harkonnen could well lose its valuable Arrakis fief—and more. Especially with the Emperor's newly announced hard-line stance against spice hoarding. *What is Shaddam thinking?*

De Vries sighed and resigned himself to the task.

To make matters worse, the Baron's thick-skulled nephew, Glossu Rabban, had already gone through the records (without permission) and removed evidence with all the finesse of a dull gravedigger's shovel; the Beast's baby brother Feyd-Rautha could have done a better job. Now the books were badly out of balance, leaving de Vries with more work than before.

Far into the evening, he hunched over his desk. He drowned his subconscious in the numbers, absorbing data. With a magnetic scriber, he made changes, altering the first level of discrepancies, smoothing over the too-obvious mistakes.

But a tugging, peripheral thought kept pulling him out of his near trance: a drug-induced vision he had experienced nine years ago, when he'd seen strange, unspecified trouble on the horizon for House Harkonnen . . . inexplicable images of the Harkonnens abandoning Arrakis, the blue-griffin banner taken down, to be replaced by the green-and-black of House Atreides. How could the Harkonnens possibly lose their spice monopoly? And what did the damnable Atreides have to do with it?

De Vries needed more information. It was his sworn duty. More important than this miserable clerical work. He pushed the ledgers away, then went to his private pharmacopoeia.

He let his fingers select bitter sapho juice, tikopia syrup, and two capsules of melange concentrate. He did not regulate the amounts he gulped. A pleasant, sweet-burning cinnamon essence exploded in his mouth. Hyperprescience, the verge of an overdose, a doorway opening. . . .

He saw *more* this time. Information he needed—*Baron Harkonnen, older and even heavier, being escorted by Sardaukar troops to a waiting shuttle*. So, the Baron *himself* would be forced to leave Arrakis, not some later generation of Harkonnens! The disaster would occur soon, then.

De Vries struggled to learn additional details, but swimming particles of light fuzzed his vision. He increased the dosage of drugs just enough to return the pleasurable sensation, but the visions did not come back, even as the chemicals rose up like a tidal wave. . . .

He awoke to find himself in the muscular arms of a pungent-smelling man with broad shoulders. His eyes came into focus a moment before his mind did. Rabban! The burly man hauled him along a rock-walled corridor, underground, beneath the Harkonnen Residency.

"I'm doing you a favor," Rabban said, feeling the Mentat stir. "You were supposed to be working on the accounts. My uncle won't be pleased to learn what you've done to yourself. *Again.*"

The Mentat could not think clearly, struggled to speak. "I have learned something much more import—"

In midsentence, de Vries was swung first to one side, then to the other, then with a splash he landed in water—*water*, of all things, here on Arrakis!

Fighting the fog of drugs, he thrashed and dog-paddled

to where Rabban knelt on a stone lip at the edge. "Good thing you can swim. I hope you haven't soiled our cistern."

Furious, de Vries crawled out and lay gasping on the stone deck, dripping puddles that would have been worth a fortune to any Fremen servant.

Rabban smirked. "The Baron could always replace you. The Tleilaxu would be only too happy to send us another Mentat grown from the same tank."

Spluttering, de Vries tried to recover. "I was *working*, you idiot, trying to enhance a vision that concerned the future of House Harkonnen." Soaked but trying to maintain his composure, the twisted Mentat pushed past the burly man and marched along the cool underground passages, then up stairs and ramps to the Baron's private suite. He pounded on the door, still dripping. Breathing hard, Rabban followed close behind.

When the Baron came to the door, floating forward with hastily strapped-on suspensors, he looked irritated. His thick, reddish eyebrows knitted on his pasty face as he scowled; the Mentat's disheveled appearance did not seem to help. "What's the meaning of coming to me at this time of night?" He sniffed. "You're wasting my water."

A mewling, bloody form lay broken on the far side of the Baron's reinforced bed. De Vries saw a pale hand twitching; Rabban pushed closer for a better view. "Your Mentat has drugged himself again, Uncle."

A lizard tongue darted across de Vries's stained lips. "Only in the line of duty, my Baron. And I have news. Important, disturbing news." Quickly, he described the drug-induced vision he had experienced.

The Baron puffed his fat cheeks. "Damn all the trouble. My own stockpiles are under constant attack by those infernal Fremen, and now the Emperor is rattling his sword, threatening dire consequences for anyone who keeps a private cache. Now my own Mentat seeks out visions of my downfall! I grow weary of it."

"You don't believe his hallucinations, do you, Uncle?" Rabban's gaze flicked uncertainly between the two men.

"Fine, then. We must prepare to suffer losses and replace what we have lost." The Baron looked over his shoulder, anxious to get back to his playmate before the boy died on the floor. "Rabban, I don't care what you have to do. Get me more spice!"

❦

DRESSED IN HIS stillsuit, Turok stood in the hot control room of a spice harvester. The huge machine groaned and creaked while it scooped material from a rich desert pit and deposited it into an onboard hopper. Screens, fans, and electrostatic fields separated melange from sand grains and purified the product.

Exhaust dust belched out of the harvester's stacks and rear pipes as heavy treads hauled the mammoth machine across an exposed spice vein. Flakes of pure melange fell into armored containers; the detachable cargo hold was ready to be whisked away at the first sign of an approaching sandworm.

Fremen like Turok occasionally volunteered to work on harvester crews, where they were valued for their desert skills. They were paid in cash, no questions asked. In doing so, Turok learned valuable information about city workers and spice crews. And information was power—so said Liet-Kynes.

Nearby, the harvester captain stood at a panel, studying screens projected by a dozen external cameras. A nervous man with a gritty beard, he worried that the spotter craft might not spot wormsign in time to save the old machine. "Use those strong Fremen eyes to keep us safe. That's what I pay you for."

Through the dusty window, Turok studied the hostile landscape, the undulating dunes. Despite the absence of movement, he knew the desert teemed with life, most of it hiding from the day's heat. He kept an eye out for deep tremors. Around the control room, three crewmen also peered through scratched and pitted windows, but they didn't have Fremen eyesight or training.

Suddenly Turok spotted a long, low mound on the distant sand, forming, growing. "Wormsign!" Using the Osbyrne direction finder by the window, he determined the exact coordinates and called them out. "The spotter craft should have signaled us five minutes ago."

"I knew it, I knew it," the captain moaned. "Damn them, they still haven't called it in!" He got on the comsystem and demanded a carryall, then broadcast to his men out on the sand. They scrambled into rover vehicles and rushed back to the uncertain refuge of the harvester.

Turok watched the sand-mound racing toward him. Shai-Hulud always came to spice operations. *Always.*

He heard a throbbing in the sky overhead, saw dust swirling around the harvester as a carryall descended. The harvester shook while the crew scrambled to make connections, locking down cables and linkage hooks.

Out on the sand, the worm raced closer, hissing through the dunes.

The harvester shuddered again, and the captain cursed over the comsystem. "This is taking too long. Get us out of here, damn you!"

"Problem with the link-up, sir," a calm voice said over the speaker. "We're disconnecting you from the hopper and taking it by cargo-sling. You're on your own."

The captain screamed at the betrayal.

Through the window, Turok saw the worm's head emerge from the sand, an ancient creature with sparkling crystal teeth and simmering flames in its gullet. The head quested one way and another as it picked up speed, a torpedo launched toward a target.

While the rest of the crew scurried about, dependent on nonfunctional rescue equipment, Turok dived into a ragged escape chute that emptied him onto the sand away from the worm. The sharp odor of freshly exposed melange burned his nostrils. He saw that his stillsuit had torn.

Struggling to his feet, Turok ran across the powdery slopes and watched the carryall lift off with the spice hopper in a sling. None of the workers had been rescued, only the spice.

Pumping his strong legs and keeping his balance on loose sand, Turok ran for his life. The other, water-fat workers would never make it.

He climbed a high dune, trying to gain distance, then stumbled along the rill. The vibrations of the monstrous harvester would mask his rhythmic footsteps for a time. He tumbled and rolled down a slipface, into the valley between dunes, then scrambled to escape the slow maelstrom as the worm circled and rose to devour its prey.

Turok heard the roar behind him, felt the crumbly ground slip. Still, he struggled in the loose sand and ran. He did not look back as the helpless spice harvester and crew fell into the cavernous gullet of Shai-Hulud. He heard the screams of men, the crunch of metal.

A hundred meters away he saw a rock formation. If he could only reach it.

🪱

BARON HARKONNEN LAY supine on a massage bed, his flabby skin hanging over the sides. Water misters sprayed his back and legs, making him sparkle like a perspiring Sumyan wrestler. Two pretty young men—dry-skinned and rangy, but the best he could find in Carthag—kneaded ointments into his shoulders.

An aide rushed in. "I'm sorry to interrupt, my Lord Baron, but we lost an entire harvester crew today. A carryall arrived in time to off-load the cargo—a full hopper—but could not rescue the men."

The Baron half sat up, feigning disappointment. "No survivors?" With a casual wave of his hand, he dismissed the aide. "Speak to no one about this."

He would order de Vries to record the loss of the machine and personnel, along with all of the spice. Naturally, the carryall crew would need to be eliminated as witnesses, and the aide who had brought him the message. Perhaps these two young men also knew too much, but they would never survive the private exercises he planned for them anyway.

He smiled to himself. People could be replaced so easily.

Peace does not equate with stability—stability is non-dynamic and never more than a hair's breadth from chaos.

— FAYKAN BUTLER, Findings of the Post-Jihad Council

Y ou will not be pleased to learn of this, my Emperor." Chamberlain Ridondo bowed stiffly while Shaddam stepped down from the dais in the small State Audience Chamber.

Does no one ever bring me good news? He fumed, thinking of all the annoying distractions that kept him from experiencing even a moment of peace.

The thin Chamberlain moved aside to let the Emperor pass, then hurried to catch up with him on the strip of red carpet. "There has been an . . . incident on Beakkal, Sire."

Though it was only early afternoon, Shaddam had terminated the rest of the day's appointments and informed the gathered lords and ambassadors that they would need to reschedule. Chamberlain Ridondo would be left with the unenviable task of rearranging the meetings of everyone involved.

"Beakkal? What do I care about that place?"

Scurrying to keep up with Shaddam's long strides, the man wiped perspiration from his high forehead. "The Atreides are involved. Duke Leto has taken us by surprise."

Elegantly attired men and women stood around the audience chamber, engaged in whispered conversation. The exotic parquet floor of facetwood and inlaid kabuzu shells gave the chamber a rich glow in the golden light of Balut crystal glowglobes. Depending on his mood, the Emperor sometimes preferred the coziness and comparative informality of this small receiving room to the Imperial Audience Chamber.

Shaddam had wrapped himself in a long scarlet-and-gold cloak studded with emeralds, soostones, and black sapphires. Beneath the lush robe, he wore a bathing suit in anticipation of the warm canals and pools beneath the Palace. He would rather be there, playing splash tag with his concubines.

As he passed a cluster of noblemen, he sighed. "What has my cousin done now? What does House Atreides have against a minor jungle world?" The Emperor stopped, stiff-backed and Imperial, while his flustered Chamberlain summarized the bold military attack on Beakkal, while a crowd of curious courtiers pressed closer.

"I believe the Duke did the right thing," said a dignified man with graying hair, Lord Bain O'Garee of Hagal. "I find it disgusting that the Prime Magistrate could allow the Tleilaxu to desecrate a memorial honoring slain heroes."

Shaddam was about to cast a withering glare on the Hagal lord when he noted murmurs of support among the other noblemen. He had underestimated the general antipathy toward the Tleilaxu, and these people were quietly cheering Leto for his boldness. *Why don't they ever cheer me when I take harsh, necessary actions?*

Another nobleman interjected. "Duke Leto has the right to respond to such an insult. It was a matter of honor." Shaddam could not remember the man's name, or even his House.

"And it was a matter of Imperial *law*," Shaddam's wife Anirul interrupted, gliding between her husband and Chamberlain Ridondo. Since the recent death of Truthsayer Lobia, Anirul had fluttered around Shaddam, as if she actually wanted to be at his side during every state function. "A man has the moral right to protect his family. Does that not include ancestors, as well?"

Some of the nobles nodded, and one man chuckled, as if Anirul had been witty. Shaddam sensed the winds of opinion. "Agreed," he said, strengthening the paternal tone in his voice. He considered how best to use this precedent for his purposes. "Beakkal's underhanded arrangement with the Bene Tleilax was clearly illegal. I wish my dear cousin Leto had gone through proper channels, but I can understand his brash actions. He is still young."

In his private thoughts, Shaddam was quick to realize how this Atreides military action could increase Leto's standing among the Great Houses. They saw the Duke as a man who dared to do what others would have been afraid to consider. Such popularity could be dangerous to the Golden Lion Throne.

He raised a ringed hand. "We will investigate this matter and issue our official opinion in due course."

Leto's actions also opened the door for Shaddam's own upcoming plans. These gathered nobles respected a swift, unwavering demonstration of justice. An intriguing precedent, indeed . . .

Anirul looked at her husband, sensing his shifting thoughts. She gave him a questioning glance, which he ignored. His smile seemed to disturb her greatly. His wife and her Bene Gesserit cronies kept too many secrets from him already, and he had every right to reciprocate.

He would call his Supreme Bashar and set his own plans in motion. The old veteran Zum Garon would know exactly how to deal with the matter, and he would appreciate a chance to show the prowess of his Sardaukar in more than just a military parade.

After all, the planet Zanovar—where the bastard Tyros Reffa lived—was not so very different from Beakkal. . . .

IN THE PRIVACY of her own apartments, Lady Anirul's sensory-pen created scratchy hieroglyphics in the air. A potted tropical plant with jet-black flowers stood beside her, exuding electric scents.

Above the desktop, Anirul's sensory-conceptual journal hovered as she wrote upon paperless pages, recording her innermost thoughts, things her husband must never discover. She scribbled in the impenetrable code language of the Bene Gesserit, the long-forgotten tongue used in the ancient *Azhar Book*.

She wrote of her sadness at the passing of Truthsayer Lobia, of the affection she had felt toward the old woman. Oh, wouldn't Mother Superior Harishka raise her eyebrows at such a naked confession of emotion! But Anirul missed her friend terribly. She had no other close companions in the Imperial Court, only insufferable sycophants who sought her favor to increase their own standing.

Lobia had been different, though. Anirul now held the old woman's memory and experiences inside of her, among the cacophony of hundreds of past generations, a forest of lives too thick to explore.

I miss you, old friend. With some embarrassment Anirul caught herself. She touched a button on the sensory-pen, watched both instrument and journal disappear like a wisp of fog into her pale blue soostone ring.

Anirul performed a series of breathing exercises. The background sounds of the Palace diminished, and she heard only her inner voice, whispering: "Mother Lobia? Can you hear me? Are you there?"

Other Memory could be unsettling at times, as if her ancestors were spying upon her from within her own skull. Though she disliked this loss of basic human privacy, usually she found their presence comforting. The conglomeration of lives formed a library-within, on the intermittent occasions when she could access it—a reservoir of wisdom and encouragement. Lobia was in there somewhere, lost among countless ghosts, just waiting to speak out.

Determined, Anirul closed her eyes and vowed to find the Truthsayer, to plunge into the clamor until she located Lobia. She went down, down . . . *deeper*.

It was like an eggshell-thin dam, waiting to be broken. She had never attempted such a radical excavation of the past-within, knowing that she risked becoming irretrievably lost in the nether realm of voices. But Anirul was the Kwisatz Mother, chosen for the secret position because she had more access to the genetic past than any living Sister. Nonetheless, this was not a journey one should risk without the support and safety net of other Sisters.

She felt a stirring, an eddy in the flow of Other Memory. *Lobia*, she called out with her mind. The turmoil intensified, as if she were approaching a roomful of noisy people. She perceived veils of swirling color in hues she had never imagined possible, filmy screens that would not permit her to enter.

Lobia! Where are you?

But instead of producing a response from a solitary voice, her agitation swelled the voices into a howling mob, screaming out warnings of disaster. It terrified her, and she had no choice but to flee.

Anirul awoke to find herself in her study again, seeing her surroundings through blurred vision. A portion of her felt as if it had remained behind, trapped deep within the collective intellect of the Bene Gesserit. She did not move a muscle as she flowed away from Other Memory, leaving their fearsome admonitions behind.

Gradually, she felt her skin tingling. When at last she could move, her vision cleared.

The voices-within sensed that something terrible and unpreventable was about to happen. Something to do with the long-awaited Kwisatz Haderach, who was only one generation away. The seed was already growing inside the womb of the unsuspecting Jessica. Other Memory warned of disaster. . . .

Anirul would rather see the Imperium itself fall before any harm came to that child.

❦

IN THE PRIVACY of her spacious chambers, the Kwisatz Mother drank spice tea and spoke in coded whispers to Reverend Mother Mohiam.

Mohiam narrowed her birdlike eyes. "Are you certain of the vision you experienced? Duke Leto Atreides is not likely to let Jessica go. Shall I journey to Caladan to protect her? His brash attack on Beakkal may have left him vulnerable to retaliation from his enemies, and Jessica might become a target. Is this what you have seen?"

"Nothing is certain in Other Memory, not even for the Kwisatz Mother." Anirul took a long, sweet sip, then set down her cup. "But you must not leave, Mohiam. You are to stay here in the Palace." Her expression became hard. "I have received word from Wallach IX. Mother Superior Harishka has chosen *you* to replace Lobia as the Emperor's Truthsayer."

If Mohiam was surprised or delighted, she let neither emotion show. Instead, she concentrated on the matter at hand. "Then how are we to keep Jessica and the baby safe?"

"I have decided that we must bring this young woman here to Kaitain for the remainder of her pregnancy. That is how we will solve the problem."

Mohiam brightened. "An excellent suggestion. We can monitor every step of the pregnancy." She smiled ironically. "Duke Leto will not like it, though."

"A *man's* wishes do not enter into this matter." Anirul sank back in her chair, heard the crinkle of the chair's velva-padded cushion. She felt enormously weary. "Jessica will give birth to her daughter here, in the Imperial Palace."

Stabilizing the present is assumed to be a form of balance, but inevitably this action turns out to be dangerous. Law and order are deadly. Trying to control the future serves only to deform it.

— KARRBEN FETHR, The Folly of Imperial Politics

Spending a day in the crowded amusement palace on Zanovar, the Docent Glax Othn had never felt so old . . . or so young. Dressed in a casual singlesuit of pale green twillcloth, he felt himself gradually begin to relax, forgetting about the mysterious threat to his ward Tyros Reffa.

He laughed with the squealing children and ate sweet confections. He played games that purportedly tested his skill, though he knew the barkers always stacked the odds in their favor. He didn't care, though it would have been nice to bring a prize back home, just as a memento. The colors and smells of this place whirled around him like a ballet for the masses, and Othn smiled.

Reffa had known exactly what the old teacher needed. He hoped the young man—who was even now on the main Taligari planet—would enjoy the suspensor opera as much as Othn was enjoying this unusual outing.

The day was long and exhausting, but stimulating. Left to his own devices, Othn would never have permitted himself such an unabashedly amusing vacation. His longtime student had taught him a valuable lesson.

Wiping sweat-dampened gray hair from his eyes, Othn looked up just as a shadow crossed the sun. Around him, the music and laughter continued. Someone screamed. He turned to see a daredevil floatdisk whisk overhead in free-form fashion, looping obstacles that stretched high into the air; the passengers held on, shrieking with mock terror.

Then more shadows darkened the sky, large and ominous. At first, the Docent did not imagine that the huge ships could be anything other than a part of the wild show.

Inside the crowded amusement park, people waited in lines for sensory-enhancement rides, mazes, holo-dances. Others tried their luck at food-vendor stands where treats could be purchased for an amusing tale or a song. Many of the people looked up. Munching the last of his crystalfruit confection, the Docent watched with curiosity instead of fear. Until the first weapons began to fire.

In the vanguard ship, Shaddam's commanding general, Supreme Bashar Garon, directed the devastating strike himself. It was his sworn duty to fire the first shot, to mark the first casualties, to draw the first blood.

An armored ornithopter swooped over the park's towering sandworm centerpiece, an articulated construction surrounded by false dunes. Explosions tore the air, weapons fire peppered the ground. Sparks accompanied flames and smoke as diaphanous structures collapsed. People screamed and ran.

The Docent's stentorian voice, made powerful by years of lecturing in halls packed with restless students, roared across the growing noise. "Shelter! Find cover!" But there was no place to hide.

Are they doing this to find Tyros Reffa?

The Supreme Bashar's Sardaukar death squad wore gray-and-black uniforms. Targeting with steely eyes, sallow-skinned Garon strafed children, melting them into unrecognizable, fused forms. It was only the beginning.

After the first shots scattered the crowds and wreaked havoc, the squadron fired on the sandworm simulacrum.

Then they used cutter beams to dismantle the gaudy center-piece into chunks of smoking metal wreckage, exposing the thick-walled melange vaults buried underneath. In accordance with Imperial orders, the advance troops had to find and retrieve the illegal spice stockpile.

Afterward, the destruction of the main cities on Zanovar could proceed.

Garon set his 'thopter down atop a pile of crisped human remains, and his soldiers streamed out, firing at anything that moved. The unarmed patrons of the amusement park ran in confusion and terror.

More Imperial gunships set down on the park grounds, disgorging soldiers who streamed into the ruins of the giant sandworm structure. The simulacrum had ostensibly been a simple amusement-park attraction that towered a hundred meters over the landscape, but the giant monument concealed underground tunnels filled with melange.

In the midst of the carnage, only one man dared approach the soldiers through the smoke and bodies, an old teacher. His face was devastated but stern, like a schoolmaster about to discipline unruly students. Zum Garon recognized the Docent Glax Othn from his premission military briefing.

Blood soaked Othn's shoulder, and the gray hair had been singed off the left side of his head. He seemed to feel no pain, only appalled anger. *So much bloodshed, just to hurt Tyros!* The Docent, who had delivered many stirring speeches during his tenure, raised his voice, "This is unconscionable!"

The Supreme Bashar, his uniform impeccably clean and unwrinkled, responded with a wry smile as knotted plumes of smoke streamed upward. Burned bodies twitched on the ground, and behind Othn a palatial structure in the amusement complex collapsed with a groan and a bang. "Teacher, you must learn the difference between theory and practice."

At a hand signal from Garon, his Sardaukar cut down the Docent before he could take another step. Dispassionately, the Supreme Bashar turned his attention back to the ruined sandworm structure to oversee the recovery operations. Surrounded by acrid fumes, he removed a private log recorder from his uniform pocket and dictated a report to Shaddam as he observed the carnage.

Immersed in the smoke and stench of the catastrophe, bands of Sardaukar loaded the gunships with contraband spice. Like swollen bumblebees, the 'thopters lumbered into the skies toward waiting transport ships. The Emperor would deliver the confiscated melange as a reward to CHOAM and the Spacing Guild. With self-righteous confidence, he would declare this the opening salvo of his "Great Spice War."

The Supreme Bashar anticipated exciting times ahead.

Operating on a tight timetable, Garon ordered his remaining ground troops to return to the large military vessels. With the recovered melange safely in hand, the rest of the annihilation could be accomplished from a distance; Garon would watch from his command chair without dirtying his hands. The squadron lifted off, oblivious to the moans of the injured, the screams of children.

The heavy battleships moved into low orbit. From there, they would finish the job of leveling the city, and then they would target a certain nearby estate.

IN REFFA'S FERN gardens, a hot breeze picked up, rippling the verdant fronds with a sound like fluttering feathers. Charence, the property administrator, switched off the fountain cascades as he walked up the slope. He had already commissioned gardeners and aquatic engineers to complete a full maintenance check of the fountain systems while his master was away on Taligari.

Meticulous in his duties, Charence took great pride in knowing that Tyros Reffa never even noticed the work he did on the estate. This was the best compliment an administrator could hope to receive. The gardens and household ran so smoothly that his master never had cause for complaint.

The Docent had assigned Charence to serve Tyros Reffa from the moment the mysterious boy had arrived on Zanovar, more than four decades ago. The loyal servant had never asked questions about the boy's parentage, or the source of his inexhaustible fortune. Charence, a focused man with plenty of responsibilities, had no time for curiosity.

As the last trickles of water drained from the fountain cascade, he stood inside the flowtree gazebo atop a flagstoned knoll. Workers in overalls carried buckets and hoses as they marched toward piping substations carefully hidden in the mushroom gardens. Charence could hear them whistling and chattering in the clear air.

He never noticed the warships overhead. The estate manager focused on the real world around him, rather than looking at the sky above. Lasgun blasts tore through the air like bolts hurled by an angry thunder god. Sonic booms of ionized air flattened the trees. Parks and lakes crackled on the horizon, vaporized into a dead plain of glass.

Eyes aching from the brilliant light, Charence looked up now, watching the myriad bolts of destruction intersect at Reffa's estate. He stood frozen, unable even to flee. He faced the storm as a locomotive of hot wind howled toward him.

Flames rolled across the landscape like red tsunamis, a stampede of white-hot incandescence that flashed the patchwork fields and forested areas into oblivion so quickly that even smoke didn't have a chance to rise.

When the shock wave passed by, it left nothing of the beautiful gardens or buildings. Not even rubble.

~

IN THE SHIMMERING city of Artesia, on the night side of the Taligari homeworld, Tyros Reffa attended the glamorous suspensor opera alone. He sat in a private box, intent

on understanding the nuances and complexities of the
show, enthralled by the color and spectacle.

All in all, he enjoyed it very much and looked forward to
sharing his experience with the Docent when he got home
to Zanovar. . . .

From a balcony, Prince Rhombur peered down into the Grand Ballroom. The preparations continued with a relentless momentum: servants, decorators, and caterers swarmed through Castle Caladan. It was like watching an army get ready for war.

Though few of his original physical systems remained, Rhombur felt anxiety in the pit of his artificial stomach. He observed unobtrusively, because if he were seen, a dozen people would assault him with endless questions about a thousand little decisions—and he had enough on his mind.

He wore a white retrotuxedo that had been fitted to cover the synthetic skin and servomechanisms that moved his replacement limbs. Despite his extensive scarring, Rhombur looked quite dashing.

Exactly as a man should, on his wedding day.

All across the gleaming floor below, servants bustled under the direction of the festival planner, an exquisitely attired off-world woman with a narrow, dark face that gave her a look of intriguing contrasts, like a Caladanian primitive vaulted into modern society. Her melodious voice cut through the clamor as she issued a steady stream of orders in formal Galach.

Servants jumped to follow her commands, setting up baskets of blossoms and sprays of colored corals, arranging ritual articles on the altar for the ceremonial priest, cleaning up spills, straightening wrinkles. Overhead, in an unobtrusive clearplaz enclosure between the beams of a curving, vaulted ceiling, a holoprojection crew set up and tested their equipment.

Immense chandeliers of the purest Balut crystal hung in tapered tiers, casting a golden glow over the congregational seating. An arrangement of exotic vine flowers climbed a pillar next to Rhombur's perch, imparting a sweet perfume of rare hibiscus violets. The aroma was a bit too strong, and with a slight twist of a control knob on a panel at his waist, he adjusted his olfactory sensor to diminish its sensitivity.

At his insistence, the Caladan ballroom looked as if it had been transported intact from the Grand Palais of Ix. It reminded him of a time when House Vernius had headed the powerful industrial world, developing innovative technology. As it would again . . .

As he stood on the high balcony, he became aware of the pumping action of his mechanical lungs, the rhythmic beating of his machine-heart. He looked at the inorganic skin on his left hand, the intricate fingerprint whorls and the naked third finger, over which Tessia would soon slip a wedding ring.

Many soldiers chose to marry their sweethearts before rushing off to war. Rhombur was about to lead the conquest of Ix and restore his family fortunes. How could he do any less than make Tessia his wife?

He flexed the thick prosthetic digits, and they did as his mind commanded, but with an ever-so-slight stiffness. Recently he had experienced dramatic improvements in his fine motor control, but he felt a slight regression today—perhaps from the stress of the occasion. He hoped he didn't do anything humiliating during the ceremony.

On a platform behind the altar, an orchestra practiced the processional from the *Ixian Wedding Concerto*, traditional music by which all Vernius noblemen had taken their marital vows. And the time-honored practice would continue, no matter how far his House had fallen from favor. The stirring music—with rhythmic, brassy sounds suggestive of large-scale industry—filled him with nostalgia and strength.

Rhombur's sister Kailea had always fantasized about such a ceremony for herself. If only she could still be here, if only things had been different and she'd made other choices. . . . Had she truly been an evil person? Rhombur wrestled with the question every day, as he dealt with the aftereffects of her misguided treachery. Despite the lingering pain, he had made up his mind to forgive her, but it was a continuing struggle.

Light flashed from above, projectors hummed, and a solido holo-form appeared in front of him. He caught his breath. It was an old animated image of his sister in a brocaded lavender dress and diamonds, when she was still a teenager . . . strikingly beautiful, with shimmering copper-dark hair. The image flickered and seemed to come alive, a smile on the generous, catlike mouth.

From the Grand Ballroom floor, the wedding coordinator gazed toward the projection and spoke into a holocom transceiver at her neck. At the coordinator's command, the image of Kailea placed its hands on its hips and the mouth moved. "What are you doing way up there? You can't hide from your own wedding. Get yourself into the dressing room for your boutonnière. Your hair looks mussed." The pretty hologram glided through open air toward the seating section, where her image would symbolically occupy one of the front-row seats.

Self-consciously, Rhombur touched his head, where manufactured hair covered the metal skullcap that protected his cranium. Chagrined, he waved to the wedding coordinator and hurried into an adjoining room, where manservants attended him.

Shortly after the Ixian fanfare sounded in the ballroom, the wedding coordinator appeared in the doorway. "This way, please, Prince Rhombur." Showing no awareness or concern because of his artificial limbs, she extended a hand. With dignified steps, she led him to a flower-decked narthex.

For the past hour, invited guests had streamed in, wearing fine clothes, pressing into the allocated seats. Uniformed members of the Atreides House Guard lined up against the stone walls, carrying purple-and-copper banners. The only conspicuous exceptions were Thufir Hawat and Gurney Halleck, who had not yet returned from their infiltration of Ix.

At the altar, Duke Leto Atreides wore a formal green jacket with a ducal chain of office hanging from his neck. Though his eyes were somber and his face was seamed with tragedy, he brightened upon seeing Rhombur. Duncan Idaho stood as Master of Arms, proudly holding the Old Duke's sword, ready to lop off the head of anyone who objected to the marriage.

Holo-relays glimmered across the ceiling, causing an image of Rhombur's father to appear beside the Prince as soon as he stepped into the aisle. Directed by transmissions from the wedding coordinator, the holographic Dominic Vernius wore a huge grin under his broad mustache, and his bald pate shone.

Momentarily overwhelmed by the sight, Rhombur swayed on his prosthetic feet and whispered, as if the holo next to him could hear him. "I have waited long enough, Father. Much too long, and I feel shame for it. My life was too comfortable before the accident that made me like this. I think differently now. Ironically, I am stronger and more decisive, better in many ways than I was before. For you, for the suffering people of Ix, and even for myself, I will retake our homeworld . . . or die in the effort."

But the holo-image, if it contained any spirit of Dominic himself, did not show it; the grin remained, as if the Ixian patriarch had not a care in the universe on his son's wedding day.

With a deep sigh of his mechanical lungs, Rhombur stepped forward into position. He was grateful to Tessia for encouraging him, for demanding that he become strong. But he no longer needed to be chided by her; as he recovered physically, reminded every day of the accident that nearly took his life, he felt more and more determined. The Tleilaxu would not get away with what they had done to his family, to his people.

Catching the gaze of Duke Leto at the altar, Rhombur realized he must look too serious for such an occasion. So, he smiled broadly, but not with the vacuous expression of the holo-Dominic beside him. Rhombur's smile was one of happiness tempered by a clear view of his place in history. This wedding day, this bond with an incredible Bene Gesserit woman, was a stepping-stone. One day, he and Tessia would occupy the Grand Palais of Ix as Earl and Lady.

Many of the guests had also dressed in Ixian finery to join the famous holo-forms filling the pews. Vivid reminders, both happy and sad. The former Ambassador to Kaitain, Cammar Pilru, was there in the flesh, though his deceased wife S'tina was present only in holo-form. Their twin sons, D'murr and C'tair, looked exactly as they had when they were growing up on Ix.

Rhombur remembered scents, sounds, expressions, voices. During rehearsal the day before, he had touched his father's hand, but had felt nothing, only static and projected electricity. *If only it could be real. . . .*

He heard a rustling behind him, and a whisper of indrawn breath from the audience. Turning, he saw Tessia gliding toward him from an arched alcove, with all the poise of a high-ranking Bene Gesserit. Vibrant and smiling, she looked like an angel in a long gown of pearlescent merh-silk, her head bowed behind an exquisite lace veil. Normally rather plain-looking, with sepia eyes and mousy brown hair, Tessia summoned an aura of self-assurance and grace today that made her thrum with an inner beauty. Everyone in the audience seemed to see in her what Rhombur had known and loved all along.

An image of Lady Shando Vernius walked beside the bride. Rhombur had not seen his mother since they'd been separated during the frantic, bloody Tleilaxu takeover of Ix. She had always expected so much from her son.

Now, the four of them came together in the center aisle, the holoprojections of Dominic and Shando on the outside, Rhombur and Tessia at the center. Behind them strutted the ceremonial priest, carrying a thick bound copy of the Orange Catholic Bible. The crowd fell into a hush. The House guards stood at attention, holding the Ixian banner high overhead. Duncan Idaho grinned, then took on a more serious expression.

Trumpets blared, and the *Ixian Wedding Concerto* resounded through the ballroom. The bride, groom, and entourage proceeded down the purple-carpeted aisle. Rhombur marched with a flawless mechanical stride, his chest puffed out in the manner of a proud nobleman.

Though space for the general audience was limited, images of the scene were transmitted across the planet, capturing every moment. The people of Caladan had always loved a spectacle.

Rhombur concentrated on moving his legs to propel himself along the purple carpet ahead of him . . . and on the loveliness of Tessia.

In the front row sat Jessica, casting occasional glances at Leto, who stood near the altar. She focused on him and narrowed her eyes, trying to determine what he was feeling. Even with her Bene Gesserit powers of observation, she had trouble penetrating Leto's closely held thoughts. Where had he learned to do that? From his father, undoubtedly. Though he was two decades in his grave, the Old Duke still exercised great influence over his son.

Reaching the altar, Rhombur and Tessia moved apart,

allowing the priest to pass between them. They then stepped together behind him, leaving the holo-forms of Dominic and Shando next to Leto, who served as best man. The wedding music ended, and the ballroom fell into an anticipatory silence.

From a golden table on the altar, the priest took two jewel-studded candlesticks and lifted them high in the air. After the priest touched a hidden sensor, a pair of candles extruded from each base and burst into flames of different hues—one purple and the other copper. As he recited the wedding invocation, he handed one set of candles to Rhombur and one to Tessia.

"We are gathered here to celebrate the union of Prince Rhombur Vernius of Ix and Sister Tessia Yasco of the Bene Gesserit." Flipping through the thick, hand-lettered Orange Catholic Bible on its pedestal in front of him, he read a number of passages, some of which had been suggested by Gurney Halleck.

Rhombur and Tessia turned and extended their candles toward each other. The colored flames merged to become an entwined fire of purple and copper. He lifted Tessia's veil to reveal her radiant, intelligent face, filled with compassion and love. Her brown hair shone with dark luster, and her wide-set eyes sparkled. Seeing his bride, he ached for her, could not believe that she had stayed with him. Rhombur felt the sting of imaginary tears his damaged body was no longer capable of producing.

Leto stepped forward, holding the rings on a crystal tray. Without breaking their loving gazes, the Prince and his bride placed wedding rings on each other's fingers. "It has been a long, hard road," he said in his synthesized voice, "for us, and for all of my people."

"I will always walk beside you, my Prince."

The triumphant, energetic recessional from the *Wedding Concerto* began, and the couple made their way back down the aisle, with Tessia's arm wrapped in Rhombur's. Leaning close, she smiled. "That wasn't so difficult, was it?"

"My artificial body is able to withstand even the most grueling of tortures."

Tessia's throaty laugh caused several members of the audience to chuckle with her, and to wonder what her whispered response was afterward.

The Ixian couple and their invited guests banqueted and danced far into the evening. On such a day, Rhombur began to believe in fresh possibilities.

But they still had heard no word from Gurney Halleck and Thufir Hawat.

ON THE MORNING after the wedding, Jessica received a message cylinder bearing the scarlet-and-gold seal of House Corrino.

A curious Leto stood beside her, rubbing his red eyes. Jessica had not counted the number of glasses of Caladan wine he had consumed the night before. "It's not often that my concubine receives a communiqué from the Imperial Court."

She cut through the seal with a fingernail and removed an Imperial scroll. Written on Corrino parchment, the message was in a Bene Gesserit cypher. Jessica tried not to show her surprise as she translated the words and relayed them to Leto. "My Duke, it is a formal summons from Lady Anirul Corrino for me to come to the Imperial Court on Kaitain. She says she is in need of a new lady-in-waiting and—" She caught her breath as she read. "My old teacher Mohiam has been appointed the Emperor's new Truthsayer. She recommended me to Lady Anirul, and she has accepted."

"Without asking me?" Leto said, anger mounting. "That seems odd . . . and capricious."

"I am subject to the commands of the Sisterhood, my Duke. You have always known this."

He scowled, surprised at himself, because he had initially been so resistant when the black-robed women had first tried to force young Jessica upon him. "I still don't like it."

"The Emperor's wife suggests that I make plans to remain there for . . . the duration of my pregnancy." Her oval face showed surprise and bafflement.

Leto took the scroll and looked at it himself, but could not read the strange symbols. "I don't understand. Have you ever even met Anirul? Why would she want you to have our baby at the Palace? Is Shaddam trying to take an Atreides hostage?"

Jessica reread the scroll, as if the answers might be hidden there. "Truly, my Duke, I do not understand."

Leto was not pleased with the summons, and felt especially troubled by a situation he could not control or understand. "Do they expect me to abandon all my duties here and just move to Kaitain with you? I am very busy."

"I . . . believe the invitation is intended for me alone, my Duke."

Startled, he looked at her. His gray eyes flashed. "But you can't just leave me. What about our child?"

"I cannot refuse this invitation, my Duke. Not only is she the Emperor's wife, but Lady Anirul is also a powerful Bene Gesserit." *And she is of Hidden Rank.*

"You Bene Gesserit always have your own reasons." The Sisters had helped Leto in the past, but he had never been able to fathom why. With a scowl, he stared at the unreadable scroll that Jessica held in her slender hands. "Is this summons from the Bene Gesserit, or is it some scheme of Shaddam's? Could this have something to do with my attack on Beakkal?"

Jessica took his hand. "I have no answers for your questions, my Duke. I only know that I will miss you terribly."

The Duke's throat tightened. Unable to speak, his only response was to pull Jessica into his arms and hold her tightly.

The fact that any family in the Imperium could deploy its atomics to destroy the planetary bases of fifty or more Great Houses need not concern us overmuch. It is a situation we can hold in check. If we remain strong enough.

—EMPEROR FONDIL III

I n light of the importance of the day's announcement, Shaddam IV had commanded that the Golden Lion Throne be moved back into the opulent Imperial Audience Chamber. Wearing a carmine robe, he sat on the heavy block of carved crystal, looking and feeling truly regal as he anticipated the reaction of the Landsraad.

After this, the unruly Houses will know they ignore me at their peril.

From behind the closed doors that led into the vast room, he could hear the murmur of impatient representatives who had been summoned here. He couldn't wait to see their faces when they learned what he had done to Zanovar.

Shaddam's pomaded red hair glistened beneath the glowglobes. He took a long drink of spice coffee from a delicate china cup, studied the fine patterns hand-painted on its surface. The precious cup would be destroyed, like everything on Zanovar. He formed his powdered face into a terrible, paternal frown. He would not smile today, no matter how pleased he felt.

Emerging from one of the secret corridors, Lady

Anirul entered the Audience Chamber, her chin held high. She walked directly toward the throne, undaunted by the magisterial decor. Shaddam muttered under his breath, cursing his lack of foresight for not closing off all entrances to the room. He would have to discuss the matter with Chamberlain Ridondo.

"My husband and Emperor." She approached the base of the dais and gazed up at the legendary throne. "Before you begin, there is a matter I must discuss with you." Anirul's bronze-brown hair was freshly coiffed and secured by a golden clasp. "Do you know the significance of this year?"

Shaddam wondered what schemes the Bene Gesserit had developed behind his back. "Why, it is 10,175. If you cannot consult an Imperial Calendar for yourself, one of my courtiers could easily have informed you of the date. Now be about your business, as I have an important announcement to make."

Anirul stood unruffled. "It is a centenary, marking the death of your father's second wife, Yvette Hagal-Corrino."

The Emperor's eyebrows shifted as he tried to follow her line of thought. *Damn her! What has this to do with my overwhelming success on Zanovar?* "If that is true, we have all year to celebrate this anniversary. Today I have a decree to announce to the Landsraad."

His meddling wife would not be swayed. "What do you know of Yvette?"

Why do women persist in matters of little import at the moment of greatest inconvenience? "I have no time for a family history quiz."

But under her steady, doe-eyed stare, he pondered for a moment, while glancing at the ornate Ixian chrono on the wall. The representatives would never expect him to begin on time anyway. "Yvette died years before I was born. Since she was not my mother, I never bothered much with her. There must be filmbooks in the Imperial Library, if you would like to learn—"

"During his long reign your father had four wives, and he

permitted only Yvette to sit beside him on a throne of her own. It is said that she was the only noblewoman he ever truly loved."

Love? What does that have to do with Imperial marriages? "Apparently, my father also had a deep affection for one of his concubines, but he didn't realize it until she decided to marry Dominic Vernius." He scowled. "Are you trying to draw comparisons? Do you want me to profess my affection for you? What sort of question are you asking?"

"It is a wife's question. It is also a husband's question." Anirul waited at the base of the dais, still looking up at him. "I want my own throne in here, beside yours, Shaddam—as your father had for his favorite wife."

The Emperor slurped half of his spice coffee to calm himself. Another throne in here? Though he'd assigned his Sardaukar spies to watch Anirul, they had not found anything incriminating yet, and probably never would. The veils of Bene Gesserit secrecy were not easily penetrated.

He weighed possibilities and options. Reminding the Landsraad that a Bene Gesserit sat by his side might be to his advantage after all, especially as he stepped up his aggressions against spice hoarders. "I shall consider it."

Anirul snapped her fingers and motioned toward an arched doorway, where two Sisters appeared from the hall shadows directing four stout male pages as they carried a throne into the audience chamber. Obviously of substantial weight, the chair was smaller than the Emperor's, but constructed of the same translucent blue-green Hagal quartz.

"Now?" The Emperor spilled spice coffee on his carmine robe as he lurched to his feet. "Anirul, I am about to conduct important business!"

"Yes—and I should be at your side. This will take only a moment." She pointed to two more pages who walked behind the throne.

Frustrated, he examined the dark stain seeping into his robe and tossed the china cup behind him, where it tinkled into shards on the checkerboard floor. Perhaps this would be the best time after all, since his announcement was sure to cause an uproar. Still, he hated to let Anirul win. . . .

Panting, the pages set the second throne on the polished stone floor with a thump, then lifted it again to carry it up the wide steps. "Not on the top platform," Shaddam said, in a voice that allowed no compromise. "Place my wife's seat on the level *below* mine, to the left." Anirul wouldn't get everything she wanted, no matter how she tried to manipulate him.

She gave him a small smile, which somehow made him feel petty. "Of course, my husband." She stepped back to scrutinize the arrangement and nodded in satisfaction. "Yvette was a Hagal, you know, and had her seat made to match Elrood's."

"We can catch up on family history later." Shaddam shouted for an attendant to bring him a fresh robe. A servant cleaned up the broken china cup, making only minimal sounds.

Gathering her skirts, Anirul sat on her new throne like an Imperial peahen settling into a nest. "I believe we are ready to entertain your visitors now." She smiled at Shaddam, but he maintained a stern countenance as he shrugged into a fresh robe, a deep blue one this time.

Shaddam nodded to Ridondo. "Let the proceedings begin."

The Chamberlain called for the frieze-plated gold doors to be swung open, on hinges that could have been used for Heighliner cargo hatches. Shaddam did his best to ignore Anirul.

Men in cloaks, robes, and formal suits streamed through the archway into the audience chamber. These invited observers represented the most powerful families in the Imperium, as well as a few lesser Houses known to hold enormous illegal melange stockpiles. As they took their positions against purple-velvet half walls, many seemed intrigued by Anirul's unexpected presence on the dais.

Shaddam spoke without rising. "Watch, and learn."

He raised a ring-bedecked hand, and the narrow armor-plaz windows around the upper ceiling became opaque. The glowglobes dimmed, and holo-images appeared in the cleared space in front of the massive crystal throne. Even Anirul had not seen the images before.

"This is all that remains of the cities of Zanovar," he said in an ominous tone.

A blackened wasteland appeared, recorded by automated Sardaukar surveillance cameras that cruised over the bubbling slag. The horrified audience gasped at images of melted structures, lumps that might have been trees, vehicles, or fused-together bodies . . . and craters that could have once been lakes. Steam rose everywhere, and fires smoldered. Twisted skeletons of buildings thrust upward like broken fingernails into a soot-smeared sky.

Shaddam had specifically asked Zum Garon to take images of the charred estate of Tyros Reffa. Seeing the devastation, he no longer had any concerns about Elrood's secret bastard son.

"Acting in accordance with long-established Imperial law, we have confiscated a large illegal melange stockpile. House Taligari is guilty of crimes against the Imperium, so their fief-holding of Zanovar has paid the ultimate price." Shaddam let the audience absorb this shocking information. He smelled the terror of the noblemen and ambassadors.

The obscure Imperial edict against stockpiling dated back thousands of years. Initially, it had applied only to the holder of the Arrakis fief, to prevent that House from embezzling spice and avoiding Imperial taxes. Later, the reasons for the edict were broadened as some noblemen became fabulously wealthy from manipulation of their hoards, starting wars or using spice to take economic and political action against other Houses. After centuries of strife surrounding this issue, all Great and Minor Houses were finally required to work cooperatively through the universal conglomerate CHOAM. Specific language was drafted into the

Imperial Code, detailing the amount of spice that any person or organization could possess.

While the images continued to play, a single bright glowglobe flickered on at the base of the Golden Lion Throne. In the pool of light an Imperial Crier read a prepared statement, so that Shaddam did not need to speak the words himself.

"Know all, that Padishah Emperor Shaddam Corrino IV will no longer tolerate illegal spice stockpiling and will enforce the Code of Imperial Law. Every House, Great and Minor, will be audited by CHOAM, in cooperation with the Spacing Guild. All outlawed spice hoards not voluntarily surrendered will be rooted out, wherever they are, and the perpetrators punished severely. Witness Zanovar. Let all be warned."

In the low illumination, Shaddam maintained his stony expression. He watched the panicked expressions on the faces of the representatives. Within hours they would race back to their homeworlds to comply, fearing his next reprisal.

Let them tremble.

As the parade of horrific images continued in the air, Anirul studied her husband. She had a closer vantage now, with no need to stand in the shadows. The Emperor had been extraordinarily tense lately, preoccupied with something more significant than his usual games of intrigue and court politics. Recently, something important had changed.

For years, Anirul had waited and observed in the patient manner of a Bene Gesserit, gathering and interpreting tidbits of information. Long ago, she had heard of Project Amal, but hadn't known what it meant—just a fragment picked up when she'd walked in on a conversation between Shaddam and Count Fenring. Upon seeing her, the men had fallen silent, and the stricken looks on their faces revealed much. She had held her silence and kept her ears open.

Finally, the remaining glowglobes brightened, and the

ion torches were lit on either side of the dais, diluting the still-playing images of blasted Zanovar. For comparison, lush and green promotional images of the planet's former beauty were projected beside the horrible devastation. Shaddam had never been a man for subtlety or restraint.

Before the audience could erupt into an uproar, two squads of Sardaukar marched forward. They stood at attention around the perimeter of the room, a chilling punctuation mark to the Emperor's startling ultimatum.

Now, he gazed dispassionately out on the assemblage, assessing the guilt or innocence he perceived in their faces. With his advisors he would study recorded images later, to see what could be learned from the reactions of these representatives.

From this moment forward, the Landsraad would fear him. No doubt he had also thrown Anirul's own plan into confusion, whatever it was. At least he hoped so. But it didn't really matter.

Even without the support of the Bene Gesserit, Shaddam would soon have his amal. Then he would need no one else.

Blood is thicker than water, but politics is even thicker than blood.

—ELROOD IX, Memoirs of Imperial Rule

Fabled Artisia, the capital of House Taligari, became a center of anguish, outrage, and demands for answers. The beloved Docent Glax Othn, who normally spoke for Taligari in matters of state, had been murdered in the blatant attack against the fief world of Zanovar. Tyros Reffa knew it—he had seen the horrific images.

Now House Taligari reeled in shock. Governmental functionaries stumbled over each other in an attempt to formulate a unified response to the outrage. Five major Zanovar cities had been obliterated, plus several surrounding estates. The open-air Senate Coliseum was a cacophony of wails, shouted questions, and declarations of vengeance.

Reffa stood unnoticed on a high tier, dressed in the same rumpled clothes he had worn for three days now, ever since learning the terrible news. His old teacher had been correct in his fears and suspicions, though Reffa had not taken them seriously. Nothing remained for him on Zanovar. While he had a few accounts and investments on Taligari, his estate, his gardens, and staff had been obliterated in a puff of steam. Just like the Docent . . .

Alarmed Taligari emissaries had gathered inside the Senate Coliseum from the eight remaining

Taligari planets. Near panic filled the air, an unruly and outraged crowd of citizens who felt helplessness and despair at the slaughter.

All eyes focused on the lead senator as he stepped to the imaging and loudspeaker podium, flanked by a pair of dour-looking representatives from other major Taligari worlds.

Because of his secret heritage, Tyros Reffa had studiously avoided any participation in politics. Still, he knew nothing would be accomplished here today. The politicians would bluster and deflect questions. In the end, formal complaints would amount to nothing. Shaddam Corrino did not care.

A tall man of commanding presence, the lead senator had a moonlike face and an expressive mouth. "Zanovar is lost," he began in the most somber of tones, his tenor voice carrying over the speaker system. He moved his hands in a variety of gestures that expanded upon his words. "Every person here has lost friends or family members in this heinous attack."

Among the Taligari people, it was traditional for gathered delegates and even common citizens to make public queries of their senators and to receive immediate answers. The people shouted, producing an overlapping drone of demands and questions.

Would the Taligarian military respond? How could they possibly hope to fight the Sardaukar, who had the power to lay waste to an entire world? Were other Taligari planets in danger?

"But why did this happen?" a man called out. "How could our Emperor commit such an atrocity?"

Reffa stood cold and speechless. *Because of me. They came because of me. The Emperor wanted to kill me, but he tried to cover it up with this monstrous excess.*

The senator lifted a message cube in the air. "Emperor Shaddam IV charges us with crimes against the Imperium and claims responsibility—claims *credit* in fact—for Zanovar. He has acted as our judge, jury, and executioner. He claims to have meted out appropriate punishment because we kept a private stockpile of melange."

Grumbles of anger, howls of disbelief. All Houses of the Landsraad maintained reservoirs of spice, just as most families retained their own stockpiles of atomics, which were forbidden to use, though not technically illegal to keep.

Another senator stepped forward. "I believe Shaddam is using us as an example for the rest of the Imperium."

"Why did my children have to die?" a tall woman shouted. "They had nothing to do with spice stockpiling."

Your children died because Shaddam does not like the fact that I was born, Reffa thought. *I got in his way, and he thought nothing of slaying millions just to kill one man. And even so, he missed the target.*

The lead senator's voice broke with emotion, then grew strong with anger. "Centuries ago the Emperor's forefather, Hyek Corrino II, granted House Taligari a holding of nine planets, including Zanovar. We have records showing that Emperor Elrood IX even visited the amusement park and joked about the smell of spice near the sandworm. It was no secret!"

Questions continued to pour in, and the senators made a gallant effort to field them. Why, after all these years, was this happening? Why had there been no warning? What could be done about the injustice now?

In the upper tier, silent during the flurry of demands, Reffa simply listened. He had come to Artisia just for the suspensor opera, had been away from Zanovar thanks to a glimmer of the old Docent's foresight. Now, having heard the tissue-thin excuses the Emperor used, he didn't believe them for a moment.

His revered teacher had always told him, "If stated reasons don't sit well with your conscience or stand the test of logic, look for deeper motivations."

He had seen scans taken by unmanned probes flying over the crisped landscape, knew that his own estate had been one of the first targets in the devastation of the planet. Had loyal old Charence even seen the flame front coming his way? Reffa's stomach burned as if he had swallowed a hot coal.

No one noticed him, just another man in the crowd. He recalled the blackened scar that remained of his home. *Shaddam probably believes he has succeeded, too. He thinks I am dead.*

Reffa stood wearing an enraged expression on his handsome, chiselfeatured face. Only once did he move, to wipe a tear from his cheek. Before the interminable public briefing reached its conclusion, he slipped out a side doorway, climbed down the sloping marble staircase, and melted into the anonymity of the city.

He had the remnants of his fortune, still a good deal of money. He had the complete freedom of movement afforded to one whom the Imperium thought dead. And now he had nothing to lose.

I am a scorpion under a rock. Now that my half brother has disturbed me, he had better beware of my sting.

Either by design or by some repellent accident of evolution, the Tleilaxu display no admirable qualities. They are abhorrent to look upon. They are generally deceptive, perhaps as part of a genetic imprint. They exude a peculiar odor, like the foul smell of disgusting, rotting food. Because I have had direct dealings with them, perhaps my analysis is not sufficiently objective. But of one fact there can be no doubt: They are extremely dangerous.

—THUFIR HAWAT, Atreides Security Commander

Inside a white capsule-car approaching the research pavilion, Hidar Fen Ajidica popped another lozenge into his mouth and chewed it. Such a vile flavor, but necessary to treat his phobia of being underground. He swallowed repeatedly to dissipate the taste, and longed for the glorious sunlight of Thalim that warmed the sacred city of Bandalong.

But as soon as he escaped here, Ajidica would have his own worlds filled with faithful, devout subjects, pursuant to the revelations he had received. His race had strayed from the sacred path, but he would put them back on it. *I am the one true Messenger of God.*

On its track, the capsule approached a wall of armor-plaz windows. Through them, he glimpsed the Sardaukar installations that provided security for the complex. Their rigorous protocols kept prying eyes away and permitted Ajidica to perform his work.

The capsule came to a stop without incident, and he took a creaking lift tube down to the main level. After decades of necessary purges, finding technicians qualified to work on complex technology had become exceedingly difficult. The Master Researcher had always preferred simpler systems, where fewer things could go wrong.

He heard the lift doors clunk shut behind him. A pale-skinned man lumbered up to the lift tube, his face smashed in, his broken body poorly reassembled onto a machine-puppet form. These bi-Ixians were one of Ajidica's own developments, a creative diversion that enabled him to utilize the bodies of executed interrogation victims. Ah, efficiency!

The horrific marionettes served to warn the restive population against rebellion. The monstrosities also performed mundane tasks: cleaning up, disposing of toxic wastes and chemicals. Unfortunately, the hybrid creatures failed to function reliably, but he kept making changes to improve them.

Ajidica passed through a bioscanner doorway that identified him by his cellular structure, then entered a room the size of a spacecraft hangar—where the new axlotl tanks were kept.

White-smocked laboratory assistants worked at instrument-laden tables. They glanced nervously at him and increased the intensity of their efforts. The air smelled metallic, scrubbed-clean with chemicals and disinfectants . . . and over it all hung a thick and distinctive cinnamon scent, reminiscent of melange.

Amal.

Coffin-sized containers held fertile women, their higher brain functions destroyed, their reflexes and senses shut down. *Axlotl tanks.* Nothing more than bloated wombs. Biological factories far more sophisticated than any machine ever built by a human hand.

Even back on their primary worlds, the Bene Tleilax grew their gholas and Face Dancers inside these "tanks." No one had ever seen a Tleilaxu woman—because none existed. Any mature female was converted into an axlotl tank, and was used to reproduce the chosen race.

For years, the Tleilaxu had quietly harvested women from the captive Ixian populace. Many thousands had died so that Ajidica could modify them to produce new substances that were biochemically similar to melange. Using the subtle language of genetics and mutations, these axlotl tanks exuded amal, and finally, ajidamal—the Master Researcher's secret of secrets.

He wrinkled his nose at the smell of the bodies, an unpleasant female odor. Tubes and wires linked each fleshy, turgid container to pulsing diagnostic instruments. He no longer saw the axlotl tanks as human; even in the beginning, they had only been *women*.

At the center of the room, two research assistants moved aside as Ajidica approached a special tank, the enhanced womb of a captured spy—the Bene Gesserit Miral Alechem. When caught attempting an act of sabotage, she had resisted divulging any information, even under severe torture. But the Master Researcher had known methods of extracting the truth before converting her to his own purposes. And, to his delight, Miral proved to have more capability as an axlotl tank than any of the Ixian stock.

After so much time, the witch's skin had taken on an orange cast. A receptacle connected to her neck contained a liter of clear liquid, her newly synthesized product. When pumped through her Bene Gesserit systems, the amal she exuded was different from that produced by any other tank. Ajidamal!

"Miral Alechem, we have a mystery. How can I adapt the other tanks to accomplish what you do?" Her flat, spiritless eyes flickered slightly, and deep within their pupils he thought he detected terror and unbridled rage. But with her vocal cords dead and her mind lost, she could not respond. Thanks to Tleilaxu technology, this womb could be forced to live for centuries. With her mind destroyed, even suicide was impossible for her.

Soon, when he and his Face Dancer minions departed from Xuttuh, Ajidica would take this valuable axlotl tank to a safe planet. Perhaps he could obtain a few more Bene Gesserit captives to see if something about them made the best tanks. For now, he had only this one, and through stimulants he had already pumped up her production levels as high as possible.

Ajidica clipped an extraction device to the receptacle and drained the liter of synthetic spice into a container, which he took with him. For several days now he had ingested a great deal of ajidamal and experienced no deleterious aftereffects, only pleasant sensations. So, he intended to take more. Much more.

Pulse racing, he hurried into his office and sealed the identity screens and defensive systems behind him. Dropping into a chairdog, he waited for the mindless, sedentary animal to conform to his body. Finally, he tilted his head back and gulped the warm, slick ajidamal, fresh from the flow of Alechem's body, like milk from a cow. He had never before consumed so much at once.

A sudden, violent fit of coughing came over him, and his stomach tried to cast out the substance in an acid upheaval. Spilling the rest of the container onto the floor, he rolled out of the twitching chairdog and doubled over. His face contorted; muscles stretched and tore. Yellow fluids poured from his mouth, vile-smelling food remnants. But his system had already absorbed the fast-acting substance.

He tumbled into euphoric convulsions that escalated until he longed for the welcome serenity of unconsciousness. Had the Bene Gesserit witch poisoned him? He clung to a furious need for revenge. With fierce Tleilaxu methods, he was sure he could make even a dreaming axlotl tank feel pain.

Countless agony-infused moments passed, until he felt a

shift in the microcosm that made up his tortured mind and body. The distress diminished, or perhaps his nerves had already been burned into cinders.

Surfacing from the nightmarish misery, Ajidica opened his eyes. He found himself on the floor of his office, with shigawire spools, filmbooks, and sample trays scattered and broken around him, as if he had flown into a mindless frenzy. The chairdog cowered in the corner, its fur ragged and pliable bones twisted and torn. The stench of his bile was overwhelming; even his body and clothes reeked. Nearby, an overturned chronometer revealed that an entire day had passed.

I should be hungry or thirsty. The stench robbed him of any such inclination, but not the rage that had kept him alive. With his long-fingered hands, he located the flat shard of a broken tray and scooped up a sample of his own vomit, which had coagulated into bead-shaped chunks.

As he hurried back onto the lab floor, Sardaukar guards and research assistants gave him a wide berth. Despite his high status, they wrinkled their noses as he passed.

He marched straight to the Miral Alechem tank, intending to hurl the bile into her face and inflict her with unimaginable indignities, though she would never know what was happening. The tank's large female eyes stared dispassionately, without focus.

With a sudden rush, new sensations and thoughts washed through his mind, an alien experience that blasted open mental blockades he had not even known existed. Vast quantities of data poured through his brain.

A side effect of the overdose of ajidamal? He saw the axlotl tanks around him in a new light. For the first time, he realized clearly that he could link every one of the tanks to the Alechem unit, so that *all* of them would produce the precious substance. With clear insight he saw how it could all fit together, and what adjustments he would need to make.

Off to one side he noticed laboratory technicians watching with their dark little eyes, whispering among themselves.

Several of them skittered away, but he shouted, "Come over here! Immediately!"

Though clearly alarmed at the bloodshot madness in his eyes, they complied. With just an assessing glance, as if each new thought were a revelation, Ajidica realized that two of these scientists would be better suited to other duties. How could he not have noticed this before? The tiniest remembered actions came to him now, petite perceptions he had been too busy to notice previously. Now it all signified something. *Amazing!*

For the first time in his life, Ajidica's eyes were completely open. His mind could now chronicle every action he'd seen, every word these men had uttered in his presence. All of the information lined up in his mind, as if he were a pre-Butlerian computer.

More data streamed into his brain through open floodgates, bits and pieces from every person Ajidica had ever met. He remembered *everything*. But how was this happening, and why? The ajidamal!

An enlightening passage from the Sufi-Buddislamic Credo came to him: *To achieve s'tori no understanding is needed. S'tori exists without words, without even a name.* It had all happened in an instant, a glimmer of cosmic time.

Ajidica no longer noticed the odor or taste of his own bile, for that was on a physical plane, and he had attained a higher state of consciousness. The large dose of artificial spice had opened untapped regions of his mind.

In a blinding new vision, he beheld the path to his own eternal salvation, by the grace of God. He was now more convinced than ever that he would lead the Bene Tleilax to holy glory—at least those worth saving. Anyone who thought differently would die.

"Master Ajidica," a tremulous voice said, "are you feeling well?"

Opening his eyes, he saw research assistants hovering around him, showing concern mixed with fear. Only one man had found the nerve to speak up. Using his heightened powers of observation, Ajidica *knew* that this was a person who could be trusted, one who would serve well in his new regime.

Rising to his feet, still holding the chunks of vomit on the shard of broken tray, Ajidica said, "You are Blin, third assistant operator of tank fifty-seven."

"That is correct, Master. Do you require medical assistance?"

"We must perform God's work," Ajidica said.

Blin bowed. "So I learned at an early age." He appeared confused, but from his body language Ajidica could tell that he wanted desperately to please his superior. With a smile that revealed sharp teeth, Ajidica said, "Hereafter you are second-in-command of my research facility, reporting only to me."

Blin's dark eyes blinked in surprise. He squared his shoulders. "I will serve in any capacity you command, sir."

Hearing a gasp of displeasure from one of the other scientists, Ajidica hurled the sample of bile at the man. "*You.* Clean my office, and replace everything that's broken. You have four hours to complete the work. If you fail, it will be Blin's first assignment to fit you with an apparatus to make you the first *male* axlotl tank."

Consumed with terror, the man hurried away.

Ajidica smiled down at Miral Alechem, a motionless hulk of repulsive naked flesh in a coffin-shaped container. Despite his enhanced abilities, he could not be certain if the Bene Gesserit spy had truly attempted to harm him, even with her buried subconscious. She did not seem aware of anything.

Now Ajidica knew that God was watching over him, a mighty presence that guided him on the path to the Great Belief—the only true path. His destiny was clear.

Despite the pain he had suffered, the overdose had been a blessing.

One can never separate politics from the economics of melange. They have walked hand in hand throughout Imperial history.

—SHADDAM CORRINO IV, *Preliminary Memoirs*

An excited spotter in Red Wall Sietch summoned Liet-Kynes to the hidden observation post high on the rugged ridge. He ascended through perilous shafts and hidden cracks, finding hand- and toeholds until he reached an exposed ledge. The air smelled like burned gunpowder.

"I see a man approaching, even in the heat of day." The spotter was a grinning boy with a weak chin and an eager smile. "Someone alone."

Intrigued, Liet followed the wiry, wide-eyed youth into the dry heat. Thermal currents shimmered from the red-and-black lava buttresses that thrust like a citadel from the dunes.

"I have summoned Stilgar as well." The spotter was full of anticipation.

"Good. Stil has the best eyes among us." Instinctively, Liet inserted plugs into his nostrils; his stillsuit was new, replacing the one the Emperor's guards had clumsily ruined.

Liet shaded his eyes from the glare of the lemon-yellow sky and stared across the undulating ocean of sand. "I am surprised Shai-Hulud hasn't taken him." He discerned a tiny speck, a moving figure that appeared no larger than an insect. " 'The lone man in the desert is a dead man.' "

"That one may be a fool, Liet, but he is not dead yet."

Turning at the voice, he saw Stilgar approaching from behind. The hawkish man knew how to move with silence and grace.

"Should we go help him? Or kill him?" The spotter's piping voice was emotionless, trying to impress these two great men. "We can take his water for the tribe."

Stilgar extended a sinewy hand, and the boy passed him an oft-repaired set of binoculars that had once belonged to Planetologist Pardot Kynes. Liet suspected the desert wanderer might be a lost member of a Harkonnen troop, an exiled villager, or some idiotic prospector.

After focusing the delicate oil lenses, Stilgar reacted with surprise. "He moves like a Fremen. Walks without pattern, his steps irregular." He increased the magnification, then lowered the binoculars. "It is Turok, and he is either injured or exhausted."

Liet reacted immediately. "Stilgar, summon a rescue party. Go save him if you can. I would rather have his story than his water."

🐛

WHEN THEY BROUGHT Turok in, his stillsuit was torn, his shoulder and right arm wounded, though the blood had coagulated. He had lost his left *temag* boot, causing the stillsuit pumps to cease functioning. Though he'd just been given water, Turok had reached the limit of human endurance. He lay back on a cool stone table, but his skin had a dusty cast, as if he had exhausted all the spare moisture that a Fremen carried.

"You walked during the *day*, Turok," Liet said. "Why would you do something so foolish?"

"No choice." Turok took another sip of the water that Stilgar offered. A little of it ran down his dusty chin, but he caught it on a forefinger and licked it. Every drop was precious. "My stillsuit no longer functioned. I knew I was close to Red Wall Sietch, but no one would have seen me after dark. I had to hope that you would come to investigate."

"You will live to fight Harkonnens again," Stilgar said.

"I did not survive merely to fight." Turok spoke with deathly fatigue. His lips were cracked and bleeding, but he refused more water. He described what had happened on the spice harvester, how Harkonnen troops had lifted off the cargo and then abandoned the crew and equipment to the sandworm.

"The spice they took will be listed as lost," Liet said, shaking his head. "Shaddam is so wrapped up with silly concerns for protocol and the garments of power that it is easy to trick him. I have seen it with my own eyes."

"For every stockpile we capture, like the one at Hadith Sietch, the Baron creates another." Stilgar looked from Turok to Liet, not liking the implication of what he was thinking. "Should we report this to Count Fenring, or send a message to the Emperor?"

"I will have nothing further to do with Kaitain, Stil." Liet didn't even write new reports; he would simply keep sending old documents that his father had written decades before. Shaddam would never notice. "This is a Fremen problem. We do not seek the help of off-worlders."

"I was hoping you would say that," Stilgar said, his eyes brightening like those of a carrion bird.

Turok accepted more water now. Faroula appeared and quietly brought the haggard man a bowl of thick, soothing herbal ointment for his sunburns. After wiping exposed areas with a damp cloth, she began to rub the cream into his skin. Liet looked at his wife fondly, watching her ministrations. Faroula was the best healer in the sietch.

She returned his glance, a confident promise of secrets to be shared later. He had fought hard to win the heart of his beautiful wife. Despite the passion they felt for one another, Fremen tradition forced a man and a woman to keep any expression of it behind the hangings of cave chambers. In public, they led almost separate lives.

"The Harkonnens are growing more aggressive—so we must unite in our resistance." Liet's mind returned to business matters. "We Fremen are a great people, scattered on the winds. Summon the sandriders to the speaking cave. I will dispatch them to other sietches to announce a grand convocation. All Naibs, elders, and fighting men will attend. In the name of my father, Umma Kynes, this will be a momentous gathering of Fremen."

He bent the fingers of one hand like a claw, and raised it high. "The Harkonnens have no idea of our combined strength. Like a desert hawk, we will dig our talons into the Baron's backside."

INSIDE THE TERMINAL building of the Carthag Spaceport, the Baron scowled and paced while preparations continued for his departure to Giedi Prime. He loathed the dry, dusty climate of Arrakis.

Pausing to catch his breath, he held on to a railing, his feet barely skimming the floor. Though by no means nimble, his suspensor belt helped the obese man maintain the impression that he was capable of doing anything he wished.

Spotlights marked the fused-sand landing field. Illumination splashed across fuel storage silos, skeletal cranes, suspensor barges, and blocky hangars constructed from prefab components—all modeled after the architecture of Harko City.

He was in a particularly foul mood this evening. His trip home had been delayed for days while he formulated a rebuttal to a notification from the Spacing Guild and CHOAM, who wanted to audit his spice-handling procedures. *Again.* He had cooperated fully with the usual audit only five months ago, and another should not have been due for at least another nineteen months. From Giedi

Prime, his lawtechs had filed a detailed letter of inquiry into the matter, which would undoubtedly delay the Guild and CHOAM, but he had a bad feeling about this. It was all tied in with the Emperor's crackdown on spice stockpiling. Things were changing, and not for the better.

As the holder of the Arrakis fief, House Harkonnen was the only Landsraad member legally entitled to any stockpiles at all, but those stocks could only be large enough to fill expected short-term demand from customers placing orders for melange, and each hoard had to be documented in periodic reports to the Emperor. It was all quite involved, and for every shipment that the Baron sent out by Heighliner, a tax was owed to House Corrino.

The customers, for their part, were only permitted to order amounts to fulfill their own short-term needs—for food additives, spice fibers, medicinal applications, and the like. For centuries, there had been no means of enforcing the prohibition against ordering too much, which led, inevitably, to hoarding. And everyone had looked the other way. Until now.

"Piter! How much longer?"

The furtive Mentat had been watching crews haul crates and supplies onto the Harkonnen frigate under the yellow-white glow. He'd appeared to be daydreaming, but the Baron knew de Vries was keeping a silent inventory, watching every object loaded aboard, ticking it off against a list inside his brain.

"I estimate another standard hour, my Baron. We have much to bring back to Giedi Prime, but these local workers are slow. If you like, I could have one tortured to increase the speed of the others."

The Baron considered the suggestion, but shook his head. "We have time before the Heighliner arrives. I will wait in the frigate lounge. The sooner I get my feet off this damned planet, the better I'll feel."

"Yes, my Baron. Shall I prepare refreshments? It helps for you to rest."

"I don't need rest," the Baron answered, more harshly than he'd intended. He disliked any implication of weakness or inability to perform his duties.

The Bene Gesserit had afflicted him with this disgusting, debilitating disease. He'd once been blessed with a perfect body, but that horse-faced Mohiam had turned it into an offensive flesh-dumpling, though it retained the sexual drive and sharp mind he'd had in his youth.

The disease itself was a closely held secret. If Shaddam ever decided the Baron was a failing leader, unable to perform the necessary functions on Arrakis, House Harkonnen would be replaced by another noble family. Thus, the Baron actively fostered the impression that his corpulence resulted from gluttony and a hedonistic lifestyle—an impression that was not difficult for him to maintain.

In fact, he decided with a smile, upon returning to Harkonnen Keep he would announce an extravagant feast there. To keep up appearances, he would encourage his guests to overindulge as much as he did.

The Baron's various physicians had suggested that he spend time in the dry desert climate, asserting that it was better for his health. But he hated Arrakis, despite the wealth he reaped from melange. He returned to Giedi Prime whenever possible, sometimes just to repair the damage his thickheaded nephew "Beast" Rabban had done while he was gone.

The workers continued their loading and the guards formed an escort cordon to the ship. Piter de Vries accompanied the Baron across the warm landing field and up the frigate ramp. On board, the Mentat prepared a tiny glass of sapho juice for himself and brought a decanter of expensive kirana brandy for his master. The Baron sat in a heavily cushioned couch, rebuilt to accommodate his bulk, and summoned the latest intelligence briefing brought by the frigate captain.

He scanned the report with a frown that deepened into

an outright scowl. Until now, the Baron had heard nothing about the outrageous Atreides attack upon Beakkal—and the surprisingly supportive Landsraad reaction. The damnable nobles had actually sympathized with Leto, even applauding his brutal retaliation. And now the Emperor had devastated Zanovar.

Things were heating up.

"These are unsettled times, my Baron, with many aggressive actions. Remember Grumman and Ecaz."

"This Duke Atreides"—the Baron raised his briefing packet, clutching it in pasty, ring-studded fingers—"has no respect for law and order. If *I* were ever to launch Harkonnen forces upon another family, Shaddam would send Sardaukar down my throat. Yet Leto gets away with murder."

"Technically, the Duke violated no laws, my Baron." De Vries paused to make detailed mental projections. "Leto is well liked among the other Houses, and he has their tacit support. Do not underestimate the Atreides popularity, which seems to grow every year. Many of the Houses look up to the Duke. They see him as a hero—"

The Baron gulped his brandy and gave a disbelieving snort. "For some unknown reason." With a grunt, he leaned back on the couch, pleased to hear the rumble of engines starting at last. The frigate rose from the glassy ground and into the blackness of night.

"*Think*, my Baron." De Vries rarely risked such a tone with him. "The death of Leto's son may have been a short-term victory for us, but now it is becoming a victory for House Atreides as well. The tragedy has generated much sympathy for the Duke. The Landsraad members will grant him leniency, and he can get away with actions no one else would dare. Beakkal is a case in point."

Irked by the success of his nemesis, the Baron blew air through his puffy lips. Outside the windows of the frigate, at the edge of orbit, he watched the atmosphere fade into starlit indigo. Exasperated, he turned back to de Vries. "But *why* do they like Leto so much, Piter? Why him, and not me? What exactly has an Atreides ever done for them?"

The Mentat furrowed his brow. "Popularity can be an important coin, if spent properly. Leto Atreides actively tries to woo the Landsraad. You, my Baron, choose to hammer your rivals into submission. You use acid instead of honey, not courting them as you could."

"It has always been difficult for me." He narrowed his spider-black eyes and swelled his chest with fresh determination. "But if Leto Atreides can do it, then by all the demons in the cosmos, I can do it as well!"

De Vries smiled. "Allow me to suggest that you consult an advisor, my Baron, perhaps even hire an etiquette instructor to reshape your actions and moods."

"I don't need a man to tell me how to hold my fork in a dainty fashion."

De Vries cut him off before his annoyance could grow. "There are many skills, my Baron. Etiquette, like politics, is a complex weaving of fine threads. It is difficult for an untrained person to keep track of them all. You are the leader of a Great House. Therefore, you must perform better than any commoner."

Baron Harkonnen remained silent as the frigate pilot guided them toward the giant Guild ship above. He finished his potent, smoky brandy. He didn't like to admit it, but knew his Mentat had spoken truly. "And where would we find such an . . . etiquette advisor?"

"I suggest obtaining one from Chusuk, which is well-known for its courtliness and manners. They make balisets, write sonnets, and are considered highly refined and cultured."

"Very well." A glint of humor flickered across the Baron's face. "And I'll want Rabban to go through the same instruction."

De Vries kept himself from smiling. "I am afraid your nephew may be beyond redemption."

"Probably. I want him to try, anyway."

"It shall be arranged, my Baron, the moment we reach Giedi Prime."

The Mentat took a sip of his sapho juice while his master poured another snifter of kirana brandy and quaffed it.

Mentats accumulate questions the way others accumulate answers.

—Mentat Teaching

W hen word came that Gurney and Thufir had at last returned from Ix and were taking a shuttle down from the Heighliner in orbit, Rhombur insisted on meeting them at the spaceport in person. He was both anxious and uneasy to hear what they had found on his once-beautiful planet.

"Be prepared for whatever news they bring, Prince," Duncan Idaho said. Immaculate in his green-and-black Atreides uniform, the young Swordmaster wore a determined expression on his round face. "They will tell us the truth."

Rhombur's expression did not flicker, but he turned his eyes toward Duncan. "I have not heard a detailed report from Ix in years, and I am eager for any news at all. It could not be worse than what I've already imagined."

The Prince walked with exaggerated care, but kept his balance and accepted no assistance. Rather than choosing more traditional honeymoon activities, his new wife Tessia had worked with him unceasingly, helping Rhombur become proficient in his cyborg body. Like an overprotective father, Dr. Yueh worried about his patient, testing functions and nerve impulse transmissions until Rhombur finally ordered the Suk doctor out of his private apartments.

Now, moving with determination and buoyed by Tessia's faith in him, Rhombur took no discouragement from the curious or pitying stares. He combated their instinctive avoidance of his freakish appearance with grins in response. His good-natured personality shamed others into accepting him.

Outside the Cala Municipal Spaceport, under skies thick with clouds, the two watched the fingernail scratch of the descending shuttle's ionization trail. As a light rain began to fall, Rhombur and Duncan drew deep breaths of the salty air, pleased to feel the dampness on their skin and hair.

The Guild shuttle aligned itself with a marked landing grid and settled into Caladan's embrace. People pushed forward to greet emerging passengers.

Dressed in the faded cloaks of down-on-their-luck merchants, Gurney Halleck and Thufir Hawat followed a line of disembarking visitors. They looked like a million others in the Imperium, but these two had defied all odds, infiltrating Ix right under the noses of the Tleilaxu. Recognizing them, Rhombur rushed forward. His hurried movements became jerky instead of smooth, but he did not care.

"Do you have information, Gurney?" Rhombur spoke in the coded Atreides battle language. "Thufir, what did you find?"

Gurney, who had experienced so much horror in the Harkonnen slave pits, looked deeply disturbed. Thufir walked on legs as stiff and leaden as Rhombur's own. The weathered Mentat took a deep breath to marshal his thoughts, choosing his words carefully. "My Lord Prince, we have witnessed much. Oh, what these eyes have seen. . . . And as a Mentat, I can never forget."

❦

LETO ATREIDES CALLED a private war counsel in one of the tower chambers. These apartments had been used by his mother Lady Helena as a personal sitting room before she'd been exiled to the Eastern Continent, but the chambers had remained unused for some time. Until now.

Servants dusted the corners and windowsills and built a roaring fire in the river-rock fireplace. Rhombur had little physical need to rest and relax, and stood waiting like a prominent piece of furniture.

Initially, Leto sat in one of his mother's embroidered cushion chairs, where she used to curl up and read daily devotions from the Orange Catholic Bible. But he thrust the chair away, selecting instead a taller wooden one. These were not comfortable times.

Thufir Hawat presented his detailed summary of what they had seen and done. As the Mentat dictated the brutal facts, his companion frequently interjected emotional comments, hammering home his revulsion and disgust.

"Sadly, my Duke," Hawat said, "we have overestimated the capabilities and accomplishments of C'tair Pilru and his supposed freedom fighters. We found little organized resistance. The Ixian people are broken. Sardaukar forces—two legions of them—and Tleilaxu spies are everywhere."

Gurney added, "They sent Face Dancers to mimic Ixians and slip into rebel cells. The resistance fighters have been massacred several times."

"We did observe widespread discontent, but no organization," Hawat continued. "However, given the proper catalyst, I project that the Ixian population will rise up and overthrow the Tleilaxu."

"Then we must provide that catalyst." Rhombur took a heavy step forward. "*Me.*"

Duncan shifted in one of the chairs, unwilling to relax. "I see tactical difficulties. The invaders have become entrenched. They won't be expecting a surprise attack after all this time, of course, but even with full Atreides military forces, it would be suicide. Especially against Sardaukar."

Gurney noted, "Why does Shaddam have Imperial soldiers inside Ix? As far as I know, it's not authorized by the Landsraad."

Leto was not convinced. "The Emperor makes his own rules. Remember Zanovar." His dark eyebrows drew together.

"We have the moral high ground, Leto," Rhombur insisted, "just like we did on Beakkal."

After having waited so long for revenge, the Prince was now filled with fire. Partly through Tessia's efforts, but more of his own volition, a new core inside him had come alive. Rhombur paced the room with precise steps, mechanical legs humming, as if his mind was so restless that it had to burn off excess energy. "I was destined to become the Earl of House Vernius, like my father before me."

He raised an arm, fist clenched, then lowered it. The servomotors and pulley musculature dramatically increased his strength. Rhombur had already demonstrated that he could crush rocks in the palm of his hand. He turned his scarred face toward the Duke, who still sat brooding in the hard chair.

"Leto, I've watched how your people view you with love, respect, and loyalty. Now, Tessia has helped me realize that for all these years I was trying to regain Ix for the wrong reasons. My heart wasn't in it, because I did not see how much it *mattered*. I was indignant at losing what was mine. I was angry at the Tleilaxu for crimes against me and my family. But what about the Ixian people? Even the poor, duped suboids who followed promises of a better life?"

"Aye, those promises led them right over a cliff," Gurney said. " 'When the shepherd is a wolf, the flock becomes only so much meat.' "

Though Rhombur stood close to the orange flames in the fireplace, he couldn't feel the heat. "I want to regain my world, not for myself, but because it's what the people of Ix *need*. If I am to be Earl Vernius, then I serve them. Not the other way around."

Hawat's memory-haunted face softened into a smile. "You have learned an important lesson, Prince."

"Yes, but putting it into practice will require considerable work," Duncan said. "Unless we have some hidden advantage or secret weapon, our military forces will be in great danger. Remember what we'll be up against."

Leto considered Rhombur's plight and acknowledged that the Vernius line would die with him, no matter what he achieved on Ix. And he felt a warm glow inside to think of Jessica's pregnancy. He himself would have another child—a son, he hoped, though she would not say. He felt a pang, knowing she would soon depart for Kaitain. . . .

The Duke had never imagined how his life would play out, how he would grow to care for Jessica after he'd first resented her presence so much. The Bene Gesserits had coerced him into keeping her here at Castle Caladan. Angered by their obvious manipulations, he had vowed never to take her as a lover . . . but he'd eventually played right into the Sisterhood's plans. They had bribed him with information about Harkonnen schemes, a new kind of battleship—

Leto sat up with a start, and a slow smile spread across his lean face. "Wait!" They all fell silent as he organized his thoughts; the only sound in the room was the crackle of the fire. "Thufir, you were present when the Bene Gesserit witches made a bargain with me to keep Jessica here."

Puzzled, Hawat tried to follow the Duke's train of thought. Then the Mentat's eyebrows raised. "They traded you information. There was an unseen ship, a vessel sporting new technology that rendered it optically invisible, even to scanners."

Leto pounded his fist on the table and leaned forward. "The prototype of that Harkonnen ship crashed on Wallach IX. The Sisters have the vessel in their possession. Wouldn't it be helpful if we could convince them to give us that technology . . . ?"

Duncan lurched to his feet. "With undetectable ships, we could infiltrate an entire force into Ix before the Sardaukar could rally to the Tleilaxu defense."

His face a mask of determination, Leto rose slowly and

said, "They owe me, by the hells! Thufir, send a message to the Mother School asking for Bene Gesserit cooperation. More than any other House, we have the right to that information, since the technology was used against us."

He looked over at Rhombur, a predatory smile cracking his stern countenance. "And then, my friend, we shall spare no effort to regain Ix."

The less we know, the longer the explanation.

— Bene Gesserit Azhar Book (renegade copy)

With a collective memory that stretched into the murky shadows of history, the ancient Mother Superior Harishka had no need for advice from her Sisters. Yet recollections from the deep past were not always applicable to the future or to the current tapestry of Imperial politics.

Harishka stood inside a stucco-walled private meeting chamber. Her most trusted advisors, well trained in subtleties and consequences, moved around the room, their robes rustling like the wings of ravens. Duke Leto's unexpected request had spurred them into a sudden and unwelcome meeting.

Acolytes brought in a selection of juices, tea, and spice coffee. The Sisters pondered, sipping beverages, but the room remained strangely silent, devoid of casual conversation. Such matters required serious contemplation.

Harishka glided to a rough stone bench and sat down. Cold and hard, it was not the sort of throne a powerful leader could have asked for, but the Bene Gesserit knew how to cope with discomfort. Her mind was sharp, her memories vivid. That was all a Mother Superior required.

The appointed Sisters settled down with a rustle of skirts. As gray-muffled sunshine filtered through the prismatic skylights, their crystal-shard eyes turned toward Harishka. It was time for the Mother Superior to speak.

"We have allowed ourselves to ignore this matter for years, and now we are forced to make a choice." She mentioned the message cylinder that had recently arrived from Caladan.

"We should not have told Leto Atreides of the no-ship's existence in the first place," said dour Reverend Mother Lanali, who managed the Mother School's map room and geographical archives.

"It was necessary," Harishka said. "He would not have accepted Jessica unless we threw him a significant bone. To his credit, the Duke has not abused the information."

"He is doing it now," said Reverend Mother Thora, who tended the orchards and was an expert in cryptography. Early in her career, she had developed a technique for implanting messages on the leaves of plants.

Harishka disagreed. "The Duke could have used the information in many ways, yet instead he chose to go through private channels, maintaining our secret. Thus far, he has not betrayed our confidence. And, I might remind you that Jessica now carries his child, as we had hoped."

"But what took her so long to get pregnant?" asked another woman. "It should have been done much sooner."

Harishka did not meet her gaze. "It makes no difference. Let us attend to the matter at hand."

"I concur," said Reverend Mother Cienna, whose heart-shaped face still bore the aura of innocent beauty that had deceived so many men in her younger years. "If anyone should be granted the power to make unseen warships, it is Duke Atreides. Like his father and grandfather before him, he is a man of impeccable credentials, a man of honor."

Lanali made a disbelieving sound. "Have you forgotten what he did on Beakkal? Wiping out the entire war memorial?"

"*His* war memorial," Cienna countered. "And he was provoked."

"Even if Duke Leto is trustworthy, what about future Atreides Dukes?" Lanali said, her words measured. "That opens up a significant unknown factor, and unknowns are dangerous."

"But there are significant *known* factors, as well," Cienna said. "You worry too much."

The youngest member of the group, slender Sister Cristane, interrupted. "This decision has nothing to do with Atreides moral character. Such a weapon, even if used for passive defense, would change the texture of warfare in the Imperium. Invisibility technology offers a huge tactical advantage to any House that possesses it. Whether you have a softness for him or not, Cienna, Leto Atreides is no more than a pawn in our master plan, as was Baron Harkonnen."

"The Harkonnens developed the terrible weapon in the first place," said Thora, finishing her spice coffee and standing to refill her cup. "Thankfully, they lost the secret and have not been able to retrieve it."

Lately, Harishka had begun to note the increasing amounts of melange the orchard-keeper consumed. Bene Gesserits could control their body chemistry, but they were strongly discouraged from extending their lifetimes beyond certain levels. Flaunting their longevity could move popular opinion against the Sisterhood.

Harishka decided to conclude this phase of the discussion. She had heard enough. "We have no choice in the matter. We must reject Leto's demand. We will send our response with Reverend Mother Mohiam when she goes to escort Jessica to Kaitain." She lifted her head. Her brain was so full of memories and free thoughts, it weighed heavily on her shoulders.

Thora let out a sigh, recalling how much work the Acolytes had done to dissect and analyze the damaged ship. "I don't know how much we could tell Duke Leto anyway. We could give him the vessel wreckage, but even *we* do not understand how the field generator works." She looked around the room, gulped more spice coffee.

Dark-haired Sister Cristane spoke up again. "Such a weapon could be catastrophic if unleashed in the Imperium. But how much more terrible if even *we* do not understand how it functions? We must learn all we can and keep the secret safely with the Sisterhood."

She had been trained as a commando to slip in and perform aggressive actions when subtler schemes failed to achieve their desired ends. Because of her youth, Cristane did not have the patience of a Reverend Mother, though at times Harishka considered such impetuousness useful.

"Absolutely correct." The Mother Superior shifted on the hard stone bench. "Certain markings on the wreckage indicate that someone named Chobyn was involved. We have since learned that an inventor by that name defected from Richese to Giedi Prime around the time this invisibility system was developed."

Thora finished her third cup of spice coffee, ignoring Harishka's disapproving frown. "The Harkonnens must have disposed of the man too soon, or they would not have had such difficulty reproducing the invisibility generator for themselves."

Harishka folded her spidery hands in her lap. "Naturally, we will begin our inquiries on Richese."

Superstition and desert necessities permeate the Fremen life, in which religion and law are intertwined.

—The Ways of Arrakis, an Imperial filmbook for children

On a day that would establish the future of his people, Liet-Kynes awoke thinking of the past. He sat at the edge of the bed he shared with Faroula, a padded mat upon the rock floor of a small but comfortable room in Red Wall Sietch.

The great Fremen convocation would begin today, a meeting of all sietch leaders to determine a unified response against the Harkonnens. Too often, the desert people had remained scattered, independent, and ineffective. They allowed clan rivalries, feuds, and distractions to come between them. Liet would have to make them understand.

His father would have been able to accomplish such a change with no more than an offhand comment. Pardot Kynes, the ecological prophet, had never understood his own power, but simply accepted it as a means to accomplish his goal of creating an Eden on Dune. His son Liet, though, was young and unproven.

Sitting on the sleeping pallet, Liet heard the low, almost imperceptible hum of machinery recirculating air in the sietch. Beside him, Faroula breathed softly, obviously awake but silent and contemplative. She liked to look at her husband with her deep blue eyes.

"My troubles have kept you from resting, my love," he said to her.

Faroula rubbed his shoulders. "Your thoughts are my thoughts, dearest. My heart feels your concern and your passion."

He kissed her hand. She rubbed her knuckles across the thin sandy beard he had grown. "Do not worry. The blood of Umma Kynes flows within you, as does his dream."

"But will the Fremen see it?"

"Our people may be foolish at times, but not blind."

Liet-Kynes had loved her for years. Faroula was a Fremen woman, the daughter of old Heinar, the sietch's one-eyed Naib. She knew her role. She was the best healer in the tribe, and her greatest work had been to heal Liet's grief-stricken soul. She knew how to touch her husband, and love him.

Still worried about the challenge of the convocation, he drew her to him and held her close on the warm sleeping pallet. But she kissed his uncertainty away, stroked his anxiety until it was gone, and imparted strength to him.

"I will be with you, my love," Faroula said, although women would not be allowed into the speaking chamber, where the Naibs of the scattered sietches gathered to hear his words. Once they left their quarters, Liet and his wife would become formal again, cultural strangers. But he understood what Faroula meant. She would indeed be with him. His heart felt glad with the knowledge.

Across the doorway hung a colorful spice-fiber tapestry, into which the women of the sietch had woven an inspiring depiction of Plaster Basin, where his father had established a bountiful greenhouse demonstration project. The tapestry showed running water, hummingbirds, fruit trees, and bright flowers. Closing his eyes, Liet imagined the ambrosia of the plants and pollens, felt damp air on his cheeks.

"I hope today I will do something to make you proud, Father," he murmured to himself, as if in prayer.

Tragically, a moisture-laden ceiling had collapsed on

Pardot and several of his assistants. Less than a year had passed since that terrible day, but to Liet it seemed much longer. He had to fill the shoes of the great visionary.

The old must always make way for the new.

Heinar, the aging Naib, might soon relinquish his leadership of Red Wall Sietch, and many Fremen assumed Liet would take his place as Naib. The Fremen word had an ancient Chakobsa meaning, "Servant of the sietch." Liet harbored no personal ambitions of any sort; he simply wanted to serve his people, fight against Harkonnens, and continue guiding the wasteland toward an eventual garden on Dune.

Liet was only half-Fremen, but from the first breaths he had taken, the first moments his heart had beaten free of his mother's womb, his soul had been Fremen. As the new Imperial Planetologist, successor to the great dreamer Pardot Kynes, Liet could not confine his work to a single tribe.

Before the last leaders arrived and the great convocation began, Liet needed to complete his daily duties as Planetologist. Though he did not value Shaddam IV as a man or an Emperor, Liet's scientific work remained a valuable part of his existence. Each moment of life was as precious as water itself, and he would not waste it.

He dressed quickly, wide-awake now. By the time dawn broke in a splash of orange across the landscape, he was outside wearing his new stillsuit. Even at such an early hour, the sand and rocks were warm, and heat devils danced over the terrain. He trudged along a rocky ridge only a few hundred meters from the sietch entrance.

In a hollow he inspected a small biological testing station, an array of sensors and data-collection devices built into the rock. Pardot Kynes had renovated the forgotten equipment years ago, and Liet's sietch members continued to maintain the raised panel of meters and control switches. The instruments measured wind velocities, temperatures, and aridity. One sensor showed an infinitesimal air-moisture reading, a trace of dew picked up by the egg-shaped collector.

Hearing a loud squeak and a frantic fluttering of wings, he turned quickly. A small desert mouse, called a muad'dib in the language of the Fremen, had been trapped by a hawk in the shiny metalplaz bowl of the solar scanner.

The little mouse tried to scramble up the slick sides of the bowl, only to be swatted back down by the swipe of a powerful talon as the hawk tried to secure its prey. The muad'dib appeared to be doomed.

Liet did not interfere. *Nature must take its course.*

To his surprise, he saw the collector begin to move as the mouse tripped a small release catch in the bowl. Its scurryings changed the angle so that reflected rays of the rising sun flashed directly into the hawk's eyes. Blinded, the bird missed with another swipe of its claw—and the desert mouse escaped into a tiny crack in the rocks.

Liet watched with amazed amusement and muttered the ancient words of a Fremen hymn that Faroula had taught him:

> *"I drove my feet through a desert*
> *Whose mirage fluttered like a ghost.*
> *Voracious for glory, greedy for danger,*
> *I roamed the horizons of al-Kulab,*
> *Watching time level the mountains*
> *In its search and its hunger for me.*
> *And I saw the sparrows swiftly approach,*
> *Bolder than the onrushing wolf.*
> *They spread in the tree of my youth.*
> *I heard the flock in my branches*
> *And was caught on their beaks and claws!"*

What was it his friend Warrick had said in agony after consuming the Water of Life? *The hawk and the mouse are the same.* A true vision, or just ravings?

As he watched the frustrated hawk fly away, rising on thermals to where it could survey the desert for any movement, Liet-Kynes wondered if the muad'dib had escaped by accident, or if it had been crafty enough to take advantage of its circumstances.

Fremen saw signs and omens everywhere. It was a common belief that the appearance of a muad'dib before making a difficult decision did not bode well. And the important meeting of sietch leaders was about to begin.

As Planetologist, though, Liet was bothered by something else. The solar scanner, installed by man, had interfered with the chain of desert life, predator and prey. While only an isolated event, Liet considered it in a much larger context, as his father would have done. Even the tiniest of human interferences, when built up over time, could lead to monumental, potentially disastrous changes.

Distressed, Liet returned to the sietch.

LEATHERY-FACED FREMEN leaders arrived from hidden settlements all across the desert. Red Wall Sietch made an ideal place for the gathering. Adjoining an extensive network of natural caves and passageways, it could easily accommodate the visitors, who brought their own water, food, and bedding.

The visitors would stay for days—weeks if necessary, until an accord could be reached. Liet would keep them here, even if he had to pound heads together to force cooperation. The desert men must coordinate their struggle, deciding on short-term targets and long-term goals. A recovered but still weakened Turok would speak to them about how the Baron was willing to sacrifice entire spice crews just to steal an unrecorded cargo of melange. Then Stilgar would describe what he and his raiders had found in the sacred caves of Hadith Sietch.

The arriving delegates had traveled great distances by sandworm, or walked in on foot; others flew at night in stolen ornithopters, which were quickly camouflaged on arrival or moved into the caves. Dressed in a new jubba cloak,

Liet-Kynes greeted each of them as they passed through the doorseal entrance into the sietch proper.

Beside him stood his dark-haired wife, with their baby daughter and the toddler Liet-chih. Worked into the silky loops of Faroula's hair were tinkling water rings, representing Liet's wealth and status in the tribe. She hovered close to him for as long as she was allowed.

Outside, the sun set in a blaze of orange, and early evening settled over the dunes. The women served the men a large communal meal in the sietch gathering chamber, traditional at the outset of such sessions. Liet sat at a low table beside Naib Heinar. In the company of the sietch leaders, Liet offered a toast in honor of the gruff old man. In response, Heinar shook his gray-haired head and declined to make a speech of his own. "No, Liet. This is your moment. Mine is past." With a hand missing two fingers from a knife duel long ago, he clasped his son-in-law's arm in a strong grip.

After dinner, as the rugged men took their places in the high-vaulted gathering chamber, Liet considered many things. He had prepared well to address this convocation— but would they choose to cooperate and resist the Harkonnens, mobilizing their desert power on Dune? Or would they flee deeper into the wastelands, each tribe fighting for itself? Worst of all, would the Fremen prefer to quarrel with each other instead of the true enemy, as they had already done too many times in the past?

Liet had a plan in mind. Finally, he stood on a high balcony overlooking the floor of the chamber. Ramallo, the old Sayyadina, stood beside him in a dusty black robe. Her dark eyes peered out of hollows in her face.

Hundreds of people stood below, hardened fighters, leaders who had risen through the ranks of their respective tribes. All shared the vision of a green Dune, all revered the memory of Umma Kynes. Additional spectators stood on benches and balconies that zigzagged up the sheer interior walls. The sour odor of unwashed desert men filled the air, along with the sharp turbulence of spice.

Sayyadina Ramallo extended her age-spotted hands in front of her face, palms turned up to say a blessing. The throng fell silent, heads bowed. On an adjacent balcony, a white-robed Fremen boy sang a traditonal lament in a lilting soprano voice, describing in ancient Chakobsa the arduous journeys of their Zensunni ancestors who had come here after fleeing Poritrin so long ago.

When the boy finished, Ramallo glided back into shadows, leaving Liet alone on the high balcony. All eyes looked at him. This was his time.

The perfect acoustics of the chamber carried Liet's voice. "My brothers, this is a time of great challenge for us. On distant Kaitain I informed the Corrino Emperor of the Harkonnen atrocities here on Dune. I told him of the destruction of the desert, of Harkonnen squads that hunt Shai-Hulud for sport."

A murmur passed through the chamber, but he had merely reminded them of what they already knew.

"In my role as Imperial Planetologist, I have requested botanists, chemists, and ecologists. I have begged for vital equipment. I have asked that a large-scale plan be enacted to preserve our world. I have demanded that he force the Harkonnens to cease their crimes and senseless destruction." He paused, letting the suspense build. "But I was dismissed summarily. Emperor Shaddam IV did not care to listen to me!"

The crowd's vocal displeasure caused the rock floor beneath Liet to tremble. Rigorously independent, the Fremen did not consider themselves true Imperial subjects. They viewed the Harkonnens as interlopers, temporary occupants who would be cast aside one day in favor of another ruling House. In time, the Fremen themselves would rule here. Their legends foretold this.

"In this great caucus we must discuss our alternatives, as

free men. We ourselves must take action to protect our way of life, regardless of the Imperium and its foolish politics."

As he spoke, searching for common ground, feeling the spark of passion within his heart, he could sense Faroula somewhere in the cool shadows nearby, listening to every word, giving him strength.

The wreckage of man's repeated attempts to control the universe is strewn along the sordid beaches of history.

—Theatre graffiti in Ichan City, Jongleur

The bright and overly decorated passenger lounge of the Wayku mass-transit ship reminded him of the surreal stage of a play, with sets that were too gaudy and colors too bright. An anonymous passenger in mid-class seating, Tyros Reffa sat alone, knowing that his life would never be the same again. The worn furniture, garish signs, and pungent refreshment drinks comforted him in an odd way, a blurring wind of distraction and white noise.

He had traveled far from Zanovar and House Taligari, far from his past.

No one noticed Reffa's name, no one cared about his destination. From the way his estate had been precisely targeted, from the Imperial spies who had scouted for him, even murderous Shaddam Corrino must believe his bastard half brother had been incinerated on Zanovar.

Why couldn't he have left me alone?

Reffa tried to block the noise of the ever-present vendors, persistent and sometimes sarcastic people in dark glasses who sold everything from spice candy to curry-fried slig. He could still hear the thrumming, atonal music that overflowed from their earclamp headsets. He ignored them utterly, and after being rebuffed for several hours, the Wayku vendors finally left him alone.

Reffa's hands were raw and chapped. He had scrubbed them repeatedly with the harshest of soaps, but still he could not get rid of the smells of death and smoke that clung to them, the gritty feel of gruesome soot beneath his fingernails.

He should never have tried to go back home. . . .

Red-eyed and weeping, he had flown his private skimmer over the blistered scar of his estate. He had broken through the restricted recovery zones, bribing officials, outrunning exhausted sentries.

Nothing remained of his beautiful, well-tended home and gardens. Nothing at all.

A few lumps of drooping stone columns, the overturned bowl of a broken fountain, but no sign of his stately manor house or beautiful fern gardens. Faithful Charence had been cremated to powder, leaving only a scarecrowish shadow on the ground, the mark of what once had been a significant human being.

Reffa had landed, stepped out onto the vile-smelling ground and been engulfed in a strangled silence. Charred stones and black glass had crunched under his boots. He bent to scoop up powder with his fingers, as if hoping he might find some hidden message in the ashes. He dug deeper, but found no living blade of grass, not even the smallest insect. Around him the world was achingly quiet, devoid of breeze and birdsong.

Tyros Reffa had never bothered anyone, content with his own pursuits, living a good life. And yet his half brother had tried to assassinate him to eliminate a perceived threat to the throne. Fourteen million people slaughtered in a bungled attempt to kill one man. It seemed impossible, even for such a monster, yet Reffa knew it was true. The Golden Lion Throne was stained with the blood of injustice, reminding Reffa of the grand soliloquy-tragedies he had once performed on Jongleur. The Imperial Palace echoed with the screams of Zanovar.

Standing under the sooty sleet on his ruined land, Reffa howled the Emperor's name, but his voice dissipated like distant thunder. . . .

And so he booked passage on the next Heighliner from Taligari to Jongleur, where in his youth he had spent happy years. He longed to be back among the student actors, the creative and passionate performers in whose company he had enjoyed peace.

Traveling unobtrusively, using false documents the Docent had long ago arranged for him in case of emergency, Reffa rode the mass-transit ship in silence. Pondering everything he had lost, he heard the ebb and flow of passenger conversations: a soostone gemologist and his wife argued about fracture patterns; four boisterous young men disagreed loudly about a recent watercourse race they had seen on Perrin XIV; a trader laughed with his rival about the humilation someone named Duke Leto Atreides had dealt to Beakkal.

Reffa wished they would all just let him contemplate what he must do. Though he had never been aggressive or violent, the scorched ruin of Zanovar had changed him. He was not experienced at seeking justice. Inside, he was in turmoil with loathing for Shaddam, and felt more than a modicum of self-hatred. *I am a Corrino, too. It is in my blood.* Heaving a deep sigh, he slumped deeper into his seat, then got up to wash his hands again. . . .

Before the brutal attack, Reffa had researched his family history, going back centuries to when the Corrinos were the model of ethics for the Imperium, to the enlightened reign of Crown Prince Raphael Corrino, as portrayed in the dramatic masterpiece, *My Father's Shadow.* Glax Othn had made Reffa into the man he was. Now, though, he had no choice, no past, no identity.

"Law is the ultimate science." This great concept of justice, first uttered long ago, echoed bitterly in his mind. It was said to be inscribed over the door to the Emperor's study on Kaitain, but he wondered if Shaddam had ever read it.

In the hands of the throne's current occupant, Imperial law shifted like quicksand. Reffa knew of mysterious deaths in his family. Shaddam's older brother Fafnir, Elrood IX himself, and even Reffa's own mother Shando, who'd been hunted down like an animal on Bela Tegeuse. He could never forget the faces of Charence, either, or the Docent, or the innocent victims of Zanovar.

He intended to rejoin his old acting troupe, under the tutelage of the brilliant taskmaster Holden Wong. But if the Emperor discovered Reffa was still alive, would all of Jongleur be at risk, too? He dared not reveal his secret.

A slight change in the Holtzmann hum told Reffa that the Heighliner had emerged from foldspace. Before long, a female Wayku voice announced their arrival and reminded passengers to purchase souvenirs.

From five overhead storage compartments, Reffa removed all of his remaining possessions. Everything. He'd had to pay dearly for the extra space, but he didn't trust direct shipment of the special items he had purchased before leaving Taligari.

Followed by a bobbing train of suspensor cases, he made his way toward the exit. Even as passengers waited in line for the descent shuttle, Wayku vendors kept trying to sell them trinkets, though without much success.

When Reffa stepped into the spaceport terminal on Jongleur, his dark mood lifted. The large facility was crowded with people full of good cheer and smiles. The atmosphere was refreshing.

He prayed he had not put another precious world at risk.

Looking around at families and friends greeting the passengers, he saw no sign of Master Holden Wong, who had promised to meet him here. Reffa's old troupe must have had a performance scheduled for that evening, and Wong always insisted on supervising everything himself. Living entirely in his world of acting, the master paid little attention to current events, probably didn't even know about the attack on Zanovar. He seemed to have forgotten to meet his guest at the dock.

No matter, Reffa knew his own way around the city. A dock adjoined the spaceport, from which a sampan water taxi carried passengers into Ichan City across a broad river dappled with a carpet of lavender algae. As the boat puttered across the slow current, Reffa stood on the deck, filling his lungs with refreshing, moist air. So different from the sour smoke and char of Zanovar.

Ahead, seen through a thin river fog, Ichan City was a jumble of ramshackle buildings and modern high-rises, crowded with rickshaws and pedestrians. From the cabin below, he heard laughter and the music of a string quartet—baliset, rebec, violin, and rebaba.

The water taxi slowed, and reversed its engines as it docked. Reffa followed other passengers onto the old city pier, a sturdy wooden structure whose planked surface was scattered with fish scales, crushed shells, and strawlike crustacean legs. Amidst seafood stands and pastry shops, merry troupes of storytellers worked alongside musicians and jugglers, providing samples of their talents and passing out invitations to evening performances.

Reffa watched a mime playing the part of a bearded god rising from the sea. Catching his eye, the mime moved closer, making oddly contorted expressions with his pasty white face. His painted grin spread even wider. "Hello, Tyros. I came to greet you after all."

Reffa recovered and said, "Holden Wong, when a mime speaks, does he impart wisdom—or reveal his folly?"

"Well said, my good friend." Wong had attained the rank of Supreme Thespian, highest of all Master Jongleurs. With protruberant cheekbones, slitted eyes, and a wispy beard, he was over eighty years old, but moved like a much younger man. He had no inkling of Reffa's parentage, or of the sudden and spiteful price placed on his head by Shaddam.

The old troupe leader put an arm around Reffa's shoulder, leaving white greasepaint marks on his clothing. "Will you attend our performance this evening? Catch up on what you have been missing all these years?"

"That, and I hope to find a place in your troupe again, Master."

Wong's deep brown eyes danced. "Ah, to have a talented actor again! For comedy? Romance?"

"I, for one, would prefer tragedy and drama. My heart is too heavy for comedy or romance."

"Ah, I am certain we shall find something for you." Wong patted Reffa on the head, this time jokingly leaving white greasepaint in his dyed black hair. "I am pleased to have you back among the Jongleurs, Tyros."

Reffa grew more serious. "I have heard you are planning a new production of *My Father's Shadow*."

"Quite so! I am just now scheduling the rehearsals for an important performance. We have not completed the casting yet, though we leave for Kaitain in a few weeks to entertain the Emperor himself!" The mime seemed delighted with his good fortune.

Reffa's eyes became intense. "I would give my soul to play the part of Raphael Corrino."

The Master Jongleur studied the younger man and detected deep fire in him. "Another actor has been selected—though he doesn't have the spark the role requires. Yes, you just might be better."

"I feel I was . . . born to play him." Reffa drew a deep breath, but he covered the smoldering expression with the skill of a master actor. "Shaddam IV has provided me with all the inspiration I need."

What can I say about Jessica? Given the opportunity, she would attempt Voice on God.

—REVEREND MOTHER GAIUS HELEN MOHIAM

It hardly seemed appropriate for a well-respected Duke and his concubine to make love in a cluttered storeroom, but time was short and Leto knew he would miss her desperately. Jessica was due to leave for Kaitain in the Heighliner that circled Caladan. She would be gone by the next morning.

Only a few steps down the corridor, cooks attended to their duties in the kitchen, banging pans, cracking mussels, chopping herbs. One of them could pop in at any moment to look for dried spices or a bag of salt. But after he and Jessica had slipped inside the cluttered room, each carrying a glass of dry claret taken during an earlier tryst in the wine cellar, Leto had blocked the door with several crates of imported bitterberry tins. He had also managed to bring the bottle with him, which he rested on a box in the corner.

Two weeks ago, after Rhombur's wedding, these unlikely liaisons had begun as a whim, an idea inspired by her imminent departure for Kaitain. Eventually, Leto wanted to make love to her in every room in the Castle, closets not included. Though pregnant, Jessica was up to the challenge, and seemed both amused and delighted.

The stately young woman set her wineglass on a

shelf, her green eyes sparkling. "Do you meet serving wenches in here, too, Leto?"

"I hardly have enough energy for you. Why would I exhaust myself further?" He moved three dusty jars of preserved lemons from the top of a large crate. "I'll need a few months alone just to regain my strength."

"I should hope so, but this must be our last time today." Jessica's tone was gentle, almost scolding. "I haven't finished packing."

"And the Emperor's wife won't be able to provide clothing for her new lady-in-waiting?"

She kissed his cheek and removed the black Atreides jacket he wore. Folding the garment carefully, she laid it down with the hawk crest showing. She then peeled his shirt off, sliding it down his shoulders to expose his chest.

"Allow me to prepare a suitable bed, my Lady." Opening the crate, Leto removed a sheet of bubbleplaz used for packing fragile items. He spread it on the floor.

"You offer all the comfort I need." Moving their wineglasses out of harm's way, she showed him that she could make do. even in a small storeroom, with nothing but bubbleplaz beneath them. . . .

As she held him afterward, Leto said, "Things would be different if I weren't a Duke. Sometimes I wish you and I could just . . ." His words trailed off.

Gazing into his gray eyes, Jessica saw his unspoken love for her, a chink in the armor of this proud, frequently aloof man. She handed him his glass of claret, took a sip of her own. "I make no demands upon you." She remembered the resentment that had gnawed at his first concubine Kailea, who had never seemed to appreciate anything he did for her.

Leto began to dress himself awkwardly. "I want to say so many things to you, Jessica. I . . . I am sorry I held a knife to your throat at our first meeting. It was only to show the Sisterhood that I could not be manipulated. I never would have used it against you."

"I know that." She kissed him on the lips. Even with the sharp edge pressed against her jugular, all those years ago, she had never felt any real threat from Leto Atreides. "Your apology is worth more than any trinket or jewel you could have given me."

Leto ran his fingers through her long bronze hair. Studying the perfection of her small nose, generous mouth, and elegant figure, he could hardly believe she was not of noble blood.

He sighed, knowing he could never marry this woman. His father had made that only too clear. *Never marry for love, boy. Think first of your House and of its position in the Imperium. Think of your people. They will rise, or fall, with you.*

Still, Jessica carried his baby, and he had promised himself that their child would bear the Atreides name and inheritance, regardless of other dynastic considerations. Another son, he hoped.

As if attuned to his thoughts, Jessica placed a finger over his lips. She understood that, with all of his pain and concerns, Leto was not ready for commitment. But it buoyed her spirit to see him struggling with his emotions—just as she did. A Bene Gesserit axiom intruded on her thoughts: *Passion clouds reason.*

She hated the constraints of such admonitions. Her teacher Mohiam, faithful and stern, had raised her under the strict guidance of the Sisterhood, sometimes doing hurtful things and inflicting harsh lessons. But for all that, Jessica still felt a pull of love for the old woman, and respect for what the Reverend Mother had achieved in her. More than anything else, Jessica did not want to disappoint Mohiam . . . but she had to be true to herself as well. She had done things for her own love, for Leto.

He stroked the soft skin of her abdomen, still flat, not yet showing the curve of pregnancy. He smiled, letting his barriers down, loving her. He allowed his hopes to show. "Before you go, Jessica, tell me . . . is it a son?"

She toyed with his dark hair but turned her face away,

wanting to be close to him but afraid she might reveal too much. "I have not allowed Dr. Yueh to perform any tests, my Duke. The Sisterhood frowns on such interference."

Leto's smoke-gray eyes were intent, and he chided her. "Come, you are a Bene Gesserit. You let yourself get pregnant after the death of Victor, and I appreciate that more than I can ever tell you." His face softened with obvious love for her, an emotion he rarely showed in front of others. She took a hesitant step toward him, wanting Leto to fold her in his arms, but he pressed for answers. "So, is it a son? You know, don't you?"

Her legs went weak, and she sat back on the crate. She flinched from his hard gaze, but she wouldn't lie to him. "I . . . cannot tell you, my Duke."

He was taken aback, the lighthearted mood gone now. "You can't tell me because you don't know the answer—or you *won't* tell me for a secret reason of your own?"

Refusing to allow herself to become distraught, Jessica gazed at him with clear green eyes. "I cannot tell you, my Duke, so please do not ask." Finding the open bottle of wine again, she poured him another glass, which he declined.

Leto turned from her, his stance rigid. "Well, I've been thinking. If it is a son, I have decided to name him Paul in honor of my father."

Primly, Jessica took a sip of her own wine. Despite the embarrassment, she hoped that a servant would interrupt them by barging into the pantry. *Why does he have to raise such matters now?* "That is your decision, my Duke. I never met Paulus Atreides, and I know him only through what you have said about him."

"My father was a great man. The people of Caladan loved him."

"I have no doubt of that." She looked away, gathering her clothes and dressing. "But he was . . . coarse. I disagree with many things your father taught you. Personally, I would prefer . . . another name."

Leto raised his aquiline nose, his pride and pain outweighing any desire for concession with her. Regardless of what he wanted, he had mastered the art of erecting fortress walls around his heart. "You forget your place."

She set her wineglass down with a heavy click that nearly broke the delicate crystal. It overbalanced on the uneven crate and spilled. Abruptly, Jessica turned to the pantry door, surprising him. "If you only knew what I've done for your love." She left, straightening her clothes.

Leto cared for her deeply, though he didn't always understand her. He followed her down the interior Castle corridors, ignoring the servants' curious stares, longing for her acceptance.

With quiet footsteps, she moved swiftly through pools of light cast by glowglobes and entered her private chamber. She knew he followed, knew he would probably grow angrier because she'd made him pursue her.

Leto stopped at the threshold of her suite, and, trembling, she whirled to confront him. At the moment she didn't want to mask her own anger, wanted to feel it and get it out. But the scars of anguish were written across his face—not simply sorrow for the tragic deaths of Victor and Kailea, but also for his slain father. It was not her place to hurt him further . . . and it was not her place, as a Bene Gesserit, to love him either.

She felt the anger drain out of her.

Leto had loved the old Duke. Paulus Atreides had taught him about politics and marriage, rigid rules that did not allow for the love between a man and a woman. His adherence to his father's teachings had turned his first concubine's devotion into murderous treachery.

But Leto had also watched his father gored to death by a drug-maddened Salusan bull and been forced to become Duke Atreides at a young age. Was it so wrong that he wanted to name his new son after Paulus? She was leaving tomorrow for Kaitain, and she might not see him for months. Indeed, as a Bene Gesserit Sister, there would be no guarantee that she would ever be allowed to return to Caladan. Especially when they discovered the sex of the baby she carried, in defiance of their commands.

I will not leave him like this.

Before the Duke could speak at the doorway, she said, "Yes, Leto. If the child is a boy, Paul will be his name. We need argue no more about it."

❦

EARLY THE FOLLOWING morning, at the hour when fishing boats departed from the Cala City docks to ply channels through distant kelp beds, Jessica awaited the time of her departure.

Just down the corridor, she heard angry words coming from the Duke's private study. The door stood ajar, and the black-robed Gaius Helen Mohiam sat in a high-backed chair just inside the room. She recognized the woman's voice from years spent under her tutelage at the Mother School.

"The Sisterhood has made the only possible decision, Duke Atreides," Mohiam said. "We do not understand the ship or the process ourselves, and we have no intention of providing clues to any other noble family—not even House Atreides. With respect, sir, your request is denied."

Jessica inched closer. Others were in the study with them. She identified the voices of Thufir Hawat, Duncan Idaho, and Gurney Halleck.

Gurney roared, "What's to prevent the Harkonnens from using it on us again?"

"They cannot reproduce the weapon, so the inventor must be unavailable—probably dead."

"The Bene Gesserit brought this to our attention, Reverend Mother," Leto barked. "You, personally, told me of the Harkonnen plot against me. For years I have put aside my pride, not using the information to clear my name—but now my purpose is more important. Do you doubt my ability to use the weapon in a sensible manner?"

"Your good name stands without question. My Sisters know this. Nonetheless, we have decided that such technology is too dangerous for any one man—or House—to hold."

She heard a crash in the study, and Leto spoke in a loud, angry voice: "You're taking my Lady, too. One affront after another. I insist that my man here, Gurney Halleck, accompany Jessica as bodyguard. For her own protection. I dare not risk her."

Mohiam sounded exceedingly rational. *A hint of Voice?* "The Emperor has promised safe passage to Kaitain and protection in the Palace. Fear not, your concubine will be well cared for. The rest is out of your hands." She rose to her feet, as if to indicate the conclusion of the meeting.

"Jessica will soon be the mother of my child," Leto said, his words carrying a deadly edge. "See that she is kept safe—or I will hold you personally responsible, Reverend Mother."

Her heart soaring at these words, Jessica saw Mohiam make a subtle body movement, shifting to a barely detectable fighting stance. "The Sisterhood is capable of protecting the girl better than any former smuggler can."

Boldly, Jessica stepped into the room, interrupting the escalating tensions. "Reverend Mother, I am ready to depart for Kaitain, if you will allow me to say my farewells to the Duke."

The men in the room hesitated, startled into an uncomfortable silence. Mohiam looked at her, making it clear that she had known Jessica was eavesdropping all along. "Yes, child, it is time."

❧

WATCHING THE DWINDLING glow from the shuttle engines, Duke Leto Atreides stood in the spaceport below, surrounded by Gurney, Thufir, Rhombur, and Duncan . . .

four men who would have given their lives for him, if he asked it.

He felt empty and alone, and thought of all the things he wished he'd had the courage to say to Jessica. But he had lost his chance, and would regret it until they were in each other's arms again.

*One cannot hide from history . . . or from human
nature.*

—Bene Gesserit Azhar Book

The ancient rock quarry was a deep bowl with
high cliff walls of chopped stone. In centuries past, blocks of variegated marble had been
removed to build new structures for the Mother
School.

Stern and professional, Sister Cristane led the
three Richesian inventors to the bottom of the
quarry. Her dark hair cropped short, her face showing more angles than feminine softness, she did
not appear to notice the cold breezes as she took
the trio of off-world scientists into a suspensorpod
that dropped like a diving bell past colored bands
of mineral impurities.

The inventors were a mixed batch. One was
boisterous and political, having achieved success
through writing excellent reports as opposed to doing superb research. His two companions were quieter and more self-absorbed, but their flashes of
inspiration had produced technological wild cards
that brought in a great deal of money for Richese.

It had taken the Sisterhood weeks to track
them down, to concoct an appropriate excuse to
bring them here. Ostensibly, these three men had
been summoned to discuss retooling the Mother
School's power systems, to develop direct satellite
links that would not interfere with the defensive

screens surrounding Wallach IX. The Richesian government had been eager to offer their creative skills to the powerful Bene Gesserit.

The pretext had succeeded. In actuality, Harishka had requested these specific inventors because of their connections to the vanished Chobyn. They might have access to the records of his work, or know something important about what he had done.

"We have traveled far from the main complex," said the meek inventor named Haloa Rund. Looking around as the suspensorpod descended, Rund noted the isolation of the quarry. It held few buildings and no noticeable rock-working technology. "What power requirements could you possibly have so far from your main complex?"

Having once studied at the Mentat School and failed, Rund still prided himself on his analytical mind. He was also a nephew of Count Ilban Richese, and had used his family connections to receive funding for eccentric projects that would have been denied to anyone else. His uncle doted on all of his own relatives.

"Mother Superior is waiting below," Cristane answered, as if that would dispel any doubts. "And we have a problem for you to solve."

Earlier, around the Mother School, Rund's two associates had been enamored with the scenery, the orchards, and the stucco buildings with terra-cotta tile roofs. Few men were ever allowed to visit Wallach IX, and they drank in all the details like tourists, happy to go wherever the Sisters wanted to take them.

The suspensorpod reached the bottom of the quarry, where the men emerged and looked around. The razor breezes were sharp and cold. Rock cliffs rose in a stairstep formation above them, like an enclosed stadium.

The wreckage of the strange vessel lay covered with electrotarps, with its hull still visible under the slanting light. Mother Superior Harishka and several black-robed companions stood next to the ship. The Richesian inventors came forward, intrigued.

"What is this? A small scout fighter?" Talis Balt was a bald, bookish man who could do even complex equations in his head. "I was given to understand the Sisterhood had no overt military capability. Why would you own—"

"This is not ours," Cristane replied. "We were attacked, but managed to destroy the vessel. It appears to have been equipped with a new form of defensive screen that makes it invisible to human eyes or scanning devices."

"Impossible," said Flinto Kinnis, the bureaucrat of the group. Though only a mid-level scientist, he had supervised highly successful technological teams.

"Nothing is impossible, Director," Haloa Rund countered, his voice stern. "The first step in innovation is to know that a thing *can* be created. After that, the rest is a matter of detail."

Reverend Mother Cienna touched a transmitter to remove a corner of the electrotarp, revealing the scratched and scarred fuselage of a small warship. "We have reason to believe this technology was developed by a Richesian named Tenu Chobyn, a person of your acquaintance. The Bene Gesserit must learn whether any of you have additional information on his operations."

Haloa Rund and Talis Balt moved toward the wreckage, fascinated by the techno-mystery. Flinto Kinnis, though, remained suspicious. "Chobyn defected from our orbital laboratory facility on Korona. He left in disgrace and took proprietary information with him. Why not ask the man yourself?"

"We believe he is dead," Cristane said simply.

Kinnis looked startled, his obvious displeasure at Chobyn's betrayal melting into confusion.

Haloa Rund turned to face the Mother Superior squarely. "Surely, this must be a dangerous secret. Why are you showing it to us?" He frowned, intrigued by the idea of advanced technological details he might glean from the wreckage, but feeling his skin crawl with uneasiness. They were far from any witnesses, and the Sisters were unpredictable. But Rund was the nephew of Count Richese, and his trip here was known. The Bene Gesserit wouldn't dare harm him or his companions . . . he hoped.

Harishka cut him off with a snap, using the full power of Voice. *"Answer our questions."*

The inventors stopped, as if stunned.

Reverend Mother Lanali spoke next, also using the implacable Voice, her heart-shaped face now looking like a storm. "You were friends of Chobyn. Tell us what you know of this invention. How do we re-create it?"

Cienna lifted the rest of the electrotarp, exposing the broken hulk. Working as a team, the clustered Reverend Mothers interrogated the Richesians in the Bene Gesserit Way, a technique that enabled them to detect minutiae. They observed the slightest flickers of doubt, untruth, or exaggeration.

Under the cold sky of Wallach IX, shielded by cliff walls, the Sisters hammered the three helpless men with every possible question in every conceivable manner, a relentless, rapid-fire debriefing to determine if enough evidence existed to reconstruct Chobyn's secret technology. They had to know.

Though the group of Richesians did not doubt the Sisters' claims about the crashed ship's capabilities, it became clear that their former comrade had been a rogue who had done the work by himself, presumably under the auspices of House Harkonnen. Chobyn had consulted with none of his colleagues, had left no known records.

"Very well then," Harishka said. "The secret is safe. It will fade and die."

Though paralyzed and unable to resist, the captive inventors still exhibited signs of dread that the witches would torture them to death in some unspeakable fashion. Cristane herself might have advocated such a solution.

Yet, if all three of these men disappeared or suffered a

too-convenient shuttle accident, Premier Ein Calimar and old Count Ilban Richese would ask too many questions. The Bene Gesserit could not afford to raise suspicion.

On the gravel, the Sisters, their faces pinched and ominous, gathered around the Richesians. The black robes of the women made them look like birds of prey.

Presently, the Bene Gesserit began to speak, lifting their whispers on the trails of the others.

"You will forget."

"You will not question."

"You will not remember."

Under controlled circumstances, trained Sisters could perform this "resonating hypnosis" to implant false memories and alter sensory perceptions. They had taken similar measures against Baron Harkonnen when he'd come to the Mother School in a fit of vengeful rage.

Cristane assisted in the chant, focusing her mental powers with those of the Reverend Mothers. Working together, they carefully crafted a new tapestry of memories, a story that Haloa Rund and his two comrades would report back to their superiors.

The three men would remember only an uninteresting conference on Wallach IX, a casual discussion of half-made plans for upgrades to the Mother School. Nothing whatsoever would come of it. The Sisters weren't particularly interested. No one would press the issue further.

The Bene Gesserit had learned all they needed to know.

The Etiquette Advisor from Chusuk took one look around the blocky Harkonnen Keep, and said with a heavy sigh, "I don't suppose we have time to do any redecorating?"

Piter de Vries ushered the rangy, foppish man into the Hall of Mirrors, where he introduced him to the Baron and Beast Rabban. "Mephistis Cru comes highly recommended from the Chusuk Academy, having trained the daughters and sons of many noble houses."

Accompanied by an army of distorted reflections in the mirrors, Cru moved as if he were a ballet dancer. His shoulder-length brown hair was frothed into lush curls that draped over a billowing robe (presumably the height of fashion on some distant world). His pantaloons were made of a shimmering fabric etched with subtle floral patterns. Cru's skin was delicately powdered, and too heavily perfumed for even the Baron's tastes.

With a gracious bow, the exceedingly proper man paused at the foot of the Baron's immense chair. "I thank you for your confidence in me, sir." The man's voice was like wet silk. Cru's full lips and even his eyes smiled, as if he imagined the Imperium could be a bright and sparkling place, if only everyone behaved with sufficient decorum. "I've read all the commentaries about you, and I agree that you simply must retool your image."

The Baron, seated in a griffin-footed chair, already regretted listening to the advice of his Mentat. Rabban stood off to one side, glowering. Two-year-old Feyd-Rautha took a few toddling steps and slipped on the polished marble floor. Landing hard on his rump, he began to cry.

Cru inhaled a deep breath. "I believe I am up to the challenge of portraying you as likable and honorable."

"You'd better be," Rabban said. "We've already sent out the invitations for a banquet."

The etiquette advisor reacted with alarm. "How much time do we have? You should have consulted with me first."

"I am not required to confer with you on any decisions I make." The Baron's voice was as hard as Arrakis rock.

Instead of being cowed by the dangerous man's simmering anger, Cru responded pedantically, "There, you see! Your sharp tone of voice, the furious expression on your face." He jabbed out with a long, pale finger. "Such things are bound to put off your peers."

"You are not one of his peers," Rabban growled.

The etiquette advisor continued as if he had not heard the remark. "Far, far better to phrase your response with sincerity and genuine apology. For instance, 'I'm so sorry I did not have the forethought to look at the problem from your point of view. However, I made the decision that I thought best. Perhaps if we work together, we might come up with a solution that is to our mutual benefit.'" Cru extended his soft hands theatrically, as if expecting applause from an audience. "Do you see how much more effective that can be?"

The Harkonnen nobleman did not agree at all, and was about to say so when the Mentat interceded. "My Baron, you agreed that this would be an *experiment*. You can always revert to your old ways later if this doesn't work."

Noting an uncomfortable nod from the fat man, Mephistis Cru began to pace back and forth, preoccupied with plans. "Relax, relax. I'm sure we'll still have enough time. We'll do what we can. None of us is perfect." He looked up at the Harkonnen patriarch and smiled again. "Let us see what a difference we can make, even under these challenging circumstances."

INSIDE THE TOWER solarium, the Baron stood supported by his suspensor belt while Mephistis Cru began the first lesson. Smoky afternoon sunlight passed through grease-smudged windows, illuminating the broad floor of what had once been an exercise room, back in the Baron's lean and healthy days.

The etiquette advisor walked around him, touching the Baron's sleeves, poking at the black-and-purple fabric lines. "Relax, please." He frowned at the large, soft bulk. "Form-fitting clothes are not for you, my Lord. I suggest billowing garments, loose robes. A magisterial cape would make you look absolutely . . . awe-inspiring."

De Vries stepped forward. "We shall have the tailors create new clothes immediately."

Next, Mephistis Cru studied the barrel-chested Rabban, with his fur-trimmed leather vest, iron-shod boots and wide belt holding his inkvine whip. Rabban's rakish hair was tousled. Cru's face barely covered an expression of dismay, but he forced himself to turn back to the Baron. "Well, let's concentrate on *you* first."

Remembering a detail, the foppish man snapped his fingers at de Vries. "Please acquire the guest list for the banquet. I intend to study backgrounds and develop specific compliments the Baron can use to gain their good graces."

"Compliments?" Rabban swallowed a guffaw as the Baron glared at him.

One of Cru's skills seemed to be an ability to ignore insults. He brought out a calibrated stick as long as his forearm and began to mark the Baron's measurements. "Relax, relax. I am as excited about this banquet as you must be. We will select only the very, very best wines—"

"Not from Caladan," Rabban interjected, and the Baron agreed.

Cru pressed his lips together for just a moment. "The *second*-best wines, then. We will commission the finest music and the most exquisite dining these lords have ever experienced. And entertainment, we must decide upon the most personally beneficial form of amusement."

"We already have a gladiatorial event scheduled," the Baron said. "It is our tradition here on Giedi Prime."

The advisor's expression melted into a look of horror. "Absolutely not, my Baron. I must insist. No gladiatorial contests. Bloodshed will foster entirely the wrong impression. We want the Landsraad to *like* you."

Rabban already looked as if he wanted to break Cru over his knee like kindling. De Vries reminded them quietly, "An experiment, my Baron."

For several uncomfortable hours, the etiquette advisor strutted around the room, rejoicing in the numerous details he had to resolve. He instructed the Baron on how to eat. He demonstrated the proper method for grasping silverware, holding it at the proper level with the elbows off the table. Cru used his measuring stick to rap the Baron's knuckles whenever he made a mistake.

Later that afternoon in the exercise room, de Vries brought in Feyd-Rautha, who squirmed and fussed. At first, Cru was delighted to see the child. "We must work hard to bring the boy up properly, as befits his station. Refined manners will reflect his noble breeding."

The Baron scowled, remembering his weakling half brother Abulurd, the child's father. "We are attempting to overcome the deficiency of Feyd's breeding."

Next, Cru insisted on watching the Baron walk. He made the big man go from one end of the solarium to the other, back and forth, studying every dainty suspensor-assisted step, making suggestions. Finally, he tapped a long finger against his lips, pondering. "Not bad. We can work with that."

Cru turned to Rabban, his face hard like a stern schoolmaster's. "But *you* need to learn the basics. We must teach you to walk with grace." His voice lilted as he spoke. "Glide through life, with each step but a gentle intrusion through the air around you. You must stop *lumbering*. It is essential not to project the appearance of an oaf."

Rabban looked ready to explode. The etiquette advisor walked over to a small case he had brought with him. Withdrawing two gelatinous balls, he held them gently in his palms, like soap bubbles. One sphere was red, the other a deep green.

"Stand still, my Lord." He balanced one ball on each of Rabban's broad shoulders, where they hovered in precarious equilibrium. "Simple stinkball toys from Chusuk. Children use them for pranks, but they are also highly effective teaching tools. They break very easily—and believe me, you *don't* want them to do that."

With an arrogant sniff, filling his lungs with the perfumes that floated around his clothes, Cru said, "Allow me to demonstrate. Simply walk across the room. Use whatever grace you can manage, but take gentle steps so as not to dislodge the stinkballs."

The Baron said, "Do what the man suggests, Rabban. It's an experiment."

The Beast strode across the floor with his usual plodding gait. He had not crossed half the distance before he dislodged the red sphere, which rolled off and burst on his leather vest. Startled by the movement, he jerked backward and lost the green stinkball, which splattered at his feet. Both spheres exuded brownish-yellow vapors that surrounded him with their foul stench.

The etiquette advisor began to chuckle. "So . . . my point is well taken?"

Cru didn't have time to take another breath before

Rabban was upon him, locking his viselike grip around the man's white-skinned throat. He squeezed the windpipe with uncontrolled fury, much as he had strangled his own father.

The foppish man squawked and struggled, but he was no match for the Beast. The Baron allowed the scuffle to go on for a few seconds, but he did not intend to grant the etiquette advisor such a quick and simple death. Finally, de Vries delivered two precise, numbing chops with the side of his hand, stunning Rabban enough that he could pull the choking, rangy man away.

Rabban's face was purple with anger, and the stink around him made the Baron cough. "Out of here, Nephew!" Feyd-Rautha had begun to cry. "And take your little brother with you." The Baron shook his head, making his jowls jiggle. "This man is right about you. You *are* an oaf. I'll thank you not to appear at the banquet."

His fists clenching and unclenching, Rabban was clearly incensed, until the Baron added, "I want you to use listening devices to spy on our guests' conversations. You'll probably have a more entertaining time than I will."

Rabban permitted himself a smug smile when he realized he would endure no further miserable etiquette training. He grabbed the child, who was wailing loudly because of the stench around his burly older brother.

The Mentat assisted Mephistis Cru as he picked himself up from the floor, his face mottled, red marks already showing on his slender throat. "I'll . . . I'll see to the menu now, my Lord Baron." With uncertain steps, in a dazed shock, the half-strangled advisor stumbled out of the solarium through a side door.

The Baron glared at Piter de Vries, causing the Mentat to shrink back. "Patience, my Baron. It's clear we still have a long way to go."

Power is the most unstable of all human achievements. Faith and power are mutually exclusive.

—Bene Gesserit Axiom

Carrying a large black bag, Hidar Fen Ajidica walked briskly past two Sardaukar guards in the underground city. The Imperial soldiers stood at attention and hardly blinked when the Master Researcher went by, as if he was beneath their notice.

Now that he had learned how to dramatically increase ajidamal production, Ajidica regularly consumed large doses of the synthetic spice; he existed in a pleasurable sense of hyperconsciousness. His intuition was sharper than ever before. The drug exceeded all expectations. Ajidamal was not only a substitute for melange; it was *better* than melange.

With his increased awareness, Ajidica noticed a tiny reptile crawling on the rough rock wall. *Draco volans*, one of the "flying dragon" lizards that had moved down from the rugged surface after the Tleilaxu takeover. With a flicker of dull, scaly skin it skittered out of sight.

Ants, beetles, and cockroaches had also found their way into the subterranean realm. He had instituted a number of eradication procedures to keep the vermin out of his antiseptic laboratories, but to no avail.

Filled with enthusiasm, Ajidica passed through

the pale orange light of a bioscanner and continued into the Sardaukar Officers' core of the military base. Without knocking, he strutted into the innermost office and dropped onto a small chairdog, holding the bag on his lap. After an uncharacteristic whine of protest, the sedentary animal conformed to the Master Researcher's body. Ajidica's eyelids slitted half-closed as a fresh burst of drug pleasure infused his brain.

A large man in a gray-and-black uniform looked up from the midday meal he'd been eating at his desk. Commander Cando Garon—son of the Emperor's Supreme Bashar Zum Garon—frequently dined alone. Though not yet forty years of age, Cando looked older than that, his brown hair frosted gray at the temples. His skin had a pale cast from spending so many years down in the caverns after being assigned here by the Emperor. The younger Garon's prominent but secret role guarding the experiments made his esteemed father proud.

The commander gave Ajidica an appraising look, spooned a gooey forkful of pundi rice and meat from packaged Sardaukar rations into his mouth. "You asked to see me, Master Researcher? Is there a problem my men must address?"

"No problems, Commander. Actually, I come to offer a reward." The little man squirmed out of the reluctant chairdog and set his satchel on the desk. "Your men have done an exemplary job here, and our long labors have finally come to fruition." The compliments tasted strange in Ajidica's mouth. "I will send a commendation directly to your father, the Supreme Bashar. In the meantime, however, the Emperor has allowed me to offer you a small reward."

Removing a sealed packet from the bag, Garon looked at it as if it might explode in his face. He sniffed, detected an unmistakable cinnamon scent. "Melange?" Garon removed several packets from the satchel. "This is far too much for my personal use."

"Enough to share among your men, perhaps? If you wish, I will see that you and your Sardaukar have as much as you need."

He met the steady gaze of Ajidica. "Are you bribing me, sir?"

"I ask nothing in return, Commander. You know our mission here, to serve the Emperor's plans." Ajidica smiled. "This substance comes from our laboratories, not Arrakis. We *manufactured* it, converted the liquid essence into solid form. Our axlotl tanks are currently operating at peak production. Soon, spice will flow freely . . . for anyone who deserves it. Not just for the Guild, or CHOAM, or the fabulously wealthy."

Ajidica snatched one of the packets himself, tore it open, and gobbled the sample. "There, to prove the substance is pure."

"I never doubted you, sir." Commander Garon opened one of the samples and sniffed cautiously at the cakey material processed from the original liquid distillate. He touched a bit of it to his tongue, then ate more. A tingle suffused his nerves, and his pale skin flushed. He clearly wanted more, but he restrained himself. "After it is tested thoroughly, I will see that this is equitably distributed among my men."

As Ajidica departed from the Officers' complex, satisfied, he wondered if this young Sardaukar commander might be of some use to him in his new regime. It was radical to trust an infidel outsider, a *powindah*. Still, Ajidica rather liked the no-nonsense soldier—provided he could be controlled. *Control.* The artificial spice might allow him to accomplish exactly that.

Content with his grand visions, Ajidica stepped into a capsule-car. Soon, he would escape to a promised world where he could grow strong, if only he could keep the Emperor and his dog Fenring at bay long enough.

Inevitably, he would have to fight the deposed Shaddam,

and the Tleilaxu corruptors who had distorted the Great Belief. For such vital challenges, Ajidica would need his own holy warriors, in addition to loyal Face Dancer servants and spies. Yes, these legions of Imperial Sardaukar could prove necessary . . . once he addicted them.

Among sentient creatures, only humans continually strive for what they know is beyond reach. Despite repeated failures they continue to try. This trait results in high achievement for some members of the species, but for others, for those who do not attain what they want, it can lead to serious trouble.

—Findings of Bene Gesserit Commission,
What Does It Mean to Be Human?

Jessica had never seen a grander residence than the Imperial Palace, the city-sized home of the Emperor of a Million Worlds. She would remain here for months, at the side of the Lady Anirul Corrino, ostensibly as a new lady-in-waiting . . . though she suspected the Bene Gesserit had other plans in mind.

Generations of the Imperial family had accumulated the material wonders of the universe and commissioned the intricate designs of the greatest craftsmen and builders. The result was a faery realm in physical form, a single sprawling building with gables, soaring rooflines, and jeweled spires that stretched toward the stars. Not even Balut's fabulous Crystal Chateau could approach such a level of ostentation. A previous Emperor, arrogant in his agnosticism, claimed that God Himself could not have resided in a more pleasing abode.

Standing here in awe, Jessica was inclined to agree. In the company of Reverend Mother

Mohiam, she worked harder than usual to control her emotions.

Dressed in conservative robes, she and Mohiam entered a sweeping parlor whose walls were sheets of priceless soo-stones; rainbow hues danced in their lustrous, milky surfaces. The brush of a fingertip caused the stones to change color temporarily.

Accompanied by watchful Sardaukar guards, a tall woman glided in to meet them. She wore an elegant white gown with a black-pearl necklace, and moved with the fluid grace of a Bene Gesserit. When she smiled warmly at the young visitor, tiny lines formed around her large doe eyes.

"Not quite like the Mother School, or cold and wet like Caladan, is it?" As she spoke, Lady Anirul looked around at the palatial extravagance, as if noticing it anew. "Another week or two, and you won't want to leave." She came forward, showing no hesitation about placing her palm on Jessica's abdomen. "Your daughter couldn't be born in a better place." Anirul seemed to be trying to sense the baby's disposition, or its gender, through her touch.

Jessica flinched away from the Emperor's wife. Mohiam looked at her oddly, and Jessica felt naked, as if her beloved yet hated teacher could see directly into her thoughts. Jessica covered her withdrawal with a hurried curtsy. "I'm sure I will enjoy my visit and your generosity, Lady Anirul. I am happy to serve you in whatever duties you think are fitting for me, but as soon as my child is born I must return to Caladan. My Duke awaits me there." Inwardly, she chastised herself. *I must not show that I care about him.*

"Of course," Anirul said. "The Sisterhood may allow that, for a time." As soon as the Bene Gesserit possessed the long-awaited Harkonnen-Atreides baby, they would have no further concern for the affairs or wishes of Duke Leto Atreides.

With Mohiam at her side, Anirul led Jessica through a dizzying maze of cavernous rooms until they reached the second-floor apartment that had been assigned to her.

Jessica held her chin high and maintained her dignity, though a wondering smile warmed her face. *If I am just to be another lady-in-waiting, why am I receiving such royal treatment?* She was given rooms near the chambers inhabited by the Emperor's wife and the Imperial Truthsayer.

"You must rest, Jessica," Anirul said, looking again at her belly. "Take care of your daughter. She is very important to the Sisterhood." Shaddam's consort smiled. "Daughters are such treasures."

Jessica felt uncomfortable with the subject. "That must be why you have five of them."

Mohiam looked quickly at Jessica. All of them knew that Anirul had given birth only to daughters because those had been her instructions from the Sisterhood. Jessica feigned weariness from her long trip, the overwhelming sights, and the amazing experiences. Anirul and Mohiam left, deep in conversation with each other.

Instead of resting, though, Jessica sealed herself in her chambers and composed a long letter to Leto.

THAT EVENING SHE attended a sumptuous dinner inside the Contemplation Tea House. A separate building in the ornamental gardens, the facility was large, with colorful woodcuts of flowers, plum trees, and mythical animals on the walls. The waiters wore distinctive uniforms, cut long and angular, with cuffs large enough to serve as pockets, and polished bells hanging from every button. Birds flew freely inside the structure, and fat Imperial peacocks strutted beneath the windows, weighed down by their long, bright feathers.

Like peacocks themselves, the Emperor and his Bene Gesserit wife displayed their own plumage. Shaddam wore a scarlet-and-gold jacket with a diagonal red sash across the front, adorned with gold piping and the Corrino golden lion. Anirul had a matching, though narrower, sash over a shimmering platinum-fiber gown.

Jessica sat in a yellow chiffeau evening gown given to her by Anirul as part of an entire new Palace wardrobe, along with a priceless blue-sapphire necklace and matching earrings. Three of Shaddam's daughters—Chalice, Wensicia, and Josifa—took their seats primly beside Anirul, while baby Rugi remained with her wet nurse. The eldest daughter, Irulan, was not there to join them.

"Lady Anirul, I feel more like an honored guest than a simple lady-in-waiting," Jessica said, touching her jewelry.

"Nonsense, you are indeed our guest for now. There will be plenty of time for tedious duties later." Anirul smiled. The Emperor ignored them both.

All through the dinner, Shaddam was silent and drank a goodly quantity of unimaginably expensive red wine. As a result, the other diners spoke little, and the meal finished quickly. Anirul made small talk with her daughters, discussing interesting subjects their tutors had taught them, or games they had played with their nannies in various park enclosures.

Anirul leaned closer to young Josifa, her large eyes wide and earnest, though her lips retained the tiny curve of a smile to show she was teasing. "Be careful with your games, Josifa. I learned there was once a child—a girl about your age, I believe—who wanted to play hide-and-seek in the Palace. The nanny said the Palace was too large for such a contest, but the little girl insisted. She ran off down the corridors, looking for a place to hide." Anirul dabbed at her mouth with a napkin. "And she was never heard from again. I expect one day our custodians will come upon a small skeleton."

Josifa looked amazed, but Chalice scoffed. "It's not true! We can tell it's not true."

Wensicia, the second-oldest daughter, asked Jessica questions about Caladan, about the ducal castle, about how much wealth the watery planet could generate. The girl's probing voice seemed businesslike and incisive, almost challenging.

"Duke Leto has all the amenities he needs, and he has the love of his people." Jessica searched Wensicia's face, saw much ambition there. "Thus, House Atreides is very wealthy indeed."

The Emperor paid no attention to his daughters at the table, nor to his wife. He didn't deign to notice Jessica much at all, either, except when she mentioned Leto—and then he seemed not to care for her opinion.

Afterward, Anirul ushered everyone toward a small auditorium in another wing of the Palace. "Come, come, all of you. Irulan has been practicing for weeks. We must be an attentive audience for her." Shaddam followed, as if begrudging another obligation of his office.

The auditorium featured hand-carved Taniran columns and artful scroll designs, as well as a high, gold-filigree ceiling, and walls covered with lush shimmer paintings of cloudy skies. On the stage stood an immense ruby quartz piano from Hagal, strung with newly tuned monofilament crystal wires.

Uniformed attendants led the Imperial party to a row of private seats with the best view of the stage, while a small audience of exquisitely dressed dignitaries filed toward lesser seats, flushed with awe to be included in such an elite gathering.

Then the Emperor's eldest daughter, eleven-year-old Princess Irulan, walked straight-backed across the stage, a lovely vision in a cerulean blue merh-silk gown. She carried herself with poise, a tall girl with long blonde hair and a face of classic patrician beauty. Gazing up at her parents in the Imperial box, Irulan gave them a formal nod.

Jessica studied this daughter of Shaddam and Anirul. The girl's every movement was precise, as if she could plan each motion with plenty of time to spare. Knowing all the ways in which Mohiam had instructed her, Jessica could see the mark of Bene Gesserit instruction on Irulan. Anirul must have been raising her with a complete grounding in the Sisterhood. This young woman was said to possess superior intellect and skills in writing and poetry, enabling her to construct complex sonnet forms. Her musical talent had marked her as a prodigy since the age of four.

"I am extremely proud of her," Anirul whispered to Jessica, who sat in her own brocaded seat. "Irulan has the potential to achieve greatness, both as a Princess and as a Bene Gesserit."

The Princess smiled at her father, as if hoping for a response on his wooden face, then turned to the audience. She perched delicately on the ruby quartz bench, her glittery dress flowing to the stage. She sat in utter stillness for a second, meditating, summoning her musical ability, then finally her long fingers danced across the soostone-inlaid keys, producing dulcet notes that danced in the air. The acoustically perfect auditorium filled with a medley of great composers.

As the magnificent sounds flowed around Jessica, she felt a wash of sadness. Perhaps her emotions were being manipulated at a visceral level by the music. How ironic that she was on Kaitain, despite having no aspirations of ever coming here, while Leto's first concubine Kailea—who had so wanted this life of luxury and spectacle—had never been able to attain it.

Jessica already missed her Duke with an ache that filled her chest and made her shoulders heavy.

She saw the Emperor's head tilt as he dozed off, and noted the disapproving sidelong glance of Anirul.

All does not glitter on Kaitain, Jessica thought.

The Sisterhood has no need for archaeologists. As Reverend Mothers, we embody history.

—Bene Gesserit Teaching

The baking red heat of a foundry bathed Mother Superior Harishka's parchment face. The bitter odors of metallic alloys, impurities, and electrical components churned inside the molten mass contained within the large crucible.

A procession of robed Sisters approached the cauldron furnace, each carrying a component of the wrecked Harkonnen craft. Like ancient islanders presenting offerings to a volcano god, they tossed broken pieces into the furious crucible.

The secret ship was being digested slowly into a viscous soup that resembled lava. The industrial thermal generators vaporized organic material, broke down polymers, and melted metals—even the space-tempered hull plates. Every scrap must be destroyed.

After altering the memories of the three Richesian inventors, Harishka had determined that no one had enough information to resurrrect Chobyn's renegade work. Once the Bene Gesserit destroyed the remnants of this lone vessel, the dangerous invisibility technology would be gone forever.

The Sisters had worked like black-robed ants, swarming over the hulk at the bottom of the rock quarry. They tore the ship apart, plate by plate, using white-hot laser cutters to chop sections into manageable pieces. The Mother Superior had no doubt that it would have been impossible to glean clues from even those fragments, yet she insisted on completing the job.

Erasure must be total and absolute.

Now, the commando Sister Cristane came forward into the acrid smoke from the roiling crucible, holding a wire-studded power generator of unknown design. To the best of their knowledge, *this* was a key part of the invisibility field projector.

The strong and implacable young woman paused to stare into the fire, unbothered by the heat that made her cheeks ruddy and threatened to singe her eyebrows. Muttering a silent prayer, she tossed the jagged component into the flames and remained where she was, watching it melt and sink, darkening the scarlet-and-orange soup as it decomposed into the mix.

Watching this, Harishka felt something stir in Other Memory, the whispers of a long-ago life, a similar experience in her ages-old genetic past. Her ancient ancestor's name surfaced . . . *Lata*.

Though language had been crude then, incapable of conveying subtleties, she had lived her life well. Lata had watched her men work with bladder bellows to pump air, increasing the temperature inside a crude stone smelter they had constructed near a lakeshore. Harishka had no names in her internal archives for that lake, or even for the land. She had watched the men smelting iron ore, perhaps from a meteorite they had found, using the metal to forge crude work blades and weapons.

Sifting through the collective memories, Harishka noted other instances of metallurgy, as her ancestors had participated in the development of copper, bronze, and then far-more-sophisticated steel. Such innovations had made kings out of warriors, and superior weapons had enabled them to conquer neighboring tribes. Other Memory connected only the female genetic line, and Harishka could recall watching wars and swordmaking from the periphery, while she gathered food, made clothes, bore children, and buried them. . . .

Now she and her fellow Sisters were using an ancient technology to destroy an awesome innovation. Unlike those long-ago warlords that she had watched through layers of past lives, Harishka decided *not* to use her new weapon, and to prevent anyone else from using it, as well.

More Sisters threw pieces of the ship into the foundry. The smoke grew thicker, but Harishka did not move from her spot near the blistering rim. After the crust of floating impurities was skimmed off, the molten metal mixture would be used to cast useful items for the Mother School. Like proverbial swords beaten into plowshares.

Although the Bene Gesserit had eliminated any possibility of the invisibility generator being rebuilt by outsiders, Harishka still felt uneasy. Her Sisters had studied the crashed ship in detail, and though they didn't understand how to reassemble the pieces, they maintained an accurate mental record of every scrap. Someday they would transfer the information into Other Memory. There, locked within the collective consciousness of the Bene Gesserit, it would remain sealed forever.

The last Sisters in the procession tossed pieces into the crucible, and the only no-ship in existence vanished forever.

It is difficult to make power lovable—this is the dilemma of all governments.

— PADISHAH EMPEROR HASSIK III,
private Kaitain journals

The Harkonnen banquet was more extravagant than any previously staged on Giedi Prime. After surviving the severe tutoring of Mephistis Cru, the Baron didn't know if he ever wanted to undergo such an ordeal again.

"This will change how you are perceived in the Landsraad, my Baron," Piter de Vries reminded him in a soothing, reasonable voice. "Remember how Leto Atreides is revered, how they applaud him for his drastic action on Beakkal. Use it to your advantage."

Upon combing through the names on the list, the etiquette advisor had been horrified to see that blood-rivals had been invited from Grumman and Ecaz. It would be like a sonic grenade waiting for the pulse of its primer. After discussion and outright argument, the Baron finally agreed to drop Archduke Armand Ecaz from the invitations, and de Vries scuttled about to make the changes, so that the banquet could proceed without problems.

The Mentat still worried that he would be executed at the conclusion of the festivities. Noting the man's obvious unease, the Baron smiled to himself. He liked to keep people off-balance, fearing for their positions and their very lives.

The evening's carefully selected guests were ferried down from orbit by a Harkonnen shuttle. Resplendent in billowing clothes that concealed both his girth and his suspensor belt, the Baron stood under the ornamental portcullis of his Keep. Gleaming in the smoky orange dusk of Harko City, the sharp iron spikes of the gate hung like dragon fangs, poised to chomp down on visitors.

As noble guests emerged from the suspensor-borne transportation barge, the Baron smiled graciously and welcomed each of them with rehearsed, exceedingly polite phrases. When he thanked them personally for coming, several men regarded him with suspicion, as if he were speaking a foreign language.

The Baron had been forced to allow the representatives an armed bodyguard, one for each nobleman. Mephistis Cru had been loath to make the concession, but the nobles had refused to come otherwise. The fact was, they simply did not trust the Harkonnens.

Even now, as the distinguished visitors stood together inside the ebony-walled reception foyer, they spoke with careful words, curious about what House Harkonnen truly wanted of them.

"Welcome, welcome, my esteemed guests." The Baron raised his ring-studded hands. "Our families have been associated for generations, yet few of us can call each other friends. I mean to add a bit more civility to interactions among the Landsraad Houses." He smiled, feeling as if his lips might break, knowing that many of these people would probably have *cheered* if Duke Leto Atreides had said the same thing. All around, he noted furrowed brows, lips pinched into frowns, eyes filled with questions.

Cru had written the remarks for him, and the words clawed at the Baron's throat. "I see this news is surprising to you, but I promise—on my honor," he continued quickly before anyone could snicker at that comment, "that I intend to ask nothing of you. I only wish to share an evening of joy and fellowship so that you might return home with a better opinion of House Harkonnen."

Old Count Ilban Richese raised his hands and applauded. His blue eyes sparkled with delight. "Hear, hear, Baron Harkonnen! I heartily endorse your sentiments. I knew you had a soft spot in you."

Stiffly, the Baron nodded his appreciation, though he had always considered Ilban Richese to be a vapid man who focused on unimportant matters, such as the inane hobbies of his grown children. As a consequence, House Richese had not adequately exploited the decline of House Vernius and the Ixian industrial empire. Still, an ally was an ally.

Luckily for House Richese, their Premier, Ein Calimar, was quite competent enough to keep the technological facilities busy even in times of adversity. The thought of Calimar made the Baron scowl, though. The two of them had conducted business on several occasions, but lately the bespectacled politician did little more than nag him about money House Harkonnen supposedly owed for the services of the Suk doctor Wellington Yueh—money the Baron never intended to pay.

"Peace and fellowship . . . such a pleasant sentiment, Baron," added Viscount Hundro Moritani, his thick mane of black hair swirling around his head, his eyebrows heavy, his eyes dark and intent. "Not something any of us expected from House Harkonnen."

The Baron tried to maintain his smile. "Well, I'm turning over a new leaf."

The Viscount always added an unsettling edge to his comments, as if a rabid dog were chained to his soul. Hundro Moritani had a habit of leading the Grumman people on fanatical, often ill-advised, strikes, flouting the rules of the Imperium and lashing out at anyone who dared challenge him. The Baron might have considered him an ally if Grumman's actions weren't so annoyingly unpredictable.

A redheaded master of arms, wearing the impressive formal badge of a trained graduate of Ginaz, stood next to the

Viscount. The other nobles had brought along muscular bodyguards, but Hundro Moritani seemed much more impressed to bring his own pet Swordmaster. Hiih Resser had been the only Grumman trainee to complete the full schooling on Ginaz. The redhead looked uneasy, though, clinging to duty like a lifeline.

The Baron considered the advantages. House Harkonnen had no devoted Swordmaster. He wondered if he should send a few of his own candidates to Ginaz. . . .

Gliding on his suspensors, taking gentle steps, he led his guests through the main levels of the Keep. The coarse facility had been decorated with bouquets of sweetly pungent off-world flowers, since available Giedi Prime floral arrangements were "disappointing," according to the etiquette advisor. As a consequence, the Baron could scarcely breathe in his own halls.

The big man gestured, wearing the flowing sleeves of a gentleman of leisure. He led the way into the reception hall, where servants carried trays of drinks in Balut crystal goblets. On a low platform, three music masters from Chusuk (friends of Mephistis Cru) played sprightly background melodies on fine balisets. The Baron flitted among the guests, joining in dull conversations with them, maintaining the illusion of civility.

And hating every moment of it.

After a few drinks laced with melange, the guests gradually relaxed and began chatting about CHOAM Directorships, animal harvests on backwater planets, or loathsome Spacing Guild tariffs and regulations. The Baron consumed two snifters of kirana brandy, double the limit Cru had attempted to impose on him, but he didn't care. These proceedings were interminable. The smile was hurting his face.

The moment dinner was announced, the Baron guided the diners into the banquet hall, eager to move on from this endless, inane conversation. Count Richese chattered incessantly about his children and grandchildren, as if anyone could keep track of them all. He seemed to hold no grudge against House Harkonnen for superseding them in spice operations on Arrakis decades ago. The noble nincompoop had lost much wealth through his incompetence and wasn't even bothered by it.

The guests took their designated seats after bodyguards had checked for booby traps. The banquet table was a plateau of darkly polished elacca wood shimmering with islands of fine porcelain and floating clusters of wine goblets. The display of food was breathtaking, the smells mouthwatering.

Beatific boys with milky skin stood behind the chairs, a designated attendant for every invited guest. The Baron had chosen these servants himself, street urchins drugged into submission and then cleaned up.

The immense host moved to a wide, customized chair at the head of the table and summoned the first course of appetizers. He had placed chronometers all around the banquet hall so he could watch every second tick by. He couldn't wait for it to be over. . . .

INSIDE THE LISTENING alcove, Rabban eavesdropped on party conversations. He had been swiveling the parabolic microphone from one blathering mouth to another, hoping to discover embarrassing gossip, accidentally divulged secrets. The sheer dullness made him want to vomit.

Everyone was on guard, careful with their words. He learned nothing at all. Rabban was frustrated. "This is even more boring than actually participating," he snapped at the Mentat, who fidgeted beside him, studying the listening devices.

Lowering his eyebrows, de Vries scowled at him. "As a Mentat, I have no choice but to memorize every single tedious moment, every line, while your simple brain will forget it all within a few days."

"I'm counting my blessings," Rabban said with a smirk.

On the high-resolution monitors, they watched the

main course being served. Rabban's thick-lipped mouth watered, knowing he'd receive only leftovers . . . but if that was the price of being excused from this chattering aviary of strutting birds, he would gladly suffer it. Even eating cold food was preferable to civility.

Behind the scenes, yet still a busybody attending to a thousand details, Mephistis Cru scampered into the spy alcove, thinking it was a dinnerware storage room. He stopped, startled to encounter Rabban and de Vries. Swallowing hard, Cru touched his neck unconsciously where thick layers of powder masked the heavy bruises from Rabban's recent stranglehold.

"Oh, excuse me," he said, finding his composure. "I didn't mean to interrupt." He nodded at de Vries, whom he erroneously considered an ally. "The banquet is proceeding quite nicely, I believe. The Baron is doing a fine job."

Beast Rabban growled, and Mephistis Cru scurried out.

De Vries and Rabban resumed their listening duties, wishing for something to happen before the night was completely wasted.

❧

"WHAT A LOVELY child!" Count Richese gushed upon seeing Feyd-Rautha. The fair-haired boy knew plenty of words and already understood how to get what he wanted. The Count extended his arms. "May I hold him?"

At the Baron's nod, a servant brought Feyd-Rautha to the old Richesian, who bounced him on his grandfatherly knee. Feyd didn't giggle, which surprised Ilban.

The Count then lifted his wineglass, while supporting Feyd with one arm. "I propose a toast to children." The guests drank to this. Grumbling to himself, the Baron wondered if Feyd might need his diaper changed, and if the old fool would be quite so happy to perform those menial duties.

At that moment, Feyd burbled a stream of nonsense words, which the Baron understood were names for his own excrement. Ilban, however, didn't know that and simply smiled and repeated the words back to the boy. He bounced Feyd again and exclaimed in a childish voice, "Look, little one! They're bringing dessert now. You like that, don't you?"

The Baron leaned forward, pleased that the meal was about to conclude, and because he had planned this part of the banquet himself, making his own decisions without listening to the guidance of the etiquette advisor. It was, he thought, a very clever idea that the guests might find amusing.

Carrying a platform large enough to hold a human body, six servants brought in a two-meter-long cake, which they placed in the middle of the table. The concoction was curved and narrow, shaped like a sandworm and decorated with powdered swirls of potent melange.

"This confection symbolizes Harkonnen holdings on Arrakis. Celebrate with me our decades of profitable work in the desert." The Baron beamed, and Count Richese applauded with all the others, though even he must not have missed the insult directed toward his family's earlier failures.

The frosting seemed to shimmer, and the Baron waited for the delightful surprise inside.

"There, look at the cake, little one!" Ilban placed Feyd on the table in front of him—an action that no doubt would have horrified Mephistis Cru.

One of the chef's assistants used a wire-knife to slice open the length of the sweet sandworm, as if he were performing an autopsy. The banquet guests crowded around to get better views, and Count Richese leaned Feyd forward.

When the cake was opened, shapes squirmed inside, long writhing forms, serpentine creatures meant to represent the sandworms of Arrakis. The harmless snakes had been drugged and stuffed inside the cake so that as they roiled and squirmed out of the frosting, they looked like a nest of tentacles. A wonderful little joke.

Feyd seemed fascinated, but Count Richese choked on a

scream. The tension of the night and the guests' suspicions about the Baron had placed everyone on edge. The Count, trying to be a hero, yanked Feyd-Rautha roughly away from the table, overturning his own chair in the process.

Feyd, who had not been afraid of the snakes, was now startled into a fit of bawling. As he wailed, bodyguards grabbed their lords and prepared to defend them.

On the other side of the table from the toddler, Viscount Moritani stood back, his black eyes glittering with an odd mixture of mirth and fury. Swordmaster Hiih Resser stood ready to protect his lord, but Moritani seemed unconcerned. The Viscount coolly adjusted a bracelet on his wrist, causing a white-hot beam from a covert lasgun to vaporize the snakes, detonating them into shreds of scaly flesh, chunks of meat, and blackened frosting.

Guests screamed. Most rushed for the doors of the banquet hall. Mephistis Cru scampered in from a back room, waving his hands and pleading for calm.

From that point on, the pandemonium only grew worse.

The more tightly packed the group, the greater the need for strict social ranks and orders.

—Bene Gesserit Teaching

Dressed in a traditional jubba cloak with the hood thrown back, Liet-Kynes stood once again on a high balcony overlooking the sietch chamber. He felt far more at home here than in the halls of Kaitain, and far more intimidated. Here he would speak of matters that affected the future of every free man on the planet of Dune.

The sessions had gone smoothly, with the exception of a disruption caused by Pemaq, the aging Naib of Hole-in-the-Wall Sietch. The conservative leader spoke against everything Liet stood for, resisting all forms of change but providing no rational alternatives. Other Fremen repeatedly shouted him down, until at last the obstinate old man had skulked off into the cool shadows, grumbling.

For days, the convocation had shifted and flowed, with some feuding members leaving the meeting in indignation, but later returning. Each night after the meetings, Faroula had held Liet, whispering her advice, helping where she could, and loving him. She kept him strong and balanced, despite his growing discouragement.

Fremen observers reported the subtle progress in their battle to tame the desert. In only a single generation, the wasteland was showing faint but definite signs of improvement. Twenty years ago, Umma Kynes had told them to be patient, that the effort might take centuries. But his dreams were already beginning to come true.

In deep arroyos at the far southern regions, cleverly concealed plantings thrived, nurtured by solar mirrors and magnifiers that warmed the air and melted frost from the ground. Stunted palm trees grew in small numbers, along with hardy desert sunflowers, gourd plants, and tubers. On some days, a few trickles of water ran freely. Water on the surface of Dune! It was an astounding concept.

So far, the Harkonnens hadn't noticed the changes, with their attention directed only toward spice operations. The planet would be recovered, one hectare at a time. Good news, all around.

Now, though, Liet heaved a sigh of anticipation. Even with all the support he had received at this convocation (much more than he had expected), there might be significant dissent this afternoon . . . after they heard his proposal.

On balconies and platforms that zigzagged up the rock walls, more than a thousand ripcord-tough Fremen returned from a midday break and took up their positions. They wore desert-stained robes and *temag* boots. Some smoked melange-laced fibers in clay pipes, as was the custom in early afternoon. With the pleasing aroma of burning spice in his nostrils, Liet-Kynes began to speak.

"Umma Kynes, my father, was a great visionary. He set our people on an ambitious, arduous course to awaken Dune. He taught us that the ecosystem is complex, that every life-form needs a niche. Many times he spoke of the ecological consequences of our actions. Umma Kynes saw the environment as an interactive *system*, with fluid stability and order."

Liet cleared his throat. "From off-planet we have brought insects to aerate the soil, which enables plants to grow more easily. We have centipedes, scorpions, and bees.

Small and large animals are spreading across the sand and rocks—kit foxes, hares, desert hawks, dwarf owls.

"Dune is like a great engine that we are oiling and repairing. One day this world will serve us in new and wondrous ways, just as we will continue to honor and serve it. My Fremen brothers, we are part of the ecosystem ourselves, an *integral* part. We occupy our own essential niche."

The audience listened attentively, with a special reverence whenever Liet mentioned the name and work of his legendary father.

"But what is our niche? Are we merely Planetologists, restoring flora and fauna? I say we must do much more than that. We need to fight the Harkonnen aggressors on a scale never before contemplated. For years, groups of us have harassed them, but never enough to cripple their rapacious operations. Today, the Baron steals more spice than ever."

Shouts of discontent passed through the chamber, accompanied by pockets of nervous whispering against the sacrilege.

Liet raised his voice. "My father failed to foresee that powerful forces of the Imperium—the Emperor, House Harkonnen, the Landsraad—would not share his vision. We are alone in this, and must *make* them stop."

The murmurings increased. Liet hoped he was awakening his people, convincing them to put aside their differences and work toward a common goal.

"What good is it to build a home if you don't defend it? We are millions strong. Let us fight for the new world my father envisioned, a world our grandchildren should inherit!"

Applause echoed in the great chamber, as well as the foot-stomping that signaled approval—especially from the rough Fremen youths, who reveled in their razzia raids.

Then Kynes heard a change in the noise. People pointed at an opposite balcony, where a wiry old man waved his crysknife in the air. Ropy hair whipped around him, making him look like a madman from the deep desert. Pemaq again.

"Taqwa!" he shouted from his balcony, an ancient Fremen battle cry that meant, "The price of freedom."

The throng fell silent, all eyes riveted on the Naib of Hole-in-the-Wall Sietch and his milky white blade. Fremen tradition held that a drawn crysknife could not be sheathed until it tasted blood. Pemaq had chosen a dangerous course.

Liet touched the handle of his own knife at his waist. He saw Stilgar and Turok making their way up a rock staircase, hurrying to the higher level.

"Liet-Kynes, I challenge you to answer me!" Pemaq bellowed. "If I do not find your response satisfactory, the time for words will be over and blood will decide! Do you accept my challenge?"

This fool could destroy all of the political progress Liet had made. With no choice in the matter, since his honor and ability to lead were at stake, Liet shouted back, "If that will silence you, Pemaq, then I accept. 'There is no man so blind as one who has made up his mind.' " A ripple of muffled laughter stirred through the audience at the skillful application of an old Fremen adage.

Angry at the rebuke, Pemaq pointed with the tip of his blade. "You are only half-Fremen, Liet-Kynes, and your off-world blood has infused you with devilish ideas. You have spent too much time on Salusa Secundus and Kaitain. You have been corrupted and are now trying to taint the rest of us with your harmful delusions."

Liet's heart hammered in his chest. Righteous anger rose, and he wanted to silence the man. Glancing back, he saw Stilgar take a guard position at the entrance to Liet's balcony.

The dissenter continued. "For decades Heinar, the Naib of Red Wall Sietch, has been my friend. I fought alongside him against the Harkonnens when they first came to Dune, after the departure of House Richese. I carried him on my back after the raid in which he lost an eye. Heinar increased the prosperity of the people under his rule—but he is old, like me.

"Now you gather support from other Fremen leaders, bringing them here to solidify your position. You speak of your father's achievements, Liet-Kynes, while citing none of your own." The defiant man trembled with fury. "Your motives are clear—you wish to be Naib yourself."

Liet blinked in surprise at the ridiculous assertion. "I deny it completely. For weeks I have spoken of important work for all Fremen, and you accuse me of petty ambition?"

Stilgar shouted then, his voice clear in the huge chamber. "It is said that if a thousand men gather in a room, one of them is sure to be a fool. I believe there are a thousand men here, Pemaq—and we have found our fool."

A few chuckles diminished the tension, but Pemaq did not relent. "You are not a Fremen, Liet-Kynes. You are not one of us. First you married Heinar's daughter, and now you intend to take his place."

"I hurl the truth back at you, Pemaq, and may it pierce your lying heart. My off-world blood comes from Umma Kynes himself, and you call that a *weakness*? Moreover, the tale of my blood-brother Warrick and how he died is known in every sietch. I gave my vow to him that I would marry Faroula and take his son as my own."

Pemaq countered in a somber tone, "Perhaps you summoned the wind of the demon in the open desert to kill your rival. I do not pretend to know the powers of off-world demons."

Tired of the foolishness, Liet turned his gaze out upon the delegates lining the chamber. "I have accepted his challenge, but he only plays games of words. If there is a duel between us, will I draw blood first, or will he? Pemaq is an old man, and if I kill him I can only dishonor myself in such a fight. Even if he dies, he achieves his aim." Liet looked across at the balcony. "Is that your plan, old fool?"

Just then, Naib Heinar, wearing his eye patch and looking as if his body were made of leather, stepped onto the balcony beside Pemaq. The dissenter reacted with surprise, then disbelief as the one-eyed Naib spoke. Heinar's raspy voice rang through the gathering chamber. "I have known Liet since the moment of his birth, and he has played no tricks against me. He has inherited the true vision of his father, and he is as much a Fremen as any of us."

He turned toward the wild-haired man beside him, who still gripped his crysknife, holding it high. "My old friend Pemaq believes he speaks on my behalf, but I say to him he must think beyond the concerns of a single sietch, to all of Dune. I would rather see Harkonnen blood spilled than the blood of my comrade, or of my son-in-law."

In the ensuing silence, Liet called out, "I will walk into the desert and face Shai-Hulud alone rather than fight a single one of you. You must either believe in me, or cast me out."

A chanting filled the chamber, begun by Stilgar and Turok, and picked up by the brash Fremen youths thirsty for Harkonnen blood. More than a thousand desert men uttered his sietch name over and over. "Liet! Liet!"

On the opposite balcony there was a sudden blur of movement, a scuffle between Pemaq and Heinar. Without saying a word, the stubborn man attempted to fall on his own naked blade, but old Heinar moved to prevent it. He snatched the crysknife out of the sweat-slippery hand of his comrade. Pemaq fell onto the balcony floor, alive but defeated.

Holding the knife, Heinar stepped back, slicing upward with a blur to cut a deep gash across Pemaq's forehead, which would leave a scar for the rest of his days. The requisite blood had been drawn. Pemaq looked up, the fury deflated from him; a line of blood dripped across his hooded brows and into his eyes. Heinar turned the crysknife around and extended it to its owner, hilt-first.

"Perceive this as a good omen, all of you gathered here," Heinar shouted into the cavern, "for it unifies the Fremen behind Liet-Kynes."

Climbing to his feet, Pemaq wiped crimson from his eyes, smearing his cheeks with streaks of blood like warpaint. He drew a deep breath to speak, as was his right; Liet braced himself, still stunned at the speed with which events had turned. But the wild-haired Fremen scowled at Heinar, then said, "I move that we elect Liet-Kynes as our Abu Naib, the father of all sietches to lead us all."

Liet reeled for a moment, but after he had composed himself, he responded, "We are at a crisis point in our history. Our descendants will look at this moment and say either that we made the correct decision, or that we failed entirely." After pausing to let this sink in, he continued. "As the awakening of Dune becomes more obvious, it will be increasingly difficult to hide our work from the Harkonnens. The Guild spice bribe becomes more important than ever, to make certain we keep all weather satellites and observation systems away from our work."

Murmurs of concurrence passed through the throng. The weeks of discussion had come down to this.

Liet-Kynes tried to keep his emotions in check. "After the treachery that resulted in the destruction of the smuggler base at the south pole, I no longer trust the middleman we have used for years, the water merchant Rondo Tuek. Though he has left the pole, he still acts as our liaison. But Tuek betrayed Dominic Vernius, and could turn on us just as easily. Why trust him any longer? I will demand a *direct* meeting with a representative of the Spacing Guild. The Fremen will no longer rely on any middlemen. From now on, the standing agreement is between us and the Guild."

Liet had always considered Dominic Vernius a friend and mentor. The renegade Earl deserved a better fate than the one arranged for him by the double-dealing water merchant. Recently, Tuek had sold his ice-mining operations to Lingar Bewt, his former right-hand man, and returned to Carthag. Considering the problem of Tuek, Liet-Kynes formed a plan to settle the matter.

Around the chamber, the Planetologist noted expressions of complete faith that he had not witnessed since the heady days of his celebrated father. This had been a long time coming, and the younger Kynes had traveled his own path. His aspirations overlapped with those of his predecessor, but went far beyond them. Where his father had envisioned only the greening of the desert wastelands, Liet considered the Fremen to be the stewards of Dune. All of it.

To achieve greatness, though, they must first free themselves from their Harkonnen shackles.

The human body is a storehouse of relics from the past—the appendix, thymus, and (in the embryo) a gill structure. But the unconscious mind is even more intriguing. It has been built up over millions of years and represents a history throughout its synaptic traces, some of which do not appear to be useful in modern times. It is difficult to find everything that is there.

—From a Secret Bene Gesserit
Symposium on Other Memory

Late at night while the auroras still burned bright, a sleepless Anirul entered the austere, chill quarters that had been used by the Emperor's former Truthsayer, Lobia. Nearly two months had passed since the old woman had died, and her chambers remained lifeless and hushed, like a tomb.

Though Lobia must be in Other Memory now, having joined the multitudes within her mind, the Truthsayer's ancient spirit had not yet surfaced. Anirul felt exhausted from the effort of trying to locate her, but something drove her on.

Anirul needed a friend and confidante, and she dared not speak to anyone else—certainly not Jessica, who knew nothing of her destiny. Anirul had her daughters, and though she was proud of Irulan's intelligence and talents, she didn't dare place such a burden of knowledge on the girl, either. Irulan wasn't ready. No, the Kwisatz Haderach breeding program was too secret.

But Lobia—if only she could be located in Other Memory—would be suitable.

Where are you, old friend? Must I shout out and awaken all those others inside me? She feared taking that step, but perhaps the benefit would be worth the risk. *Lobia, talk to me.*

Empty boxes were stacked along one wall of the unheated apartment, but Anirul had avoided packing the dead Truthsayer's meager possessions and sending them back to Wallach IX. Since Gaius Helen Mohiam had preferred a different set of rooms for herself, these quarters could remain empty for years in the sprawling Palace before anyone noticed them.

Anirul walked through the dim, austere rooms, breathing the chill air as if hoping to feel spirits stirring about. Then, taking a seat at a small rolltop desk, she activated her sensory-conceptual journal from the soostone ring on her hand. The diary hovered in the air, visible only to her. This seemed an appropriate, contemplative place for Anirul to organize her private thoughts.

She was sure Lobia would approve. "Wouldn't you, old friend?" The sound of her own voice startled her, and Anirul fell silent again, surprised that she had begun talking to herself.

The virtual diary lay open in front of her, waiting for more words. She calmed herself, opened her mind, using Prana-Bindu techniques to stimulate her thoughts. A long, slow breath eased out of her nostrils, barely visible in the frigid air.

A chill coursed her spine. Shivering, Anirul adjusted her metabolism until she could no longer feel the cold. Four unadorned glowglobes near the ceiling dimmed and then brightened, as if a mysterious power surge had rippled through the air. She closed her eyes.

The room still smelled like Lobia, a comforting mustiness. The late Truthsayer's psychic energy lingered as well.

Removing an innocuous-looking ink plume from its receptacle on the desk, Anirul held it with both hands, pressing it between her palms and concentrating. Lobia had used
this instrument often when sending coded transmittals to
the Mother School, where she had been an instructor for
years. The old woman's fingerprints were on the pen, along
with discarded skin cells and bodily oils.

But the ink plume was a primitive method of writing and
would not serve for this sensory-conceptual journal. In its
place Anirul summoned a sensory-pen and raised it in front
of the ethereal pages.

In the night stillness, in this place where Lobia had
spent so much of her life, Anirul wanted to describe her
friendship with the remarkable Truthsayer, documenting
the wisdom she had learned from her. With brisk strokes
she entered a coded date on the paperless page.

Then her hand hesitated. Her turbulent thoughts became murky, blocking the flow of words she wanted to
write. She felt like a child in the Mother School, given a
difficult assignment but unable to marshal her thoughts because the Proctor Superior was staring at her, scrutinizing
her every move.

The glowglobes dimmed again, as if shadows were passing in front of them. Turning abruptly, Anirul saw no one at
all.

Refocusing her tired mind, she turned back to her journal and set about completing what she'd come here to do.
She managed only two sentences before her thoughts
drifted away like chime kites caught on the wind.

The apartment was filled with the faintest of ghostly
whispers.

She could imagine Lobia sitting beside her, imparting
wisdom, counseling her. In one of their many conversations, the old woman had explained how she had come to
be selected as a Truthsayer, how she had shown more ability
than hundreds of other Sisters. In her heart, however, Lobia
would have preferred to remain at the Mother School,

tending the orchards, a duty now ably performed by Reverend Mother Thora. Regardless of her personal wishes, a Bene Gesserit performed the duties assigned to her. *Such as marrying the Emperor.*

Lobia had found time in her assignment to give scolding lectures to Sisters stationed in the Palace, even to Anirul herself. While doing so, the cantankerous woman would wag her withered-stick forefinger to emphasize each point. With Anirul's eyes closed, the memory of Lobia's laugh drifted back—a cross between a cackle and a snort that came at odd moments.

The two women had not been close in the beginning of their relationship, and had in fact experienced some friction over access to the Emperor. Anirul found it disquieting and frustrating whenever she saw her husband and Lobia engaged in extensive private conversation. Sensing this, Lobia had told her with a wrinkled smile, "Shaddam loves his reins of power far more than he could ever love any woman, my Lady. It is not *me* he is interested in; it is what I have to tell him. The Emperor worries about enemies at every turn and wants to know if they are lying to him, scheming to take his power, his wealth, even his life."

As the years went by and Anirul gave him no male heir, Shaddam had grown even more distant toward her. Before long, he would probably dispose of her and secure another wife who would dutifully bear him a son. His father Elrood had done that enough times.

But, unknown to Shaddam, Anirul had already introduced an undetectable agent into her husband during their infrequent sexual sessions. After five daughters, he would never conceive another child. The Emperor was sterile—now that he and Anirul had served the Sisterhood's purposes. Shaddam IV had been with enough other women that he should have been able to guess his condition, but the man would never consider that something might be wrong with *him*, not when he could blame someone else. . . .

As all of this came back to her, Anirul opened her eyes and scribbled furiously with the virtual pen. But again she paused, thinking she heard something. Someone talking in the corridor outside? Stealthy footsteps? She listened carefully, but heard nothing more.

She rolled the virtual writing implement in her hand . . . and heard the noises again—louder this time—as if people were *inside* the room with her. Whispers rose to incomprehensible sentence fragments and then drifted off. Nervously, Anirul left the desk and searched the empty closets, the largest trunks, anyplace where someone might be hiding.

Again, nothing.

The voices grew louder, and with a start Anirul finally recognized a new clamor from Other Memory, an increasingly unruly surge. She had never experienced such an outpouring before, and wondered what had triggered it. Her own search? The turmoil of her troubled thoughts? This time the voices seemed to be *around* her, as well as inside.

The echoes rose in volume, as if she were in a chamber filled with argumentative Sisters, but she could see none of them and could not understand their garbled, overlapping conversation. Each one had something to say, but the words were confusing, contradictory.

Anirul considered fleeing Lobia's empty apartment, but thought better of it. If the multitude-within was trying to contact her, attempting to say something important, she needed to learn what it was. "Lobia? Are you there?"

In response, the storm of words shifted like a ghostly cloud. Voices faded and grew louder, like poorly tuned com-signals struggling through a raging static discharge. Some of the long-dead women screamed to be heard over the others, but still Anirul could not comprehend. They seemed to be calling out the various names of the Kwisatz Haderach in many languages.

Suddenly all sound diminished inside her head. Anirul's head rang with a disquieting silence, and she felt a sick cramping in her stomach.

She stared at the sensory-conceptual journal still hovering above the desk. The previous time that she had detected agitation in Other Memory, she had also been writing in her journal. At that time, she had probed deeply into that realm, only to find herself blocked by a swirling mist.

The two experiences were different, but she received the same message from each. Something was wrong in the clamorous throng of her female ancestors. This time the incomprehensible voices were even more disturbed, coming unbidden.

If she did not discover why, her life—or, worse, the Kwisatz Haderach program, which was her entire reason for existence—might be in grave danger.

*Once you have explored a fear, it becomes less terrify-
ing. Part of courage comes from extending our knowledge.*

— DUKE LETO ATREIDES

As an afternoon wind picked up over the sea
of Caladan, Leto leaned his elbows on a
balcony table. He liked to sit out in the salty air,
watching lines of thunderclouds roll across the
choppy waves. The great storms at sea were at
once terrifying and glorious, bringing to mind the
turmoils in the Imperium, and in his heart. Reminding him of how insignificant a mere Duke was
against forces greater than himself.

On the other side of the table, facing the stone
wall instead of the sea, Prince Rhombur did not
feel the cold with his cyborg body. Rather, he studied an ornate board of cheops, a strategy game of
pyramid chess that Leto had often played with his
father. "It is your move, Leto."

The Duke's mug of strong tea had grown cold,
but he took a drink anyway. He moved his vanguard piece, a cymek warrior set up to ward off the
approach of his opponent's black priest.

"I mean it's your move in another sense, too."
Rhombur stared past him at lines in the ancient
stone-block walls. "The Bene Gesserit have turned
down your request for the invisible ship, but we
cannot stop there. Now that Thufir and Gurney
have returned with their report, we have all the

information we need. The time has come for genuine action to recapture my place on Ix." He gave a boyish grin on his scarred face. "And with Jessica gone, you need something useful to occupy yourself."

"You may be right." Leto stared off to sea, not smiling at the joke. Ever since the skyclipper explosion, he had looked for a dramatic goal to keep himself steady. The punitive strike on Beakkal had been a good first step, but not enough. He still felt only a fraction of a man . . . like Rhombur.

"Still, I must consider the welfare of my own people first," Leto said, thoughtfully. "Many of my soldiers would die in an attack on Ix, and we need to bear in mind the security of Caladan as well. If the attack were to fail, the Sardaukar would be down our throats here. I want to save your world, not lose my own."

"I *know* it'll be dangerous. Great men take great risks, Leto." Rhombur hit his fist on the table with more force than he'd intended. The pieces on the cheops board jumped as if an earthquake had rocked their tiny world. Then, looking down at his prosthetic hand, he raised it carefully from the table. "Sorry." His expressions were more dramatic than before, more emotionally charged. "My father, mother, and sister are dead. I am more machine than flesh, can never have children. What in the hells do I have to lose?"

Leto waited for him to finish. The Prince was building up a head of steam, as he often did when the subject of Ix came up. The only good result of the terrible tragedy of the skyclipper explosion was that it seemed to have galvanized his mind and made it more clear. He was much more forceful now, with clear-cut goals and timetables he wanted to meet. He was a man—a *new* man—on a mission.

"Emperor Shaddam's conditional amnesty was an empty gesture, and I was lulled into complacency by accepting it. For years! I kept convincing myself that things would get better if I just waited. Well, my people can wait no longer!"

He made as if to slam his fist on the tabletop again, but when Leto flinched, Rhombur stopped himself. His face softened, taking on a pleading expression. "It's been too damned long, Leto, and I just want to *go*. Even if all I do is slip inside and find C'tair. Together, we could foster an uprising from the downtrodden populace."

Rhombur stared at the cheops board, with its multiple levels and complexities that mirrored life in so many ways. He reached out with his prosthetic hand, pressed his fingers together, and picked up a delicately carved Sorceress game piece, which he moved across the board.

"Ix will repay you every solari for the military campaign, plus a generous interest rate. In addition, I could have Ixian technicians come to Caladan and go over all your systems—industry, government, transportation, fishing, farming—and provide your people with advice on how to improve them. Systems are the key, my friend, along with the latest technology, of course. We would provide the necessary Ixian machines, too—at no charge for an agreed-upon period of time. Say ten years, or even twenty. We could work it out."

Knitting his eyebrows, Leto studied the board and made his move, sliding a Heighliner piece up a level to capture his opponent's Navigator.

With only a casual glance at the board, Rhombur said, "Every House in the Landsraad—including House Atreides—will benefit from the overthrow of the Tleilaxu. Ixian products, once considered the most reliable and ingenious in the universe, now break down, since quality control is laughable in the Tleilaxu-run manufactories. And who can trust Tleilaxu products, even when they do work?"

Since the return of the spy team, Leto had continued to ponder the many questions the information had raised. If the Tleilaxu were not driven back, they would undoubtedly use their foothold to create mischief throughout the Imperium. What were they doing with the Ixian armament factories? The Tleilaxu could form new armies and equip them with the latest military technology.

And why were the Sardaukar there? A terrible thought occurred to Leto. Under the traditional balance of power in the Imperium, House Corrino and its Sardaukar were the approximate equal, militarily, of the combined Great Houses of the Landsraad. What if Shaddam intended to tip that balance in his favor by allying himself with the Tleilaxu? Is that what they were doing on Ix?

Leto turned away from the board. "You are right, Rhombur. No more games." His face became serious. "I no longer care about court politics or appearances, or how history might judge me. Justice is my main concern, and the future of the Landsraad, including House Atreides."

He captured another of Rhombur's cheops pieces, but the cyborg Prince didn't seem to notice. Leto continued, "However, I want to be sure you are not intending to make an extravagant but empty gesture, as your father wanted to do. His ill-fated atomic attack on Kaitain would have sent traumatic ripples through the Imperium, and it would have gained House Vernius nothing."

Using neck servos, Rhombur nodded his heavy head. "It would have brought howling avengers down on me—and on you as well, Leto, by association." Then he made a quick move in the game, a strategic blunder, enabling Leto to move another level up the cheops pyramid.

"A good leader must pay attention to details, Rhombur." The Duke tapped the pyramid chessboard, chiding him. "Great plans count for nothing if all the threads don't hold together."

Rhombur flushed. "My skills at the baliset are better than at games."

Leto took another sip of his cold tea, then sloshed the liquid over the balcony edge. "This will not be simple, or straightforward. Yes, I think the rebellion must begin from within, but there will also be an overt attack from the outside. Everything must be coordinated precisely."

The wind picked up as the squall approached. Out on the water, coracles and fishing boats puttered back to the dock, trying to beat the oncoming rain. In the village below, men worked to stow loose components, tie down sails, and anchor their craft against the storm.

A servant hurried out to take the empty teacup and the tray of sandwiches she had brought an hour before. A matronly woman with frizzy, straw-colored hair, she frowned at the ominous storm clouds. "You must come in now, my Duke."

"Today I feel like staying out until the last possible moment."

"Besides," Rhombur piped up, "I haven't beaten him yet."

Leto gave an exaggerated moan. "Then we'll be out here all night."

After the servant retreated, throwing a disapproving frown over her shoulder, Leto fixed Rhombur with a determined gaze. "While you work with the Ixian underground, I will mobilize military forces and prepare for a full-scale assault. I won't let you go alone, my good friend. Gurney Halleck will accompany you. He's a great fighter and smuggler . . . and he's already been inside Ix."

Gray daylight glinted off the metal cap on Rhombur's skull as he nodded. "I would not turn down his assistance." He and Gurney often played baliset together, and sang. The Ixian nobleman often practiced for hours at a time to help his coordination, using his cyborg fingers to strum the gentle strings adeptly, though his singing voice never improved. "Gurney was also a friend of my father's. He'll want revenge almost as much as I do."

Leto's black hair whipped in the wind. "Duncan will provide you with covert equipment and weapons. A camouflaged combat pod hidden in the Ixian wilderness can cause a lot of damage, if used properly. Before you go, we'll work out a precise date and time for our full military assault from the outside, to coordinate it with your uprising from within. You punch the enemy in the belly, and while he's bent over, my troops will deliver the finishing blow."

Rhombur moved another game piece as they discussed troop movements and weaponry. After all this time, the Tleilaxu would not expect an outright frontal attack, but their Sardaukar allies would be another story.

Leto reached forward to pick up a perfectly detailed Sardaukar captain and moved it from the base of the pyramid all the way to the top. "I love to see you enthralled with plans, Rhombur. It occupies your mind, focuses your thoughts."

He toppled Rhombur's most important piece, the Corrino Emperor sitting on a tiny representation of the Golden Lion Throne. "And when you don't pay attention to your game, it's far easier for me to win."

The Prince smiled, rippling a scar on his cheek. "You're a formidable foe, indeed. It is my great honor, and good fortune, that we're *allies* on the field of battle."

Man participates in all cosmic events.
— EMPEROR IDRISS 1, Legacies of Kaitain

For each day Jessica spent at the Imperial Court, Lady Anirul found something even more extravagant to show her. The young concubine was ostensibly a lady-in-waiting to serve the Emperor's wife, but Anirul treated her more like a guest, rarely giving her anything important to do.

In an evening's entertainment at the Hassik III Center for the Performing Arts, Jessica rode with the Emperor and his lady in a private coach. The exquisite enameled vehicle was drawn by enormous Harmonthep lions, whose creamy fur and wide paws were more suited to traversing rugged mountains than the streets of the most glorious city in the Imperium. As crowds lined the boulevards, the trained animals padded along, their muscles rippling in the pastel light of sunset. For public events such as this, teams of manicurists maintained the saberlike claws, while groomers shampooed the lions' fur and brushed their manes.

Attired in a scarlet jacket and gold trousers, Shaddam sat stony-faced in the front of the shielded carriage. He did not strike Jessica as having a particular fondness for plays or operas, but his advisors must have pointed out the benefits of portraying himself as a cultured ruler. Anirul and Jessica, clearly subordinate, rode in the rear seat.

During Jessica's time on Kaitain, the Emperor

had not spoken more than a few sentences to her; she doubted he even remembered her name. She was, after all, merely a lady-in-waiting, pregnant, and of little interest. The three eldest Imperial Princesses—Irulan, Chalice, and Wensicia—traveled in a less ornate and unshielded vehicle behind them. Josifa and Rugi remained with caretakers.

The Imperial coaches pulled up in front of the column-studded edifice of the Hassik III Center, a cavernous building designed with acoustic enhancements and prismatic windows. Spectators could see and hear performances from the most creative talents in the Imperium, without missing a whisper or nuance, even sitting in the most distant seats.

Veined-marble arches with flanking fire-fountains marked an entrance reserved for the Emperor and his retinue. The fountains spewed feathery arcs of perfumed oils; blue flames consumed much of the fuel before the droplets fell into the lozenge-shaped reflecting pools.

Hassik III, one of the first rulers to settle on Kaitain after the destruction of Salusa Secundus, had taxed his subjects nearly into bankruptcy in order to rebuild a governmental infrastructure. Members of the Landsraad, vowing not to be outdone by House Corrino, had built their own monuments in the growing city. Within a generation, unremarkable Kaitain had become an awesome spectacle of Imperial architecture, museums, and bureaucratic self-indulgence. The Performing Arts Center was only one example.

Preoccupied, Anirul looked up at the imposing building, then turned her round eyes toward Jessica. "When you become a Reverend Mother, you will experience the wonders of Other Memory. In my collective past"—she raised a slender hand, devoid of rings or other jewelry, and made a graceful, all-encompassing gesture—"I remember when this was built. The first performance here was an ancient and rather amusing play: *Don Quixote*."

Jessica raised her eyebrows. In class, Mohiam had drilled her for years, teaching her culture and literature, politics and psychology. "*Don Quixote* seems an odd choice, my Lady, especially after the tragedy on Salusa Secundus."

Anirul looked at her husband's profile as he gazed out the coach window; Shaddam was engrossed in the brassy fanfare and the crowds waving pennants in his honor. "Back then, Emperors permitted themselves to have a sense of humor," she said.

The Imperial party stepped from their coaches and passed through the arched entryway, followed by a train of attendants who carried a long whale-fur cape for the Emperor. Ladies-in-waiting draped a similar, though less impressive, fur-lined shawl around Anirul's shoulders. The retinue entered the Center for the Performing Arts with slow precision, so that the spectators and news imagers could capture every detail.

Shaddam marched up a cascade of polished stairs to the spacious Imperial box, close enough to the stage that he would be able to see the pores on the actors' faces, if he bothered to pay attention. He seated himself in a cushioned wingseat that had been sculpted to smaller proportions in order to make the Emperor look large and dominating.

Without a word to her husband, Anirul sat on his left, and continued her conversation with Jessica. "Have you ever seen a performance by a registered company of Jongleurs?"

Jessica shook her head. "Is it true that Master Jongleurs have supernatural powers, enabling them to wring raw emotions from even the hardest heart?"

"The Jongleur talent appears to be a resonance-hypnosis technique similar to what the Sisterhood uses, except these players use it merely to enhance their performances."

With a toss of her bronze hair, Jessica said, "Then I look forward to experiencing the enhanced play." Tonight they would see *My Father's Shadow*, one of the finest post-Butlerian pieces of literature, a work that had done much to secure Crown Prince Raphael Corrino's place in history as a revered hero and respected scholar.

Escorted by Sardaukar guards, valets entered the Imperial box and offered goblets of sparkling wine to the Emperor, then to his wife and her guest. Anirul handed one of the fluted glasses to Jessica. "A fine Caladan vintage, part of the shipment your Duke sent as a gift, to thank us for watching over you." She reached over to touch Jessica's slightly rounded belly. "Though I dare say, he didn't seem pleased to have you come here, based upon what Mohiam told me."

Jessica flushed. "I'm sure Duke Atreides has enough business to distract him from wistful thoughts about a mere concubine." She maintained a placid expression, so as not to show the pain of missing him. "I'm sure he has some grand ambition planned."

The valets vanished with their wine just as the orchestra struck up the overture and the play began. Shimmering floodlights bathed the stage, tuned yellow to imply sunrise. The set had no markings, props, or curtains. The acting troupe marched out in a phalanx and found their marks. Jessica studied the lush costumes, the fabric embellished with splendid mythological designs.

Shaddam sat in his chair, not quite bored, but Jessica guessed that would come soon enough. Following tradition, the performers waited until the Emperor nodded for them to proceed.

Behind the stage, a technician activated a bank of solido hologenerators, and suddenly the props and sets shimmered into visibility—a towering castle wall, a throne, a thick stand of trees in the distance.

"Ah, Imperium, glorious Imperium!" exclaimed the lead actor playing Raphael. Carrying a long scepter topped by a faceted glowglobe, he had thick, dark hair that flowed to the center of his back. His stocky, muscular body gave him a commanding presence. The face had a porcelain beauty that stirred Jessica. "My eyes are not strong enough and my brain not spacious enough to see and learn about all the wonders that my father rules."

The actor lowered his head. "Would that I could devote my life to study, so that I might die with even a glimmer of understanding. In that way I could best honor God and my forefathers, who have made the Imperium great, who have stamped out the scourge of thinking machines." He raised his head, and with a piercing gaze looked squarely at Shaddam. "To be born a Corrino is more blessing than any man deserves."

Jessica felt a chill on her skin. The actor's delivery was rich and sonorous, yet he had altered the traditional words slightly. From her studies, she was certain that she remembered every line of the classic play. If Lady Anirul noticed the modified soliloquy, though, she said nothing of it.

The female lead character, a beautiful woman named Herade, rushed onstage to interrupt the Crown Prince's reverie and inform him of an assassination attempt upon his father, the Padishah Emperor Idriss I. Shocked, young Raphael sank to his knees and began to weep, but Herade clutched his hand. "No, no, my Prince. He is not yet dead. Your father survives, though he has suffered a grievous head wound."

"Idriss is the light that makes the Golden Lion Throne shine across the universe. I must see him. I must rekindle that ember and keep him alive."

Herade said, "Then let us make haste. The Suk doctor is with him already." Solemnly, they left the stage together. Within moments, the holo-scenery shifted to an interior room.

As he watched from his box, Shaddam leaned back with a heavy sigh.

In the play, Emperor Idriss failed to recover from his injury or awaken from his coma, yet life-support systems kept him alive. Idriss remained in the Imperial bed, tended round the clock. Raphael Corrino, de facto ruler and rightful heir to the throne, grieved for his father but never formally took his place. Raphael never sat in the Imperial throne, but always seated himself on a smaller chair. Though he commanded the Imperium for years, he never called himself anything other than Crown Prince.

"I shall not usurp my father's throne, and woe to any parasite who considers it." The actor stepped closer to the Imperial box. The faceted glowglobe atop his staff was a shimmering jewel like a cold geological torch.

Jessica blinked, trying to assess precisely which lines the actor had altered, and why. She saw something strange in his movements, a certain tension. Was he only nervous? Perhaps he had forgotten his lines. But a Jongleur would never forget his lines. . . .

"House Corrino is more powerful than the ambition of any individual. No one man can claim to own that heritage for himself." The actor rapped his staff on the stage. "Such hubris would be folly, indeed."

Now Anirul began to notice the mistakes herself and flashed a glance at Jessica. Shaddam just looked sleepy.

The actor portraying the enlightened Raphael took a second step forward, just below the Emperor's box, while the other Jongleurs faded back, giving him center stage. "We all have parts to play in the grand performance of the Imperium."

He then digressed completely from the script and recited from a Shakespeare play, words even more ancient than My Father's Shadow. "All the world's a stage, and all the men and women merely players. They have their exits and their entrances, and one man in his time plays many parts."

Raphael reached to his breast and yanked off a ruby brooch. The gem had been ground down so that it looked like a lens. "And Shaddam, I am much more than an actor," he said, startling the Emperor into awareness. He slammed the faceted ruby into a socket on the staff, and Jessica realized it was a power source.

"An Emperor should love his people, serve them, and work to protect them. Instead, you chose to become the

Butcher of Zanovar." The glowglobe atop his staff blazed intensely bright. "If you wanted to kill me, Shaddam, I would gladly have given my life for all the people of Zanovar."

Sardaukar stepped forward to the edge of the stage, not certain what to do.

"I am your half brother Tyros Reffa, son of Elrood IX by Lady Shando Balut. I am the man you tried to murder when you destroyed a planet, slaying millions of innocents—*and I challenge your right to House Corrino!*"

The staff blazed, like a sun.

"That's a weapon!" Shaddam bellowed, standing up. "Stop him, but take him alive!"

The Sardaukar rushed forward, clubs and blades drawn. Reffa looked startled, waving his jeweled staff. "No, this isn't how I meant for it to happen!" The Sardaukar were almost upon him, and Reffa seemed to reach a sudden decision. He adjusted the gem. "I only wanted to make my case."

A beam shot out from the prop, and Jessica lurched to one side. Lady Anirul toppled her own chair, throwing herself to the floor. The focused glowglobe had emitted a deadly laser blast. A nearby Sardaukar guard crashed into the Emperor's chair, knocking Shaddam aside while the fiery blow shattered the guard's chest into cinders.

The audience screamed. The Jongleur acting company fled to the rear of the stage, looking at Reffa in astonishment.

Ducking behind props to avoid a volley of Sardaukar fire, Tyros Reffa swung his faceted glowglobe, slicing with the laser as if it were a long, hot knife. Abruptly, the burst of blinding light sputtered out, the power source in the ruby brooch drained.

Sardaukar guards poured across the stage and surrounded the man who claimed to be Elrood's son. Attendants dragged the shaken but uninjured Emperor to safety behind the ruined Imperial box. A young theater usher assisted Anirul, her daughters, and Jessica. Emergency response teams rushed in to extinguish the smoldering fires.

In the corridor outside the Imperial box, a Sardaukar officer strode forward, his face grim. "We have captured him, Sire."

Shaddam looked stunned and ruffled. A pair of valets brushed off his Imperial cape, while another smoothed his pomaded hair. The Emperor's green eyes turned cold, more angry than frightened by his brush with death. "Good."

Plucking at his chest, Shaddam rearranged the glittering medals he had awarded himself for past accomplishments. "See that you arrest every person involved here. Somebody made a huge blunder with these Jongleurs."

"It will be done, Sire."

The Emperor finally looked over at his wife and Jessica, who stood nearby with his daughters, all unharmed. He showed no relief, just processed the information.

"Well . . . in a sense, perhaps I should reward the man," the Emperor mused, trying to lighten the tension. "At least we don't have to watch any more of that dull play."

The mysterious Bene Gesserit Mother School
had been a peculiar experience for the three
Richesian inventors, but Haloa Rund could not
say exactly why. For some reason, the trip to
Wallach IX seemed unreal.

The return shuttle approached the laboratory
satellite of Korona. Rund sat meekly in a passenger
seat, wondering if the Bene Gesserit would actually commission their large-scale project from his
uncle, Count Ilban Richese. The Sisterhood could
certainly afford to pay for technical assistance with
their power systems; the work would be a boon for
the Richesian economy.

Oddly, though, Rund couldn't remember exactly what he and his companions had actually
done on Wallach IX. It had been an exhausting
trip, with many meetings. They had worked up detailed plans and suggestions for the Sisters . . . hadn't
they? Director Kinnis and bookish Talis Balt must
still have the plans in their crystalboards. A stick-
ler for schedules, Kinnis tracked the activities of
all his lab employees to the nanosecond, using dictation cards that he always kept in his pocket.
Whatever the bureaucrat didn't have on his crystalboards, Talis Balt would surely remember.

But something inside Rund's mind seemed slippery. Every time he tried to remember any specific conversation or particular design proposal he had made, his grasp of the subject slid sideways. He had never been so distractible before. In fact, he had always been obsessively focused, thanks in part to his minimal Mentat background.

Now, as their ship docked against the orbiting satellite, he had a vague memory of looking over facilities on Wallach IX. He and his colleagues had been inside the famed School, and he must have been paying attention. He did remember a sumptuous banquet the Sisters had thrown for them, the best meal he'd ever eaten. But he couldn't recall any of the items on the menu.

Neither Balt nor Kinnis seemed perturbed, already discussing completely different work. The men didn't mention the Bene Gesserit at all, focused instead on improving the manufacturing techniques for valuable Richesian mirrors in the orbital laboratory.

As he and his colleagues disembarked into the Korona research facility, Rund felt as if he were awakening from a bad dream. He turned around, disoriented, realizing that none of them had any luggage or personal articles with them. Not now, anyway. Had they packed any?

Glad to be back in the satellite lab facility, and eager to plunge into his continuing research and development work, he found himself tempted to forget anything to do with the Sisterhood. He resented the lost time . . . but wasn't sure precisely how long he had been gone. He would have to check.

Walking beside Rund through the metal corridors, Flinto Kinnis and Talis Balt blinked in the harsh light. Struggling to think back to the Bene Gesserit banquet, Rund sensed fragments of thoughts filtering into the edge of his consciousness, like water seeping through a crack in a dike. He tried to use some of the Mentat techniques he had attempted to learn, long ago, but each time it was like grasping a moss-slicked rock. He wanted to know more. If the break became larger, perhaps the troublesome memory block would crumble away.

A cold feeling of dread weighed on him, and he began to feel dizzy. This wasn't right. His ears rang. *Did the witches do something to us?*

He began to lose his balance on rubbery legs. Before his companions could help him, Rund slumped onto the cool metal deck. His ears kept ringing.

Leaning over the fallen man, Talis Balt wrinkled his smooth forehead. "What is it, Haloa? You want a medic?"

Kinnis pursed his lips. "Perhaps a furlough, Rund? I'm sure your uncle would allow it." He seemed to be reassessing schedules in his mind. "I doubt the Bene Gesserit were serious about contracting our services anyway."

Confused and alarmed, Rund seized on the comment. "Our services for *what*, Director?" The recent days were foggy shadows. How could he have forgotten so much so soon? "Do you remember?"

The bureaucrat sniffed. "Why, for their . . . project, of course. What does it matter? A wasted effort, if you ask me."

To Rund's mind, it seemed that his eyes had turned inward, revealing flashes of a Bene Gesserit woman, her lips phrasing harsh questions that echoed in his head. He saw her mouth opening and closing in slow motion, uttering strange words, her long fingers moving hypnotically.

He used Mentat mnemonics, focusing techniques. Moment by moment, the crack in the mental dike widened. He remembered tan cliffs, a rock quarry . . . a crashed ship, a specific comment. *"You were friends of Chobyn."*

Abruptly, the mental block crumbled and broke, revealing everything. *"Tell us what you know of this invention. How do we re-create it?"* Still seated in the corridor, Rund began shouting commands. "Bring me a holorecorder, now. I need to get these details down."

"He's gone crazy," Director Kinnis lamented. "Something snapped."

But Talis Balt snatched one of the dictation cards from the bureaucrat's pocket and handed it to his colleague. Rund grabbed it. "This is important! No time for questions before I lose contact."

Without looking at either of his companions, he activated the voice pickup and spoke into it in a breathless rush. "Tenu Chobyn . . . his secret projects were of much concern to Premier Calimar. He disappeared . . . defected to House Harkonnen. Too many gaps in the records he left behind. Ah, now we know what he was working on! A generator for an invisibility field."

Balt knelt next to him, his smooth brow furrowed. Kinnis looked as if he still wanted to call for medics and drugs, and a relief ship to take the inventor down to Richese. Kinnis didn't like problems that unsettled the workforce, but he had to take a light touch with the Count's nephew.

More images flooded into Rund's mind, and his words came out rapid-fire. "He used his field generator to make a warship invisible . . . Harkonnens crashed it into the Mother School. That is why we were brought to Wallach IX, to help them understand the incredible technology—"

Flinto Kinnis had heard enough. "Nonsense, we were summoned to discuss work on a . . ."

"I'm sure I have everything in my notes," Balt added, but then frowned.

"Do you remember the quarry?" Rund demanded. "The women who interrogated us? They did something to erase our memories."

Clutching the plaz dictation card, the impatient inventor chattered everything he could remember. A curious crowd began to gather in the satellite corridor, and as Rund painted images from his restored memory, Kinnis and Balt could not tear themselves away. Detail after detail hammered at their doubts, but still they could not remember.

Obsessed, Rund demanded more dictation cards and spoke into them for hours, refusing any food or water, until finally he lay on the floor of the corridor, exhausted. His work had only just begun.

He who laughs alone at night does so in contemplation of his own evil.

—Fremen Wisdom

Because water was so precious on Arrakis, Rondo Tuek's moisture-extraction factories at the antarctic cap had made him a wealthy water merchant. He had the means to purchase everything a man could desire.

Yet he lived in abject terror, doubting he would ever feel safe again, no matter where he fled.

Tuek holed up inside his mansion in Carthag, an elegant home filled with beautiful objets d'art he had collected. He had spent a great deal of money to install a state-of-the-art security system, and to acquire a wide range of personal defensive weapons. For guards, he had hired off-world mercenaries with no family ties to any of the victims of his treachery.

He should have felt safe.

After he had revealed the location of the long-hidden smuggler base, Tuek's life had taken a sharp downturn. For many years he had kept the presence of Dominic Vernius secret, accepting bribes from him and helping his smugglers acquire items they needed. He had felt no guilt about playing both sides, so long as his profits kept coming in. Later, seeing an opportunity to make a purseful of solaris, Tuek had fingered the fugitive to Count Hasimir Fenring. Well-armed Sardaukar troops had descended upon the smuggler base.

He'd never suspected that the renegades had hoarded atomic weapons. Cornered, Dominic Vernius had triggered a stone-burner, vaporizing his base, his men, and an entire regiment of the Emperor's soldiers. . . .

Considering the possibility of a beautiful female assassin, Tuek had dismissed his concubines and slept alone. Ever alert to the possibility of poisons, he prepared his food himself and tested every morsel with the finest Kronin poison snoopers. He no longer walked unprotected into the city, fearing a sniper attack.

Now the unpredictable Fremen, without explanation, had tersely ended their business relationship with him, and would no longer use him as an intermediary with the Spacing Guild. For years, he had worked as a go-between, delivering spice bribes from the Fremen to the Guild.

Did the Fremen suspect what he had done? On the other hand, why should they care about a band of smugglers? Still, if they insisted on eliminating his participation, Tuek could have no compunction against reporting their illegal activities to Kaitain. Perhaps Shaddam IV would reward him handsomely, just as Count Fenring had done.

But deep-seated fear kept the water merchant trapped within his heavily guarded house. *I have made too many enemies.*

He tried to find comfort in the soft cushions and silks that surrounded him. The hypnotic hum of outrageously expensive fountains should have lulled him to sleep, but it did not. He told himself for the thousandth time that he was being unduly concerned.

LIET-KYNES AND Stilgar, along with three other Fremen commandos, easily bypassed the security systems. They could cross open expanses of sand and leave no recognizable tracks. This was no challenge to them.

After cutting the throats of two mercenary guards, the

Fremen slipped into the water merchant's mansion and glided down the well-lit corridors. "Tuek should have hired better men," Stilgar whispered.

Liet had drawn his crysknife, but the milky dagger remained unblooded this night. He intended to save his violence for the man who most deserved it.

Years ago, young Liet had joined Dominic Vernius and his smugglers down at the south pole. Dominic had been a great friend and teacher, well liked by his men. But after Liet had left them and returned to the sietch, Rondo Tuek had betrayed the renegades. The water merchant was without honor.

Tonight, Tuek would receive a different kind of payment: the Fremen gift of justice. . . .

They hurried silently down stone corridors, melting into shadows, approaching the merchant's sleeping quarters. It had been a simple matter to obtain detailed plans of the mansion from former servants, town-Fremen whose loyalty remained with their sietches.

Even though he had never met Dominic Vernius, Stilgar followed Liet, who was now the Abu Naib of all Fremen. Any razzia commando would have been happy to join this mission. Fremen understood the concept of vendetta.

In deep darkness, they broke into Tuek's bedchamber and sealed the door behind them. Their blades were drawn, their footsteps as quiet as oil trickling across rock. Liet could have brought out his maula pistol and shot the traitor in his bed, but it was not his intention to murder the man. Not at all.

Tuek awoke with a start, and sucked in a loud breath to scream, but Stilgar leaped upon him like a wolf. The two thrashed on the slick sheets; Stilgar clamped down on the man's throat and lips to prevent him from calling out.

The water merchant's wide-set eyes rolled from side to

side, filled with terror. He squirmed, but the commandos held his short legs, pinned his hands to the bed to prevent him from triggering alarms or reaching for hidden weapons.

Stilgar said in a sharp whisper, "We don't have much time, Liet."

Liet-Kynes glared at the captive. Years ago, as a young Fremen emissary, Liet had journeyed to the ice-mining facilities to deliver the monthly spice bribe, but it was clear that Tuek did not recognize him now.

As a practical matter, Stilgar symbolically cut out Tuek's tongue so his screams were reduced to gurgling sounds because of the blood pooling in his mouth.

As the man retched and spat gouts of scarlet, Liet pronounced the Fremen sentence upon him. "Rondo Tuek, we take your tongue for the treachery you have spoken."

With the tip of his crysknife, Liet gouged out the man's eyes, one at a time, and placed the staring white orbs on a bedstand. "We take your eyes for witnessing things you should not have seen."

Tuek writhed and struggled in horror and agony, trying to scream, but he only succeeded in spitting more blood. Two of the Fremen commandos frowned at the wasted moisture.

With the edge of the blade, Liet first carved off the treacherous man's left ear, then his right, placing the flaps of skin beside the tongue and eyeballs on the bedside table. "We take your ears for listening to secrets not meant for you."

All the commandos participated in the final step: chopping off Tuek's hands with a hollow sound of cracking bones. "We take your hands, with which you collected bribes, selling out a man who trusted you."

At last they released the merchant to flop and bleed on his bed—alive, but perhaps better off dead. . . .

Before the Fremen left, they drank deeply of the trickling

water in the ornamental fountain in Tuek's bedchamber. Then they slipped silently back into the dark streets of Carthag.

From this point on, Liet-Kynes would deal with the Spacing Guild directly and establish his own terms.

A thought derived from intensity of feeling is localized in the heart. Abstract thought must be localized in the brain.

—Bene Gesserit Dictum, The Principles of Control

Rhombur wore a well-tailored uniform and dramatic purple cape lined with copper merhsilk. His movements were smooth enough now, and the garments so well made that he could disguise his cyborg body from anyone not looking too closely. Proud to be at his side, Tessia took his arm and accompanied him through the military hangars at the fringe of the Cala Municipal Spaceport.

Inside the largest aircraft bay, they met Leto and Thufir. The battering and clanging of maintenance crews filled the building with a tumult that made Rhombur cringe.

"The first step is nearly ready, Prince Rhombur," Hawat announced. "We have purchased passage on a Heighliner for you and Gurney, but you will follow such a convoluted and time-consuming route that when you arrive at Ix, no one will be able to trace your origin."

Wiping grease from his hands and shoving a crystal databoard into his pocket, Duncan Idaho hurried over to greet them. "Leto, our fleet is almost ready for inspection. We have completed full checkouts on twenty-six war frigates, nineteen troop dropships, one hundred combat 'thopters, and fifty-eight single-man fighters."

Thufir Hawat mentally recorded the numbers, calculated the number of solaris the Spacing Guild would charge to transport the entire force, and compared it to the available finances of House Atreides. "For such an extensive operation, we will need to secure a loan from the Guild Bank, my Duke."

Leto dismissed the concern. "My credit is solid, Thufir. This is an investment we should have made long ago."

"And I will pay back every solari, Leto . . . unless I fail to recapture Ix for House Vernius—in which case, I'll be bankrupt, or dead." Noticing the flash of Tessia's sepia eyes, Rhombur added quickly, "It's difficult to overcome my old ways of thinking, I fear. But I've waited long enough. I wish Gurney and I could leave tomorrow. We'll have a lot of work to do underground."

Leto had eyes for the sleek forms of his military aircraft. They walked past crews that were testing engines, refueling, checking control panels. The men of the Atreides House Guard snapped to attention and saluted their Duke.

"Why so many 'thopters and single-man fighters, Duncan? This isn't an air or ground battle. We will have to fight our way through tunnels into the underground city."

Duncan pointed to the various craft. "Our assault relies heavily on the frigates and troop dropships to deploy nearly a full legion of men as rapidly as possible. However, the 'thopters and the single-man fighters will hit first, and hard, to take out Sardaukar sensor towers and crack open the shielded hatches that lead through the cliff walls." He scanned the cluster of dart-shaped, fast fighters. "If our troops can't get past the surface defenses quickly, the underground takeover is doomed."

Leto nodded. Thufir Hawat kept a careful mental inventory of the shields, explosives, lasguns, hand weapons, rations, fuel, and uniforms. This kind of major, single-strike assault posed as many business problems as tactical ones. As it was, he would be taking away most of the forces he normally kept in place to defend Caladan. It was a balancing act.

However if the Emperor decided to retaliate against the Atreides homeworld by sending Sardaukar, no amount of defensive strength would be adequate. Since the Emperor's dire warning about illegal spice stockpiles, and his astonishingly vicious assault on Zanovar, many Houses were tightening their security. Some noble families had voluntarily surrendered long-held spice hoards, at great cost to themselves, while others vehemently denied any involvement in contraband melange.

Leto had sent a message to Kaitain, volunteering to submit to a CHOAM audit—a message that had not been answered. Innocence was no assurance of safety, since records (and even stockpiles themselves) could always be falsified. Thufir cited the example of House Ecaz, whom he considered to be innocent of charges in a recent flare-up. After an infiltrator destroyed a hidden spice stockpile on Grumman, Viscount Hundro Moritani railed against Ecaz—his archenemy. Shortly afterward another spice hoard was exposed, this one on Ecaz. Indignant, Archduke Armand Ecaz claimed it had been planted there by House Moritani, simply to frame the Ecazi people. As proof, he offered several already-executed Grumman "saboteurs." The Emperor was investigating while the two sides hurled charges and countercharges at each other.

A liveried Courier poked her head into the daylit frame of the hangar. Breathless, she trotted inside and asked directions of one of the mechanics, who pointed toward the Duke and his companions. Leto stiffened, recalling all the times in the past when flushed Couriers had delivered urgent messages. Never once, as far as he could remember, had they brought good news.

The woman approached Leto briskly, bowed, and asked to see his ducal ring to verify his identity. Satisfied, she handed him a message cylinder, after which he dismissed her with a minimum of courtesy. Rhombur and Tessia took a step back, giving Leto space in which to read and consider the communiqué. Duncan and Thufir both stared at him, steeling themselves.

"It is an official notice from Kaitain. There has been an assassination attempt on the Emperor," Leto said, his voice low, then he paled. "And Jessica was in the line of fire!" His knuckles whitened as he clenched the open cylinder; his gray eyes flicked from side to side as he absorbed the details. "According to this, a madman went berserk during a play."

Rhombur looked at Tessia in dismay. "Vermilion hells! Jessica was supposed to go to Kaitain for *protection*."

"Is she injured?" Duncan asked.

"Jessica wrote this second note," Leto said, clearly relieved, removing a new sheet of paper. He read it and passed it on to Thufir Hawat, not caring if his Mentat saw the private thoughts of his concubine.

Leto stood in turmoil, feeling his stomach knot. Sweat broke out on his brow. Against his better judgment, he had come to love her and now placed so many of his hopes on her unborn child.

"I am sure there is far more to the story than the official announcement reveals. But still, Jessica was clearly *not* the target, my Duke," Hawat pointed out. "If any assassins had meant to kill her, they must have had ample earlier opportunities. Security was far greater with the Emperor present. No, your Lady was just . . . in the way."

"But she would have been no less dead if she had taken a lasgun blast." Leto's face was stormy; his heart wrenched. "Lady Anirul requested—no, *demanded*—that Jessica go to Kaitain for the remainder of her pregnancy. Would I have had to worry about her life if she'd remained here at Castle Caladan?"

"I think not," Duncan said, as if promising his own protection.

Around them in the hangar bay, work resumed, its sounds drowning out their low conversation. Leto felt helpless and ready to lash out. *Jessica could have been killed!* He would fight ferociously to defend her. *Losing her would devastate me*.

His first instinct was to go immediately to the Heighliner in orbit, and arrange for the first available transportation to Kaitain. Just to be by her side, he would abandon these military preparations—let the others here finish them—and stand ready to tear apart any would-be assassins who dared to cross his path.

But when he saw Rhombur looking at him, Leto remembered the complex interworkings of their secret plans, as well as what Thufir and Gurney had reported about the horrors on Ix. Yes, Leto was a human being, a man, but first and foremost he was the Duke. Despite his anguish and his longing for Jessica, he could not ignore his duty and leave his best friend Rhombur, and millions of Ixian people, to suffer for it.

"The Padishah Emperor has many enemies and is making new ones every day. He clamps down, seizes stockpiles, threatens to destroy other worlds just as he did Zanovar," Rhombur said. "He continues to clench his fist."

Tessia's expression became contemplative. "Shaddam's power comes directly from his birthright. He has the Throne . . . but does he have the skill?"

Leto shook his head, thinking of all the innocent victims that already littered the Emperor's twisted, blundering path. "I believe his Great Spice War is going to backfire on him."

Laws are dangerous to everyone, innocent and guilty alike, because they have no human understanding in and of themselves. They must be interpreted.

—States: The Bene Gesserit View

Under the usual cloudless blue sky, yet another Imperial garden party took place on the patchwork quilt of lawns, greenhouses, and arboretums on the Palace grounds. The squeals of exuberant noble children and the pleasant chatter of courtiers drifted on gentle breezes.

Jessica felt that these people had no *reality* in their existence. Ennui seemed to be their greatest risk. Even decadence must grow dull after a time. She wondered how the business of government ever got done. As a lady-in-waiting, she certainly had nothing to do, though the court Bene Gesserits seemed to be watching her all the time.

Had she been on Caladan with Leto, Jessica could have been engaged in monitoring the House finances, checking the disposition of the fishing fleets, tracking weather patterns across the great oceans. She could have been helping Leto heal from his deep grief and channel his anger into productive action. But here, she was confronted with nothing more challenging than lawn games.

As Jessica negotiated a crushed-stone path that meandered past crimson jewel bougainvillea and trumpet-shaped morning glory, the delicate scents reminded her of Caladan. On the Atreides world, dense meadows of starflowers north of the Castle thrived in the spring mists. On one warm day, far from the eyes of Thufir Hawat, Leto had taken her to an isolated clearing high above the rugged shoreline. There, on a cushion of thick starflowers, he had made love to her, and afterward they had spent half an hour looking up at the clouds. How she missed her Duke. . . .

But she must wait another four and a half months until her baby was born. Jessica was not allowed to question such things. But, silently, she could wonder.

Mohiam, the teacher who knew her so well, would be gravely disappointed when she discovered the secret of the young woman's rebellion. Jessica feared seeing the betrayal and disappointment on the Reverend Mother's face when she held up a newborn baby *boy*. Could they kill the Duke's son, out of spite?

But she squared her shoulders as she walked on. *I can always bear a daughter later, as many as the Sisterhood might want of me*.

Jessica spotted young Princess Irulan dressed in an elegant black playsuit that accented her long blonde hair. She sat on a polished stone bench, intent on a filmbook open on her lap. Looking up, Irulan noticed her. "Good afternoon, Lady Jessica. Have you been eliminated from the tournaments?"

"I am not a game player, I'm afraid."

"Neither am I." Irulan made a graceful gesture with her hand. "Will you sit?" Anirul, while remaining aloof in the Bene Gesserit way, still paid a great deal of attention to her eldest daughter. The Princess was serious and intelligent, even more so than her younger sisters.

Irulan held up her filmbook. "Have you read *Lives of the Heroes of the Jihad?*" She acted much older than her years, seemed hungry to learn. It was said that the Princess harbored aspirations of being a writer one day.

"Of course. Reverend Mother Mohiam was my teacher. She made me memorize the whole thing. There is a statue of Raquella Berto-Anirul on the grounds of the Mother School."

Irulan raised her eyebrows. "Serena Butler was always my favorite."

Jessica sat on the sun-warmed stone bench. They watched children run by, kicking a red ball in front of them. The Princess put away her filmbook and changed the subject. "You must find Kaitain quite different from Caladan."

Jessica smiled. "Kaitain is so beautiful and fascinating. I learn new things every day, see amazing sights." She paused, then admitted, "It is not my home, however."

Irulan's classic beauty reminded Jessica of herself at that age. She was only eleven years older than the Princess; the two of them might have been sisters, by appearance. *This one is exactly the type my Duke should marry, in order to gain stature for his House. I should hate her, but I do not.*

The Emperor's wife, wearing a long dress of mauve cloth with a golden collar and filigree sleeves, emerged from the garden path behind her. "Oh, there you are, Jessica. What are you two plotting?"

Irulan replied. "We're just talking about how amazing Kaitain is."

Anirul allowed herself a momentary flash of pride. She noted the filmbook, knew that Irulan had been studying while others played court games. In a conspiratorial tone she said to Jessica, "Irulan seems more dedicated to learning the labyrinth of leadership than my husband is." She extended a ring-bedecked hand to Jessica. "Come, I have things to discuss with you."

Jessica followed the Emperor's wife through a topiary garden, whose shrubs had been trimmed into soldier shapes. Anirul plucked a small, out-of-place twig from the uniform of one of the shrub-soldiers. "Jessica, you are different from the hangers-on at court, who constantly gossip and vie for social position. I find you refreshing."

"Surrounded by so much splendor, I must seem rather plain."

Anirul chuckled. "Your beauty requires no enhancement. I, on the other hand, am expected to dress in a certain way." She displayed the rings on her fingers. "This blue soostone, however, is more than a ring."

She pressed the gem, and a shimmering journal appeared in front of her, the pages dense with information. Before Jessica could read any of the holo-scribed words, Anirul deactivated the projection.

"Since privacy is so rare at Court, I have found my diary to be an extremely useful tool for contemplation. It enables me to analyze my thoughts, and to sift through Other Memory. You will know about it, Jessica, when you become a Reverend Mother."

Jessica followed her on stepping-stones that crossed a small water garden, where oversize lilies and aquatic flowers floated. Anirul continued, "I consider my journal a responsibility, in case anything should happen to prevent my memory transference at the end of my life." Her words left much unsaid: In these critical last days of the long-planned secret breeding program, she, as the Kwisatz Mother, needed a written chronicle for those who would follow her. She dared not risk having her life and experiences vanish into an abyss of unrecorded history.

Anirul fingered her soostone ring. "I would like to give you a journal of your own, Jessica. An old-fashioned bound book. In it, you may preserve your thoughts and observations, your most personal feelings. You will come to a better understanding of yourself and those around you."

As they walked around a fountain, Jessica felt a mist on her skin, like the breath of a child. Unconsciously, she touched her belly, feeling the life inside there. Growing.

"My gift is already in your apartment. You will find an old blank book inside a small rolltop desk that belonged to my dear friend Lobia. Write in your diary. It could be a new friend for you in our lonely, crowded Palace."

Jessica paused, not sure how to respond. "Thank you, my Lady. I shall make my first entry this evening."

There are some men who refuse to accept defeat under any circumstances. Will history judge them heroes, or fools?

—EMPEROR SHADDAM IV,
Revised Official Imperial History (draft)

In bygone glory years, Cammar Pilru had been the Ixian Ambassador to Kaitain, a man of stature whose duties took him from the glittering cavern cities to the Landsraad Hall and the Imperial Court. A distinguished and sometimes beguiling man, Pilru had tirelessly sought favorable concessions for Ixian industrial products by slipping payments to one official or another, giving away valuable luxury items, bartering favor for favor.

Then the Tleilaxu had invaded his world. House Corrino had ignored his pleas for assistance, and the Landsraad turned a deaf ear to his complaints. His wife had been killed in the attack. His world and his life were destroyed.

Once, in what seemed another lifetime, the Ambassador had wielded considerable influence in financial, business, and political circles. Cammar Pilru had made friends in high places, kept many secrets. Though he was not inclined to engage in extortion, the mere *perception* that he might use a bit of information against another person gave him substantial power. Even after the passage of so many years, he remembered each detail, and others remembered much of it as well. Now it was time to use that information.

The Warden of the Imperial Prison on Kaitain, Nanee McGarr, was a former smuggler and rogue. Judging by her broad, swarthy appearance, some made the assumption that she was a man, and an ugly one at that. Originally from a high-gravity planet in the Unsidor system, she was squat and at least as muscular as a big Anbus wrestler. McGarr had served almost a year in an Ixian prison tunnel before bribing a guard to let her escape. Officially, she remained at large.

Years later, upon glimpsing McGarr in the Imperial city, Ambassador Pilru had recognized her from confidential Ixian arrest notices. After Pilru had privately revealed to her that he knew—and planned to keep—her secret, the Warden was in his pocket. For twenty long years he had remained on Kaitain, an exiled ambassador from a renegade House, and he had never found a need to call in that favor.

Then an actor had boldly tried to assassinate the Emperor, making shocking claims concerning the actor's lineage. Those assertions had been outrageous enough to plant seeds in Ambassador Pilru's mind. He desperately needed to see this prisoner who might be the son of Elrood IX and the Imperial concubine Shando Balut, a woman who had later become the wife of Earl Dominic Vernius.

If true, Tyros Reffa was not only the half brother of Shaddam IV—but also of Prince Rhombur Vernius. It was a staggering thought, a double-revelation. A Prince of Corrino and of Vernius locked up in prison, right here on Kaitain! Rhombur thought himself the last survivor of his Great House, and believed that his bloodline would end with him.

Now there might be a slim chance, at least through the maternal line. . . .

Shaddam would never grant him access to Reffa, so instead the Ambassador decided upon another avenue. Despite the decline of House Vernius, Warden McGarr would not want her past crimes revealed. It could only lead to deeper investigations. In the end, the Ambassador didn't even have to raise the threat, and she made arrangements for him. . . .

When darkness began to settle over the metropolis of Corrinth, Pilru took a forest trail along the western perimeter of the Palace grounds. He crossed an ivory rock bridge over a stream and disappeared into shadows on the other side. In his pockets he carried certain medical tools, sample vials, and a small holorecorder, all concealed in a nullentropy pouch strapped against his stomach.

"This way," a gravelly voice said from the direction of the stream. In the dimness, Pilru saw the boatman he was supposed to meet, a hunched figure with pale, glistening eyes. The motor made a faint purr, holding the craft steady against the current.

After Pilru climbed aboard, the flat-bottom boat rode low in the water. The boatman used a tall tiller to guide them as the simple craft traversed a maze of waterways. Around them thorn hedges rose high, forming ominous silhouettes against the darkening sky. There were many dead ends in these labyrinthine canals, traps for the uninformed. But the crouching pilot knew the route.

The boat rounded a bend, and the hedges here appeared taller, the sharp thorns longer. Ahead, Pilru saw dim lights at the base of a large structure of gray stone. A double-doored metal gate over a water lane led into the penal facility. Lights shone on the other side of the lattice ironwork.

Set atop high poles flanking the gate were the heads of four executed prisoners—three men and a woman. Their skulls, still draped in bloody flesh and then coated with a preservation polymer, had been hollowed out and fitted with glowglobes, so that an unsettling ghoulish light shone through the eye sockets, mouths, and nostrils.

"Traitor's Gate," the boatman announced, as the metal doors creaked open and the small boat hummed through.

"A lot of famous prisoners enter this way, but not many come back out."

A guard on a dock waved them over, and Pilru climbed from the swaying boat. Without asking to see his ambassadorial credentials, the man led him through a dismal corridor that smelled of mold and rot. From somewhere, Pilru heard screams. Perhaps they were echoes from the Emperor's much-feared torture chambers . . . or simply recordings to maintain an excruciating sense of anxiety among the prisoners.

Pilru was guided to a small cell rimmed by a glowing orange containment field. "Our royal suite," the guard announced, dimming the containment field and allowing the Ambassador to step through. The cell stank.

Rivulets of moisture ran down a rock wall at the rear of the cell onto the bed and the rough stone floor, where lumps of fungus grew. Inside, a man in a tattered black coat and filthy trousers lay on a bunk. The prisoner sat up warily as they approached. "Who are you? My lawtech, at last?"

The guard said to Pilru, "Warden McGarr says to give you one hour. Then you either go . . . or you stay."

Tyros Reffa dangled his booted feet over the edge of the bed. "I have studied the guidelines of the justice system. I know the Imperial Law Code letter for letter, and even Shaddam is bound by it. He is not following—"

"The Corrinos are bound by whatever law they choose." Pilru shook his head. He had learned this personally, when he'd decried the injustices on Ix.

"I am a Corrino."

"So you say. You don't have legal representation yet?"

"Almost three weeks, and no one else has spoken to me." He looked agitated. "What happened to the rest of the acting troupe? They know nothing about this—"

"They are arrested as well."

Reffa hung his head. "For that, I am truly sorry. And for the death of the guard. I did not intend to attack, but only to speak my piece." He looked at his visitor. "So who are you, then?"

Standing close so that he could keep his voice low, Pilru identified himself by name and title. "Woefully, I am a government servant without a government. When Ix fell to invaders, the Emperor did nothing about it."

"Ix?" Reffa looked at him with a touch of pride. "My birth-mother was Shando Balut, who later married Dominic Vernius of Ix."

The Ambassador squatted, careful not to let his clothes touch anything unsavory. "If you are truly who you say, Tyros Reffa, then you are technically a Prince of House Vernius, along with your half brother Rhombur. You are the only two living members of a once-great noble family."

"I am also the only male Corrino heir." Reffa did not seem afraid of his potential fate, only indignant at his treatment.

"So you say."

The prisoner crossed his arms. "Detailed genetic tests will prove my claim."

"Exactly." The Ambassador removed a medical kit from the nullentropy container strapped to his stomach. "I have brought a genetic extraction kit with me. Emperor Shaddam means to keep your true identity hidden, so I am here without his knowledge. We must be extremely cautious."

"He has certainly performed no analyses himself. Either he already knows the truth, or he is not interested." Reffa sounded disgusted. "Does Shaddam just intend to hide me here for years, or quietly execute me? Did you know that the real reason for his attack on Zanovar was to eliminate me? All those people dead—but I wasn't even there."

Pilru, who had developed his diplomatic skills over the years, managed not to show surprise at the startling assertion. An entire planet sterilized to strike at one person? But then, he could very well believe Shaddam might have tried to take care of the perceived threat to his throne in that way.

"Anything is conceivable. Nevertheless, it serves the Emperor's purposes to deny your existence. That is why I must take samples in order to perform a full and objective analysis—somewhere far from Kaitain. I need your cooperation."

He could see an expression of hope on Reffa's face. The gray-green eyes brightened, and he sat up straight. "Of course." Mercifully, he did not ask for additional details.

Pilru opened a slender black case to reveal a gleaming autoscalpel, and a capsule syringe, along with some small vials and tubes. "I will need enough material for several genetic tests."

The prisoner submitted. Quickly the Ambassador collected blood, semen, skin scrapings, fingernails, and epithelial cells from the inside of Reffa's mouth. Everything necessary to provide absolute proof of Reffa's parentage, no matter how Shaddam tried to cover it up.

Assuming that Pilru successfully got the specimens off-planet, of course. He was playing a dangerous game here.

When all the samples were taken, Reffa's broad shoulders sagged, as if he had finally accepted that he would never get out of this prison alive. "I don't suppose I will ever be granted my day in court?" He looked like an innocent little boy.

The beloved old Docent Glax Othn had always taught him to hold justice sacred. But Shaddam, the Butcher of Zanovar, considered himself above Imperial law.

"I doubt it," the Ambassador said with brutal honesty.

The prisoner sighed. "I wrote a speech for the court, a grand statement in the tradition of Prince Raphael Corrino, the role I played in my last performance. I was going to use all of my skills to make people weep for the lost golden age of the Imperium and make my half brother recognize the error of his ways."

Pilru paused, then removed a tiny holorecorder from his

nullentropy pouch. "Deliver your speech now, Tyros Reffa. To me. And I will see that others hear it."

Reffa sat straight, drawing a magnificent cloak of dignity around himself. "I would be pleased to have any audience at all." The recorder began to hum.

AFTERWARD, WHEN THE guard returned, Ambassador Pilru stood shaken, tears streaming down his face. As the hazy containment field opened on one side, the guard said, "So? Are you staying with us? Should I find you an empty cell?"

"I'm coming." Flashing a farewell glance at Reffa, Pilru hurried out. The Ambassador's throat was dry, his knees weak. He had never before experienced the full power of a trained Jongleur.

Standing as tall and proud as an Emperor, Elrood's bastard son looked at Pilru through the orange haze of the field. "Give my greetings to Rhombur. I wish . . . we could have met."

The key to discovery lies not in mathematics, but in the imagination.

— HALOA RUND, early laboratory journals

His body still ragged and unrested, Rund hunched over an electronic drawing table, staring at doodles and magnetic lines on the flat screen. Scrolling down the list of his notes, using the few Mentat memory-recovery tricks he had learned a long time ago, he had reconstructed, in exact order, every question the Bene Gesserit had asked, every detail he had seen of the wrecked ship.

Now that he knew such an invisibility field *could* exist, he had only to find the path to re-create it. The challenge was formidable.

Talis Balt and Director Kinnis stood to one side of the austere laboratory room. "Director, I have been pondering for hours," Balt said. "Haloa's claims sound . . . correct to me, though I can't say exactly why."

"I don't remember anything," the Director said.

Rund said without looking up, "My mind has been through the rigors of Mentat training. Maybe I have some ability to resist Bene Gesserit mind tricks."

"But you failed as a Mentat," Kinnis reminded him, his voice heavy with skepticism.

"Nevertheless, it changed the neural pathways in my brain." He remembered an adage from the school: Patterns tend to repeat themselves, for success or failure. "My mind developed pockets of resistance, mental muscles, auxiliary storage areas. Perhaps that is why their coercion didn't take hold completely." His kindly old uncle would be proud of him.

Balt scratched his scalp, as if trying to dig up any remaining roots of hair. "I suggest we take the time to go over Chobyn's laboratory again."

The Director looked impatient. "We already did that after he defected. Chobyn was just a low-level researcher, from an unimportant family, so he did not have a very large space. We have used it for storage since his departure."

Rund erased the sketches on his drawing screen. Without asking Kinnis for permission, he hurried toward the old work area. . . .

Inside the long-abandoned laboratory, he stared at a list of requisitioned parts and fragments of notes. He went over administrative-surveillance holophotos taken of Chobyn—but nothing important presented itself.

The renegade inventor had been altering classic Holtzman equations developed millennia ago. The most brilliant modern scientists didn't completely understand how Tio Holtzmann's esoteric formulae worked—only that they *did* work. Rund couldn't understand what Chobyn had done, either.

His brain was afire, operating at a higher efficiency than he had imagined possible. Flinto Kinnis stood amidst the activity, doing his best to supervise, while Rund went over the entire laboratory space, ignoring the other people. He tapped floorplates, walls, and ceilings. Every square centimeter.

Kneeling at a juncture between the floor and the outer hull of the orbiting station, he noticed a crack that flashed in and out of view, a camouflaged portion, no more than a tiny flicker, a dust grain in the eye. Rund stared until his eyes ached, remembering how a stern Mentat teacher had taught him to *observe*. He sped up his perceptions, slowing down time, *and caught the next flicker.*

At the precisely correct moment, Rund stepped *through* the wall.

He found himself inside a claustrophobic alcove, smelling of metal and stale air. With another flicker, the wall sealed itself behind him. He could barely turn around in the tight room. Darkness crashed down, as if he had gone blind. His breathing became labored. Every surface was frosty.

Fumbling in the blackness, he found thin sheets of ridulian crystal, plan screens, shigawire spools packed with data. He called out, but his words bounced back at him. He could not hear or see anything of the main room.

When the wall flickered again, Rund stumbled out, unnerved but excited. Director Kinnis stared at him. "It is a secret, shielded room, but the field seems to be breaking down. Chobyn has left much information inside."

Kinnis squeezed his hands together. "Excellent, we must retrieve it. I intend to get to the bottom of this." He turned to one of the tall technicians. "The moment another flicker occurs, go inside and bring out anything you find."

The technician poised like a hunting cat, chose his time perfectly, and jumped forward to vanish into the wall. The room disappeared again.

But as Rund and Kinnis waited in the old lab for minutes, then half an hour, the man did not come back out. They could hear no sound, nor could they pry open the alcove again, despite repeated pounding on the white structural plates.

A work crew came in with cutting tools and ripped through the wall, but they found only the standard airspace between the station walls. Even scanners showed nothing unusual in the area.

While the technicians grew more desperate, Haloa Rund stared off, his mind lost in a near-Mentat projection. Based on a variation of the Holtzman equations, he assumed that the invisibility field had folded space itself in a ripple around the hidden chamber.

When the opening flickered again and stayed open, the technician slumped back out through the opening, his face pale and eyes flat, his fingernails torn and bleeding, as if he had tried to claw his way out. Two men rushed forward to help him, but the technician was dead, apparently suffocated or frozen from his strange journey. Where had the "flicker" taken him?

Afraid, no one moved to retrieve the data inside the still-open alcove, until Rund shouldered his way forward as if in a trance. Kinnis made only token protests, his eyes hungry for the cache of information.

Expecting the barrier to phase back into place at any second, Rund tossed out plan screens, shigawire spools, sheets of ridulian crystal, while technicians scrambled to retrieve them. As if mentally attuned to the weird field generator, Rund stepped back into the safety of the laboratory only moments before the wall phased back again, as solid as before.

Talis Balt stared at the hoarded notes. "It will require quite an investment to exploit this work properly."

The dead technician already forgotten, Director Kinnis looked as if he might be trying to decide how to take credit for the work. "I will convince Premier Calimar that we need extensive funding. Very extensive. Rund, you speak to Count Ilban. Between them, they should be able to figure out how to obtain a great deal of money."

"Revenge." Has language ever created a more delicious word? I repeat it to myself when I go to sleep at night, confident it will give me pleasant dreams.

— BARON VLADIMIR HARKONNEN

The government of Richese needed a large, but unofficial, influx of solaris in order to finance redeveloping Chobyn's invisibility field. And Premier Ein Calimar knew where to get all the funds he wanted.

He arrived on Giedi Prime, angry that he had to keep pressing for his long-overdue payment from House Harkonnen. Instead of being taken directly to the looming Keep where he had always met the Baron before, guard Captain Kryubi led Calimar deep into the oppressive heart of Harko City.

A thin man, fastidiously dressed, Calimar steeled himself, trying not to lose his nerve. The Baron always played psychological games. The Premier had to finish these negotiations and survive them. For some unknown reason, the Harkonnen lord had decided to inspect his waste-recycling plants this morning, and the Premier was informed that the meeting must be conducted there, or not at all. Calimar wrinkled his nose at the thought of it.

Inside the huge industrial building the air was moist, warm, and redolent with odors that he would have preferred never to experience. Behind his gold-rimmed spectacles, his eyes stung. He could feel the stench permeating his synthetic fabric suit and knew that this outfit would have to be burned once he returned to his plush offices in Triad Center. But he would not return without the money the Baron owed House Richese.

"This way," Kryubi said, his firm lips adorned with a thin mustache. He led Calimar up an endless series of metal steps to a network of catwalks. These high walkways overlooked pungent sewage vats, like sinister aquariums for bottom-feeders. *How did a man as fat as the Baron ever get up here himself?*

Calimar panted most of the way, trying to keep up with the captain, and finally noticed metal lift platforms installed at convenient locations. *So, he is trying to put me in my place already.* His nostrils narrowed, and he gritted his teeth to bolster his confidence. He would need to be tough and treat the Baron with firm determination.

The first time fastidious Calimar had come to Giedi Prime, the Baron had calmly allowed him to sit in a room with an unseen dead body nearby. While the Premier had made his embarrassing request for quiet financial assistance, the odor of rot in the air presented an unspoken threat.

This time, Calimar would turn the tables on the fat man. Years ago, the Baron had offered to help the faltering industries of Richese, on condition that he receive the secret ministrations of a Suk doctor. Afterward, the Baron had paid only part of what he'd agreed, then subsequently ignored Richese's repeated demands. The doctor, Wellington Yueh, had been able to identify his patient's disease, but had no way of curing it. No one could do that.

And so the Baron had used that as a justification to ignore paying the rest of the fee. But now, with Korona Director Flinto Kinnis's excited assurances that they would potentially develop an invisibility generator, Calimar needed large amounts of seed capital. The initial research work would be expensive, but with their rival Ix closed off and operating far below optimum capacity, Richese had a chance to win back its powerful economic position.

The Baron must pay what he owed, even if Calimar had to blackmail him into fulfilling his obligations. . . .

The Premier proceeded across the catwalk to where the enormous man tottered near the rails high above the sewage vats. Kryubi told him to go forward alone, which made Calimar wary. *Does the Baron intend to kill me?* Such an action would cause an uproar in the Landsraad. No, House Richese had too much damaging information on the Harkonnens, and their lord knew it.

Calimar noticed that the Baron wore specially designed nose plugs and filters against the reek of the sewage plants. Without similar protection, the Premier didn't want to know how many toxins he might be inhaling with each breath. He removed his gold-rimmed eyeglasses and wiped the lenses, but an oily, streaky film remained.

"Baron Harkonnen, this is an . . . unorthodox place for our meeting."

The Baron looked at the swirling currents of lumpy sludge as if he were peering into a kaleidoscope. "I have business to attend to, Calimar. We will talk here, or no-where."

The Premier recognized the unspoken message, gross disrespect from a gross man. In response, he made his voice as gruff as possible. "Indeed, Baron. And as adults, as well as leaders of our respective worlds, we have obligations to meet. You, sir, have not met yours. Richese provided the services you requested. You are obligated to pay the remainder of the agreed-upon fee."

The Baron scowled. "I don't owe you anything. Your Suk doctor didn't cure me."

"That was never part of our agreement. He examined you and diagnosed your disease. You must pay."

"I refuse," the Baron said, as if that ended the matter. "Now you may leave."

Taking a deep breath that made him gag, the Premier

pressed on. "Sir, I have repeatedly tried to be reasonable, but considering your criminal refusal to pay, I feel totally justified in altering the conditions of our agreement. Hence, I am upping the price." Calimar named an exorbitant sum of solaris, and added, "Richese is fully prepared to take the matter to Landsraad Court, where our lawtechs and attorneys will prove our case. We will reveal the origin of your disease and describe your continued degeneration and weakness. Perhaps we will even present evidence of a growing mental instability."

The Baron's face purpled with rage, but before he could explode, they were interrupted by the arrival of three guards. They escorted a rangy man who wore exquisite, well-tailored clothes and billowing pantaloons.

Mephistis Cru did his best to ignore the alarming odors around him and stepped forward. "You summoned me, my Lord Baron?" He looked from side to side and frowned, then with a disapproving gaze he looked down at the vat.

The Baron shot a sidelong glare at Premier Calimar, then turned back to Cru, and said, "I have a delicate question to ask you, a matter of decorum." His jowly face focused into an expression of deadly anger. "I trust you can provide me with a satisfactory answer?"

The advisor stood straight and proud. "Of course, my Baron. I am here to serve."

"Ever since the debacle of my gala banquet, I've been wondering. Would it be polite for me to throw you into this sewage death trap myself, or should I have a guard do it, so that I don't dirty my hands?"

Cru took an alarmed step away as Kryubi gestured for the guards to block off his retreat. "My . . . I don't understand, my Lord. I gave you only the best—"

"No clear answer, eh? Very well, I think I'll have the guards do it." The Baron motioned with a pudgy hand. "That's probably the most polite alternative, anyway."

Suddenly the etiquette advisor could think of nothing civil to say. He screamed surprisingly foul words that even the Baron found offensive. Uniformed guards grabbed the rangy man by the arms and in a smooth, mechanical gesture, swung him over the catwalk. Cru's elegant garments fluttered as he fell. He managed to twist himself in the air before splashing into the deep vat of human waste.

As Cru struggled and kicked, trying to stroke his way through the quagmire of sewage, the Baron turned toward his shocked visitor. "Pardon me, Premier. I wish to watch this and enjoy every moment of it."

Coughing, Mephistis Cru somehow made it to the slick, rounded edge of the vat, where he clutched the rim and vomited onto the clean floor, missing the sewage pond entirely. Guards wearing polymer gloves met him there and grasped his arms.

When they hauled Cru up over the rim, he wept with relief and terror. The advisor was sobbing, shaking, covered in brown slime and feces. He wailed up at the high catwalks, begging forgiveness.

The guards attached small weights to his ankles and tossed him back into the stinking muck.

Calimar watched these events with horror, but refused to be intimidated. "I've always found it enlightening to witness the depths of your cruelty, Baron Harkonnen." He forced firmness into his voice as the unfortunate victim continued to thrash below. "Perhaps we can continue with more important matters?"

"Oh, be silent a moment." The Baron pointed down at the flailing figure, surprised that Cru still had enough strength to keep his head out of the goo.

Calimar refused to be put off. "Many years ago, Emperor Elrood ousted my master Count Ilban Richese from Arrakis *because he appeared weak.* When your own half brother Abulurd appeared weak, you removed him and assumed control of spice operations before Elrood could take action himself. The Landsraad and the Emperor have no fondness for impotent leaders. Once they learn of your debilitating disease, and how it was inflicted upon you by a witch, you will become the laughingstock of the Imperium."

The Baron's spider-black eyes turned to sharp obsidian. Below, the etiquette advisor sank beneath the sewage, but somehow emerged again to gasp a breath. He spat and coughed and splashed.

The Baron was only too aware of how mercurial the Corrino Emperor had been lately. Calimar had his rival by the testicles, and both men knew it. The Baron could rage all he wanted, but he had no doubt that the Richesians would do exactly as they threatened. In a conciliatory tone, he said, "I cannot pay so much. Surely we can come to some more reasonable accommodation?"

"We agreed upon a price, Baron, and you could have paid it at any time. But no longer. Now, your own folly has increased the cost."

The Baron choked on his reply. "If I emptied all the treasury houses on Giedi Prime, I could never provide you with so many solaris!"

Calimar shrugged. Mephistis Cru's head was now submerged, but his arms flopped again. Even with the weights on his ankles, he managed to keep himself afloat for a few more agonizing minutes.

The Premier made a final countermove. "We have already filed our grievance in Landsraad Court. A hearing is set for two weeks. We can easily rescind that action, but only if you pay us *first*."

The Baron scrambled for a solution, but knew he had no choice—for now. "Spice. I can pay you in spice! I have enough melange set aside to pay your damnable price, and I can provide it immediately. That should be a solid enough coin for a foul blackmailer like you."

"Your insults mean nothing. The Harkonnen griffin has no teeth." Calimar emitted a small laugh, then grew more circumspect. "However, after the bloodbath on Zanovar, and given Shaddam's continued threats against illegal spice stockpiles, I am hesitant to accept payment in that form."

"It is the only way you'll get paid. You can accept melange now, or wait until I acquire sufficient financing for an alternate form of payment." The Baron flashed an insidious smile. "It may take months."

"Very well." Calimar judged this was the best he could obtain, since his adversary needed to save face in some small manner. "We will arrange for the secret transfer of your stockpile to our laboratory moon of Korona, where it will be guarded and kept safe." The Premier allowed himself to feel smug. "I'm glad the matter is now over, though I am sorry to have to do this."

"No you're not," the Baron snapped. He maintained a stony countenance. "Now get out of here, and don't ever try to blackmail me again."

Calimar did his best to conceal his nervousness as he negotiated the catwalk and scampered down the stairs. . . .

His insides roiling, the Baron resumed his concentration on Mephistis Cru. This foppish man, so concerned with formalities and fancy perfumes, had surprising strength. It was admirable, in a way. Even with the weights on his ankles, he still hadn't drowned.

Finally, tired of the show, the Baron ordered Captain Kryubi to turn on the vat's chopper blades. As the thick, lumpy liquid began to swirl, Mephistis Cru tried to swim even more frantically.

The Baron only wished he could have added Premier Calimar to the mix.

> *There are more tragedies in history than triumphs.*
> *Few scholars want to study a long litany of events*
> *that turned out well. And we Atreides have left more*
> *of our mark on history than we ever intended.*
>
> —DUKE PAULUS ATREIDES

Holding a wicked-looking dagger in his left hand and a shorter kidney-stabber in his right, Duncan Idaho lunged at Leto.

Scrambling backward into the banquet hall, Leto spun to cover his vulnerable spots with a shimmering half shield. The Swordmaster's reflexes had already slowed, adjusting the blade's speed so that the tip could slide through the dampening barrier.

Leto surprised Duncan by making an unorthodox move. He threw himself directly toward his younger opponent. This increased the relative speed of Duncan's knife with respect to Leto's shield, and the blade skittered off the buzzing protective wall.

Leto brought up his short sword, but the young Swordmaster sprang out of the way, leaped atop the banquet table, and ran backward with catlike grace.

The faceted eyes of the stuffed Salusan bull's-head and the matador portrait of the red-garbed Duke Paulus seemed to watch the duel with interest.

"Those candlesticks were a wedding gift to my parents," Leto said with a laugh. "If you break them, I'll take the cost out of your hide."

"You won't be able to touch my hide, Leto." Duncan performed a blatantly insulting backflip on the table.

While the Swordmaster was still in midair, Leto swept his dagger arm sideways, knocking down one of the long candlesticks himself and rolling it under Duncan's feet. The Swordmaster lost his balance, sprawling on his backside. Jumping up onto the table, Leto ran forward, short sword in hand, ready to conclude this practice duel. It would be his first victory.

But Duncan was no longer there.

The Swordmaster kept rolling and flung himself off the far edge of the table, then scuttled crablike beneath the heavy furniture and sprang up behind Leto. The Duke backed off, facing his opponent, both of them grinning.

Duncan jabbed with his knives, dancing on the fringe of the half shield's protection, but Leto deftly parried with short sword and dagger. "You're distracted, Duke Atreides. You miss your woman too much."

Indeed, I do. But I will never allow it to show. Their blades struck, skittered, scraping edge against edge. *Not even to you, Duncan.*

Leto feinted with the short sword, then brought up his fist, moving his bare hand through the shield and grabbing Duncan's loose green tunic just to prove that he could touch his opponent. Surprised, the Swordmaster yanked free by slashing at Leto's eyes with the kidney-stabber, coming close to touching, but not too close. Duncan sprang down onto a dining chair, tottering the heavy seat but maintaining his balance as he stood on tiptoes.

Through the doorway to the banquet hall, a servant entered with a tray of refreshments, her face open and innocent. Offhandedly, Leto gestured for her to leave them alone, and Duncan chose that moment to dive toward him. He did not use knives this time, instead crashing shield against shield to knock Leto to the tabletop. It was all the servant could do to scuttle back out of the banquet hall without dropping her tray.

"Never heed distractions, Leto." Duncan caught his breath and backed off. "Your enemies will concoct diversions to make you focus your attention where it does not belong. Then they will strike."

Panting, Leto lay back, felt the sweat trickling through his dark hair. "Enough! You've bested me again." He switched off his half shield, and the Swordmaster proudly sheathed his two blades, then helped the Duke to his feet.

"Of course I've bested you," Duncan said. "But you tricked me a few times. Very interesting tactics. You're learning, sir."

"Some of us can't afford to spend eight years on Ginaz. And my offer still stands to bring your companion Hiih Resser to Caladan. If he fights with half your skill, he would be a welcome addition to the Guard at House Atreides."

Duncan looked troubled. "I have heard only a little from him since his return to House Moritani. I was afraid the Grummans might kill him when he got home, but he seems to have survived. I think he's now even part of the Viscount's personal guard."

Leto wiped sweat from his brow. "Obviously, he's stronger and smarter than he was before. I just hope he isn't corrupted."

"It's not easy to corrupt a Swordmaster, Leto."

Thufir Hawat stood at the doorway to the banquet hall, observing. Now that the training session was over, the Mentat stepped forward and gave a slight bow, his sinewy form making distorted reflections on the blue-obsidian walls. "I concur with your Swordmaster, my Duke, that you are becoming a better fighter. However, I would like to add my insight on tactics by reminding you that distractions and diversions can work both ways."

Leto sat heavily on one of the dining chairs while Duncan set the toppled, undamaged candlestick upright on the table. "What do you mean, Thufir?"

"I am your Security Commander, my Duke. My primary concerns are to keep you alive and to protect House

Atreides. I failed you when I did not prevent the skyclipper explosion, just as I failed your father in the bullring."

Leto turned to look at the stuffed head of the monstrous, multihorned creature that had killed the Old Duke. "I already know what you're going to say, Thufir. You do not want me to join the fighting on Ix. You'd rather I did something safe instead."

"I want you to take the role of a *Duke*, my Lord."

"I absolutely concur," Duncan said. "*Rhombur* must be physically present in the heat of battle so that the people can see him, but *you* need to face the Landsraad. Personally, I think that might be an even tougher fight."

Glowering, Leto looked at his two military advisors. "My father was on the front lines of the Ecazi Revolt, and so was Dominic Vernius."

"Those were different times, my Duke. And Paulus Atreides did not always heed advice." Hawat glanced meaningfully up at the monstrous Salusan bull's-head. "You must make this a victory in your own manner."

Leto raised his short sword over one shoulder, holding the hilt loosely as if he held a dagger, and hurled it. The blade spun in the air.

The Mentat's hooded eyes widened, and Duncan gasped as the blade plunged into the bull's black, scaly throat. The sword had skewered the beast and stuck there, quivering.

"You are right, Thufir. I am more interested in results than in grandstanding." Pleased with himself, Leto turned back to his advisors. "We must make certain all the Imperium learns the Atreides lesson of Beakkal. No warning. No mercy. No ambiguity. I am not a man to be trifled with."

There are no facts—only observational postulates in an endlessly regenerative hodgepodge of predictions. Consensus reality requires a fixed frame of reference. In a multilevel, infinite universe, there can be no fixity; thus, no absolute consensus reality. In a relativistic universe, it appears impossible to test the reliability of any expert by requiring him to agree with another expert. Both can be correct, each in his own inertial system.

—Bene Gesserit Azhar Book

I n Lady Anirul's wing of the Imperial Palace, Reverend Mother Mohiam glided into Jessica's apartment without knocking.

Sensing the older woman's presence, Jessica looked up from the rolltop desk, where she had been writing in the bound-parchment journal Anirul had given her. She laid her inkplume down and shut the volume. "Yes, Reverend Mother?"

"A fact has just been brought to my attention by our operative Tessia," Mohiam said in the tone of a displeased schoolteacher. It was a voice Jessica had heard many times from the Proctor Superior. Mohiam could show compassion and kindness when she was pleased with her student, but she was also ruthless.

"We waited for you to conceive an Atreides daughter, pursuant to your orders. It is my understanding that you have been the Duke's lover for three years? *Three years* gave you ample opportunity to become pregnant! I can only presume that you intentionally refused our instructions. I would like to know why."

Though her heart lurched, Jessica locked onto Mohiam's gaze, without wavering. She'd been expecting this, but still she felt like a little girl again, crushed by the disappointment her teacher had always been able to wield. "I am sorry, Reverend Mother."

As Jessica watched the wrinkled lips move, she remembered how Mohiam had observed her, studied her every movement as she tested her with the deadly gom jabbar. The poison needle, the box of pain. With that needle at Jessica's neck, Mohiam could have killed her in a fraction of a second.

"You were ordered to bear a child. You should have allowed yourself to become impregnated the first time you slept with him."

Jessica managed to keep her voice firm, without cracking or stammering. "There are reasons, Reverend Mother. The Duke was bitter about his concubine Kailea, and suffered many political problems abroad. An unexpected child at that time would have been a great burden upon him. Later, he was distraught over the death of his son Victor."

The older woman showed no sympathy whatsoever. "Upset enough to alter his sperm count? You are a Bene Gesserit. Surely I have taught you better than this? What were you thinking, child?"

Mohiam has always been expert at manipulating my emotions. She is doing it now. Jessica reminded herself that the Sisterhood took pride in understanding what it meant to be human. *What more human act could I have committed than to bear a child for the man I love?*

She refused to back down, speaking in a way that was sure to take her old teacher by surprise. "I am not your student anymore, Reverend Mother, so you will kindly not address me in such a condescending manner."

The response took Mohiam aback. She stood silently.

"The Duke was not ready for another baby, and he had

access to his own contraceptive measures." *Not a lie, just a diversion.* "I am pregnant now. What is the point in chastising me? I can have as many daughters as you like."

The Reverend Mother emitted a harsh laugh, but her face grew gentler. "Headstrong girl!" She backed out the door, a mixture of emotions playing across her face. She took a calming breath and glided away down the hallway. Her secret daughter had a stubborn, defiant streak. Mohiam decided it must be from the Harkonnen blood in her veins. . . .

IN THE DRY, artificially cooled air of the Residency at Arrakeen, Lady Margot Fenring watched with the sharp eyes of a Bene Gesserit as the Fremen housewoman methodically packed things for the extended trip to Kaitain. The woman, Mapes, had no sense of humor and virtually no personality, but she worked hard and followed instructions.

"Bring my immian-rose dresses, the peach and saffron wardrobe, and the full lavender gown for regular daily appearances at Court," Margot commanded. "And also those transforming silkfilm garments for the nights, after Count Fenring returns from his business trip." As she spoke, she concealed a slip of Imperial parchment from the eyes of her servant.

"Yes, my Lady." Without a smile or a scowl, the dried husk of a woman folded the slippery, sexy undergarments and packed them with all the other items for Margot's departure to Kaitain.

Almost certainly, this hardened desert woman understood much more about Lady Fenring than she let on. Years ago, in the dark of night, Mapes had led her to a hidden sietch in the mountains, taking her to see their Sayyadina, the Fremen equivalent of a Reverend Mother. Afterward, the entire sietch had disappeared. Mapes had never said another word about the incident and avoided all questions.

Now Count Fenring had departed again, and Margot knew her husband had secretly gone to the closed world of Ix, though he believed he kept all of his furtive movements and errands hidden from her. She let him maintain his little delusions, because it strengthened their marriage. In a universe of secrets, Margot kept many of her own, too.

"Have an early dinner prepared," Margot ordered. "And be ready to depart with me in two hours."

Her sinewy arms straining, Mapes sealed the fully packed suitcases and lifted them toward the door without using the attached suspensors. "I would prefer to remain here, my Lady, rather than taking the journey across space."

Margot frowned at her, brooking no further discussion. "Nevertheless, you shall accompany me. Many ladies at Court will be curious to see a woman whose every breath, every meal, has been impregnated with spice. They will see your blue-within-blue eyes and think them pretty."

Mapes turned away. "I have work to do here. Why should I waste time with pretentious fools?"

Margot's laugh was light. "Because it would do the courtiers good to see a woman who knows how to work. Now *that* will be an exotic sight for them!"

Scowling in response, the houseservant trudged off with the two suitcases.

When Mapes had passed out of sight, Margot again touched the slip of Imperial parchment that had been sent to her by Courier. She ran her fingertips over the uneven coded bumps, searching for further subtleties in the brief message from Lady Anirul.

"We need your eyes here in the Palace. Jessica and her baby were nearly killed in an assassination attempt on the Emperor. We must keep them safe. Make excuses, but come quickly."

Margot slipped the note into a pocket of her dress, then busied herself with final details.

Politics is the art of appearing candid and completely open, while concealing as much as possible.

— States: The Bene Gesserit View

Since his appointment as Imperial Spice Minister, Count Hasimir Fenring had spent more time aboard Heighliners than ever before. He'd left Margot in Arrakeen that very morning, where she had been packing for a vacation on Kaitain. He indulged his lovely wife in her little holidays and pleasure trips.

But Fenring had important work to do, taking care of the Emperor's business. On Ix, Hidar Fen Ajidica should have everything completed by now, ready for the most vital test of all.

During these tedious trips with all their stops and delays, Fenring kept his deadly skills honed. Only a few moments ago, in the frigate's private ablutions room, Fenring had pulled on black gentleman's gloves, locked the door, and strangled one of the irritating Wayku vendors.

"There is great skill in concealing one's hostility," an ancient sage had said. How true that was!

Fenring had left the singlesuit-clad body in a sealed toilet enclosure surrounded by the Wayku's own overpriced, poorly made souvenir products. No doubt when another attendant discovered the corpse, he would take the trinkets and try to sell them to some unsuspecting passenger. . . .

His frustrations sated for now, the Count rode a

shuttle through misty clouds down to Ix, accompanying a few traders and approved suppliers of industrial resources. The small ship landed amidst the heavily guarded bustle of the new Xuttuh Spaceport, a large open overhang on the edge of a canyon.

Standing on bilious yellow tiles, Fenring sniffed the distinctive odor of many Tleilaxu. He shook his head in dismay. The construction skills of the gnome-men were woefully lacking, and evidence of inept workmanship was abundant. A public address system announced the arriving and departing shuttles. A few much taller outsiders delivered supplies and dickered with research managers over price structures. No Sardaukar were visible.

Pushing toward the security barricades, Fenring shouldered two Tleilaxu Masters out of his way, ignoring their protestations, then skirted a puddle of water beneath a dripping rock ceiling.

After he entered his high-level access codes and proved his identity, rushed messages were dispatched to the research complexes below. Fenring didn't hurry; Hidar Fen Ajidica would not have time to hide everything.

Inside the deep access tunnels, he smiled broadly as a Sardaukar officer hurried toward him, his black-and-gray commander's uniform in disarray. "We did not expect you, Count Fenring."

The young leader of the Imperial legions, Commander Cando Garon, raised an arm as if to salute the Spice Minister. Instead, Fenring grabbed the officer's beefy hand and shook it briskly with one of the gloved hands he'd used to strangle the vendor. "You should never expect me, Commander Garon, but you should always be *prepared* for me, hmmm?"

The soldier accepted the slight rebuke with grace and turned to escort the Emperor's man toward the deep facilities.

"By the way, Commander, your father is well. The

Supreme Bashar is doing the most important work of his career."

The younger Garon raised his eyebrows. "Is that so? We are isolated here, and I rarely receive word from him."

"Yes, hmmm, the Emperor is keeping him busy destroying planets. Zanovar is his latest handiwork. It's completely lifeless."

Fenring watched for any reaction, but the young Commander simply nodded. "My father is always thorough. As Shaddam commands. Please give him my regards upon your return to Kaitain."

A private railcar took them across the grime-streaked cavern metropolis. "I am here for a new series of tests. Surely the Master Researcher is ready to begin? He was to have made certain, ahhh, arrangements."

Garon sat stiffly in his seat. "We shall have to ask him. So far, sir, the synthetic spice production is proceeding remarkably well. The Master Researcher seems quite satisfied and enthusiastic." Garon stared straight ahead, rarely looking at his companion. "Quite generously, he has provided me and my men with samples of the synthetic melange. It appears to be a complete success."

This surprised Fenring. What was Ajidica doing, testing amal on the Sardaukar legions without authorization? "Commander, the substance has not yet been fully approved."

"There have been no ill effects, sir." Clearly, the Sardaukar leader had no intention of turning down future supplies of the drug for himself or his men. "I have already sent a message to the Emperor, and I believe he is pleased with what we have done. Amal greatly improves our stamina and efficiency. My soldiers are quite satisfied with it."

"Satisfaction is not part of your mission, Commander. Is it, hmmm-ah?"

When the railcar docked in the research complex, a

silent Garon escorted him into the facility, though Fenring had been here many times. It seemed as if the Sardaukar officer had been ordered to keep an eye on him.

But when Fenring entered the main office, he stopped in complete surprise. *Commander Cando Garon* himself stood next to a smirking Ajidica. Fenring looked at the man who had escorted him: The two were identical, down to the last detail.

"Garon, meet Garon," the Master Researcher said. The officer next to Ajidica stepped forward to shake his duplicate's hand, but the Sardaukar who had accompanied Fenring—presumably the *real* Garon—wanted no part of this charade. He stepped back, avoiding contact with the impostor.

"Just a little Face Dancer trick." Ajidica displayed a mouthful of sharp teeth in his smile. "You may leave now, Commander. Thank you for accompanying Count Fenring." With a scowl, the soldier departed.

Ajidica folded his small hands together, but did not gesture for the Count to sit in a chairdog by the desk. Fenring took a seat anyway, looking suspiciously at the surrogate Sardaukar.

"We have been laboring around the clock, Count Fenring, to produce commercial quantities of amal. All difficulties have been resolved, and the new substance works marvelously."

"So, you consume it yourself, hmmmm? And you gave it to the Emperor's Sardaukar as well? You have overstepped your authority, Master Researcher."

With a dark twinkle in his eyes, Ajidica answered, "It falls precisely within my authority as chief of amal research. The Emperor himself gave me the mission to develop a perfect melange substitute. That cannot be accomplished without testing."

"Not on the Emperor's men."

"They are more alert than ever before. Stronger, more energetic. You must be familiar with the old platitude, 'happy troops are loyal troops.' Aren't they, Commander Garon?"

With the faintest rustle of sound, the Garon duplicate shifted his appearance to match Ajidica's, but wearing a baggy Sardaukar uniform. Then he metamorphosed into Emperor Shaddam Corrino, again filling the clothing. The flow of muscles and skin was disorienting, and the resulting resemblance astounding. The reddish hair and dark green eyes were perfect, as was the facial expression of barely contained distaste. Even the Emperor's voice, as he announced in an authoritative tone, "Bring in my Sardaukar. Kill everyone in the laboratory!"

Next the Emperor's nose grew in length until it resembled a Poritrin carrot. As Ajidica beamed at his creation, the Face Dancer shifted once more, this time into the form of a mutated Guildsman, with portions of his deformed body stretching and ripping the clothing.

"Count Fenring, meet Zoal, the partner you demanded for a Heighliner navigation test. With him, you can infiltrate the Spacing Guild's security on Junction."

Fascinated and eager, Fenring set aside his concerns. "And this Face Dancer understands that I am in charge of the mission? That my orders are not to be questioned?"

"Zoal is highly intelligent and has many capabilities," Ajidica said. "He is not trained to kill, but will follow any other instructions you might have, without hesitation."

"How many languages do you speak?" Fenring asked.

"How many are required, sir?" Zoal said, in a voice bearing an accent that Fenring could not quite identify. The faint nasal tone of Buzzell, perhaps? "I will absorb whatever we may need. But I am forbidden to carry weapons."

"It is programmed into Face Dancers," the Master Researcher added.

Fenring frowned, not sure he believed this. "Then I will handle the violence myself, hmmm-ah." He ran his gaze up and down the laboratory-bred creature, then turned to the research chief. "He appears to be exactly what I need. The evidence appears quite positive so far, and the Emperor is quite impatient to proceed. Once we verify that Navigators can use amal, our spice substitute will be ready for distribution throughout the Imperium."

Ajidica tapped his fingers on a tabletop. "Such a test is merely a formality, Count. Amal has already been proven to my full satisfaction."

Secrets within secrets. Privately, Ajidica had continued to experience messianic, prescient visions of leading immense military forces against the infidel Great Houses.

Zoal had many siblings, Face Dancers grown here in the axlotl tanks, mutable creatures loyal only to him and to his grand, concealed plan. On expendable ships, he had already dispatched more than fifty Face Dancers to scout uncharted planets and establish beachheads for his future empire. Some of these ships journeyed far beyond the mapped star systems of the Imperium, searching for ways that Ajidica could spread his influence. It would take time. . . .

Inside the shielded office, Count Fenring began to describe his complicated plan to infiltrate Junction, discussing how they would penetrate Guild security. Zoal listened, absorbing the details. Ajidica was not concerned.

The Face Dancer already had overriding orders. When the time came, the shape-shifter would know exactly what to do.

Make your points aggressively.
— SHADDAM CORRINO IV,
Building Strength in the New Imperium

O f all the state duties Emperor Shaddam had to endure, executions were the least objectionable, especially in his current mood.

In the center of Petition Square he sat upon a jewel-studded throne so high that he looked like a grand priest on a ceremonial ziggurat. The sun shone through the blue skies, perfect weather for the Emperor, sunny days for the whole Imperium.

The next victim was dragged forward in chains and left to stand at the base of a black cube of impregnable gnarl-granite, beside several bodies. The Imperial guards had employed a variety of execution methods: garroting, laser beheadings, precision-stabbing, dismemberment, disemboweling, and even a spike-gloved fist driven under the ribs to pull out a quivering heart. With each death the crowd applauded, as required.

Crisply uniformed guards lined the steps of the dais. The Emperor had wanted to station an entire regiment around the square, but had decided against it. Even after Tyros Reffa's bold assassination attempt, he did not wish to show the least bit of nervousness. Shaddam IV did not need more than an honor guard and shimmering shields around his chair.

I am the rightful Emperor, and my people love me.

Lady Anirul sat on a high-backed wooden chair on a lower step to the left, clearly a subordinate position. She had insisted on being seen with her husband, but he had discovered how to turn the tables on her by positioning the chairs to emphasize how little his wife meant in the Imperial scheme. Of course she had figured out his little show, but would not complain.

As a deadly symbol of state, Shaddam now held the tall staff topped with its faceted glowglobe, the same murderous prop Reffa had used during the play. The Emperor's weapons specialists had been most intrigued by the ingenious device. His people had recharged the compact ruby power source, and he intended to use it to good effect.

While Shaddam studied his new toy, the next criminal was slain by a soldier. The Emperor looked up sharply just as the victim slumped to the paving stones. Frowning in disappointment, he chastised himself for not paying closer attention. From the blood gushing out of the man's throat, Shaddam guessed his larynx and trachea had been ripped out—a Sardaukar specialty.

Breezes rippled across Petition Square, and the crowd grew restless, sensing that something more interesting was coming. They had already watched twenty-eight executions in four hours. Some of the performers in the Jongleur theatrical troupe had demonstrated their true acting abilities with pleas for mercy and protestations of their innocence. Actually, he believed them for the most part, but that didn't matter. It had made for wonderful high drama, before the Sardaukar disposed of them in diabolical ways.

In recent weeks, during the uproar following Reffa's attack on the Imperial box, Shaddam had seized his opportunity. Quickly and deviously, he had arranged for the arrest of five political enemies—uncooperative ministers and ambassadors who had brought unwelcome news or had not convinced their leaders to cooperate with various Imperial edicts—and he had implicated all of them in the assassination plot.

Hasimir Fenring would have admired the intricacies of Shaddam's schemes, the convoluted machinations of politics. But the Count was off on Ix now, wrapping up details for full-scale production and distribution of amal. Fenring had insisted on completing one more important test himself, in order to prove that the effects of the artificial substance were identical to genuine melange. Shaddam paid little attention to the details, mindful only of the results. And so far everything seemed perfect.

For himself, he had learned how to make decisions without Fenring's input, or interference.

Remembering how Viscount Moritani had ignored an Imperial command to make peace with Ecaz years before, Shaddam had added the Grumman Ambassador to the list of convicted criminals (much to the Ambassador's shock). It had been easy to prepare incontrovertible "evidence," and the deed was done before any protest could be organized by House Moritani.

The Viscount's disruptive influence would not be easily tamed, despite several regiments of Sardaukar peacekeeping troops the Emperor had stationed on Grumman to quell the ongoing dispute with House Ecaz. The Viscount still misbehaved at unexpected times, but perhaps this message would cow him just a little longer.

A pair of Sardaukar briskly marched the Grumman Ambassador to the center of the square. The prisoner's arms were bound behind his back and his knees wrapped so that he could not bend. Standing before the black cube of granite, the convicted man made his final speech—a fairly uninspired one, Shaddam thought. Impatiently, the Emperor raised one hand in a signal, and a soldier opened fire with a lasgun, slicing the body in half from crotch to crown.

Pleased with the gruesome festivities so far, Shaddam leaned back to relax, waiting for the most important show of the day. The noise of the crowd increased.

As Padishah Emperor, the "shah of all shahs," he expected to be treated as a revered leader. His word was law, but when surprises like Tyros Reffa interfered with his rule, he did not rest easily. It was time to squeeze harder, to set another example.

Shaddam twirled the tall staff so that bright sunlight shimmered from the faceted glowglobe. He pounded the heel of the rod on the smooth step in front of him. Lady Anirul did not flinch, staring ahead as if lost in her own thoughts.

The audience watched Supreme Bashar Zum Garon march into the execution square leading Tyros Reffa, the man who claimed to be a son of Elrood. In a few moments, that problem would be gone as well.

From her chair, Lady Anirul spoke in a directed whisper, so that her words were clear to Shaddam without raising her voice. "Husband, you deny that this man is your half brother, yet his claim has been heard by many people. He has planted seeds of doubt, and there are mutterings of discontent."

Shaddam scowled. "No one will believe his claim, if I tell them not to."

Looking directly at the man on the high throne, Anirul remained skeptical. "If his assertion is false, why do you refuse to run genetic tests? The populace will say you have murdered your own blood."

It will not be the first time, Shaddam thought. "Let them talk—and we will listen closely. It shouldn't take long to silence any voices of dissent."

Anirul made no further comment, but turned to watch as Reffa was prodded toward the block of gnarl-granite. His stocky, muscular body moved stiffly. The luxurious dark hair had been shorn away, leaving his head covered with a spiky mass of carelessly chopped stubble.

Reffa was forced to stand near the butchered bodies of other victims, all of whom had been given a few moments to speak their final words. Shaddam had made certain, though, that his purported half brother would receive no such opportunity. The court doctors had surgically fused the prisoner's lips together. Though he strained and worked his jaw, Reffa could not force out words, nothing more than pitiful mewling sounds. His eyes were wild with fury.

Wearing an expression of supreme disdain, the Emperor stood atop the ziggurat platform and motioned for the shields to be shut down around his chair. He held the scepter weapon in front of him. "Tyros Reffa—impostor and assassin—your crime is worse than any of the others." His booming voice was enhanced by the amplifiers in a medallion hanging at his neck.

Reffa struggled, screaming inside, but he had no mouth. The bright red skin of his fused lips looked as if it was about to tear.

"Because of the audacity of your claim, we grant you an honor you do not deserve." Shaddam withdrew the prismatic ruby power source and inserted it into the socket in the staff. The power glowed and surged, shooting to the top of the rod and igniting the faceted glowglobe. "I will attend to you *personally*."

A purple beam struck Reffa full in the chest, incinerating his torso and leaving a huge, bloody hole. Shaddam, with his jaws clenched in a rictus of Imperial wrath, bent the staff so that the beam continued to char the body even after it toppled to the foot of the black granite.

"When you challenge us, you speak out against the entire Imperium! Thus, the entire Imperium must observe the consequences of your folly."

With the staff's power source drained, the beam gave out. The Emperor gestured for his Sardaukar to continue. In unison, they fired on the corpse, their blazing beams cremating the body of Elrood's bastard son. The lasguns vaporized organic tissue and even bone, leaving only a smear of black ashes which swirled in the thermal currents, and finally blew away.

Shaddam stood stoic and firm, inwardly delighted. Now,

no evidence whatsoever remained. No one could prove Reffa's genetic link through Elrood to Shaddam. The problem was disposed of. Completely.

Good-bye, Brother.

The most powerful man in the universe raised his hands, seizing the crowd's attention. "Now there is cause for celebration! We declare a holiday across the Imperium, and feasts for everyone."

In a much better mood, Shaddam took his wife's arm and stepped down from the dais. Row upon row of Sardaukar soldiers escorted them back into the lavish interior of the Imperial Palace.

Pay your spies well. One good infiltrator is more valuable than legions of Sardaukar.

—FONDIL CORRINO III, "The Hunter"

Rhombur sat on an examination table in a warm pool of afternoon sunshine that poured through a high window. He could detect the warmth on his cyborg limbs, but it was a different sensation from his memories of human nerve signals. Many things were different. . . .

Dr. Yueh, his long hair secured in a silver Suk ring, held a scanner over the artificial knee joints. His narrow face remained intent. "Flex the right one now."

Rhombur sighed, "I intend to go with Gurney whether or not you give me medical clearance."

The doctor showed neither amusement nor annoyance. "May Heaven save me from ungrateful patients."

As Rhombur bent his prosthetic leg, the scanner blinked green. "I feel physically strong, Dr. Yueh. Sometimes I don't even think about my replacement parts. It's what is natural for me now." Indeed, even with his scarred face and polymer skin, the joke around Castle Caladan (started by Duncan Idaho) was that the Prince was still better-looking than Gurney Halleck.

Yueh visually checked the cyborg mechanics as Rhombur walked about the room, did chin-ups, and completed a clattering tuck-and-roll across the floor. A muscle on the left side of the doctor's jaw twisted as he spoke. "I believe you've been greatly helped by your wife's aggressive therapy."

"Aggressive therapy?" Rhombur asked. "She calls it 'love.'"

Yueh shut down his scanners. "You have my approval to go with Gurney Halleck on this difficult mission." Concern etched the weathered features of the Suk doctor's face, wrinkling the diamond tattoo on his forehead. "It will be dangerous for anyone sneaking into Ix, however. Even more so because of who you are. I do not want to see my lovely handiwork destroyed."

"I'll try not to let that happen," Rhombur said, taking on a determined expression. "But Ix is my home, Doctor. I have no other choice. I am prepared to do what is necessary for my people, even if the Vernius bloodline must . . . end with me."

Rhombur saw the doctor's eyes flicker with deep pain, but no tears. "You may not believe this, but I understand. A long time ago, my wife Wanna was seriously injured in an industrial accident. I found a specialist in artificial human control functions—very primitive compared with what you have, Prince. He replaced Wanna's hips, spleen, and uterus with synthetic parts, but she could never have children. We had planned to wait . . . but we waited too long. Of course Wanna is beyond childbearing age now, but back in those days it was quite traumatic for us." He busied himself putting away his medical instruments.

"Similarly, Prince Rhombur, you are the last of House Vernius. I am sorry."

⌖

WHEN LETO SUMMONED him to his personal study, Rhombur suspected nothing. After clomping into the room he stopped and stared with astonishment at a familiar man standing by a stone-framed window.

"Ambassador Pilru!" Rhombur always felt a surge of affection when he saw this public servant who had so tirelessly, though fruitlessly, fought for the Ixian cause over the past two decades. But he had just seen the man at his recent wedding to Tessia. Rhombur felt a sudden twist in his heart. "Is there news?"

"Yes, my Prince. Surprising and troubling news." Rhombur wondered if it had to do with the Ambassador's son, C'tair, who had been continuing the fight on Ix.

As Rhombur settled into a rigid stance, the dignified diplomat paced the office, ill at ease. He activated a holo-projector at the center of the room, displaying the image of a ragged, dirty man.

Leto's voice had an edge. "This is the man who attempted to assassinate Shaddam. The one who almost killed Jessica in the Imperial box."

Pilru looked quickly at him. "Entirely by accident, Duke Leto. Many aspects of his plan were . . . naive and ill conceived."

"And it now seems that certain aspects of his 'maniacal attack' were a bit exaggerated by the official Imperial report," Leto said.

Rhombur remained confused. "But who is he?"

The Ambassador halted the image and turned purposefully to him. "My Prince, this is—or was—Tyros Reffa. The Emperor's half brother. He was executed four days ago, by Imperial decree. Apparently, there was no need for a trial."

Rhombur shifted his weight. "But what does this have to do with—"

"Very few people know the truth, but Reffa's claim was indeed legitimate. He was truly Elrood's bastard son, raised quietly by House Taligari. Shaddam apparently considered him a threat to the throne, however, and concocted an excuse for his Sardaukar to annihilate Reffa's home on Zanovar. Shaddam also killed fourteen million additional people in the cities on Zanovar, just for good measure."

Both Rhombur and Leto were shocked.

"That is what triggered Reffa's brash attempt at revenge."

Handing a set of printed documents to Rhombur, the Ambassador continued. "This is the genetic analysis proving Reffa's identity. I extracted the samples myself, in his prison cell. There can be no question. This man was a Corrino, by blood."

Rhombur scanned the sheaf of papers, still wondering why he had been called to this meeting. "Interesting."

"There is more, Prince Vernius." Pilru gazed intently at the scarred man's face. "Reffa's mother was Elrood's concubine, Shando Balut."

Rhombur looked up quickly. "Shando—!"

"My Prince, Tyros Reffa was *your* half brother as well."

"That can't possibly be true," Rhombur protested. "I've never been told anything about a brother. I . . . never even met the man." He kept looking over the analysis report, rereading it, searching for something to free him from this terrible reality. "*Executed?* You're sure?"

"Unfortunately, yes." Ambassador Pilru chewed at his lower lip. "Why couldn't Elrood have just made Tyros Reffa a noukker—an officer in the Imperial Guard—like most other Emperors have done with the sons of their concubines? But no, Elrood had to whisk the child away as if he was something *special*, opening up all of these problems."

"My brother . . . if only we could have helped him." Rhombur dropped the documents onto the floor. He rocked back on his heavy cyborg legs, his face a mask of anguish. The Prince of House Vernius paced the stone floor.

In a measured tone, Rhombur announced, "This only steels my resolve to oppose the Emperor. Now he has made it personal between us."

Money cannot purchase honor.
　　　　　　—Fremen Saying

I t came out of the sky like a screaming black bird and swooped low, a jet-powered 'thopter with a ferocious sandworm painted on its nose, a round maw open wide to reveal sharp crystal teeth.

In an isolated dry lake bed surrounded by rock buttresses that kept the area free of Shai-Hulud, four robed Fremen dropped to their knees and cried out in terror. The covered litter they had been carrying tilted and fell over.

Refusing to cower, Liet-Kynes stood tall instead, arms folded across his chest. His sandy hair and desert-stained cloak whipped in the breeze thrown by the aircraft. "Get up!" he yelled at his men. "Do you want them to think we are frightened old women?" The Guild representative had arrived precisely on time.

Chagrined, the Fremen righted the cargo-litter on the sand. They smoothed their robes and tightened the fittings of their stillsuits. Even at this hour of the morning, the desert was like a furnace.

Perhaps the Guild had painted the sandworm with specific intent, knowing that the Fremen revered the sandworms. But Liet knew something about the Guild himself, which enabled him to overcome his fear. *Information is power, especially knowledge of an enemy.*

He watched the jet-powered 'thopter as it circled,

its wings tucked tightly against its hull. Gunholes had been cut into the fuselage beneath the ports. The engines made an ear-piercing whine as the craft set down on a dune ridge a hundred meters away, kicking up sand. From silhouettes against the plaz windows, he counted four men inside. But one of them was not quite a man.

The craft's front folded open, and an open-topped vehicle rolled down a ramp, bearing a bald man who foolishly wore no stillsuit in the desert air. Sweat glistened on his pale, water-fat face. A square black box had been fitted to the front of his throat.

From the waist down, his body was an unclothed mass of amorphous, waxy flesh, as if it had been melted and hideously regrown. Fleshy webs joined his fingers. His yellow, protruberant eyes seemed alien, as if transplanted from an exotic, dangerous creature.

Some of the superstitious Fremen muttered and made warding signs, but Liet silenced them with a sharp glance. He wondered why this off-worlder made a point of revealing his repulsive body. *To put us off guard, perhaps.* He judged the representative to be a game player, seeking to elicit reactions, hoping to frighten and intimidate in order to improve his bargaining position.

The representative stared at Liet and ignored the other Fremen. His metallic voice came from the synthesizer at his throat. "You show no fear of us, not even of the sandworm on our aircraft."

"Even children know that Shai-Hulud does not fly," Liet said. "And anyone can make a painting."

The deformed man gave a narrow smile. "And my body? You do not find it repulsive?"

"My eyes have been trained to look for other things. A beautiful person may still be repugnant inside, and a malformed body may contain a perfect heart." He leaned closer to the open vehicle. "Which sort of creature are you?"

The Guildsman laughed, a tinny reverberation from his

throat. "I am Ailric. You are the troublesome Liet-Kynes, son of the Imperial Planetologist?"

"*I* am Imperial Planetologist now."

"So you are." Ailric's alien yellow eyes scanned the litter. Liet noticed that his pupils were almost rectangular. "Explain to me, *half*-Fremen, why does an Imperial servant seek to prevent satellite surveillance of the deep desert? Why is it so important to you?"

Sidestepping the intended insult, Liet replied, "Our arrangement with the Guild has been in force for centuries, and I see no reason to discontinue it." He waved an arm, and his men uncovered the litter, revealing brown pouches of concentrated melange essence, piled high. "However, the Fremen would prefer to deal without intermediaries. We have found such men to be . . . unreliable."

Ailric lifted his chin, narrowing his nostrils. "In that case, Rondo Tuek is now in a potentially threatening position to you, able to reveal your bribe to the authorities. No doubt he has already made plans to betray you. Are you not concerned?"

Liet could not keep the pride from his voice. "That problem has already been dealt with. Tuek is of no concern."

Ailric considered him for a long moment, trying to read nuances in Liet's tanned face. "Very well. I defer to your judgment."

As the Guild representative studied the spice payment laid out in front of him, Liet could see him mentally counting bags, calculating value. This was an enormous sum, but the Fremen had no choice but to keep the Guild satisfied. It was especially important to maintain their secret now, since they were replanting so many regions of Dune, to follow the ecological dream of Pardot Kynes. The Harkonnens must never know.

"I will accept this as a down payment for our continued cooperation," Ailric said. He watched Liet closely. "But our price has doubled."

286 Brian Herbert and Kevin J. Anderson

"Unacceptable." Liet raised his bearded chin. "You have no middleman to pay now."

The Guildsman narrowed his yellow eyes, as if to conceal a lie. "It costs more for me to meet with you directly. And Harkonnen pressure has increased. They complain about their existing satellites, and demand better surveillance from the Guild. We must fabricate more and more elaborate excuses. It costs money to keep the Harkonnen griffins at bay."

Liet looked at him dispassionately. "Twice is too much."

"One and a half times, then. You have ten days to pay the additional sum, or services will be cut off."

Liet's companions grumbled, but he just stared at the strange man, considering the predicament. He kept his emotions in check, not permitting his anger or alarm to show. He should have known the Guild was no more trustworthy, no more honorable than any other outsider.

"We will find the spice."

No other people have mastered the genetic language as well as the Bene Tleilax. We are right to call it "the language of God," for God Himself has given us this great power.

—Tleilaxu Apocrypha

Hasimir Fenring had grown up on Kaitain, inside the Imperial Palace and cyclopean government structures. He had seen the cavern cities of Ix and the monstrous sandstorms of Arrakis. But never had he experienced anything as majestic as the Guild Heighliner maintenance yards on Junction.

Carrying a tool kit and wearing grease-stained overalls, Fenring looked like a mere maintenance worker not worth a second glance. If he played his part well enough, no one would ever notice him.

The Spacing Guild employed billions of people. Some of them conducted the monumental operations of the Guild Bank, whose influence spread across all planets of the Imperium. Vast industrial complexes such as this Heighliner yard required hundreds of thousands of support workers.

Fenring's overlarge eyes drank in countless details as he and the Face Dancer hurried along the main concourse in the midst of hordes of workers, with crowded walkways overhead and lifts going up and down. Zoal had chosen to wear nondescript features, giving him the bland appearance of an unremarkable man with a sagging face and rugged eyebrows.

Few non-Guild people ever saw the inner workings of Junction. Docking cranes towered skyscraper-high, studded with emerald and amber lights, like stars in an inky night sky. The grid-blocks of the city stretched out in geometric patterns, a stitchery of civilization across an uninteresting landscape. Concave receiving dishes, clinging like creeper plants to the exteriors of structures, absorbed electromagnetic signals from space. Metallic wharves reached toward the sky, outstretched claw girders ready to clamp on to arriving shuttlecraft.

The two infiltrators approached a towering archway that marked one of the work zones. They entered the complex, mingled with labor crews. Ahead hung the immense shape of one of the largest Heighliners ever built, a vessel constructed during the last days of Vernius rule on Ix. This and one other craft—also currently undergoing maintenance in orbit—were the only two remaining Dominic Class vessels, a controversial design that boasted increased cargo capacity, which proportionately decreased Imperial tax revenues.

But after the Tleilaxu takeover on the machine planet, construction of new Heighliners had dropped dramatically because of production and quality-control problems. As a consequence, the Guild had to maintain their existing fleet with greater care.

Fenring and his Face Dancer companion rode sequential lift platforms along the curved hull of the metropolis-sized spaceship. Swarms of workers crawled like parasites over the plates, sealing, scouring, inspecting the metal. Micrometeorites and radiation storms produced tiny fractures in a hull's lattice structure; once every five years, each Heighliner went into drydock in the Junction maintenance yards, for an overhaul.

The two men passed through an access tunnel to the inner hull of the great ship, and finally into the cavernous hold. No one paid attention to them. Inside the vessel's

shell, armies of workers inspected and revamped the docking clamps used by family frigates, cargo haulers, and passenger shuttles. Others scurried in and out of the decks
nestled within the Heighliner's inner skin.

Rising like a spider on a thread, a lift took Fenring and
Zoal to the upper restricted zone where the Navigators'
tanks were located. Soon they would encounter heightened
Guild security—and the real challenge would begin.

The Face Dancer looked at Fenring, his expression unreadable. "I can assume the mask of any victim you choose,
but remember *you* must do the killing."

Fenring carried several knives tucked into his coveralls,
and he certainly knew how to use them. "A simple division
of responsibilities, hmmm?"

Zoal set a brisk pace, with Fenring hurrying to keep up.
The shape-shifter confidently made his way along dim, low-
ceilinged corridors. "The blueprints show that the Navigator's chamber is this way. Follow me, and we will be done
before long."

They had studied Heighliner blueprint holos left behind
in the subterranean assembly facilities on Ix, where the
ships had originally been built. Since this giant vessel
would not be ready to depart for several more weeks, no
Navigator occupied the tank, and the spice supply had not
yet been replenished. Security would not be at its tightest
yet.

"Around this corner." Zoal kept his uninflected voice
low. He took out a ridulian handboard and fingered through
sheets of shimmering crystal, illuminating a rough diagram
of the Heighliner's upper levels.

As they approached a guard stationed at the far end of
the corridor, Zoal put on a deeply puzzled expression and
pointed to lines on the handboard. Fenring shook his head,
feigning disagreement. They walked toward the guard, who
stood stiffly at attention, his stunner at his hip.

Fenring raised his annoyed voice as they drew closer.
"This is not the right level, I tell you. We're in the wrong

section of the Heighliner. Look here." He jabbed his fingers at the crystal sheets.

Playing his part like a Jongleur, Zoal flushed. "Listen to me, we followed the directions step by step." He glanced up, pretending to notice the guard for the first time. "Let's ask him." He pushed forward, closing the distance.

Glowering, the guard jerked a thumb toward Fenring. "You're both in the wrong section. No unauthorized access."

With a sigh of disgust, Zoal held up the Heighliner drawing on his handboard, pushing it toward the guard's face. "Well then, can you direct us?" Fenring pressed close on the other side.

The guard peered at the crystalboard. "Here's your problem. This isn't—"

With flawless grace, Fenring slipped his long, slim knife through the man's ribs and deep into his liver, then twisted the blade and pushed higher into the lungs. He avoided major blood vessels to minimize bleeding, but the wound was sufficiently fatal.

The guard gasped and twitched. Dropping his handboard, Zoal grabbed the victim in a brutally strong grip. Fenring withdrew his slender knife and stabbed again, this time under the sternum and up into the heart.

Zoal stared into the guard's face as he eased the slumping body to the deck. Then the Face Dancer twitched. His features became liquid, as if made of soft clay, and shifted into a new mask. His appearance was now identical to the guard's. Zoal drew a deep breath, twitched his head to one side, then stared at the dead man's face. "I am finished."

They dragged the corpse into an unoccupied closet and sealed the door. Fenring waited while the Face Dancer changed clothes with the murdered guard, applying enzyme sponges to dissolve the worst of the bloodstains. Afterward, they used the ridulian handboard to consult an accurate schematic of the upper Heighliner levels and located a disposal chute that dropped into the heated reactor chamber. The guard's ionized ashes would never be found.

Together, they proceeded into the security area. The Count carried his tool kit and this time feigned a look of aggrieved distress, as if he had been given an impossible work assignment. The impostor marched him along, gruffly acknowledging other guards on the higher levels. They succeeded in finding an unoccupied operations chamber behind the Navigator's tank.

The spice compartment was, as expected, empty. Quickly, Fenring removed the canisters of super-compressed amal pellets, dense tablets of synthetic spice shaped exactly like their melange counterparts. In such a potent form, the spice would be vaporized to create a rich gas, thick enough that a Navigator could feel its full effects and envision safe paths through foldspace.

Fenring sealed the container into the spice-supply compartment, then applied a counterfeit approval label. It might cause some confusion when the spice-stockers found the chamber already loaded, but they would not think too hard upon finding an *excess* of melange. With luck, no one would complain.

The conspirators slipped back out. Within an hour, they had departed from the Heighliner yards and moved to the next stage of their plan.

"I hope the vessel in orbit will be just as easy to break into, hmmm?" Fenring said. "We need two test ships, to be absolutely sure."

The Face Dancer looked at him. Zoal's ability to mimic the guard's features was eerie. "It may take a bit more finesse, but we'll get in."

❦

AFTERWARD, WEARY BUT exhilarated from completing the second half of their mission, they stood under the cloudy skies and twinkling lights of the Junction spaceport.

They hid among piled dump boxes at the edge of the loading zone; Fenring wanted to avoid conversation with Guild workers who might ask too many questions.

He could easily have hired a mercenary or a professional commando to complete this covert mission, but Fenring liked to perform dirty work himself, when it interested him. This kept his abilities honed and provided him with pleasure.

During a moment of guarded peace, the Count soothed himself with thoughts of his lovely wife, Margot. He was anxious to return to the Imperial Palace, where he would see and learn what she'd been up to. She should have arrived on Kaitain several days ago.

Zoal interrupted his reverie. "Count Fenring, I must compliment you on your skills. You have done your part well."

"A compliment from a Face Dancer, hmmm?" Pretending to relax, Fenring leaned against a corroded metal dump box that would soon be hauled up to a Heighliner. "Thank you."

Seeing a blur, he instinctively jerked to one side just as a flash came toward him, a knife thrown with deadly accuracy. Even before the point of his first weapon missed its target and clanged against the metal cubicle, the Face Dancer snatched another blade hidden in his uniform.

But Count Hasimir Fenring was more than equal to the challenge. His senses and reactions tuned to an extremely high level, he drew his own knives and dropped into a fighting stance, his expression feral. "Ahhh, I thought you were supposed to be untrained in bladework?"

The Face Dancer wore a hard, predatory expression. "I have also been trained to lie, but apparently not well enough."

Fenring held his knife. He had more experience in assassin's work than this shape-shifter could ever imagine. *The Tleilaxu have underestimated me. Another mistake.*

In the dim light of the spaceport, Zoal's features flickered and shifted once more. His shoulders became broader, his face narrow, his eyes overlarge, until Fenring was looking into a nightmarish reflection of himself, but in the Face Dancer's clothing. "Soon I will play a new role as Imperial Spice Minister and boyhood friend of Shaddam IV."

The entire plot fell into place for Fenring, how this Tleilaxu creature would mimic him, passing himself off as a confidant of the Emperor's. Although Fenring doubted Zoal could fool Shaddam for long, the shape-shifter needed only to get close to the Emperor for a few moments in private—where he could kill him and then take over the Golden Lion Throne, as ordered by Ajidica.

Fenring admired the audacity. Considering the botched decisions Shaddam had made of late, perhaps this simulacrum might not be an altogether unwelcome alternative.

"You'd never fool my Bene Gesserit wife. Margot notices the subtlest details."

Zoal smiled, an uncharacteristic usage of Fenring's ferret-like facial features. "I believe I am up to the challenge, now that I have observed you closely."

The Face Dancer lunged, and Fenring parried with one of his own knives. Their daggers clashed again, and the combatants used their bodies as weapons, slamming each other against the dump boxes.

His back against the wall, Fenring kicked out, trying to break Zoal's shin, but the changeling dodged and brought his blade point up in a flash. Fenring swung his right forearm, deflected the knife from his eye, then rolled away from the dump boxes.

Sweat poured from both fighters. Zoal had a nick under his chin, which dripped scarlet. The Count's coveralls had been slashed in several places, yet the shape-shifter had not succeeded in injuring him. Not even a scratch.

Still, Fenring very nearly underestimated the Face Dancer, who elevated his abilities and fought with renewed frenzy. His knife attacks became a blur. This was a danger Fenring had not contemplated: The shape-shifter was mimicking the Count's formidable fighting skills, learning from him, stealing tricks.

The Count considered what to do and when to do it, never letting his guard down. He needed to come up with a new move, one this laboratory-bred creature would never expect. He thought of trying to capture the shape-shifter alive in order to interrogate him, but that would be too risky. He couldn't let their mission here be exposed.

He heard the whine of a shuttle in the background, but didn't dare look. The smallest lapse would be fatal. Fenring let himself stumble and fall backward, pulling the shape-shifter down with him. The Count self-consciously grunted as if in pain and dropped his own knife; it clanged and skittered out of reach under one of the dump boxes.

Thinking he had wounded his quarry, the kneeling Zoal raised his blade, prepared to deliver the killing blow.

But Fenring had surveyed the ground first and landed near the place where the Face Dancer's first thrown knife had fallen. In a single fluid movement, he snatched up the forgotten dagger before Zoal could bring down his own weapon. Fenring plunged the tip into the Face Dancer's throat. He kicked Zoal away from him before the shape-shifter's severed jugular could spray blood all over his clean clothes.

The Face Dancer's body sprawled in the shadows between dump boxes. Fenring backed away, looking around to make certain no one had seen or heard anything. He did not want to answer questions; he just needed to be far from here.

Slumped on the ground, Zoal seemed to melt, his features losing precise focus until he had transformed into a hairless, smooth-faced mannequin with no distinctive qualities: waxy skin and smooth fingers without the whorl of fingerprints.

This Tleilaxu plot was particularly intriguing. Fenring would hoard that knowledge as if it were a prized treasure.

DUNE: HOUSE CORRINO   295

He would consider how best to use it against Hidar Fen Ajidica.

Breathing hard, but still *breathing*, Fenring stuffed the Face Dancer's body into one of the dump boxes and sealed the hatches. Within weeks, the bizarre cadaver would arrive on some distant world, much to the surprise of the cargo's intended recipient. . . .

Fenring glanced toward the spaceport lights and saw that the orbital shuttle was just setting down. He would take a roundabout passage back to Kaitain, leaving no traceable path. Of secondary concern, he needed to avoid traveling on either of the two Dominic Class Heighliners, just in case the Navigators had unfortunate reactions to synthetic spice. Fenring did not intend to be part of the test himself.

Exhilarated, he hurried to the spaceport and joined a crowd of workers and third-class passengers boarding the shuttle. As he rode the shuttle toward the Heighliner that orbited Junction, he kept to himself and answered no questions, though two of his fellow passengers asked him why he wore such a rich smile on his face.

A secret is most valuable when it remains a secret. Under such circumstances, one does not require proof in order to exploit the information.

—Bene Gesserit Dictum

Shortly after arriving on Kaitain, as ordered by the Baron, Piter de Vries padded through the corridors of the Imperial Office Complex. His Mentat mind easily kept track of every turn in the maze of connected government buildings.

It was midmorning, and he still tasted the sweetness of imported fruit in his mouth from breakfast on board the diplomatic frigate. More delicious, though, was the incriminating knowledge that he had been instructed to deliver anonymously. Shaddam would probably soil his Imperial trousers when he learned of it.

He brought out a message cube from beneath his clothing and concealed it in a wall alcove behind an idealized bust of the Emperor, one of many scattered throughout the Palace.

A side door in the Office Complex opened, and a ruddy-faced, intense man stepped into the corridor. De Vries recognized the Harkonnen Ambassador, Kalo Whylls. In his mid-thirties, Whylls looked barely old enough to shave; he had obtained his position through family connections. None of the information Whylls sent back to Giedi Prime ever proved to be of any value; he was ineffective, unschooled in how to use his position to become a competent spy.

"Why, Piter de Vries!" Whylls hailed in a syrupy voice. "I didn't know you were in the Palace. The Baron sent me no notification. Are you coming to make a courtesy call?"

The Mentat feigned surprise. "Perhaps soon, Mister Ambassador, but at the moment I have an important appointment. Business for the Baron."

"Yes, time is short, isn't it?" Whylls agreed with a broad smile. "Well, I must hurry off, too. We both have so many vital things to do. Let me know later if I can help in any way." The Ambassador bustled down the corridor in the opposite direction, obviously trying to look important.

On a scrap of instroy paper, the Mentat sketched a map and wrote directions, to be given to an Imperial Courier who would pick up this hidden message cube and take it directly to Shaddam. A bombshell.

This would be a suitable revenge for the Richesian blackmail.

❦

IT MUST WORK.

Haloa Rund supervised while laboratory metalworkers completed the casing of a prototype invisibility generator, based upon sketches and equations the renegade inventor Chobyn had left behind.

In one of his sealed shigawire spools, Chobyn had called this a "no-field"—making an object both "here" and "not here" at the same time. During every waking moment, Rund thought about the amazing concept.

He still had not deciphered the intermittently failing invisibility mechanism in the rogue inventor's old laboratory chamber. Judging from fragments of schematics, he had determined that the minimum diameter for projecting the no-field was one hundred fifty meters. With this in mind, Rund didn't see how the device could disguise a small laboratory room—until he discovered that most of the field extended asymmetrically outside the Korona station into space.

Upon hearing of the project, and after complete funding

had been supplied by the Richesian government, Count Ilban Richese had sent a message to his nephew, congratulating him for his ingenuity and foresight. The old man promised someday to come up to Korona where he might see the work firsthand, though he doubted he would understand it. Premier Calimar sent his own supportive communication, encouraging the inventors.

For decades this artificial moon had concealed the proprietary technology for manufacturing mysterious and valuable Richesian mirrors. No other House had been able to duplicate the science of the mirrors, despite numerous attempts at industrial espionage. If a no-field breakthrough occurred, though, Korona's facilities might begin to produce an even more valuable technology.

The all-out research and development effort was extremely expensive and required the brainpower of the best scientists, diverting them from other duties. Recently Premier Calimar had delivered full funding in the form of a large melange stockpile that would be stored on the satellite station, where it could be liquidated for cash as necessary. Melange storage vaults now accounted for six percent of Korona's usable volume.

The political clout of Director Flinto Kinnis had increased because of the ambitious project, but Haloa Rund didn't care. Chobyn's generator was an exceedingly complex problem, enough to demand his complete attention.

The inventor worried about nothing else.

✧

WHEN SHADDAM OPENED the message cube, he canceled all further appointments and locked himself in his private study, fuming. An hour later, he summoned Supreme Bashar Zum Garon. "It seems that my Sardaukar have more work to do." He could barely suppress his rage.

The old veteran Garon, resplendent in his uniform, stood at attention, listening for further orders. "We are at your command, Sire."

After all the express warnings and after the severe example Shaddam had set on Zanovar, House Richese had the temerity to do this? Premier Calimar believed he could just *ignore* an Imperial decree and keep his own illegal melange stockpile? The surreptitious message provided incontrovertible proof that an illegal quantity of spice was stored inside the artificial moon of Korona.

At first he had been suspicious of similar claims. Ecaz and Grumman had done their best to cast suspicion on each other, pointing fingers, exaggerating accusations. But their proof had been flimsy, their motives transparent.

"It is time to set another example, to show the citizens of the Imperium that they cannot ignore Corrino laws." Shaddam paced the floor.

As his anger simmered, the Emperor's better sense came into play. The core motivation behind his first attack on Zanovar had been to erase Tyros Reffa. However, his larger scheme was to leave the Imperial economy completely vulnerable to his impending monopoly on synthetic spice. He had to take the next step, increase the stakes. Richese would be the second scapegoat.

He would notify Guild investigators and CHOAM auditors of his upcoming measure. After the alleged stockpile was removed from Korona (and used as a payoff to buy Guild and CHOAM support), other political factions would gather behind the throne as well.

Since Hasimir Fenring had not yet returned from Ix, Shaddam would have to make another important decision by himself. No matter. The Emperor knew what to do, and a response could not wait. He gave the Sardaukar commander his orders.

The Great Spice War was about to heat up.

It has been demonstrated in every epoch of history that if you want profits you must rule. And to rule, you must blunt the edge of the citizenry.

— EMPEROR SHADDAM CORRINO IV

Flushed with the Ajidamal pulsing through his thoughts, Hidar Fen Ajidica had a lizard's-eye view of the corpses in the dining hall. Twenty-two of the most meddlesome Tleilaxu Masters lay slumped over the tables, poisoned. *Dead.*

Inspired by the revelations he had received from God, he was about to redraw the lines of power in the Imperium.

And among the bodies, a bonus: the pretentious Master Zaaf himself, who had arrived the day before on an unexpected inspection tour. With piquant slig stew spilled all over himself, Zaaf lay supine, his eyes bulging and mouth open, a most undistinguished state of death for the Master of Masters. The fast-acting toxin slipped into the food by Face Dancer cooks had sent Zaaf and his dinner companions into paroxysms within minutes, and their gray skin had turned a sickly scarlet, as if scalded from the inside out.

When the Master Researcher stood in the doorway, admiring his accomplishment, he had noticed a *Draco volans* in the rafters, one of the little lizards that seemed immune to pest-control measures. Only a few centimeters long, it had scaly appendages on either side of its body that permitted it to glide through the air like a Terran flying squirrel.

Seeing the lizard, Ajidica had decided to exercise the sparkling new powers that had come to him after consuming so much ajidamal. Now his mind's eye seemed to be *inside* the diminutive dragon. From a perch in the rafters, he gazed down on the results of the slaughter through reptilian eyes. One of the bodies twitched, then fell as still as the rest.

Nearly two dozen dead Masters . . . it was a good start, as far as he was concerned. The Tleilaxu heretics must be removed before the Great Belief could resurface properly under Ajidica's firm guidance.

He smiled as his thoughts raced through the myriad possibilities in his remarkable level of consciousness. Ajidica hardly slept at all anymore, and spent much of each day romping through his own marvelous mind as if it were an amusement park of new experiences and delights. He could hold ninety-seven simultaneous lines of thought in balance, ranging from mundane to complex subjects. He had the ability to study each mosaic of information as if it were a filmbook on a library shelf.

Ajidamal was even better than melange, even more intense. With it, Guild Navigators might be able to fold space into other universes, no longer restricted to one. One of his ninety-seven balanced lines of thought moved to the forefront. By now, Count Fenring and Zoal would have substituted ajidamal for melange in at least two Heighliners, and the Navigators should be about to use it. Fenring himself must be as dead as these victims here. The Face Dancer would have done his work well, and would return soon to report the details. . . .

With his imagined lizard eyes, the Master Researcher surveyed the sprawled, blotchy corpses. There could be no turning back from his holy mission now. His other Face Dancers would replace the old-guard Masters, and everything would appear normal. Then he could send them to Kaitain. . . .

From here, the Face Dancer replica of Master Zaaf would

send word to Bandalong that he had decided to remain on Xuttuh for several months—which was the amount of time Ajidica needed to complete his plans. Any others who got in the way would also be consumed, like insects caught on the tongue of a flying lizard.

He imagined his tongue darting out, snapping up bugs and swallowing them. Darting and snapping, darting and snapping. He tasted their bitter, crunchy little bodies. The flying dragon hopped from the rafter and sailed slowly over the corpses, as if on an aerial inspection mission.

With a blink of his eyes, Ajidica dragged his consciousness away from the lizard and returned to his own body, which stood in the doorway. His mouth had a bitter taste, and his tongue felt raw and sore.

In an excited voice, he summoned his Face Dancers from the kitchen. They arrived promptly, ready for orders. "Dispose of the bodies. Then prepare for a journey."

As the shape-shifters set about their task, Ajidica searched for the little lizard. The elusive creature, however, was nowhere to be seen.

WITH A THRILL of amazement, a sunken-eyed C'tair Pilru found the gruesome bodies at the disposal site. The hated invaders were not covered with enough garbage to conceal them fully.

Slinking through shadows long after the strict curfew, C'tair had arrived just as a groundtruck departed, throwing rock dust into the air behind it. No one had seen him. He often frequented the subterranean dumping areas, searching for salvage items that he might adapt to his needs.

But this! Dead Tleilaxu Masters, more than twenty of them. High-ranking officials every one, and they had been murdered! Their normally pallid skins were a scalded-red color. He drew the only possible conclusion his weary mind could formulate. Here was proof that the resistance movement continued on Ix.

Someone else is killing the Tleilaxu.

C'tair scratched his head, disarranging his ragged hair. He looked around in the low starlight from the projected sky, not certain what to do next, wondering who his mysterious allies were.

Not long ago, a pair of Atreides men had promised that rescuers would arrive soon, like knights on white horses. In anticipation of this, other resistance groups must be mobilizing. He only hoped he lived long enough to see the glorious liberation of Ix.

Rhombur was coming! At last!

Not to be outdone, C'tair went into darkened subterranean chambers in search of lone Tleilaxu. He had become hardened over the long, desperate years. By the end of the night, seven more Tleilaxu joined the bodies at the disposal site.

Any road followed precisely to its end leads precisely nowhere. You must climb the mountain just a little . . . enough to test that it's a mountain, enough to see where the other mountains are. From the top of any mountain, you cannot see that mountain.

—EMPRESS HERADE,
consort to Crown Prince Raphael Corrino

He had avoided this duty for half of his life, but now the departure could not come soon enough for Rhombur Vernius. He made no attempt to conceal his cyborg body—in light of his mission to Ix, he considered it a badge of honor.

Following concise descriptions from Thufir Hawat's perfect memory, Dr. Yueh made cosmetic modifications to disguise the sophisticated mechanical enhancements, making them look like primitive, clumsy devices. Rhombur hoped he could pass himself off as one of the part-human, part-machine monstrosities the Tleilaxu called "bi-Ixians."

For weeks, Gurney and Rhombur had discussed strategy with the Duke and his highest-ranking military men. "The success or failure of this mission ultimately falls on my shoulders," Rhombur said, as he stood awaiting a shuttle that would take him and Gurney to the Heighliner. "I'm not a kid collecting pretty rocks anymore. I need to remember everything my father ever taught me. By the age of seven, I had to memorize all the military codes, and I learned about every great battle House Vernius had ever fought."

"This struggle will be something for us to write songs about, something for your children to memorize," Gurney Halleck said with an encouraging smile. Then, from the way his expression stiffened, it was clear he regretted his remark.

Breaking the uncomfortable silence, Rhombur said, "Yes, it will be something for all Ixians to tell their children and grandchildren."

The necessary bribes had been paid: The Spacing Guild would again interfere with Tleilaxu defense scanners long enough for their camouflaged combat pod to slip into a hidden access port. This particular pod had been designed so that it could be dismantled for its parts, many of which had dual purposes as weapons themselves. The sleek gray pod sat on struts in a loading dock, while Atreides men hurried to make the link-ups that would connect it to the shuttle.

Thufir and Duncan arrived to bid the two men farewell. Duke Leto had not appeared yet, and Rhombur refused to board the shuttle until he could embrace his friend. The liberation of Ix could not begin without an Atreides blessing.

The night before, Rhombur had recharged his cyborg components, but his mind remained exhausted from lack of authentic sleep. His thoughts continued to press through questions. Tessia had worked her wonders, though, rubbing the tense muscles in the remaining flesh of his body, miraculously soothing him. Her dark brown eyes seemed full of pride and anticipation. "My love—my *husband*, I promise that our next night spent together will be in the Grand Palais."

With a small chuckle, he said, "Not in my old rooms, though. You and I deserve more than a boyhood bed-chamber!" He gave a mighty heave of his chest and shoulders, simultaneously dreading and looking forward to seeing Ix again.

The timetable was in place. Everything would adhere to a strict schedule because the separate prongs of the attack could not rely on communications while en route. There would be no room for error, or delay . . . or doubts. Duke Leto was counting on him and Gurney to soften up the Tleilaxu from within, to expose their underbelly, after which the Atreides military would deliver a hammerblow from the outside.

Turning, he saw Leto. The Duke's black jacket was uncharacteristically wrinkled; the nobleman's chin and cheeks were shadowed with dark stubble. Poorly concealed behind his back, he held a large parcel gift-wrapped in gold paper with a ribbon on top. "You can't leave without this, Rhombur."

Accepting the package, the Prince determined from sensors in his arm that it was surprisingly light. "Leto, the combat pod is already so packed there's barely enough room for Gurney and me."

"You'll want to take this anyway." A rare smile broke through his normally hard expression.

Fumbling to tear the wrapping paper with his mechanical fingers, Rhombur got it open. Inside the box he found a much smaller case. The hinged lid opened easily. "Vermilion hells!"

The fire-jewel ring was just like the one he had worn before the skyclipper explosion—a ring that had represented his authority as the rightful Earl of House Vernius. "Fire-jewels aren't easy to come by, Leto. Each stone has its own personality, its own unique appearance. Where did you get this? It looks just like the one I used to have. Of course, it couldn't be the same one."

Leto's gray eyes twinkled as he draped a brotherly arm around the Prince's artificial shoulders. "This *is* your ring, my friend, regenerated from a tiny fragment of the jewel that was found fused into the flesh of your hand."

Rhombur's remaining organic eye blinked as if to drive back tears. This ring symbolized the glories of Ix, as well as the terrible losses he and his people had suffered. But his imaginary tears stopped, and his face hardened. He slipped the fire-jewel ring onto the third finger of his prosthetic right hand. "Perfect fit."

"And more good news," Duncan Idaho added. "According to the spaceport center, the Heighliner on this route is the last Dominic Class vessel ever manufactured on Ix, newly refurbished from Junction. Sounds like a good omen to me."

"Indeed, I will take it as that." Rhombur hugged each of his friends before heading for the private shuttle, accompanied by Gurney Halleck. Behind them, Leto, Duncan, and Thufir called out, "Victory on Ix!"

To Rhombur's ears, it sounded like a statement of fact. He vowed to succeed . . . or die trying.

We could be dreaming all the time, but we do not perceive those dreams while we are awake because consciousness (like the sun obscuring stars during the day) is much too brilliant to allow the unconscious content so much definition.

—Private Journals of
KWISATZ MOTHER ANIRUL SADOW-TONKIN

Haunted from within her own mind, Lady Anirul could not sleep.

Once roused, the voices of countless generations allowed her no rest. The intruders from Other Memory demanded her attention, begging her to look at historical precedents, insisting that their lives be remembered. Each one had something to say, a dire warning, a cry for attention. All of it inside her head.

She wanted to scream.

As the Emperor's consort, Anirul lived in greater luxury than the vast majority of the lives within her had ever experienced. She had access to servants, fine music, the most expensive drugs. Her combined chambers, filled with beautiful furniture, were large enough to encompass a small village.

At one time Anirul had thought being the Kwisatz Mother had been a blessing, but the possession of her mind by a multitude from across the chasms of time was consuming too much of her as the moment of Jessica's delivery drew closer. The voices-within knew that the end of the breeding program's long road was at last near.

Restless on her oversize bed, Anirul flung the slippery sheets away; the fabric tangled and oozed to the floor as if it were a living invertebrate. Naked, Anirul walked to the gold-inlay doors. Her skin was buttery and smooth, massaged daily with lotions and salves. A diet of melange recipes, as well as a few biochemical tweaks she accomplished internally using Sisterhood training, kept her muscles toned and her body attractive, even if her husband no longer noticed her.

In this room she had allowed Shaddam to impregnate her five times, but he rarely visited her bed anymore. The Emperor had, quite correctly, given up hope that she would ever bear him a male heir. Now sterile, he would have no more children: not by her, nor by any of his concubines.

Though her husband suspected she had taken other lovers during their years of marriage, Anirul required no personal entanglements to satisfy her needs. As a skilled Bene Gesserit, she had access to means of pleasuring herself with all the intensity she could desire.

Now, what she desired most was a restful, deep sleep.

She decided to go out into the quiet night. She would wander the huge Palace, and maybe the capital city beyond, in the vain hope that her legs could carry her away from the voices.

She grasped the door handles, then realized that she wore no clothes. In recent weeks, Anirul had overheard courtiers chattering about her unstable personality, rumors probably started by Shaddam himself. If she were to stride naked into the corridors, that would pour more fuel on the flames of gossip.

Cinching a turquoise robe around herself, she tied an intricate knot that no one but a Bene Gesserit could release without a knife. Shoeless, she stepped onto the tile floor and headed from her rooms.

She had often walked barefoot back at the Mother

School on Wallach IX. The chill climate provided a rigorous environment for young Acolytes to learn endurance, to discover how to control their body heat, perspiration, and nerve responses. One time, Harishka—who was Proctor Superior of the school at the time, not yet Mother Superior—had led her young women into the snowy mountains, where she instructed all of them to remove every garment and trudge four kilometers through ice-crusted snow to the top of a windswept peak. Once there, they had meditated for an hour in the nude before climbing back down to their clothes and warmth.

Anirul had nearly frozen to death that day, but the crisis had driven her to a better understanding of her metabolism, and of her own mind. Even before putting her garments back on, she had made herself warm and comfortable, with no need of anything else. Four of her Acolyte classmates hadn't survived—failures—and Harishka had left their bodies up in the snow, where they would remain as grim reminders for later students. . . .

Now as Anirul wandered the Palace corridors, ladies-in-waiting emerged from their rooms and rushed to her side. Not Jessica, though; she kept the pregnant young woman sheltered, protected, unaware of her personal turmoil.

With her peripheral vision Anirul saw the shadow of a guard slipping away from a lady's quarters—and was irritated that her women would waste time on trysts during their on-duty hours, especially since they were well aware of her frequent bouts of insomnia.

"I am going to the animal park," she announced, not even looking at the women scurrying to follow her. "Send word ahead, and instruct the conservator to grant me access."

"At this hour, my Lady?" said an attractive young maidservant, as she buttoned up her bodice. She had blonde hair in ringlets and delicate features.

Anirul shot her a hard glare, and the maid seemed to shrivel. This one would be dismissed in the morning. The

Emperor's wife could not abide anyone challenging her whims. With all the responsibility on her shoulders, Anirul was becoming less tolerant, and much less patient. A bit like Shaddam.

Outside, the night sky was a wash of swirling auroral lights, but Anirul hardly noticed. Her growing entourage followed her across garden terraces and elevated boulevards until she arrived at the artificially forested enclosures set aside as the Imperial Zoo.

Previous rulers had used the animal park for their private enjoyment, but Shaddam could care less about biological specimens from distant worlds. In a "gracious gesture," he had opened the park to the general public, so that they might experience "the magnificence of all creatures under the dominion of House Corrino." His other alternative—expressed privately to his wife—had been to slaughter the animals and save the minor expense of feeding them.

Anirul stopped at the entrance to the animal park, a slender crystalline arch. She saw lights switching on, heavy glowglobes that shone brightly and disturbed the sleeping animals. The conservator must be running from one set of controls to another, preparing the zoo for her arrival.

Anirul turned to her ladies-in-waiting. "Remain here. I wish to be alone."

"Is that wise, my Lady?" said the blonde maidservant, again annoying her mistress. No doubt Shaddam would have executed the girl on the spot.

Anirul gave her another withering look. "I have dealt with Imperial politics, young woman. I have encountered the most unpleasant members of the Landsraad, and I have been married to Emperor Shaddam for two decades." She frowned. "I can certainly handle a few *lesser* animals."

With that, she marched into the beautifully manicured faux wilderness. The zoo always had a calming effect on her. She saw cages with force-field bars that were habitats for tufted saber-bears, ecadroghes, and D-wolves. Laza tigers lounged on electrically heated rocks, warming themselves even without sunlight. One lioness munched lazily on bloody strips of raw meat. Nearby, tigers raised their slitted eyes and regarded Anirul sleepily, too well fed to be ferocious anymore.

In a large tank, Buzzell dolphins swam about. With enlarged brains, the creatures were intelligent enough to perform simple underwater tasks. The dolphins streaked by like silvery blue knives; one returned to peer through the glass, as if recognizing her as a person of significance.

While strolling among the animals, Anirul felt a rare moment of internal peace. Chaos did not bother her here in the drowsy quiet of the Imperial Zoo. She heard nothing but her private thoughts. Anirul heaved a long sigh, then drew a deep breath, drinking in the delicious solitude.

She knew her sanity could not survive the continually growing inner storm that afflicted her. As Kwisatz Mother and the Emperor's wife, she had vitally important duties. She needed to concentrate. She especially needed to watch Jessica and her unborn child.

Has Jessica caused this turmoil? Do the voices know something I do not? What about the future?

Unlike most other Sisters, Anirul had access to *all* her memories. But, following the death of her good friend Lobia, she had excavated too deeply, gone too far in her search for the old Truthsayer inside her head. In the process, she had triggered an avalanche of lives.

In the stillness of the zoo, Anirul thought again of Lobia, who had given her so much advice when she had been alive. Anirul wanted to hear the old woman's voice rising above all the others, a voice of reason in the mystic throng. Mentally, she called out for her lost friend, but the Lobia-within did not emerge.

Suddenly, hearing the call, the ghost-voices assaulted her again, so tumultuously that they echoed in the air around her. Memories grew louder, lives and thoughts, opinions and arguments. Voices shouted her name.

She screamed back at them, telling them to be quiet. . . .

Inside the zoo, the Buzzell dolphins thrashed in their tank, bumping their bottle-noses against the thick plaz. The Laza tigers let out echoing roars. The saber-bear bellowed and fell upon its companion in the enclosure, triggering a fierce battle of teeth and claws. Captive birds began to shriek. Other animals howled in panic.

Anirul dropped to her knees, still screaming at the voices-within. The guards and servants rushed to help her. They had been watching at a safe distance, disobeying her request for privacy.

But as they tried to lift her to her feet, the Emperor's wife spasmed, flailing her arms. One of her jeweled rings struck the face of the blonde maidservant, slashing her across the cheek. Anirul's eyes were wild, like those of a rabid animal.

"Emperor Shaddam will not like this," one of the guards said, but Anirul was beyond hearing anything at all.

Diplomats are chosen for their ability to lie.
—Bene Gesserit Saying

In the Kaitain ambassadorial quarters, Piter de Vries sat at his writing desk, composing a note.

Blood dripped from the ceiling, pooling and congealing in a thick puddle on the floor, but the Mentat paid it no heed. The steady metronome of falling droplets sounded like a ticking clock. He would clean up the mess later.

Since delivering his anonymous message that informed the Emperor of Richese's illegal spice stockpile, de Vries had remained at the Imperial Court, setting up complex plans to advance the position of House Harkonnen. He had already heard grumblings about Shaddam's intended punishment of Richese. De Vries relished the thought of appropriate revenge.

He also meant to hoard any knowledge he gathered, eventually doling it out to the Baron in measured doses. In this manner he would prove his continued worth and keep himself alive.

While spying at court, he had picked up an interesting tidbit the Baron might appreciate, far more important than mere political or military moves against House Richese. For the first time, Piter de Vries had seen Jessica across a crowded room, a lovely woman six months pregnant with another Atreides heir. That opened up so many possibilities. . . .

"My dear Baron," he wrote, using a coded Harkonnen language, "I have discovered that the concubine of your enemy, Leto Atreides, currently resides in the Imperial Palace. She has been taken under the wing of the Emperor's wife, ostensibly as a lady-in-waiting, though I cannot fathom the reason for this. She seems to have no duties. Perhaps it is because this whore and Anirul are both Bene Gesserit witches.

"I would like to propose a scheme that could have many repercussions: pride and satisfaction for House Harkonnen, pain and misery for House Atreides. What more could we desire?"

He pondered again, watching the blood drip from the ceiling. A message cylinder lay open beside him on the writing desk. He scribbled again. "I have managed to keep myself hidden from her. This Jessica intrigues me."

With a smile he recalled how Leto's concubine Kailea and their firstborn son Victor had both been killed in the past year. The Harkonnens had hoped this double-tragedy might drive the Duke mad and destroy the backbone of House Atreides forever. Unfortunately, against all odds, Leto seemed to have recovered. His recent attack on Beakkal indicated that he was more aggressive and decisive than ever.

But how much more could the damaged, bitter man tolerate?

"Jessica intends to stay here and give birth to her child in the Palace. Though she is constantly watched by the other witches, I believe I may be able to discover an opportunity to slip in and kill the newborn infant, and, if you wish, the mother as well. My Baron, think of how that would wound your mortal enemy! But I must proceed with great care."

He finished writing in smaller letters, so that his entire message could fit on a single sheet of *instroy* paper. "I have therefore arranged a legitimate reason to remain here on

Kaitain, so that I might keep watch on this intriguing woman. I will send you regular reports."

He signed the note with a flourish and sealed it inside the message cylinder, where it would be dispatched on the next outbound Heighliner to Giedi Prime.

Dispassionately, he gazed up at the ceiling, where he had hidden a body behind the panels. The inept Harkonnen ambassador, Kalo Whylls, had put up more of a struggle than expected, so de Vries had slashed him a few extra times, leaving him a patchwork of gaping wounds, with his lifeblood draining out of him. Quite a mess.

Turning back to the items on his desk, de Vries examined a document obtained from the Imperial Minister of Forms, a simple transmittal to the Kaitain bureaucracy. No one would question it. Smiling with his sapho-stained lips, the Mentat dutifully finished writing an official decree, which he would deliver to the Emperor's Chamberlain, informing them that the previous Harkonnen Ambassador had been permanently "recalled" to Giedi Prime. Piter de Vries filled in his own name as the man temporarily designated to take his place.

When all was in order, he stamped the document with the Baron's official seal. Then he got ready for the next step. . . .

At heart we are all travelers—or runners.

—EARL DOMINIC VERNIUS

Inside his sealed tank on the top level of the enormous Dominic Class Heighliner, Steersman D'murr swam in orange spice gas.

Unaccountably troubled, and waiting for his Guild crew to complete the loading and unloading procedures, he felt time flow differently for him. His Heighliner had been in stationary orbit over Caladan longer than usual, due to an article that required special handling and a great deal of secrecy.

A combat pod. Interesting.

Normally, D'murr concerned himself with steering the great ship safely from one star system to another. It was his practice to ignore trivial details, human aspirations, since all the universe was his to hold and use.

Indulging in a moment of uncharacteristic curiosity, however, he tapped into the comsystem, flashed through records and transmissions, and eavesdropped on two Flight Auditors on a lower deck. Duke Leto Atreides had paid a substantial fee for this cargo, which required surreptitious delivery to Ix.

D'murr's roundabout route through foldspace took him from world to world, to an endless parade of planets across the Imperium. On this run, one of his destinations was Ix, formerly a routine stopover for travelers from Caladan visiting their allies on the industrial planet. Now, though, much had changed.

Why are the Atreïdes going to Ix? And why now?

He listened to whispered conversations on the restricted Guild levels, gleaning additional information that the route supervisors would never reveal to outsiders because of strict neutrality agreements. For the Spacing Guild, this was business as usual. Two Atreides men would accompany the small craft to Ix, traveling under false documents. One was Prince Rhombur Vernius, in disguise.

D'murr absorbed the new information and found that his reactions were strange and extreme, even unbalanced. Elation? Fear? *Rhombur.* Unsettled, he consumed more of the melange in his tank, but instead of the expected sense of release, he felt as if the once-welcoming universe had become a dense forest of shadowy trees and indistinct paths.

Since becoming a Navigator, D'murr had never reacted this way to haunting memories, the detritus of his human past. The spice gas made his head ring, his brain crackle. He felt strangely out of synch, disoriented. He sensed large-scale, conflicting forces at work, threatening to rip the fabric of space. Out of desperation, he drank more deeply of melange.

D'murr decided the next foldspace leap would smooth the disruptive wrinkles around him. The journey always comforted him, restored his place in the cosmos. He inhaled more spice gas, felt it burn within him, hotter than usual.

After sending a terse, impatient inquiry to the Guild crew, he finally received word that the loading process had been completed. *It is time.* The hangar-bay doors and loading-dock ports swung closed.

Anxiously, D'murr began his preparations and high-order mental calculations. Envisioning a safe path required only a few moments, and the Holtzman-jump would take less than that.

D'murr never slept, spent most of his time in contemplation, drifting in his tank. Thinking back to his times as a young man, times as a *human*.

Ideally, Navigators should retain no such memories. Steersman Grodin, his superior on Junction, said it took longer for some candidates to shed their atavistic fetters. D'murr did not want his performance hindered. He had already achieved the rank of Steersman and looked forward to each journey through foldspace with great anticipation. And now, with some concern.

He worried that this continued flood of recollections and nostalgia might make him begin to revert to something different, something hideous and useless, something primitive and human. But he had *evolved* past that. All other states of existence, including humanity, were far beneath him.

But was he *devolving* now? Could that explain the troubling sensations? He had never felt so . . . peculiar. The spice gas around him seemed only to enhance his long-buried memories of Ix and the Grand Palais, of his parents, of the Navigation test that he had passed and his twin brother had failed.

A buzzer sounded inside the navigation chamber, and D'murr saw a ring of bright blue lights overhead. The signal to proceed.

But now I am no longer ready.

From the depths of his disturbance, D'murr felt a single, powerful surge of internal strength, as if he were desperately trying to raise himself from a sickbed. It was a distant call.

"C'tair," he whispered.

❧

CONCEALED BENEATH AN abandoned Ixian school, C'tair Pilru stared at the blackened parts of his rogo transmission machine. Since it had been damaged more than two years ago when he'd made his last contact with his brother, he had found some replacement parts and repaired the device as much as he could. But the remaining silicate crystal rods were of questionable quality, scavenged from technological waste dumps.

In that last transmission, C'tair had begged his Navigator brother to find help for Ix. That thread of hope had frayed, until now. Rhombur must be on his way. The Prince had promised. Help would soon arrive.

With a flick of a whiplike tail, a small lizard scurried from one dark corner to another, disappearing into a pile of scrap parts. C'tair stared after the tiny reptile, seeing its gray-green body vanish. Before the Tleilaxu came, there had been no pests—no insects, lizards, or rats—in subterranean Ix.

The Tleilaxu brought other vermin in with them.

C'tair located the milky white rod he had set aside earlier. His last one. He turned it over in his hands, felt its coolness, and stared at a hairline crack along one side. Someday, if House Vernius rose in his lifetime, C'tair would have access to new components, and he could resume contact with his brother. As children, the twins had been remarkably close; they often completed each other's sentences.

But now they were so far apart—in time, distance, and physical form. D'murr was probably parsecs away, sailing through foldspace. And even if C'tair could reconstruct the unorthodox transmitter, it might not be possible to reach him.

He clung to the silicate crystal rod like a filament of hope, and to his surprise it began to glow in his hands with a warm incandescence. The hairline crack brightened and seemed to disappear altogether.

A voice enveloped him, sounding like D'murr. "C'tair..." But it couldn't possibly be. Looking around, he saw no one with him. He was alone in this dismal hiding place. A shudder coursed through his body, but the crystal rod grew warmer. And he heard more.

"I am about to fold space, my brother." D'murr sounded as if he were speaking through thick liquid. "Ix is on my route and Prince Rhombur is aboard. He is coming to you."

C'tair could not comprehend how his brother's voice could possibly have reached him. *I am not a rogo transmitter! I am only a person.*

And yet . . . Prince Rhombur was coming!

IN MEMORY, D'MURR was inside his twin's mind long ago as C'tair picked through the smoldering rubble of an Ixian building destroyed in the initial Tleilaxu attack. How many years had it been? Twenty-one? Out of that rubble a hallucination of Davee Rogo had emerged, the crippled genius who had befriended the twins and shown them his wondrous inventions. Back in peaceful, halcyon times. . . .

But that ghostly image had been transmitted by D'murr's uncontrolled human side—a powerful force that had refused to succumb to the changes in his body and mind. D'murr had not been fully aware of what he had done, what concepts his subconscious had developed in tandem with his connection to his twin. Using information provided by the apparition, C'tair had then been able to build the cross-dimensional transmission device, enabling two-way conversation between a pair of very different, but genetically linked, life-forms.

Even then, D'murr's subconscious mind had wanted to remain in contact with his home and memories.

Inside his tank, he now stopped moving his stunted arms and legs. Within the fraction of a second that he stood on the precipice of foldspace, he recalled the excruciating physical pain caused by each transmission with C'tair—as if his own Navigator persona had been fighting the human side, trying to subdue it.

But now he activated the Holtzman generator and lunged blindly between dimensions, taking the Heighliner with him.

DEEP BENEATH THE crust of Ix, C'tair held the flickering crystal rod until it grew ice-cold against his fingers, and D'murr's voice faded. He shook off his surprised paralysis and called his brother's name. No response came, only staticky, popping sounds. D'murr had sounded so strange, almost sick.

Suddenly, ringing through his skull, C'tair heard a wordless, primal scream in the very depths of his soul. His brother's outcry.

And then nothing.

One moment of incompetence can be fatal.

—SWORDMASTER FRIEDRE GINAZ

The Heighliner emerged from foldspace at the wrong point and plummeted into the atmosphere of Wallach IX.

Navigator error.

As large as a comet, the ship crashed into the envelope of air, scraping and roaring. Its outer hull turned molten from the friction. The passengers didn't even have time to scream.

For centuries, the Bene Gesserit planet had been guarded by security screens that could vaporize any unauthorized vessel. The immense craft was already doomed by the time it struck the first overlapping energy-defense shield.

The out-of-control Heighliner sizzled in the atmosphere, its metal skin ripped away like the soft layers of an onion. Shrapnel smoked through the air and slammed into the landscape like a cannonade, leaving Heighliner components strewn across a thousand-kilometer swath.

The Navigator had no chance to send a distress signal or offer any sort of explanation before the whole craft was obliterated.

AS DATA FROM the defense shield poured in, identifying the doomed ship, Mother Superior Harishka composed a high-priority message to be sent to Junction. Unfortunately, its delivery would have to await the next Heighliner, by which time the Spacing Guild might already know about the disaster.

In the meantime, within hours of the early-morning crash, Sister Cristane was dispatched with a team of Aco-lyte workers to the wild, poorly charted site. The Sisters converged on a mountainous region where the largest sec-tion of the Heighliner had impacted.

Her dark eyes squinting against the frigid whiteness, Cristane surveyed the collision scars on the winter-etched mountainside. Snow and ice had melted around clumps of slag and twisted wreckage. Wisps of steam still curled up from the largest metallic masses. Using cutters and welders, her work crew might find a few scraps of bodies fused into the debris, but Cristane didn't know if it would be worth the effort. There could be no survivors here.

All her life, she had been trained to respond to emergen-cies, but now she could do nothing more than observe. This Heighliner had been doomed the moment it emerged from foldspace.

Cristane was not yet a Reverend Mother, so she didn't have the multigenerational memories her superiors experi-enced. But during their meeting to plan a response to the crash, Mother Superior had claimed that in thousands of years, none of the Sisters-within had ever witnessed an ac-cident like this.

Historically, Navigators had made a few minor miscalcu-lations, but serious mishaps were extremely rare—only a handful had been recorded since the formation of the Spacing Guild, well over ten thousand years ago. During the final battle of the Butlerian Jihad, there had been much risk using the first foldspace ships, before the prescient qualities of melange had been discovered. But since that time, the Guild had a sterling safety record.

The implications of this tragedy would have repercus-sions throughout the Imperium, for centuries to come.

WHEN THE GUILD inspection and recovery team arrived two days later, the men descended upon Wallach IX in swarms. Thousands of workers brought in heavy equipment. Laborers set about cutting up the wreckage and whisking away samples for analysis. The Sisters wanted to keep their secrets, and so did the Guild, which left behind no scraps of their vessel for any outsider to inspect.

Cristane sought out the man in charge of Guild operations. Square-bodied in his pale green singlesuit, he had close-set eyes and wide lips. Studying him, she saw how overwhelmed he was by the tragedy. "Do you have any suspicions, sir? Any explanation for this?"

He shook his head. "Not yet. It will take time to analyze everything."

"What else?" Despite her youth, the commando Sister carried herself well, with authority. She spoke with enough inflection of Voice that the man answered reflexively.

"This was one of only two vessels in the Dominic Class, constructed during the last days of House Vernius, with an impeccable safety record."

Cristane regarded him with her large eyes. "Do you have any reason why this Heighliner design might suddenly have become unreliable?"

The Guildsman shook his head, yet could not resist the command of Voice. His face contorted as he tried not to reply. But he lost the effort. "We have not yet had time to assess the details. I . . . should reserve further comment at present."

As the effects of Voice wore off, he seemed flustered at what he had revealed. He fled Cristane's presence.

The commando Sister ran the possibilities through her mind. She watched as armies of laborers dismantled the Heighliner piece by piece. Soon all of the tangible wreckage would be gone, leaving only ugly scars on Wallach IX.

Fate and Hope only rarely speak the same language.
—Orange Catholic Bible

Inside the pavilion's demonstration room, Hidar Fen Ajidica stood at the dome-shaped enclosure. His mind sang with energy, and possibilities rippled around him like rainbows.

He checked the sealed sample chamber daily in order to monitor the progress of the new captive sandworm inside, another one that had survived here for a few months. He enjoyed feeding it additional ajidamal, which the creature devoured voraciously. During the years of experimentation, the tiny sandworm specimens had died promptly once they were taken from Arrakis. But so far this one had survived, even thrived. Ajidica had no doubt it was because of the synthetic spice.

With ironic humor, he had named the worm after the late Tleilaxu leader. "Let us take a look at you, Master Zaaf," he said with a cruel smile. Just that morning, he had consumed an even larger dose of ajidamal himself, tapped directly from the tank-trapped body of Miral Alechem. He felt the drug's workings now, the wild expansion of his consciousness and enhancement of his mental functions.

Glorious!

Pressing a button at the base of the tiny sandworm's dome, the euphoric Master Researcher watched the foggy plaz clear. The sand became visible inside the enclosure. Dust had been thrown against the sides of the dome, as if the little beast had thrashed about in a frenzy.

The worm sprawled motionless atop the sand, its body segments split open, its round mouth agape. Pinkish slime oozed from between its gaping rings.

Flipping open an exterior panel on the dome, Ajidica read the life monitor frantically. His eyes bulged in disbelief. Despite regular doses of ajidamal, the worm had died horribly.

Fearless of the risk, he reached inside to retrieve the flaccid shape of the creature. The carcass felt soft and loose, and its rings peeled apart like sections of rotting fruit in his fingers, sloughing from its main body. The worm looked as if it had been flayed by an inept dissection student.

But Ajidica had been feeding it the same drug he had taken himself, in varying forms. Suddenly he did not feel so euphoric. He seemed to be plunging into a dark abyss.

Each man is a little war.

— KARRBEN FETHR, The Folly of Imperial Politics

S*pice.* What Fremen could fail to find it, when necessary? The Guild had demanded more melange, and the desert people had to pay the price, or lose their dreams.

On his belly behind the crest of a towering dune, Stilgar peered through binoculars toward the abandoned village of Bilar Camp. Broken, bloodstained hovels lay at the base of a shifting mountain of sand, blocked from the rear by a small mesa that held a hidden cistern, which was now filled with sealed containers of contraband spice. The Baron's spice.

Stilgar adjusted the oil lenses, and images sharpened in the crystalline dawn. A squad of blue-uniformed Harkonnen troops went about their business as if confident that no one would dare spy on them. All Fremen considered this place cursed.

While Stilgar watched, a large carryall set down near the abandoned village. He recognized the aircraft, with its retractable wings tucked against its body: a heavy-lift vehicle used to transport spice-harvesting factories out to melange-rich sands and haul them to safety when the inevitable sandworm approached.

He counted thirty Harkonnen soldiers, more than twice the number of raiders he had with him.

Nonetheless, the odds were acceptable. Stilgar's team would have the advantage of surprise. Fremen style.

Two soldiers used an arc-light device to repair the underside of the carryall. In the still air of morning, the hum of activity carried up the dune face. Nearby, the low rock-and-brick walls of the haunted village looked rounded, their edges softened by years of hard weathering.

Nine years ago, the villagers of Bilar Camp had been horribly poisoned by bored Harkonnen scouts. The scouring desert winds had erased most, but not all, marks of the catastrophe. The Bilar Camp villagers had died ripping their own bodies apart, maddened by the poison in the water supply. Fingernail scratches and bloody handprints could still be seen on a few protected walls.

The water-fat Harkonnens believed that superstitious desert dwellers would never come back to such a cursed place. The Fremen knew, though, that this evil had been committed by *men*, not desert demons. Liet-Kynes himself had witnessed the horrors with his revered father. Now, as the Abu Naib who led all Fremen tribes, Liet had sent Stilgar and his men on this mission.

Along the other side of the dune, Stilgar's commandos crouched, each holding a slick sandboard. Wearing desert-stained robes, fitted so that the sun would not expose the gray stillsuit fabric beneath, the raiders put their face masks in place. They sipped from catchtubes at their mouths, building energy, readying themselves. Maula pistols and crysknives were strapped to their waists; stolen lasrifles were attached to the sandboards.

Ready.

Stilgar found himself amused at the ineptitude of the Harkonnens. For weeks he had watched their activities, and he knew exactly what they intended to do this morning. *Predictability is death*—it was an old Fremen saying.

Liet-Kynes would pay the increased Guild spice bribe directly from hidden Harkonnen stockpiles. And the Baron could lodge no complaints.

Below, the carryall repair had been completed. The uniformed soldiers worked together in a brigade line to remove rocks covering the cistern, exposing a reinforced container. They chatted casually, with their backs turned to the high dune. They hadn't even posted perimeter guards. Such arrogance!

When the Harkonnens had nearly finished uncovering the cistern, into which they would unload more stolen spice from the carryall's cargo hold, Stilgar made a chopping motion with his hand. The commandos mounted their slick-bottomed sandboards, thumped over the edge onto the steep slope, and careened down the smooth dune face like a racing wolfpack. At the front, picking up speed and riding with bent knees, Stilgar unclipped his lasrifle. The other Fremen did the same.

Hearing the humming whine of sand friction beneath the boards, the preoccupied Harkonnen soldiers turned, but too late. Purple knives of disruptive light cut their legs out from under them, melting flesh and mangling bones.

Stilgar's raiders jumped off their boards and fanned out to secure the big carryall. Around them, the mutilated soldiers screamed and moaned, thrashing their cauterized stumps. Because of Fremen marksmanship, all of the men still had their vital organs and their lives.

A young soldier with pale wisps of beard looked in terror at the dark-robed desert men and tried to scramble backward across the bloody sand, but he could not move without legs. These Fremen seemed to fill his heart with more fear than did the sight of the blackened stumps of his legs.

Steeling his resolve, Stilgar ordered his men to bind the Harkonnens and wrap their wounds in sponges and sealing cloths to preserve the moisture for the sietch deathstills. "Gag them, so we need not hear their childish crying." Soon the whimpering voices were silenced.

Two commandos inspected the carryall, then raised their hands in a signal. Stilgar bounded up a gangplank on the heavy aircraft to a narrow interior platform that ringed the modified cargo hold. The spacious enclosure was lined with heavy plating. Overhead, four grappling hooks dangled on chains.

This carryall had been stripped of its decks and equipment, fitted instead with armor. It reeked with the odor of cinnamon. The upper hold was already full of unmarked melange containers that the soldiers had been about to hide inside the cistern. The lower hold was empty.

"Look here, Stil." Turok pointed down at the craft's underbelly, at its unpainted crossbeams and fittings of new construction. He touched a toggle beside him, and the armored belly spread apart, open to the desert. Quickly, Turok climbed a metal stairway into the pilot's cabin and fired up the big engines, which surged to life with a powerful rumble.

Holding a handrail, Stilgar felt a faint vibration, the sign of a well-maintained ship. This workhorse craft would be a good addition to the Fremen fleet. "Up!" he shouted.

Turok had worked on spice crews for years and was proficient in operating all types of equipment. He punched the jet sequence. The carryall lifted with a powerful surge, and Stilgar clutched the handrail to keep his balance. The dangling chains and heavy hooks clattered above the open cargo doors; soon he could see the top of the uncovered cistern below.

While Turok hovered the big carryall, Stilgar disengaged the chains and dropped down the thick hooks. Below, the raiders scrambled over the smooth walls of the reinforced cistern and secured grappling hooks to lifting bars. The chains grew taut, the heavy engines groaned, and the entire spice-filled cistern ripped free of the rock platform, rising until it fit inside the open cargo hold. The carryall doors shut beneath it like the mouth of a gluttonous snake.

"I believe the Emperor has called it a crime to keep so much spice." Stilgar smiled as he shouted up to his companion. "Is it not good to assist the Corrinos in their quest for justice? Perhaps Liet should ask Shaddam to give us a commendation."

Chuckling at the irony, Turok brought the lumbering vessel back around and hovered just above the ground. The remaining Fremen climbed aboard, dragging the squirming, maimed Harkonnen captives with them.

The laden aircraft rode low in the sky, but accelerated as it headed out over the open desert, toward the nearest si-etch. Seated against a vibrating bulkhead, Stilgar studied his exhausted men, and the doomed prisoners who would soon be thrown into the deathstills. He exchanged satisfied grins with his men, who had removed their face masks to reveal weathered, bearded faces. In the low light of the carryall's interior, their blue-within-blue eyes glowed.

"Spice and water for the tribe," Stilgar said. "A good haul for one day."

Beside him, one of the Harkonnen soldiers moaned and opened his eyes. It was the young, terrified man who had looked at him before. In a moment of mercy, deciding this one had suffered enough, Stilgar drew his crysknife and slit the soldier's throat, then covered the wound to absorb the blood.

The other Harkonnens did not receive a similar kindness.

It is astonishing how foolish humans can be in groups, especially when they follow their leaders without question.

—States: The Bene Gesserit View,
All States Are an Abstraction

The Imperial fleet arrived at Korona without warning, the next blow in Shaddam's Great Spice War. With eight battle cruisers and fully armed frigates, it was a show of force even more fearsome than the one that had blackened the most populous cities of Zanovar.

The military vessels converged upon the artificial moon for an on-site investigation. Over the comsystem, Supreme Bashar Zum Garon issued his ultimatum. "We are here by order of the Padishah Emperor. You, House Richese, are charged with possessing an undocumented stockpile of melange, strictly against the laws set forth in Imperial and Landsraad courts." The hardened commander then waited for their response. *Let's see how guilty they act.*

Desperate pleas erupted from the control rooms of Korona, echoed moments later by appeals from the Richesian government below.

The Supreme Bashar, staring out from the flagship bridge, accepted none of the transmissions. He spoke into a loudspeaker system. "By order of his Awesome Majesty Shaddam IV, we will search for contraband melange. If found, the spice will be confiscated, and Korona station will be summarily destroyed. Thus the Emperor has commanded."

Two battle frigates slipped into the artificial laboratory moon's receiving bays. The Richesian fools attempted to re-seal the airlock doors, so two cruisers fired upon other docking bays, blasting open the hatches and spewing air, cargo, and bodies into space.

As docking collars clanged together and grappling claws forced open the sealed hull of the moon, Garon transmitted a further warning. "Any resistance will be met with extreme measures. You have precisely two hours to evacuate Korona. If we find evidence sufficient to warrant the annihilation of this facility, any person remaining on the station at that time will die."

From the flagship bridge, Garon stepped into a lift that carried him down to the disembarkation level. Korona did not have sufficient defenses to resist the Sardaukar. No one did.

The veteran commander led a full regiment into the orbiting laboratory. Through the metal corridors, alarms rang, lights flashed, sirens echoed. Inventors, technicians, and lab workers scrambled toward evacuation ships. At the hub of a walkway system, the Supreme Bashar gestured for his soldiers to separate into teams and begin their search. They understood that it might be necessary to torture a few employees to determine the location of the stockpile.

A florid-faced man stumbled like a cannonball out of a lift tube, rushing from his administrative center to meet the Sardaukar vanguard. He flailed his hands. "You can't do this, sir! I am Laboratory Director Flinto Kinnis, and I tell you that two hours is not enough time. We don't have sufficient ships. We need to recall vessels from Richese just for the *people*, not to mention all the research materials. It will take at least a day to evacuate."

Garon's weathered face showed no sympathy. "The Emperor will not have his orders questioned or resisted in any manner." He nodded to his soldiers, who opened fire, slicing the shocked bureaucrat apart even as he spluttered more objections.

The troops moved deeper into the giant laboratory station.

During one of their private dinners together, Shaddam had taken Zum Garon into his confidence and explained his intent. The Emperor understood that many civilians could die in this invasion, and he was perfectly willing to make another extreme example like Zanovar, and another, until his rule was secure.

"The only thing I require," Shaddam had said, holding up one finger, "is for you to retrieve *all* the contraband spice you find. A large enough reward of spice will minimize Guild and CHOAM complaints." He smiled, pleased with his plan. "Then use atomics to destroy the whole station."

"Sire, using atomics goes beyond the line—"

"Nonsense. We'll be giving them a chance to evacuate, and I am simply obliterating a metal structure out in space. I understand Korona is quite an orbital eyesore." To Shaddam's frustration, Garon did not look entirely convinced. "Don't concern yourself with legal nuances, Bashar. The point I am trying to make is best punctuated with nuclear explosives. It will frighten the Landsraad more than a thousand smaller warnings."

Zum Garon had lived many harsh years on Salusa Secundus, and had fought in the Ecazi Revolt. He knew that Imperial orders were meant to be carried out, never questioned—and he had raised his talented son Cando to believe the same thing.

Within half an hour, the first group of evacuation ships blundered their way down to the surface. Scientists scrambled to retrieve experimental records and irreplaceable notes from research projects. But many who wasted time gathering such items soon found themselves stranded when all the available shuttlecraft had departed.

Below, in Triad Center, Premier Ein Calimar bellowed impotently into the comsystem, demanding that he be given time to contact the Landsraad court. Beside him, Count Richese wrung his hands and pleaded, but to no effect. Simultaneously, the Richesians struggled to launch surface-based rescue ships, though with the clock ticking down, the Sardaukar leader doubted they would arrive in time.

Troops ransacked laboratory chambers, searching for the alleged melange stockpile. Near the armored core of Korona, they encountered two frantic inventors, a bald scientist with sloping shoulders and an intense man whose eyes flicked back and forth as if his mind was working at high speed.

The intense inventor stepped forward, trying to look reasonable. "Sir, I am working on a vital research project and I must transport all my notes and delicate prototypes. This work cannot be reproduced elsewhere, and has repercussions for the future of the Imperium."

"Denied."

The inventor blinked, as if he hadn't heard correctly.

Beside him, the bald man narrowed his gaze. "Let me speak." He gestured to a pyramid of sealed crates, where workers stood with anti-grav lift trucks, but no place to go. "Supreme Bashar, my name is Talis Balt. My colleague Haloa Rund does not exaggerate the importance of our work here. Also, look at this valuable stockpile. You can't allow it to be destroyed."

"Is that melange?" Garon said. "I have orders to remove any and all spice."

"No, sir. Richesian mirrors, nearly as valuable as spice."

The officer pursed his lips. Tiny chips of Richesian mirrors could power large scanning devices. The hoard of reflective units here would be sufficient to power a small sun.

"Talis Balt, I regret to inform you that your Director was a casualty of this operation. Therefore, I appoint *you* to be in charge of Korona." Balt's jaw went slack as he absorbed the import of the Supreme Bashar's words.

"Director Kinnis?" he asked in a weak voice. "Dead?"

Garon nodded. "You have my permission to remove all of the Richesian mirrors you can place aboard my ships in time—provided you tell me where to find your illegal spice hoard."

Haloa Rund still seemed appalled. "What about my research?"

"I cannot sell equations."

Balt squirmed, obviously considering whether or not to lie. "I assume your men will ransack laboratories and destroy sealed chambers until you find it. Therefore, I will save us all the misery." He told the Bashar where to look.

"I am pleased to see that you have made the correct decision, and that you have verified the presence of melange." Touching a button on his uniform, Garon sent a signal back to his ship. Moments later, low-ranking soldiers ran aboard, carrying suspensor pallets laden with containers of atomics. He turned back to the bald scientist. "You may move what you can aboard our battle cruisers, and I will permit you to keep half of what you load."

Appalled at the situation but smart enough not to argue, Balt set to work. A bemused Garon watched the efforts of workers as they moved crates of the fragile mirrors. Clearly, they would not rescue even a tenth of the treasure. Haloa Rund rushed back to his laboratory, but the Sardaukar Bashar left instructions that he not be allowed to clutter the ships with useless "prototypes."

Garon directed his men to the melange-storage area, where soldiers with holorecorders documented the illegal stockpile, taking evidence before moving the spice, just in case the Emperor needed it. Shaddam hadn't stipulated this precaution, but the Bashar knew evidence was evidence.

As Zum Garon monitored the operations, Sardaukar infantry entered the moon's core, bearing their first load of nuclear warheads. He looked at his chronometer. Less than an hour remained.

TALIS BALT SCURRIED back and forth, close to dropping from exhaustion. Sweat glistened on his bald pate; he and his crew had already loaded a surprising number of the expensive mirrors aboard the Sardaukar flagship.

On a Korona cargo dock, Haloa Rund sat hunched and weeping beside hastily packaged crates that had been blasted open with hand weapons. When he had insisted on carrying them toward the docked flagship, two soldiers had opened fire, destroying the no-field machinery inside.

As time ran out and the Supreme Bashar ordered a retreat from the doomed satellite, Talis Balt stood on the loading dock, waiting to get away.

Calmly, Garon informed the bald inventor that he would have to remain behind. "I am sorry, but it is illegal for us to permit civilian passengers to ride aboard an Imperial military warship. You must find your own way off the moon."

With little time remaining, Rund's family connections with Count Ilban Richese would not help him. And the atomic weaponry could not be deactivated.

TEN MINUTES BEFORE the appointed time, all Imperial battle cruisers and support ships detached themselves from the satellite, leaving the damaged docking-bay doors open to the hard vacuum of space. Aboard the flagship, Supreme Bashar Garon watched his troops wrap up their operations with military precision.

Though the hoard of melange had not been as extensive as the Emperor had been led to believe, the cargo compartments belowdecks contained many crates of Richesian mirrors, as well as the spice stockpile. The Sardaukar would immediately present the confiscated melange to Guild representatives on board the waiting Heighliner. A shameless bribe, but effective.

ON THE SURFACE of the planet, Premier Calimar looked into the sky at the satellite moon, an artificial structure so large that it dwarfed the fleet of Sardaukar ships moving away from it. His stomach was knotted, his heart near frozen with fury at the injustice of Shaddam's action.

How had the Emperor learned about the spice hidden on Korona? After Baron Harkonnen had quietly paid him, Calimar had kept the stockpile absolutely secret. Certainly the information could not have come from the Harkonnens, because that would only direct questions back at them. . . .

When the atomics erupted on Korona, bright light seared through the Richesian sky. However, instead of dimming as time went on, the fireball continued to build in a chain reaction that ignited the remaining Richesian mirrors, spreading the fragments in a cloud of broken, powerful crystals that rained through the atmosphere like shards from a supernova.

Below, the Richesians of an entire continent stared into the firestorm that showered across the sky. Priceless mirrors fell like tiny asteroids, screaming and searing through the air.

Calimar bit back an outcry, but he could not stop staring. The awful light grew brighter. Many Richesians watched in mesmerized horror, unable to believe what was happening.

Within the next few days, as the retinal damage progressed, fully a quarter of Richese's population would go blind.

I feel the invulnerable and sliding thrust of space where a star sends lingering beams across the undistance called parsecs.

—The Apocrypha of Muad'dib,
All Is Permitted, All Is Possible

Lost in emptiness, the Heighliner tumbled out of control.

Gurney Halleck knew something was wrong the instant they emerged from foldspace. The giant vessel lurched as if it had run into thick turbulence.

Placing a hand on a blade concealed inside his drab traveling clothes, Gurney looked beside him to make sure Rhombur remained safe. The cyborg Prince anchored himself to a wall, which had now become the floor. "Are we under attack?" He wore a cloak and cowled hood, as if he were a pilgrim. Loose woolweave fabric covered his mostly artificial body so no one would notice the extraordinary differences in his anatomy.

The cabin door of their private passenger quarters slid halfway open, then jammed in its track. Outside in the main corridor, a service panel sparked as a power surge rippled through the frigate's systems. The decks tilted as gravity generators went off-line, shifting the center of mass. Lights flickered. Then, with a creaking shudder, the passenger frigate righted itself as the Heighliner rolled.

Gurney and Rhombur struggled to the jammed cabin door and tried to push it the rest of the way open. With one powerful mechanical arm, Rhombur shoved the blockage aside, scraping metal.

The two men slipped into the corridor where panicky passengers scurried about, some of them injured and bleeding. Through widely spaced portholes, Gurney and Rhombur could see the havoc in the Heighliner cargo hold outside, where ships were tilted and smashed. Some drifted free, sprung from their docking clamps.

On every deck, communications boards lit up as hundreds of passengers demanded explanations. Black-uniformed Wayku stewards hurried from lounge to lounge, calmly instructing everyone to wait until further information was received. The attendants looked sleek and aloof, but showed an edge of strain from this unprecedented situation.

Gurney and Rhombur headed to the crowded main lounge, where frightened passengers were gathering. From the half-hidden expression on Rhombur's hooded face, Gurney could see he wanted to calm these people, to take charge. To prevent this, he gave a subtle hand signal, warning the Prince that they must keep their identities secret and draw no attention to themselves. Instead, the Prince worked to discover for himself what had happened, but the ship's systems offered little information.

Rhombur's waxy face was furrowed in deep concentration. "We don't have time to delay—we're on a very precise schedule. The whole battle plan could fall apart if we don't do our job."

After an hour of unanswered questions and mounting panic, a Guild representative finally sent a holo-emissary into the frigate lounge. His image appeared inside the primary gathering points of all vessels within the hold.

From his uniform Rhombur recognized the Guildsman's rank as Flight Auditor, a relatively important administrator who maintained accounting records, and cargo and passenger manifests, and interfaced with the Guild Bank regarding payments for interstellar passage. The Flight Auditor had extremely wide-set eyes, a high forehead, and a thick neck; his arms appeared too short for his torso, as if the parts had been mismatched during his genetic assembly.

He spoke in a flat voice with an annoying tic that made him sound like a buzzing insect. "We have, nnnn, experienced difficulty in translocation of this vessel and are currently trying to reestablish, nnnn, contact with our Navigator in his chamber. The Guild is investigating the matter. We have, nnnn, no further information at this time."

The passengers began to shout out questions, but the projection either couldn't hear them or didn't care to reply. He stood straight-backed and expressionless. "All maintenance and major repairs to Guild ships must be done, nnnn, at Junction. We currently have no facilities to complete major repairs here. We have not yet been able to determine our precise location, nnnn, though preliminary measurements show we are in uncharted space, far beyond the Imperium."

The collective inrush of the passengers' breath sounded like a heavy-duty air exchanger. Gurney scowled at Rhombur. "Guild representatives might be good at mathematical studies, but apparently they have no training in *tact*."

Rhombur frowned. "A lost Heighliner? I've never heard of such a thing. Vermilion hells! This ship is one of the best Ixian designs."

Gurney gave him a rueful, scar-faced smile. "Nevertheless, it's happened." He quoted from the Orange Catholic Bible. " 'For mankind is lost, even with the righteous path laid out for him.' "

Rhombur surprised him by responding with the second half of the verse. " 'Yet no matter how far we stray, God knows where to find us, for He can see the whole universe.' "

The Ixian Prince lowered his voice and guided Gurney

away from the grumbling conversation and sour stench of fear-sweat inside the crowded lounge. "This Heighliner design was built under the direction of my father, and I know how these ships work. One of my duties as the Prince of House Vernius was to learn everything about ship manufacture. The quality controls and safety features were extraordinary, and Holtzman engines never fail. That technology has proven reliable for ten thousand years."

"Until today."

Rhombur shook his head. "No, that's not the answer. It can only be a problem with the Navigator himself."

"*Pilot* error?" Gurney lowered his voice to avoid eavesdroppers, though the passengers were doing a fine job of feeding their own panic. "This far outside the boundaries of the Imperium, if our Navigator has failed, we'll never find our way home."

Other Memory is a wide, deep ocean. It is available to help the members of our order, but only on its own terms. A Sister invites trouble when she tries to manipulate the internal voices to her own needs. It is like trying to make the sea one's own personal swimming pool—an impossibility, even for a few moments.

—The Bene Gesserit Coda

At last back in his apartments on Kaitain after planting his test samples in two Heighliners, Count Hasimir Fenring rolled out of bed and gazed around the opulent room. He wondered how soon he would hear results; he certainly couldn't *ask* the Guild, so he would have to be very discreet in his inquiries.

Through sleep-bleary eyes, he saw gold filigree on the walls and ceiling, reproductions of ancient paintings, and exotic chin-do carvings. This was a far more stimulating place than dry Arrakis, scabrous Ix, or utilitarian Junction. The only finer beauty he wanted to see was the exquisite face of lovely Margot. But she had already arisen and left their bed.

After his roundabout journey from Heighliner to Heighliner, he had arrived after midnight, exhausted. Despite the late hour, Margot had used her seductive skills on him, techniques to both arouse and relax. Then, he had fallen asleep, lulled by the comfort of her arms. . . .

The Count had been out of touch with the

Imperium for nearly three weeks, and he wondered how many blunders Shaddam had made in the meantime. Fenring would have to arrange a private meeting with his childhood friend to discuss matters, though he would keep the tale of the Face Dancer assassin secret, for now. The Spice Minister intended to get his own personal revenge against Ajidica, and he would savor it greatly. Only afterward would he tell Shaddam, and they would both chuckle with pleasure.

First, though, he had to learn if the Master Researcher's work was successful. Everything depended on amal. If the tests proved Ajidica's claims false, Fenring would show no mercy. If the amal worked as promised, though, he would have to learn every aspect of the process before he began the torture.

Two of his suspensor-borne suitcases still sat on a broad dressing table. The bags were open. He sighed, stretched, and walked away from the bed. Yawning, he strolled into the adjacent bathing spa, where the withered maidservant Mapes bowed, though only slightly. The Fremen woman wore a white housedress that left her tanned, scarred arms bare. Fenring didn't much care for her personality, but she was a good worker and tended to his needs, albeit humorlessly.

He removed his shorts and dropped them on the floor. Mapes retrieved them with a scowl and tossed them into a laundry shredder on the wall. He donned the usual protective goggles, used his voice to command the spa jets. Powerful bursts of warm water surrounded his body, lifting him into the air, massaging him on all sides. On Arrakis, such luxuries were not possible, even for the Imperial Spice Minister. He closed his eyes. So soothing . . .

Abruptly he jolted to awareness as peripheral details took on relevance. He had left his suspensor-borne luggage on the floor the night before, intending to unpack in the morning. Now the bags were *open* on a dressing table.

He had hidden a test sample of the amal in one of the suitcases.

Hurrying into the bedchamber, still naked and wet, he found the Fremen housekeeper removing clothing and toiletries from the bags, putting articles away. "Leave that until later. Mmm-m-m. I will call you when I need you."

"As you wish." She had a throaty voice, as if grains of storm-blown sand had scarred her vocal cords. She looked with disapproval at the puddles he dripped on the floor, disgusted by the waste rather than the mess.

But the secret luggage compartment was empty. Alarmed, Fenring called after her, "Where is the pouch I had in here?"

"I saw no pouch, sir."

He searched feverishly through the bags, scattering items onto the floor. And broke into a sweat.

Just then, Margot entered, carrying a breakfast tray. She eyed his naked form with raised eyebrows and a smile of approval. "Good morning, dear. Or should I say, good afternoon?" She glanced at the wall chronometer. "No, you still have another minute." She wore a shimmering parasilk dress with pale yellow immian roses sewn into it, tiny flowers that remained alive in the fabric and gave off a delicate, sweet scent.

"Did you remove a green pouch from my suitcase?" A skilled Bene Gesserit in her own right, Margot would have easily located the secret compartment.

"I assumed you brought it for me, darling." Smiling prettily, she placed the breakfast tray on a side table.

"Well, hmmm, this time it was a difficult trip, and I—"

She pretended to pout. Margot had noticed a tiny symbol in one fold of the pouch, a character that she deciphered as the letter "A" in the Tleilaxu alphabet.

"Where did you put it, hmmmm?" Despite Ajidica's reassurances, Fenring was not at all convinced the Tleilaxu synthetic melange wasn't harmful, or even poisonous. He preferred to use others as test subjects, not himself or his wife.

"Don't worry about that right now, my dear." Margot's gray-green eyes danced seductively. She began to pour spice coffee for them. "Do you want breakfast before or after we resume where we left off last night?"

Pretending lack of concern, though Margot would note every flicker of uneasiness in his body, Fenring grabbed a black casual suit from the walk-in closet. "Just tell me where you put the pouch, and I'll get it myself."

Emerging from the closet, he saw Margot lifting a coffee cup to her lips.

Spice coffee . . . the hidden pouch . . . the amal!

"Stop!" He rushed toward her and knocked the cup out of her hands. Hot liquid splattered all over the handwoven carpet, and stained her yellow dress. The still-living immian roses flinched.

"Now you've wasted all that spice, dear," she said, startled but coolly trying to regain her composure.

"Surely you didn't pour all of it in the coffee, hmmm? Where's the rest of the spice you found?" He calmed himself, but knew he had already revealed far too much.

"It's in our kitchen." She regarded him with Bene Gesserit scrutiny. "Why are you behaving this way, dearest?"

Without explaining, he poured the remaining cup of spice coffee back into the pot and hurried out of the room with it.

❦

GRIM-FACED, SHADDAM stood at the entrance to Anirul's chambers, with his arms crossed over his chest. A ponytailed Suk doctor stood beside him. The Truthsayer Mohiam refused to let them enter the bedroom suite. "Only Bene Gesserit medical practitioners can tend to certain ailments, Sire."

The slope-shouldered doctor spat his words at Mohiam.

"Do not assume that the Sisterhood knows more than a graduate of the Suk inner circle." He had ruddy features and a wide nose.

Shaddam scowled. "This makes no sense. After my wife's bizarre behavior at the zoo, she needs special attention." He pretended concern, but was more interested in hearing his Supreme Bashar's debriefing as soon as the Imperial Sardaukar fleet returned from Korona. Oh, what an account that would be!

Mohiam remained firm. "Only a qualified Medical Sister can deal with her, Sire." Her voice took on a smoother undertone. "And the Sisterhood will provide such services without charge to House Corrino."

The Suk doctor began to snap at her, but the Emperor silenced him. Suk services were very expensive, more than Shaddam wanted to spend on Anirul. "Perhaps it would be best, after all, if my dear wife is tended by one of her own."

Beyond the tall doors, Lady Anirul slept fitfully, and occasionally burst out long streams of meaningless words and odd sounds. Though he didn't admit it to anyone, Shaddam was quietly pleased that she might be going mad.

🝔

A SMALL, FEISTY woman in a black robe, Medical Sister Aver Yohsa carried only a small shoulder satchel as she bustled into the bedchamber, ignoring Sardaukar guards and protocol.

Lady Margot Fenring locked the apartment to prevent interruption and looked over at Mohiam, who nodded. Efficiently, Yohsa gave the Kwisatz Mother an injection at the back of her neck. "She is being overwhelmed by the voices within. This will dampen Other Memory, so she can rest."

Yohsa stood at the bedside, shaking her head. She drew conclusions quickly, with complete confidence. "Anirul may have probed too deeply without the support and guidance of a companion Sister. I have seen such cases before, and they are most serious. A form of possession."

"She will recover?" Mohiam asked. "Anirul is a Bene Gesserit of Hidden Rank, and this is a most delicate time for her duties."

Yohsa did not mince words. "I know nothing of her rank or duties. In medical matters, especially questions involving the intricate workings of the mind, there are no simple answers. She has suffered a seizure, and the continuing presence of these voices has had a . . . disturbing . . . effect on her."

"See how peacefully she sleeps now," Margot said in a soft voice. "We should leave her. Let her dream."

THE SLEEPER DREAMED of the desert. A solitary sandworm fled across the dunes, trying to escape a relentless pursuer, something as silent and implacable as death. The worm, though immense, seemed minuscule in the vast sea of sand, vulnerable to forces much greater than itself.

Even inside the dream, Anirul felt the blistering hot sands against her raw skin. Thrashing in her bed, she kicked off her silky coverings. She longed for the coolness of a shady oasis.

With a jolt, she found herself inside the mind of the sinuous creature, her thoughts traveling through nonhuman neural pathways and synapses. She *was* the worm. She felt the friction of silica beneath her segmented body, igniting fires in her belly as she made a frantic attempt to escape.

The unknown pursuer drew closer. Anirul wanted to dive into the safe depths of the sand, but she could not. In her nightmare there was no sound, not even the noise of her own passage. She let out a silent scream through a long throat lined with crystal teeth.

Why am I fleeing? What do I fear?

Suddenly she sat up, her eyes fire-red and filled with abject terror. She had fallen onto the cool floor. Her body was bruised and abraded, soaked with perspiration. The mysterious disaster was still out there, approaching, but she could not understand what it was.

Humans are different in private than in the presence of others. While the private persona merges into the social persona in varying degrees, the union is never complete. Something is always held back.

—Bene Gesserit Teaching

As the sun set behind him, Duke Leto Atreides stood with Thufir Hawat and Duncan Idaho on either side of him, facing the expectant crowd that was gathered on a rocky area along the shore. Another spectacle to impress the populace before his troops went off to war.

While Rhombur and Gurney were gone, waiting was the hardest part.

Accompanied by liveried guards and representatives of Caladan's major towns, Leto looked behind him, lifting his gaze toward the magnificent monument he had commissioned, one that would serve as a lighthouse and more. On an outthrust spit of land that bounded a narrow cove, the towering stone image of Paulus Atreides stood as a guardian of the coastline, a colossus visible to all ships approaching the docks. The statue, resplendent in matador costume, rested a paternal hand on the shoulder of the innocent, wide-eyed Victor. Paulus's other hand held a self-feeding brazier filled with flammable oils.

The Old Duke had died in the bullring years before Victor's birth, and so the pair had never actually met. Still, these two had been a tremendous influence on Leto: his political philosophy shaped by the unbending leadership of his father, and his compassion grown from love for his son.

Leto's heart had a hollow feeling. Every day as he occupied himself with the business of running House Atreides, he felt alone without Jessica. He wished she could be with him now, to participate in the formal dedication of this spectacular new monument, though he supposed she might disapprove of the extravagance lavished on the memory of his father. . . .

So far, he had received no message from Rhombur and Gurney, but by now he could only hope they had arrived safely on Ix and were beginning their dangerous work. House Atreides would soon be embroiled in much more than the unveiling of statues.

A temporary scaffold rose behind the statues. Two muscular youths scrambled to the top of the platform and waited above the brazier, torches in hand. Selected from a local seining crew, the acrobatic boys normally spent their days clambering around in the rigging like flying crabs. Their proud parents, as well as the captains of their boats, waited below with an Atreides honor guard.

Leto drew a deep breath. "All people of Caladan owe a debt of gratitude to those immortalized here: my father, the beloved Duke Paulus, and my son Victor, whose life was cut so tragically short. I have ordered the creation of this memorial so that all ships entering and leaving our harbor can remember these revered heroes."

The business of being a Duke. . .

Leto raised his hand in a signal, and the last dying sunlight flashed off the signet ring on his finger. From their precarious position, the youths lowered their firebrands to the brazier, igniting the oils. Blue flames roared high without crackling or smoking, a silent torch in the palm of the statue's giant hand.

Duncan held the Old Duke's sword in front of him as if it were a royal scepter. Thufir remained grim and emotionless.

"Let the eternal flame never be extinguished. May their memories burn brightly forever."

The crowd cheered, but the applause could not warm Leto's heart as he remembered the quarrel he'd had with Jessica about naming their unborn child after his father. He wished she had been able to meet the old man, perhaps even to talk philosophy with him. Then maybe she would have a better opinion of Paulus, rather than focusing her ire on his policies, which Leto refused to change.

He raised a gray-eyed gaze to the implacable, idealized face of Paulus Atreides beside the achingly beautiful statue of the boy. The glow from the eternal torch cast a halo around their giant-sized features. Oh, how Leto missed his father, and his son. And Jessica most of all.

Please let my second child have a long and meaningful life, he thought, not entirely sure to whom he prayed.

ACROSS THE IMPERIUM, on another balcony watching another sunset, Jessica thought about her Duke. She stared across the glorious architecture of the Imperial city, lifted her gaze to the competing colors of aurora curtains shimmering against the dusk.

How she longed to be with Leto. Her whole body ached for him.

Earlier in the day, Reverend Mother Mohiam and the newly arrived Medical Sister Yohsa had tested and prodded her, then assured Jessica that her pregnancy was proceeding normally as she entered her final trimester. In order to make certain the child was developing well, Yohsa had wanted to perform a sonogram, using machines that would send harmless pulses into Jessica's womb and take holo-images of the baby growing inside. Technically, such procedures did not violate the Bene Gesserit strictures against tampering with children *in utero*, but Jessica had flatly refused the test, afraid it would reveal too much.

Seeing the surprised, annoyed expression on the Medical

Sister's face, Mohiam took Jessica's side, showing rare compassion. "There will be no sonograms, Yohsa. Like all of us, Jessica has the ability to determine for herself if anything has gone wrong during the gestation period. We trust her."

Jessica had looked up at her mentor and fought a stinging sensation in her eyes. "Thank you, Reverend Mother." Mohiam's gaze had searched for answers, though Jessica would not provide them, voluntarily or otherwise. . . .

Now the Duke's concubine sat alone on the balcony, blanketed in the Imperial sunset. She thought of the skies on Caladan, of the storms that came swiftly across the sea. Over the past several Standard Months, she and Leto had exchanged numerous letters and gifts, but such tokens were not nearly enough for either of them.

Though Kaitain held many treasures to amaze visitors, Jessica wanted to be back on her ocean world with the man she loved, at peace, leading her former life. *What if the Sisterhood exiles me after our son is born? What if they kill the baby?*

Jessica continued to make entries in the bound journal Lady Anirul had given to her, jotting down impressions and ideas, using a coded language of her own devising. She recorded her innermost thoughts, filling page after page with plans for her unborn son, and for her relationship with Leto.

In this process, however, she avoided writing about an increasingly unsettled feeling that she did not understand and which she hoped would go away. What if she had made a terribly wrong decision?

We depend entirely upon the benevolent cooperation of the unconscious mind. The unconscious, in a sense, invents the next moment for us.

—Bene Gesserit Precept

When Anirul awakened, she discovered that the Medical Sister had been monitoring and adjusting her medication to keep the disturbed clamor of Other Memory from overwhelming her.

"Good color in your skin, alertness in your eyes. Excellent, Lady Anirul." Yohsa smiled gently, reassuringly.

Anirul managed to sit up on her bed, overcoming a wave of weakness. She felt almost recovered, almost sane. For now.

Margot Fenring and Mohiam scurried into the bedchamber, wearing anxious expressions that would have earned them a scolding rebuke if she had been feeling better.

Margot changed the polarity of the filter field at a private patio door, allowing bright sunlight into the room. Anirul shielded her eyes and sat up straighter in bed so that the warm, golden sunlight splashed across her skin. "I can't spend my life in darkness."

To her intent Bene Gesserit listeners, she explained the nightmare of the desert sandworm fleeing an unseen, unknown pursuer. "I must determine what this dream means, while the terror is still fresh in my mind." The skin on her face began to feel hot in the sunlight, as if she had been sunburned by her vision.

The Medical Sister tried to interrupt, but Anirul shooed her away. Frowning in brittle disapproval, Yohsa left her alone with the other two women, closing the door behind her a bit more forcefully than necessary.

Anirul walked barefoot to the terrace, into full sunlight. Instead of recoiling from the heat, she stood naked and unself-conscious, absorbing the rays of the sun on her bare skin. "I journeyed to the brink of madness, and came back." She experienced a strange longing to roll on . . . hot sand.

The three Sisters stood beside a waving immian rosebush at the terrace. "Dreams are always triggered by conscious events," Mohiam said, paraphrasing a Bene Gesserit teaching.

Contemplating, Anirul picked one of the tiny yellow immian roses from the bush beside her; as the sensitive flower flinched, she lifted it to her nose to smell the delicate scent. "I think it has something to do with the Emperor, spice . . . and Arrakis . . . Have you heard of Project Amal? One day I walked into my husband's study while he was discussing such a project with Count Fenring. They were arguing about the Tleilaxu. Both of them fell awkwardly silent, as guilty men always do. Shaddam told me not to meddle in affairs of state."

"All men behave strangely," Reverend Mother Mohiam observed. "That has long been known."

Margot frowned. "Hasimir keeps trying to hide the fact that he spends so much time on Ix, and I often wonder why. Just an hour ago, he ruined a dress that I wore especially for him, knocked a cup of spice coffee out of my hands before I could sip from it, as if it were poison. I used some melange I found in a secret luggage compartment." She narrowed her eyes. "It was in a pouch with a marking on it, the Tleilaxu symbol for 'A.' Amal, perhaps?"

"Quietly, the Emperor has been sending military resources to Ix, while keeping that information hidden from the Landsraad. Fenring . . . Ix . . . Tleilaxu . . . melange," Anirul said. "No good can come of this."

"And Shaddam has declared open war on spice hoarders," Mohiam said. Even in the brightness of day, her wrinkled face seemed to absorb new shadows. "All roads lead to melange."

"Perhaps the sandworm in my dream was fleeing from a storm of upheavals in the Imperium." Still naked in the sunlight, Anirul stared across the Palace grounds. "We must contact Mother Superior right away."

Simplicity is the most difficult of all concepts.

—Mentat Conundrum

The Emperor sat alone in one of his private banquet halls, mercifully without his wife. He smiled with anticipation as the lavish six-course meal was brought in for him. At the moment he wanted no troubles, no politics, not even old war stories from Supreme Bashar Garon. Just a private, luxurious celebration. The briefing about Korona, and the detailed holo-images of the explosion, had been enough to give him quite an appetite.

The first serving tray was a scrolled silver platter carried by a pair of nubile young women. Fanfare blared, announcing the three skewers of lightly seasoned slig cubes, cooked to perfection, that graced the tray. The serving girls removed one skewer at a time, plucked off each cube of meat, and took turns placing the morsels onto Shaddam's Imperial tongue. The savory meat was as tender as moist cheese, with sensuous flavors that snapped his taste buds awake.

Sardaukar marksmen held weapons ready, prepared to react instantly if one of the women attempted to use a blunted skewer as an assassination device.

A golden-skinned young man in a creamy white toga poured a goblet of rich claret. Shaddam sipped the wine in between bites as the two girls awaited his pleasure, holding more cubes of meat. He drew a deep breath, smelling the carefully chosen scents that wafted around the servants. *Decadent.* This was what it meant to be Emperor. He sighed and gestured for the next dish.

The second course consisted of succulent broiled crustaceans, many-legged but eyeless creatures that were found only in underground springs on Bela Tegeuse. The sauce was butter, salt, and garlic, nothing more, but it tasted delicious. Two wenches used tiny platinum forks to pry out the crustaceans' sweet, white flesh and feed it to the Emperor.

Before the next dish could be brought, however, Count Hasimir Fenring stormed into the banquet hall, elbowing aside the guards as if impervious to their weapons.

Shaddam wiped his mouth with a napkin. "Ah, Hasimir! When did you return from your travels? You've been gone a long time."

Fenring could barely keep the strangled quality from his voice. "You destroyed *Korona,* hmmm? How could you do such a thing without consulting me first?"

"The Landsraad members can complain all they want, but we caught the Richesians red-handed."

Shaddam had never seen his friend so angry. He switched to the private code they had developed as boys, so the servants could not eavesdrop. "Calm yourself, or would you prefer that I never summon you to Kaitain again? As we've discussed, we needed to improve the market advantage of amal by eliminating melange. This got rid of another major stockpile."

Fenring moved forward with a prowling gait, grabbed a chair beside the Emperor's, and sat himself down. "But you used atomics, Shaddam. Not only did you attack a Great House, but you used forbidden *atomics!*" He brought his hand down on the table surface with a loud smack.

Shaddam gestured with his fingers, and the serving girls whisked away the Tegeusan crustaceans. Too late, a serving boy hurried in with a flagon of golden mead, but Shaddam waved him away and signaled for the third course.

The Emperor decided not to raise his voice. "The Great Convention forbids the use of atomics only against *people*, Hasimir. I used atomics to destroy a man-made structure, a laboratory moon where Richese had stored an illegal spice hoard. I was fully within my rights."

"But hundreds of people died, maybe thousands."

Shaddam shrugged. "They were given notice. If they chose not to evacuate in time, how can I be held responsible? You just don't like me to take actions without your advice, Hasimir." Fenring simmered, but the Emperor smiled maddeningly. "Ah look, here comes the next course." Two strong men walked in carrying a thin stone slab on which slumped an Imperial peacock roasted in herbs, its browned skin still crackling from the heat.

Servants rushed forward with a clean plate, silverware, and a crystal goblet for Count Fenring.

"Did you at least get a legal opinion before the attack, hmmm? To make certain your interpretation would stand up in Landsraad Court?"

"It seems obvious enough to me. Supreme Bashar Garon took holoimages of the whole scene on Korona. The evidence is incontrovertible."

With an exaggerated sigh of forced patience, Fenring said, "Would you like me to *obtain* an opinion, Sire? Shall I consult with your lawtechs and Mentats?"

"Oh, I suppose—go ahead." With gusto, Shaddam dug into the first slices of juicy peacock meat, licking his lips after swallowing. "Try some, Hasimir."

The Count picked at the roast bird on his silver plate, but didn't taste anything.

"You worry too much. Besides, I am the Emperor, and can do as I please."

Fenring looked at him with large eyes. "You are the Emperor because of support from the Landsraad, CHOAM, the Spacing Guild, the Bene Gesserit, and other powerful forces, hmmm-ah? Should they all grow displeased, you would be stripped of everything."

"They wouldn't dare," Shaddam said, then lowered his voice. "Now that I am the only male Corrino."

"But there are plenty of eligible noblemen who would love to marry your daughters and continue the dynasty!" Fenring pounded the table again. "Let me find a way to salvage this, Shaddam. I think you will need to appear before the Landsraad, hm-m-m, in two days time. They will be in an uproar. You must state your reasons, and we'll pull together all the support we can manage. Otherwise, mark my words, there will be a revolt."

"Yes, yes." Shaddam concentrated on his food, then snapped his fingers. "Will you stay for the next course, Hasimir? It's seared boar steaks from Canidar. Just arrived by Heighliner this morning, fresh."

Fenring pushed his plate away and stood up. "You have given me much work to do. I must begin immediately."

Law always moves in the direction of protecting the strong and oppressing the weak. Dependence upon force corrodes justice.

—CROWN PRINCE RAPHAEL CORRINO,
Precepts of Civilization

Though he loathed the arrogant Premier Calimar, Baron Harkonnen had never expected Shaddam to use atomics against House Richese. *Atomics!* When the news reached him on Arrakis, he had mixed feelings, and a good deal of fear for his own security. In the face of the Emperor's appalling zeal, no one was safe, especially not House Harkonnen, which had so much to hide.

Buoyed by his suspensor belt, the Baron paced his strategy room in the Carthag Residency, looking through a convex wall of armor-plaz windows. Blazing desert sunshine streamed in, tempered by filtering films on the two-centimeter-thick windows.

Muffled by barriers and humming security systems, he heard preparations for the military parade that was scheduled to occur soon in the main square. Just beyond his field of vision, troops assembled in the afternoon heat, each fully armed man in a blue dress uniform.

With grand fanfare, the Baron had returned to the harsh planet accompanied by his nephew. Brutish Rabban, in one of his rare moments of intelligence, had suggested that they remain here close to the spice operations, until "the troubling Imperial matters" were resolved.

The Baron slammed a fist against one of the windows, causing the plaz to quiver. How much more did Shaddam intend to do? It was madness! Fully a dozen Landsraad families had voluntarily surrendered fortunes in hoarded spice, pathetically contrite in order to avoid further demonstrations of Imperial wrath.

No one is safe.

It was only a matter of time before CHOAM auditors came sniffing around Harkonnen spice operations on Arrakis . . . which could well be the end of the Baron and his Great House. Unless he managed to hide everything.

Exacerbating his problems, the damnable Fremen kept preying on his secret stockpiles, locating many of the largest caches! The desert vermin were opportunists, exploiting the Imperial crackdown, knowing the Baron could report none of their raids because then he would have to admit his own crimes.

Outside, giant banners bearing the blue Harkonnen crest streamed down the sides of tall buildings, oceans of limp cloth hanging in the hot air. Griffin statues had been erected around the Carthag Residency, towering monsters that seemed ready to defy even the great sandworms. The mandatory crowds were assembled in the square, wretches chased from their begging stations and dingy homes so that they could cheer on cue.

Normally the Baron preferred to spend his wealth on personal diversions, but now he took a page from the Emperor's book. With finery and gaudy spectacles, he would cow the indigent population. It made him feel a little better after the embarrassing banquet debacle. Henceforth, he had no intention of attempting to follow the Atreides model for inspiring goodwill. Baron Vladimir Harkonnen wanted his subjects to *fear* him, not to *like* him.

A Guild Courier fidgeted at the open doorway to the

strategy room, showing the edge of her patience. "Baron, my Heighliner will depart in less than two hours. If you have a package for the Emperor, I must take it soon."

Angered, the big man whirled, and the momentum kept him moving gracelessly on his suspensors. He caught himself against a wall. "You will wait. An important part of my message will be images from the parade we are about to host."

The Courier's hair was short and wine-colored, her features hard and unattractive. "I will remain only as long as time permits."

With a grunt of displeasure, the Baron floated in an exaggerated posture of dignity back to his writing table. Grumbling to himself, he could not think of the proper way to phrase the rest of his message, and wished Piter de Vries were here to help. But the twisted Mentat remained on Kaitain, spying on his behalf.

Perhaps he should have kept that etiquette advisor alive. For all his preposterous training, Mephistis Cru had known how to compose a polite turn of phrase.

With pudgy fingers the Baron scrawled another sentence, then sat back, thinking how best to explain the recent rash of "accidents" and lost spice-excavation equipment on Arrakis, with which he had hidden his embezzling activities. In a recent Imperial transmittal, Shaddam had expressed concern about the problem.

For once, the Baron was glad the Spacing Guild had never managed to put up adequate weather surveillance satellites here. This enabled him to assert that brief, vicious storms had occurred, when in actuality they had not. But perhaps he had gone too far . . . and too many clues pointed toward his activities.

These are dangerous times.

"As I have reported to you before, Sire, we have been plagued by Fremen unrest," he wrote. "The terrorists destroy equipment, then steal our cargoes of melange and disappear into the desert before a proper military response can be mounted." The Baron pursed his lips, trying to select the proper tone of contrition. "I admit that we have perhaps been too lenient with them, but now that I am back on Arrakis, I will personally supervise our retaliation efforts. We will grind down the unruly natives and make them bow under Harkonnen command, in the glorious name of your Imperial Majesty."

He thought his words might be a bit too extravagant, but decided to let them stand. Shaddam was not a man to complain about excessive compliments.

The Fremen rogues had recently stolen an armored spice transport and another stockpile hidden in an abandoned desert village. How had the filthy guerrillas known to strike there?

The Courier continued to fidget at the doorway, but the Baron ignored her. "I promise you this unrest will no longer be tolerated, Sire," he wrote. "I will send regular reports of our success in bringing the traitors to justice."

With a flourish, he signed the letter, sealed it in the message cylinder, and slapped the ornate tube into the Courier's palm. Without a word, the wine-haired woman spun about and made her way through the halls, heading toward the Carthag Spaceport. The Baron shouted after her, "Stand by on the Heighliner for transmitted images to go with that message. My parade is about to begin."

Next, he summoned his nephew to the strategy room. Despite Rabban's many flaws, the Baron had in mind a job the "Beast" could perform well. The big-shouldered man strode in, carrying his much-used inkvine whip. In a gaudy blue uniform with gold tassels and lapels decked with clusters of medals, he had dressed as if he meant to be the center of the military display in the main square rather than an observer from a high balcony.

"Rabban, we must show the Emperor how angry we are over these recent Fremen activities."

The thick lips smiled cruelly, as if the Beast already anticipated what he would be told to do. "Do you want me to round up some suspects and interrogate them? I'll make them confess to whatever you like."

Outside, the blare of trumpets cracked through the dry air, announcing the arrival of the Harkonnen troops.

"Not good enough, Rabban. I want you to select three villages, I don't care which ones. Point your fingers at a map, if you like. March in with commandos and raze the settlements to the ground. Level every building, kill all the people, leave only black spots in the desert. Maybe I'll write up a decree explaining their supposed crimes, and you can scatter copies among the carnage, so the rest of the Fremen rabble can read it."

Again, trumpets blew outside in the square. The Baron accompanied his nephew out onto the observation platform. A sullen crowd filled the square, unwashed bodies whose stench reached him even here, three floors up. The Baron could only imagine how unbearable the smell must be down there in the heat.

"Entertain yourself," the Baron said, twiddling his ring-studded fingers. "One day your brother Feyd will be old enough to accompany you on these . . . instructive exercises."

Rabban nodded. "We'll teach those lawless bandits who wields the real power here."

The Baron responded in a distracted tone. "Yes, I know."

The soldiers lined up in their ceremonial uniforms, lovely muscular men—a sight that never failed to stimulate the Baron. The parade began.

*Every man has the same final destination: death at
the end of life's road. But the path we travel makes all
the difference. Some of us have maps and goals.
Others are just lost.*

— PRINCE RHOMBUR VERNIUS,
Ruminations at a Fork in the Road

Trapped on the stranded Heighliner, Gurney
Halleck stared out the frigate porthole at
the airless void of the cargo hold. Hundreds of
ships hung precariously in their berths, clustered
together, some smashed and upended. Aboard
those craft, many people must be injured or dead.

Next to him, still wearing the concealing
cloak and cowl, Rhombur studied the Heighliner's
framework, reassembling details from a blueprint
in his mind.

Two hours earlier, another holoprojection of the
oddlooking Flight Auditor had appeared inside each
ship. "We have, nnnn, no additional information.
Please stand by." Then the images had dissolved.

The Heighliner held numerous cargo ships and
transport frigates, some of which were filled with
foodstuffs, medicines, and trading goods, enough
to keep the tens of thousands of passengers alive
for months. Gurney wondered if they would remain marooned out here until starving people began to attack each other. Already, some passengers
were nervously gorging themselves on personal
supplies.

Gurney remained far from despair, though. In his younger days he had survived Harkonnen slave pits and had escaped from Giedi Prime by concealing himself in a shipment of blue obsidian. After that, he could tolerate going astray on a spaceship. . . .

Abruptly, Rhombur lunged to his feet with his baliset and turned his scarred face toward his companion. "This is driving me mad." The sinews of the Prince's neck stood out so that Gurney could make out the polymer connections where human muscles had been grafted onto prosthetic parts. "The Guild is full of administrators, bureaucrats, and bankers. The support staff on a Heighliner performs only menial duties. None of them has much expertise in these vessels or the Holtzman engines."

"What are you getting at?" Gurney looked around. "How can I help?"

Rhombur's gaze took on the rigid, expectant stare of a leader, eerily similar to the countenance of Dominic Vernius, which Gurney remembered so well. "I have spent my life like the passengers on this Guild ship, waiting for someone else to solve my problems, expecting the situation to fix itself. And I won't do it any longer. I must try, no matter the result."

"We have to keep our identities secret in order to complete our mission."

"Yes, but we can't help Ix unless we can get there." Rhombur went to the nearest observation porthole, staring out at the other ships trapped there. "I'm willing to wager that I know more about the intricacies of this ship than any other person aboard. Emergency situations call for strong leadership, and the Spacing Guild doesn't staff its regular passenger vessels with strong leaders."

Gurney placed their balisets in a storage locker, but did not bother to lock it. "Then I am at your side. I've sworn to protect you and assist you in any way."

Rhombur looked out a large window at the convoluted

catwalks and structural girders that formed the giant ship's framework. His gaze acquired an unfocused quality, as if he were trying to recall subtle details. "Come with me. I know the way to the Navigator's chamber."

❦

WITH MANY OF his ingrained memories recovered after the tragedy of his accident, Rhombur recalled a plethora of access codes and the locations of unmarked hatches that laced the Heighliner's inner hull decks like boreholes in wormwood. Though the programming had been installed decades ago during the construction of the vessel, Dominic Vernius had always left secret access points for his family as a routine precaution.

Guild security men were doing their best to keep passengers aboard their individual ships, while allowing a limited number of people to wander into the gallerias and assembly areas within the hull decks. But in the midst of turmoil and frightened passengers, security could not watch every path.

Rhombur's cyborg legs did not tire, and Gurney followed with his rolling gait. The cowled Prince marched along a damaged but still-serviceable catwalk. Even making use of lift platforms and caged-in conveyors, it took the pair hours to reach the upper high-security decks.

When he activated a hatch and stepped into a garishly lit chamber, Rhombur startled seven Guild representatives in the midst of an urgent conference around a heavy table. The Guildsmen sat up, their normally dull eyes flashing silver. Most of them looked subtly altered from the human norm. One man had puffy ears and a narrow face, another had tiny hands and eyes, and yet another had stiff limbs, as if he lacked knees and elbows. Based upon their distinctive lapel badges, the Ixian Prince identified route administrators, a roly-poly Guild Banker, a legate to CHOAM, an ancient Guild Mentat, and the fish-eyed Flight Auditor who had served as holo-spokesman.

"How did you get in here?" the roly-poly Banker demanded. "We are in the middle of a crisis. You must return to your—"

A flurry of guards rushed in, blades drawn. One man carried a stunner.

Rhombur stepped forward, with Gurney at his side. "I have something important to say . . . and to *do*." Arriving at a crucial decision, he put a hand to the hood that covered his head. "As a nobleman, I invoke the Guild's code of secrecy."

The guards took several steps closer.

Slowly, Rhombur pulled down his hood to reveal the metal plate on the back of his skull, the lumpy burn marks and poorly healed lacerations on his face. As he opened the robe, the Guildsmen could see his bulky armored arms, his prosthetic legs, the life-support systems woven into his clinging garments.

"Let me see the Navigator. I may be able to help."

The seven Guild representatives around the table looked at each other and spoke in a clipped language, shorthand for thought impulses and words. The Prince strode to the edge of their table. His limbs thrummed with power, and the pumps in his chest drew in breaths, filtered them, and metabolized oxygen, adding chemical energy to the battery packs that powered his artificial organs.

The elderly Guild Mentat regarded the cyborg intruder, with hardly a glance at Gurney Halleck. Holding up one hand, palm out, the Mentat gestured for the security men to leave. "We require privacy."

When they were gone, the aged man said, "You are Prince Rhombur Vernius of Ix. We learned of your presence on this craft, and of the . . . fee . . . that you paid to keep it secret." His rheumy eyes studied the mechanical enhancements of Rhombur's body.

"Do not be concerned for your secret," said the Flight Auditor. He placed his too-short arms on the table. "Your identity is, nnnn, safe with us."

Gazing around the table, Rhombur said, "I understand how this Heighliner was constructed. In fact, on its maiden voyage I watched a Navigator guide it through foldspace, to move it from the caverns of Ix." He paused, letting his words sink in. "But I suspect our predicament has nothing to do with the Holtzmann engines. You would know that as well as I do."

Like a lightning thought that skittered around the table, the Guildsmen abruptly sat straighter, putting together the implications of Rhombur's identity, his disguise, and his destination.

"Know this, Prince," the pudgy Banker added, "the Guild would not object to seeing House Vernius restored to Ix. The Bene Tleilax have no vision or efficiency. Heighliner production and quality have fallen off drastically, and we have been forced to reject some ships because of inadequate workmanship. This has harmed our revenues. The Spacing Guild would benefit from your return to power. In fact, the entire Imperium would be well served if you were to—"

Gurney interrupted. "Nobody said anything about that. We're just travelers maintaining a low profile." He looked sharply at Rhombur. "And, at the moment, this ship isn't going anywhere."

Rhombur nodded. "I need to see the Navigator."

THE CHAMBER WAS a large, round-walled aquarium sealed with armored glass and filled with the cinnamon-orange fog of melange gas. The mutated Navigator, with webbed hands and atrophied feet, should have floated without gravity inside the chamber. Instead, the creature's distorted form lay slumped and motionless in the spice fog, its shrunken eyes glassy and unfocused.

"The Navigator collapsed while folding space," explained the Flight Auditor. "We don't know, nnnn, where we are. We cannot rouse him."

The Guild Mentat coughed, and said, "Traditional navigation techniques are unable to pinpoint our location. We are far beyond the edge of known space."

One of the route administrators shouted into a speaking screen on the wall. "Navigator, respond! Steersman!" The creature twitched on the floor, proving that he was still alive, but no words came from the puckered, fleshy mouth.

Gurney looked around at the seven Guildsmen. "How are we going to help him? Are there any medical facilities for . . . these creatures?"

"Navigators require no medical attention." The Flight Auditor blinked his wide-set eyes. "Melange gives them life and health. Nnnn. Melange makes them more than human."

Gurney rolled his lumpy shoulders. "Melange isn't doing enough right now. We need this Navigator to recover so we can return to the Imperium."

"I want to go inside the chamber," Rhombur said. "Perhaps I can rouse him. He might be able to tell me what went wrong."

The Guildsmen looked at each other. "Impossible." The plump Banker gestured with a stubby-fingered hand toward the murk of spice. "Such a concentration of melange would be fatal to anyone not adapted to it. You cannot breathe the air."

Rhombur placed a prosethetic hand on his own barrel chest, where the cyborg bellows of his mechanical diaphragm caused him to inhale and exhale in a precise rhythm. "I do not have human lungs."

The realization made Gurney laugh with astonishment. Even if concentrated melange damaged organic tissues, Dr. Yueh's artificial metabolizers should protect Rhombur, for a short while at least.

In the sealed chamber, the Navigator stirred again, on the verge of death. Finally, the odd-looking group of Guildsmen agreed.

The Flight Auditor evacuated the sealed umbilical corridor behind the Navigator's tank, knowing that some of the potent gas would leak out when the hatch was opened. Rhombur clasped Gurney's hand, careful not to squeeze hard enough to break his friend's bones. "Thank you for your faith in me, Gurney Halleck." He paused, thinking of Tessia, then turned to the hatch.

"When this is over, we'll have to add a few more verses to our epic song." The troubadour warrior clapped the Ixian on the shoulder, then ducked back into the protected corridor with the Guildsmen, who sealed the entrance.

Rhombur approached the rear access panel that the bloated form of the Navigator could no longer pass through. Before proceeding, he increased the filtration levels of his cyborg breathing mechanism and decreased his respiration requirements. Drawing upon his body's power cells, he hoped to function for a time without having to inhale the melange gas.

He disengaged the lock of the access hatch and broke the seal with a hiss. Then he yanked open the round doorway, crawled inside, and closed it behind him to retain as much of the orange fog as possible. His organic eye stung, and the olfactory receptors, still functional in his nostrils, screamed against the potent reek of acrid aromatic esters.

The Prince took a tentative step forward, walking with leaden feet, as if immersed in a slow, drug-induced dream. Ahead, through shifting visibility, he spotted the Navigator's naked, fleshy form—not human anymore, but some sort of atavistic mistake, a creature that had never been meant to reproduce.

Rhombur bent to touch the soft skin. The Navigator turned his massive head and tiny inset eyes toward him. The shriveled mouth twitched and opened to exhale rusty clouds of gas without a sound. He blinked at Rhombur as if assessing possibilities, sorting through memories and groping for primitive words with which he could communicate.

"Prince . . . Rhombur . . . Vernius."

"You know my name?" Rhombur was surprised, but remembered that Navigators possessed prescient powers.

"D'murr," the creature said in a long, low whisper. "I was . . . D'murr Pilru."

"D'murr? I knew you as a young man!" None of the Navigator's features was recognizable.

"No time . . . Threat . . . outside force . . . evil . . . drawing closer . . . beyond the Imperium."

"A threat? What kind of threat? Is it coming here?"

"Ancient enemy . . . future enemy . . . cannot remember. Time folds . . . space folds . . . memory fails."

"Do you know what's wrong with you?" Rhombur's words buzzed as he forced them through his enhanced larynx without drawing breaths. "How can we help you?"

"Tainted . . . spice gas . . . in tank," D'murr struggled to say. "Prescience fails . . . navigation error. Must escape . . . return to known space. *The enemy has seen us.*"

Rhombur had no idea which enemy he meant, or if the injured D'murr was having delusions. "Tell me what to do. I want to help."

"I can . . . guide. First, spice gas must be . . . changed. Remove poison. Bring fresh spice."

Rhombur stood back, uneasy about the strange, unidentified threat. He didn't understand what could be wrong with the melange gas, but at least he understood how to fix the problem. He had no time to lose. "I'll have the Guildsmen exchange the spice in your tank, and you'll be fine soon. Where is your backup supply?"

"None."

Rhombur felt cold. If the Guild had no spice stockpile aboard the marooned Heighliner, they had no hope of finding melange out here in deep, uncharted space.

"No . . . backup supply on board."

How long can one man fight alone? Far worse, though, to stop fighting completely.

—C'TAIR PILRU, private journals (fragment)

Seated on an organic sofpad inside her snow shelter, Sister Cristane considered her predicament. A cold blue glowglobe floated just beneath the low ceiling. She wore a hooded orange syndown jacket, clingtrousers, thick boots.

This was only her first day on the mountain, far from the Heighliner crash site . . . far from anything at all. As part of her commando training, to stay in top physical and mental condition, she was required to go on regular wilderness hikes, pitting her survival skills against the elements.

Before dawn, she had begun hiking up the six-thousand-meter Mount Laojin, winding her way along wooded ridges, high meadows, rugged talus slopes, and finally negotiating a rocky glacier. She had brought along a small pack, minimal supplies, and her wits. It was a typical Bene Gesserit test.

An unexpected weather shift had caught her in a white-out on a boulder-strewn moraine, an open expanse with steep snow-covered cliffs above—ripe for an avalanche. Cristane had hollowed out a snow cave and crawled inside with her gear. She could adjust her metabolism enough to keep herself warm, even here.

Breathing steam, letting a thin film of perspiration glisten on her skin under the blue glowglobe, she took deep, relaxing breaths. At a double-snap of her fingers, the light went out, immersing her in eerie moon-white darkness. The blizzard roared on outside, a relentless onslaught that scraped against her small enclosure.

She had been intending to enter a meditational trance, but suddenly the drone of the blizzard grew quieter, and she heard the unexpected vibration of an ornithopter. Within moments, the excited voices of women and the sounds of digging came from outside the shelter.

The snowdrift broke away, exposing her shelter to the cold wind. Familiar faces peered inside. "Leave your gear here," one Sister said, looking at Cristane. "Mother Superior needs to see you right away."

The young Bene Gesserit emerged from the shelter into the ragged end of the blizzard. The rocky peak of Mount Laojin was bedecked with a thick blanket of new snow. A large ornithopter perched on a flat area upslope, and she trudged through soft whiteness toward it.

Mother Superior Harishka leaned out of the 'thopter hatch, waving her rail-thin arms. "Hurry, child. We can just get you to the spaceport in time for the next Heighliner."

Cristane climbed in, and the two women sat side by side as the aircraft lifted off in a flurry of blown snow. "What is it, Mother Superior?"

"An important assignment." With dark almond eyes, the old woman peered at her. "You are being sent to Ix. We have already lost one operative there and now we have received disturbing information from Kaitain. You must learn what you can about the secret operations of the Tleilaxu and the Emperor. They have been scheming together on Ix."

Harishka placed a dry, wrinkled hand on the commando's knee. "Discover the nature of Project Amal, whatever that is."

WRAPPED IN A protective trance that reduced her metabolism to near zero, Sister Cristane huddled inside an orbital dump box as it braked through the atmosphere and cruised down to the surface of Ix, accompanied by a parade of sonic booms. Everything had happened very quickly.

A Bene Gesserit makeup specialist had followed her onto the Heighliner, where she was disguised as a male for her protection, since no one had ever seen a Tleilaxu female. In addition, before she had fallen ominously silent, the Bene Gesserit spy Miral Alechem had reported the disappearance of Ixian women on the Tleilaxu-controlled industrial planet.

Now, using an electronic device she carried, the young commando guided the plummeting box several kilometers off course. After it skidded across an alpine meadow, finally coming to a halt, she worked her way out, sealed the container behind her, and shouldered her backpack, which contained weapons, food, and warm-weather survival gear.

Wearing infrared contact lenses, she managed to gain entry to a ventilation shaft. Engaging the suspensor mechanism on her belt, Cristane climbed inside, and dropped—with no idea where the shaft led. In the darkness, she fell slowly, deeper and deeper into the planetary crust.

Finally, with frayed nerves and reflexes, she crawled into the subterranean world. She was on her own.

Among the crowded, subdued population, she could easily distinguish the once-proud Ixians from the suboids, Tleilaxu overlords, and Sardaukar soldiers. The true Ixians spoke little to each other, kept their eyes averted, and shuffled along aimlessly.

For two days, she explored narrow connecting tunnels, gathering information. In a short while, the efficient Cristane developed a mental map of the city's comprehensive air-circulation system, while discovering ancient security systems, most of which were no longer operable. She wondered where Sister Miral Alechem might be now. Had the other Bene Gesserit infiltrator been killed?

One evening, Cristane watched a black-haired man steal packages from an unlit loading dock, hiding them inside a clogged vent. Though she wore infrared lenses, it struck Cristane as extraordinary that he was able to move about with no illumination. The man knew the area extremely well, suggesting a long time spent here.

As the furtive figure stashed packages, she studied him closely, detecting subtleties. This Ixian walked with a purpose, confident but wary. When he came close to her hiding place, she used the power of Voice and whispered from the darkness. "Do not move. Tell me who you are."

Paralyzed by the tone, C'tair Pilru was unable to flee. Though he struggled to clamp his mouth shut, his lips moved of their own volition. In a low, agitated voice, he provided his full name.

His mind spun as he tried to sort possibilities. Was this a Sardaukar guard, or a Tleilaxu security investigator? He could not tell.

Now he heard a soft voice, and felt the warmth of someone's breath on his ear. "Do not fear me. Not yet." A *woman*.

She forced him to reveal the truth. He told of his years spent fighting to restore Ix, how he had cared for Miral Alechem and how she had been taken by the vile Tleilaxu . . . and how Prince Rhombur would arrive soon. Cristane sensed that C'tair had more to say, but his words drifted off into a long silence.

For his part, he perceived the strange woman moving around him, but couldn't see her, and still he was unable to move. Would she speak again, or would he feel a blade piercing his ribs and heart?

"I am Sister Cristane of the Bene Gesserit," she said, at last.

C'tair felt a lifting of the mental shackles that had restrained him. In the light cast by a passing groundtruck he was surprised to see what appeared to be a slender man with close-cropped, dark hair. A disguise.

"When has the Sisterhood ever concerned itself with Ix?" C'tair demanded.

"You spoke eloquently of Miral Alechem. She was also a Sister."

C'tair could hardly believe this. In the darkness, he touched her arm. "Come with me. I will show you a safe place to stay."

Darting in and out of shadows, he guided her through the once-beautiful city. In the low illumination of artificial night, Cristane's wiry body showed few feminine curves. She could pass as a man if she were careful enough.

"I am glad you're with me," he told her, "but I fear for your life."

An ignorant friend is worse than a learned foe.

—ABU HAMID AL GHAZALI,
Incoherence of the Philosophers

Wandering alone through the corridor outside her apartment, trying to escape the persistent attentions of Medical Sister Yohsa, Lady Anirul bumped into Count Hasimir Fenring just as he rounded a corner at a brisk pace.

"Mmmm, pardon me, my Lady." When he looked at the Emperor's wife, his flickering eyes assessed her weakened condition. "So good to see you up and about. Good, very good. I heard about your illness, hmmm, and your husband has been so worried."

Anirul had never liked this slippery little man. Suddenly, a chorus of voices in her mind encouraged her, and she could withhold her feelings no longer. "Maybe I would have a true *husband* if you did not interfere so much, Count Fenring."

Recoiling in surprise, he said, "Whatever do you mean, hmmm-ah? I spend most of my time away from Kaitain, on business. How could I possibly interfere?" His large eyes narrowed, analyzing her further.

Impulsively, she decided to jab and parry with words, then watch for his reaction to learn more about him. "So tell me about Project Amal and the Tleilaxu. And Ix."

Fenring's face showed just the hint of a flush.

"I'm afraid you must be suffering a relapse. Shall I call a Suk doctor?"

She glared at him. "Shaddam doesn't have the foresight and intuition to develop such a scheme by himself, so it must have been your idea. Tell me, why are you doing this?"

Though the Count appeared ready to lash out at her, he made a visible effort to calm himself. Automatically, Anirul adopted a subtle fighting stance, a barely perceptible shifting of her muscles. A well-placed toe-kick could disembowel him.

Fenring smiled even as he studied her closely. From living with Margot, he had learned to watch for minute details. "I am afraid your information is incorrect, my Lady, mm-m-m?" Although he carried a neuroknife in his pocket, Fenring now wished for a more substantial weapon. He took a half step backward, and said in his calmest tone, "With all due respect, perhaps my Lady is imagining things." He bowed stiffly and left in a great hurry.

As Anirul watched him scurry away, the clamor of voices increased inside her skull. Finally, through the haze of drugs, after searching for so long, she heard old Lobia's familiar voice rising above the others. "That was very human of you," the dead Truthsayer scolded, "very human, and very foolish."

As he disappeared into the maze of corridors, Fenring pondered damage control. In these unstable times, the Sisterhood could significantly undermine Shaddam's power base if they chose to turn against him.

If the Emperor falls, I go down with him.

For the first time Fenring considered that it might be necessary to kill Shaddam's wife. Quite accidentally, of course.

❦

INSIDE THE LANDSRAAD Hall of Oratory, noblemen and ambassadors had begun to speak openly of revolt. Representatives from Great and Minor Houses stood in line for the podium, where they shouted red-faced or spoke with cold venom. The emergency session had already lasted a night and most of the following day without respite.

Emperor Shaddam, though, was totally unconcerned. He sat unruffled in the elaborate seat reserved for him within the Great Hall. The nobles fumed and talked among themselves, an ill-tempered, rowdy assemblage. Shaddam was disappointed to see their uncouth behavior.

He lounged in the immense chair, his manicured hands folded on his lap. If this meeting went as planned, the Emperor wouldn't need to say a word. He had already requested more Sardaukar troops from Salusa Secundus, though he doubted they would be necessary to control this minor civil unrest.

Somewhat recovered from her recent episodes, but still looking dazed, Lady Anirul sat in her subordinate seat, wearing a formal black aba robe, as he had requested. Beside her stood the Imperial Truthsayer Gaius Helen Mohiam in a matching robe. Their presence clearly implied that the powerful Sisterhood still supported Shaddam's reign. It was high time the witches followed through on their duties and veiled promises.

Before the opening complaints from the Landsraad were heard, Shaddam's lawyers stepped forth and presented his position, citing appropriate precedents and technicalities.

Next, a primary envoy from the Spacing Guild took the podium. The Guild had transported Shaddam's warships to Richese for the attack on Korona, and they defended their decision to do so, referencing legal precedents of their own. Thanks to Shaddam's benevolence, the Guild had reaped half of the recovered spice stockpile from Korona, and they would stand by House Corrino.

Shaddam sat with regal confidence.

The President of CHOAM stepped forward after this, a man with stooped posture and a silvery gray beard. His voice carried loud and far. "CHOAM supports the Emperor's right to enforce order in the Imperium. The law against stockpiling melange has long been a part of the Imperial Code. Though many of you complain vociferously, every House is aware of it." He looked around the assemblage, waiting for any voices of dissent, then continued.

"The Emperor issued repeated warnings that he intended to enforce this law. Yet, even after he took action against Zanovar for the same crime, Richese foolishly ignored the rule." The CHOAM President jabbed a sharp-nailed finger out toward the delegates.

"What evidence is there against House Richese?" a nobleman shouted.

"We have the word of a Corrino Emperor. That is sufficient." The CHOAM President let his words hang in a confrontational pause. "And, in private session, we have seen holo-images of the Richesian stockpiles before they were confiscated."

The President started to leave the podium, then stepped back, and added, "The Emperor's legal position is solid, and you cannot censure him to cover your own crimes. If any of you violate the stockpiling edict, you do so at your own peril. It is the Imperial prerogative to use any means necessary to maintain political and economic stability, supported by the rule of law."

Shaddam suppressed a smile. Anirul glanced at him, then back across the Great Hall and the throng of unruly Landsraad representatives.

Finally, Chamberlain Beely Ridondo boomed his sonic staff to restore order. Gazing out at the nobles, he announced, "These proceedings are formally open. Now, who dares to speak against the Emperor's actions?"

Shaddam's loyal staff members rose to their feet with scrolls and scribing pens, ready to take down names. The implication was clear.

The simmering discontent settled to a murmur, and no one came forward to be the first. The Emperor made a public show of patting his wife's hand, knowing he had won. For now.

Never attempt to understand prescience, or it may not work for you.

—Navigator's Instruction Manual

Rhombur staggered out of the swirling spice gas, choking and coughing. His artificial lungs sounded ragged, too overworked to process the massive melange exposure. Spice residue thrummed through his mind, making it difficult to interpret the combined visual impulses of his organic eye and its prosthetic companion. He lurched two steps, leaned against a wall.

Wearing a filter mask, Gurney Halleck pushed his way forward to help him. He guided the Prince back into a corridor, where the air was clean. An anxious Flight Auditor used a compact air jet to blast the powdery coating of melange from Rhombur's clothes. Touching a control on the side of his neck, the cyborg Prince activated an internal mechanism that purged his lung filters.

One of the route administrators grasped him by the shoulder. "Can the Navigator still function? Can he guide us out of here?"

Rhombur tried to speak, but in his muddled state of mind he didn't know how coherent his words sounded. "The Navigator is alive but weakened. He says his spice gas is tainted." He took a deep mechanical breath. "We need to replace the melange in his tank with a fresh supply."

Hearing this, the Guildsmen spoke quickly

among themselves. The rotund Banker seemed the most alarmed. "The concentration of melange in a Navigator's chamber is high. We don't have the resources."

The aged Mentat stood as if in a trance, checking data in his head, running through his memorized ship rosters. "This Heighliner carries over a thousand vessels, but none are listed as spice transports."

"Still, there must be a great deal of melange scattered in small portions throughout the ships in the hold," Gurney said. "What about all the passengers' personal possessions, all the dining galleys? We have to look everywhere."

The Banker agreed. "Many noble families consume spice daily to maintain their health."

"Such supplies are not reported on passenger manifests, so we cannot be certain of the quantity available," the Mentat-Guildsman said. "In any event, dealing with all the passengers could take days."

"We will find a way to move faster. The Navigator is very afraid," Rhombur said. "He says a great enemy is drawing closer. We are in danger."

"But from what?" the Flight Auditor said. "Nnnn, I don't understand what could possibly be a threat to us out here."

The Mentat said, "Perhaps another intelligence, something . . . not human?"

"The Navigator may be hallucinating," one of the route adminstrators pointed out, sounding hopeful. "His mind is damaged."

The Banker disagreed. "We cannot gamble on this. He has prescience. Perhaps we are in the path of a huge cosmic event, a supernova or something else, that will swallow us with it. We have no choice but to demand that all private passenger ships surrender their melange. We'll get the Wayku and the security men started immediately."

"It won't be enough," said the old Mentat-Guildsman.

Impatient with the bickering and endless discussion, Rhombur spoke in a commanding tone and insisted, "Nevertheless, we will make it work."

THE MISSION WENT slowly. Despite the Heighliner's obvious need, passengers were reluctant to surrender their precious melange, not knowing how long they might be stranded out here in uncharted space. To force the issue, the Guildsmen enlisted security forces to scour ship after ship.

But it was taking too long.

Gurney Halleck went on his own to the upper Heighliner deck, where he stood inside a plaz-walled enclosure. He had trudged from docking section to docking section, searching, listening, attempting to spot something none of the others would think to look for.

While gazing out upon the congregation of vessels inside the hangar bay, he scrutinized every hull plate, every ship configuration, every serial number and insignia. The Guild Mentat had mentally reviewed all of the cargo manifests, and the other officials had accepted his assessment with dismay and resignation.

But they failed to ask Gurney's question: What if there was an *undeclared* cargo of spice?

He was no expert on spacecraft, but he studied the streamlined frigates, the sharp-angled military craft, the cube-shaped orbital dump boxes. Some ships proudly displayed the colors of noble families on their hulls; other nondescript vessels were battered and dirty from age and overuse. Gurney focused on those in particular, raking his gaze from one to the next, remembering his smuggler past when he had made unobtrusive journeys inside Heighliner holds himself.

With growing anticipation, he moved to the next observation deck for a better vantage. Finally, he spotted a small ship tucked behind a much larger frigate that bore the crest of House Mutelli. The dingy vessel was an outdated pinnace, a commercial craft used to haul salvage and other unimportant cargoes.

Gurney studied the stains on the hull, looked at the enlarged engine compartments and repairs that had been made to the superstructure. He *knew* this unusual craft. He had seen it before.

It was exactly what he'd been looking for.

⌇

ACCOMPANIED BY GUILD security forces, Gurney and Rhombur led the way under a huge hull-support buttress to the old pinnace. When the group demanded entrance, the captain and crew refused to acknowledge. However, before berthing aboard a Heighliner, every vessel had to submit certain override codes to Guild manifest personnel.

The pinnace hatch finally cracked open and the security men thundered aboard, Gurney surged to the front of the group. The ragtag pinnace crew had armed themselves and taken up assault stations, ready to fire upon the intruders. But Gurney raised his arms, putting himself directly in the crossfire. "No! No weapons! Either side!"

He gazed around at the scruffy men who looked like down-on-their-luck salvage workers. Marching deeper into the corridor, he glanced from one unfamiliar face to another—until finally he recognized a squat, stubble-cheeked man chewing on a stimleaf plug. "Pen Barlowe, you don't need your weapons with me."

The defiant expression on the rugged man's face melted into a look of wonder. He spat out the end of his sodden plug and stared, openmouthed. "That inkvine scar. Gurney Halleck, is it you?"

The Guild security men waited anxiously, not sure what was happening.

"I knew if I looked hard enough among the ships here, I was sure to find one of my old comrades." He came forward to greet his smuggling companion.

Pen Barlowe began to laugh loudly, braying like a pack animal, and pounded him on the back. "Gurney, Gurney!"

Gurney Halleck gestured back in the direction of the

cyborg Prince, who approached in his cloak and cowl. "There's someone you need to meet. Allow me to introduce . . . Dominic's son."

Several smugglers gasped, for even those who had not served with Dominic Vernius knew of his legendary exploits. Rhombur thrust out his synthetic arm and clasped Pen Barlowe's free hand in the half handshake of the Imperium. "We need your help, if you're a friend of Gurney's."

Barlowe gestured toward his men. "Stand down, fools! Can't you see there's no emergency here?"

"I need to know your true cargo, my friend," Gurney said gravely. "Is this vessel carrying what I think it is? Unless you've changed your ways since I left the smugglers, you may have the key to saving us all."

The swarthy man looked down, as if considering whether to retrieve the stub of his stimleaf plug from the deck and stuff it back into his mouth. "We heard the call, but thought it was some kind of trick." He met Gurney's gaze and shifted nervously on his feet. "Yes, we've got an undeclared cargo, and it's illegal to haul . . . dangerous, even, with the Emperor's crackdown . . ."

"We are all relying on Guild confidentiality here, myself included," Rhombur said. "These are extraordinary circumstances—and we are far beyond the reach of Imperial law."

Gurney studied his comrade, not letting his gaze waver. "You have melange aboard, Barlowe, to be sold to black marketeers at a fine profit." He narrowed his eyelids. "But not today. Instead, you'll buy us all our lives."

Barlowe glowered. "Yes, we have sufficient spice aboard for an Emperor's ransom."

Rhombur smiled, crinkling his scarred face. "That could be enough."

THE SMUGGLING CREW looked on, their faces stricken, as the Heighliner security men hauled container after unmarked container of compressed spice up to the top levels. Taking several Guildsmen aside, Gurney negotiated for some compensation for the smugglers. The Guild was notoriously frugal, and the amount they agreed to pay was not nearly full value, but the smugglers were in no position to argue.

In the midst of all the activity, Rhombur stood outside the Navigator's tank, trying to attract the attention of D'murr. The mutated human lay slumped and barely breathing. "We must hurry!" he called back to the others.

Crewmen worked feverishly, draining the tainted spice from the tank. Afterward, other men converted containers of packed melange into aerosol and fed fresh gas into the chamber in long, orange streamers. They hoped that this batch of uncontaminated spice would be enough to revive the Navigator and give him the ability to guide the Heighliner back into familiar space.

"He has not moved in over an hour," said the Flight Auditor.

Rhombur cleared the area again and went back inside the sealed chamber. Orange spice gas curled and flowed into the tank from vents high in the chamber. Moment by moment, visibility decreased, but the Ixian Prince plodded toward the center of the Navigator's tank, to the hulk of what once had been a dark-haired, handsome young man like his twin C'tair. Long ago they had both flirted with Rhombur's sister, Kailea Vernius.

He recalled the twins, children of Ambassador Pilru. Everyone had been happy in those glory days of Ix. It all seemed like a dream, even more so because of the spice now seeping into his consciousness.

D'murr had been so proud to pass his examination to become a Guild Navigator, while C'tair had been devastated at his failure and remained behind on Ix. Always on Ix . . .

A past so distant it might never have happened . . .

Rhombur spoke in a soothing tone, as if he were a medical practitioner. "We are replenishing your spice, D'murr." Kneeling, he saw the Navigator's glassy eyes. "We have found pure melange. Whatever was wrong will be fixed."

The creature no longer appeared even remotely human. Distorted and atrophied, his body looked as if it had been remade by a sadistic sculptor of flesh. The bloated hulk stirred weakly and flopped, as helpless as a fish on a hot dock. D'murr's face twisted, his strange mouth forming an odd expression. He sucked in mouthfuls of the potent spice gas.

Rhombur's thoughts floated, and the movements of his mechanical arms and legs seemed slow, as if inhibited by thick liquid. The cyborg's artificial lungs labored. He needed to get out of the tank soon. "Will this help? Can this new spice let you see through foldspace and bring us home?"

"Must," D'murr said, exhaling curls of smoke. "We are in danger . . . the enemy . . . has seen us. Approaches. Wants to destroy."

"Who is the enemy?"

"Hatred . . . extinguish us . . . for what . . . we are." D'murr managed to bring his twisted body more upright. "Flee . . . as far as possible . . ." He turned, his tiny eyes surrounded by folds of waxy flesh. "I see the way now . . . to bring us . . . home."

The Navigator seemed to be consuming all of his strength for one last gesture. D'murr squirmed closer to the vents that sprayed dense melange gas. He drew in a deep breath. "Must hurry!"

Instead of rushing to the hatch to escape, Rhombur helped him grasp the controls. The faltering Navigator powered up the Holtzman engines and, with a sudden jerk, the Heighliner shifted and then spun over, righting itself in space.

"Enemy . . . is near."

And the great ship *moved*—or seemed to.

Feeling a lurch in his stomach, Rhombur grasped the tank wall and sensed the transition as the powerful Holtzmann field folded space, wrapping it around the Heighliner in a precise manner.

The Navigator completed his sacred assignment.

The Heighliner winked into view above the planet Junction. D'murr had instinctively brought them back into the Imperium, back to Guild headquarters, to his only home since he had left Ix as a young man.

"Safe," D'murr announced weakly.

Touched by the tremendous effort of the Navigator, Rhombur went back to him, ignoring for the moment his own need to escape. D'murr had used the last of himself to rescue everyone aboard. "C'tair—" With a long, hissing sigh that sounded as if his entire body were deflating, the Navigator slumped to the floor of his chamber and did not move. With the cyborg Prince crouched beside him, surrounded by potent melange gas, D'murr died.

Rhombur could say no farewells now, and knew he needed to leave the chamber before the melange overwhelmed him. His vision reeling, the organic parts of his body burning from saturation with spice, Rhombur staggered back toward the hatch. D'murr's body dissolved into the orange spice fog and disappeared from sight.

Justice? Who asks for justice in a universe crawling with inequity?

— LADY HELENA ATREIDES,
Private Meditations on Necessity and Remorse

Like shadows, four sisters in isolation approached Castle Caladan from the sea. They rode aboard a leaky fishing trawler, rather than a formal processional barge. It was early evening, and a pall of fading daylight lingered beneath a cloudy sky.

Standing on the deck of the boat and gazing toward the cliff face and the Castle above it, the Sisters wore capes and loose-fitting jerkins made of the blackest cloth. Flexible gloves, leggings, and boots covered every centimeter of their skin. A fine woven mesh of ebony fibers, sewn around the rims of their hoods, shrouded their faces.

During the long voyage across the ocean on the trawler, the Sisters had kept to themselves. The boat captain had received an extravagant fee from them, a partial compensation for the whispers and fear the reclusive women engendered among his superstitious crew. The captain turned south and skirted the shoreline, heading for a village dock from which his passengers would have a more comfortable walk up to the Castle.

One of the women in black stared through her gauzy face-mesh at the towering new statue of Duke Paulus Atreides on a spit of land, holding bright flames in a brazier on his uplifted palm. She seemed to have become a statue herself, profiled against the ruddy sky of late afternoon.

Without a word of thanks to the captain, the four Sisters disembarked onto the dock and walked through the old town. Villagers mended nets, boiled pots of shellfish, and tended greenwood fires in smokehouses, watching the visitors with curiosity. Exotic and mysterious, the Sisters in Isolation were rarely seen away from their fortress nunneries on Caladan's eastern continent.

The Sister at the head of the group wore cobwebs of silver embroidery stitched into ideograms around the fringes of her robes, fabric tattoos that swirled across the silkweave veil. She glided with determined steps along the steep roadway that led to the edifice of Castle Caladan.

By the time the four reached the portcullis gate, full dusk filled the sky with a muted purple of gloaming. Uneasy Atreides guards blocked their passage. Without speaking, the woman in silver embroidery separated from the others and drew very close to the men, where she stood calmly, enigmatically.

A young soldier rushed to the Castle to fetch Thufir Hawat. When the Mentat emerged from the courtyard beyond the gate, he adjusted his formal uniform to create an intimidating presence. With Mentat eyes he studied the women, but could glean no information from their muffled figures. "The Duke has retired for the evening, but he will open his doors to the populace for two hours tomorrow morning."

The lead woman reached up to her fine woven veil. Hawat analyzed her movements, saw how the silver embroidery threads on her black dress were not simply decoration, but a form of sensor net enclosing the person within it . . . Richesian technology. Taking a step back, he touched the dueling dagger at his hip, but did not draw it.

Calmly, she plucked the stitches that bound the silken veil to her hood, ripped the fabric, and pulled away the mask that had altered her features. "Thufir Hawat, would you deny me access to my rightful home?" Her identity revealed, she blinked in the dim light and met his gaze without wavering. "Would you forbid me to see my own son?"

Even the unflappable Mentat was taken by surprise. He bowed slightly, then gestured for her to accompany him into the courtyard, but he did not greet her with any form of welcome. "Of course not, Lady Helena. You may enter." He motioned for the guards to let the hooded Sisters pass.

When they were inside the courtyard, Hawat told them to wait, and commanded the guards, "Perform a thorough weapons scan on these women while I notify the Duke."

LETO ATREIDES SAT on a dark wooden chair in his receiving hall. He had pulled on a dress jacket as well as the golden chain and medallion that signified his rank as a Duke of the Landsraad. He wore such trappings only on grimly formal occasions. Such as this one.

Even without confirmation from Rhombur and Gurney, he could not delay his plans. He'd spent the day in military preparations, and despite Duncan Idaho's brash confidence, Leto knew the battle for Ix would be an unpredictable and dangerous undertaking.

He had no time, no patience, and no love for his exiled mother.

Glowglobes surrounded him, but did not drive back the shadows in his heart. Leto felt a chill that had nothing to do with the cold mists of evening. He had not seen Helena in twenty-one years, not since her insidious involvement in the death of her own husband, the Old Duke.

When she entered, Leto did not rise from his seat. "Close the doors," he said, his voice iron. "We require privacy. And leave those other women to wait in the corridor."

Lady Helena's auburn hair had become streaked with gray, her skin drawn tight over facial bones. "They are my attendants, Leto. They have accompanied me from the eastern continent. Surely you can offer them some hospitality."

"I'm not in a hospitable mood, *Mother*. Duncan and Thufir, you two remain with me."

Duncan Idaho, still proudly holding Paulus's sword, waited by the lower step of the ducal platform. With a troubled expression, he looked from Leto to his mother, and then to the stony expression of suppressed anger on Hawat's leathery face.

The warrior-Mentat escorted the still-hooded personal attendants out of the room, then swung the heavy doors shut with a sound that echoed throughout the hall. He remained inside, at the door.

"So, I see you haven't forgiven me, my son." Helena frowned petulantly. Thufir prowled forward from the tall doors, a weapon in human form. Duncan tensed.

"How can you suggest there is something to forgive, Mother, if you maintain there was never any crime?" Leto shifted on his seat.

Helena's dark eyes bored into her son's, but she did not respond.

Duncan was concerned and perplexed. He barely remembered the wife of the beloved Old Duke. She had been a stern and domineering presence when he'd been but a boy who had escaped from the Harkonnens.

Pale with suppressed rage, Leto said, "I had hoped you would remain in your nunnery, continuing to feign grief while reflecting on your culpability. I thought I made it clear you are no longer welcome in Castle Caladan."

"Eminently clear. But while you remain without an heir, I am the only shred of your bloodline on Caladan."

He leaned forward, his gray eyes flashing with fury. "The Atreides dynasty will endure, have no fear, Mother. My concubine Jessica is even now on Kaitain, soon to give birth to my child. Therefore, you may return to your fortress nunnery. Thufir will be pleased to arrange your passage."

"You do not yet know why I have come," she said. "You

will hear me out." It was a tone of parental authority that Leto remembered from his childhood, and it stirred old memories about this woman.

Confused, Duncan again looked from face to face. He had never been told why Lady Helena had gone away, despite his many questions.

Leto sat like a statue. "More excuses, more denials?"

"A request. Not for me, but for your distaff bloodline, the family Richese. During the Emperor's heinous attack on Korona, hundreds of Richesians were killed, many thousands blinded. Count Ilban is my father. In the name of humanity I demand that you offer assistance. With the wealth of our"—her face reddened—"*your* House, you can provide aid and medical supplies."

Leto was surprised to hear such a request from her. "I know of the tragedy. Are you asking me to defy the Emperor, who has found Richese guilty of breaking Imperial law?"

She clenched her black-gloved fist and lifted her chin into the air. "I am suggesting that you help the people who need it most. Is that not the Atreides way, the way of honor? Is that not what Paulus taught you?"

"How dare you lecture me!"

"Or is House Atreides simply to be remembered for acts of aggression, such as the brutal strike against Beakkal? Destroy anyone who offends you?" She sneered. "You remind me of the Grumman Viscount. Is that to be the legacy of House Atreides?"

Her words stung, and he leaned back in the stiff wooden chair, trying to cover his discomfort. "As Duke, I do what I must."

"Then help Richese."

Further argument was pointless. "I shall consider it."

"You will guarantee it," Helena shot back.

"Return to the Sisters in Isolation, Mother." Leto stood from his chair, and Thufir Hawat moved forward. Duncan gripped the Old Duke's sword and instinctively closed in on her from the other direction. She recognized his blade, and then studied Duncan's face, without knowing who he was. He had changed much from the nine-year-old child she had known before her exile.

After a moment of tension, Leto waved them back. "I am surprised you would try to teach me compassion, Mother. However much I loathe you, though, I agree with the need for action. House Atreides will send aid to Richese—but only on condition that you leave here immediately." His expression grew even harder. "And speak to no one of this."

"Very well. Not another word, my son."

Helena spun about and marched back toward the exit so quickly that Hawat barely got there in time to open the heavy doors. After she and her three shadowy companions flitted through the halls and out into the deepening night, Leto mumbled a farewell, barely above a whisper. . . .

Duncan approached the Duke, who sat motionless, stunned. The Swordmaster's face was ashen, his eyes wide. "Leto, what was that all about? What is this breach between you two that has never been explained to me? Lady Helena is your *mother*. People will talk."

"People always talk," Thufir said.

Duncan climbed up the steps to the ducal chair. Leto gripped the carved wooden armrests with white-knuckled hands. His ducal signet ring pushed a dent into the wood.

When he finally glanced at his Swordmaster, his eyes were murky, like smoke. "House Atreides has many tragedies and many secrets, Duncan. You know how we concealed Kailea's culpability in the skyclipper explosion. You yourself took Swain Goire's place as head of my House Guard when we sent him into exile. My people must never know the truth about that . . . or about my mother."

Duncan was not certain where the discussion was leading. "What truth about her, Leto?"

The Mentat came forward with a warning expression. "My Duke, it is not wise—"

Leto raised a hand. "Thufir, Duncan deserves to know. Because of the accusations cast upon him as a child that he had tampered with the Salusan bulls, he needs to understand this."

Hawat lowered his head. "If you must, though I advise against it. Secrets do not diminish when they are spread among many ears."

Slowly and painfully, Leto described Lady Helena's involvement in the death of Paulus, how she had arranged for the drugging of the Salusan bull that had killed the revered Old Duke.

Duncan gaped, without speaking.

"I was sorely tempted to order her execution, but she is my mother, despite everything. She is guilty of murder—but I will not be responsible for matricide. Hence, she is to remain with the Sisters in Isolation until the end of her days." He sank a heavy chin onto his clenched fists. "And Swain Goire said to me, on the day I sentenced him to guard her, that I would one day be remembered as Leto the Just."

Duncan sat on the step, dropping heavily onto it while holding the revered sword between his knees. Blustery, generous Duke Paulus had accepted the young lad into the Atreides household and given him work in the stables. Then Duncan, a mere child of nine, had been wrongfully accused of involvement by Stablemaster Yresk, who was himself implicated in the bullring tragedy.

Now the layers of secrecy became clear, the reasoning unfolded, and it felt as if a floodgate had burst open. For the first time in many years, Swordmaster Duncan Idaho wept.

Many creatures bear the outward form of a man, but do not be fooled by appearances. Not all such life-forms can be considered human.

—Bene Gesserit Azhar Book

Since his uncle the Baron rarely let him have free rein, Beast Rabban decided to cause as much mayhem as possible, now that he had been given the opportunity.

He studied the crude and incomplete maps of settlements around the Shield Wall. Squalid town-folk lived there, people who survived by scaveng-ing and by stealing Harkonnen property in the middle of the night. In punishment for the Fremen raids on spice stockpiles, the Baron had told his nephew to obliterate three such villages. Rabban chose the targets, not quite at random, but because he didn't like their names: Licksand, Thinfare, and Wormson.

Not that it made much difference to him. People all screamed pretty much the same.

The first village he simply firebombed from the sky. With a group of attack 'thopters, his men swooped low and dropped incendiaries into dwell-ings, schools, and central markets. Many people died at once, while the remainder ran about like furious insects on a hot rock. One man even had the audacity to shoot up at them with an antique maula pistol. Rabban's sidegunners used the vil-lagers for target practice.

The devastation was swift and complete, but Rabban found it ultimately unsatisfying. He decided to take more time with the other towns. . . .

❦

ALONE IN HIS quarters at the Carthag Residency, Rabban had worked long hours before the raids to compose a terse proclamation explaining why these people must all be killed and their villages destroyed in retaliation for Fremen crimes. Upon showing his handiwork proudly to his uncle, however, the Baron scowled and tore up the note, then wrote a proclamation of his own, using many of the same words and phrases.

After each attack, those leaflets (printed on flameproof *instroy* paper) were scattered among the smoldering remains of the obliterated village. Other Fremen would descend like vultures upon the ruins, no doubt trying to pick cheap jewelry from the charred bones. Thus, they would learn why the Baron had decreed such brutal punishment. They would feel the blame. . . .

❦

FOR THE SECOND village, Thinfare, Rabban marched in with ground troops. They all wore shields and carried hand weapons. A few held back with flamecannons in case they needed to finish the massacre in a hurry, but the Harkonnen troops fell upon the hapless villagers with swords and daggers, slashing right and left. Beast Rabban joined in the slaughter with a broad grin on his face.

Back on Giedi Prime, in the giant prison city of Barony, Rabban had often trained children to become victims of the hunt. He had selected the most resourceful and most determined boys to become his special prey during amusing outings at the isolated Forest Guard Station.

He didn't necessarily find that murdering children was more satisfying than killing adults, who were often far more creative and more earnest in groveling for their lives.

Children didn't have sufficient imagination to comprehend the fate they were about to suffer, and rarely showed enough genuine fear. Also, many children had an innocent faith in God, a naive belief in a protector who would save them. They believed and they prayed up to the last moments of their lives.

In the village environment, however, Rabban discovered a new technique with children that gave him more pleasure. It was emotionally satisfying, igniting a warm flame in his heart. He liked to watch the faces of anguished parents as he tortured and then slew their own children in front of them. . . .

In the third village, Wormson, Rabban discovered that he could increase his victims' abject terror by distributing the Baron's dire proclamation *prior to* his attack. That way, the captives knew exactly what lay in store for them before the shooting began.

At times like these, Beast Rabban was proud to be a Harkonnen.

T he guildsman lay retching on a makeshift bed, writhing in pain, his face contorted. *Poisoned by spice.*

Four Junction Specialists stood around the patient, consulting with each other, but none had any idea how to treat him. He thrashed and spat, his face greasy with perspiration.

They had placed the seriously ill Heighliner Coordinator in a sterile room that served more as a medical laboratory than a hospital. High-level Guild workers consumed so much melange that they rarely had any need for doctors, and thus their available hospital facilities were minimal. Even if the Spacing Guild had bothered to summon a Suk practitioner, though, the doctor would probably have been incapable of treating any human with a metabolism as distorted as this one's.

"Questions but no data," one of the four Specialists said. "Does anyone understand what happened here?"

"His body reacted to melange," said another man who had patches of blue hair on his head and bushy eyebrows that nearly covered his eyes.

"Why would a Guildsman suddenly find his daily melange incompatible with his metabolism? That is absurd," said a third. Though they all looked different, the Specialists sounded identical, as if a four-part entity were conversing with itself.

On the bed, the victim shuddered with a particularly violent convulsion. The Specialists paused, then looked at each other.

Lights flashed to indicate an incoming file, and a screen on the research room wall lit up with a new summary analysis. One Specialist scanned down the information. "Verified. The melange itself was tainted." He scrolled down. "The spice he consumed is chemically incorrect, and his biochemistry rejected it."

"How can melange become *tainted*? Was this an intentional poisoning?"

The Specialists consulted each other, studied more information. Around them, lights shone bright and harsh, reflecting off the sterile white walls and making them look like pale ghosts. The four stood at a distance, watching the Heighliner Coordinator struggle and writhe. He seemed unaware of the presence of anyone in the room with him.

"Will he live?" one asked.

"Who can say?"

"This may be the second incident," the blue-haired Specialist said. "We know the Navigator aboard the recently lost Heighliner suffered from tainted spice gas, too."

"Interrogation of the passengers is still proceeding. News of the problem is not yet general knowledge in the Imperium."

"It is the *third* incident," corrected another Specialist. "This also explains the crash on Wallach IX. There must be a serious deficiency with melange in the Imperium."

"But we have found no common source of the problem. This man ate a significant amount of spice that was traced back to a merchant on Beakkal. The Prime Magistrate may have been disposing of his illegal hoard, because of the

Emperor's ultimatums. The two Navigators, however, got their spice from *different* sources, standard Guild stockpiles."

"We have a mystery here."

"The spice must flow."

"All melange harvesting and processing is under the Emperor's control. We need to enlist the aid of House Corrino."

In grim unison, the Specialists turned to the broad, filtered window and stared out toward the bleak Navigator's Field. There, a mechanical crane was erecting a commemorative plaque to honor the two dead Guild Navigators from the recent Heighliner accidents. Another Navigator in a sealed tank flew over the Field, heading for his departure on a long Heighliner run. The meditating Navigator hovered over the expanse of nameless plaques and communed with the ancient heart of the Spacing Guild, the Oracle of Infinity.

On the hospital bed, the poisoned Guildsman screamed so loudly that blood sprayed from his mouth. Convulsions stretched him like a torture victim on a medieval rack. Standing beside his bed, the four Specialists heard muscles break, vertebrae snap . . . and watched him die.

"We must call Shaddam IV," the specialists said in unison. "We have no choice."

The manner in which you ask a question betrays your limits—those answers you will accept, and those you will reject or confuse with misunderstanding.

— KARRBEN FETHR, *The Folly of Imperial Politics*

After the lesson of Zanovar, and then Korona, Shaddam IV felt that matters were finally on a proper course. Now, if only he could find a way to cut off the regular flow of spice from Arrakis, he would have the Imperium in the palm of his hand. . . .

Master Researcher Ajidica had sent another glowing report confirming that his amal had passed all of the rigorous testing protocols. Accompanying the communication was a separate message from Sardaukar Commander Cando Garon, the diligent son of the Supreme Bashar, reaffirming everything Ajidica had said. The Emperor couldn't have asked for better news.

Shaddam wanted the synthetic melange in full production. *Now*. He saw no further reason to wait.

Attired in gray-and-black Sardaukar jodhpurs and a military shirt with epaulets, he sat back at his extravagant desk and stared at a live holo of the Landsraad Council, which continued to hold tedious hearings to explore the legalities of the atomic attack he'd made against Richese. Clearly, though, his opposition did not have enough support for censure or a vote of no confidence. Why couldn't they just give it up?

Count Fenring had been upset ever since returning from Ix and Junction, but the man had worried too much about the Landsraad members. Shaddam wasn't concerned. Everything seemed to be going very well.

In his message, Master Researcher Ajidica had made an odd aside to inquire about the Spice Minister's health. Perhaps Hasimir was feeling too much stress. Maybe he needed to go back to Arrakis. . . .

Looking up, Shaddam saw Chamberlain Ridondo enter the private study in an uncharacteristic state of agitation and nervousness. Ridondo rarely became flustered with any but the most delicate conundrums of Court politics. "Sire, a Spacing Guild emissary insists upon seeing you."

Though annoyed, Shaddam knew he could not turn the emissary away. In matters involving the Guild, even an Emperor had to tread lightly. "Why could he not have arranged an appointment ahead of time? Does the Guild not have access to Imperial Couriers?" He snorted to cover his discomfort at the situation.

"I . . . do not know, Sire. Nevertheless, the envoy is right behind me."

A tall albino man with muttonchop sideburns swept into the office. He did not introduce himself or give his rank. The Guildsman selected a comfortable suspensor chair—when he sat upon it, he appeared even taller, because of the length of his torso—and gazed down at the Emperor.

Shaddam withdrew an elacca wood toothpick from a dispenser and casually began to trace the edges of his teeth. The wood had a naturally sweet flavor. "What is your title, sir? Are you the leader of the Spacing Guild, or someone who scrubs exhaust cowlings? Are you the Premier, the President, the Chief? What do you choose to call yourself? What is your rank?"

"What is the relevance of the question?"

"I am the Emperor of a Million Worlds," Shaddam said,

picking rudely at his teeth. "I wish to know whether I am wasting my time with an underling."

"You are not wasting your time, Sire." The Guildsman's face, narrow at the forehead and wider at the chin, looked as if it had been pounded into this peculiar shape and drained of all color. "It is not yet general knowledge, Sire, but the Guild has recently suffered two major Heighliner disasters. One crashed onto Wallach IX with the loss of all passengers and crew."

Shaddam sat up in surprise. "And . . . was the Bene Gesserit school damaged?"

"No, Sire. The Heighliner crashed into a very remote area."

Shaddam did not hide his disappointment. "You said there were two accidents?"

"Another Heighliner was lost in deep space, but the Navigator managed to bring it back to Junction. Our preliminary analysis suggests that both disasters were caused by tainted spice in the Navigator tanks. Then, a third data point—one of our Guildsmen consumed a large amount of melange traced to Beakkal, which poisoned him. We have confiscated all other remnants of the melange we purchased from Beakkal and it is all similarly tainted. The chemical structure is somewhat peculiar, enough to cause these mishaps."

Shaddam threw his toothpick aside. How would a backwater jungle planet get "spoiled" spice? Unless they were contaminating it themselves? Then he pounced. "Beakkal isn't supposed to have spice to sell. You've found another illegal stockpile? How much?"

"That, Sire, is currently under investigation." The Guildsman passed an entirely white tongue over colorless lips. "While searching for fiscal anomalies, we discovered that the Prime Magistrate of Beakkal has recently *spent* far more melange than his treasury could possibly *own*. He must have a spice hoard."

Shaddam surged with anger, and then anticipation, as he considered another punitive strike. When would the Great Houses ever learn? "Continue your research, sir, and I shall deal with the Beakkal matter in my own way."

In fact, he was looking forward to it.

This time, however, he planned a different response. He considered discussing the idea with Hasimir Fenring first, but decided instead to let it be a surprise. To everyone.

❧

ANIRUL BARELY MADE it to her bed after a pleasant dinner alone with her daughters and Jessica. She had been thinking to herself how much Irulan was blossoming into a beautiful young woman, intelligent and cultured, the perfect Princess . . . and then the universe had gone sour around her.

The voices in Anirul's head had returned, and even the sympathetic presence of Lobia-within could not hold them at bay. Anirul collapsed to her knees, dry heaving, and crawled into her bedchamber. Jessica had walked her to the room, and then in alarm had summoned Medical Sister Yohsa; Margot Fenring and Mohiam also rushed in to help.

After examining Lady Anirul, Yohsa quickly gave her a powerful sedative. Only half-awake, the Kwisatz Mother lay wheezing and perspiring, as if she had run a very long distance. Yohsa looked on, shaking her head. Jessica stood over her, wide-eyed, until Mohiam shooed her out of the room.

"I know her sandworm nightmare has been recurring," Margot Fenring said from the foot of the bed. "Perhaps she thinks she is out in the desert at this very moment."

Mohiam peered with hard eyes at the disturbingly ill woman, who seemed to be fighting sleep, struggling to avoid it. Anirul's eyes alternately opened wide, then grew heavy-lidded.

The Medical Sister said, "I was not able to reduce the

Other Memory flow soon enough. The gates of Anirul's past lives have been thrown open inside her mind. She may be driven to suicide or to some other form of violence. She could even be a threat to any of us. We must watch her closely."

The fundamental rule of the universe is that there is no neutrality, no pure objectivity, no absolute truth that is divorced from the pragmatic lessons gained in application. Before Ix became a great power in the invention and manufacture of technology, scientists routinely concealed their personal prejudices behind a facade of objectivity and purity of research.

— DOMINIC VERNIUS, *The Secret Workings of Ix*

The prime magistrate of Beakkal had made a mistake. A very serious one.

Six months earlier, Tleilaxu researchers—desperate to obtain Atreides and Vernius genetic samples from an ancient war memorial—had paid a bribe with an outrageously large amount of spice that showed up on no official records. It had seemed a good idea at the time, a boon to Beakkal's economy.

After Duke Leto's vengeful attack, the Prime Magistrate began using that spice to pay Beakkali debts. After passing through several hands, some of it found its way to the Spacing Guild . . . and poisoned a Heighliner Coordinator, which triggered an investigation that was reported to the Emperor himself.

When he sent in his Sardaukar fleet, Shaddam did not comprehend the irony that Beakkal no longer had in its possession the melange they were accused of stockpiling. More ironic still, the Prime Magistrate never realized that the

Tleilaxu had not paid him in genuine melange, but had instead given him a cargo of their unproven synthetic spice. . . .

A Heighliner dropped off the Imperial fleet at the transfer-station of Sansin, a nearby asteroid center and the hub of commerce in the Liabic star system, which included Beakkal and its blue primary sun.

Commanded by Supreme Bashar Zum Garon, the heavy warships remained at the transfer station: battle cruisers, monitors, crushers, and troop-carriers, all set to proceed toward Beakkal in a blistering display of power. Shaddam had ordered the Sardaukar to make their intentions obvious first . . . and to take their time.

When the jungle world's defensive satellite network detected their approach, planetary alarms went off. The Beakkali people panicked; many took to underground shelters, while others fled into the forest depths.

In a futile effort, the Prime Magistrate ordered his private military force to launch warships, and form a defensive network in orbit. The ships lifted off, hastily crewed with available personnel. Additional troops scrambled to their planetary garrisons, preparing a second wave of defense. Long-stored weapons were retrieved, uniforms thrown on.

"We were caught unawares when Duke Leto Atreides attacked us," the Prime Magistrate said in a public announcement. "We have seen how Emperor Shaddam laid waste to Zanovar and destroyed the Richesian moon." He sensed the fear of his people. "But *we* will not stand by meekly and allow ourselves to be slaughtered! Perhaps our world cannot withstand a full Sardaukar assault—but we will make them pay dearly for it."

Still stationed at Sansin, the Imperial fleet moved with ominous deliberation. In a typically brief statement, the Supreme Bashar broadcast, "By order of Emperor Shaddam IV, this planet is hereby placed under siege for the crime of stockpiling melange. This blockade will remain in force until such time as your fief holder confesses to his crimes, or proves his innocence." He transmitted no further warning, no ultimatum.

The lumbering Sardaukar fleet gave the targeted population more than a day to grow increasingly frightened. During that time, the Prime Magistrate delivered five speeches, some of them indignant, others pleading for mercy from the wrath of Shaddam.

❦

BEHIND BARRICADED DOORS, the Beakkali leader and his council of ministers met to discuss the problem. A stocky man with a red mustache and a lush, blond beard, the Prime Magistrate sat in the elevated center cutout of a round conference table, with the ministers arrayed around him. Attired in the dark green toga of his office, he rotated his chair so that he could look at whoever was talking, but most of the time he just stared off into space. An impending sense of doom hung over him.

The ministers wore tight trousers and white tunics with rune symbols on the collars, reflecting their rank and public identity. "But we don't have a melange stockpile! It's all gone," said one minister, a woman with a raspy voice. "We have been . . . accused, but the Emperor can't prove we were ever hoarding. What is his evidence?"

"What difference does it make?" another said. "He *knows* what we did. Besides, we should have paid taxes to the Emperor. A bribe is still income, you know."

The ministers argued around the table, voices high-pitched with emotion. "If House Corrino is really after taxes, can't we just figure the value of the melange and offer to pay a large fine? In installments, of course."

"But the edicts against spice stockpiling encompass more than tax avoidance. They go to the core of cooperation between the Great and Minor Houses, preventing any House from becoming too independent from the others, too dangerous to the stability of CHOAM."

"As soon as the Sardaukar establish a cordon, they will trap us here and starve us out. Our world is not self-sufficient."

Smelling the sweat of his fear, the bleary-eyed Prime Magistrate looked at a tracking screen that showed the position of the approaching Imperial fleet.

"Sir, two big supply ships just arrived at the Sansin transfer station, fully loaded with foodstuffs," reported a minister behind him. "Perhaps we should commandeer them. They belong to a rather obscure House Minor, nothing to worry about. It could be our last chance for a long time."

"Do it," the Prime Magistrate said, rising to signify the end of the meeting. "That's something, anyway. Now let's see what we can do to find more good fortune."

JUST BEFORE THE arrival of the menacing fleet, Beakkali troops boarded and confiscated the two loaded supply ships at the asteroid transfer station, taking them like a pair of fat plums just waiting to be picked.

When the Sardaukar forces subsequently went into orbit around Beakkal, they did not engage the local defense forces. Instead, the Supreme Bashar instructed his ships to maintain their distance as ominous guardians that would refuse to grant any vessel access to Beakkal or to the nearby asteroids.

A man of emotional ups and downs, the Prime Magistrate was energized by the success of the operation. "We can wait them out," he declared in yet another speech, this one on an outdoor acoustics stage. In his usual green toga, he had shaved his beard as a symbol of austerity. "We have supplies, we have workers, and we have our own resources. We have been falsely accused!"

The gathered crowd cheered, but with an undertone of extreme anxiety.

"The Emperor will be long in his tomb before we surrender." The Beakkali leader raised a fist in the air, and his people clapped in support.

Overhead, the Sardaukar forces settled in to wait, a noose tightening around the planetary equator.

Error, accident, and chaos are persistent principles of the universe.

— Imperial Historical Annals

We haven't played shield-ball in years, Hasimir," Shaddam said as he leaned over the device, pleased that his score was one point higher than Fenring's. They were in the Emperor's private quarters, on the top level of the Imperial Palace.

Distracted, the Count moved away from the gaming table and went to the balcony. In years past, he and Shaddam had developed numerous schemes together, many of them plotted during shield-ball competitions . . . such as the original idea for creating a spice substitute. Now, knowing the treachery of the Tleilaxu Master Researcher and his murderous Face Dancer, Fenring regretted the entire plot. The Heighliner tests, too, seemed a total disaster.

But the Emperor wanted to hear none of it. "You're imagining things," he said. "I have received a report from the Guild itself, and they have discovered tainted spice originating from an illegal stockpile on Beakkal. They are convinced this insidious poisoning is the cause of the recent accidents. Not your amal."

"But we cannot be sure, Sire, hmmm? The Guild will not release the designations of the lost Heighliners. I find it suspicious that two large vessels experienced traumatic mishaps after I—"

"What connection could there possibly be between Beakkal and Ajidica's amal research?" He sounded exasperated. "None!" The Master Researcher's glowing reports, along with the repeated reassurances of Commander Cando Garon, had him completely convinced about the impending availability of synthetic spice. "Have you, personally, in all your inspections of the Tleilaxu work, ever seen specific evidence that the amal does not work as Ajidica claims?"

"Not . . . as such, Sire."

"Then stop looking for excuses, Hasimir, and let me play." The game mechanism buzzed, and the Emperor withdrew a guiding rod. The hard ball bounced and crackled through the elaborate labyrinth of components. Shaddam scored again and laughed. "There, I challenge you to beat that."

Fenring's eyes flashed. "You've been practicing, Shaddam, hmmm? Not enough Imperial matters to occupy you?"

"Now, Hasimir, don't be a sore loser."

"I haven't lost yet, Sire."

Overhead, the night skies of Kaitain shimmered with pastel auroras. The Padishah Emperor had recently ordered the launch of satellites containing rare gases that were ionized by particles from the solar wind, enhancing the colors that rippled across the constellations. He liked to light up the sky.

Fenring returned to the shield-ball device. "I am pleased that you chose not to crush Beakkal like Zanovar. A siege is much more appropriate, since the evidence was not exactly, hmmm-ah, *compelling* enough for a more emphatic response. In all likelihood, Beakkal has already spent their hoard on other things."

"The evidence is sufficient, especially when you consider the contamination that likely caused the Heighliner accidents." Shaddam gestured toward the game device, but Fenring still did not take his turn. "Just because they've spent their entire illegal stockpile doesn't mean they didn't flaut Imperial restrictions in the first place."

"Hmmm, but if you retrieve no large reward of melange, you can't bribe CHOAM and the Guild to support your policies. Not a good investment of violence, hmmm?"

Now Shaddam smiled. "Now you see why I've had to be much more subtle in this case."

Fenring's eyes widened in concern, but he refrained from commenting on Shaddam's skill at subtlety. "How long is this blockade going to go on? You've made your point, scared them down to their bones. What more do you need?"

"Ah, Hasimir, watch and learn." Shaddam paced around the table like an excited little boy. "Soon it will become obvious that the blockade is imperative. I am not doing this simply to prevent House Beakkal from obtaining outside supplies. No, there's much more to it. I won't destroy their world—I'll let them do it themselves."

Fenring grew more alarmed. "Perhaps, ahhh, you should have consulted me before setting your plans in motion, Sire?"

"I can make magnificent plans of my own, without your help."

Though Fenring disagreed with that assessment, he decided not to argue. Pensively, he turned to the game, dropped another ball into play, manipulated the rods with deft fingers, and intentionally achieved a low score. Now was not the time to demonstrate his superior abilities to the Emperor.

With mounting excitement, Shaddam continued, "You see, when my Sardaukar informed Beakkal of the imminent siege, the Prime Magistrate sent ships scrambling to Sansin in order to stockpile foodstuffs. Like a pirate, he commandeered two fully loaded supply ships that were just waiting there. As I knew he would."

"Yes, yes." Fenring tapped his fingers on the table, surprised that Shaddam didn't jump back to the game and take his own turn. "And your ships stood by and let him gather sufficient cargo to last Beakkal for perhaps six months. A rather inept way to administer a siege, hmmm?"

"He fell into my trap," Shaddam said. "The Prime Magistrate will begin to realize the real plan soon enough. Ah, yes. Quite soon."

Fenring sat back, waiting.

"Unfortunately, the two supply ships he stole were loaded with contaminated grains and dehydrates. Tit for tat, considering what they did to the spice they sold to the Guild."

Fenring blinked. "Contaminated? With what?"

"Why, with a terrible biological agent that I just happened to be sending for study under controlled conditions to a distant planet. For security reasons the plague-infested supplies were unmarked and placed in nondescript vessels so that they could be transported without causing alarm."

Fenring's skin crawled, but Shaddam fairly gushed with pride at his cleverness. "Now that the Prime Magistrate has *stolen* this cargo and taken it to Beakkal, he has brought with him a biological agent that will defoliate the jungle belt. Crops will wither and die, forests will fall into skeletons. Within days we will begin to see the effects. Tsk, tsk. Such a tragedy."

Fenring had thought the use of atomics on Korona and the unexpected blinding of so many Richesians already went far beyond the pale. Even by his standards, it was all too much. An entire planetary ecosystem! "I don't suppose this decision can be reversed?"

"No. And luckily my Sardaukar cordon just happens to be there, and can enforce a strict quarantine. We can't afford to spread this unfortunate plague to innocent planets, now can we?" Shaddam let out a long, vicious laugh. "See, I've outsmarted even you, Hasimir."

Fenring suppressed a groan. The Emperor seemed to be gaining momentum, but in the wrong direction.

RICHESIAN PREMIER EIN Calimar watched Duke Leto's relief ships land at the Triad Center Spaceport, bringing much-needed aid for the victims of the Korona explosion. He had thought he was beyond weeping.

The Atreides crews provided shipments of expensive medicinals, as well as fish products and pundi rice. Richese was not a poor world, but the destruction of the laboratory moon—not to mention the obliteration of the secret Holtzmann invisibility project and most of their stock of mirrors—was a monumental setback to their economy.

Old Count Richese, surrounded by his tribe of children and grandchildren, went to the visitor's gallery of the spaceport for the ceremonial function of greeting the supply ship crews. Four of his daughters and one grandson had been blinded in the falling rain of activated Richesian mirrors, and his nephew Haloa Rund had been killed on Korona itself. As members of the noble family of Richese, they would be among the first to receive help.

The Count was resplendent in thick robes of state, his chest weighted by dozens of medals (many of them handmade trinkets from his family). The old man raised both hands. "It is with deepest gratitude that we accept this assistance from my grandson Duke Leto Atreides. He is a fine nobleman, with a good heart. His mother always said so." Ilban's face creased with a maudlin smile of gratitude, and tears sparkled in his grief-reddened eyes.

Within hours, prefabricated distribution centers were set up, interlocked tentments built in court areas around Triad Center. Atreides soldiers worked to keep the crowds in line and performed triage to find the patients who needed help the most. From a rooftop garden spot where he would not be interrupted, Premier Calimar observed it all, avoiding contact with the relief forces.

Duke Leto was doing his best, and would be commended

for it. But as far as Calimar was concerned, the Atreides had come too late to be treated as true saviors. The Tleilaxu had arrived first.

Very soon after the crowds had been burned and blinded by the debris, Tleilaxu organ merchants had descended on Richese, bringing shipments of artificial eyes. Though clearly opportunistic, the genetic wizards had been welcomed nonetheless, for they offered more than hope, more than consolation. They brought tangible cures.

Out of habit, Calimar pushed his gold spectacles up on his nose. He no longer needed the glasses, but their presence comforted him. He stared across the spaceport landing field to where Atreides troops unloaded supplies. He didn't blink, merely drank in the details with his new metal Tleilaxu eyes. . . .

There is much of ruin in everyday life. Even so, we need to see beyond the wreckage to the magnificence that once was.

— LADY SHANDO VERNIUS

Concealed with his men in the cool crevices of a rock formation, Liet-Kynes watched a flat salt pan through binoculars. Heat and bright light rippled off the powdery gypsum, creating mirages. He handed the binoculars to the Fremen beside him, then peered into the distance with his bare eyes.

At precisely the appointed time, a black ornithopter swooped out of the sky, flying so high they could not hear the whir of articulated wings until the last moment. The vessel landed in a cloud of stirred dust and sand. This time the vehicle had no egregious sandworm painted on the front.

Liet smiled tightly. *Ailric has decided the Guild will play no more games. At least, not the obvious ones.*

The 'thopter engines whined to a stop, and Liet's sharp eyes detected nothing out of the ordinary. He glanced at the desert men with him, and they all nodded.

After the front of the 'thopter folded open and the ramp thumped onto the hard ground, Liet led his men out of concealment. They strode forward, brushing dust from their stillsuits and straightening

422 *Brian Herbert and Kevin J. Anderson*

their camouflaged robes. As before, four Fremen carried a heavy litter of spice, melange that had been processed and condensed from the *ghanima*, or spoils of war, captured during the raid on the Harkonnen stockpile at Bilar Camp.

They had met the Guild's outrageous demands.

This time when the wheeled vehicle rolled down the ramp, the deformed representative wore a modified stillsuit—one that was of poor workmanship and not well fitted. The bottom of Ailric's slick gray suit was loose, wrapped around his fused mass of lower-body flesh.

The Guildsman didn't realize how ludicrous he looked in the outfit. Rolling closer to the Fremen, he acted as if he were an experienced man of the desert. Opening his face mask with a flourish, Ailric remarked in his synthesized voice, "I have been ordered to remain here on Arrakis for a time, since Heighliner travel has become increasingly . . . uncertain."

Liet did not respond; Fremen tended to avoid pointless banter. Ailric shifted to a stiffer, more formal position. "I did not expect to see you again, half-Fremen. I thought you would choose a pureblood desert man to act as intermediary from now on."

Liet smiled. "Perhaps I should take your water for my tribe, and let the Guild send another representative. One who does not tire me with insults."

The Guildsman's alien gaze focused on the litter, which the Fremen bearers set down on the sand near the ornithopter. "You have it all?"

"Every gram you specified."

Ailric rolled his vehicle closer. "Tell me, half-Fremen, how is it that simple desert people can afford so much?"

Liet-Kynes would never tell an off-worlder that the Fremen harvested melange themselves and also stole from the Harkonnen overlords. "Call it a blessing from Shai-Hulud."

The Guildsman's laugh was a tinny reverberation from the voice box. *These Fremen must possess hidden resources that we have never suspected.* "And how will you come up with the payment next time?"

"Shai-Hulud will provide. He always does." Knowing the Guild didn't want to lose his lucrative business, he pushed back a little. "Be warned that we will tolerate no further increases in the bribe."

"We are satisfied with the current arrangement, half-Fremen."

Liet rubbed his chin thoughtfully. "Good. Then I will tell you something of great importance to the Spacing Guild, and it will cost you nothing. You may use the information as you wish."

The rectangular pupils in the Guildsman's eyes glistened with curiosity and anticipation.

Liet paused to build suspense. In a misguided attempt to harm the Fremen, Beast Rabban had obliterated three squalid villages on the fringe of the Shield Wall. Though Fremen often looked with disdain upon the peoples of the pan and graben, men of honor could not tolerate such outrages. The victims had not been Fremen, but they were innocents. Liet-Kynes, Abu Naib of all the desert tribes, would set in motion a particular revenge against the Baron.

With the assistance of the Spacing Guild.

Knowing how Ailric would react, he announced, "The Harkonnens have amassed several large spice stockpiles on Arrakis. The Emperor knows nothing of them, nor does the Guild."

Ailric took a quick, hissing breath. "That *is* interesting. And how does the Baron obtain this spice? We monitor his exports closely. We know precisely how much melange the Harkonnen crews harvest, and how much is shipped off-planet. CHOAM has reported no discrepancies."

Kynes gave him a taunting smile. "Then the Harkonnens must be smarter than the Guild or CHOAM."

Ailric snapped, "And where are these stockpiles? We must report them immediately."

"The Harkonnens move the locations frequently, to

confuse searchers. Nevertheless, such stockpiles could be found with a little effort."

Under the pounding desert sun, the Guildsman considered this for a long moment. All spice came from Arrakis. What if the Harkonnens were the source of the contamination that had caused two Heighliner accidents and poisoned several Guildsmen on Junction? "We shall look into the matter."

Though he had never been pleasant, Ailric was even edgier than usual. He watched his men load the rich spice payment into the black ornithopter, knowing that the sheer value of this treasure made even extreme risks acceptable. He would test this melange carefully, certify its purity. Ailric's commission from handling the enormous Fremen bribe was worth the unpleasantness of staying in a hellish place such as this.

Liet-Kynes did not bother with further conversation. Abruptly, he turned and left. His men flowed over the sand behind him.

There are those who envy their lords, those who long for positions of power, memberships in the Landsraad, ready access to melange. Such people do not understand how difficult a task it can be for a ruler to make simple decisions.

— EMPEROR SHADDAM CORRINO IV, autobiography (unfinished)

In all his years of service to House Atreides, Thufir Hawat had rarely looked so troubled. The Mentat glanced from side to side at the servants and cooks going about their afternoon tasks. "This is a deeply serious situation, my Duke. Perhaps we should find a more private place in which to discuss these matters of strategy?"

Leto paused in the warm clutter of Castle Caladan's kitchens, breathing in the mingled odors of spices, rising bread, simmering sauces, and other foods in various stages of preparation. A roaring fire in a stone fireplace drove away even the damp chill with its cheery orange glow. "Thufir, if I have to worry about Harkonnen spies in my own kitchens, then we shouldn't eat any of the food."

The master chefs and bakers worked in short-sleeved tunics, aprons cinched around their generous waists as they concentrated on the evening's meal, oblivious to the war council meeting in their midst.

Frowning, the Mentat nodded, as if Leto had

made a serious proposal. "My Duke, I have long advocated that you use a personal poison snooper over each dish."

As usual, Leto waved away the suggestion. He stopped at a long metal table framed by narrow drainage gutters where young apprentice cooks cleaned a dozen fat butterfish that had been brought up from the docks that morning. Leto gave the fish a cursory inspection, nodded his approval. He watched one young woman as she sorted through fresh mushrooms and herbs. She gave him a shy, flirtatious smile, and when he offered her a slight grin in return, she blushed furiously and went back to her duties.

Duncan Idaho followed the two men. "We do need to consider all possibilities in the overall plan, Leto. If we make the wrong choice, we doom our people to certain death."

Looking at his Mentat and Swordmaster, Leto's gray eyes grew hard and flinty. "Then we must not make the wrong choice. Has our Courier returned from Junction yet? Do we have any further information?"

Duncan shook his head. "All we can say for certain is that the Heighliner carrying Gurney and Prince Rhombur was misrouted somehow, for a time, but later returned to the Guild stronghold. All passengers disembarked and were held for questioning. The Guild is not saying whether all of them have now been sent to their scheduled destinations."

Hawat made a gruff sound deep in his throat. "So they could still be stranded on Junction, even though we expected them to reach Ix more than a month ago. At the very least, Gurney and Rhombur were delayed. Already, the plan is not as we expected."

"Plans rarely are, Thufir," Leto said. "But if we quit every time one went awry, we'd never accomplish anything."

Duncan smiled. "A Swordmaster teacher said a very similar thing to me on Ginaz."

Thufir pursed his sapho-stained lips. "True, but we cannot rely on platitudes. Too many lives are at stake. We must make the right decision."

Bakers braided loaves of fresh dough with care, buttered the surfaces, and added bitterseeds one at a time, as if setting jewels in a royal crown. Leto doubted the workers were paying special care because he happened to be there; they always put forth a meticulous effort.

With Jessica, Rhombur, and Gurney away, Leto considered it necessary to grasp some semblance of a normal life. He had busied himself by spending extra hours in the courtyard meeting with his subjects, concentrating on his ducal duties, even sending help to Richese for the victims there. Despite the grand and secret schemes that were even now drawing like a knot around the Imperium, he tried to reassure all of his Castle staff that the normally serene life on Caladan would continue.

"Let us consider the scenarios, my Duke," the Mentat said. He did not add his opinion at the moment; that would come during the arguments later. "Suppose Rhombur and Gurney do not reach Ix, and they are unable to stir the internal revolution as we had hoped. In that case, if the Atreides troops prematurely engage in a frontal attack, none of the Tleilaxu defenses would be weakened, and our men could be slaughtered."

Leto nodded. "Don't you think I know that, Thufir?"

"On the other hand, what if we delay our response? Rhombur and Gurney might even now be rallying the oppressed people. Knowing the exact timetable for our arrival, suppose the Ixians rise up and attempt to overthrow the invaders, expecting our reinforcements . . . but House Atreides troops do not arrive as we've promised?"

Duncan looked agitated. "Then they will be massacred— and so will Rhombur and Gurney. We can't just abandon them, Leto."

Deep in thought, the Duke studied both of his advisors. His loyal men would follow him on whatever path he chose. But how to make such a choice? He watched a matronly chef preparing a fine custard confection in a nest of flaky crust; it had been one of Rhombur's favorite desserts, back when he had all of his natural bodily functions. The sight of the pastry brought a sudden tear to Leto's eye, and he turned back, knowing his answer.

Leto said, "My father taught me this: Whenever I find myself faced with a difficult choice, I must follow the course of *honor*, setting aside all other considerations."

He stood motionless, staring at the diligent workers in the Castle kitchens. A lot was riding on this decision. But for an Atreides Duke, there was, after all, no real alternative. "I have made my promises to Prince Rhombur, and therefore to the people of Ix. I am bound to go through with this plan. And so we must do everything in our power to assure that we succeed."

He turned and led the Swordmaster and the Mentat out of the kitchens, back to where they could continue their work.

Survival demands vigor and fitness, and an under-standing of limitations. You must learn what your world asks of you, what it needs of you. Each organism plays its part in keeping the ecosystem operational. Each has its niche.

— IMPERIAL PLANETOLOGIST LIET-KYNES

Though it was the primary headquarters of the Spacing Guild, Junction was not a world where any visitor would choose to live.

"I don't know how much more of this waiting I can take," Rhombur groused. "I want to be on Ix!"

Restricted to a passenger-recreation area that was far from the majestic Heighliner yards and maintenance docks, he and Gurney Halleck walked along a barren blakgras field. Rhombur thought it must be the site of an out-of-session Navigator school, but no one would answer any questions. The midday sun cast dim, murky light.

Despite repeated pleas and attempted bribes, the two would-be infiltrators had been unable to send a message to Caladan. The Guild had completely isolated all passengers from the lost Heighliner, kept them prisoners here on Junction, as if trying to bottle the news of the troubled ship and the dead Navigator. In all likelihood, Duke Leto knew nothing about it. By now, he must assume that both of his operatives were inside Ix, already rallying the disenchanted populace. House Atreides was counting on them.

But unless Rhombur could accomplish something soon, that assumption could be a serious danger to Atreides forces.

With his mental turmoil, the cyborg Prince's stride was jerky. Gurney could hear the clicking of the mechanical parts. Hundreds of other passengers from the rescued Heighliner milled about on the blackgras grounds; now that they were safe, the stranded travelers grumbled with a steady stream of complaints, infuriated at the inconvenience. Junction was escape-proof: They could not get off the planet until the Guild took them.

" 'One comes to know God only through patience,' " Gurney quoted, a passage his mother used to read from the Orange Catholic Bible. "They have no reason to hold us much longer. The investigation must be almost concluded."

"What do they expect to learn from isolated passengers? Why won't they let us contact Leto? Damn them!" Rhombur lowered his voice.

"If you could send a message, would you tell the Duke to delay the strike?" he asked, already knowing Rhombur's answer.

"Never, Gurney. *Never.*" He stared across the bleak field. "But I do want to be there when it happens. We have to make this work."

Though the Prince had been an unacknowledged hero of the Heighliner disaster, Guild representatives now treated the two men as ordinary, waylaid human cargo, to be transferred to another ship that would take them to their previously guaranteed destination (presumably with their camouflaged combat pod intact). For a full month they had been held on the austere world, interrogated about every event, every moment, on the lost Heighliner. The Guild seemed very concerned about the origin of the poisoned melange, but Rhombur and Gurney had no more answers to give.

As a small display of protest, the two men refused to shave; Gurney's beard was pale and patchy over his inkvine scar, while the Ixian Prince's was thicker and a little longer on the fleshy side of his face, which gave him bragging rights.

The gray, bulge-shaped building that housed the visitors contained a curious mixture of metal-barred cells, offices, and studio apartments. Surveillance comeyes were everywhere in various states of concealment. Guildsmen watched the passengers constantly.

All of the buildings in this zone looked ancient, showing evidence of numerous repairs and alterations. With no ornamentation whatsoever, the structures were designed for function and practicality.

Through hidden speakers, a droning voice seemed to come from everywhere at once. "All passengers are hereby released. Proceed to the central processing terminal to arrange for transport to your original destination." After a pause, the voice added an afterthought, as if from a script, "We are sorry to have inconvenienced you."

"I'll make certain our combat pod gets loaded, if I have to carry it on my own shoulders," Gurney said.

"I might be better equipped for such labors, my friend— if it comes to that." Rhombur took powerful mechanical strides toward the central processing terminal, ready to go back home, back to the battleground, at last.

The War for Ix was about to begin.

For weeks, C'tair Pilru and the disguised Bene Gesserit Cristane worked together in the dark underground passages of Ix. The wiry, androgynous Sister's intensity and determination were matched only by C'tair's vehement hatred of the Tleilaxu.

Drawing upon skills learned during decades of hiding and preying on the Tleilaxu, C'tair taught her to navigate the back routes for shelter and food. He knew how to disappear into labyrinthine alleys where neither the Tleilaxu nor the Sardaukar ventured.

For her part, Cristane was a fast learner and deadly with her hands. Though her mission was to obtain information on Tleilaxu research activities—especially any mention of the mysterious Project Amal and how it might relate to spice—she relished the opportunity to aid C'tair in creating mayhem for its own sake.

"You saw something in the research pavilion," she said. "I must get inside there and find out what experiments the Tleilaxu are performing. That is my assignment."

In a dim tunnel one evening, they had captured one of the invaders to find out what was taking place inside the sealed laboratory complex. But even with the harshest and most sophisticated Bene Gesserit interrogation techniques, the captive had revealed nothing . . . probably because he didn't know. Efficiently, Cristane had killed him in disgust.

Later, C'tair killed a lab bureaucrat himself. He wondered if he and his new comrade should start keeping score. With her help, and the knowledge that Prince Rhombur was on his way at last, C'tair showed little restraint. The flames of his vengeance burned brightly.

He knew, too, that his brother D'murr was dead.

Cristane had told him of the Heighliner disaster over Wallach IX, as well as the second ship that had disappeared into uncharted space. With a shudder, he recalled his Navigator brother's strange last contact, D'murr's inhuman cry of anguish and despair—and then nothing. By the leaden feeling in his heart, he had already sensed the loss of his twin. . . .

One night, lying in one of his shielded bolt-holes, C'tair stirred fitfully on the thin sleeping pallet, unable to sleep, grieving for everyone and everything he had lost.

Cristane, breathing deeply on an adjacent bed, seemed to be in a meditative sleep. Suddenly he heard her voice in the darkness. "Bene Gesserits are trained not to show emotion, but I recognize your suffering, C'tair. We have endured losses, each of us." Her words filled the shadows between them.

"I was a child on Hagal, orphaned in many ways. My stepfather abused me, damaged me . . . and the Sisterhood spent many years healing my wounds, toughening my scars, making me into what I am." Her voice sounded strained; she had never spoken of such things to a man before. Cristane didn't really know why, but for once in her life, she wanted someone to *know* her.

When he moved over onto her bed, she allowed him to put an arm around her rigid shoulders. He wasn't sure of his own intentions, but it had been so long since he had let down his guard, even for a moment. Cristane grew quiet. Her skin was softly sensual, but he tried not to think about it. She could have seduced him easily, but she did not.

"If we find a way into the research pavilion, is there a chance we could help Miral?" he asked in the quiet darkness. "If only to end her suffering?"

"Yes . . . provided I can get inside."

She gave him a brief, dry kiss, but his mind was already on Miral and the ephemeral relationship they had shared before she was taken so cruelly from him. . . .

FURTIVELY, THE COMMANDO Sister paused before the protected doorway. Beyond the bioscanner barriers lay the large central gallery of the lab complex, with its high, catwalk-laced ceiling and sprawling rows of tanks on the floor. If she succeeded in infiltrating the research pavilion, Cristane knew she would probably have to kill the captive Bene Gesserit Sister to free her from any misery she might be suffering.

C'tair had dressed Cristane in stolen Tleilaxu clothes and treated her face and hands with harsh chemicals to make her appear like the gray-skinned men. "There, now you look as awful as they do." Fortunately, no one she encountered in the corridors asked her any direct questions; she could duplicate their guttural accents, but knew only a few words in their secret language.

Concentrating, employing the most sophisticated Bene Gesserit skills, Cristane adjusted her internal body chemistry so that the crude bioscanner would identify her as a Tleilaxu. Taking a deep breath, she stepped into the orange static of the energy field, attempting to get inside to the laboratory floor.

Her skin tingled as cellular probes examined her. Presently, she felt a release and stepped through. With rapid and efficient steps, she made her way toward one side. Her eyes drank in the horrific details of strange tank enclosures, experiments the Tleilaxu were performing on female bodies. The air was heavy with the reek of soured melange wafting up from brutalized flesh.

Suddenly, an alarm roared through the walls. The bioscanner doorway behind her flickered bright orange. Cristane had confused the unit long enough to pass through, but now she was trapped inside the lab.

Running as fast as she could, looking from one slack female face to another, Cristane finally found the bloated form, the gruesome remnants of Miral Alechem. She heard excited Tleilaxu voices behind her—thin, squealing shouts— and the patter of slippered footsteps. She also heard the heavier footfalls of Sardaukar boots and shouted military commands.

"Forgive me, my Sister." Cristane thrust an explosive wafer beneath one of Miral's shoulder blades, hiding it between the tubes and pump-lines that kept her alive. Then the Bene Gesserit commando dodged between flaccid axlotl tanks, reached another aisle and ran as fast as she could.

So many women, so many spiritless faces. . . .

Sardaukar guards blocked her way. Cristane fled in another direction, dropping a few more explosive wafers with brief detonation delays. She knew it was only a hopeless stalling tactic. She steeled herself for a fight to the death, even against Sardaukar. She might be able to kill a few of them.

C'tair would have been proud of her.

A stunner caught Cristane in the spine, spinning her around, making her nerves crackle. She tumbled onto her back, fell hard, and couldn't move. . . .

As the Emperor's soldiers closed in, an explosion ripped the air, vaporizing Miral Alechem and destroying a whole section of axlotl tanks around her. While fires raged and the smoke thickened, fire-suppression systems dumped dry chemicals into the air like a sinister fog. Paralyzed, Cristane couldn't see more than a tiny field of view.

The dark, rodent eyes of a Tleilaxu Master peered down at her. He shook with rage. "You ruined my best axlotl tank, the one I need the most." Cristane had been trained by the Sisterhood, enough to understand parts of their guttural private language. The tonalities, the expressions on their grayish faces, filled in the details she did not know.

"Four tanks were destroyed, Master Ajidica," another Tleilaxu man said in a whining voice.

Cristane shuddered, incapable of speaking. At least she had freed her Sister and several other women from their degradation.

Leaning close to examine the prisoner, the Master touched Cristane's treated skin. "You are not one of us."

Guards tore her clothing, revealing Cristane's slender, pale-skinned form. "A female!" Ajidica ran his fingers over her compact breasts as he contemplated putting her in immediate pain for what she had done to his special axlotl tank, the only one that had produced ajidamal on its own. But by now he had others.

"A strong female of childbearing age, Master Researcher," one of his assistants said. "Shall we hook her up?"

Ajidica thought of the powerful biological agents and personality destroying chemicals he might use. "We must interrogate her first, before we do too much damage to her mind." Leaning close to Cristane, he whispered, "You'll suffer a long time for this."

She felt someone lifting her and moving her. The air reeked of sour spice. While she lay outwardly helpless, she ordered her body to break down the gaseous components in the air of the laboratory and analyze them.

The spice . . . No—not real melange. It is something else. . . .

Strong hands hooked her up to a pumping apparatus on an empty table. She wondered how long she would remain conscious. As a Bene Gesserit, she could resist the drugs and poisons, for a while at least. *Victory on Ix!* She clung to the words C'tair had passed on to her, wishing she might have shouted them aloud, but she could not speak.

Cristane felt herself merging into the diabolocal Tleilaxu mechanism, learning secrets she had never wanted to discover. . . .

Hasimir Fenring's fingers curled into claws
when he thought of the treacherous
Ajidica and his Face Dancer assassin—but before
he could return to Ix, he had to deal with other
disasters here on Kaitain.

Such as cleaning up Shaddam's messes.

The Emperor's private law library contained no
filmbooks, texts, scrolls, or written opinions.
However, with seven Court Mentats and five
lawtechs, Fenring and Shaddam had instant access
to more information than could be found within a
building ten times its size. They had only to sort
through all that data to glean the relevant items.

Looking arrogant and Imperial, Shaddam IV
had posed his question, and now the Mentats
stood eerily silent in front of him, sifting through
the volumes of knowledge in their minds. Their
lips shone from fresh doses of sapho juice; their
eyes gazed into the distance. Lawtechs stood ready
to record any clause or precedent they might cite.

In one corner of the room, a giant alabaster

statue of a twisted sea horse spewed a wide flow of water from its stone mouth. The fountain provided the only noise in the chamber.

Fenring began to pace impatiently in front of the sea horse. "Normally, it is accepted procedure to obtain a legal opinion *before* one does something that might cause an open revolt in the Imperium, hmmm? This time you don't have a reward of melange to give to the Guild and CHOAM."

"We found a loophole for my use of atomics, Hasimir. We'll find a way out of the Beakkal matter as well."

"Oh, so you are not bound by the Great Convention because your plague attacks *plants* instead of *people*, hmmm? Absurd!"

Shaddam looked quickly at his seven Mentats, as if the suggestion might be a genuine possibility. Unanimously, the men shook their heads and continued to ponder in deep Mentat mode.

"Many Houses agree with my position," the Emperor said, pursing his lips. "Beakkal brought this upon themselves, through no direct action of House Corrino. How can you speak of revolt?"

"Are you deaf and blind, Shaddam? There is talk of direct warfare against you, of overthrowing your regime."

"On the floor of the Landsraad Hall?"

"Whispers in the corridors."

"Get me names and I will deal with them." The Emperor drew a deep breath and exhaled it in a long sigh. "If only I had great heroes, loyal men like the ones who helped my father years ago."

Fenring's eyes shone with wicked irony. "Hmmm, as in the Ecazi Revolt? It seems to me that Dominic Vernius and Paulus Atreides were involved in that."

Shaddam scowled. "And better men, like Zum Garon."

Muttering, the legal Mentats shared information with one another, since each of them had reservoirs of data that the others did not possess. Still, no answers surfaced.

Shaddam lowered his voice and fixed his eyes on the water rushing from the sea horse statue. "Once we have amal, these petty squabbles will be irrelevant. I want you to return to Ix and personally supervise full-scale production. It is time to proceed, so that we can wrap up this matter."

Fenring paled. "Sire, I would rather wait for the final analysis from the Guild about the tainted spice in the Heighliners. I am still not convinced—"

Shaddam's face reddened. "Enough delays! By the hells, I don't believe you'll ever be convinced, Hasimir. I have heard from the Master Researcher, who would not dare to lie to me, and from my Sardaukar commander there. Your Emperor is satisfied with the results—that is all you need to know." He became slightly more conciliatory and gave Fenring a paternal smile. "We will have plenty of time to tweak the formula afterward, so stop your worrying. Everything will turn out well for us." He clapped his childhood friend on the back. "Now, get this issue settled."

"Yes . . . Sire. I will depart for Ix immediately." Despite his uneasiness, he was eager to get back to confront the Master Researcher about Zoal. "I have, hmmm-ah, *business* of my own with Ajidica."

<hr/>

TWO FRESH REGIMENTS of Sardaukar recruits from Salusa Secundus marched in thunderous lockstep down the broad boulevard in front of the Palace. The Emperor found them impressive and comforting. These soldiers, led by battle-hardened veterans, would shore up his home defenses, enough to make the Landsraad squirm.

Within view of the troops, Shaddam made yet another formal procession to the Hall of Oratory wearing full Imperial regalia. He had invoked his sovereign privilege to summon an unscheduled emergency session of the Landsraad; his advisors would document which of the noble Houses did not bother to send representatives.

He sat inside his velva-padded coach, pulled by Harmonthep lions. Ahead, the Great Hall towered like a mountain, surpassed in size only by the Palace behind him. Under Kaitain's always-perfect skies, he rehearsed his words. Like sharks tasting a diluted droplet of blood, the Landsraad Council would sniff out the smallest trace of weakness.

I am Emperor of a Million Worlds. I have nothing to fear!

When the procession arrived at the rainbow of flags above the Landsraad Hall, the trained lions knelt, folding their paws beneath them. Sardaukar guards formed a gauntlet of uniforms so the Emperor could pass unhindered through the towering doors. He had not brought his ailing wife with him this time, nor did he feel the need for the moral support of his advisors, the Guild, or CHOAM. *I am the leader. I can do this myself.*

With appropriate fanfare, criers announced his arrival. The cavernous chamber was filled with private boxes, raised chairs, and long benches, some gaudily decorated, others austere and rarely used. Duke Leto's concubine Jessica sat next to the official ambassador from Caladan, as if to reinforce the presence of House Atreides. Shaddam tried to spot empty seats that might indicate absent Houses.

Applause rippled through the hall, but the reception sounded a bit strained. As "Protector of the Imperium" and his numerous other titles were called out, Shaddam took time to rehearse again. Finally, he stepped up to the podium.

"I am here to inform my subjects of a grave matter." Discreetly, he had ordered that the speaker system be specially amplified only during his speech, so now his words boomed out. "As your Emperor, it is my duty and responsibility to enforce the laws of the Imperium with impartiality and firmness."

"But without due process of law!" shouted one dissenter, a tiny voice in the immensity of the Landsraad Hall.

Sardaukar guards, especially the enthusiastic new recruits, were already pushing through the aisles to identify the speaker, who was trying, ineffectually, to melt into the sea of faces.

Shaddam frowned, pausing just long enough that the audience noticed him falter. *Not good.* "As my esteemed ancestor, Crown Prince Raphael Corrino, once said, 'Law is the ultimate science.' Know this, all of you—" He clenched his fist, but pursuant to Fenring's advice tried not to look too aggressive, hoping to maintain a fatherly appearance. "*I* am the law in the Imperium. *I* approve the codes. *I* have the right and the responsibility."

In the audience, other representatives drew away from the heckler, and the Sardaukar descended on him. Shaddam had given the troops explicit instructions to avoid shedding blood, however—at least during his speech.

"Some noble families have been punished because they chose to ignore Imperial law. No one here can claim that the guilty parties on Zanovar or Richese were unaware of their illegal actions." He pounded his fist on the lectern. The microphone carried the vibrations like thunder around the hall. Mutters rippled through the audience, but no one dared to speak out.

"If laws are not upheld, if perpetrators suffer no consequences for their crimes, the Imperium will degenerate into anarchy." Self-justification burned in him. Before he could grow angrier, he commanded the holoprojections to begin. "Observe Beakkal. All of you."

Three-dimensional images filled the governmental chamber, an ominous montage of withering jungles and blighted forests. Unmanned surveillance pods, dropped by the Sardaukar fleet in orbit, had sent imager-drones flying over the thick jungles to capture the spread of the biological scourge.

"As you can see, this scofflaw world is suffering the ravages of a terrible botanical plague. As your Emperor—for the protection of all—I dare not allow them to break the quarantine I have imposed."

Beautiful green leaves changed to brown and then purplish-black. Animals starved; tree trunks turned gelatinous and toppled.

"We must not risk the spread of this blight to other worlds. *Loyal* worlds. Therefore, thinking only of the safety of my subjects, I have placed a cordon around this defiant planet. Even after the plague dies out, the ecosystem of Beakkal will take centuries to recover." He made no attempt to sound distraught at the prospect.

Since the siege, the Beakkali people had instituted frantic measures, burning jungles or spraying corrosive acids in an attempt to isolate the defoliating plague. But nothing worked. It continued to spread, to metastasize across the planet. Smoke curled into the sky. Wildfires raged.

Next he played holorecordings of the Prime Magistrate pleading for help, delivering speech after speech to the Sardaukar, all falling upon deaf ears. Supreme Bashar Garon allowed no one to escape.

After Shaddam completed the sickening display, leaving the assemblage in stunned silence, Archduke Armand Ecaz requested permission to speak in opposition. Considering the rough treatment the heckler had received, Shaddam was surprised to see that the well-liked Archduke had the courage to stand forth.

Then the Emperor remembered a recent report, that House Ecaz had captured and publicly executed twenty Grumman "saboteurs," members of guerrilla teams purportedly sent in to plant fake spice stockpiles to implicate their rivals. Perhaps the loose-cannon Viscount Moritani saw Shaddam's preoccupation as an opportunity for him to strike again with impunity. He decided he wanted to hear what the Archduke had to say.

"With all due respect, Your Most Imperial Majesty," the tall silver-haired nobleman said in a strong voice from the floor, "I accept your enforcement of Imperial laws, and the quarantine of Beakkal. You are the greatest embodiment of justice in the Known Universe. You yourself did House Ecaz a great service, Sire, when you defended us against unwarranted Grumman aggression ten years ago.

"But I pose this question so that you may have an opportunity to answer directly, so that my esteemed colleagues in this assembly will have no cause to speak in ignorance." Shaddam stiffened as the Archduke gestured around the hall.

"Because of the horrors inflicted upon us by thinking machines during the Butlerian Jihad, the Great Convention forbids all biological weaponry, just as it restricts the use of atomic weapons. Perhaps you might speak to this fact, Majesty, because some of those here do not understand how it is that you have unleashed such a pestilence upon Beakkal without breaking the strictures."

Shaddam could find no fault with the way the Archduke had phrased his question. In the Imperium there was a long tradition of polite dissent and discussion among the noble families, including even all-powerful House Corrino.

"You misunderstand the facts regarding Beakkal, Archduke. I released no plague upon Beakkal at all. That was not my doing."

More muttering, but Shaddam pretended not to hear it.

"But what is the *explanation*, Sire?" Armand Ecaz pressed. "I simply wish to increase my understanding of the law of the Imperium, so that I may better serve House Corrino."

"An admirable goal," Shaddam said in a clipped voice, amused at the shrewd phrasing. "After I received disturbing evidence of an illegal spice hoard on Beakkal, my Sardaukar fleet approached with the intention of imposing a blockade, until such time as the Prime Magistrate answered the charges against him. However, the panicked Beakkali population engaged in an act of piracy, hijacking two supply ships that were loaded with contaminated cargo and being sent to a safely isolated biological research station. *I* had no hand in the theft of those ships. *I* did not disseminate this scourge. The Beakkalis themselves brought about the death of their world."

Louder muttering throughout the hall now, with an undertone of uncertainty.

"Thank you, Sire," Archduke Ecaz said, and returned to his seat.

Later, as he exited the Landsraad Hall of Oratory, Shaddam felt exceedingly pleased with himself, and moved with a youthful spring in his step.

The conquerors despise the conquered for allowing themselves to be beaten.

—EMPEROR FONDIL III, "The Hunter"

I x, at last.

Camouflaged from sensors, the Atreides combat pod looked like just another meteor in its red-hot descent. Piloting the stealth craft, hoping the unresponsive Guild would honor the previous agreement to keep their secret, Gurney Halleck set the controls for the polar regions of the machine world. Beside him, Prince Rhombur sat silently, remembering.

Home again, after twenty-one years. He wished Tessia could be there with him.

Before leaving the Heighliner, when the two infiltrators had sealed themselves into the small combat pod, the Flight Auditor with wide-set eyes had bidden them farewell. "The Guild is watching you, Rhombur Vernius, but we can offer you no assistance, nnnn, no *overt* assistance."

Rhombur had smiled. "I understand. But you can wish us luck."

The Flight Auditor was taken aback. "If such things matter to you, nnnn, then I will do so."

Now, as the pod plunged through the choppy ocean of air, Gurney grumbled that too many Guild members knew their identity and suspected their covert mission. To his knowledge, a Guild pledge of secrecy had never been broken, but they *did* accept bribes.

Prouder and stronger than ever before, Rhombur said to him, "Think of how interstellar commerce has suffered since House Vernius lost control of Ix. Do you think the Guild would rather keep the Tleilaxu in power here?"

Gurney's inkvine scar turned angry red. With the pod's hull beginning to heat up, he continued the line of descent, gripping the control bar in both hands. "The Spacing Guild is no one's ally."

Rhombur's waxy face showed no flush of emotion. "If they started revealing their passengers' secrets, their credibility would crumble." He shook his head. "The Guild will know what we're up to as soon as they start transporting Atreides forces to Ix anyway."

"I know all that, but I can't help worrying. Too many things can go wrong. We've been cut off from Duke Leto, held incommunicado on Junction for a month. We don't know if the plan is still on schedule. We are all running headlong into the dark. 'The man without concerns is the man without aspirations.' "

Rhombur held on as the spherical vessel bounced and careened. "Leto will do as he promised. And so will we."

They landed hard in an isolated wilderness in the northern latitudes of Ix. The pod came to a rest nestled in folds of snow, surrounded by ice and barren rock. Undetected. The secret tunnel there had been intended for Vernius family members trying to escape a subterranean disaster. Now, though, it was Rhombur's best opportunity to break back into the world that had been taken from him.

Working together in the cold night, the infiltrators broke down and rearranged the components of their combat pod. Detachable parts of the hull were designed to be reassembled into various forms. Numerous weapons could be removed and distributed to allies; plasteel honeycombs were filled with packaged foods.

Under the starry blackness, the men waited inside a makeshift, thin-walled shelter while Gurney planned the long, steep trudge downward. He was eager for action. While he enjoyed discussing strategy and playing baliset back at Castle Caladan, the former smuggler was a fighter at heart and not entirely happy unless he could be doing something in service to his liege—be it Dominic Vernius, Duke Leto, or Prince Rhombur. . . .

"I may be ugly, but at least I'll pass inspection as a human. You"—Gurney shook his head, looking at the Prince's cyborg parts—"will have to come up with a better story in case questions are asked."

"I look enough like a bi-Ixian." Rhombur raised his artificial left arm and moved his mechanical fingers. "But I would rather be welcomed as the rightful Earl Vernius."

All the time Rhombur had spent as an exile, and the recent pain he had suffered, had made him a better leader. He empathized with his people rather than taking them for granted. Now he wanted to earn their respect and loyalty, as Duke Leto had done with the people of Caladan.

During Rhombur's upbringing in the Grand Palais, while innocently collecting rocks and tapping his fingers in boredom through class after class, he had blithely expected to be the next head of House Vernius—never dreaming that he would have to *fight* for the position. He, like his sister, had accepted the role into which he'd been born.

But there was so much more to being a leader. And he had suffered much to learn this difficult lesson.

First, the murder of his mother Shando—who he now knew had given birth to another child, Emperor Elrood's bastard son. Then, after so many years of hiding, Dominic Vernius had committed atomic suicide, taking a number of Sardaukar with him. And Kailea . . . driven to madness and treachery, trying to grasp what she believed to be hers by right.

Soon there would be more bloodshed, when he and

Gurney triggered a subterranean revolution and Atreides forces came in to finish off the invaders. The Ixian people would have to fight again, and many would die.

But every drop of blood, Rhombur vowed, would be well spent, and his beloved world would be free again.

The universe is always one step beyond logic.

—LADY ANIRUL CORRINO, personal journal

Castle Caladan and the nearby military barracks were abuzz with activity. Atreides soldiers drilled and packed for the big expedition,
eager to depart. They cleaned their weapons and
inventoried explosives and siege machines, making ready for an all-out battle.

To coordinate such a complex operation, they
had prepared for months, and Duke Leto had ordered the House Guard to hold back no effort. He
owed that much to Rhombur—and he would risk
whatever was necessary.

Rhombur and Gurney could be dead by now. Leto
had heard nothing, no word, no calls for help, no
news of success. *Or they could already be in the middle of a brewing revolution.* After the Heighliner
mishap, the pair of infiltrators had vanished into
resounding silence. There had been no further
word from Ix. *Even so, we will do our utmost. And
hope.*

But if Rhombur did not succeed and Atreides
troops were defeated by the Tleilaxu and the
Emperor's Sardaukar, then Leto would suffer enormous repercussions here. Caladan itself might be
forfeit. Thufir Hawat was uncharacteristically nervous.

Leto, though, was completely committed. In
his mind, he had already passed the point of no

return. He would take the gamble, throw every effort into this fight, even if it left peaceful Caladan vulnerable for a short while. It was the only way he could restore Rhombur, and restore his own heart of honor.

The plans were proceeding like a juggernaut.

Amid the thousands of decisions that needed to be made, Leto avoided watching the final steps and went instead to the main docks below the Castle. As the noble leader of his Great House, he had duties at home—more enjoyable ones, though he wished Jessica could be with him.

The large fishing fleet was returning, boats that had been trolling around the reefs during the past two weeks of hot weather. Once each year, the fleet came in with their seasonal catch of grund, small bluish-silver fish that were captured by the netful. As part of a traditional festival, the delicious grund were washed and salted, then boiled in large batches. The tiny fish were spread out on plank tables, and people feasted on them. The Duke loved the Caladan delicacy as much as the coarsest fisherman did.

Rhombur had even more of a taste for grund than Leto did, and this was the first such celebration the Ixian Prince had missed in years. Leto tried to drive away his sense of foreboding. The waiting had ground down his patience.

Away from the bustling preparations for war, he stood at the end of a dock, watching the first trawlers approach. Already, crowds had gathered on the shingle beach, while merchants and chefs hurried to set up tables, cauldrons, and stalls in the old village plaza.

Leto heard minstrels playing along the shore. The music made him smile and reminded him of how often Rhombur and Gurney had practiced their balisets side by side, trying to outdo one another with outrageous lyrics and satirical songs.

But even though the Duke tried to enjoy a moment of peace, Duncan Idaho and Thufir Hawat spotted him and approached through the dense, noisy crowd. "You should have personal guards with you at all times, my Duke," the Mentat warned.

"You need to answer questions and make decisions about weaponry," Duncan added. "The fleet is scheduled to depart very soon." As Swordmaster, he would lead the Atreides military forces to Ix, just as he had commanded the strike against Beakkal.

In Leto's position, the head of House Atreides was required to avoid the actual fighting, though he wished he could be at the head of his troops. Instead, following Thufir's advice, Leto would act as the political spearhead on Kaitain, where he would make the formal announcement explaining his actions. "*That* is the job of a Duke," the grizzled Mentat had insisted.

Now, Leto gazed up the steep roads that led to the top of the cliff. From this angle, he could see the top levels of the Castle. "This is a good time for a major assault. While Beakkal festers in that awful plague, Emperor Shaddam is distracted with his own schemes. We'll crush the Tleilaxu on Ix before he knows what we're doing."

"I've seen images of those jungles," Duncan said. "No matter what excuses Shaddam makes, I don't doubt for a moment that he intended for it to happen."

Leto nodded. "Destroying Beakkal's ecosystem goes far beyond any revenge I could have demanded for their crimes. Still . . . the situation on Beakkal gives us another opportunity." He watched the first large fishing boats tie up to the docks. A rush of eager helpers swarmed forward to grab ropes and help steady the grund nets.

"I provided generous medical aid to Richese after my cousin attacked *them*. Now it is time to show the Landsraad that House Atreides can be benevolent to those who are not my relatives." He smiled. "Thufir, before our primary forces depart secretly for Ix, I want you to gather a fleet of cargo ships. Accompany them with a military escort. I, Duke Leto Atreides, will send relief supplies to plague-ravaged Beakkal and ask nothing in return."

Duncan was appalled by the suggestion. "But Leto! They tried to sell your ancestors to the Tleilaxu."

"And we need our House Guard to stay here to defend Caladan while our forces strike Ix," Hawat added. "This campaign has already depleted our resources."

"Send only a minimal military escort, Thufir, just enough to show that we're serious. As for the Beakkalis, we've already punished them for their poor judgment at the Senasar War Memorial. We have nothing to gain by holding a grudge against an entire population. The Beakkalis have seen how hard we can be. Now it is time to show them our benevolent side. My mother—who is not wrong all of the time—reminded me that a leader must show compassion as well as firmness."

He pressed his lips together, remembering conversations he'd had with Rhombur about leadership and how political considerations, though important, must be balanced with the needs of common citizens.

"Mark my words," Leto said, "I do this for the *people* of Beakkal, not for their politicians. This is not a reward for the actions of the Prime Magistrate, nor is it to be construed as forgiveness or even acceptance of an apology."

Thufir Hawat frowned. "Does this mean you do not wish me to accompany our troops to Ix, my Duke?"

Leto gave his old advisor a sly smile. "I'll need your diplomatic skills at Beakkal, Thufir. There will be tense moments when you reach the Imperial blockade. The planet is under strict quarantine, but I'm betting that the Emperor has not given explicit orders to destroy anyone who makes no attempt to land. Exploit that gray area."

Both the Mentat and the Swordmaster looked at him as if he had gone insane. Leto continued, "You're sure to draw the attention of the Sardaukar and maybe of Shaddam himself. In fact, it could be quite a spectacle."

Beside him, Duncan brightened as he understood the real plan. "Of course, a diversion! The Emperor can't fail to notice such a dramatic crisis. While Thufir faces down the

Imperial blockade, no one will think of paying attention elsewhere, and it will draw all the Sardaukar there. We will have our forces in position on Ix before anyone can send word to Kaitain. The Sardaukar on Ix will be operating without orders. The relief mission is just a diversion."

"Exactly. But one that could do some good for the people of Beakkal, while increasing my standing in the Landsraad. After I throw Atreides support to the military operation on Ix, I will require all the allies I can summon."

On the crowded docks, huge cranes groaned as they hoisted bulging fish-filled nets out of holds. In the harbor beyond, trawlers lined up, awaiting their turn; the port facilities could not accommodate them all at once.

When Duncan hurried up the hill to the barracks of the House Guard, Leto remained behind to participate in the festival. Hawat insisted on staying with his Duke as bodyguard.

Load after load of swollen nets crammed with millions of the silvery grund were lifted to shore. The odor of fish filled the air. Muscular laborers hefted the squirming catch into vats and tubs filled with salt and water, while chefs used slotted shovels to scoop out the grund from the vats into steaming cauldrons of seasoned broth.

Leto thrust his arms up to his elbows into one of the tubs, grabbing the little fish and passing them to the helpers down the conveyer line. Everyone cheered his contribution. He loved this part of his work.

Thufir Hawat strolled stiffly through the dense crowds, constantly on the alert for any assassin who might be lurking among the fisherfolk.

Leto, meanwhile, sat at an outdoor plank table to enjoy a savory meal of grund. The people applauded as he stuffed a handful into his mouth, and then they all joined in the feast.

It was the last moment of peace he would experience for some time.

> *Who knows what detritus of today will survive the eons of human history? It might be the slightest thing, a seemingly inconsequential item. Yet somehow it strikes a resonant chord, and survives for thousands of years.*
>
> —MOTHER SUPERIOR RAQUELLA BERTO-ANIRUL,
> founder of the Bene Gesserit

Following a fitful night in her fourth set of unfamiliar apartments, Lady Anirul lurched out of bed and made it to the doorway. The voices followed her, like shadows in her skull. Even the ghost Lobia had joined the clamor, and she offered no assistance, no refuge.

What are you all trying to tell me?

The ever-vigilant Medical Sister Yohsa approached, arms loose at her sides, body poised in a combat stance to prevent Anirul from passing her. "My Lady, you must return to bed and get your rest."

"There is no rest in there!" Anirul wore a loose-fitting nightgown that clung to her perspiration-damp skin, and her copper-brown hair stuck out in all directions. Lines and shadows etched her features around bloodshot eyes.

Previously, under Anirul's frenetic direction, servants had transferred her immense bed and heavy furnishings from one room to another, seeking a sufficiently quiet place. But nothing gave her relief.

Yohsa kept her voice calm. "All right, my Lady. We will find some other place for you—"

Swaying as if on the verge of fainting, Anirul made a quick, aggressive move and shoved the Medical Sister off-balance. The little woman stumbled over a table and sent an expensive ornate vase crashing to the floor. Leaping past her, Anirul fled down the tiled hallway, knocking a breakfast tray out of a maidservant's hands.

Running wildly, Anirul turned a corner, her bare feet slipping on the polished floor, and crashed into Mohiam, scattering a pile of loose papers and ridulian crystal sheets the Truthsayer had been carrying. Reacting quickly, Mohiam abandoned her documents and gave chase, but lost ground. Within moments, a panting Yohsa caught up with her.

Ahead of them, wild-eyed Anirul opened the door to a service stairway. She surged through, but caught a foot on the hem of her sleeping gown. Crying out, she tumbled down the stairs.

The pursuing Bene Gesserits arrived in a rush at the top of the stairs, just as Anirul, bruised and bleeding, struggled to sit up on the landing below. Mohiam hurried down and knelt beside the Emperor's wife. Under the guise of helping to steady her, the Reverend Mother gripped Anirul's arm and placed another hand around her waist, thus preventing her from escaping again.

Yohsa bent to study the injuries. "Her breakdown has been a long time coming. And I fear it will only grow worse." The Medical Sister had already administered increasing doses of powerful psychotropic drugs in unsuccessful attempts to suppress the storms of Other Memory.

Mohiam helped the injured Sister to her feet. Anirul's gaze darted around in the shadowy stairwell as if she were a cornered animal. "The voices within cannot be silenced. They want me to join them."

"Don't say that, my Lady." Mohiam added a soothing form of Voice, which seemed to have no effect on Anirul. The Medical Sister placed a quicknit amplifier patch on

Anirul's wounded forehead. Together, they raised the Emperor's wife, slowly leading her back to her rooms.

"I hear them clamoring in my head, but they utter only sentence fragments in a variety of languages—some familiar and some alien. I cannot understand what they are trying to tell me, why they are so alarmed." Anirul's voice throbbed with anguish. "Lobia is in there, too, but even she cannot rise above the others and help me."

The Medical Sister poured spice tea from a ready pot on a credenza in the room. After she collapsed on an antique Raphaelian couch in her parlor, Anirul turned her hazel-eyed gaze to the dark figure of Mohiam. "Yohsa, leave us. I need to speak with the Imperial Truthsayer. Alone."

The Medical Sister became stern, but finally, grudgingly, she agreed to leave them alone. Lying on the sofa, Anirul inhaled a long, shuddering breath. "Secrets can be such a great burden."

Studying her carefully, Mohiam took a sip of spice tea and felt the melange flow smoothly into her awareness. "I have never thought of it that way, my Lady. I consider it a great honor to be entrusted with important information."

Lady Anirul took a sip of tepid tea and frowned, as if it contained a foul-tasting medicine. "Soon Jessica will give birth to a daughter who is destined to bear our long-awaited Kwisatz Haderach."

"May we live to see that occur," Mohiam said, as if uttering a prayer.

Now Anirul seemed entirely reasonable, and conspiratorial. "But I have grave concerns as the Kwisatz Mother. I alone see and remember all aspects of our breeding program. Why is Other Memory so disturbed, and why *now* when we are so close to accomplishing our goal? Are they trying to warn us of some impending danger to Jessica's child? Is a disaster about to occur? Is the mother of the Kwisatz Haderach not going to be what we expect? Or is it something about the Kwisatz Haderach himself?"

"Only two more weeks," Mohiam said. "Jessica is due to deliver soon."

"I have decided that she must be told at least part of the truth, so that she can better protect herself and the child. Jessica must understand her destiny, and her importance to us all."

Mohiam swallowed more tea while trying to cover her surprise at the suggestion. She felt a great affection for her secret daughter, who had also been her student for years on Wallach IX. Jessica's future, her destiny, was greater than either Mohiam's or Anirul's. "But . . . to reveal so much, Lady Anirul? And you want me to tell her?"

"You are her birth-mother, after all."

Yes, Mohiam agreed, the girl must be told at least a part of the truth. Even in her tormented state, Lady Anirul was right about that. *But Jessica does not need to know the identity of her father. That would be too cruel.*

During his trip back to Ix, leaving the Emperor to reap the political problems he had
sown, Count Hasimir Fenring thought of subtle,
malicious, and exceedingly painful deaths he would
like to inflict upon Hidar Fen Ajidica for the
treachery he had attempted with his Face Dancer.

But none satisfied him.

As he gave the appropriate hand signals to
guards and descended to the grotto levels beneath
the Ixian surface, he chided himself for not having
seen the signs sooner and taking appropriate action against the turncoat Tleilaxu. The scheming
Master Researcher had made too many excuses for
a long time, and Emperor Shaddam had been completely duped. Amazingly, several Tleilaxu Masters
had recently appeared at court on Kaitain, as if
they belonged there—and Shaddam tolerated it.

But the Count knew the bitter truth. Despite
more than twenty years of planning, research, and
excessive funding, Project Amal was an utter failure. No matter what the Guild believed, Fenring
was convinced the two Navigators had failed because of the artificial spice, not some imagined
Beakkali plan.

Foolishly, Shaddam had assumed that the synthetic spice was already in his grasp, and had acted accordingly. True, most of the evidence available to the Emperor pointed to long-awaited success, but Fenring remained uneasy. Despite the tissue-thin legal justifications, Shaddam's Great Spice War had greatly damaged his political relations with the noble Houses. Now it would take decades to recover from all of the blunders . . . if they could recover at all.

Perhaps it might be better if he and his lovely Margot took steps to protect themselves from the approaching storm, while leaving the Emperor to the wolves. Shaddam Corrino would suffer for his own mistakes; Count Fenring did not need to sink into the depths with him. . . .

Now, in the doorway of his private administrative office, Hidar Fen Ajidica stood waiting for Fenring with pride and arrogance, as if his small body could not contain his high opinion of himself. Rust-brown smears marred the front of his white lab coat.

At a sharp gesture from the Master Researcher, the Sardaukar guards slipped away, leaving him alone with Fenring in the office. Clenching and unclenching his fists, the Count forced control upon himself. He did not want to murder the little man too quickly. As he entered, Fenring made a point of closing the door behind them.

Ajidica stepped forward, his rodent-black eyes flashing with haughty self-importance. "Bow to me, Zoal!" He chattered additional commands in an incomprehensible guttural language, then switched to Imperial Galach. "You have sent no word, and will be punished for your lapse."

Fenring could barely stop himself from laughing at the man's assumption, but made a smirking little bow that seemed to mollify Ajidica. Then he lashed out and grasped the front of the Master Researcher's robes. "I am not your Face Dancer! I have already marked you for death. The question is how and when, hmmm?"

Ajidica's grayish skin turned even paler as he realized his awful mistake. "Of course, my dear Count Fenring!" His voice became raspy as the Spice Minister tightened his stranglehold. "You have . . . you have passed my test. I am so pleased."

In disgust, Fenring flung him down. Arms and legs akimbo, Ajidica crashed hard onto the floor. Fenring wiped a hand on his own jerkin, feeling soiled after touching the treacherous creature. "It is time to salvage what we can from this disaster, Ajidica. Perhaps I should drop you from the balcony of the Grand Palais, so that all the people can watch, hmmm?"

In a strangled voice, the Master Researcher called for guards. Fenring heard footsteps come running, but he was not concerned. He was the Imperial Spice Minister and a close friend of Shaddam's. The Sardaukar would obey his orders. He smiled as an idea took shape in his mind.

"Yes, hmmm, I shall declare Ix free at last and become its great liberator. Along with the Sardaukar, I will decry the years of Tleilaxu oppression, hmmm-ah, destroy all evidence of your illegal amal research, and then I—and Shaddam, of course—will emerge as heroes."

The Master Researcher scrambled to his feet, looking like a cornered rat with very sharp teeth. "You cannot do this, Count Fenring. We are so close, now. So close. The amal is *ready*."

"The amal is a failure! Both Heighliner tests were disasters, and you may be thankful that the Guild still hasn't figured out what we've done. Navigators can never use the synthetic spice. Who knows what other aftereffects your substance will have?"

"Nonsense, my amal is perfect." Ajidica reached into the folds of his robe, as if for a hidden weapon. Fenring crouched to attack, but the scientist only brought out a rust-colored tablet, which he popped into his mouth. "I have consumed extraordinary doses myself, and I feel magnificent. I am stronger than ever. I see the universe more clearly." He tapped his forehead so hard that it left a mark on the skin.

The door burst open and a squad of Sardaukar filed in, led by young Commander Cando Garon. The men moved with feral grace, less regimented than usual.

"I have tripled spice rations for all the Sardaukar stationed here," Ajidica said. "They have been consuming amal for six months now. Their bodies are saturated with it. See how strong they look!"

Fenring studied the faces of the Imperial soldiers. He did see a wolfish intensity there, a hardness in their eyes and a coiled danger that sang through their muscles. Garon bowed slightly to him, showing minimal deference.

"Maybe the amal was too potent for those test Navigators, and the mixture should have been adjusted," Ajidica continued. "Or perhaps they should be trained differently. No need to dispose of all our progress because of some minor piloting error. We have invested too much. The amal works. *It works!*"

Ajidica became feverish and fidgety, as if close to a seizure. With jittery, palsied movements he scrambled past Fenring and elbowed the Sardaukar out of his way. "Here, Count, you must see this. Let me convince you. The Emperor needs to consume some of my product himself. Yes, we must send samples back to Kaitain." He raised his hands as he strutted into the corridor, a little man with delusions of grandeur. "You can't understand everything. Your mind is . . . infinitely small."

Fenring struggled to keep up as Ajidica scurried ahead. The soldiers followed silently.

The main floor of the research pavilion always disgusted him, though the Count understood the necessity for the Tleilaxu axlotl tanks. Brain-dead females lay like cadavers hooked up to bubbling life-support systems, no longer human, their bodies bloated and force-fed. Captive wombs, they were little more than biological factories that produced whatever organic substances or abominations the genetic wizards programmed into their reproductive systems.

Curiously, the receptacles attached to their bodies—usually containing the amal they had produced—were empty. Though still alive, the tanks seemed to be off-line. All except for one.

Ajidica led him to a naked young woman only recently hooked up to an axlotl system. She was androgynous and flat-chested, with short, dark hair. Her closed eyes had sunken into her face. "Note this one, Count. Very healthy, very fit. She will produce well for us, though we are still re-configuring her uterus to produce the chemical compounds necessary for the amal precursor. Then we can link the other tanks to her and produce more."

Fenring found nothing erotic about the helpless lump of flesh, as different from his own beautiful wife as a woman could possibly be. "Why is she so special?"

"She was a spy, Count. We captured her poking around, disguised as a male."

"I'm surprised all the females around here don't disguise themselves and hide."

"This one was a Bene Gesserit."

Fenring could not cover his astonishment. "The Sisterhood knows about our operations here?" *Damn that Anirul! I should have killed her.*

"The witches have some inkling of what we're up to. Therefore, we do not have much time." Ajidica kneaded his hands together. "You see, you cannot execute me now. You dare not bring all this work to a halt. The Emperor must have his amal. We can work out our minor differences later."

Fenring raised his eyebrows. "You call the destruction of an entire Heighliner with the loss of all passengers a 'minor difference'? You say I should just forget your Face Dancer's assassination attempt on me? Hmmm?"

"Yes! Yes, I do. In the scheme of the entire universe, such events are insignificant." Insanity flashed in the little man's eyes. "I cannot let you cause problems now, Count

Fenring. The importance of my work goes beyond you, or House Corrino, or the Imperium itself. I just need a little more time."

Fenring turned, intending to snap orders at the Sardaukar—but saw a strange quality in their eyes as they looked at Ajidica, a zealous devotion that astonished him. Of all things, he had never suspected the loyalty of *Sardaukar* would be questionable. These men were obviously addicted to the synthetic spice, their bodies crackling with the power of artificial melange. Had the Master Researcher brainwashed them, too?

"I will not let you stop me." Ajidica's threat was clear. "Not now."

Inside the research pavilion, Tleilaxu workers took notice and came closer. Some of them might be Face Dancers as well. Fenring's stomach sank, and for the first time in his entire life he felt the cold grip of true fear. He was alone here.

Over the years, he had often belittled Ajidica's abilities, but now he saw that the Master Researcher had managed to put an astonishing plan in place. Surrounded, Fenring realized that he might never get off this planet alive.

Waiting. Time passes slowly, more than a lifetime, it seems. When will our nightmare end? Each day drags on, though hope endures. . . .

—C'TAIR PILRU, fragment from his secret journals

The man-machine stood outside the shambles of an Ixian weapons manufactory. During the decades of Tleilaxu occupation, the assembly lines that produced complex machinery and technological marvels had been poorly maintained, abandoned, or used for other purposes. The invaders were not knowledgeable enough to keep sophisticated systems running smoothly, and the skilled Ixian workers passively resisted in every way.

Just days before, the last groaning and shuddering stations on the production line had seized up. Engines smoked, components ground together and broke down. During the emergency, the workers had just watched.

The underground world had been slowly sliding into disorder and decay. Repair technicians halfheartedly removed the ruined assembly-line components, but the Tleilaxu overlords had no replacement parts. Workers at other machines tried to look busy, while prowling Sardaukar guards and Tleilaxu Masters kept a close watch. Surveillance pods drifted overhead, searching for anything out of the ordinary.

Prince Rhombur hid in plain sight. He stood

like a statue in front of the bustling facility. Ixian workers glanced at him, then looked away without seeing, without recognizing. Years of oppression had deadened their minds and senses.

His scarred face and the metal skullcap were exposed, like badges of honor. The prosthetic skin on his artificial limbs had been peeled away to reveal pulleys, electronics, and mechanical enhancements, a better approximation of the clumsy bi-Ixian monstrosities. Gurney had even dirtied him up. While Rhombur could not pretend to be completely human, he *could* masquerade as something far less than he was.

Chemical smoke poured toward the cavern ceiling, where air-exchangers absorbed and filtered the particulates. But even the best purification systems could not remove the traces of innocent people living in fear.

Rhombur's eyes, both the real and the synthetic, examined everything around him. He felt revulsion, nausea, and anger to see the ruin of this once-wondrous city, and could hardly endure any more. With zero hour fast approaching for the arrival of Atreides forces, he hoped he could seed the revolution quickly enough to make a difference.

When he began to move, Rhombur took slow, jerky steps, wandering aimlessly like one of the Tleilaxu's reanimated bi-Ixians. Rhombur made his way under a darkened overhang beside the broken-down factory.

Unnoticed among the work crew and guards, Gurney Halleck signaled him. Beside the inkvine-scarred man stood the broken shadow of someone Rhombur remembered from a shared youth. In astonishment at the man's stark appearance, he whispered, "C'tair Pilru!"

This had once been a vibrant young man, dark-eyed and small in stature like his twin D'murr. But in some ways C'tair's changes seemed even more horrifying than the Navigator's alterations. The eyes were fatigue-laden and sunken; the dark hair stuck out in unwashed spikes.

"My . . . Prince?" His voice was whispery and uncertain.

He had suffered too many hallucinations and broken dreams. Appalled to see the horrific changes in the heir to House Vernius, C'tair seemed ready to break down.

Gurney squeezed his arm in a viselike grip. "Careful, both of you. We must not draw attention to ourselves. We dare not stay here in the open for long."

"I . . . have a place," C'tair said. "Several places."

"We must spread the word." Rhombur's voice was low, determined. "Inform those who have given up and those who have retained a spark of hope for all these years. We will even enlist the aid of the suboids. Tell everyone that the Prince of Ix has returned. Freedom is no longer an improbable hope—the time is now. Let there be no question: We are about to retake Ix."

"It is very dangerous for anyone to say such things aloud, my Prince," C'tair said. "The people live in terror."

"Pass the word anyway, even if it causes the monsters to seek me out. My people need to know that I am back and that the long, dark nightmare of Ix will soon be over. Tell them to be ready. Duke Leto's forces arrive soon."

Rhombur reached out with a powerful prosthetic arm and embraced the emaciated freedom fighter. Even to the Prince's clumsy nerve sensors, C'tair felt skeletal. He hoped Leto would not delay.

Making a sport of war is a move toward sophistication. When you govern men of military temper, you must understand their passionate need for war.

— SUPREME BASHAR ZUM GARON,
Imperial Sardaukar Commander

On the day of departure for Ix, the Atreides troops went to their ships with an air of euphoria. But the reality of war would soon set in.

Swordmaster Duncan Idaho and the Mentat Thufir Hawat accompanied Leto as he stood atop a speaking tower that overlooked the spaceport field. Caladan had not witnessed such a gathering since the fateful skyclipper procession. Row upon row of military vessels glinted in the morning sun. Uniformed, fiercely loyal Atreides soldiers stood in ranks, a sea of men ready to mount the transports, destroyers, monitors, and battle cruisers.

For over two decades, the Tleilaxu usurpers and their Sardaukar allies had entrenched themselves on Ix. Many spies had died trying to get inside that world—and if Rhombur and Gurney had been captured and tortured, the Atreides assault force might have lost their element of surprise. Leto knew he could forfeit everything with this gamble, but he did not consider calling off the attack. Not for a moment.

Under Hawat's separate command, eighteen supply ships were ready to depart with a small armed escort. The Mentat's bold move would be the obvious one, but a diversion. His relief fleet would appear between Beakkal and the Sansin transfer station, where they would broadcast Leto's humanitarian offer. Presumably, the Sardaukar officers in the blockade would send messages to the Emperor, and in turn Shaddam would focus his attention on the quarantined world. The Imperial military would be drawn there. Meanwhile, no doubt, Landsraad delegates in the Hall of Oratory would extol the generosity of Duke Atreides.

At about that time, Duncan Idaho's assault would strike Ix like a hammer.

Crowds on the landing field pressed against the ribbons strung along the perimeter, colorful strands that fluttered in a light wind. People cheered and waved black-and-green pennants bearing the heraldic hawk crest, the ancient sigil of House Atreides.

Sweethearts, wives, and mothers called out to the soldiers assembled on the field, encouraging them. In a flurry of activity, many of the young men rushed back to the barricades for goodbye kisses. Often, it didn't even matter if they knew the pretty women seeing them off; it was simply a reassurance that someone cared about their safety and wished them well.

Duke Leto could not help but think of Jessica, separated from him for months, living in luxury in the Imperial Palace. Very soon now, she would bear his child, and he longed to be with her. That was the best advantage of his going to Kaitain. . . .

Leto had taken great care to dress himself in a scarlet matador's uniform similar to the one his father had so proudly worn for bullfights. It was a significant symbol, one easily recognized by the citizens of Caladan. When Leto wore red, the crowd saw not an echo of bloodshed (from which the Atreides Red Dukes had drawn their appellation long ago) but of pageantry and glory.

The boarding ramps opened, and subcommanders shouted

their men into ranks. One troop broke into a familiar Atreides battle song. As they shouted off-key into the hubbub, other soldiers took up the refrain, and soon all the uniformed men had joined in the chorus, a resounding celebration of defiance, determination, and love for their Duke.

The song concluded, and just before the first ranks began to board the warships, Leto stepped to the edge of the tower. The troops fell silent, waiting for his send-off speech.

"In the Ecazi Revolt many years ago, Duke Paulus Atreides fought side by side with Earl Dominic Vernius. These great men were war heroes and fast friends. Much time has passed since then, and many tragedies have occurred, but we must never forget one thing: *House Atreides does not abandon its friends.*"

A surge of cheering swept through the crowd. Under other circumstances, the general populace might not have cared about the renegade family. For the common folk of Caladan, Ix was a distant world they would never visit, but they had taken Prince Rhombur into their hearts.

"Our soldiers will retake the ancestral home of House Vernius. My friend Prince Rhombur will rescue the Ixian people and restore their freedom."

On Caladan and many other Imperial planets, the people had learned to hate the Tleilaxu. Ix was undoubtedly the most heinous example of their misbehavior, but there were numerous other instances. For centuries the gnomish men had gotten away with too much, and now it was time to administer Atreides justice.

Leto continued, "We do not pick and choose when to be moral, when to follow the correct path and assist others who need us. And that is why I have sent my Mentat Thufir Hawat on a mission of his own."

He surveyed the crowd. "Not long ago, we had to take stern action against the Prime Magistrate of Beakkal—but now that Beakkal's people are suffering from a terrible plague that is devastating their world, should we simply ignore them because I had a quarrel with their government?" He raised a fist in the air. "*I say no!*"

The people cheered again, though a bit less enthusiastically this time.

"Other Great Houses are content to watch the Beakkali population die, but House Atreides will challenge the Imperial blockade and deliver much-needed relief supplies, just as we did for Richese." He lowered his voice. "We would want others to do the same for us, would we not?"

Leto was confident they understood the principle and the choice. After gaining stature in the Landsraad with his aggressive response to the original Beakkali insult, he had shown a more compassionate side by assisting the victims on Richese. Now he would prove the strength of his heart. He remembered a quote from the Orange Catholic Bible: "It is easy to love a friend, hard to love an enemy."

"I will travel directly to Kaitain alone, where I will talk with my cousin the Emperor and deliver a formal speech to the Landsraad." He paused, and felt emotion well up inside. "I will also see my beloved Lady Jessica, who is about to give birth to our first child."

Whoops and whistles erupted; Atreides pennants waved. The people had long perceived their Duke and his activities at Castle Caladan as myth and legend. The commoners needed such images.

Finally, he raised a hand in benediction, and the roar of the crowd and soldiers nearly deafened him. Beside him on the observation tower, Duncan and Thufir watched as the soldiers boarded their assigned ships, marching in perfect ranks. Such a military display would have impressed even Emperor Shaddam himself.

Leto felt an inner warmth as waves of confidence and good expectations from his people washed over him. He vowed not to disappoint them.

The face of the Imperium was about to shift.

*The man who sees an opportunity and does nothing is
asleep with his eyes open.*

—Fremen Wisdom

Back home on Giedi Prime, Glossu Rabban
enjoyed being in charge of Harkonnen
Keep. From the high, stone-walled fortress, he
could command the servants, announce his own
gladiatorial tournaments, and keep the population
under firm control. It was his privilege as a noble
of the Landsraad.

Better still, he had no wily Mentat to breathe
down his neck or criticize him for everything he
tried to do. Piter de Vries was playing his diplomatic spy games on Kaitain. And Rabban's uncle
had remained on Arrakis to monitor the complex
spice operations under the threat of CHOAM inspections and audits.

Which left the Beast alone and in charge.

He was technically the na-Baron, the heir apparent to House Harkonnen, though the Baron
had often threatened to change his mind and cede
control to young Feyd-Rautha. Unless Rabban
could find some way to prove himself invaluable.

He stood in the Keep's east wing at the animal
pens, where the stench of the hounds hung dense
and feral in the corridors. Wet fur and blood,
saliva and feces, piled up and grew old as the animals thrashed in their pit enclosure below the
walkway. With gleaming black eyes, the dogs

fought for a glimpse of daylight or a scrap of fresh meat, snapping at imaginary enemies with their long fangs. Like the alpha male of the pack, Rabban growled back at the hounds, curling his thick lips to expose uneven white teeth.

Squatting, he reached into a cage at the edge of the walkway and yanked out a squirming simian rabbit. The creature's eyes were huge and round, its ears floppy. Its prehensile tail twitched, as it feared for its life, yet longed for affection. Rabban's strong fingers gripped the folds of soft skin and warm fur so tightly that the creature trembled. He held it high to let the hounds see the morsel of food.

In the kennel pit, the animals began to bark and snarl, leaping high. Their claws skittered on slimy stone walls, but the hounds fell short of the kennel edge. The furry creature in Rabban's grip flinched and kicked, trying to escape from the nightmare of snapping jaws.

A voice interrupted from behind, shockingly close. "Maintaining your image, Beast?"

The interruption startled him so much that he inadvertently released his grip. The simian rabbit dropped, flailing, toward the pit. One leaping hound—a big gray Bruweiler—snatched it from the air and tore the scrap of food to bloody shreds before the doomed victim could even make a squeak.

Rabban whirled to see the dark-haired, fiery-eyed Viscount Hundro Moritani standing behind him. The man's big-knuckled hands were propped on his scale-armored jodhpurs; broad epaulets flared on his surcoat made of crimson overlapping silkscales.

Before Rabban could splutter a reply, Captain Kryubi, head of the Harkonnen House Guard, hurried up at a brisk pace, followed by an agitated-looking aide, who also wore the shoulder pads and lapel crest of House Moritani.

"I'm sorry, m'Lord Rabban," Kryubi said, out of breath. "The Viscount proceeded without my permission. While I was attempting to locate you, he—"

The Grumman leader just smiled.

Rabban waved Kryubi to silence. "We'll deal with that

later, Captain, *if* this turns out to be a waste of my time." Feeling slightly off-balance, he turned his broad shoulders and looked Moritani straight in the eye. "What do you want?" Technically, the Viscount outranked him in the Landsraad, and the man had already proven his vengeful temper against House Ecaz as well as the Swordmasters of Ginaz.

"I want to offer you a chance to join me in an enjoyable strategic game."

Trying to regain his composure, Rabban grabbed another simian rabbit from the cage. He held the creature by the back of its neck so that no matter how it flipped its prehensile tail, it could not get a grasp on Rabban's wrist.

"I thought only House Harkonnen would enjoy the irony as much as I," Moritani continued. "I also thought you would be willing to seize the opportunity Duke Leto's poor planning has presented to us."

Rabban dangled the rabbit over the hound pen. The dogs snapped and growled, trying to reach the tantalizing treat, but the Beast held it far out of their reach. The terrified, writhing rabbit released its bladder, and a stream of urine rained down into the pen, but the dogs didn't seem to mind. When Rabban felt the creature had reached the peak of its fear, he flung it with disgust to the dogs. "So explain yourself. I'm waiting. What does House Atreides have to do with this?"

The Viscount raised his bushy eyebrows. "I believe that you have even less love for Duke Leto Atreides than do I."

Rabban glowered. "Any fool knows that much."

"At this very moment, Duke Leto is on his way to Kaitain. He is scheduled to speak before the Landsraad."

"So? Do you expect me to rush to Kaitain for a front-row seat?"

The Viscount smiled patiently, like a parent waiting for a child to understand a point. "His Mentat, Thufir Hawat, has apparently gone to deliver supplies to Beakkal.

And"—Moritani held up his index finger—"without any fanfare, Leto has dispatched virtually all House Atreides troops and ships on a secret military mission."

"To where? How did you find out about this?"

"I found out about it, Beast Rabban, because one cannot move a force of that size, filling so many Guild ships, without attracting notice from even the most incompetent of spies."

"All right," Rabban said. The wheels in his mind spun, but found no traction. "So you know about it. Where is this Atreides task force going? Is Giedi Prime in danger?"

"Oh, not Giedi Prime—House Atreides is much too civilized for an underhanded action like that. In fact, I'm not concerned about their target, so long as it's not you or me."

"So why should I care?"

"Rabban, if you do your mathematics correctly, you will realize that these careful and coordinated Atreides movements leave Leto's beloved Caladan protected by only a skeleton force. If we make a concentrated military strike now, we could strip him of his ancestral home."

The simian rabbits in the cage squeaked and squirmed, and Rabban kicked the mesh bars, but that only served to heighten their agitation. Kryubi stood back, his thin mustache wrinkling as he pursed his lips in contemplation. The guard captain would not speak or offer tactical advice unless Rabban specifically requested it.

The nervous-looking aide hurried to Moritani's side. "My Viscount, you know that it is not wise. Striking a planet without giving fair warning, without first filing a dispute with the Landsraad, and without formally challenging an opposing noble House goes strictly against the rules of kanly. You know the forms as well as anyone, sir. You—"

"Silence," the Viscount said without raising his voice even slightly. The aide clamped his mouth shut with an audible click. But Rabban had wanted to hear the answers to the aide's objections, because the agitated man was raising questions he himself hadn't wanted to ask for fear of looking like a coward.

"May I?" Moritani asked, and reached into the rabbit cage. He grabbed a squirming ball of fur and held it up over the pit. "Interesting. Do you ever place bets on which hound will get the prey?"

Rabban shook his head. "This is just feeding."

The Viscount let go. Again the large gray Bruweiler outleaped his companions and snatched the rabbit out of the air. Rabban decided to cull that aggressive dog and turn it loose in the next gladiatorial event.

"Rules are for old men who prefer to walk in the wheel ruts of history," the Viscount said. He had brutally attacked his archrival House Ecaz by carpet-bombing the entire capital peninsula, killing the Archduke's eldest daughter and rekindling a feud that had simmered for generations.

"Indeed, and you've faced years of Imperial sanctions for breaking the rules," Rabban said. "Sardaukar troops stationed on your world, commerce interrupted."

The Grumman lord didn't seem to care a bit. "Yes, but that's all over now."

Years ago, when Duke Leto had tried to broker a peace between Moritani and Ecaz, he had shown bias in favor of House Ecaz, might even have been betrothed to a daughter of the Archduke at one time. But vengeance didn't enter into Moritani's proposal as much as simple exploitation of an opportunity.

"Still, I am forbidden from moving many troops because of Shaddam's strictures. I brought as many as I could comfortably slip away from the observers—"

"Here? To Giedi Prime?" Rabban was alarmed.

"Just a friendly visit." Moritani shrugged. "It occurred to me, however, that House Harkonnen can launch as much military force as it wishes with no added scrutiny. So I ask you now, will you join me in this daring enterprise?"

Rabban took a deep breath, shocked into momentary

silence. Kryubi shuffled his feet uneasily, but said nothing. "You want Harkonnen troops to join yours? Grummans and Harkonnens attacking Caladan—"

"At the moment, Caladan has almost no defenses," Moritani reminded him. "According to our intelligence report, only a few youths and old men with small weapons remain. But we must act quickly, for Leto won't leave his doors wide-open for long. What have you got to lose? Let's go!"

"Duke Leto may also be counting on the rules of kanly, to which all Houses are bound, sir," Kryubi said in a dry voice. " 'The forms must be obeyed.' "

The nervous aide straightened his lapel crest and beseeched his master, "My Lord Viscount, this action is too rash. I beg you to reconsider—"

With a sharp and vicious move of his shoulder, Hundro Moritani knocked his own aide sprawling over the edge and down into the kennel pit. Unlike the rabbits, the aide had time to scream as the hounds attacked him.

The Grumman smiled at Rabban. "Sometimes, one must act unexpectedly in order to secure the greatest benefit."

The aide stopped squirming below, and the hungry animals tore his body apart. Rabban could hear the wet, ripping sound of meat, the sharp cracks of leg bones being broken open for their fresh, hot marrow.

He nodded slowly, ominously. "Caladan will be ours. I like the sound of that."

"Under joint occupation," Moritani said.

"Yes, of course. And how do you propose that we defend our prize once we take it? As soon as the Duke returns, he'll have his force—assuming he doesn't lose it somewhere."

Moritani smiled. "To begin, we make certain no messages leave Caladan. After our forces are successful, we restrict shuttle transport to and from any arriving Heighliners."

"And we set up a surprise party for Duke Leto when he comes back!" Rabban said. "We ambush him as soon as he lands."

"Exactly. We can work out the details together. We may also need to bring in reinforcements after the fact, a full occupation force to subdue the populace."

The coarse Harkonnen heir set his thick lips in a firm line. The last time he had taken matters into his own hands, he had crashed the only existing no-ship on Wallach IX. He'd attempted to attack the smug Bene Gesserit witches who had contaminated the Baron with their disease. Back then, Rabban had thought his uncle would be proud of him for acting independently. Instead, the plan had not gone well, and the priceless ship had been lost. . . .

This time, however, he knew his uncle wouldn't hesitate, given such an opportunity to strike against the mortal enemies of House Harkonnen. Cautiously, he looked over at the Viscount. Captain Kryubi gave a silent but well-considered nod of assent.

"So long as we use unmarked ships, Viscount," Rabban said. "We make it look like a big trade delegation or something . . . anything but a military force."

"You have brains, Count Rabban. I think we will work well together."

Rabban beamed at the compliment. Hopefully this bold decision would show his uncle how smart the Beast really was.

They shook hands on the deal. Below, the sounds of feeding faded, and the bristling muscular hounds looked up from their kennel, hoping for more.

Does knowledge increase a person's burden more, or ignorance? Every teacher must consider this question before beginning to alter a student.

— LADY ANIRUL CORRINO, private journal

Beneath another glorious Imperial sunset, Mohiam crept up behind Jessica, who sat beside a small pool in an ornamental garden. For a long moment, the Truthsayer observed her secret daughter. The young woman carried her advanced pregnancy well, comfortable with the new awkwardness of her body. The baby would be born soon.

Jessica reached forward to swirl her fingertips in the pool, blurring her reflection. She spoke out of the corner of her mouth. "I must be very entertaining, Reverend Mother, for you to stand there watching me."

Mohiam wrinkled her lips in a small smile. "I expected you to sense I was here, child. After all, who taught you to observe the world around you?" She came to the edge of the pool and held out a memory crystal. "Lady Anirul has asked me to give this to you. There are certain things she would have you know."

Jessica took the glittering object, studied it. "Is the Lady well?"

Mohiam's tone was guarded. "I believe her condition will improve considerably once your daughter is born. She is most concerned about the child, and this is causing her great distress."

Jessica looked away, afraid Mohiam might see her flush. "I don't understand, Reverend Mother. Why should the baby of a Duke's concubine be of such importance?"

"Come to a place where we can sit. In private." They walked toward a solar-operated carousel that a previous Emperor had installed for his amusement.

Jessica wore a maternity dress in Atreides colors that reminded her of Leto. The bodily changes from her pregnancy had unleashed many conflicting emotions inside her, shifting moods she could barely control even with her Bene Gesserit training. Each day she had poured her loving thoughts into the bound parchment journal Anirul had given her. The Duke was a proud man, but Jessica knew in her heart that he missed her.

Mohiam took a seat on the gilded carousel bench, and Jessica joined her, still holding the memory crystal. Activated by their weight, the mechanism began to spin slowly. Jessica watched the changing garden view as it passed in front of her. On a nearby post draped with bougainvillea, a dangling glowglobe flickered on, though the sun had not yet dropped below the horizon.

Since her arrival on Kaitain, especially after Tyros Reffa's surprise stunt in front of the Imperial Box, Jessica had been watched constantly by hovering Bene Gesserit guardians. Though she gave no sign of annoyance, Jessica could not have failed to notice their doting protection.

Why am I so special? What does the Sisterhood want with my baby?

Jessica turned the memory crystal over in her hands. It was octagonal, glimmering with lavender facets. Mohiam brought out a companion crystal and held it. "Go ahead, child. Activate it."

Jessica rolled the sparkling device between her palms and then cupped it in her hands, warming it with her body heat, moistening it with her perspiration to energize the custom memories stored inside.

As she looked into it, staring with focused attention, the

crystal began to project image beams that intersected across her retinas. Beside her, Mohiam activated the companion crystal.

Jessica closed her eyes and felt a bone-deep hum, like that of a Guild ship entering foldspace. When she opened her eyes again, her vision had changed. She seemed to be inside the Bene Gesserit Archives, far from Kaitain. Deep within the translucent cliffs of Wallach IX, the walls and ceilings of the huge library facility reflected prismatic illumination, shuttling light across billions of jeweled surfaces. Immersed in a sensory projection, she and Mohiam stood together at the virtual entrance. The illusion felt incredibly real.

Mohiam said, "I will be your guide, Jessica, so that you can understand your importance."

Jessica stood silently, intrigued yet intimidated.

"When you left the Mother School," Mohiam began, "had you learned everything there was to know?"

"No, Reverend Mother. But I had learned how to obtain the information I needed."

When Mohiam's image took Jessica by the hand, she seemed to feel the older woman's strong grip and dry skin. "Quite so, child, and this is one of the important places to look. Come, I will show you amazing things."

They passed through a tunnel into darkness that expanded around Jessica. She sensed, but could not see, an immense black chamber with walls and ceiling far beyond reach. Jessica wanted to cry out. Her pulse raced. She used her training to slow it down, but too late. The other woman had noticed.

Mohiam's dry voice broke the silence. "Are you frightened?"

" 'Fear is the mind-killer,' Reverend Mother. 'I will allow it to pass over me and through me.' What is this darkness, and what can I learn from it?"

"This represents what you still do not know. This is the universe you have not yet seen and which you cannot possibly imagine. At the beginning of time, darkness reigned. In the end, it will be the same. Our lives are but pinpoints of light in between, like the smallest stars in the heavens." Mohiam's voice came close to her ear. "*Kwisatz Haderach.* Tell me what that name means to you."

The Reverend Mother let go of her hand, and Jessica felt herself float off the ground, blind in the saturated blackness. She shivered, fought panic. "It is one of the Sisterhood's breeding programs. That is all I know."

"This black pit of hidden knowledge around you contains every secret in the universe. The fears, hopes, and dreams of humanity. All that we have ever been and can ever achieve. *This* is the potential of the Kwisatz Haderach. He is the culmination of our most exacting breeding programs, the powerful male Bene Gesserit who can bridge space and time. He is the human of all humans, a god in man-form."

Unconsciously, Jessica held her hands over her rounded belly, where her unborn child—the Duke's son—curled in the security of her womb, where it must be as dark as this chamber.

Her old teacher's voice was brittle, as dry as sticks. "Hear me, Jessica—after thousands of years of careful Bene Gesserit planning, the daughter you carry is destined to give birth to the Kwisatz Haderach. That is why such care has been taken to ensure your safety. Lady Anirul Sadow-Tonkin Corrino is the Kwisatz Mother, your sworn protector. It is by her command that you now learn your place in the events unfolding around you."

Jessica was too overwhelmed to speak. Her knees buckled in the weightless blackness. For the love of Leto, she had defied the Bene Gesserit. She was carrying a *son*, not a daughter! And her Sisters did not know.

"Do you understand what has been revealed to you, child? I have taught you many things. Do you grasp the importance?"

Jessica's voice was small. "I understand, Reverend Mother."

She didn't dare admit her transgression now, could think of no one in whom she could confide her terrible secret, especially not her stern teacher. *Why didn't they tell me before?*

Steeling herself, Jessica thought of Leto, and of his anguish following the death of Victor, caused by the treachery of his concubine Kailea. *I did it for him!*

Despite the Bene Gesserit strictures against being swayed by emotions, Jessica had come to believe that her superiors had no right to interfere with the love between a man and a woman. Why were they so afraid of it? Nothing in her training answered this question.

Had Jessica single-handedly destroyed the Kwisatz Haderach program, ruining millennia of work? Confusion, anger, and fear mixed within her. *I can always have other daughters.* If it was so important, why hadn't she been told earlier? *Damn them and their schemes!*

She sensed her teacher behind her and recalled a day on Wallach IX when she had been forced to undergo a test of her own humanity. Reverend Mother Mohiam had held a poisonous gom jabbar at her creamy neck. One slip, and the deadly needle would have penetrated her skin, killing her instantly.

When they discover I am not carrying a daughter...

The intensely black room spun slowly, as if connected to the carousel in the Imperial garden. She lost her sense of direction and place, until she realized she was following Mohiam through shadows into a tunnel of light. The two women emerged into a large, bright room. The floor beneath them was a projection screen filled with a dizzying forest of words.

Mohiam said, "These are names and numbers depicting the genetic programs of the Sisterhood. See how they all branch from a core bloodline? This is the line that culminates, inexorably, in the Kwisatz Haderach, at its pinnacle."

The floor glowed. The Reverend Mother gestured, demonstrating where Jessica fit in. The young woman saw her own name, and above that a name designating her birth-mother, *Tanidia Nerus*. Possibly real, or more likely a code designation. The Sisterhood held so many secrets. The bonds between birth-parents and children did not exist among the Bene Gesserit.

One name, among others, surprised Jessica . . . Hasimir Fenring. She had seen him in the Imperial Court, a strange man always whispering in the Emperor's ear. On the chart, his bloodline approached the desired pinnacle, but tapered off to a genetic dead end.

Noting her scrutiny, Mohiam said, "Yes, Count Fenring was very nearly our success. His mother was one of us, carefully chosen. But his breeding ultimately failed. He became a talented but useless experiment. To this day, he does not know his place among us."

Jessica sighed, wishing her own life could be less complicated, with straightforward answers instead of deceits and mysteries. She wanted to give birth to Leto's son—but now she knew an ancient house of cards had been built upon this one birth. It was not fair.

She could not endure this sensory projection for much longer. Her burdens were already immense and so very private that she could discuss them with no one. She needed time to think, a desperate feeling. She wanted to be away from the scrutiny of Mohiam.

Finally, the memory crystal stopped glowing, and Jessica found herself once more on the slowly spinning carousel bench in the Imperial garden. High over their heads, stars encrusted the roof of the night sky. She and Reverend Mother Mohiam sat in a pool of glowglobe illumination.

Inside her belly, Jessica felt the baby kick, harder than ever before.

Mohiam extended her hand, palm open, over the concubine's protruding stomach and smiled as she, too, felt the unborn baby kick. Her normally flat eyes twinkled. "Yes, it is a strong child . . . one with a great destiny."

We are trained to believe and not to know.

—Zensunni Aphorism

Dressed in a wide-sleeved ambassadorial day-coat in order to fit in with the Imperial Court, Piter de Vries stood furtively at the back of the crowd, scrutinizing dignitaries as they watched the proceedings in the Imperial Audience Chamber. A Mentat could learn a great deal in the thick of activity.

He had crept close, unobtrusively, until Duke Leto's pregnant concubine stood in front of him in the company of Margot Fenring, young Princess Irulan, and two other Bene Gesserit Sisters. He could smell the Atreides whore, saw the golden light playing off her bronze hair. *Beautiful.* Even pregnant with Leto's whelp, she remained desirable. Using his diplomatic credentials, de Vries had positioned himself so that he could observe Jessica and pick up any bits of conversation that might prove useful in planning the bold act he had in mind.

High on his Golden Lion Throne sat Shaddam IV, listening to the Lord of House Novebruns, who had formally requested that the fief of Zanovar be transferred away from House Taligari to his own holdings. Though the Emperor's Sardaukar had turned the main cities on Zanovar into blackened scars, Lord Novebruns believed he could still mine the area for valuable raw materials. To strengthen his case, the enterprising nobleman greatly overestimated the resulting tax revenues his new income would generate for House Corrino. Noticeable in their absence, the disgraced House Taligari had not even been permitted to send an emissary to the discussion.

De Vries found it all very amusing.

On Shaddam's left, Lady Anirul's matching, though smaller, throne remained empty; Chamberlain Ridondo had made the usual excuses that the Emperor's wife was not feeling well. A gross understatement, and everyone at court knew it. According to rumor, she had gone quite mad.

Piter de Vries found that even more amusing.

If the Lady Anirul had suffered some sort of mental breakdown, if she was in fact violent, it would be particularly effective (and virtually untraceable to House Harkonnen) if the twisted Mentat could somehow convince *her* to strike out against the Atreides whore. . . .

For months now, following the unfortunate demise of his predecessor Kalo Whylls, de Vries had served as the interim Harkonnen Ambassador. During that time, he had lurked in the Palace shadows, rarely speaking to anyone, maintaining a low profile. Day after day he observed the activities of the Court and analyzed the interactions of various personalities.

Oddly, the pregnant Jessica was constantly surrounded by other Sisters like clucking hens, which made no sense at all. What were they up to? Why should they be so overprotective?

It would not be easy to get to her, or to the Duke's baby. He preferred to kill Jessica while she was still pregnant, thereby accomplishing both murders in a single stroke. But so far he had seen no opportunity. And the Mentat had no intention of sacrificing his own life for the Baron's benefit. He wasn't *that* loyal to House Harkonnen.

Peering over the shoulder of a man in front of him, de Vries spotted Gaius Helen Mohiam standing in her usual position off to one side of the Emperor, where she could be called upon to perform her Truthsayer duties.

Even at this distance, with the intervening people and activities, Mohiam locked gazes with him, a dark-eyed venomous stare. Many years before, de Vries had used a stunner on her so that the Baron could impregnate her with the daughter the Bene Gesserit had demanded of him. The Mentat had gloated then, and ever since had harbored no doubt Mohiam would kill him if ever given the chance.

Suddenly, he felt other eyes on him and saw more of the robed women lurking in the crowd, pressing closer. Uneasy, he backed into the swirl of the crowd, away from Jessica.

❦

LIKE ALL TRUTHSAYERS, Gaius Helen Mohiam considered the interests of the Bene Gesserit to be paramount, above even those of the Emperor. Now the Sisterhood's highest priority was to protect Jessica and her child.

The furtive presence of the Harkonnen Mentat caused Mohiam great concern. Why did Piter de Vries take such an interest in Jessica? He skulked around the perimeters, obviously spying on her. This was an especially sensitive time, with the day of her delivery fast approaching. . . .

Mohiam decided to take another step to keep the Mentat off-balance. Suppressing a smile, she flashed a hand signal to a Sister at the rear of the audience chamber, who in turn whispered in the ear of a Sardaukar guard. Mohiam could use an obscure legal precedent still on the books. A true Mentat probably had them memorized already, but de Vries was no true Mentat. This one had been created—and twisted—in Tleilaxu tanks.

The uniformed soldier marched into the crowd while Lord Novebruns continued his audience with the Emperor, explaining mineral resources and excavation techniques. The guard grabbed de Vries's collar as he tried to slither toward the back of the Audience Chamber. Three guards came to assist, stifling the Mentat's struggles and objections as they hauled him toward a side entrance. The scuffle was over in moments, causing only minimal disturbance during the Lord's impassioned speech. The court proceedings continued. On his throne, the Emperor looked bored.

Mohiam slipped through an alcove and circled around to meet the struggling prisoner in the corridor. "I have requested a full review of your ambassadorial credentials, Piter de Vries. Until this security check is completed, you will not be allowed in the Audience Chamber while the Padishah Emperor is discussing matters of state."

De Vries froze as he pondered the assertion. His narrow face took on a look of disbelief. "Preposterous. I am the formally charged Ambassador of House Harkonnen. If I am not allowed in the Emperor's presence, how can I possibly perform my services in the Baron's name?"

Mohiam leaned closer to him, her eyes narrowed to slits. "It is highly unusual for a Mentat to be placed in an ambassadorial position."

De Vries looked at her, assessing what he considered to be a petty power play. "Nevertheless, all the proper forms have been completed and approved. Kalo Whylls was recalled, and the Baron trusts me to take his place." He attempted to straighten his clothing.

"If your predecessor was 'recalled,' how is it that no travel documents were ever filed? How is it that Whylls himself never signed the order rescinding his appointment?"

De Vries smiled with stained lips. "There, so you see evidence of his incompetence? Is it any wonder that the Baron wished to place a more reliable person in such an important position?"

She gestured to the guards. "Until this matter can be thoroughly investigated, this man is not to appear inside the Audience Chamber, or anywhere within view of

Emperor Shaddam." She gave a condescending nod to the Mentat. "Unfortunately, such a process may take months."

The guards acknowledged the Emperor's Truthsayer and glared at de Vries, as if he might be a threat. At her command, they left the two alone in the corridor.

"I am tempted to kill you now," Mohiam snapped. "Do a projection, Mentat. Without your concealed neural stunner, you have no chance against my fighting abilities."

De Vries rolled his eyes comically. "Am I supposed to be impressed by the bluster of a schoolyard bully?"

Now she got down to business. "I want to know why you are on Kaitain—and why you have been hovering so close to Lady Jessica."

"She is a most attractive woman. I notice all the beauties of the court."

"Your interest in her is excessive."

"And your games are tiresome, witch. I am on Kaitain merely to handle important business for Baron Vladimir Harkonnen, acting as his legitimate emissary."

Mohiam did not believe him for a moment, but he had dodged her question and spoken no outright lie. "How is it that you have filed no motions, attended no committee meetings? I would say you are not much of an Ambassador."

"And I would say that an Emperor's Truthsayer should have more important things to do than monitor the comings and goings of one minor representative of the Landsraad." De Vries looked down at his fingernails. "But you are right—I do indeed have vital duties. Thank you for reminding me."

Mohiam detected subtleties in his body language that showed he was lying. She gave him a scornful smile as he walked off a bit too quickly. She was convinced of his intention to harm Jessica, and perhaps the child. Mohiam had put him on notice, though. She hoped de Vries would try nothing foolish.

If, however, he failed to heed her warning, she would be happy for an excuse to eliminate him.

～

OUT OF THE damnable witch's sight, de Vries removed his torn coat and flung it at a passing servant in a white housecoat and trousers. When the man leaned down to retrieve the garment, the Mentat kicked him in the back of the head, just hard enough to render him unconscious without killing him. One had to keep in practice.

He snatched his coat from the floor, leaving no evidence, and stalked toward his office. Why—*why!*—did the witches consider Jessica so special? Why had the Emperor's wife summoned Leto's concubine here to the Imperial Court, just to give birth to a brat?

Facts slid around in his mind, clicked into place. Mohiam herself had been assigned as the breeder cow when, twenty years ago, the witches had blackmailed House Harkonnen into giving them a daughter. So the Baron had raped her, quite obligingly. Piter de Vries had been there himself.

That daughter would be almost exactly Jessica's age.

In the hallway outside the office that he had commandeered from Kalo Whylls, de Vries stopped in his tracks. His mind locked into the intense focus of a first-approximation analysis. He leaned against a stone wall.

He assessed Jessica's facial features, looking for the faintest echoes of parentage. A great rush of information assailed him. The twisted Mentat slumped to the floor, with his back to the wall, and made an extraordinary connection in his mind:

Lady Jessica is herself the Baron's daughter! And Mohiam is the birth-mother!

Snapping out of the trance, he noticed a concerned diplomatic aide approaching, but he struggled to his feet and waved her off. Stumbling into his office, he passed his secretaries without a word and disappeared into the main room. His brain continued to hum, whirling from one probability to another.

Emperor Shaddam played his own political games, but didn't see the intrigues right before his eyes. With a satisfied smile the Mentat realized what a wonderful weapon this new theory could be. *But how best to use it?*

Before allowing yourself to celebrate, take the time to ascertain whether good tidings are actually the truth, or simply what you want to hear.

— Advisor to FONDIL III (no name given)

After a long and tedious session with Lord Novebruns and the other supplicants in his throne room, Shaddam was exhausted, anxious to get back to his offices to sip a quiet drink—perhaps even some of Duke Leto's fine Caladan wine. Later, he might go down to the labyrinthine Imperial steam pools beneath the Palace, where he could play with his concubines . . . though he did not feel in a particularly amorous mood.

He was astonished to find Hasimir Fenring waiting for him in the office.

"Why aren't you on Ix? Didn't I send you there to supervise production?"

Fenring hesitated just a moment, then smiled. "Hmmmm-ah, I had important matters to discuss with you. Personally."

Shaddam looked around furtively. "Is something wrong? I insist that you tell me the truth. My decisions depend on it."

"Hmmm." Fenring paced the room. "I bring you good news. Once it is released, we won't hold any more secrets. In fact, we will want the entire Imperium to know." He smiled, his overlarge eyes gleaming. "My Emperor, it is perfect! I have no more doubts. Amal is all we could have hoped for."

Taken aback at Fenring's enthusiasm, Shaddam sat down at his desk and grinned. "I see. Very well, then. All of your doubts were unwarranted, as I suspected."

Fenring bobbed his large head. "Indeed, I have looked closely at all of Master Researcher Ajidica's facilities. I watched the production in the axlotl tanks. I have tasted the amal myself, and have performed a number of tests, all of which were successful." He fumbled in the front pocket of his formal frock coat and withdrew a small packet. "See, I have brought back a sample for your own use, Sire."

Uneasy, Shaddam took the packet. He sniffed. "Smells like melange."

"Yes, hmmm. Taste it, Sire. You will see how excellent it is." Fenring seemed just a bit too eager.

"Are you trying to poison me, Hasimir?"

The Spice Minister reeled backward in surprise. "Your Majesty! How can you think such a thing?" He narrowed his eyes. "Naturally, you must realize I have had ample opportunities to murder you over the years, hmmm?"

"That's true enough." Shaddam held the sample up to the light.

"I will taste it myself, if that will put you at ease." Fenring reached forward, but Shaddam took the packet away.

"Enough, Hasimir. That is all the reassurance I need." The Emperor touched a bit of the powdery substance to his tongue, then some more, and finally upended the entire portion into his mouth. In supreme ecstasy, he let the amal dissolve on his tongue, feeling the familiar tingle of melange, the energy, the stimulus. He smiled broadly. "Very good. I can't tell any difference. This is . . . incredibly good."

Fenring bowed, as if taking credit for the whole project.

"Do you have any more? I would like to start using it myself, to replace my daily spice." Shaddam looked in the packet as if searching for tiny crumbs in the corners.

Fenring took a half step away. "Alas, Sire, I was in a

great hurry and could bring only this tiny amount. However, with your blessing, I will tell Master Researcher Ajidica that he may continue full-fledged production without further doubts from the crown, hmmm? I think that will speed things up considerably."

"Yes, yes," Shaddam said, waving his hands. "Go back to Ix and make sure there are no further delays. I've waited long enough for this."

"Yes, Sire." Fenring seemed very anxious to get away, but the Emperor hardly noticed.

"Now if only I can find a way to eliminate the spice from Arrakis," Shaddam mused, "then the Imperium will have no choice but to come to me for amal." He tapped his fingers on the desk, already deep in thought.

Fenring bowed at the door to the Emperor's private offices and departed.

Once in the hall, the Face Dancer maintained his impersonation until he could get far enough from the Palace. Other Tleilaxu remained at the Kaitain court, planted there by Ajidica himself, but the Face Dancer would be glad to return to Xuttuh.

Shaddam had heard the news he wanted to hear, and Master Ajidica could now continue his work unhindered. The Master Researcher's great plan was nearing its fruition.

*When you feel the pressures of limitations, then you
begin to die . . . in a prison of your own choosing.*

— DOMINIC VERNIUS, *Ecaz Memoirs*

Deep in the suboid warrens, C'tair led Rhombur and Gurney to a large, rock-hewn room.
Long ago it had been an overflow storage chamber,
but with dwindling food supplies there were now
many such empty areas. During the first night
there, Rhombur and Gurney had kept out of sight,
discussing strategy. Because of the Heighliner delay, now they had less time than they had hoped.

In a whispered rush of words under the faltering
light of a waning glowglobe, C'tair told Rhombur
about the sabotages he had committed over the
years, how surreptitious Atreides assistance had
helped him strike crippling blows against the invaders. But Tleilaxu cruelty, as well as an increase
in illicit Sardaukar troops stationed here, had
stolen all hope of release from the Ixian people.

Rhombur had no choice but to report the sad
news that his Navigator brother, D'murr, had died
from tainted spice, although he had lived long
enough to save a Heighliner full of people.

"I . . . I knew something had gone wrong,"
C'tair said in a bleak voice, not wanting to say
anything about Cristane. "I was talking to him just
before it happened."

Hearing of C'tair's experiences, the Ixian Prince
could not conceive how this solitary terrorist, this

intensely loyal subject, had survived so much despair. The strain had nearly driven him mad, yet this man continued his work.

But things would change. On Ix, Rhombur had plunged into his new obsession with fiery-eyed enthusiasm. Tessia would have been glad to see it.

Before the break of artificial dawn the next day, he and Gurney slipped back up to the surface, dismantled the rest of the camouflaged combat pod, and carried down the hidden weaponry and armor components. It would be enough for a small armed uprising, provided the material could be distributed effectively.

And provided they could find enough fighters.

INSIDE THE PRIVATE rock-walled chamber, Rhombur stood like a figurehead. For days, word had been spread that he was back. Now awed people, carefully screened by C'tair and Gurney, found excuses to be away from their assignments and trickled in to see him, one by one. The very presence of the returned Prince gave them hope. They had heard promises for years, and now the rightful Earl Vernius had returned.

Rhombur looked out at the huddled workers still waiting to enter the chamber. Many of them were wide-eyed; others had tears on their faces. "Look at them, Gurney. They are my people. They will not betray me." Then he had formed a wan smile. "And if they *do* turn against House Vernius, even after what the Tleilaxu have done here, then perhaps it is not worth such a struggle to win back my home."

The furtive people continued to arrive, reaching out to shake the mechanical hand of the cyborg Prince as if he were a holy resurrection. Some dropped to their knees, others stared him in the eyes as if challenging his ability to bring freedom back to the downtrodden people.

"I know you have been disappointed many times before," Rhombur said in a voice that sounded much older, much more confident than Gurney had heard before. "But this time you will have victory on Ix." As he spoke, the people listened attentively. Rhombur felt wonder at this, and a tremendous sense of responsibility.

"For the next few days you must watch and wait. Prepare for your opportunities. I don't ask you to endanger yourselves . . . not yet. But you will know when the time is right. I can provide no details, because the Tleilaxu have many ears."

The nervous gathering muttered, fewer than forty people looking sidelong at their companions as if they might find shape-shifters in their midst.

"I am your Prince, the rightful Earl of House Vernius. Trust me. I will not let you down. Soon you will be liberated, and Ix will return to the way it was when my father Dominic ruled the planet."

The people gave a low cheer, and someone shouted, "Will we be free of the Tleilaxu *and* the Sardaukar?"

Rhombur turned to face the man. "The Emperor's soldiers have no more right to be here than the Tleilaxu." His face became grim. "Besides, House Corrino has committed its own crimes against the Vernius family. Observe."

Gurney stepped forward and activated a small holo-projector. The solido image of a gaunt, beaten man appeared, sitting in dank shadows.

"Before she married my father, Lady Shando Vernius was a concubine of Emperor Elrood IX. Unknown to us until recently, she also bore the old Emperor an illegitimate son. Under the name of Tyros Reffa, the boy was raised in secret by the gentle Docent of Taligari. Reffa was therefore my half brother, a member of House Vernius through the distaff line."

Mutters of surprise rippled through the chamber. The Ixians all knew of the deaths of Dominic, Shando, and Kailea, but they had not guessed there might be another member of the family.

"These words were recorded in the Imperial prison by

our Ambassador-in-Exile, Cammar Pilru. This is the last speech Tyros Reffa ever made, before Emperor Shaddam Corrino executed him. Even I never met my own half brother."

He played Reffa's impassioned words to growing moans of anger and outrage. Apparently the man had not previously known his connection to House Vernius, but that did not matter to the rebellious people as they listened. When the image faded, people came forward as if to embrace the air in which the holograms had been projected.

Afterward, even with the power with which the doomed Reffa delivered his words, Rhombur spoke his own piece, finding strength and passion that would have made a Master Jongleur proud. He did more to inflame rebellious thoughts than any reasoned plan another man could have put together. In the emotion-packed sentences, Prince Rhombur pleaded for *justice*.

"Now go forth and tell others," he urged. Their time had been curtailed here, and the Prince had to take greater risks in his work. "Be careful, but enthusiastic. We don't dare reveal our plans to the Tleilaxu and the Sardaukar. Not yet."

Hearing the names of their hated enemies, several Ixians spat on the stone floor. In a grim mutter of outrage that built to a barely controlled crescendo, the recruits cried, "Victory on Ix!"

Quickly, C'tair and Gurney whisked the Prince away through side tunnels, to hide him before the wrong people noticed the disturbance and came to investigate.

🐗

DAYS LATER, STILL full of questions and uncertainties, the two infiltrators watched a chronometer and prepared themselves for a labor shift to change, so that they could slip out and talk to other potential rebels. A faint glowglobe flickered overhead in their small rock chamber.

"Everything's going as well as we could have hoped, given our shortened timetable," Rhombur said.

"Still, Duke Leto is operating in a blackout of information," Gurney said. "I wish we'd had a way of contacting him, to tell him that we're going ahead."

Rhombur responded with a quote from the Orange Catholic Bible, knowing his companion's fondness for the scripture. " 'If you have no faith in your friends, then you have no true friends.' Rest assured, Leto won't let us down."

The men tensed as they heard a commotion in the hall, followed by furtive footsteps. Then C'tair appeared, his work shirt and hands bloodied. "I need to change quickly, and clean up." He looked back and forth, fearing detection. "I was forced to kill another Tleilaxu. He was just a lab worker, but he had cornered one of our new recruits and was interrogating him. I know he would have given away our plan."

"Did anybody see you?" Gurney asked.

"No. But our recruit fled, leaving me with the mess to clean up." C'tair hung his head, shook it, then raised his chin again, his eyes proud but sad. "I will kill as many as necessary. Tleilaxu blood cleanses my hands."

Gurney was concerned. "This is bad news, our fourth near discovery in only three days. The Tleilaxu are bound to be suspicious."

"That's why we dare not delay," Rhombur said. "Everyone must know the timetable, and be ready. I will lead them. I am their Prince."

Gurney's inkvine scar reddened as he scowled. "I don't like this."

C'tair began wiping his hands and scrubbing under the fingernails. He seemed resigned to the danger. "We Ixians have been massacred before, but our determination will prevail. Our prayers will prevail."

The search for an ultimate, unifying explanation for all things is a fruitless endeavor, a step in the wrong direction. This is why, in a universe of chaos, we must constantly adapt.

—Bene Gesserit Azhar Book

The Ishaq Hall of magnificent documents was lost among the extravagant monuments on Kaitain. During his youth Shaddam had spent much time in elaborate diversions in the city, but he'd had little interest in old papers and manifestos. Still, an official Imperial visit to the hoary old museum seemed an appropriate diversion now.

Why is the Guild so upset?

In preparation for Shaddam's arrival, the Ishaq Hall had been swept clean of surveillance devices. For this one day, all teachers, historians, and students had been forbidden to enter the building, thus permitting the Emperor full access. Even so, he was accompanied by his retinue of guards and so many court functionaries that the echoing corridors felt crowded.

Though the Guild had requested this secret meeting, Shaddam had arranged for the appropriate time and place.

Long ago, when Emperor Ishaq XV designed and built the museum, it was one of the most spectacular constructions in the burgeoning Imperial city. But in the intervening millennia, the Hall of Magnificent Documents had been swallowed by ever more impressive architecture; now it was difficult to find it among the congestion of governmental structures.

The Senior Curator greeted the Emperor and his retinue with embarrassing enthusiasm and gushing formality. Shaddam mumbled appropriate responses as the obsequious man proudly displayed a number of ancient handwritten journals, the personal diaries of past Corrino Emperors.

Considering all the time-consuming duties that required his attention, Shaddam couldn't imagine any skilled ruler having the luxury to write such ponderous musings for the sake of posterity.

Like Ishaq XV, who had tried to inscribe his name in the chronicles of the Imperium by constructing this once-impressive museum, every Padishah ruler sought a special place in history. With amal, Shaddam vowed to attain his fame through something greater than a handwritten diary or a dusty old building.

What can the Guild possibly want of me? Have they learned more about the tainted spice from Beakkal?

Though he still hadn't decided what to do with Arrakis, as soon as he succeeded in monopolizing spice commerce with his inexpensive substitute, Shaddam intended to lay the foundation for future generations of House Corrino.

During the tour, the Hall Curator showed him constitutional documents, oaths of conditional independence and declarations of planetary loyalty dating back to when the growing Imperium was consolidating itself. A carefully preserved parchment of the first Guild Charter, supposedly one of only eleven extant copies in the universe, sat bathed under filter lights and a protective shield. One display case held a copy of the *Azhar Book*, the Bene Gesserit volume of secrets written in a long-forgotten language.

Finally, standing before a pair of tall locked doors, the Curator stepped aside. "In here, Your Majesty, we hold our greatest treasure, the cornerstone of Imperial civilization." His voice grew whispery with awe. "We have the *original document* of the Great Convention."

Shaddam tried to look impressed. He knew the legalities of the Great Convention, of course, and had studied the precedents, but he had never taken the time to read the actual wording. "You have made arrangements for me to view it alone, at my leisure?"

"Of course, Sire. In a completely private and secure chamber." The Curator's eyes flickered with concern and overprotectiveness. Shaddam wondered what the man thought he might do. If an Emperor ripped the document to shreds, would that not be a historical event in itself? A smile stole across his lips.

Shaddam knew, though few others did, that this "hallowed relic" was not actually the original, but was instead a clever forgery, since the original had been lost in the atomic blaze on Salusa. But it was a symbol, and people could be fanatical about such things. Shaddam pondered this as the doors swung wide and he stepped into an isolated room, moving with proud Imperial grace, but not speed. He felt mounting dread.

The Spacing Guild has rarely demanded anything of me, and now they insist on this secret meeting. What do they want? The Guild had received exorbitant bribes after each attack on a spice-hoarding world, and they had seemed satisfied with them.

He stepped into the windowless chamber and looked at the shrine-podium that displayed the fraudulent document, complete with singed brown edges to maintain the fiction that it had been rescued from the Salusan holocaust. He wished Hasimir Fenring were there with him, instead of away on Ix again. With problems compounding in his Great Spice War, Shaddam needed good suggestions. He heaved a deep sigh. *I am on my own.*

In due course, especially now that Fenring had disavowed all his misgivings, Shaddam planned to announce his amal to the unsuspecting CHOAM and the Guild. No doubt the economic fallout would be chaotic, but the

Emperor was strong, and with the secret of synthetic spice he could endure any sanctions. But he would have to block the regular channels of melange.

Arrakis, what to do with Arrakis . . . ?

He would either destroy the desert planet or station Sardaukar there on a permanent basis to prevent the Guild from obtaining their own spice. This was essential during the transition, in order to force the Imperium into purchasing his amal. . . .

As soon as the doors sealed behind him, a secret entrance slid aside in the far left wall. A tall man with pink eyes and a dandelion puff of white hair took a step into the room, but hesitated and glanced around suspiciously. He wore a Guild protective suit made of polymer leatheryl, rigged with tubes and pulleys that connected to a pressurized tank on his back. Spice gas seeped through evaporators around his collar, so that the Guild Legate's face was wreathed in a halo of pungent, orange melange gas.

He came closer, albino eyes sharp, locking onto the Emperor's features. Behind him followed five companions, smaller Guildsmen in identical suits, but without melange packs. They were hairless, pale-skinned dwarfs, their bone structures distorted as if someone had turned their skeletons to clay and then squeezed. They carried speaking grids and recording apparatus.

Shaddam stiffened. "This is supposed to be between us, alone, Legate. I have brought no guards." In the confined space, the Emperor picked up the strong cinnamon odor of spice.

"Neither have I," said the Guild Legate in a phlegmy voice, softened by the thick melange. "These men are extensions of me, parts of the Guild. All of the Guild is closely interconnected—whereas you are alone to represent House Corrino."

"The Guild would be wise not to forget my position." He caught himself, not wanting to begin any blustery displays that might bring repercussions, subtle or overt. "You requested this meeting. Please get to the point quickly, as I am a busy man."

"We have reached conclusions regarding the flawed spice that led to serious Navigator errors and the death of a Guildsman. We now know the source."

Shaddam's brow furrowed. "I thought you said the contaminated melange came from Beakkal. I have that place under quarantine already."

"Beakkal merely sold it to us." The Guild Legate was grim. "Spice comes from Arrakis. Spice comes from the Harkonnens." The albino sucked in another breath of the curling vapors around his face. "From our operatives there, we have learned that the Baron has gathered large, illegal stockpiles of melange. We know this is true, yet he has not decreased his shipments."

Shaddam simmered with anger. The Guildsman had to know this was a particularly sensitive subject for him.

"On audit, we have completed a study of Harkonnen records. The Baron has documented his spice production with particular thoroughness. The amounts seem to be correct."

Shaddam had trouble following this. "If his records are correct, then how did the Baron compile his hoard? And what does this have to do with tainted spice?"

For some unknown reason, the small, identical Guildsmen shifted their position around the albino Legate. "Consider, Sire. If the Baron steals a percentage of each spice harvest, yet continues to ship the appropriate amount according to manifest documents, then obviously he must be 'cutting' the export shipments. He must be skimming away pure melange and diluting it with supposedly inert materials. Thus the Baron keeps the skimmed melange for himself, while providing weakened spice for Navigator use. Given the evidence, there can be no other conclusion."

The Legate adjusted controls on his complicated polymer leatheryl suit and drew a long breath of orange vapor.

"The Spacing Guild is prepared—in Landsraad Court—to accuse the Baron Harkonnen of malfeasance, of causing the Heighliner disasters. If convicted, he would be forced to pay enough reparations to drive House Harkonnen into bankruptcy."

Shaddam could not stop a grin from spreading across his face. He had been waiting for a solution to the Arrakis problem, and now this appeared, like a miracle. The idea was clear in his mind—and it would take care of *everything*. He could not have concocted a better scenario had he tried. The Guild's blatant charges were a golden opportunity—perhaps a bit premature, but no matter.

He finally had the excuse he needed to lock down his monopoly. With the recent glowing report by Hasimir Fenring, as well as similar communications from Master Researcher Ajidica and Sardaukar commander Cando Garon, he was utterly confident in the viability of his synthetic spice.

Based on the Legate's accusation, Shaddam could turn his Imperial sword of justice against Arrakis, with full Guild cooperation. Before anyone knew what was happening, the Sardaukar would wipe out all spice production in the desert, leaving House Corrino with absolute and total control of the only remaining source of spice: amal. This economic revolution would occur faster than he had ever dreamed.

The mutated dwarfs moved around, watching their superior, awaiting his commands.

Shaddam turned to the Guild Legate. "We shall confiscate all spice from House Harkonnen, starting with Arrakis, and then search every other world the Baron holds." He smiled paternally. "As before, I am primarily concerned with enforcing Imperial law. And, as before, the Guild and CHOAM shall share the spoils of every illegal stockpile we uncover. I will keep none for myself."

The Guild Legate bowed his head into the curling melange mist. "That is most satisfactory, Emperor Corrino."

More for me than for you, Shaddam thought. He had

been waiting for this all along—how could he ignore such an opportunity? Once he obliterated the only known source of natural melange and began widespread distribution of amal, the few crumbs of recovered spice would become irrelevant.

"While maintaining my blockade around Beakkal, I shall send a large Sardaukar force to Arrakis." He arched his eyebrows. If he could avoid the mandated costs of transport for such a huge military operation, he could reap even greater benefits. "Naturally, I expect the Guild to provide Heighliners for this operation."

"Of course," the Legate promised, playing right into Shaddam's hands. "As many as you require."

Life improves the capacity of the environment to sustain life. Life makes needed nutrients more readily available. It binds more energy into the system through the tremendous chemical interplay from organism to organism.

—IMPERIAL PLANETOLOGIST PARDOT KYNES

Under the command of Thufir Hawat, the Atreides relief ships approached the blockade around the quarantined planet of Beakkal. The Mentat commander issued no threats, but did not waver in his course. The flotilla carried only minor defenses, weapons that could not have driven off even a ragtag band of pirates.

Facing them, the immense Sardaukar warships bristled with weaponry in a titanic show of Imperial power.

As Hawat's supply carriers proceeded toward the cordon, two Corrino corvettes streaked across open space toward them. Even before the Sardaukar captains could issue blustery threats, Hawat opened a comlink. "Our ships fly under the colors of Duke Leto Atreides, on a humanitarian mission. We bear food supplies and medical aid for plague-ravaged Beakkal."

"Turn back," a gruff officer responded.

Either of the corvettes could have decimated the Atreides flotilla, but the Mentat did not flinch. "I see that your rank is Levenbrech. Tell me your name so that I may commit it to permanent memory." His stare at the comscreen was unflinching. Such a minor officer would never make any significant decisions.

"Torynn, sir," the Levenbrech said in a sharp, formal voice. "Your House has no business here. Turn your fleet around and return to Caladan."

"Levenbrech Torynn, we can help the people below survive while they replant their crops with resistant strains. Would you deny food and medicines to a starving populace? That is not the stated purpose of this blockade."

"No ships may get through," Torynn insisted. "A quarantine is in place."

"I see, but I do not understand. Neither, apparently, do you. I will speak with your commanding officer."

"The Supreme Bashar is otherwise occupied," the Levenbrech said, trying to sound implacable.

"Then we shall occupy him further." Hawat ended the transmission and signaled for his ships to continue forward, not hurrying, not deviating.

The two corvettes tried to head off the procession, but the Mentat sent quick orders in Atreides battle language, and the entire flotilla spread out and flowed around the warships, as if they were rocks in a stream. The Levenbrech continued to signal, growing more frustrated when Hawat simply ignored his commands.

Finally, Torynn called for reinforcements. Thufir knew the Sardaukar would never forgive the minor officer for failing to stop a group of unarmed, sluggish cargo ships.

Seven larger vessels broke away from the orbital net at Beakkal and approached the Atreides ships. The Mentat knew this was a dangerous moment, because Supreme Bashar Zum Garon, an old veteran like Hawat himself, would be on edge, certain that this was a trap or a feint designed to leave the planet undefended. Hawat's weathered face showed no emotion. This was a feint indeed, but not one the Sardaukar would expect.

Finally, the grim Bashar spoke directly to him. "You have

been ordered to turn back. Comply immediately, or you will be destroyed."

Thufir could feel the members of his crew growing uneasy, but he held firm. "Then you will no doubt be relieved of your command, sir, and the Emperor will spend a long time dealing with the political repercussions of firing upon peaceful, unarmed vessels bearing humanitarian supplies to a suffering population. Shaddam Corrino has made thin excuses to cover your blatant aggressions. What will his justification be this time?"

The heavy brows furrowed on the craggy face of the old military man. "What is your game, Mentat?"

"I do not play games, Supreme Bashar Garon. Few people bother to challenge me, because a Mentat always wins."

The elder Garon snorted. "You would have me believe that House Atreides sends assistance to *Beakkal*? Not eight months ago, your Duke bombed this place. Has Leto grown soft?"

"You do not understand Atreides honor, any more than your Levenbrech understands the principles of quarantine," Thufir said in a chiding tone. "Leto the Just metes out punishment when warranted, and gives aid where needed. Are these not the principles by which House Corrino established its rule after the Battle of Corrin?"

The stern Bashar did not respond. Instead, speaking in a clipped code, he issued an order. Five more ships broke away from orbit and surrounded the Atreides flotilla. "We deny you passage. The Emperor's orders are clear."

Thufir tried another tactic. "I am certain His Imperial Majesty Shaddam IV would not prevent his cousin from making amends to the people of Beakkal. Shall we ask him directly? I can wait, while you delay . . . and while people die on the world below."

No other Landsraad family would dare challenge the Emperor's blockade, especially in Shaddam's obviously volatile state of mind. But if Thufir Hawat succeeded here in Leto's name, other Houses might well be shamed into providing aid, feeding the people of Beakkal, giving them strength to fight against the botanical plague. Perhaps they would view it as a passive act of censure for the Emperor's recent actions.

The Atreides Mentat continued, "Send a message to Kaitain. Tell the Emperor what we intend to do here. There is no chance for us to be personally contaminated if we use orbital dump boxes to deliver our cargo. Give Emperor Shaddam the opportunity to demonstrate the benevolence and generosity of House Corrino."

As Sardaukar warships tightened around the Atreides flotilla, Supreme Bashar Garon said, "You will divert to Sansin, Thufir Hawat. Keep your cargo ships there and await further instructions. Even now, a Heighliner is preparing to depart from the transfer station. I will go myself to the Imperial Palace and present your request to the Emperor."

The warships herded Hawat's cargo vessels toward the asteroid supply station. Grudgingly, the Atreides flotilla followed.

The warrior Mentat shot a last comment at the recalcitrant Bashar. "Waste no time, sir. People are rioting on Beakkal, and we have food right here. Do not deny it to them for long."

In truth, though, Thufir was content enough that his diversion would occupy these Imperial forces.

THE ATREIDES FLOTILLA waited at Sansin for a full day after Supreme Bashar Garon departed. Then, choosing an appropriate moment, Hawat sent another coded communication to his supply vessels, and they withdrew from the transfer station and headed confidently back toward Beakkal, ignoring the renewed protests of the Sardaukar fleet.

Another officer demanded that he stop. "Cease your

advance or we will consider you a threat. We will destroy you." Apparently the disgraced Levenbrech Torynn had been relieved of command.

The military blockade responded with a flurry of activity, but Hawat knew that if the Supreme Bashar himself was not willing to fire upon them, none of the lower-ranking officers would take the risk.

"You have no such orders. Our supplies are perishable, and the people of Beakkal are starving. Your unconscionable delay has already cost thousands—perhaps millions—of lives. Do not compound your crime, sir."

The panicked officer sent other messages and powered up his weapons, but Hawat drove his ships right through their net. Even with the fastest Courier, it would be days before they received a response from Kaitain.

In orbit, the Atreides ships hovered over the most-afflicted population centers. Fuselage bays opened, and self-propelled dump boxes dropped into the atmosphere, giant unmanned cubes tumbling and braking. Simultaneously, Thufir transmitted a message to the citizens below, extolling the mercy of Duke Leto Atreides and telling them to accept these gifts in the name of humanity.

He had expected an appalled Prime Magistrate to respond, but in a comlink response the Mentat learned that riots had already cost the politician his life. His frightened successor insisted that he bore no grudge against House Atreides, especially not now.

The Sardaukar blockade ships would probably prevent the now-empty Atreides ships from departing the system, but Thufir would deal with that in due course. He hoped he had done what was necessary, causing the appropriate stir on Kaitain.

Now he could afford to wait. According to Duke Leto's timetable, the Atreides assault forces would even now be descending upon Ix.

When a newly arrived Courier skimmer rushed from the Sansin complex and was intercepted by the Sardaukar flagship, Hawat assumed it was the return of Supreme Bashar Garon.

An hour later, in his vanguard ship, the warrior Mentat was surprised to receive the news that the Emperor had not deigned to give a response about what he called the "minor Atreides matter" at Beakkal. Instead, he had recalled his Supreme Bashar. Intercepting a radio message between ships, Thufir learned that it was for a "major new strike."

Thufir Hawat's mental projections had not foreseen this. His mind spun, without locking onto a solution. A major new strike? Was this a reference to Ix? Or an Imperial retaliation against Caladan? Had Duke Leto already lost?

Every extrapolation suggested by his complex mind gave him cause for alarm. The timing was terrible.

Perhaps Leto had been lured into disaster after all.

It is not always the same thing to be a good man and a good citizen.

—ARISTOTLE of Old Earth

Though Duke Leto Atreides rarely made formal trips to Kaitain, his arrival at the Imperial Palace aroused little interest. The magnificent structure was a flurry of high-level diplomatic and political activity. No one paid attention to yet another Duke.

Accompanied by a small retinue of servants, Leto rode in a diplomatic transport toward the reception wing of the Palace. The air smelled of trumpet flowers and aromatic enhancers that concealed vehicle exhausts. Though burdened by concerns—for Duncan and the Atreides soldiers, for Thufir and his bluff against the Beakkal blockade, and for the frightening silence from Rhombur and Gurney—Leto maintained the calm demeanor of a professional diplomat and leader on an important mission.

Despite the pressures, though, he eagerly looked forward to seeing Jessica. Their baby was due in mere days.

Liveried guards ran alongside the elegant floater-car. The vehicle was at least three centuries old, with red-velva seats. The golden lion hood ornament swiveled to the left and right, opening its jaws, baring its teeth, and even roaring whenever the black-mustachioed driver touched the horn pad.

The Duke was not particularly impressed by the gadgetry. With his speech to the Landsraad, he would soon be throwing fuel on the fire. Shaddam would be furious about the attack on Ix, and Leto feared the damage would be irreparable. But he was willing to sacrifice all that to do the right thing. He had ignored the injustice for too long. The Imperium must never think him soft and indecisive.

Along the route of crystal-paved boulevards, Corrino banners fluttered in a gentle breeze. Immense buildings stretched to a cloudless blue sky, too perfect for Leto's tastes. He preferred the changing weather of Caladan, even the beauty and unpredictability of storms. Kaitain was too tame, having been transformed into a caricature world taken from a fantasy filmbook.

The floater-car slowed at the Palace reception gate, and Sardaukar guards waved them through. The mechanical lion roared again. Ominous weapons were plainly in view, but Leto had eyes only for the arrival platform. He caught his breath.

Lady Jessica stood waiting for him in a golden parasilk dress that clung to her rounded body, emphasizing her abdomen—but even such elegance could not overshadow the radiance of her beauty as she smiled at him. Four Bene Gesserit Sisters hovered around her.

As Leto stepped onto the oiltile pavement, Jessica hesitated and then hurried toward him, her walk still graceful, despite her ungainly size. Jessica paused, as if concerned that embracing him in public might not be proper. Confident in himself, though, Leto cared nothing for appearances. He closed the gap between them and gave her a long, passionate kiss.

"Let me have a look at you." He pulled back to admire her. "Ah, you are as lovely as a sunset." Her oval face had tanned from time spent in the Palace gardens and solarium. She wore no jewelry, and did not require it.

He placed his callused palm against her stomach and held it there, as if trying to feel the baby's heartbeat. "It appears I arrived with no time to spare. You were barely showing at all when you left me alone on Caladan."

"You are here to deliver a speech, not a baby, my Duke. Will we be able to spend time together?"

"Of course." His tone grew more distant as he noticed the scrutiny of the Bene Gesserit, as if they were taking notes on his performance. At least one of them showed signs of disapproval. "After my speech to the Landsraad, I may need to go into hiding." He gave her a wry smile. "Therefore, your company would be most welcome, my Lady."

At that moment, Emperor Shaddam emerged from the Imperial residence, walking briskly in a straight line as guards, attendants, and advisors swarmed around him like gnats: Sardaukar officers, gentlemen in tailored suits, ladies with high-coiffed hairdos, servants guiding suspensor-borne suitcases and trunks. From the hangar wing of the reception gate, a spectacular processional barge drifted forward, piloted by a tall man who was almost completely hidden beneath loose, fluttering robes, as if he were a living banner.

The Emperor looked ready for war. He had forsaken his whale-fur cape and chains of office for a crisp gray Sardaukar uniform outlined with silver braids, epaulets, and a Burseg's black, gold-crested helmet. He was scrubbed and polished, from his skin to the medals on his chest to his shiny black boots.

Spotting the Duke, Shaddam walked over to him, excessively pleased with himself. Jessica bowed formally, but the Emperor paid no attention to her. Like Leto, Shaddam IV had hawklike facial features and an aquiline nose. And like Leto, he harbored important secrets. "I apologize that pressing matters prevent me from receiving you more formally, Cousin. The Sardaukar forces require my presence for a major operation."

An immense war fleet awaited him on the staging grounds—so many ships laden with soldiers and matériel that three Guild Heighliners had been retained to transport them, along with two more escort Heighliners in a show of bravado and strength from the Guild itself.

"Is it anything I need concern myself with, Sire?" Leto tried to keep the questions and anxiety from his face. Was Shaddam playing games with him?

"I have it all under control."

Leto tried to cover his relief. "I had hoped you would be present for my speech in the Landsraad Hall tomorrow, Sire." In fact, he had expected to face down the Emperor there, aided by a groundswell of popular support from the other nobles. *A major Sardaukar operation? Where?*

"Yes, yes, I'm sure your announcement will be very important. The opening of a new fishery or some such thing on Caladan? Unfortunately, duty calls me away." His baritone voice was pleasant, but his green eyes gleamed with cold cruelty.

The Duke gave a formal bow and took a step backward to stand at Jessica's side. "When I deliver my words to the Landsraad, Sire, I will be thinking about you. I wish you success on your mission. You can review my remarks at your leisure when you return."

"At my *leisure*? I have an Imperium to manage! I have no leisure, Duke Leto." Before he could answer, Shaddam noticed the jewel-handled knife sheathed at Leto's waist. "Ah, is that the blade I gave you, at the end of your Trial by Forfeiture?"

"You told me to carry it with me as a reminder of my service to you, Sire. I have never forgotten."

"I remember." Finished with the conversation, Shaddam turned back toward the processional barge that would take him to the waiting war fleet.

Leto sighed. Since the Emperor's attention was not on him, the new military operation must not involve Ix, Beakkal, or Caladan. Therefore, it was to the Duke's advantage that Shaddam would not be present when he made his announcement and justification for the Atreides assault on

Ix. Rhombur would be firmly seated in the Grand Palais before anyone in the Imperial government could mount a response.

He smiled as Jessica escorted him into the Palace. *Perhaps everything will work out, after all.*

He had never been averse to taking risks, but now C'tair actually relished them. It was time to be overt.

During his work shifts, he whispered into the ears of strangers as they labored alongside him, selecting those who appeared the most oppressed. One by one, the bravest among them took up the rallying cry.

Even suboid workers, whose minds were too dim to comprehend political implications, came to understand how they had been betrayed by the Tleilaxu. Years ago, the invaders had seduced them with promises of a new life and freedom— but their lot had only grown progressively worse.

Finally, the oppressed population had more than a vague hope. Rhombur had truly returned! Their long nightmare would be at an end. Soon.

WAITING IN A tiny alcove where he was supposed to meet his companions, Prince Rhombur heard a scuffle down the corridor and powered up his synthetic limbs, ready to fight. Leto's troops were due to arrive within hours, and C'tair had already slipped up to the surface, crawling through cramped ducts and emergency shafts so that he could plant the last few smuggled explosive wafers at key places in the Sardaukar surface defenses. A few well-timed blasts would leave the port-of-entry canyon unprotected against the arriving Atreides army.

But all their work would be for naught if Rhombur was discovered here too soon. The noise grew closer.

Then scarred Gurney Halleck lurched into the alcove carrying a broken body. The corpse looked barely human, with smooth, waxy features, lifeless eyes, and a doll-like head that lolled on a snapped neck.

"Face Dancer, posing as a suboid. I thought he showed too much curiosity in me. I took a chance, deciding he had to be more than one of your feebleminded workers."

He dropped the dead shape-shifter in a heap on the stone floor. "So I broke his neck. Good thing, too. 'The hidden enemy is the greatest threat.' " He looked intently at Rhombur and added, "I think we have a serious problem. They know about us now."

TO COUNT FENRING'S surprise the Master Researcher made no overt move against him, but he still felt like a prisoner.

Never taking his safety for granted, the Count remained alert, playing along until he could find an opportunity to escape. He had seen many disturbing behaviors and side effects among the people who had consumed too much synthetic melange, including the Sardaukar. Very bad . . .

The diminutive Tleilaxu scientist, increasingly erratic and unpredictable in his behavior, spent an entire morning in his office showing numbers to the Imperial Spice Minister, demonstrating production enhancements and the quantities of amal that his axlotl tanks could produce, to keep his program going for just a little while longer. "The Emperor will have to dole it out carefully at first, as rewards for those who are most loyal to him. Only a few should receive this blessing. Only a few are worthy."

"Yes, hmmm." Fenring still had many questions about the synthetic melange, but saw too much danger in asking them. He sat across the desk from Ajidica, examining hardcopy documents and mini-holos the Master Researcher passed across to him.

Ajidica was filled with uncontrollable nervous energy. He had a glazed, defiant look on his pinched face, combined with a supreme haughtiness, as if he considered himself a demigod.

All of Fenring's instincts screamed warnings, and he just wanted to kill the man and be done with it. Even guarded carefully, a deadly fighter like Count Hasimir Fenring could find a thousand ways to commit murder—but he would never escape unscathed. He saw the fanatical loyalty, the hypnotic control the Master Researcher had over his personal guards and ferociously devoted staff . . . even, most disturbingly, on the Sardaukar troops.

Other changes were happening as well. In recent days, the Ixian populace had grown unruly and dissatisfied; incidents of sabotage had increased tenfold. Graffiti had blossomed on the walls like Arrakeen flowers in the morning dew. No one knew what had triggered it after so much time.

Ajidica's response had been to squeeze even harder, further restricting the minimal freedoms and rewards the people retained. Fenring had never approved of the draconian tactics the Tleilaxu employed against the Ixians; he considered it shortsighted politics. Day by day, the unrest increased and pressure built, as if a lid had been clamped on a boiling pot.

The Master Researcher's office door slammed open, and Commander Cando Garon marched in. The young Sardaukar leader had tangled hair and a rumpled uniform with dirty gloves, as if he no longer bothered with a military dress code. In his strong grip he dragged a small, weak creature, one of the suboid workers.

Garon's eyes were dark and dilated, flicking about with rapid movements. His jaw was clenched, his lips curled in feral displeasure mixed with triumph. He looked more like a ruthless bully than the commander of disciplined Imperial troops. Fenring felt a flutter of uneasiness in his chest.

"What is this?" Ajidica snapped.

"I believe it's a suboid," Fenring said dryly.

The Tleilaxu researcher scowled with distaste. "Take that filthy . . . creature out of here."

"First, listen to him." Garon tossed the pale worker to the floor.

The suboid scrambled to his knees and looked from side to side, not comprehending where he was or what kind of trouble he was in.

"I told you what to do." Garon kicked the weak man in the hip. "Say it."

The suboid fell over, gasping in pain. The Sardaukar commander lunged at him, grabbing one of his ears with a gloved hand. He twisted until blood dripped from it. "Say it!"

"The Prince has returned," the suboid said, then repeated it over and over, like a mantra. "The Prince has returned. The Prince has returned."

Fenring felt hairs prickle on the back of his neck.

"What is he talking about?" Ajidica asked.

"Prince Rhombur Vernius." Garon nudged the suboid, ordering him to say more. Instead, the simpleminded man whimpered and repeated the phrase.

"He's talking about the last survivor of the renegade Vernius family, hmmmm?" Fenring pointed out. "He *is* still alive, after all."

"I know who Rhombur Vernius is! But it has been so many years. Why should anyone care about him now?"

Garon slammed the suboid's head against the hard floor, making him scream in pain.

"Stop!" Fenring said. "We need to interrogate him further."

"He knows nothing more." Garon balled his gloved fist and pounded the helpless man's back. Fenring could hear ribs and vertebrae crack. The wild commander punched again, an out-of-control pile driver.

The suboid drooled blood onto the floor, twitched, and died.

Sweating and agitated, the Sardaukar commander straightened. His eyes were bright and feral, as if looking for something else to kill. Blood had spattered all over his uniform, and he didn't seem to mind.

"Just a suboid," Ajidica said, with a sniff. "You're correct, Commander—we would have gotten no further information anyway." The Master Researcher thrust a small hand into his robes and withdrew a tablet of compressed synthetic spice. "Here you are." He tossed it to Garon, who snatched the tablet out of the air with lightning-fast reflexes and gobbled it, like a trained dog receiving a treat.

Garon's wild-eyed gaze focused on Fenring. Then the officer strode toward the door, leaving the bloody mess on the floor. "I'll go find others to interrogate."

Before he could depart, loud alarms rang out. Fenring leaped to his feet, while the Master Researcher looked around, more in annoyance than in fear. He had not heard such sirens in the twenty-two years that he had resided on Ix.

From the rhythm of the alarm, Commander Garon knew what was happening. "We are under attack, from the outside!"

THE ATREIDES MILITARY fleet dropped through the atmosphere and slammed into the Sardaukar defensive grid. Attacking warships descended into the port-of-entry canyon, where hundreds of grottoes were covered by heavy doors used for deliveries and exports.

C'tair's sabotage bombs went off, startling the Sardaukar and knocking out their main sensor nets and installations.

The surface-to-air guns went dead as control decks shorted out. The bored Tleilaxu perimeter guards could not respond to the astonishing attack that had appeared out of nowhere.

The Atreides ships launched explosives, melting armor plates and blasting rock. Sardaukar scrambled to mount a defense, but after so many years of complacency their weapon stations were designed to quell internal disturbances and intimidate would-be infiltrators.

Led by Duncan Idaho, the fleet arrived exactly on schedule. Transports landed and soldiers boiled out, their swords drawn for close-in shield fighting where lasguns could not be used. They howled a war cry for their Duke and for Prince Rhombur.

The battle for Ix had begun.

There is no mystery about the source from which love draws its savage power: It comes from the flow of Life itself—a wild, torrential, outpouring that has its source in the most ancient of times. . . .

— LADY JESSICA, journal entry

When Jessica's labor began, the Bene Gesserit were ready for her. Few understood the full reasons, but every one of the Sisters knew this long-awaited child was important.

The sunny birthing room had been laid out in accordance with Anirul's exacting specifications. Careful attention was paid to ancient Feng Shui practices, as well as to lighting and air-flow patterns. Philaroses, silver orchids, and Poritrin carnations grew inside suspensor-borne planter globes above the bed. The room on the top level of the Imperial Palace was open to the eyes of the universe, reaching nearly to the fluffy underlayers of weather-control clouds.

Jessica lay back, concentrating on her body, and her environment, and most of all on the child anxious to come out of her womb. She avoided eye contact with Reverend Mother Mohiam, afraid her guilt would show on her face. *I have challenged her before, resisted her dictums . . . but never in a matter of such consequence.*

Soon, the Sisters would know her secret.

Will the Reverend Mother kill me for my betrayal? In the hours after the birth, Jessica would be completely vulnerable. In her old teacher's eyes, failure would be a greater crime than outright treachery.

Between labor spasms, Jessica inhaled the flowers' sweet scents and thought of far-off Caladan, where she wanted to be with her Duke and their child. "I shall not fear . . ."

Mohiam sat nearby, watching her prize student attentively. A drained-looking Lady Anirul had insisted on coming to the birthing room, despite Medical Sister Yohsa's stern admonitions. Who could resist the command of the Kwisatz Mother at such a time? Heavily medicated, Anirul claimed to have made a temporary peace with the clamor in her head.

Jessica tried to rise out of deference, but the Emperor's wife wagged a stern finger at her. "Put on the birthing gown we have provided for you. Lie back and concentrate on your muscles. Prepare your mind and body, as you have been taught. I will not have anything go wrong with this delivery. Not after waiting for ninety generations!"

Yohsa came closer, touched Anirul's arm. "My Lady, she has just begun dilating. We will call you when the hour approaches. It will be some time yet before she—"

Anirul cut her off. "I have already borne five daughters to the Emperor. This young woman will heed my advice."

Jessica dutifully removed her clothes and donned the long kai-sateen gown Anirul had provided. It was so light and smooth that she barely felt it against her skin. As she climbed back onto the curved birthing bed, Jessica felt a tingle of anticipation that overcame her worries. *When I leave this bed, I will have a son, Leto's son.*

For nine months she had nurtured and protected this baby. Until twelve days ago, when a sensory-projected Reverend Mother Mohiam had shown her the truth of the Kwisatz Haderach program, she had thought only of her love for her Duke, and how much he needed another son after the tragic death of Victor.

At Anirul's side, Mohiam wrinkled her lips in a smile. "Jessica will do well enough, my Lady. She has always been my finest student. Today, she will show the worth of all the training I have given her."

Overwhelmed by the thought of what these powerful women might do, Jessica wished Leto could be with her now. He would never allow harm to come to her or their child. They had spent the previous evening together, and she'd been grateful just to hold him again in her bed, her skin touching his. To Jessica, such gentle comfort mattered more than moments of high passion.

By the soft light of glowglobes in their chambers, Jessica had noticed a change in the Duke. He had become his old self again, the hard but powerful Leto Atreides she loved, more alive than he had been in a long time.

But he was scheduled to speak to the Landsraad today. The Duke of a Great House had far more important duties than hovering anxiously at the bedside of his concubine.

In the birthing room now, surrendering to the natural processes of her body, Jessica lay back and closed her eyes. She had no option but to cooperate with the Bene Gesserit and hope. *I can bear another child, a daughter next time. If they let me live.*

Jessica knew she had preempted their plans by moving the male birth up by a full generation. Still, genetics was an uncertain science, the gambling dice of a higher, undefined power. *Could my son be the one anyway?* It was a frightening, exhilarating possibility.

Opening her eyes, she saw two Medical Sisters move in like sentinels on either side of her bed. Whispering to each other in a language even Jessica did not understand, they checked diagnostic equipment while touching probes and sensors to her skin. At the foot of the bed with Yohsa, Lady Anirul watched everything, her doe eyes deeply sunken above her hollow cheeks. Like a person risen from her deathbed, the Emperor's wife instructed the women in every detail, making them nervous and irritated.

Yohsa's concern was divided between Jessica and Lady Anirul. "Please, my Lady, this is simply a routine delivery.

There is no need for your attentions. Return to your own chambers and rest. I have a new prescription for you, to quiet the voices of Other Memory." Yohsa reached into her pocket.

Anirul waved the smaller woman aside. "You understand nothing. You have already given me too many drugs. My friend Lobia is trying to warn me of something . . . from deep inside. I need to listen, not plug my ears."

Yohsa's voice took on a scolding tone. "You should never have probed so deeply without companion Sisters."

"Are you forgetting who I am? This is a matter that involves my Hidden Rank. *You will not challenge me.*" Grabbing a surgical lasknife from a tray, she spoke in a menacing tone. "If I tell you to plunge this into your own heart, you will do it." The other Medical Sisters stepped back, not knowing what to make of this.

Anirul glared at Yohsa, her doe eyes ablaze. "If I determine that your continued presence endangers the success of the project, I will kill you myself. Be careful, very careful."

Mohiam, however, glided closer and intervened. "Have the voices given you advice, my Lady? Can you hear them now?"

"Yes! And they are louder than ever before."

With a quick movement, Mohiam pushed the endangered Medical Sister beyond the reach of the agitated woman. "Lady Anirul, it is your right and duty to shepherd this special birth, but you must not interfere with these women."

Still holding the lasknife, her body twitching as if she were fighting Other Memory for control of her mind and muscles, Anirul took a seat on a suspensor chair beside Jessica. The other two Medical Sisters stood off to one side, but at a hand signal from Mohiam they resumed their work.

Amidst this chaos, Jessica took calming breaths and cycled through techniques that Mohiam had taught her. . . .

Anirul tried to quell her raging anxiety, so that her dangerous emotions would not contaminate the birthing room.

Feral thoughts raced through the Kwisatz Mother's troubled mind, struggling to be heard over the internal and external disorder. She bit the knuckles of one hand. If anything went wrong in the next few hours, the Kwisatz Haderach program could be set back for centuries, and possibly ruined for all time.

It must not happen.

Anirul suddenly looked down at the lasknife in surprise, then set it on a nearby table, but still within reach. "I am sorry, child. I did not mean to upset you," she murmured. Presently she continued in a prayerlike tone, "At this most important time, you must use Prana-Bindu skills to guide the baby through your birth canal." She looked at the shining implement on the table. "I will cut your daughter's umbilical cord myself."

"I am ready to begin," Jessica announced. "I will intensify my labor now." *How they will hate me when they see.*

She exercised precise Bene Gesserit control over her body, over every birthing muscle, and exerted pressure. What would Lady Anirul do? Her eyes bore the signs of madness, but was the Emperor's wife capable of murder?

Jessica vowed to remain alert and ready to protect Leto's son in any way possible.

The Emperor still speaks by the authority of the people and their elected Landsraad, but the great council is becoming more and more a subordinate power and the people are fast turning into an uprooted proletariat, a mob to be aroused and wielded by demagogues. We are in the process of transforming into a military empire.

— **PREMIER EIN CALIMAR**
of Richese, speech to the Landsraad

A swift and impressive display of force. Shaddam was quite pleased with the effect. Arrakis— and the Imperium—would never be the same again.

Unannounced and unexpected, an armada of Guild ships appeared in the skies over the desert world. Five Heighliners, each more than twenty kilometers long, took their places in orbit, within sight of the Harkonnen capital of Carthag.

An astonished Baron Harkonnen stood on the Residency's shielded balcony and stared up into the night sky. A borealis display of ionization discharges rippled overhead in patterns that made his corpulent flesh crawl. "Damnation! What is going on up there?"

Buoyed by his suspensor belt, the Baron held himself steady to keep from drifting. Deep in his gut, he regretted that he had not returned to Giedi Prime as he'd intended the week before.

A hot breeze crept like a plague through the

dark streets. High above him, the bright, reflected shapes of Heighliners spread out in low orbit, like jewels floating on a black sea. The Carthag City Guard sounded alarms, rousing troops from the barracks and locking down the populace under a state of martial law.

An aide rushed in, even more afraid of the spectacle in the sky than of his Harkonnen master. "My Lord Baron, a Guild envoy has sent a message from the Heighliners. He wishes to speak to you."

Indignantly, the fat man puffed out his cheeks. "I am most curious to know what in the hells they think they are doing above my planet." Melange production had exceeded the Emperor's expectations, even despite the amount of spice he surreptitiously skimmed. House Harkonnen should have nothing to fear, even with Shaddam's recent incomprehensible petulance and volatility. "There must be some mistake."

The aide switched on a comscreen, and adjusted controls until he made the proper connection. Harsh words grated across the speaking mesh. "Baron Vladimir Harkonnen, your crimes have been exposed. The Guild and the Emperor will decide your punishment. You are subject to our combined judgment."

The Baron was accustomed to denying his culpability in criminal matters, but in this instance he was so astounded that he could not even stammer an excuse. "But . . . but . . . I don't know what—"

"This is not a dialogue," the voice said, louder and harsher. "This is a *pronouncement*. CHOAM auditors and Guild representatives are being sent down to scrutinize every aspect of your spice operations."

The Baron could barely draw a breath. "Why? I demand to know what I am accused of doing!"

"Your secrets will be exposed and your mistakes punished. Until we decree otherwise, the flow of spice throughout the Imperium will be cut off. You, Baron Harkonnen, must provide the answers we seek."

Panic set in. He had no idea what had triggered this absurd saber rattling. "I . . . who are my accusers? What is the evidence?"

"The Guild will now cut off your communications and shut down all spaceports on Arrakis. Effective immediately, we are suspending the operation of spice harvesters in the field. All 'thopters are grounded." The comsystem in front of him began to smoke and spark. "This message is ended."

From overhead, the armada of Guild ships broadcast intense pulses that disabled the circuitry and navigational systems on all vessels in the Carthag Spaceport. Inside the Baron's residency, glowglobes dimmed and then brightened as they were bombarded. Some fizzled and exploded, showering plaz fragments on his head.

He covered his face and shouted into the comsystem, but there was no response. Even local comlinks had broken down. In blind rage, he bellowed—though no one except those in his immediate presence could hear (and they wisely fled).

The Baron could not demand any further explanation, or summon help from anyone.

THE UNDERBELLIES OF three Heighliners opened, and the main Sardaukar fleet detached from their docking clamps. Battle cruisers, corvettes, marauders, bombers—every military vessel the Emperor could gather on short notice. In mounting this operation, Shaddam understood that he was leaving other parts of his Imperium vulnerable, but he had too much to gain, in one unexpected master stroke. Not even the Guild understood his true aims.

Wearing a dress uniform emblazoned with commander-in-chief insignia, the Emperor sat on the bridge as his flagship descended toward Arrakis. This would be the culmination of decades of planning, an unexpectedly quick finish to the overall amal project. For once, he would lead his troops into victory himself, for the magnificent end of the Great Spice War. His Project Amal was ready, and now he would remove Arrakis from the equation.

The Sardaukar had been instructed to follow his direct orders, though Supreme Bashar Garon would supervise the actual maneuvers. Shaddam needed someone he could trust to act without question, because there *would* be many questions. Standing stiffly beside him, the weathered Sardaukar veteran did not know the Emperor's plan or understand the desired outcome of this confrontation. But he would follow his superior's command, as always.

Using the holocaust weapons they had demonstrated on Zanovar, the Sardaukar warships were about to eliminate all spice on Arrakis, a necessary step in the shaping of Shaddam's new Imperium. Afterward, *he* would have the only remaining answer. Amal. With this one attack, Shaddam Corrino IV would strengthen the Golden Lion Throne and crush the monopolies and trading conglomerates that had hobbled his rule.

Ah, if only Hasimir could be here to see my victory. The Emperor reminded himself how he had proven time and again that he didn't need an advisor pestering him, contradicting his ideas, constantly trying to take credit.

As his flagship flew closer to the fringe of atmosphere, the Emperor leaned forward in his command chair to stare at the cracked brown planet. *Ugly place.* Would further devastation even be noticeable here? He saw an incomplete ring of satellites, ineffective weather observers that the Guild had grudgingly put into orbit after years of insistence from the Baron himself. They monitored only Harkonnen-controlled areas, while providing no information at all about the deep desert and polar regions.

"Time for target practice," he announced. "Send out your marauders and destroy those satellites. Every one." He tapped his fingers on the padded arm of the command chair. He had always loved playing soldier. "Let us blind the Baron even further."

"Yes, Your Imperial Majesty," said Zum Garon. Moments

later, small attack ships swarmed from the Heighliners and spread out like hordes of locusts. With precise shots, they vaporized one satellite after another. Shaddam savored each tiny explosion.

From the ground, his fleet must look terrifying. The Guild assumed he only meant to establish a firm military presence here, to soften up any Harkonnen defenders so that the Sardaukar could confiscate illegal melange stockpiles. Already Landsraad nobles—those few who knew he had brought a fleet here—were calling in favors, shifting positions, trying to become the next recipient of the Arrakis fief and its spice industry.

A soon-to-be *worthless* spice industry.

Oh, how Shaddam looked forward to the next act in his grand play. He thought back on the dry and outdated drama, *My Father's Shadow*, which had extolled the virtues of Crown Prince Raphael Corrino, a deluded fool who had never formally accepted the Imperial throne.

Shaddam had considered becoming a patron of the arts himself, though his accomplishments could not be limited to cultural ones. An Imperial biographer would document his military and economic victories, and a team of writers would create enduring literary works to enthrall later generations with his greatness. It was all so simple, once an Emperor received the absolute power he deserved.

After the desert planet was no more than a charred ball, the Spacing Guild—and everyone else who relied upon melange—would be wrapped around his finger. He decided to call this campaign the Arrakis Gambit.

For such a fabulous triumph it was worth taking extravagant risks.

Greatness must always be combined with vulnerability.

— CROWN PRINCE RAPHAEL CORRINO

Ready to face another turning point in his life, Duke Leto marched into the Landsraad Hall of Oratory. Even with the Emperor off on some war game, Leto was prepared to deliver what might well be the most important speech of his noble career.

He recalled the last time he had appeared before this august assembly. He had been very young, the newly installed Duke of House Atreides following the untimely death of his father. After the overthrow of Ix by the Tleilaxu, Leto had been brash, decrying the invaders and condemning the Landsraad for ignoring the pleas of Earl Vernius. Instead of being impressed, the representatives had laughed at the immature young nobleman . . . much as they had scoffed at the protestations of Ambassador Pilru for so many years.

But this afternoon, as Duke Leto led his proud procession down the entrance promenade, delegates cheered and shouted his name. Applause swelled in the vast Hall, making him feel stronger, more sure of himself.

Though they had no means of communicating with one another now, the disparate parts of his overall plan had to proceed with perfect timing. Already, Thufir Hawat had made his successful move against the blockade at Beakkal, and the separate attack would proceed on Ix, even without confirmation from the two infiltrators. Leto knew his own role here on Kaitain. If the scheme went as planned, if Rhombur and Gurney were still alive, the liberation of Ix would be complete and the new Earl Vernius would be secure in his ancestral home before anyone could object. . . .

But only if everything happened at once.

Immediately before entering the Hall of Oratory, Leto received a rushed notification from one of the nameless Bene Gesserit Sisters who fluttered like ravens around the Imperial court. "Your concubine Jessica has gone into labor. She is being cared for by the best Medical Sisters. There is nothing to fear." The Acolyte gave him a small smile along with a reflexive bow as she backed away. "Lady Anirul thought you might wish to know."

Feeling unsettled, Leto strode toward the speaking platform. Jessica was about to have his child. He should be with her in the birthing room. The Bene Gesserit might not approve of a man's presence there, yet under other circumstances, without all these pressing affairs of state, he would have defied them.

But this was a matter of protocol; his speech had to be given *now*, while Duncan Idaho led the troops into the caverns of Ix.

As the court crier read his name and titles, Leto tapped his fingers on the lectern and waited for the cheers to die down. Finally, a silence of expectation blanketed the chamber, as if the delegates suspected he might have something interesting—and even bold—to say.

His popularity and stature in the Landsraad had been building for years. No other nobleman, including those much wealthier than he, would have risked such an impetuous and unexpected move.

"You all know the plight of Beakkal, ravaged by a botanical plague that threatens to destroy its ecosystem.

Although I had my own dispute with the Prime Magistrate, that matter has been settled to my satisfaction. My heart, like yours, aches for the suffering Beakkali people. Therefore, I have dispatched ships filled with relief supplies, in hopes that Emperor Shaddam will allow us to pass the blockade and deliver vital aid."

Applause rippled through the Hall, reflecting admiration mixed with surprise.

"But that is only one small part of my activities. More than twenty years ago, I appeared before you to protest the illegal Tleilaxu conquest of Ix, the proper fief of House Vernius—friend to House Atreides and friend to many of you.

"Receiving no help from the Emperor, Earl Dominic Vernius chose to go renegade. He and his wife were hunted down while the vile Tleilaxu invaders secured their hold on Ix. Since that time Prince Rhombur, the rightful heir, has lived under my protection on Caladan. For years, the Ixian Ambassador-in-Exile has implored you for help, but not one of you lifted a finger in assistance." He waited, watched, and listened to the uncomfortable stirring in the cavernous hall.

"Today, I have taken unilateral action to correct that injustice."

He let the ominous statement sink in with his listeners, then continued in a resounding voice. "Even now, as I speak to you, Atreides military forces are attacking Ix, with the intention of restoring Prince Rhombur Vernius to his proper place. Our aim is to drive out the Tleilaxu and liberate the Ixian people."

A gasp rippled through the throng, followed by anxious, murmurous conversation. None of them had expected this.

He forced a brave smile and changed his approach. "Under oppressive and inept Tleilaxu rule, the production of essential Ixian technology has drastically decreased. The Landsraad, CHOAM, and the Spacing Guild all know this. The Imperium needs good Ixian machines. Every nobleman here will benefit from the restoration of House Vernius. Let no one deny it." He looked around the sea of faces, daring anyone to disagree.

"I came to Kaitain to speak with the Padishah Emperor, but he is preoccupied with another military matter." Leto saw mostly blank faces and shrugs, but a few nods from those who seemed to know something. "I have no doubt that my dear cousin Shaddam will support the restoration of House Vernius to its former position in the Imperium. As Duke Atreides, I have taken action for Justice, for the Imperium, and for my friend, the Prince of Ix."

As Leto concluded, waves of reaction passed through the Landsraad Hall. He heard cheers, a few angry shouts—and, above all, confusion. Finally, the tide turned. One by one, delegates rose and began to applaud. Within moments the Hall erupted in a standing ovation.

Waving and nodding to them in appreciation, Leto paused as he caught the gaze of a dignified, gray-haired man in the audience who had no impressive uniform or rank, no box or reserved seat: Ambassador Cammar Pilru. The Ixian representative looked up at Leto with something like reverence. And he began to weep.

The expectation of danger leads to preparation. Only those who are prepared can expect to survive.

—SWORDMASTER JOOL-NORET, Archives

It was a long journey back to Caladan. The Heighliner threaded its way along a route in the Imperium, stopping at planet after planet. Among other vessels, the Heighliner's cargo bay held the small Atreides relief flotilla, with Thufir Hawat aboard the flagship.

After completing his diversionary humanitarian mission to Beakkal, Thufir wanted to be back home in the gray-stone towers of Castle Caladan, high on a cliff overlooking the sea.

His feint against the Sardaukar blockade had been as successful as he could have hoped. He had ruffled the Emperor's feathers and also delivered the relief supplies. After Shaddam had summoned his commander away, the Atreides flotilla had waited near Beakkal for nine days until another Heighliner arrived to take them on the scheduled route to Caladan.

First out of the hold, a handful of Atreides ships dropped into the cloudy skies of Caladan and were quickly swallowed up in the swirling weather patterns that covered the ocean. Behind the small flotilla, merchant vessels and passenger frigates descended to the spaceport on their regular business runs.

Thufir felt as if he could sleep for three days

straight. He had not rested well on this trip, because of all he had needed to accomplish, and because of his concerns about Duncan's primary assault on Ix. It should be happening at this very moment.

But he would not take that much-needed rest. Not yet. With the Duke away on Kaitain, and most of the Atreides military forces dispatched to Ix, he wanted to make absolutely certain that the remaining military personnel and equipment were set up properly for the defense of the planet. Caladan was too vulnerable.

When his few escort ships settled down at the miltary base adjacent to the Cala Municipal Spaceport, the Mentat was astounded to find no vessels at all, only a few elderly men and women in uniforms, little more than a maintenance staff. A reserve lieutenant told him that Duke Leto had decided to throw everything into the fight for Ix.

Seeing this, Thufir had an uncertain, exposed feeling.

AS THE HEIGHLINER cruised in parking orbit, more ships dropped out in the continuing bustle of space commerce. Later that day, when the immense Guild vessel crossed over the sparsely populated Eastern Continent, a large group of unmarked craft disembarked at the last moment, taking high orbital positions, far from prying eyes. . . .

Even with a pilot as skilled as Hiih Resser, the wings of the scoutship thumped and bounced as it cut through the cold storm currents of Caladan's upper atmosphere. The redheaded Swordmaster sat behind the controls of a rapid-reconnaissance ship, sent from the hastily gathered Grumman-Harkonnen fleet.

Resser peered down through patchy gaps in the clouds as he soared away from the planet's nightside, racing the sunset and gaining upon the daylight that lingered over the water.

His lord, Viscount Moritani, was willing to sacrifice everything in a sudden attack. Glossu Rabban, though a brute himself, was more conservative, wanting to know where the force would make its surprise attack and what their chances of success were. Though Resser had sworn his loyalty to the Viscount, after many rigorous oaths and testings, he preferred Rabban's point of view. Resser frequently disagreed with his lord, in principle, but after years of Swordmaster training he knew his place. His loyalty could not be questioned. He clung to his honor.

As did Duncan Idaho.

Resser remembered the years that he and Duncan had spent on island-dotted Ginaz. They had been fast friends from the beginning and had ultimately fought their way to victory, becoming Swordmasters themselves.

When other students from Grumman had been cast out of Ginaz because of a black dishonor committed by the Viscount, Resser had stayed behind, the only one from his House to complete the training. After graduating and returning to Grumman, he had assumed he would be disgraced and perhaps even executed. Duncan had implored Resser to come to Caladan, to join House Atreides, but the redhead had refused. Bravely, he had gone home anyway. He had kept his honor, and survived.

Because of his fighting and leadership skills, Resser had risen rapidly through the Grumman ranks, attaining the position of Special Forces Commander. For this mission to Caladan, he was second-in-command only to the Viscount himself. But he preferred to work hands on. Resser flew the scoutship himself, and when it came time to fight he would be in the thick of it.

He didn't look forward to opposing Duncan Idaho, but had no choice. Politics made razor cuts through relationships. Now, as he remembered all the things young Duncan had told him about his beloved and beautiful Caladan, Resser plunged beneath a raft of gray clouds until he could see the landscape, the cities, and the weaknesses of the planet.

He flew in, racing quickly over Cala City, across the river deltas and the lowlands filled with pundi rice farms. He noted the murky swamp of kelp beds out in the shallow waters and the black molars of reefs surrounded by white breakwaters. Resser recognized what he saw. Duncan had told him everything.

As they had sat together reading letters from home, Duncan had shared delicacies sent to him from House Atreides. He had talked about what a good man the Old Duke had been, how Paulus had taken Duncan under his wing as a boy and raised him in the Castle, where the newcomer had proven his loyalty.

Resser heaved a deep sigh, and flew on.

The scoutship flew fast and low, while the redhead drank in the details with his trained eyes. He saw what he needed to, then flew back to the hidden fleet to make his report, unable to reach any other conclusion. . . .

Later, when he stood at attention in front of the Viscount, he announced, "They have left themselves completely vulnerable, my Lord. Caladan will be an easy conquest."

ALONE AND CONCERNED, Thufir Hawat stood by the new statues that Leto had erected on the rocky promontory . . . towering figures of Old Paulus and young Victor Atreides, holding aloft the brazier of an eternal flame.

Out on the calm water, many little boats puttered about, sifting through the kelp, dragging nets, and hunting larger fish. It seemed peaceful. The clouds were patchy as the sun lowered toward the horizon.

The warrior Mentat also saw a single ship flying high and fast. Obviously a reconnaissance craft, a scout. Unmarked.

Detailed projections, first and second order. Thufir predicted what might be occurring, knew he could do little to defend Caladan against an outright attack. He still had a few warships from the escort flotilla, but nothing else remained of the Atreides home defense. Leto had gambled everything on his Ixian campaign . . . too much, perhaps.

The unmarked scoutship streaked overhead, gathering all of the damning information a spy would need. Looking up at the stony visage of Duke Paulus and then down at the innocent face of Victor, the Mentat of House Atreides was reminded of his past mistakes.

"I dare not fail you again, my Duke," he said aloud to the colossus. "Nor can I let Leto down. But I wish I had some answer, some way to protect this beautiful world."

Thufir gazed across the ocean, saw the ragtag fleet of fishing boats scattered at random across the waters. This conundrum would require all of his Mentat skill to solve, and he hoped that would be enough.

*They have hindered and hunted me for the last time
with their village-provost minds! Here, I make my
stand.*

—Attributed to the renegade EARL DOMINIC VERNIUS

Shortly after noon, precisely on time, alarms
rang out in the underground city. It was a
joyous sound for Prince Rhombur Vernius. "It's
starting! Duncan is here!"

In the shadows of a suboid warren, the Ixian
heir looked over at Gurney Halleck, whose glass-
splinter eyes shone in his lumpy face. " 'We gird
our loins, sing our songs, and shed blood in the
name of the Lord.' " He smiled and began to move.
"No time to lose."

C'tair Pilru, haggard and red-eyed, leaped to his
feet. He hadn't slept in days, and seemed to live
more on adrenaline than nourishment. His
planted explosives would have just gone off at the
port-of-entry canyon, opening the way for Atreides
troops to force their way inside.

C'tair called, "It is time to break out the
weaponry and rally anyone who will follow us. The
people are ready to fight back, at last!" His drawn
face had the angelic, ethereal look of a man who
had transcended the need for fear or reassurance.
"We follow you into battle, Prince Rhombur."

Gurney's inkvine scar flickered as he scowled.
"Take care, Rhombur. Don't give our enemies too
easy a target. You would be a big prize for them."

The cyborg Prince strode toward a low doorway. "I will not hide while others fight my battles, Gurney."

"At least wait until we secure part of the city."

"I will announce my return from the steps of the Grand Palais." Rhombur's tone invited no discussion. "I won't be satisfied with anything else." Gurney grumbled, but fell silent, considering how best to protect this proud, stubborn man.

C'tair led the way to a concealed armory, a small ventilation-equipment room that they had converted to their own purposes.

Rhombur and Gurney had already distributed components broken down from the sophisticated Atreides combat pod. They had smuggled weaponry, explosives, shields, and communications devices into the hands of zealous rebel volunteers.

C'tair grabbed the first weapons he could lay his hands on—two grenades and a stun-club. Rhombur attached a rack of throwing knives to his belt, then hefted a heavy two-handed sword with one of his powerful cyborg arms. Gurney selected a dueling dagger and a long sword. All three strapped on body-shields and activated them, producing the familiar, comfortable hum. *Ready.*

They left the lasguns untouched. At close quarters, with shields activated, they didn't want to risk setting off a deadly lasgun-shield interaction, which could vaporize the underground city.

While alarms continued to sound, some of the Tleilaxu production-facility doors closed in an automatic lockdown; others jammed in their tracks. Rumors in the past few days had already alerted the Ixians to what might happen, but many of them still could not believe that the arrival of Atreides saviors was at hand. Now they were overjoyed.

C'tair bellowed for support and ran through the tunnels. "Forward, citizens! To the Grand Palais!"

Many of the workers were afraid. Some felt a cautious hope. Suboid labor crews ran about in confusion, and C'tair shouted until they took up the chant. "For House Vernius! For House Vernius!"

He hurled his first grenade into a knot of screaming Tleilaxu factory administrators; it exploded in the cavern with a thunderous boom. Then he used his stun-club to thrash any of the gray-skinned men in his way.

As Rhombur charged forward like a railcar, a fléchette dart whizzed close to his head, but it was deflected by his shield. Spotting a Tleilaxu Master crouching off to one side, the Prince hit him in the chest with a thrown knife, then sliced another invader with his heavy sword. He pushed onward, into the mêlée.

Shouting, Rhombur rallied whatever rebels he could find. From the tunnel opening, he and Gurney handed weapons to eager fighters and directed them to fresh stashes of supplies. "Now is our chance to purge Ix of these invaders forever!"

Fighting his way to the center of the cavern floor, Gurney bellowed commands, worrying that these poorly organized revolutionaries would be cut to ribbons by the professional Sardaukar.

The holo-sky flickered on the grotto ceiling as explosions ripped through control substations in the stalactite buildings. The most magnificent structure, the inverted cathedral of the Grand Palais, hung like a Holy Grail for Rhombur to obtain. In the upper levels, uniformed Atreides troops rushed across high walkways behind a dark-haired Swordmaster, with blades raised.

"There's Duncan!" Gurney gestured toward the walkway overhead. "We need to get up there."

Rhombur fixed his gaze on the Grand Palais. "Let's go."

Following C'tair, shouting and attacking ferociously, the improvised band swelled with volunteers as they surged across the cavern floor. The rebels commandeered an empty cargo barge, a heavy anti-grav platform designed for ferrying off-world materials through the port-of-entry canyon and down to lower construction facilities.

Gurney climbed onto the barge's control deck and turned on the suspensor engines. They made a high-pitched whine. "Aboard! Aboard!"

Fighters scrambled onto the barge platform, some unarmed but willing to fight with their fingernails if necessary. When the vehicle began to rise in the air, a few rebels were crowded off the edge and tumbled to the floor. Others jumped up to grab handrails, dangling until comrades hauled them onto the deck.

The barge lifted while Sardaukar swarmed about below it, trying to form into regiments. A spray of fléchette needles erupted from their sidearms, ricocheting off walls, striking bystanders. Body-shields slowed or deflected some of the projectiles, but most of the innocent citizens were unprotected.

From their high vantage on the cargo barge, the wild rebels opened fire upon their enemies below. Unlike the Emperor's soldiers, the Tleilaxu Masters wore no body-shields. C'tair, in a frenzy, found a projectile weapon and fired it.

As the barge floated higher on its suspensors, Imperial soldiers directed their weapons upward, not even knowing who had taken the vessel. The Sardaukar seemed to be blood-maddened. One of the suspensor engines blew out, causing the platform to tilt. Four hapless rebels slipped and tumbled to their deaths on the stone floor far below.

Gurney wrestled with the reluctant controls, but Rhombur nudged him aside and added power to the remaining engines. The skewed barge rose toward the plaz-walled balconies of the former Grand Palais. The Prince stared upward, saw places from his youth, remembered how his family had celebrated their privileged lives.

He wrenched the guidance controls, and the overloaded platform diverted toward one of the broad windows, a balcony and observation deck where celebrations had once been held for the wedding anniversary of Dominic Vernius and his beautiful Lady Shando.

Rhombur drove the barge straight through the window, like a stake into a demon's heart, smashing the ornate balcony. Shards and other debris fell around them, and screams mixed with defiant cheers. The barge's suspensor engines faded as Rhombur shut down power, and the sluggish craft ground to a halt.

C'tair was the first to leap onto the checkerboard floor into the midst of panicky Tleilaxu and a handful of Sardaukar guards who scrambled to defend themselves. "Victory on Ix!" The freedom fighters took up the cry and surged forward with more enthusiasm than weaponry.

Accompanied by Gurney Halleck, Rhombur stepped off the barge for his triumphal return to the Grand Palais. Standing in the debris-strewn hall, surrounded by battle cries and gunfire, he felt as if he had finally come home.

WITHIN THE CEILING levels, Duncan Idaho led Atreides troops into the brunt of the clash, and the elite Sardaukar responded savagely. The Imperial soldiers crammed what seemed to be melange wafers into their mouths—an overdose of spice?—and raced into the fray.

Like animals gone berserk, the Sardaukar hurled themselves into hopeless offensives against overwhelming odds. At close quarters, shields crackling, they discarded their long-range weapons and charged into the Atreides force, using well-timed knives, swords, and even bare hands to penetrate defensive shields. Each time the Sardaukar subdued one of Duke Leto's fighters, they disabled his shield and ripped him apart in an instant.

Commander Cando Garon, his uniform torn and bloodied, waded in against Duncan's troops. Though a long sword hung at his hip, Garon declined to use it; instead, he wielded a more personal kindjal, jabbing back and forth with the wicked dagger tip. He pierced eyes, severed jugular veins, and simply *ignored* the Atreides assaults around him.

A brash Caladan lieutenant slipped in from the side,

dipped the point of his sword through the Commander's shield, and stabbed it into the meat of Garon's shoulder. The Sardaukar Commander stopped in his tracks, shook his head as if to clear the gnats of pain from his spice-frenzy, and plunged back into the mêlée with an even greater ferocity, oblivious to his attacker.

Wailing with bestial voices, the Sardaukar soldiers rushed forward, a tidal wave of uniforms in no formation whatsoever. Pell-mell and primitive, they were still effective, and deadly.

The Atreides ranks began to buckle under the onslaught, but Duncan yelled at the top of his lungs. He raised the Old Duke's sword to rally them. The blade felt powerful, infused with the spirit of its original owner. He had used it on Ginaz—and today it would lead the Atreides forces to victory. Had Paulus Atreides lived, the Old Duke would have been proud to see the achievements of the scamp he'd taken under his wing.

Hearing the Swordmaster's strong voice, Leto's men pushed forward with a clash of humming shields and a clatter of blades. Given the overwhelming Atreides numbers, it should have been a wholesale rout—but the wild-eyed Sardaukar did not give up ground easily. Their faces were flushed, as if the men had been pumped up with intense stimulants. They refused to surrender.

As the furious assault progressed, Duncan saw no sign of imminent victory, no hope that this would end soon. Somehow, despite their disorganization, the Sardaukar rallied yet again.

He knew that this would be the bloodiest day in his life.

WHILE THE FIGHTING raged in the underground caverns, Hidar Fen Ajidica stormed toward the high-security research pavilion, hoping it would serve as a sanctuary. Running beside him, Hasimir Fenring debated whether this might be his opportunity to find a hidden exit and escape. He decided he had no choice but to follow along and let the Tleilaxu researcher destroy himself—as the crazed little man seemed intent on doing.

Inside the vast laboratory, shielded from the eyes of outsiders, Fenring wrinkled his nose at the decayed-human stench that bubbled up from rows of axlotl tanks. Hundreds of Tleilaxu workers moved about, monitoring tanks, taking samples, adjusting metabolic control mechanisms. The ongoing battle outside frightened them, but they attended to their duties with unwavering dedication, fearing for their lives if they faltered even for an instant. The slightest fluctuation, the simplest misstep, could throw all the delicate tanks out of the range of acceptable parameters and ruin the vital amal program. Ajidica had his priorities.

The Sardaukar troops stationed closest to the research pavilion had been given more ajidamal and been pulled from their usual duties. Now they rushed helter-skelter into the fray outside the lab complex, screaming wildly.

Fenring did not fully understand, or like, what he saw. No one seemed to be leading the troops at all.

His gaze darting around, Ajidica gestured to the Count. "Come with me." The little man's eyes were now a startling shade of scarlet, their whites having turned bright red as seeping hemorrhages blossomed in his sclera. "You are the Emperor's man and should be at my right hand when I make announcements regarding our future." He gave a predatory grin, and blood trickled from his gums, as if he had just feasted on raw flesh. "Soon you will worship me."

"Hmmm, first let me hear what you have to say," Fenring answered carefully, recognizing the dark glint of insanity in the researcher's demeanor. He considered breaking the gnomish man's neck right then—it would take only a swift, simple blow—but too many loyal laboratory workers were nearby, staring at them, waiting for news.

The two of them climbed a steep metal stairway to a

high catwalk over the crowded laboratory floor. "Hear me! This is a test from God!" Ajidica cried to the listeners below, his voice booming into the open space. Blood sprayed from his mouth as he spoke. "I have been given a marvelous opportunity to show you our future."

The researchers gathered on the floor, listening to him. Fenring had heard the little man's delusional pronouncements before, but now Ajidica seemed to have gone completely mad.

A huge comscreen on one wall showed a steady stream of battle images from holoprojectors mounted around the subterranean world. Atreides forces, allied with the rabble of Ix, were taking control of sector after sector.

Oblivious to the tide of combat, the frenzied Master Researcher held up both hands, clenched into fists. Blood dribbled between his spidery fingers and small knuckles, and ran in scarlet streams down along the tendons of his forearms. He opened his hands to reveal the bright flowers of blood that had blossomed in the center of his palms.

Are those supposed to be stigmata? Fenring thought. *An interesting bit of showmanship. But is it real?*

"I created ajidamal, the secret substance that will open the Way for the faithful. I have dispatched Face Dancers to unexplored corners of the galaxy to lay the foundations of our magnificent future. Other Tleilaxu Masters are even now at the Imperial Court on Kaitain, ready to make their move. Those who follow me will be immortal and all-powerful, blessed for eternity."

Fenring reacted with surprise to that information. Blood spilled from an open wound that appeared in the center of Ajidica's forehead, running down across his brows to his temples. Even his eyes wept thick crimson.

"Heed me!" By now Ajidica's words had built into a shriek. "*Only I* have the true vision. *Only I* understand God's wishes. *Only I*—" And as he yelled, a gout of blood erupted from his throat. His frantic gestures degenerated into a seizure and his body flopped down onto the catwalk. His skin, pores, and breath reeked of cinnamon and rot.

Appalled, Fenring backed away, studying the Master Researcher, watching his death throes. The little man's gray-skinned body was wet and red, with more bleeding from his nostrils and ears.

Fenring frowned. Unquestionably, the long-standing, expensive project was a miserable failure. Even the Sardaukar, regularly dosed with synthetic melange, had been *changed* . . . and not for the better. The Emperor could no longer risk continuing this program.

Fenring stared with disbelief at the comscreen. Atreides military forces were crushing Tleilaxu defenses and berserk Sardaukar regiments, and Fenring found himself watching every aspect of his long-term plan fall apart.

The only way to salvage his future would be to make certain that all blame fell squarely upon Master Researcher Hidar Fen Ajidica.

Leaking blood from a hundred wounds, the little man continued to writhe on the catwalk, screaming grand pronouncements and curses, until he rolled and thrashed to the edge. Finally, Ajidica plummeted off and smashed into an axlotl tank below . . . with only the slightest nudge of assistance from Count Fenring.

Everyone is a potential enemy, every place a potential battlefield.

—Zensunni Wisdom

Another labor spasm hit. The contractions grew more painful, tighter, stronger.

It took all of Jessica's Bene Gesserit training to control her body, to focus her muscles and guide the baby through the birth canal. She didn't care about Mohiam's disappointment now, or how this unexpected boy-child would throw the Sisterhood's centuries-long breeding program into chaos. She could think only of the process of giving birth.

At the side of Jessica's bed, Lady Anirul Corrino sat in a suspensor chair. Her face was gray and drawn, as if she were using all her mental abilities to maintain her focus and hold the gossamer strands of her sanity. In one hand, she gripped the surgical lasknife again. Ready. Watching, like a predator.

Jessica surrounded herself in a meditative cocoon. She held her secret tight for just a few moments more. The baby would come soon. A son, not a daughter.

Both Reverend Mother Mohiam and Lady Margot Fenring had remained during the hours of her labor, and now they stood attentively just behind Anirul, ready to lunge if she threatened violence. Even though she was the Kwisatz Mother, they would not allow her to harm Jessica's baby.

Out of the corner of her eye, between deep breaths, Jessica noticed a flicker of Mohiam's hand, a special signal meant for her. *Tell Anirul you want me to cut the umbilical cord. Let me be the one to hold the laknife.*

Jessica pretended a quick spasm to give herself time to consider this. For years, Proctor Superior Mohiam had been her instructor on Wallach IX. Mohiam had indoctrinated her young student in the Sisterhood, had given Jessica explicit orders to conceive a *daughter* by Leto Atreides. She remembered Mohiam holding the gom jabbar at her neck, the poisoned needle ready for a swift and deadly prick. The penalty for failure.

She would have killed me then, if I had not met the Sisterhood's esoteric standard of humanity. She could just as easily kill me now.

But was that in itself a *human* thing for Mohiam to do? The Bene Gesserit zealously prohibited the emotion of love—but wasn't it *human* to feel love and compassion? In the present situation, would Mohiam be any less dangerous than Anirul?

No, it is more likely they will kill my baby.

It seemed to Jessica that love was something a machine could not experience, and humans had defeated thinking machines in the Butlerian Jihad, millennia ago. But if humans were the victors, why did this remnant of nonhumanity—the savagery of the gom jabbar—thrive in one of the Great Schools? Savagery was as much a part of the human psyche as love. One could not exist without the other.

Must I trust her? The alternative is too terrifying. Is there any other way?

Between pushes, Jessica lifted her sweaty head from her pillow and said in a soft voice, "Lady Anirul, I would like . . . Margot Fenring to cut the baby's umbilical cord." Mohiam recoiled in surprise. "Would you hand the laknife to her, please?" Jessica pretended not to notice her old mentor's agitation and displeasure. "It is my choice."

Anirul appeared distracted, as if she had been listening

to the internal voices, still trying to understand them. She looked down at the surgical tool clutched in her hands. "Yes, of course." Glancing over her shoulder, she handed the potential weapon to Lady Fenring. The anguish in Anirul's face subsided for a moment. "How far along?" She leaned close to the birthing bed.

Jessica attempted to adjust her body chemistry to quell a sharp bolt of pain, but it had no effect. "The baby is coming."

Instead of looking at the observers in the room, she detached herself and studied several tame honeybees that moved between the floating planter globes over her head. The insects crawled inside the enclosures and pollinated the flowers. *Focus. . . . Focus. . . .*

After several moments, the spasm subsided. When her vision cleared, she saw to her surprise that Mohiam now held the surgical lasknife after all. She felt a moment of terror for her baby. The weapon itself was irrelevant, though. *They are Bene Gesserit. They need no cutting instrument to kill a helpless child.*

The labor pains came closer together. Fingers touched her, slid inside her vagina. The plump Medical Sister nodded. "She is fully dilated." And, with a touch of Voice: *"Push."*

Reflexively, Jessica responded, but the effort only intensified the pain. She cried out. Her muscles clenched. Concerned voices moved into the background, and she had trouble comprehending their words.

"Keep pushing!" Now it was the second Medical Sister.

Something inside fought against Jessica, as if the baby himself was taking control, refusing to come out. How could this be possible? Didn't it defy the natural way of things?

"Stop! Now, relax."

She couldn't identify the source of the command, but obeyed. The pain became excruciating, and she suppressed a scream, using every skill Mohiam had taught her. Her body responded with biological programming as deep as her DNA.

"The baby is strangling on its cord!"

No, please, no. Jessica kept her eyes closed, focused inward, trying to guide her precious child to safety. Leto must have his son. But she couldn't envision the right muscles, couldn't feel any changes. She perceived only darkness and an intense, overwhelming gloom.

She felt the soft hand of a Medical Sister reach inside her, poking and probing to untangle the baby. She tried to control her body, to work her muscles, to direct her mind down into each cell. Again Jessica had the peculiar sensation that the tiny child was resisting, that he didn't want to be born.

At least not here, not in the presence of these dangerous women.

Jessica felt small and weak. The love she had wanted to share with her Duke and their son seemed so insignificant in comparison with the boundless universe and all it encompassed. The Kwisatz Haderach. Would he be able to see everything even before his own birth?

Is my child the One?

"Push again. Push!"

Jessica did so, and this time felt a change, a smooth flow. She clenched her entire body, straining as long as she could, and then pushed again, and again. The pain subsided, but she reminded herself of the peril all around her.

The baby came out. She felt him go, sensed hands reaching out, taking him away . . . and then all of her strength faded for a moment. *Must recover quickly. Need to protect him.* After three deep breaths, Jessica struggled to sit. She felt weak, deeply fatigued, sore everywhere.

The women gathered at the foot of her birthing bed said nothing, hardly moved. A hush had fallen over the sunlit room, as if she had given birth to a monstrous deformity.

"My baby," Jessica said, cutting the ominous silence. "Where is my baby?"

"How can this be?" Anirul's voice was high-pitched, on the ragged edge of hysteria. She let out a keening cry. "No!"

"What have you done?" Mohiam said. "Jessica—*what have you done?*" The Reverend Mother did not show the anger Jessica had feared so greatly; instead her expression showed defeat and utter disappointment.

Again, Jessica struggled to get a glimpse of her child, and this time she saw wet black hair, a small forehead and wide-open, intelligent eyes. She thought of her beloved Duke Leto. *My baby must live.*

"Now I understand the disturbance in Other Memory." Anirul's face became a mask of unbridled rage as she glared at Jessica. "They *knew,* but Lobia couldn't tell me in time. I am the Kwisatz Mother! Thousands of Sisters have worked on our program for millennia. Why did you do this to our *future?*"

"Don't kill him! Punish me for what I did, if you must— but not Leto's son!" Tears streamed down her cheeks.

Mohiam placed the baby in Jessica's arms, as if ridding herself of an unpleasant burden.

"Take your damned son," she said, in the coldest of tones, "and pray that the Sisterhood survives what you have done."

Humanity knows its own mortality and fears the stagnation of its heredity, but it does not know what course to take for salvation. This is the primary purpose of the Kwisatz Haderach breeding program, to change the direction of humankind in an unprecedented manner.

— LADY ANIRUL CORRINO, her private journals

Just outside the imperial birthing room, the man disguised as a Sardaukar guard wore expertly applied makeup to conceal his saphostained lips. At the back of the thin man's creased trousers, just beneath the uniform jacket, a faint blood splotch could still be seen. Hardly noticeable at all . . .

With heightened speed and senses, Piter de Vries had slipped a knife beneath the real guard's coat into his left kidney as the man walked to his post; then he had moved quickly to salvage the uniform. He took pride in his work.

Within only a few minutes, de Vries had dragged the dead man into an empty room, donned the gray-and-black uniform, and rapidly applied smears of enzyme chemicals to eliminate bloodstains. He composed himself, then assumed his station outside the birthing room.

The dead guard's companion looked at him skeptically. "Where's Dankers?"

"Who can say? I got pulled from lion-tending duty to stand here while some lady-in-waiting has a brat," de Vries said, his voice gruff with disgust. "I was told to come here and replace him."

Grunting as if he didn't care, the other guard checked his ceremonial dagger and adjusted the strap of a neuro-stun baton on his shoulder.

De Vries had another blade sheathed beneath his jacket sleeve. He also felt the sticky wetness of the bloody shirt against his back and rather liked the sensation.

They heard a sudden outcry, surprised and anguished voices inside the birthing room. Then a bawling baby. De Vries and the guard looked at each other, and the Mentat's sense of danger heightened. Perhaps the pretty mother, the Baron's secret daughter, had died in childbirth. Oh, but that would be too much to hope for—too simple. Now he heard only low tones of conversation . . . and the continuing cry of the baby.

Duke Leto's infant offered so many possibilities . . . the Baron's own secret grandchild. Maybe de Vries could take the baby hostage, use it to make the beautiful Jessica submit to him as a love slave—and then kill them both before he tired of her. He could toy with the Duke's woman for a while. . . .

Or, the child itself might be even more valuable than Jessica. The newborn was both Atreides and Harkonnen. Perhaps the safest course of action would be to remove the brat to Giedi Prime to be raised beside Feyd-Rautha—what a fabulous revenge against House Atreides that would be! An alternative Harkonnen heir, if Feyd turned out to be as much of a clod as his older brother Rabban? Depending upon how he played out the situation, de Vries might gain leverage against the Sisterhood, against two Great Houses, and against Jessica herself. All in a day's work.

He salivated, considering the delicious possibilities.

The women's voices grew louder, and the birthing-room door slid open smoothly. With a rustle of clothing, three witches walked into the corridor—the foul Mohiam, the Emperor's unsteady wife, and Margot Fenring, all of them dressed in black aba robes and preoccupied with a hushed, muttered argument.

De Vries held his breath. If Mohiam looked in his direction, she might recognize him, in spite of the makeup and stolen uniform. Fortunately, the women were too upset about something to notice anything as they hurried down the corridor.

Leaving the mother and child unprotected.

After the witches rounded a corner, de Vries said gruffly to his companion, "Should check inside to make sure everything's all right." Before the guard could decide upon a response, the Mentat slithered into the birthing room.

The loud cries of a baby came from the bright area ahead, and more female voices. He heard the guard hurrying to join him, boots clicking on the floor. The door closed behind them.

With a swift, silent movement, de Vries spun and cut the Sardaukar's throat before the man could utter a sound. The vicious slash of the knife made a whistling sound in the air and splattered gouts of red on the wall.

After easing the uniformed body down to the floor, the Mentat prowled deeper into the delivery room. He touched the neuro-stun baton against his wrist, activating the field.

At a wall-mounted workstation he saw two short Medical Sisters tending a baby, taking cellular and hair samples and studying the screen of a diagnostic machine. Their backs were to him. The taller woman scowled down at the baby, as if it were an experiment gone wrong.

Hearing a buzzing sound, the shorter, heavier woman started to turn. But de Vries leaped forward and swung the stun-baton like a bat. It caught her in the face, smashing her nose and sending crackling impulses through her brain.

Before she hit the floor, her companion stepped in front of the baby and raised her arms in a defensive posture. De Vries struck with the stun-baton. She blocked the blows—only to find both of her arms paralyzed. His blow to her neck was so hard that he heard her vertebrae shatter.

Panting, exhilarated, he stabbed both motionless forms, just to make sure. No point in taking chances.

The baby boy lay on the table, kicking and crying. Nicely vulnerable.

On the other side of the birthing room, he saw Jessica lying on a wide bed, exhausted from the delivery, her eyes bleary with analgesics. Even haggard and sweat-streaked, she looked beautiful and fascinating. He thought about killing her, so that Duke Leto could no longer have her.

Only seconds had passed, but he could spare no more time. When he reached for the baby, Jessica's eyes widened with shock. Her expression changed to one of misery and anguish.

Oh, this is much better than killing her.

She reached out, struggling to sit. She was going to crawl off the bed and come after him! Such devotion, such maternal distress. He smiled at her—but through his makeup and disguise, he knew she would never recognize him again.

Deciding to take what he had before anyone interrupted, the Mentat tucked the stun-baton and dueling dagger into his uniform belt. While Jessica dragged herself off the bed, he bundled the baby in a blanket, his movements calm and efficient. She could never reach him in time.

He saw a seep of crimson spreading across her kai-sateen birthing gown. She staggered, then fell to the floor. De Vries held up the baby, taunting her, then fled out into the corridor. Even as he ran down a stairway, trying to stifle the wailing infant, his mind spun through possibilities.

There were so many of them. . . .

⁕

MARCHING OUT OF the Hall of Oratory after his well-received speech, Leto Atreides held his head high. His father would have admired that performance. This time, he had gotten it right. He had not asked anyone's permission for what he had done. He had *notified* them, and his actions were *irrevocable*.

When he was out of sight of the assemblage, his hands began to shake, though he had held them steady all through the oration. He knew from the applause that the majority of the Landsraad genuinely admired his actions. His deeds might well become legendary among the nobles.

Politics, however, had a way of taking strange twists and turns. The gains of one moment could be lost in the next. Many delegates might have applauded only because they'd been caught up in the moment. They could still reconsider. Even so, Leto had made new allies today. It only remained to determine the extent of his gains.

Now, though, it was time to see Jessica.

At a rapid pace he crossed the flagstone-paved ellipse. Once inside the Palace, he bypassed the grand staircase and instead caught a lift tube to the birthing room. Perhaps his child was already born!

But as he stepped out on the top floor, four Sardaukar guards blocked his path with weapons drawn. An alarmed crowd milled in the corridor behind them, including a number of black-robed Bene Gesserits.

He saw Jessica slumped in a chair, wrapped in an oversize white robe. The sight of her so weak, so drained, shocked him. Her skin was damp with sweat, translucent with pain.

"I am Duke Leto Atreides, the Emperor's cousin. The Lady Jessica is my bound concubine. Let me through." He thrust his way past, employing moves Duncan Idaho had taught him to knock aside threatening blades.

When Jessica saw him, she pushed aside the clinging arms of her Bene Gesserit Sisters and tried to stand. "Leto!"

He caught her and embraced her, afraid to ask about the baby. Had it been stillborn? If so, what was Jessica doing here outside the birthing room, and why all the security?

Reverend Mother Mohiam stepped close, her face a mask of anger and distress. Jessica tried to say something, but broke down in tears. He noticed blood on the floor under her. Leto's words were cold, but he had to voice the question. "My child has died?"

"You have a son, Duke Leto, a healthy child," Mohiam said curtly. "But he has been kidnapped. Two guards and two Medical Sisters are dead. Whoever took the boy wanted him very badly."

Leto could not absorb the terrible news all at once. He managed only to hold Jessica more tightly.

For long lifetimes marked by the hulks of ruined planets, man was a geological and ecological force without knowing it, with little awareness of his own strength.
— PARDOT KYNES, *The Long Road to Salusa Secundus*

The stranglehold of Heighliners over Arrakis tightened until Baron Harkonnen felt unable to breathe. All afternoon, Sardaukar warcraft continued to stream from the underbellies of the Guild transport ships. He had never been so afraid.

The Baron knew, intellectually, that Shaddam would never incinerate Arrakis, as he had done to Zanovar—but it was not beyond the realm of possibility for the Emperor to obliterate Carthag. And him with it.

Perhaps I should leave in one of my ships. Quickly.

But no more shuttles could take off. All spacecraft had been grounded. The Baron had no way to escape, except on foot, into the desert. And he wasn't quite *that* desperate—not yet.

Standing inside the plaz observation bubble of the Carthag Spaceport, he watched an orange contrail against the darkening sky: the descent of a shuttle from one of the Heighliners. On short notice, he had been instructed to come and meet it. The unprecedented situation rankled him.

That damnable Shaddam loved to play soldier, strutting around in his uniform, and now he was behaving like the biggest bully in the universe. The Baron's orbital observation satellites had already been destroyed in an offhand action. *What in all the hells does the Emperor want of me?*

Standing in the bleak light of dusk, the Baron scowled. By sending out runners, he had mustered a meager company of troops onto the demarcated receiving area of the space-port. The day's residual heat rippled from the fused-silica pavement, evaporating chemicals and oils that impregnated the field. Around him, the embargoed vessels sat with their systems shut down.

On the horizon, where the colors of sunset blazed like a distant fire over the sandy edge of the world, he could see a blur of dust. Another one of those cursed sandstorms.

The small shuttle landed. Preparing to meet it, the Baron felt like a trussed animal. The additional troops he had brought from Giedi Prime could never deal with an invasion on this scale. If only he had more time, he might summon Piter de Vries from Kaitain to act as his emissary, to negotiate a diplomatic end to what surely must be a simple misunderstanding.

Floating forward on suspensors to greet the CHOAM and Guild entourage, he forced a smile onto his jowly face. An albino Guild Legate stepped down from the elaborate shuttle craft, wearing a spice-infuser suit. Close behind him came the weathered Supreme Bashar and an ominous-looking CHOAM Mentat-Auditor. The Baron flicked his spider-black eyes toward the Mentat and knew this man would be the real problem.

"Welcome, welcome!" He could barely keep the unset-tled look of dismay from his face; a careful observer would certainly notice his nervousness. "I will of course cooperate in every possible way."

"Yes," announced the albino Guild Legate, inhaling deeply of diffused spice gas that seeped from his thick collar, "you *will* cooperate in every way." The trio wore arrogance like second skins.

"But . . . you must first explain to me the infraction you

believe I have committed. Who has falsely accused me? I assure you there has been some sort of error."

The Mentat-Auditor came close, with the Supreme Bashar at his side. "You will grant us access to all financial and shipping records. We intend to inspect every spice harvester, legal storehouse, and production manifest. We shall ascertain if there has been an error."

The Guild Legate followed close behind. "Don't try to hide anything."

Swallowing hard, the Baron guided them out of the spaceport. "Of course."

He knew that Piter de Vries had carefully doctored his records, combing through every document, every report, and the twisted Mentat was normally very thorough. But the Baron felt cold inside, certain that even the most careful manipulations would not stand up to the close scrutiny of these demonic auditors.

With a pained smile, he gestured them onto a transport platform that would carry them to the Harkonnen Residency. "May I offer refreshments?" *Perhaps I can find a way to slip poison or mind-fogging drugs into their drinks.*

The Supreme Bashar gave a deprecating smile. "I think not, Baron. We heard about your social prowess at the gala banquet on Giedi Prime. We can't allow Imperial business to be delayed for such . . . pleasantries."

Unable to think of any further excuses, the Baron led them into Carthag.

❦

OUT IN THE desert, Liet-Kynes and Stilgar had watched the Heighliners arrive, ship after ship appearing out of foldspace in the night sky. The vessels created an ionization cloud in the air that drowned out most of the stars.

Liet knew, however, that this was a storm generated by politics, not an awesome natural phenomenon. "Great forces move beyond us, Stil."

Stilgar sipped the last drops of pungent spice coffee that Faroula had brought to the men, where they sat on the rocks below Red Wall Sietch. "Indeed, Liet. We must learn more about it." By tradition, Faroula had prepared the strong drink for them at the end of the hot day, before hurrying her young son Liet-chih into the sietch communal play areas. Baby Chani still spent the days with a nursemaid.

Within hours, Fremen housekeepers and servants who lurked in the Harkonnen Residency began to send distrans reports: organically encoded messages implanted on the sonic patterns of homing bats. With each piece of the puzzle, the news grew more interesting.

Liet was delighted to learn that Baron Harkonnen himself had his head on the chopping block. Details were sparse, and tensions ran high. Apparently the Spacing Guild, CHOAM, and the Emperor's Sardaukar had come to investigate certain irregularities in spice production.

So, the Guildsman Ailric listened to my words. Let the Harkonnens stew.

Now, standing in one of the sietch communal rooms, Liet scratched his sandy beard where the stillsuit catchtube had made an indentation. "The Harkonnens have been unable to hide the effects of our raids . . . or of the secret we leaked. Our small revenge has caused larger repercussions than we had hoped."

Stilgar checked the cryskknife in its sheath at his waist. "Using this event as a fulcrum, we might just succeed in ejecting the Harkonnens from our desert."

Shaking his head, Liet responded, "That would not free us from Imperial control. If the Baron is ousted, the Dune fief would simply be transferred to another Landsraad family. Shaddam thinks it is his right to do so, though the Fremen have lived and suffered here for hundreds of generations. Our new lords might not be better than Harkonnens."

Stilgar's hawkish face tightened. "But they could not be worse."

"Agreed, my friend. And here is my idea. We have destroyed or taken some of the Baron's spice hoards. Those actions were costly annoyances to him. But now we have the opportunity to strike an embarrassing blow while the CHOAM auditors are present. It will be the Harkonnens' downfall."

"I will do whatever you ask, Liet."

The young Planetologist reached out to touch the other man's muscular arm. "Stil, I know you dislike the towns, and Carthag most of all. But the Harkonnens have established another hidden storehouse of melange there, right in the shadow of the spaceport. If we were to target that hoard, set fire to the warehouse where it is stored, the Guild and CHOAM could not help but see. The Baron will be mortified."

Stilgar's blue-within-blue eyes widened. "Such challenges are always enjoyable, Liet. It will be dangerous, but my commandos are most pleased not only to hurt our enemies, but to *humiliate* them."

⬥

AS THE MENTAT-Auditor stared at shipping records, he did not blink, did not move his head. He simply absorbed the data and documented discrepancies on a separate scribing pad. The list of errors grew longer with each hour, and the Baron became more and more concerned. So far, however, all of the "mistakes" they had discovered were relatively minor—enough to earn him a few penalties, but certainly not enough to warrant his summary execution.

The Mentat-Auditor had not yet found what he was looking for. . . .

The explosion in the warehouse district took them all by surprise. Leaving the auditor at a tableful of documents, the Baron raced to the balcony. Response teams rushed across the streets. Flames and dust rose in a pillar of brownish-orange smoke. Without moving to get a better look, the Baron realized exactly which of the nondescript ramshackle warehouses had been the target.

And he cursed silently.

The Mentat-Auditor stood beside him on the balcony, observing with intent eyes. On his other side, Supreme Bashar Garon squared his shoulders and bristled. "What is in that building, Baron?"

"I believe . . . it is just one of my industrial warehouses," he lied. "A place where we store leftover construction materials, components for prefabricated dwellings shipped from Giedi Prime." *Damnable hells! How much spice was inside there?*

"Indeed," the Mentat-Auditor said. "And is there a reason why the warehouse might have exploded?"

"A buildup of volatile chemicals or a careless worker, I would imagine." *It's those cursed Fremen!* He didn't have to fabricate a confused expression.

"We will inspect the area. Thoroughly," Zum Garon announced. "My Sardaukar will assist your relief efforts."

The Baron quailed, but with no legitimate excuse he could not argue. Those desert scum had blown up one of his melange hoards, and the debris would be evidence to be used against him by this Mentat-Auditor and CHOAM. They would easily prove that the warehouse had been full of spice, and that House Harkonnen had kept no records of such a stockpile.

He was doomed.

He raged inside, infuriated that the Fremen would choose to strike *here* and *now*, at a time when he would not be able to gloss over the event. He would be caught red-handed, with no defense and no excuse.

And the Emperor would make him pay dearly.

Why should we find it odd or difficult to believe that disturbances at the pinnacle of government are transmitted to the lowliest levels of society? Cynical, brutal hunger for power cannot be concealed.

—CAMMAR PILRU,
Ixian Ambassador-in-Exile, Speech to the Landsraad

On Ix, even after their numbers had been more than halved, the Sardaukar fought on. Oblivious to pain or grievous wounds, the drug-frenzied Imperial fighters showed no fear for their own lives.

One of the uniformed Sardaukar drove a young Atreides fighter to the ground, reached a gloved hand through his shield, and switched off the controls. Then, like a D-wolf, he bared his teeth and ripped out the man's throat.

Duncan Idaho could not understand why the Emperor's elite corps would so ferociously defend the Tleilaxu. Clearly, young Commander Cando Garon would never surrender, not even if he were the last man alive atop a mountain of dead comrades.

Duncan reassessed his strategy, focusing on the goal of his mission. While projectile fire spattered around him like sparks from a bonfire, he raised a hand and bellowed in Atreides battle language, "To the Grand Palais!"

The Duke's men disengaged from the maddened Sardaukar and pushed around them, forming a phalanx with Duncan at the lead. He carried the Old Duke's sword and slashed at any enemy who came within reach.

Boots slapping on stone, they raced through the ceiling tunnels, negotiating honeycombed passageways toward the stalactite administrative buildings. A lone, defiant Sardaukar soldier, his uniform torn and bloodied, stood in the middle of a skyway bridge that spanned the open grotto. When he saw Duncan's men charging toward him, he clasped a grenade to his chest and detonated it, blowing up the bridge. His body tumbled through the enclosed sky, along with a rain of fire and structural wreckage.

Appalled, Duncan signaled for his men to back away from the severed bridge, while he looked for another route to the inverted pyramid of the Ixian palace. *How do we fight against men like this?*

Trying to spot a new aerial walkway, he watched as a transport barge crashed into one of the Grand Palais balconies, obviously driven by a madman. Rebels surged off the platform and into the royal structure, shouting defiance.

Duncan led his men over a second bridge and finally entered the upper levels of the Grand Palais. Tleilaxu bureaucrats and scientists fled for shelter, wailing and pleading for mercy in Imperial Galach. A few Atreides soldiers took potshots at the unshielded forms, but Duncan called his men together. "Don't waste your efforts. We can clean up the garbage later." They ran ahead through the once-grand but now spartan rooms.

Atreides fighters had spread into the crustal levels of the city, and some had taken lift tubes down to the cavern floor, where fierce fighting continued. Battle cries and screams echoed through the cavern, mixing in the air with the stomach-twisting stench of death.

Duncan's squad reached the main reception chamber and marched onto an inlaid checkerboard floor. There they encountered a surprising confrontation between ragtag passengers from the crashed cargo barge and furious Sardaukar guards. Broken crystalplaz and synstone wreckage lay strewn around the grounded barge in the middle of the reception floor.

At the center of it all, he saw Rhombur's unmistakable cyborg form, along with the troubadour Gurney Halleck, both men struggling to hold their own. Gurney's fighting style had no finesse, nothing that would have impressed the Swordmasters of Ginaz, but the former smuggler had an instinctive prowess with a weapon.

When Duncan's men rushed forward, howling the names of Duke Leto and Prince Rhombur, the desperate battle turned in their favor. Suboids and Ixian citizens fought with renewed strength.

A side passage burst open, and several blood-spattered Sardaukar ran forward, firing weapons and shouting. Their hair was in disarray and their faces streaked with scarlet, but they kept coming. Commander Cando Garon led them in a suicide attack.

Through the bloodlust, Garon noticed the cyborg Prince and charged directly at him with blind fury. In each hand, the Commander carried a sharp blade, already slicked with thick crimson fluid.

Duncan recognized the son of the Emperor's Supreme Bashar, saw murder in his eyes, and launched himself into motion. Years ago, he had failed to stop the attack of the frenzied Salusan bull that had killed Old Duke Paulus, and he had sworn not to let himself fail again.

Rhombur stood beside the crashed barge, directing the freedom fighters, and didn't see Garon rushing toward him. Rebels streamed off the barge platform, picking their way over the rubble, grabbing weapons dropped by fallen Sardaukar. Behind Rhombur, the blasted-open wall of the Grand Palais was a yawning hole that overlooked the city grotto.

Running at full speed, Duncan crashed into Garon,

striking him on the side. Their body shields collided with a report like a thunderclap and a momentum exchange that hurled Duncan backward.

But the impact also diverted Garon, who staggered toward the gaping hole in the window wall, slipping on debris on the floor. Deflected from his target, the ravening Sardaukar Commander saw a chance to kill more of the enemy and collided with three shouting Ixian rebels who stood too close to the edge of the smashed balcony. He spread his strong arms and, like a bulldozer, swept the astonished victims over the precipice.

Garon went over the side, too—but he managed to grab a broken protruding girder that had once separated broad sheets of crystalplaz. He caught himself and dangled, his face pulled into a rictus of ferocious effort, his lips skinned back from his teeth. The tendons in his neck stood out like cords ready to snap. He held on with one hand, as if sheer defiance could counteract the relentless pull of gravity.

Seeing the leader of the Sardaukar and knowing Garon was the son of Shaddam's Supreme Bashar, Rhombur bounded over to the brink on his cyborg legs. He bent down, grasping the broken wall for support and reached down with his prosthetic mechanical arm. Garon merely snarled up at the proffered assistance.

"Take it!" Rhombur said. "I can pull you to safety—and then you must surrender your troops. Ix is mine."

The Sardaukar Commander made no move to grab his hand. "I would rather die than be rescued by you. My shame would be a far worse death, and facing my father in disgrace would be greater pain than you could imagine."

The cyborg Prince anchored himself with his legs and reached down to grab Cando Garon by the wrist, squeezing a viselike hold. He remembered losing his entire family, and his own body in flames during the skyclipper explosion. "There is no pain I cannot imagine, Commander." He began to haul the struggling man up, despite his protestations.

But the Sardaukar used his free hand to grab at his own

waist, and drew a razor-knife. "Why don't you let yourself fall with me, and we'll die together?" Garon smiled wickedly, then slashed with the thrumming blade. It struck sparks off of Rhombur's mechanical wrist tendons, hitting the metallic, synthetic bone cylinders, but could not cut deeply enough.

Undaunted, Rhombur lifted the young officer close to the edge where he could be saved. Duncan rushed forward to help.

His face insane with determination, Cando Garon slashed again with the powerful cutting tool—this time cutting cleanly through Rhombur's pulleys and support joints, severing the cyborg hand. As Rhombur reeled backward, looking at the sparking and smoking stump of his artificial arm, the Sardaukar Commander tumbled away without a scream, without so much as a whisper.

Rapidly, the remaining Atreides forces and the enthusiastic rebels secured the Grand Palais. Duncan breathed a sigh of relief, but remained wary.

After witnessing Cando Garon's suicidal plunge, the suboids and rebels delighted in throwing captured Tleilaxu over the brink, a grim reflection of the days when the hated overlords had so ruthlessly executed alleged resistors.

Catching his breath, Duncan shook with exhaustion. The battles continued below, but he took a moment to greet his companion. "Well met, Gurney."

The lumpy-faced man shook his head. "A rather messy meeting, if you ask me." He swiped sweat from his brow.

Too weary and ragged to celebrate the long-awaited victory, C'tair Pilru sat on a lump of broken plastone and touched the checkerboard floor, as if trying to recapture childhood memories. "I wish my brother could be here." Recalling the last time he had stood inside the Grand Palais, the son of a respected ambassador, he wished for the stolen years back. It had been a time of elegance and finery, of grand receptions, and of flirtations and intrigues for the hand of Kailea Vernius.

"Your father still lives," Rhombur said. "I would be most pleased to have him restored to service as a respected Ambassador for House Vernius." Gently, with precise control of his intact cyborg hand, he squeezed C'tair's sagging shoulders. The Prince looked at his still-glowing stump, as if dismayed that he would have to be repaired and face rehabilitation again. But Tessia would help him. He couldn't wait to see her once more.

Haggard but grinning, C'tair looked up. "First we must find the sky controls so that you can make an announcement and put your final mark on this day." Breaking into the Tleilaxu-controlled palace, he had done the same thing many years before, transmitting sky-images of Rhombur's defiant words. Now he led the way with the Prince, Duncan, and a dozen men accompanying them. Outside the control room, they discovered two Tleilaxu dead on the floor, their throats cut. . . .

Rhombur did not know how to operate the equipment, so C'tair helped him scan his face into the system. Moments later, they projected the Prince's giant image from the grotto ceiling. His amplified voice boomed out, "I am Prince Rhombur Vernius! I now hold the Grand Palais, my ancestral home, my *rightful* home. Here I intend to stay. Ixians, throw off your shackles, subdue your oppressors, take back your freedom!"

When he finished, Rhombur heard a roar of renewed cheers from below, while the battle continued to rage.

Gurney Halleck met him in a hallway. "Look what we've found." He led the Prince to an immense armored storage room, which the Atreides had cut open with lasguns. "We had hoped to root out incriminating records, but instead we discovered this."

Cases were stacked from floor to ceiling. One had been pried open to reveal an orange-brown powder, a dusty substance that reeked of cinnamon. "It looks and tastes like melange, but look at the label. It says AMAL, in the Tleilaxu alphabet."

Rhombur glanced from Duncan to Gurney. "Where did they get so much spice, and why are they hoarding it?"

In a low voice, C'tair murmured, "I have already . . . seen what occurs in the research pavilion." He looked haggard. Realizing that the others had not heard him, he repeated it, louder, then added, "Now it begins to make sense. Miral and Cristane . . . and the spice odors."

His companions looked at him, quizzically. C'tair's eyes and the slump of his body showed the effects of the years on him. Men of less determination would have given up long ago.

He shook his head vigorously, as if to clear a buzzing from his ears. "The Tleilaxu were using Ixian laboratories to attempt to create some form of synthetic melange. Amal."

Duncan glowered. "This scheme is more than just Tleilaxu villainy. Its shadow extends all the way to the Golden Lion Throne. House Corrino has been behind the suffering of all Ixians and the destruction of House Vernius."

"Artificial spice . . ." Rhombur considered this, and it made him angry. "Ix was destroyed—my family murdered—for *that?*" He recoiled at the very idea, realizing the vast economic and political implications.

Scratching his inkvine scar, Gurney Halleck frowned. "D'murr said something about tainted spice in his tank—was this what killed him?"

Voice throbbing with excitement, C'tair said, "I suspect the answers are in the research pavilion."

A man cannot drink from a mirage, but he can drown in it.

—Fremen Wisdom

After assessing the reconnaissance information obtained by Hiih Resser's scoutship, the joint Harkonnen-Moritani assault force descended into the skies of Caladan. Beast Rabban was surrounded by firepower, but he still felt nervous.

He flew his own ship at the vanguard of the cobbled-together fleet, ostensibly leading the charge, though he wisely hung close to the heavy assault vessel piloted by the Grumman Swordmaster, Resser. Viscount Moritani commanded the foremost troop carrier, ready to secure Caladan from the ground, terrorize the villagers, and lock down control of the Atreides cities. They intended to stop Duke Leto from ever setting foot on the planet again.

As he flew down through the clouds, ready for the adrenaline rush of destruction, Rabban wondered how House Harkonnen and House Moritani would divide the spoils of this conquest for "joint occupation." His barrel stomach twisted with a knot of queasiness. The Baron would have demanded the lion's share of benefits from this operation.

Rabban grasped the controls of his attack ship with sweaty fingers, remembering when he had secretly fired upon the two Tleilaxu transports within a Heighliner hold, attempting a too-subtle blow against the untrained young Duke Leto Atreides. Personally, Rabban preferred to be more overt than that.

If Caladan was truly as exposed as Resser's scoutship suggested, then this whole operation would be over within an hour. The Harkonnen heir couldn't believe Duke Atreides would have made such an error in judgment, even for only a few days. But his uncle had often said that a good leader must constantly remain on the lookout for mistakes and be prepared to exploit them at a moment's notice.

The attackers would take control of the Castle and city as well as the spaceport and adjacent military base. By maintaining their hold on a few key places, the Grumman-Harkonnen forces could quickly secure their conquest and then prepare to ambush any Atreides forces returning home. In addition, Giedi Prime and Grumman were prepared to send full-scale reinforcements, once this preliminary operation was completed.

But Rabban worried about long-term political repercussions: a Landsraad protest by Duke Leto might be followed by joint military operations and/or sanctions and embargoes. It could be a dicey situation, and Rabban hoped he hadn't made another bad decision.

En route, before they had launched their forces, Hundro Moritani had sat on the command bridge of his troop carrier, dismissing the concerns. "The Duke doesn't even have an heir. If our position here is secure, who other than the Atreides would risk challenging us? Who would bother?" Rabban detected the ragged edge of madness in the Viscount's tone, and in the fiery glimmer behind his eyes.

Swordmaster Resser broke in over the comchannel, "All ships are prepared to proceed with the attack. It is your lead, Lord Rabban."

Drawing a deep breath of the cockpit's reprocessed air, Rabban dropped through the blanket of mist. The ships followed him like a stampede of deadly animals, ready to trample anything that got in their way.

"We have the coordinates for Cala City," Resser said. "It should be appearing in front of us momentarily."

"Damn this cloud cover." Rabban leaned forward to squint through the cockpit window. When the obscuring mist finally cleared, he could see the bay and the ocean, the rocky cliffs holding tall Castle Caladan . . . and the large city, spaceport, and military base beyond.

Then cries of surprise and confusion erupted across the comchannels. Below, in the ocean surrounding Cala City, Rabban saw dozens—no, *hundreds!*—of battleships on the water, and floating defensive platforms that moved across the waves in a mobile fortress. "It's a gigantic fleet!"

"Those ships were not there yesterday," Swordmaster Resser said. "They must have been moved in overnight to defend the Castle."

"But on the *water?*" The Viscount could not believe what he was seeing. "Why would Leto disperse such important firepower *on the water?* That hasn't been done for . . . centuries."

"This is a trap!" Rabban cried.

Just then, Thufir Hawat called in every single warship that had accompanied his escort of relief carriers to Beakkal. The armed air-and-space vessels zoomed over the Castle parapets, then split up and circled around, performing aerial maneuvers in an intimidating show of strength. Dozens of hangar doors in the military base slowly opened, implying that many more attack craft had not yet been launched.

"Leto Atreides lured us here!" Rabban pounded the control panel. "He wants to crush us and subject our Houses to Landsraad punishment."

Cursing the Viscount for talking him into this ill-advised assault, Rabban yanked his controls and sent his vanguard vessel streaking back into the clouds. Over the comchannel he gave orders for all Harkonnen vessels to break off the attack. "Retreat. *Now*—before our ships are identified."

From his command bridge, Viscount Moritani shouted

orders that the Grumman soldiers should strike anyway. But in the lead, Hiih Resser concurred with Rabban. Choosing not to hear the orders of the Viscount, he issued instructions for his ships to pull out and rendezvous in orbit.

Below, the floating fortresses on the water and the highly maneuverable battleships began to raise big guns toward the targets in the sky. It seemed obvious that alarms had been sounded, that the defensive forces were ready to retaliate.

Rabban flew faster, praying that he could get out of this situation before he caused further humiliation and damage to House Harkonnen. The last time he had made such a mistake, the Baron had exiled him to miserable Lankiveil for a full year. He didn't want to imagine what his punishment would be this time.

The fleet would reconvene on the dark side of the planet and then head out of the system, hoping that they could meet with the next inbound Heighliner. Rabban knew that was the only way he could save his own skin.

STANDING OUT ON the rocky point by the lighthouse statues, Thufir Hawat directed the maneuvers from a portable comconsole. He instructed his few airships to make another aggressive overflight for good measure. But the disguised attackers were already on the run, surprised and embarrassed.

He wondered who they were. None of the enemy ships had been hit, so no wreckage had been left behind. It would have been preferable to defeat them in a military engagement and take evidence, but he had done everything possible under nearly impossible circumstances.

From history, Thufir knew this tactic had been used during the Butlerian Jihad and before. Such a trick could not be used often—perhaps not again in the near future—but it had served its purpose for now.

He looked up at the clouds and watched the last of the would-be invaders disappear. They probably assumed

Atreides forces intended to pursue them, but the Mentat didn't dare leave Caladan undefended again. . . .

The next day, after receiving confirmation that the intruders had boarded a Heighliner and left the system for good, Thufir Hawat called in the scattered fishing boats in the waters around the Castle. He thanked the captains for their service and instructed them to return all hologenerators to the Atreides armories, before resuming their fishing runs.

It is not easy for some men to know they have done evil, for reasoning and honor are often clouded by pride.

— LADY JESSICA, journal entry

As he fled through the imperial palace carrying the kidnapped baby, Piter de Vries made decisions based on instinct and split-second assessments. Mentat decisions. He did not regret taking advantage of a brief and unexpected opportunity, but he wished he could have planned an actual escape route. The infant squirmed in his hands, but he tightened his grip.

If de Vries could make it out of the Palace, the Baron would be so pleased.

After bounding down a steep service stairway, the interim Harkonnen Ambassador kicked open a door and lunged into a narrow, alabaster-arched hallway. He paused to recall his mental map of the labyrinthine Palace, determining where he was. Thus far, he had taken random turns and passages in order to be unpredictable, and to avoid curious courtiers and Palace guards. After an instant of introspection, he recognized that this corridor led toward the study and play rooms used by the Emperor's daughters.

De Vries stuffed a corner of the blanket into the infant's mouth to suppress its crying, then reconsidered as the baby began to thrash and choke. When he removed the cloth, the child wailed even louder than before.

He sprinted through the structural nucleus of the Palace, his feet whispering across the floor. Closer to the Princesses' quarters, the walls and ceiling were of pitted crimson rock imported from Salusa Secundus. The simple architecture and lack of adornment stood in stark contrast with the opulent sections of the sprawling residence. Though they were Imperial offspring, Shaddam lavished few fineries on his unwanted daughters, and his wife Anirul seemed to be raising them in Bene Gesserit austerity.

A series of plaz windows lined the hallway on both sides, and the Mentat glanced into each room as he ran past. This Atreides brat counted for little. If the situation took a dramatic downturn, he might need a Corrino daughter hostage instead to improve his bargaining position.

Or would the Emperor even care?

During his months of careful observation and planning, de Vries had set up two separate hiding places in the Imperial Office Complex, accessible through tunnels and passageways that linked it with the Palace. His ambassadorial credentials granted him the access he needed. *Run faster!* He knew ways of contacting groundcar drivers, and thought he might reach the spaceport, even under alarms and crackdowns.

But something had to be done to quiet this child.

Rounding a turn he nearly bumped into a boyish-faced Sardaukar soldier, who obviously thought the uniformed de Vries was another guard. "Hey, what's the matter with the baby?" Then a voice crackled in his com-ear.

Trying to distract him from the transmission, de Vries said, "Trouble upstairs! Just getting him to safety. I guess we're baby-sitters now." With his left hand, he shoved the wrapped infant into the other man's face. "Here, take him."

When the surprised soldier faltered, de Vries used his other hand to slam a dagger into his exposed side. Without bothering to make certain the soldier was dead, de Vries ran on with the baby in one arm and the dagger in his free hand. He realized, belatedly, that he was leaving too much of a trail behind.

Just ahead, he saw a flash of blonde hair. Someone had looked out of a room and ducked back inside, behind the hall windows. One of Shaddam's daughters? A witness?

He sidestepped to the room, ducked inside, but didn't see her. The girl must be hiding behind furniture or under the filmbook-strewn desk. Some toys that belonged to little Chalice were scattered about, but the nursemaid must have taken the child away. Still, he sensed a presence. Someone was hiding.

The oldest daughter . . . Irulan?

She might have seen him murder the guard, and he could not allow her to notify anyone. His disguise would keep her from identifying him later, but that wouldn't help if he was caught with the brat in his hands, scarlet stains on his uniform, blood on his knife blade. Warily, he strode deeper into the chamber, his muscles coiled. He noticed a doorway on the opposite wall, slightly ajar.

"Come out and play, Irulan!"

At a noise behind him, he whirled.

The Emperor's wife moved with uncharacteristic awkwardness, not the smooth, gliding manner so typical of the witches. She did not look well.

Anirul saw the baby and recognized it as Jessica's newborn son. Then startled realization flashed across her face as she noticed the Mentat's smudged makeup, the too-red lips. "I know you." She detected murder in the disguised man's eyes—a willingness to do anything.

All the voices-within shouted warnings simultaneously. Anirul grimaced in pain and grabbed her temples.

Seeing her falter, de Vries lashed out with the dagger, as swiftly as a venomous serpent.

Though fogged by the clamor tormenting her, the Kwisatz Mother went into a blur of motion, darting to one side with suddenly restored Bene Gesserit grace and lethal fighting skills. Her speed surprised him, and de Vries was thrown off-balance for just an instant. His knife failed to connect with flesh.

From within her sleeve Anirul removed a favored weapon of the Sisterhood and grabbed de Vries by his sinewy neck. She held a poison gom jabbar at his throat, the silver needle tip glittering with poison.

"You know what this is, Mentat. Surrender the child, or die."

<hr/>

"WHAT'S BEING DONE to find my son?" Duke Leto stood beside Chamberlain Ridondo, looking at the carnage inside the birthing room.

Ridondo's high forehead glistened with perspiration. "There will be an investigation, of course. All suspects will be interviewed."

"*Interviewed?* You make it sound so polite." The two Medical Sisters lay butchered on the floor. Closer to the door, a Sardaukar had been stabbed to death. Nearby, Jessica had struggled groggily on the birthing bed. So close. *The assassin could have killed her too!* He raised his voice. "I am talking about *now*, sir. Has the Palace been sealed off? My son's life is at stake."

"I assume the Palace Guard is taking care of all security matters." Ridondo tried to sound placating. "I suggest we leave it in the hands of professionals."

"*You assume?* Who is in charge here?"

"The Emperor is not currently present to command the Sardaukar, Duke Leto. Certain lines of authority must be—"

Leto stormed out into the corridor, where he spotted a Levenbrech. "Have you sealed off the Palace and all surrounding buildings?"

"We are handling the matter, sir. Please do not interfere."

"Interfere?" Leto's gray eyes flashed. "An attack has been

made upon my son and his mother." He looked at the security name tag on the officer's lapel. "Levenbrech Stivs, under the Emergency Powers Act I am assuming command of the Palace Guard. Do you understand?"

"No, my Lord, I do not." The officer rested his hand on a stun-baton at his waist. "You have no authority to—"

"If you draw that weapon against me, you are a dead man, Stivs. I am a Duke of the Landsraad and blood cousin of Emperor Shaddam Corrino IV. You have no right to countermand my orders, especially not in *this* matter." His features hardened, and he felt the hot flow of blood in his arteries.

The officer hesitated, looked over the angry Duke's shoulder at Ridondo.

"The kidnapping of my son on Palace property is *an attack against House Atreides,* and I demand my rights under the Landsraad Charter. This is an emergency military situation, and in the absence of the Emperor and his Supreme Bashar, my authority exceeds any man's."

Chamberlain Ridondo took a moment to think. "Duke Atreides is correct. Do as he says."

The Sardaukar guards seemed impressed by the Atreides nobleman and his quick, firm grasp of command. Stivs barked into a com-unit on his lapel, "Seal off the Palace, all surrounding buildings, and the commons. Begin a thorough search for the person who has kidnapped the newborn son of Duke Leto Atreides. During this crisis, the Duke is temporarily in charge of the Palace Guard. Follow his orders."

With a quick motion, Leto removed the officer's com-unit and secured it to the lapel of his own red uniform. "Get yourself another one." Breathing hard, he pointed down the corridor. "Stivs, take half of these men and search the north section of this level. The rest of you, come with me."

Leto accepted a stun-baton but kept one hand on the jeweled hilt of the ceremonial dagger the Emperor had given him years earlier. If his son had been harmed in any way, a mere stun-baton would not be sufficient.

WITH ANIRUL'S GOM jabbar pressed against his throat, Piter de Vries froze in place. Just a prick, a tiny scratch, and the poison would kill him instantly. Anirul's hands trembled too much for the Mentat's comfort.

"I cannot defeat you," he said in the barest of whispers, careful not to move his larynx. His fingers loosened their hold on the blanket-wrapped child. Would that be enough to divert her attention? Make her hesitate for just an instant.

In his other hand he held the bloodied dagger.

Anirul tried to separate her own thoughts from the ever-increasing clamor within. While four of her daughters were too young to understand, the eldest—Irulan—had watched her mother's physical and mental degeneration. She was sorry that Irulan had to see that, wished she could have spent more time with her daughter, raising her to be a prime Bene Gesserit.

Knowing a murderer was loose in the Palace, the Emperor's wife had come to the study and play rooms to make certain her children were safe. It had been the brave, impulsive act of a mother.

The Mentat flinched, and she pushed harder with the needle, attuned to his every impulse. A diamond of perspiration glistened on his forehead and rolled slowly down his powdered temple. The little tableau seemed to last forever.

The baby squirmed in his arms. Even though this was not the infant the Sisterhood had anticipated for their all-important plans, it was still a link to a web more complex than even Anirul could comprehend. As the Kwisatz Mother, her life had been focused on bringing about the final steps in the breeding program, first arranging for the birth of Jessica herself, and then her baby.

The genetic linkages had become increasingly pure after millennia of refinement. But in human birth, even with the powers and talents of Bene Gesserit breeding mothers, nothing could be guaranteed. Odds and percentages prevailed, never certainty. After ten thousand years, was it possible to be accurate to within a single generation? *Could this baby be the One?*

She looked into the child's alert, intelligent eyes. Even so newly born, the little fellow had a presence about him, a steadiness in how he held his head. She felt a stirring inside her mind, a rumbling, unintelligible cacophony. *Are you the One, the Kwisatz Haderach? Have you arrived a generation early?*

"Perhaps . . . we should discuss this," de Vries said, barely moving his mouth. "An impasse serves neither of us."

"Perhaps I should waste no more time and just kill you."

The voices kept trying to tell her something, to warn her, but in the turmoil she couldn't understand. What if she had been *sent* to these rooms in the Palace, not to check on her own daughters, but to save this special child?

She heard a babble of voices like an oncoming tsunami— and remembered her intense dream of a worm fleeing across the desert from a silent pursuer. But the pursuer was no longer quiet. It was a multitude.

A clear voice broke through the cacophony: old Lobia, with her wry, all-knowing voice, speaking in a soothing tone. Anirul saw the words coming from the kidnapper's sapho-stained mouth, a wavering reflection in the window-plaz fronting the hallway.

You will join us soon. Her moment of shock caused her to jerk back. The gom jabbar slipped from her grasp and tumbled toward the floor. Inside her head, Lobia's voice screamed out a desperate warning, breaking through the background noise. *Beware the Mentat!*

Before the silver needle could even strike the tiles, de Vries had already brought the dagger up in a blur, slicing through black robes and deep into her flesh.

As the first gasp exploded from Anirul's mouth, he struck again, and a third time, like a heat-maddened viper.

The gom jabbar hit the floor with a sound like shattering crystal.

Now the voices roared around Anirul, louder and clearer, drowning out the pain. "The child has been born, the future changed. . . ."

"We see a fragment of the plan, a tile of the mosaic."

"Understand this—the Bene Gesserit plan is not the only one."

"Wheels within wheels—"

"Within wheels—"

"Within wheels—"

Lobia's voice sounded louder than all the rest, more comforting. "Come with us, observe more . . . observe it all."

Lady Anirul Corrino's dying lips trembled with what might have been a smile, and she knew suddenly that this one child would reshape the galaxy after all and change the course of humanity more than the hoped-for Kwisatz Haderach ever could.

She felt herself falling to the floor. Anirul could not see through the mists of her approaching death, but she understood one thing with absolute certainty.

The Sisterhood will endure.

❦

EVEN AS THE Kwisatz Mother collapsed beside her poison needle, de Vries was running back out into the hallway with the hostage baby. They slipped through a side passageway.

"You'd better be worth all this trouble," he muttered to the wrapped infant. Now that he had killed the Emperor's wife, Piter de Vries wondered if he would ever get out of the Palace alive.

All proofs inevitably lead to propositions that have no proof. All things are known because we want to believe in them.

—Bene Gesserit Azhar Book

Aboard his orbiting flagship, Emperor Shaddam Corrino had no intention of returning to Kaitain while the audit of Harkonnen spice operations on Arrakis continued. And once CHOAM declared the Baron guilty, he had something else in mind. Something drastic. This was his window of opportunity and he could not ignore it.

From his private cabin, Shaddam watched events unfold exactly as he had hoped. Though he wore a military uniform, his opulent Imperial quarters were filled with amenities unfamiliar to the austere Sardaukar.

Sealed behind the opaque cabin doors, he summoned the Supreme Bashar to join him for a gourmet meal—ostensibly to discuss strategy, but in truth the Emperor just liked to hear war stories about the old soldier's military campaigns. In Zum Garon's early years, he had been a training-prisoner on Salusa Secundus, a slave picked up during a raid on a distant planet. Though poorly armed and untrained, Garon had shown so much bravery and fighting skill that the Sardaukar had drafted him into their ranks. The man was quite a success story, and his son Cando seemed to be following in the old veteran's footsteps, commanding the secret legions stationed on Ix.

Relaxing for a moment after the meal, Shaddam looked across the table at Garon's craggy face. The Supreme Bashar had eaten only sparingly of the exotic dishes and had been a disappointing dinner companion. Garon seemed preoccupied with the siege of Arrakis.

The cluster of Guild ships continued to lock down all activity on the deserts below, and Shaddam waited with the eagerness of a malicious gossip to learn what embarrassing errors and cover-ups the inspectors had found.

In this matter, CHOAM and the Spacing Guild were convinced they were the Emperor's allies, integral parts of a crackdown on House Harkonnen. The Emperor could only hope he'd be able to eradicate the only natural source of melange before they suspected the truth. Then they would have to come to him for amal.

When a shuttle bearing the Guild Legate and the CHOAM Mentat-Auditor arrived from Carthag, Sardaukar escorts brought the two visitors to Shaddam's opulent cabin. Both men reeked of melange.

"We are finished, Sire."

Shaddam poured himself a glass of honey-sweet Caladan wine. Across the table, Zum Garon sat with rigid military posture, as if he were about to be interrogated. The Guild Legate and Mentat-Auditor remained silent until the cabin door was sealed shut.

The Mentat stepped forward first, holding out a scribing pad onto which he had transferred the mental summary of his results. "Baron Vladimir Harkonnen has committed a profusion of transgressions. He has allowed numerous purported 'mistakes' to remain uncorrected. We have proof of his missteps, as well as details that show he attempted to conceal his manipulations from us."

"As I suspected." Shaddam listened while the auditor gave him a synopsis of the illegal activities.

Garon allowed his anger to show. "The Emperor has

already established that he is willing to enact severe punishment for such misdeeds. Does the Baron not know of Zanovar, or Korona?"

Shaddam took the summary pad from the Mentat-Auditor and scanned the text and numbers. None of it would mean much to him unless he sat for hours with an interpreter—something he had no intention of doing. He had been convinced of the Baron's guilt from the outset.

"We have clear evidence of crimes against the Imperium," the Legate said, sounding oddly uneasy. "Unfortunately, Sire . . . we did not find what we sought."

Shaddam held up the scribing pad. "What do you mean? Does this not show how House Harkonnen broke Imperial law? Does he not deserve to be punished?"

"It is true that the Baron stockpiled spice, doctored production numbers, and avoided Imperial taxes. But we have tested sample after sample of the spice in Harkonnen shipments and cargo facilities. Every scrap of melange is pure, with no evidence of tainting." The albino Legate hesitated. Shaddam looked impatient.

"This is not what we expected, Sire. We know from our analysis that the Navigators in our lost Heighliners died from contaminated spice gas. We also know that samples taken from the liquidated Beakkal stockpile of melange were chemically corrupt. Therefore, we had expected to discover impurities here on Arrakis, inert substances used by the Baron to extend the quantity of melange while diluting its quality—thereby introducing the subtle poisons that resulted in several disasters."

"But we found nothing of that nature," the Mentat concluded.

The Supreme Bashar leaned forward, his hands locked in a double fist. "Nevertheless, we still have enough evidence to remove House Harkonnen."

The Guild Legate inhaled deeply, bowing his nose close to the diffuser collar. "Quite so, but that will not answer our questions."

Shaddam formed his lips into what he hoped was a concerned frown. He wished Fenring could be here to watch this, but even now his Spice Minister should be preparing the initial shipments of amal. Pieces were fitting into place nicely.

"I see. Well, nevertheless, the Bashar and I will determine a suitable response," he said. Within a few days, the matter would be moot. He stared down at the Mentat's scribing pad. "We must study this information. Perhaps my personal advisors can offer a theory to explain the altered spice."

Knowing his Emperor's moods, and sensing that the two guests were dismissed, Zum Garon rose from the table and began to usher them out.

After the door sealed again, Shaddam turned to his Supreme Bashar. "As soon as the shuttle has returned to its Heighliner, I want you to sound battle stations throughout the fleet. Dispatch my warships and take up positions within direct firing range of Carthag, Arrakeen, Arsunt, and every other population center on the planet."

Garon received this bombshell with a stony expression. "Just like on Zanovar, Sire?"

"Precisely."

ISSUING NO WARNING, the Sardaukar armada descended from the Heighliners until they scraped the atmosphere of Arrakis. Their weapons ports opened and glowed with a readiness to strike. Shaddam sat on the command bridge, issuing orders and making pronouncements into a holorecorder, more for his memoirs and posterity than for anything else.

"Baron Vladimir Harkonnen has been found guilty of high crimes against the Empire. Independent CHOAM auditors and Guild inspectors have uncovered incontrovertible evidence to support this judgment. As I demonstrated on Zanovar and Korona, my law is the law of the Imperium. Corrino justice is swift and complete."

The Guild would undoubtedly assume he was bluffing at first, but they were in for a rude surprise. With his forces already dispersed, once the rain of destruction began, it would take his Sardaukar little time to blacken the desert world, and obliterate all melange.

Guild Navigators required huge quantities of spice. The Bene Gesserit were steady customers as well, consuming increasing amounts each year as their numbers grew. Most of the Landsraad was addicted. The Imperium could never do without the substance.

I am their Emperor, and they will do as I say.

Even without the advice of Count Fenring, he had thought this over carefully, considering all possibilities. Once he destroyed Arrakis, what could the Guild do? Leave in their ships and strand him here? They wouldn't dare. Then they would never receive a single gram of synthetic spice.

He signed off and began the countdown to full bombardment.

Things will be different in the Imperium after this.

My life ended the day the Tleilaxu invaded this world.
All these years of fighting back, I have been a dead
man, with nothing more to lose.

—C'TAIR PILRU, secret journals (fragment)

Skirmishes continued underground among the Ixian manufactories and technological centers. The suboids, their anger and frustration unleashed, tore uniforms from slain Sardaukar soldiers, grabbed weapons, and fired indiscriminately, destroying the few remaining production lines.

Behind Rhombur, a Tleilaxu statue erected to honor the invaders had been decapitated in the fighting, and fragments of its alloy head lay scattered about on the pavement. "This will never end."

Allied with Ixian rebels, Atreides troops had succeeded in retaking the stalactite buildings, the tunnels, and the Grand Palais itself. Pockets of frenzied Sardaukar fought on the open cavern floor, where House Vernius had once built Heighliners. The bloodshed did not seem to ebb.

"We need another ally," C'tair suggested. "If we can prove that flawed artificial spice resulted in the deaths of two Navigators—including my brother— the Spacing Guild will stand with us."

"They have already said as much," Rhombur said. "But we had thought to complete this action without their interference."

Gurney looked concerned. "The Guild isn't here, and we can't bring them fast enough."

C'tair's dark eyes gleamed—bloodshot, but full of determination. "*I* might be able to."

He led them to a small warehouse that appeared abandoned. Rhombur watched while C'tair lovingly removed the hodgepodge construction of his rogo transmitter from a locked storage container. The strange device appeared stained and singed, with evidence of frequent repairs. It was studded with crystalline power rods.

His hands trembled as he held it. "Even I don't know exactly how this thing works. It's configured to the electrochemistry of my own mind, and I was able to communicate with my twin brother. We shared a bond once. Although his brain changed and passed far beyond any definition of humanity, I could still understand him."

Memories of D'murr welled up in him like tears, but he drove them back. His hands trembled on the controls.

"Now my brother is dead, and our rogo is damaged. This is the last crystal rod, one that was somehow . . . repaired in my last communication with D'murr. Perhaps . . . if I use sufficient power, I can send at least a whisper to other Navigators. They might not understand all of my words, but they may hear the urgency."

Rhombur was overwhelmed by everything happening around him. He had not envisioned anything like this, and said, "If you can bring the Guild here, we will do our best to show them what Shaddam has been doing behind a cloak of secrecy."

C'tair squeezed Rhombur's artificial arm so hard that the cyborg sensors detected the pressure. "I have always been willing to do whatever is necessary, my Prince. If I can help, it would be my greatest honor."

Rhombur saw a strange determination in the man's eyes, an obsession that went beyond rational thought. "Do it."

C'tair grabbed electrode leads and attached sensors to his scalp, the back of his head, and his throat. "I don't know the capacity of this device, but I intend to use all the energy I can pump through it, and through me." He grinned. "This will be a shout of triumph and a cry for help, my loudest message to the outside."

When the rogo was fully powered, C'tair took a deep breath for courage. In the past, he always spoke aloud during transmissions to D'murr, but he knew his brother did not actually hear the words. Instead, the Navigator picked up the *thoughts* that accompanied the speech. This time, C'tair would say nothing out loud, and would instead concentrate all of his energy on projecting his thoughts across the vast distances.

Pressing a transmit button, he sent a fusillade of thought, a volley of desperate signals directed to any Guild Navigator who could hear, a cosmic mayday. He didn't know whether the rogo or his brain would fail first, but he felt them connecting . . . and reaching out.

C'tair's jaw clenched, his lips drew back, and his eyes squeezed shut until tears flowed from them. Sweat poured from his forehead and temples. His skin turned ruby red. Blood vessels bulged at his temples.

This transmission was exponentially more powerful than anything he had ever attempted with D'murr. But this time he did not have the inexplicable mental connection of his twin.

Rhombur saw C'tair dying from the effort, literally killing himself in a great final attempt to use the transmitter. The haggard rebel screamed soundlessly inside his skull.

Before they could disconnect him, the rogo transmitter sparked and burned. The machine overloaded, and its circuits fused. The crystal rods shattered into black snowflakes. C'tair's face bore a strangled expression; his features tightened as if in unspeakable pain. Synapses melted inside his brain, preventing him from uttering a sound.

With his one remaining hand, Rhombur yanked the sensor leads from the rebel's head and neck, but C'tair collapsed to the floor of the storage chamber. His teeth chattered, his body twitched, and his smoking eyes never opened again.

"He's gone," Gurney said.

In a deep well of sadness, Rhombur cradled the fallen rebel, this most loyal of all people who had ever served House Vernius. "After such a long fight, sleep in peace, my friend. Rest well on free soil." He stroked the cooling skin.

The cyborg Prince stood, his scarred face more grim than ever, and made his way out of the storage chamber, followed by Gurney Halleck. Rhombur did not know if C'tair's transmission had succeeded, or how the Guild might respond to the call across space, if they heard it at all.

But unless they received reinforcements soon, the day's battle might be for naught.

The Ixian nobleman spoke in a deep, implacable voice to the Atreides fighters around him. "Let us finish this."

To produce the genetic alteration of an organism, place it in an environment which is dangerous but not lethal.

—Tleilaxu Apocrypha

After the messy death of Hidar Fen Ajidica, Count Fenring saw the Atreides troops actually winning their battle against the Imperial Sardaukar.

A most disturbing development.

It astonished him that after so many years Duke Leto Atreides would authorize such a blatant military move. Perhaps the family tragedies that would have crushed any other man had actually galvanized him into action.

Still, it was a brilliant surprise strategy, and these Ixian facilities would be an impressive economic prize for a Great House like Atreides, even after decades of Tleilaxu mismanagement and detrimental maintenance. Fenring couldn't believe Duke Leto would just blithely hand them over to Prince Rhombur.

On the comscreen of the research pavilion, Fenring watched Atreides soldiers approaching the complex. That left him with little time to accomplish what was necessary. He had to erase all evidence of Project Amal and his own culpability.

The Emperor would seek a scapegoat for the research debacle, and Fenring was determined that he would not fill that role. Master Researcher

Ajidica had failed spectacularly and now lay smashed among the bovine bodies of brain-dead women. Several bloated axlotl females, still connected to tubes in their coffinlike boxes, had fallen around the little man in a parody of bizarre sexuality.

Ajidica's stigmata-studded body might serve one final purpose. . . .

The remaining Tleilaxu scientists were frightened. The Sardaukar had rushed to the main battle and abandoned them here in the research pavilion. Knowing the Count was the Emperor's official representative, the Tleilaxu looked to him for advice. Some of them might even believe he "Fenring" was the Face Dancer replica Zoal, as Ajidica had originally planned. Maybe they would follow his orders, at least for a short time.

Fenring stood on the catwalk and raised his hands in much the way Ajidica had done before his histrionic demise. Foul odors bubbled up from the smashed axlotl tanks, including the thick stench of human waste products.

"We are left defenseless," he shouted, "but I have an idea that may save you all, hmmm?" The surviving researchers stared up at him with uncertainty bordering on hope.

Fenring knew the layout of the research pavilion, and his eyes flicked back and forth. "You are all too valuable for the Emperor to risk losing you." He directed the scientists to a secure laboratory chamber that had only one exit. "You must take shelter there and remain hidden. I will bring reinforcements."

He counted twenty-eight researchers, though a few others must be trapped in outlying administrative buildings. Ah well, the mobs would take care of them.

Fenring scuttled down from the catwalk to the main floor. When the doomed scientists had crowded into the single chamber, he stood in the doorway smiling. "No one can get to you here. Shhhh." He nodded and then sealed the door. "Leave it to me."

The foolish little men didn't even imagine something

was amiss until he had walked halfway across the broad floor of the pavilion. He ignored their muffled shouts and fist-hammerings. Those researchers probably knew every detail about the amal program. To keep them from talking, he might have been inconvenienced by having to kill each one of them. This way, he could take care of the problem much more efficiently, with minimal effort. As Imperial Spice Minister he was, after all, a busy man.

The lab floor and the support systems for the axlotl tanks were filled with canisters of biological hazards, flammable substances, acids, and explosive vapors. He donned a breathing filter apparatus from an emergency station on one wall. A man of many talents, he moved through the chamber like a dervish, dumping fluids, mixing liquids, releasing deadly gases. He paid little heed to the twitching female bodies in disarray on the floor, grossly reengineered by the Tleilaxu to produce synthetic spice.

So close. Ajidica's plan had almost worked.

Fenring stopped by the sightless husk of the fertile young woman who had been Cristane, the Bene Gesserit commando. He studied her naked flesh; her abdomen bulged outward, the uterus stretched into a factory designed to serve Tleilaxu purposes. Nothing more than a machine now, a chemical facility.

As he gazed upon Cristane's waxy face, Fenring thought of his remarkably beautiful wife Margot, still on Kaitain, no doubt gossiping at Court and sipping tea. He looked forward to getting back to her and relaxing in her arms.

This Sister Cristane would never send her damning report back to Wallach IX, and Fenring would not let any details slip, not even to his wife. He and Margot loved each other deeply, but that didn't mean they would share *all* of their secrets.

Fenring heard military activity outside the buildings as Atreides forces encountered the remaining floor-level Sardaukar. The Imperial troops would hold them off for a while, long enough.

He strolled to the high-arched outer chambers and turned back to look at the chaos in the laboratory: smashed canisters, puddled noxious fluids, bubbling gases, bodies, tanks. From here, he could no longer hear the desperate pounding of the Tleilaxu scientists locked inside their death trap.

Count Fenring tossed an ignitor over his shoulder, deep into the facility. The gases and chemicals burst quickly into flames, but he had time to depart with his usual lounging gait. Concussions boomed behind him.

The laboratories burned in his wake—destroying the axlotl tanks, the amal research, and all evidence—but Fenring didn't bother to hurry.

THE RESEARCH PAVILION exploded as Duncan Idaho and his men penetrated the Imperial barricades, allowing the Atreides soldiers to charge forward.

A tremendous boom echoed through the facility, and everyone took cover. Debris spouted through the roof of the pavilion like a volcanic eruption; the inner walls collapsed. Within moments, the lab complex became an inferno of melted glass, plasteel, and flesh.

Duncan held his men back from the growing fire. His heart sank to know that all proof of the Tleilaxu crimes was being incinerated. Roiling brown-and-orange vapors spewed upward, toxic smoke that could kill them as surely as the flames themselves.

The Swordmaster saw a lean, broad-shouldered man stride out, totally unconcerned. His silhouette was muscular against the orange wall of heat. The man removed a breathing apparatus from his face and tossed it aside. He held a short fighting sword, such as the Sardaukar carried. Duncan raised the Old Duke's blade in a defensive posture, stepping forward to block this man's passage.

Count Hasimir Fenring came forward without hesitation. "Aren't you going to cheer the fact that I've escaped, hmmm? Cause for celebration, I'd say. My friend Shaddam will be overjoyed."

"I know you," Duncan said, remembering his months of political instruction on a sun-drenched island on the Ginaz archipelago. "You're the fox who hides behind the Emperor's cape and commits dirty work for him."

Fenring smiled. "A fox? I've been called a weasel and a ferret before, but never a fox. Hmmm. I have been held here against my will. Those evil Tleilaxu researchers meant to perform terrible experiments on me." His large eyes widened. "I even foiled a plot that was intended to replace me with a Face Dancer duplicate."

Duncan stepped closer, his sword half-raised. "It will be interesting to hear your testimony in front of an investigation board."

"I think not." Fenring seemed to be losing his sense of amusement. He slashed out with his short sword, as if swatting a fly, but Duncan parried quickly. The blades clanged, and the short sword was deflected upward, but Fenring maintained his grip on its hilt.

"You dare to raise a blade against the Emperor's Spice Minister, against Shaddam's closest friend?" Fenring was frustrated, though still slightly amused. "You'd best step aside and let me pass."

But Duncan pressed forward, taking a more aggressive stance. "I am a Swordmaster of Ginaz, and I have fought many Sardaukar today. If you are not our enemy, then throw down your weapon. You would be wise not to face me as an opponent."

"I killed men before you were even born, pup."

The laboratory fire continued to build. The hot air stank of roiling chemicals. Duncan's eyes stung and watered. Atreides soldiers closed in to protect their Swordmaster, but he waved them off, honor-bound to fight this one by himself.

The Count pressed his attack. He usually killed through devious means, rarely in open combat against a worthy opponent. Still, he possessed many fighting skills that Duncan had not previously encountered.

Lunging toward his rival, the Swordmaster growled through clenched teeth. "I have seen too many casualties in this fight already, but I am not averse to adding you to their number, Count Fenring." He swung with the Old Duke's sword, and his blade crashed against his opponent's up-thrust weapon.

Duncan fought with the finesse of a well-trained Swordmaster, but with an edge of brutality. He did not stand on ceremony or chivalrous principles, unlike many of the swordplay instructors Fenring had heard about or actually met in combat.

The Count held up the blade to defend himself, and Duncan swung down, concentrating great strength into a single blow. The Old Duke's sword rang, and a notch appeared on the blade. But Fenring's weapon thrummed in his hand—and shattered from the blow. The momentum knocked him into a wall.

Fenring scrambled to recover his balance, and Duncan lunged forward, ready to deal the coup de grace, but alert for anything. This fox had many tricks.

Options flashed through Fenring's mind. If he wanted to elude the sharp point of his adversary's blade, he could turn and run back into the raging fire of the laboratory building. Or he could surrender. His choices were indeed limited.

"The Emperor will ransom my life." He threw down the hilt of his broken sword. "You wouldn't dare murder me in cold blood while all these men are watching, hmmm?" Still, Duncan took a menacing step forward. "What about the famous Atreides code of honor? What does Duke Leto stand for, if his men are free to kill a person who has already surrendered, hmmm?" Fenring held up both empty hands. "You wish to slay me now?"

Duncan knew the Duke would never approve of such a dishonorable action. He watched the laboratory burn and heard the continuing shouts of violent combat outside in the grotto. No doubt Leto could find ways to use this political prisoner to stabilize the Imperial turmoil after the battle for Ix.

"I serve my Duke before I serve my own heart." At a signal from the Swordmaster, Atreides men came forward and secured restraints to the prisoner's wrists.

Duncan leaned close to him, his breath hot. "In the aftermath of this war, Count Hasimir Fenring, you may wish I had let you die here."

The Spice Minister looked at him as if he knew a dark secret. "You haven't won yet, Atreides."

*It is no secret that we all have secrets. However, few
of them are as veiled as we intend them to be.*

—PITER DE VRIES,
Mentat Analysis of Landsraad Vulnerabilities,
private Harkonnen document

U nder the leadership of Duke Atreides, the
Imperial guards spread out in search patterns throughout the Palace grounds. Leto was anguished to leave a weak and exhausted Jessica
alone, but he could not wait beside her while his
newborn son was in danger.

He shouted orders and tolerated no hesitation.
As he stormed through opulent corridors and confusing mazes of prismatic mirrors, he thought of the
ferocity of gaze-hounds who fought to protect their
young. Duke Leto would prove that a wronged father could be just as formidable an enemy.

They have taken my son!

Haunted by memories of Victor, he swore by
House Atreides that no harm would come to this
child.

But the Imperial Palace was the size of a small
city, and had been designed with countless hiding
places. As the fruitless search continued, Leto
tried not to despair.

PITER DE VRIES was accustomed to having blood
on his hands, but now he truly feared for his life.

Not only had he kidnapped a noble child, he had killed the Emperor's wife.

After he had left Anirul's body behind him, he sprinted down the corridors, his stolen Sardaukar uniform disheveled and spotted with blood. His heart pounded and his head ached, but despite his extensive training, the Mentat could not reassess and develop a new plan for escape. The makeup on his face was smeared, revealing vivid sapho stains on his lips.

The blanket-wrapped infant squirmed in his arms, occasionally crying, but for the most part remained surprisingly silent. Set into a fresh pink face, the young eyes burned with a strange intensity, as if this baby understood something beyond the capacity of a normal infant. He was so much different from the fussy, often-annoying, little Feyd-Rautha.

De Vries tucked the blanket tighter around the tiny body, tempted for a moment to turn the wrappings into a garrote. Suppressing the urge, he ducked into a dimly lit chamber filled with alcoves of trophies and statuettes, a room designed to show off prizes earned by some long-forgotten member of House Corrino who had apparently been a talented archer.

With sudden shock, he looked up to see the silhouette of a black-robed woman who stood like a specter of death in the doorway, blocking escape.

"*Stop!*" barked Reverend Mother Gaius Helen Mohiam, using the full power of Voice.

Her command seized his muscles, paralyzed him in his tracks. Mohiam glided into the trophy room, the diffuse light shining like furnace flames on her fury. "Piter de Vries," she said, recognizing him through the smeared makeup. "I suspected a Harkonnen hand behind this."

Struggling to crack the invisible restraint of her command, his mind spun. "Come no closer, witch," he warned through gritted teeth, "or I will kill the child." He managed to flex his arms and reassert a minimum of bodily control, but she could always paralyze him again with another utterance.

De Vries knew about Bene Gesserit fighting abilities. He'd just dueled with the Emperor's wife and had been surprised to defeat her. But Anirul had suffered from some kind of illness; the mental debility had given him an edge. Mohiam would be a much more formidable opponent.

"If you murder the baby, you will die with him," she said.

"You intend to kill me anyway. I see it in your eyes." De Vries took a small step forward, brash and defiant, to demonstrate that he had broken her Voice spell. "Why should I not assassinate the Duke's heir and bring more misery to House Atreides?"

He took a second step, clutching the infant to his chest like a shield. A quick jerk of his muscles could snap the small neck. Even with her Bene Gesserit reflexes, Mohiam could not be certain of stopping him.

If he could just bluff his way past her and escape through the doorway of this forgotten room, he could *run*. Even holding a child, his muscles could carry him faster than this used-up woman would ever be able to go. Unless she had a weapon under that robe other than a poison needle, something she could throw or shoot. Still, he had to try something. . . .

"This infant is vital to the Bene Gesserit, isn't he?" de Vries said, stealing a third step. "Part of a breeding scheme, no doubt?" The Mentat watched for any jitter of her facial muscles, instead saw her long fingers flex. Those nails could become razor-sharp claws to slash his eyes, rip out his throat. His heart pounded.

He raised the baby a little higher to protect his face.

"Perhaps if you give me the child, I will allow you to pass," Mohiam said. "I'll let the Sardaukar hunters deal with you in their own way."

She closed the distance and de Vries stiffened, every reflex at the ready, his eyes watching. *Should I believe her?*

She touched the blankets with strong fingers, her gaze locked on the Mentat's, but before she could draw the child into her grasp, de Vries whispered hoarsely, "I know your secret, witch. I know the identity of this child. And I know who Jessica really is."

Mohiam froze as if he had used Voice against her himself.

"Does the whore know she's the daughter of Baron Vladimir Harkonnen?" When he saw her startled reaction to this revelation, he spoke more rapidly, knowing his deduction had been correct. "Does Jessica realize that she is *your* daughter as well—or do you witches keep such things secret from your children, treating them like puppets in some genetic master plan?"

Without answering, Mohiam snatched the infant from him. The twisted Mentat stepped back, head held high. "Before you move against me, consider this. Once I learned these things, I compiled full documentation and sealed it where it would be transmitted to Baron Harkonnen and the Landsraad in the event of my death. Won't Duke Leto Atreides be amused to learn that his beautiful little lover is the daughter of his mortal enemy, the Baron?"

Mohiam set the wrapped baby down next to one of the archery trophies, in a velva-lined alcove under a saffron-colored light.

He continued in a rush, intent on convincing her. "I made copies of these documents and secreted them in various places. You cannot stop the message from going out if I am killed." De Vries took a confident step toward the door and his avenue of escape. "You *dare* not harm me, witch."

With the baby safe, Mohiam turned back to face him. "If what you say is true, Mentat . . . then I must let you live."

De Vries gave a sigh of relief; he knew the Reverend

Mother could not risk the revelations. Even the slightest chance that he was not bluffing would be enough to stall her so he could get away.

Suddenly, Mohiam lunged at him with the full fury of a wounded panther. She struck out in a blur of kicks and punches. De Vries stumbled backward, trying to defend himself, raising a forearm to intercept a vicious slash with her foot.

His wrist snapped from the impact, but after a quick, icy gasp, he mentally blocked the pain and swung with his other arm. Mohiam threw herself on him again, and he could not counter—or even see—every phase of her attack, a flurry of jabs and kicks and slashing blows.

A hard heel landed at the center of his stomach. A steely fist slammed into his sternum. He felt ribs crack, internal organs rupture. He tried to scream at her, but only blood came out, staining his lips a brighter shade of red than the makeup-smudged sapho.

He lashed out with his foot, trying to crush her kneecap, but Mohiam slipped to the side. De Vries raised his intact arm to block a driving kick, but this only resulted in another broken wrist.

He turned to run, forgoing the fight, leaping toward the doorway and his escape route. Mohiam reached the door first. Her hard heel flashed upward in a blur and drove into his throat. The swift kick snapped the Mentat's neck like dry kindling. Piter de Vries fell dead to the floor, his expression one of astonishment.

Mohiam stood still, catching her breath. She recovered in only a moment. Then she turned to gather the rescued Atreides baby.

Before walking out of the trophy room, she stood over the crumpled corpse on the floor and allowed a sneer to cross her face for a delicious moment before erasing it. She spat on his dead face, remembering how he had leered over her during the Baron's rape.

Mohiam knew there was no documentation of the secrets de Vries had discovered. *None*. All of his terrible revelations had died with him.

"Never lie to a Truthsayer," she said.

*An Emperor's slightest dislike is transmitted to those
who serve him, and there it is amplified into rage.*

—SUPREME BASHAR ZUM GARON,
Commander of Imperial Sardaukar Troops

Before Shaddam could order his Sardaukar
fleet to unleash their planet-destroying
weapons, the Guild broke through to his secure
comchannels and demanded clarifications and explanations.

Standing on the command bridge of his flagship,
the Emperor did not give them the satisfaction of
an answer, nor even a justification of his actions.
The Guild, and indeed the entire Imperium, would
have their answers soon enough.

Beside him, Supreme Bashar Garon stood at the
control station, logging acknowledgments from
the warship commanders. "All weapons ready,
Sire." He looked down at the screen, then at his
Emperor, who studied him. The weathered old veteran's
face was implacable. "Awaiting your order to
fire."

Why can't all my subjects be like him?

After being ignored, the Guild Legate transmitted
a solido hologram image onto the flagship
bridge. Tall and imposing, larger than life, he said,
"Emperor Shaddam, we insist that you cease this
posturing. It serves no purpose."

Irritated that the Spacing Guild had been able
to penetrate his security, Shaddam frowned at the

holo-image. "Who are you to decide my Imperial purpose? I am the *Emperor*."

"And I represent the Spacing Guild," the Legate replied, as if the two things were of comparable importance.

"The Guild does not determine law and justice. We have pronounced our judgment. The Baron is guilty, and we will impose the penalty." Shaddam turned to Zum Garon. "Give the order, Supreme Bashar. Proceed with the full bombardment of Arrakis. Destroy every living thing on the planet."

ON A LEDGE outside the cool, dry tunnels of Red Wall Sietch, the boy Liet-chih woke up, restless. Only four years old, he rolled off the mat on which he had been lying and looked around. The night was warm, with barely a breeze. His mother Faroula rarely let the children sleep outside, but she and the other Fremen had activities in the darkness, on an open shelf of rock.

He saw shadowy shapes moving in well-practiced silence—desert people bustling about with efficient movements, making no unnecessary noise. Barely visible in the moonless starlight, his mother and her companions opened small cages of distrans bats, releasing the creatures to fly high and far, carrying messages to other sietches.

Behind the Fremen workers, doorseals held moisture inside the hidden warrens of the sietch, where some communal chambers held production areas—looms for weaving spice fiber, stillsuit assembly tables, plastique-molding presses. Those machines were silent now.

Faroula looked at Liet-chih and, with eyes accustomed to the darkness, saw that her son was safe. She reached inside her cage for another tiny black bat; she could hear it fluttering against the bars. Holding the creature gently in her hands, she stroked the downy fur of its little body.

Suddenly, with a murmur of alarm, two of the Fremen women made warding signs at the sky with their hands. Faroula tilted her head to look up, and in surprise released the squirming bat before she was ready. On black wings, it soared off into the shadows in search of insects.

Overhead, against the stars, Liet-chih saw a bright cluster of lights, hot and blue, descending closer. Ships! Immense ships.

His mother grabbed the boy roughly by the shoulders, while the Fremen women broke open the doorseal and rushed back inside, hoping the mountain walls would offer a small measure of safety.

❧

STRANDED IN HIS Carthag Garrison, Baron Harkonnen realized the fate that hung over his head. And he could do nothing about it. No communications. No spaceships. No short-range vehicles. No defenses.

He smashed furnishings and threatened his aides, but nothing helped. He bellowed up at the sky, "Damn you, Shaddam!" But the Imperial flagship could not hear him.

He had grudgingly expected to pay heavy fines and penalties for the discrepancies those maddening CHOAM auditors had discovered. If the charges were serious enough, he had feared that House Harkonnen might lose its siridar fief on Arrakis and subsequent control over spice-harvesting operations. There had even been a slim but terrifying chance that Shaddam might order the Baron's summary execution, as another "lesson" to the Landsraad.

But never this! If those warships opened fire, Arrakis would become a charred rock. Melange was an organic substance, of mysterious derivation in this environment, and surely it could not survive such a conflagration. If the Emperor went through with this insanity, Arrakis would be of little interest to anyone, no longer even on Heighliner routes. By the hells, there would be no Heighliner travel at all, anywhere! The whole Imperium depended on spice. It made no sense. Shaddam *had* to be bluffing.

The Harkonnen lord remembered the blackened cities of Zanovar, and knew the Emperor was capable of carrying out his threats. He had been shocked at Shaddam's response against Richese's laboratory moon, and he had no doubt that the Emperor had been behind the botanical plague on Beakkal.

Was the man insane? Undoubtedly.

With his transmission systems obliterated, the Baron was incapable of even pleading for his life. He could not cast the blame on Rabban, and Piter de Vries remained on Kaitain, out of reach, probably relaxing in luxury.

Baron Vladimir Harkonnen was all alone, facing the Emperor's wrath.

"STOP!" THE GUILD Legate's booming voice was amplified by a full order of magnitude. The Supreme Bashar actually hesitated. "I don't know what game you are playing, Shaddam." The Legate's pink eyes were hot with malice. "You dare not damage melange production to salve your petty pride. The spice must flow."

Shaddam sniffed. "Then perhaps you need to enact a few new austerity measures. And unless you cease this open defiance of Imperial rule, I shall take punitive measures against the Spacing Guild as well."

"You are bluffing."

"Am I?" Shaddam stood up from his command chair and glared at the image.

"We are not amused." In the clustered Heighliners over Arrakis, the appalled Guildsmen must be scrambling.

Turning calmly to Garon, the Emperor barked, "Supreme Bashar, I gave you an order."

The Legate's image wavered, as if with shock and disbelief. "This course on which you embark is beyond the right of any ruler—Emperor or not. Because of it, the Guild henceforth withdraws all transportation services. You and your fleet will not be given passage home."

Shaddam felt a stab of ice. "You would never dare, not after you hear what I—"

The Legate cut him off. "We decree that you, Padishah Emperor Shaddam.IV, are now stranded here, the king of nothing more than a wasteland, accompanied by a military force that has nowhere to go and nothing to fight."

"You decree nothing! I am the—" He stopped as the holo-image of the Legate faded and the comsystem filled with static.

"All communication has been cut off, Sire," Garon reported.

"But I still have something to say to them!" He had been waiting for the right moment to make his announcement about the amal, to gain the upper hand. "Reestablish contact."

"Trying, Your Majesty, but they have it blocked."

Shaddam saw one of the Heighliners above them disappear as it folded space. The Emperor was bathed in perspiration, drenching his ceremonial uniform.

This was one scenario he had not envisioned. How could he make promises or issue ultimatums if they severed communications? Without a way to send messages, how could he win back their cooperation? How could he tell them about amal? If the Guild trapped him at Arrakis, his victory would amount to nothing.

The Spacing Guild could very well maroon him and then convince the Landsraad to gather a military force against him. They would gladly install someone else on the Golden Lion Throne. After all, House Corrino only had daughters as heirs.

On the comscreen, a second Heighliner disappeared, followed by the remaining three. Nothing but empty space remained overhead.

In a state of near panic, Shaddam felt the overwhelming immensity of the situation. He was far from Kaitain. Even if the technicians with him could cobble together a means of traveling through space with pre-Guild technology, he and his forces would not arrive back home for centuries.

Supreme Bashar Garon's expression turned hard. "Our

forces are still ready to fire, Your Majesty. Or should I instruct them to stand down?"

If they were all stranded, how long would it be before the disenfranchised Sardaukar troops banded together in a mutiny?

Shaddam raged at the dead comscreen that had linked him with the Guild representative. "I am your Emperor! I alone decide policy for the Imperium!"

No answer came. No one was even there to hear.

The natural destiny of power is fragmentation.
— PADISHAH EMPEROR IDRISS I, Landsraad Archives

I n the skies above Ix, space itself shimmered, then opened to reveal an armada of more than a hundred Guild Heighliners, called from all across the Imperium, including the five Heighliners Shaddam had taken to Arrakis.

The magnificent vessels overshadowed the forests, rivers, and craggy ravines on the Ixian surface. Smoke from the destruction in the subterranean battlefield below curled out of emergency purification vents. For the huge ships, it was a return home, since every one of the vessels had been constructed here, most of them under the supervision of House Vernius.

UNDERGROUND, THE SURVIVING Sardaukar, the strongest fighters, had taken last-stand defensive positions, back-to-back, near the center of the cavern grotto, with no intention of surrendering. The frenzied Imperial soldiers would make the new conquerors pay dearly for victory.

Surrounded by Atreides guards, the captive Count Hasimir Fenring looked self-satisfied, as if he felt that he alone maintained control of the situation. "I am a victim, I assure you, hmmm? As Imperial Spice Minister, I was dispatched here by the Emperor himself. We had heard rumors of illegal experiments, and when I discovered too much, Master Researcher Ajidica tried to kill me."

"I'm sure that is why you greeted our arrival with such enthusiasm," Duncan said, holding up the Old Duke's notched sword.

"I was frightened, hmmm? All the Imperium knows the ruthlessness of Duke Leto's soldiers." Duncan's men glared at the Count, as if they wanted to arrange for Tleilaxu medical experiments on Fenring himself.

Before Duncan could respond, a signal rang in his com-ear. He pressed a finger to the transceiver and listened. His eyes widened at the news. He smiled at Fenring without explanation, then turned to Rhombur. "The Guild has arrived, Prince. Many Heighliners are in orbit around Ix."

"C'tair's message!" Prince Rhombur said. "They heard him!"

Before Fenring could manage another thin excuse, the air within the grotto rumbled. A clap of thunder like a world exploding cracked through the cavern.

Above the huge open area where the Sardaukar were making their final stand, the fabric of the air stretched, and tore. A Heighliner appeared where there had been only empty space moments before.

The sudden displacement of such a huge volume of atmosphere sent an overpressure wave like a storm through the grotto, knocking people back, throwing them against the stone walls. Without warning, the huge vessel was simply *there*, hovering on suspensors, barely two meters above the ground in the center of the grotto. The ship struck down some of the rallied Sardaukar directly beneath it and scattered the rest, effectively rendering the last Imperial soldiers helpless.

For Rhombur, the sight brought back memories of years past, when he and young Leto, along with the Pilru twins and Kailea, had watched the departure of a newly constructed Dominic Class Heighliner. The Navigator had simply folded space and piloted the ship away from the Ixian underground—out into the open universe.

The reverse had occurred just now. The Heighliner had been returned by a talented Steersman piloting the ship with such precision that he could direct it with pinpoint accuracy to a location in a large bubble within the crust of the planet.

Silence fell after the awe-inspiring arrival of the giant vessel. The scattered clashes of swords went quiet; even the rioting suboids ceased their shouting and destruction.

Then, the Guild commandeered the grotto skyspeakers and a deep voice boomed out, leaving no room for doubt. "The Spacing Guild celebrates the victory of Prince Rhombur Vernius on Ix. We welcome a return to normal machine production and technological innovation."

Standing beside Gurney and Duncan, Rhombur looked up at the great ship as if he couldn't believe the words he had just heard. It had been so long . . . more than his lifetime, it seemed. Tessia would find her own place here, too.

The smug and confident look on the face of Count Hasimir Fenring had dissolved. Now the devious Spice Minister simply looked defeated.

Brutality breeds brutality. Love breeds love.
—LADY ANIRUL CORRINO, journal entry

A dead guard, his uniform soaked with blood from a stab wound in his side, lay across the corridor on one of the lower levels of the Palace.

Leaving the latest victim to the men behind him, Duke Leto jumped over the slain soldier and ran faster, knowing he must be close to the person who had taken his son. He walked through a spreading pool on the floor and left diminishing red footprints as he rushed on. He drew the jeweled ceremonial dagger from his belt, with every intention of using it.

In a chamber in the Princesses' study and play area, he found another corpse: a Bene Gesserit. Just as he was trying to identify her, two Sardaukar beside him let out stunned gasps. Leto caught his breath.

It was Lady Anirul, wife of Emperor Shaddam IV.

Reverend Mother Mohiam, also wearing black robes, appeared in the doorway. She looked at her fingers, then down at the waxy face of the dead woman. "I arrived too late. I could not help her . . . I could salvage nothing."

With a clatter of boots and equipment, several men in Leto's squad fanned out to search nearby rooms. Leto stared, immediately wondering if Mohiam herself had murdered the Emperor's wife.

Mohiam's birdlike eyes flicked across the faces

of the men, recognizing their questions. "Of course I did not kill her," she said, with firm conviction and just a touch of Voice. "Leto, your son is safe."

Looking across the room, he saw the baby, wrapped in blankets on a cushion. The Duke stepped forward, his knees weak, surprised at his own hesitation. The newborn was red-faced and alert. He had wisps of black hair like Leto's own and a chin reminiscent of Jessica's. "Is this my son?"

"Yes, a *son*," Mohiam responded in a flat, somehow bitter tone. "Exactly what you wanted."

He didn't understand what she meant by her tone, but didn't care. He was just happy to have the child safe. He picked up the baby, cradling it in his arms, remembering how he had held Victor. *I have another son!* The child's bright eyes were open wide.

"Support his head." Reaching out, Mohiam adjusted the baby in Leto's arms.

"I know well enough how to do it." He remembered Kailea telling him the same thing after the birth of Victor. His heart wrenched at the thought. "Who was the kidnapper? Did you see?"

"No," she said without the slightest hesitation. "He fled."

Gazing down the bridge of his nose at the Reverend Mother, Leto asked in a suspicious tone, "And how is it that my son came to be here, and the kidnapper conveniently escaped? How did you find the baby?"

The robed Sister looked suddenly bored. "I found your boy on the floor here, beside the body of Lady Anirul. Do you see her hands there? I had to pry her fingers loose from the child's blankets. Somehow she saved him."

Leto looked at her, not believing. He noted no blood on the blankets or marks on the baby.

One of the Sardaukar came up and saluted. "Sorry to interrupt, sir. We have located the Princess Irulan, and she is unharmed." He pointed toward the adjacent study room, where a guard stood beside the eleven-year-old girl.

The guard made clumsy attempts to comfort Irulan. Wearing a dress of alternating brown and white damask with the Corrino crest on one long sleeve, Irulan was visibly shaken, but she seemed to be dealing with the tragedy better than the guard was. How much had she seen? The Princess looked at the Reverend Mother with an impenetrable Bene Gesserit expression, as if the two of them shared one of the Sisterhood's damnable secrets.

Her beautiful young face a stiff mask, Irulan walked into the chamber as if the milling guards were not even there. "It was a man. He wore a Sardaukar disguise, and makeup on his face. After killing my mother, he ran. I could not see his features well."

Leto's heart went out to the Emperor's daughter, who stood as motionless as one of the many statues of her father. He thought she showed remarkable poise and coolheadedness. Though clearly shocked and filled with sadness, she maintained control of herself.

Irulan stared down at her mother's body as one of the guards covered it with a gray cloak. No tears came to the girl's bright green eyes; her classically beautiful face could have been an alabaster sculpture.

He knew the feeling well, a similar lesson his own father had taught him. *Grieve only in private moments, when no one can observe you.*

Irulan's eyes met Mohiam's, as if together they were erecting battlements. The Princess seemed to know more, something she kept between herself and the aging Reverend Mother. Leto would probably never know the truth.

"The criminal will be found," the Duke vowed, holding his son closer. The guards spoke on their com-units and continued the search throughout the Palace.

Mohiam looked at him. "Lady Anirul gave her life to save your son." Her expression became pinched, resentful. "Raise him well, Duke Atreides." She touched the baby boy's blankets and pushed him against Leto's chest. "I am sure Shaddam will not rest until he sees justice done to the man who killed his wife." She stepped back, as if dismissing him. "Go, see your Jessica."

Reluctant and suspicious, but recognizing his priorities, Leto proudly carried the infant out of the chambers and headed back to the birthing room, where Jessica awaited him.

Irulan looked steadily at Mohiam, but not even a hand signal flickered between them. Unknown to anyone, even Mohiam, the Princess had hidden behind a slightly ajar door and watched her mother sacrifice herself for the sake of the newborn baby. She was amazed that such a powerful and reserved woman had placed so much importance on this *Atreides* infant, born of a mere concubine. What possible reason could there be?

Why is this child so special?

Despite the day's momentous victory, Prince Rhombur Vernius knew that many years of struggle remained ahead in order to effectuate a complete restructuring of Ixian society. But he was up to the task.

"We'll bring in the best investigators and forensics experts," Duncan said, looking at the still-smoldering wreck of the laboratory complex. "The ventilation is clearing the air, but we still can't go inside the research pavilion. After the fire goes out, they will comb through every ash for evidence. Something must be left, and with any luck it will be enough to bring Count Fenring—and the Emperor—to justice."

Rhombur shook his head, holding up a prosthetic arm and looking at the ragged wrist stump. "Even if we are completely victorious here, Shaddam may find some way to worm out of his guilt. If he has that much at stake here, he will try to manipulate the Landsraad against us."

Duncan gestured toward the dead who lay all around, and at white-uniformed Atreides medics who were tending to the wounded. "Look how many Imperial troops have been killed here. Do you think Shaddam can ignore it? If he cannot cover it up, he will make some excuse for the Sardaukar presence on Ix and accuse *us* of treason."

"We did what we had to do," Rhombur said with a firm shake of his head.

"Nevertheless, House Atreides has taken military action against the Emperor's soldiers," Gurney said. "Unless we can find some way to turn this against him, Caladan may be forfeit."

STRANDED AND HELPLESS over Arrakis, outraged that his plans had been ruined, and his Imperial presence humiliated before all the Sardaukar, Shaddam issued the most difficult order he had ever given. With jaw clenched and lips curled, he finally turned to old Zum Garon.

"Tell the fleet to stand down." He drew a deep breath, narrowing his nostrils. "I rescind the order to fire."

As the Imperial warships drew away from the planet into a higher orbit, he looked at his bridge officers in search of a solution. The Sardaukar remained expressionless, but Shaddam could tell that they blamed him for their situation. Even if he landed on the desert planet's surface, the Emperor would meet only with disdain from Baron Harkonnen.

I am being made into the laughingstock of the Imperium.

After an uncomfortable silence, he cut off any questions from the officers by snapping, "Await further orders."

In the end, they waited a full day.

All communications systems on Arrakis remained nonfunctional. Although the Sardaukar fleet could still use its ship-to-ship transmitters, they had no one but themselves to talk to. *Marooned.*

He locked himself in his private cabin, unable to believe what the Guild had done to him. At any second, he expected the Guild fleet to return so they could see how contrite their Emperor had become.

But with the passage of each hour, his hopes began to wane.

Finally, when he was certain the Sardaukar were on the verge of revolt, a single Heighliner returned, appearing high above the huddled Imperial warships.

Shaddam had to restrain himself from shouting curses at the vessel or demanding that the Guild return him to Kaitain. Every defense or argument that came to mind sounded childish and weak. And so he let the Guild speak first, to make their demands. He hoped he could tolerate their requirements.

The bottom cargo hatch of the Heighliner cracked open, and a single ship descended. A message came to the bridge of the flagship. "We have dispatched a shuttle to retrieve the Emperor. Our representative will bring him back to this Heighliner, where we will continue our discussions."

Shaddam wanted to rage at the Legate, to insist that no one, not even the Spacing Guild, was in a position to *demand* his appearance at a meeting. Instead, the humiliated ruler swallowed hard and tried to sound as Imperial as possible. "We shall await the arrival of the shuttle."

The Emperor had just enough time to change into formal scarlet-and-gold robes, applying all the trappings and badges of office that he could locate on short notice, before the shuttle arrived. He stood in the landing bay to greet the shuttle, a regal figure that should have made entire populations tremble. Uncomfortably, he thought of long-forgotten Mandias the Terrible, whose dusty tomb was hidden in the Imperial necropolis.

He was utterly astonished to see Hasimir Fenring step out of the small Guild ship and gesture him aboard. The Count's expression warned him not to say a word. At the Emperor's side, Supreme Bashar Garon stood waiting, as if expecting to accompany Shaddam as a personal bodyguard. But Fenring motioned the old veteran back. "This will be a private meeting. I'll see what I can do to talk the Emperor and the Guild through this, hmmm?"

Shaddam seethed with rage and embarrassment, and knew the worst was yet to come. . . .

When the shuttle departed again, the two sat in comfortable chairs, gazing through large portholes at a starstudded universe. For ten thousand years, House Corrino had ruled this vast realm. Below them, the cracked brown globe of Arrakis looked austere and ugly, a wart in an empire of jewels.

Shaddam suspected their conversation on board would be recorded by eavesdropping Guild spies. Knowing that, Fenring spoke in code, using a private language the two friends had developed as boys. "Everything on Ix is a disaster, Sire. And I see you haven't done any better here." He rubbed his chin thoughtfully. "Ajidica deceived us . . . as I said he would, hmmm?"

"What about the amal? I tasted it myself! All the reports told me it was perfect—the Master Researcher, my Sardaukar commander, even you!"

"That was a Face Dancer, Sire, not me. Amal is a total failure. Test samples caused the two recent Heighliner accidents. I myself watched our Master Researcher die in convulsions from an overdose of the substance. Hmmm."

Shaddam's head jerked back involuntarily, and all color drained from his face. "My God, when I think of what I almost did to Arrakis!"

"Amal poisoned your Sardaukar legions on Ix, too, hindering their ability to defend us against the Atreides attackers."

"Atreides! On Ix? What—"

"Your cousin Duke Leto has used his military to restore Rhombur Vernius to the Grand Palais. The Tleilaxu—and your Sardaukar—have been completely overthrown. In any event, I destroyed all of our research and production facilities. No evidence remains to implicate House Corrino."

Shaddam purpled, unable to comprehend how completely he had been defeated. "Let us hope."

"By the way, you will have to inform your Supreme Bashar that his son was killed in the fighting."

"More disasters." The hawk-faced Emperor, looking haggard and weary, groaned. "So there is no spice substitute? Nothing?"

"Hmmm, no. Not even a remote possibility."

The Emperor sank back in his chair and watched the Heighliner grow huge in front of them.

Fenring showed obvious disgust. "If you had succeeded in your foolhardy plan to devastate Arrakis, you would have brought an end not only to your reign, but to the entire *Imperium*. You would have thrown us back to pre-Jihad space travel." His voice took on a scolding tone and he extended a finger. "I have warned you time and again not to make such decisions without consulting me first. It will be your downfall."

The Heighliner swallowed the tiny shuttle like a whale eating a single krill. No Guild representative came to receive the Padishah Emperor, nor did anyone escort him from the shuttle.

While he and Fenring sat alone, waiting for contact, the Navigator activated the Holtzmann engines and folded space, taking the disgraced ruler back to Kaitain, where he would face the consequences of his decisions.

Vengeance may come through complex schemes or outright aggression. In some circumstances, revenge can only be achieved through time.

—EARL DOMINIC VERNIUS, *Renegade Journals*

On Kaitain weeks later, unmoved by anything but anger, Shaddam Corrino IV watched the conclusion of the bastard Tyros Reffa's recorded speech. He cursed under his breath.

Behind the closed doors of the Emperor's private office, Cammar Pilru waited for Shaddam to comment. The Ixian Ambassador had seen the oration numerous times, and still it wrenched his heart.

Shaddam, though, remained cold. "I see I was right to have his damnable mouth fused shut before I executed him."

Upon returning to the Palace, the Padishah Emperor had sequestered himself. Outside the grounds, Sardaukar tried to keep order in the face of numerous demonstrations. Some demanded that Shaddam abdicate, which might have been a viable solution if he'd had an acceptable male heir. As it was, his eleven-year-old daughter Irulan had already received numerous marriage proposals from the heads of powerful Houses.

Shaddam wanted to kill all the suitors . . . perhaps his daughters, too. At least he didn't have to worry about his wife anymore.

Following their numerous military embarrassments, even the once-loyal Sardaukar were upset with him, and Supreme Bashar Zum Garon had lodged a formal complaint. Garon's son had died in the Ixian debacle, but even worse in the old Bashar's estimation, the Imperial soldiers had been betrayed. Not defeated, but *betrayed*. This was an important distinction in his mind, for the Sardaukar had never, in their long history, tasted defeat. Garon demanded that this potential blemish be formally erased from the record. He also wanted a posthumous commendation for his son.

Shaddam didn't know how to deal with it all.

Under other circumstances, he would never have given this pathetic and now self-important Ixian diplomat a moment of his time. But Ambassador Pilru still had his damnable connections and was riding the wave of Rhombur's victory.

Feeling strong again after all the years of abuse and neglect, Pilru dropped a hard sheet of ridulian crystal in front of Shaddam's frowning face. "It was most unfortunate, Sire, that you did not have the opportunity to perform a thorough genetic analysis on Tyros Reffa, if only to disprove his claim that he was also a member of House Corrino. Many members of the Landsraad, indeed many noblemen of the Imperium, question this."

He tapped the data on the crystal sheet, which Shaddam no doubt found incomprehensible. Pilru had been ignored, insulted, and dismissed for decades, but now that would change. He would make certain that the Emperor paid reparations to the Ixian people and that he offered no resistance to the restoration of Vernius rule.

"Luckily, I was able to obtain samples from Reffa in his prison cell." Pilru smiled. "As you can see, this is incontrovertible genetic proof that Tyros Reffa was indeed a son of Emperor Elrood IX. You signed your own brother's death warrant."

"*Half* brother," Shaddam snapped.

"I could easily arrange to have his recording and the test results distributed quietly among the members of the Landsraad, Sire," Ambassador Pilru said, holding up the crystal sheet. "I'm afraid the fate of your *half* brother wouldn't remain quiet for long."

He had, of course, removed all details of the mother's identity from the test results. No one needed to know the bastard's connection to the long-dead Lady Shando Vernius. Rhombur had the secret, and that was enough.

"Your threat is all too clear, Ambassador." Shaddam's eyes burned bright through the shadows of defeat that had settled around him. "Now, what do you want of me?"

⁂

WHILE SHADDAM WAITED in his private receiving hall for the arguments and proceedings to begin, he had very few moments of pleasure. Now he understood why his old father had felt the need to drink so much spice beer. Even Count Fenring, his companion in misery, could not cheer him up, with so many political millstones around the Imperial neck.

However, an Emperor could also make others miserable.

Fenring paced beside him, fidgeting and full of feral energy. All doors except the main entrance had been sealed, all witnesses removed. Even the guards had been instructed to wait in the halls.

Shaddam was eager. "They will be here any moment, Hasimir."

"It still seems a bit . . . childish, hmmm?"

"But gratifying, and don't pretend to disagree." He sniffed. "Besides, it is the privilege of being an Emperor."

"Enjoy it while you can," Fenring murmured, then turned away from Shaddam's glare.

They both watched the double bronze doors, which guards swung open slowly. Sardaukar soldiers brought in a familiar, awful-looking machine with a good deal of clanking, creaking, and clattering. Hidden cutter blades whirred inside the monstrosity, and sparks crackled from circuit ports.

Years ago, Tleilaxu prosecutors had brought the horrible execution device to Leto Atreides's Trial by Forfeiture, hoping to vivisect him with it, draining his blood and slicing open his tissues to take numerous genetic samples. Shaddam had always thought the machine had a great deal of potential.

Fenring looked at it, pursing his lips in contemplation. "A device designed only to maim, to hurt, to exert pain. If you ask me, Shaddam, it is clearly a machine with a human mind, hmmm-ah? Perhaps it is a violation of the Butlerian Jihad."

"I am not amused, Hasimir."

Behind the machine marched six captive Tleilaxu Masters, shirtless because of their well-known tendency to conceal weapons in their sleeves. These were the Tleilaxu representatives who had come to the Imperial Court in recent months, held here after the failure of Project Amal. Before word could get out about Ajidica's demise, Shaddam had ordered their capture and detention.

Count Fenring himself held a deep grudge, suspecting that at least one of these Tleilaxu was a Face Dancer, a shape-shifter who had mimicked him in order to deliver a falsely optimistic report about the success of the artificial spice. It had only been a delaying tactic by Ajidica, to forestall Imperial retaliation long enough for the Master Researcher to escape. But it had failed.

For his part, Shaddam didn't look at any of the captives as individuals, and indeed the gnomish men all appeared very much alike. "Well?" he shouted at them. "Stand by your machine. Don't tell me you aren't aware of its purpose?"

With despondent expressions, the captive Tleilaxu Masters took up positions around the diabolical-looking device.

"You Tleilaxu have caused me a great many problems. I am about to face the greatest crisis in my reign, and I think you all should shoulder some of the blame." He looked at their faces. "Choose one among you, so that I can see this device in operation, and after the demonstration the rest of you will dismantle it right here."

Guards stepped forward, holding hand tools. The glowering, gray-skinned men looked at each other, remaining silent. Finally, one man reached forward to activate the power source on the angular plates of the execution machine. The cumbersome contraption surged to life with a roar that startled the Emperor and the guards.

Fenring merely nodded, realizing that half of the effectiveness of this machine was its ominous nature. "It seems they are having trouble choosing, hmmm?"

"We have chosen," one of the Tleilaxu announced. Without a word or gesture, the six Tleilaxu Masters all climbed up and jumped into a hopper on top of the execution contraption. They tumbled inside, throwing themselves into the embrace of the choppers, cutters, and slicers. As a final, malicious joke, gouts of blood, fragments of flesh, and small pieces of bone sprayed the Emperor and Fenring. The Sardaukar scrambled away.

Shaddam spluttered and grabbed for a cape to wipe the gore off of himself. Fenring did not seem terribly put off as he smeared a gobbet away from his eyes. The vivisection machine continued to cough and grind. The Tleilaxu had made no screams, no outcries.

"I believe that takes care of the Face Dancer question," the Emperor announced in a not-quite-satisfied tone.

After weeks of turmoil, the shock waves of uncovered plots and tangled secrets still swept across Kaitain. All that remained was for the last few fires to be put out, the political fallout assessed, favors exchanged, and debts called in.

Impressively attired in the Old Duke's ceremonial red uniform, with buttons and medals gleaming, Leto Atreides sat on an elevated platform at the center of the Hall of Oratory. This historic meeting would be part censure, part inquisition . . . and part bargaining session.

Emperor Shaddam Corrino faced the room alone.

On the platform beside Leto sat six Guild representatives and an equal number of Landsraad noblemen, including the newly restored Prince Rhombur. The banners of Great Houses were draped all around, an array of crests and colors like rainbows after a storm, including the purple and copper of Vernius—formally replacing the flag that had been taken down and publicly burned after Dominic Vernius had gone renegade. Largest of all was the golden lion banner of House Corrino in the center, flanked on either side by the equally large banners of the Spacing Guild and the moiré checkerboard of CHOAM.

Plush black and maroon booths held the noblemen, ladies, prime ministers, and ambassadors of all the Great Houses. Not far from Leto sat the official Atreides delegation, including his concubine Jessica and their new son, only a few weeks old. With them sat Gurney Halleck, Duncan Idaho, Thufir Hawat, and a number of brave Atreides officers and troops. Tessia was there as well, looking at her husband. Rhombur flexed his new replacement hand, which Dr. Yueh had attached, scolding his patient all the while.

The accusers' table had been reserved for grim-faced representatives from the savaged Houses of Ix, Taligari, Beakkal, and Richese. Premier Ein Calimar sat straight-backed, watching the proceedings with his metal replacement eyes, purchased from the Tleilaxu.

More widely reviled than ever as a result of their actions, the Bene Tleilax were not represented at all. The token members of the race who had been at the Imperial Court seemed to have vanished. Leto did not look forward to hearing the long record of their crimes and moral atrocities, but he could already tell that the hated little men would receive the brunt of blame and punishments.

At the first morning bell, the elderly CHOAM president rose in front of the lectern. "During this time of upheaval, many terrible mistakes were made. Others were barely averted."

Oddly, neither Baron Harkonnen nor even the official House Harkonnen ambassador was in attendance at the hearings. After the debacle on Arrakis, apparently the Baron had difficulty arranging passage off-world, and his twisted Mentat had disappeared from the Palace. Leto was sure the Harkonnens had had something to do with at least part of the turmoil.

Meanwhile, many rival families crouched here like

vultures, hoping to feast upon the fat holdings of Arrakis, but Leto did not doubt that House Harkonnen would keep its fief—though barely. The Baron would be required to pay stiff fines, and had probably placed bribes in the right places.

There had already been enough upheavals in the Imperium.

For hours the preliminaries were read, with lawtech Mentats reciting long descriptions and summaries from the Imperial Law Code. The questions and charges were extensive. The audience began to grow bored.

Finally, Rhombur was called forward. The cyborg Prince stood in full Ixian military uniform with an officer's cap on his scarred head. He took his position at the podium and locked his mechanical legs into place. "After many years of oppression, the Tleilaxu invaders are now gone from my world. We have achieved victory on Ix."

The delegates applauded, though none of them had responded to Dominic Vernius's requests for help years ago.

"I formally request a full reinstatement of Great House privileges for the Vernius family, who were forced by treachery to go renegade. If we are returned to our former role in the Imperium, every House here will benefit."

"I second that!" Leto shouted from his seat at the main table.

"The throne approves," Shaddam said loudly, unasked. He looked over at Ambassador Pilru, as if they had reached a prior agreement. When none of the other representatives raised any objection, the audience bellowed its approval, passing the measure by acclamation.

"So noted," the CHOAM president said, not even bothering to ask for dissenting opinions or further discussion.

Rhombur's scarred face managed a grin, though the restoration of House Vernius was a mere formality, since the Prince could never beget an heir. He raised his chin. "Before I leave the podium, I believe certain honors are in order." Lifting a rack of colorful medals from the lectern, holding them up to the light, he said, "Would someone step up here and pin all of these on me, please?"

The audience laughed, a brief respite from the tension and tedium.

"Only a jest." His face grew serious. "Duke Leto Atreides, my faithful friend." Leto walked onto the stage, accompanied by thunderous applause. The rest of the Atreides delegation joined him: Duncan Idaho, Thufir Hawat, Gurney Halleck, and even Jessica, holding her baby.

While the Duke stood at attention, beaming with pride, Rhombur pinned a medal onto the Old Duke's jacket, a swimming helix of precious metals, immersed within liquid crystal. He presented similar honors to the Atreides officers, as well as to the long-faithful Ambassador Cammar Pilru. The Ambassador also received a posthumous medal for his valiant son, C'tair Pilru, as well as for the Navigator D'murr, who had brought all the passengers of his lost Heighliner back to safety. Finally, Rhombur removed the last medal from the rack and looked at it, perplexed. "Did I forget someone?"

Leto took the gleaming award and pinned it on Rhombur's own chest. Then, in the midst of a cheering din, the two men embraced.

From the podium, Leto gazed down at the Emperor. No ruler in the long history of the Imperium had ever suffered such an ignominious defeat. He wondered how Shaddam could possibly survive—but the alternatives were not clear-cut. After so many thousands of years, even political rivals would not lightly abandon stability in the Imperium, and no faction had clear support. Leto had no idea how the hearings would turn out.

Finally, Shaddam IV was called upon to speak in his own defense. The Landsraad Hall fell into uneasy murmurings. Chamberlain Ridondo directed an Imperial fanfare to play loudly enough to drown out their noise.

Showing no uncertainty, holding his head high, the

Emperor of the Known Universe stood, but did not go to the podium. In a voice that was hoarse (probably from days of shouting at his staff), he delivered a scathing speech that blamed the Tleilaxu and his own father for developing the ill-fated artificial spice project. "I do not know why Elrood IX did business with such despicable men, but he was old. Many of you remember how volatile and irrational he became near the end of his life. I deeply regret that I did not discover his mistake sooner."

Shaddam claimed he had never fully understood the ramifications and had assigned Sardaukar troops to Ix only to keep the peace. As soon as he learned of the existence of amal, he had sent his Imperial Spice Minister, Count Hasimir Fenring, to investigate—and Fenring had been held hostage. The Emperor hung his head in a too-careful expression of sorrow.

"The word of a Corrino must mean something, after all." Shaddam said all the proper words, though few of the attendees looked as if they believed what he said. Delegates whispered among themselves and shook their heads. "Slippery as a greased slig," Leto heard one of them say.

In spite of all the forces aligned against him, Shaddam remained a proud man. He stood on the shoulders of powerful, highly respected ancestors dating all the way back to the Battle of Corrin. His representatives at court had worked behind the scenes to salvage his position, and certain concessions would undoubtedly be granted.

Leto stared at the ceiling, his thoughts in turmoil. Old Paulus had always taught him that there were ugly necessities in politics.

Coming to a decision, the Duke spoke to the assemblage before returning to the main table, deviating slightly from the agenda. The CHOAM president frowned, but allowed him to have the floor. "Years ago, at my Trial by Forfeiture, Emperor Shaddam stepped forward and spoke on my behalf. I find it appropriate to return the favor at this time."

Many members of the audience reacted with surprise.

"Hear me out. The Emperor, through his . . . ignorance, nearly brought ruin to the Imperium. However, if this assembly were to take rash countermeasures, this could bring even more turmoil and suffering. We must consider *the good of the Imperium*. We dare not degenerate into chaos, as our civilization did during the Interregnum centuries ago."

Pausing, Leto locked eyes with the Emperor, whose expression betrayed warring emotions. "At this point, the Imperium needs stability more than anything else, or we face the very real risk of civil war. With wiser counsel and strict controls, I believe Shaddam can reassert his prudence and rule with benevolence."

Leto stepped around the lectern. "Know this. We all owe many obligations to the Imperial House. Every family of the Landsraad must mourn the loss of Shaddam's beloved wife Anirul—and I more than most, since the Great Lady gave her life to protect my newborn child, the heir to House Atreides."

He raised his voice to be heard over the crowd. "I suggest that the Landsraad and the Guild select many new advisors to assist the Padishah Emperor in his rule from this day forward. Emperor Shaddam Corrino IV, do you formally agree to work with the chosen representatives, for the good of all people, of all worlds, of all holdings?"

The beaten ruler knew he had no choice. Rising to his feet, he replied, "I accept what is best for the Imperium. As always." He stared at the floor, wishing he could be anywhere but there. "I pledge to cooperate fully and learn how to better serve my people." He had to admit a certain grudging admiration for Duke Leto, but it irked him how this Atreides cousin had risen so far, while he, the Emperor of a Million Worlds, had been forced into this embarrassing position.

Duke Leto stepped to the edge of the platform, never removing his gaze from Shaddam, who stood alone in his private area. Leto yanked the jeweled ceremonial knife from his own belt. The Emperor's eyes widened.

Leto flipped the knife around and extended it hilt-first to Shaddam. "More than two decades ago you gave this weapon to me, Sire. You supported me when I was falsely accused by the Tleilaxu. Now, I believe you have a greater need for it. Take it back, and rule wisely. Think of Atreides loyalty whenever you look at it."

Grudgingly, Shaddam accepted the ceremonial weapon. *My time will come again. I do not forget my enemies.*

The secret worlds of the Bene Tleilax have long been the source of twisted Mentats. Their creations have always raised the question of which is more twisted, the Mentats or the source?

—Mentat Handbook

To the Baron Harkonnen, Giedi Prime was beautiful, even in comparison with spectacular Kaitain. Smoky skies turned the sunset into torchlight. The blocky buildings and dramatic statues gave the Harkonnen capital a solid, implacable appearance. The very air, with its odors of industry and crowded population, smelled comforting and familiar.

The Baron had never thought to see this place again.

Once the ominous Heighliners and the Emperor's Sardaukar fleet had departed from Arrakis, the desert world had trembled liked a kangaroo mouse that had barely escaped a predator.

According to the official story from the Palace, the Emperor had merely been bluffing, and never actually intended to damage melange operations. The Baron was not entirely convinced of this, but decided not to speak his mind. Shaddam IV had taken extreme, ill-advised actions before, like a petulant child who did not know his limits.

Insanity!

In his damaged garrison capital, the Baron had slammed around in search of scapegoats; all of his

Fremen house workers had mysteriously vanished. It had taken him weeks just to get transport back to civilization. Rabban—with a variety of excuses— hadn't been too quick to send a frigate.

Shaken by the infuriating Landsraad scrutiny and censures, the uneasy nobleman had fled to Giedi Prime to lick his wounds. Though he had been forced to miss the drawn-out proceedings against the Emperor, he had sent Couriers and messages, expressing his outrage at Shaddam's misguided threat to destroy all life on Arrakis—"in reaction to a few minor bookkeeping errors." He was skilled at shadings of truth, at massaging information to make himself look the least culpable. As the de facto Harkonnen ambassador, Piter de Vries should have been on Kaitain to take care of such matters.

He would have to send gifts quietly to Kaitain and act humbled and repentant, hoping the politically hamstrung Emperor would choose not to lash out at House Harkonnen. The Baron would make amends and pay even more substantial bribes than he'd already expended, probably amounting to all of the spice he had managed to stockpile illegally.

But the twisted Mentat had vanished without even bothering to send a message. The Baron hated unreliability, especially in an expensive Mentat. During the turmoil following the siege of Arrakis, as well as the revolt on Ix, there must have been ample opportunity for de Vries to kill Duke Leto's woman and their baby. Reports were guarded, but it seemed that, while there had been a brief scuffle shortly after the birth, the Atreides baby was safe and healthy.

The Baron wanted to wring de Vries's neck, but the Mentat was nowhere to be found. Damn the man!

As darkness fell, the fat Harkonnen lord glided on suspensors back inside Harkonnen Keep. He had much to do in preparation for his own legal defense, should CHOAM pursue the matter of his "indiscretions." He wanted to be ready, though he had spoken the words all the Imperium wanted to hear. "I assure you that melange production will continue, as always. *The spice will flow.*"

His nephew Rabban was no help at all when it came to record keeping and technicalities. The brute was proficient at bashing skulls together, but nothing that required finesse. Certainly his chosen nickname of "Beast" did little to foster the image of a judicious statesman or skilled diplomat.

In addition, expensive repairs were necessary to rebuild the infrastructure of Arrakis, especially the spaceports and communication systems damaged by the Guild embargo. It was all so hard to do by himself, and he seethed again, angry that his supposedly loyal Mentat was not there to serve him.

Cursing his misfortune, he returned to his private chamber, where slaves had laid out a banquet: succulent meat dishes, rich pastries, exotic fruits, and the Baron's expensive kirana brandy. He paced, nibbled, and brooded.

Since being trapped in bleak Carthag for so many days, unable even to send a transmission or summon a Courier, he had felt desperate for the finer things in life. Now he liked to snack all day long, just to reassure himself. He licked frosting off his fingers.

His body was soft and perfumed, having been bathed by fine serving boys, oiled, and massaged, until finally his tensions were beginning to relax. He was exhausted and sore, weary from the pleasures in which he had immersed himself.

Rabban lumbered into the chamber unannounced. Feyd-Rautha toddled along beside his big brother, wearing an intelligent but mischievous expression on his cherubic face.

The Beast thought he and the Viscount Moritani had managed to cover up their bungled attack on Caladan. The Baron, though, had learned of it almost immediately, and had kept silent about it. The idea did indeed show a surprising amount of initiative, and might have worked, but he would never want to admit that to his nephew. The Beast seemed to have covered his tracks well enough to keep any fallout away from House Harkonnen, and so the Baron would keep silent and let his nephew stew about it, worrying that he would be found out.

Now, Rabban shouted to two slaves who plodded along behind him. They carried a long, bulky package covered in bright wrapping and ribbons. "This way. The Baron will want to open it himself. Hurry up, you fools." With a show of bravado, Rabban yanked the inkvine whip from a clip at his belt, and threatened to lash the slaves. Neither of the tall, bronze-skinned men flinched, though their arms and necks bore bright scars from previous whippings.

The Baron looked with disdain at the object, which appeared to be nearly two meters long. "What is this? I'm expecting no package."

"A gift for you, Uncle, just arrived by Courier. There's no marking on the outside." He poked the wrapping with a blunt finger. "You'll have to open it and see who it's from."

"*I* have no intention of opening it." The Baron stepped back warily. "Has it been scanned for explosives?"

Rabban made a rude snort. "Of course. For all types of booby traps and poisons. We found nothing. It's completely safe."

"Then what is it?"

"We . . . couldn't exactly determine that."

The Baron took another small step backward, propelled by momentum and the assistance of his suspensors. He had not survived this long without a suspicious nature. "Open it for me, Rabban, but make sure Feyd remains well clear of you." He had no intention of losing both heirs in one assassination attempt.

Rabban gave his little brother a small shove. Feyd stumbled toward the Baron, who snatched the child by the shirt collar and yanked him to safety. Rabban himself kept his distance from the package, and snapped to the two slaves. "You heard the Baron. Open it!"

Feyd-Rautha wanted to see what was inside and fussed when the Baron held him back. The slaves tore at the packaging. Since they were not allowed to hold knives or any sharp objects, they were forced to use their fingers to break the seals.

Remaining where he was, Rabban bellowed, "Well? What is it?"

Feyd struggled against the Baron's grip. Finally the fat man released his fingers, letting the toddler make his way to the package that lay torn open on the floor.

The child looked inside and laughed. The Baron floated over on his suspensors. Curled up in the box he saw the mummified body of Piter de Vries, surrounded by metallic moldings that must have prevented scanners from determining exactly what the contents were. His lean face was unmistakable, though his cheeks and eyes were sunken in death. The twisted Mentat's papery lips still showed sapho stains.

"Who sent this?" the Baron roared.

Now that the danger seemed to be past, Rabban strutted forward. He bent a molding aside and pried a note from de Vries's stiff fingers. "It's from the witch Mohiam." He held it in front of his close-set eyes and read slowly, as if even the four words were difficult for him. " 'Never underestimate us, Baron.' " Rabban crumpled the note and threw it to the floor. "They killed your Mentat, Uncle."

"Thank you for explaining that." The Baron wrenched moldings aside and tipped the box over so that the mummy tumbled out. He then delivered a vicious kick to the body's rib cage. Now, in this most difficult time that required delicate political maneuvers just to ensure the survival of House Harkonnen, he needed a scheming Mentat more than ever.

"Piter! How could you be so stupid, so clumsy as to get yourself killed?"

The corpse did not answer.

On the other hand, de Vries had begun to outlive his usefulness. He had, admittedly, been an adequate Mentat, devious and full of sophisticated ideas. But he'd also had a penchant for drugs that distorted his perceptions, and a tendency toward showing too much initiative and acting on his own. . . .

The next one would have to be watched more closely. The Baron knew the Tleilaxu had already grown other gholas from the same genetic stock: serial versions of Piter de Vries, fully trained as Mentats and twisted with specialized conditioning. The genetic wizards had known it was only a matter of time before the Baron finally lost his temper and carried out his repeated threats to kill de Vries.

"Send a message to the Tleilaxu," he growled. "Have them rush me another Mentat."

Inevitably, the aristocrat resists his final duty—which is to step aside and vanish into history.

—CROWN PRINCE RAPHAEL CORRINO

According to a public Proclamation by Emperor Shaddam, the funeral pyre would be more magnificent than any seen before in the Imperium.

Lady Anirul's body, swathed in her finest whale-fur robes and adorned with worthless replicas of her most expensive jewelry, lay atop a bed of green crystal fragments, like jagged monster-teeth made of emeralds.

Shaddam stood at the head of the pyre, gazing across the ocean of faces. The sweeping crowd of mourners had gathered from across the Imperium to watch this final farewell to their ruler's wife. The grieving Emperor wore regal garments in muted colors to portray an atmosphere of subdued splendor.

Feigning sadness, he bowed his head. All of his daughters hovered near the front row of the crowd, by the bier, sniffling and mourning in earnest. Baby Rugi cried at all the right times. Only Irulan stood formal and reserved.

This display would pull at the heartstrings of every member of the audience, but Shaddam felt no sorrow at her death. Given time, his wife would have driven him to assassinate her anyway.

Trying not to look defeated, he let his mind

wander while priests intoned their tedious chants, reading from the Orange Catholic Bible and going through more ritual than Shaddam had seen during his own coronation or his marriage to this Bene Gesserit witch, whose primary allegiance was not to him. Still, this ceremony was what the populace expected, what they enjoyed in their perverse fashion.

And now, shackled with the restraints imposed on him by the hostile Landsraad, Guild, and CHOAM, Shaddam could not flout any rules. The forms must be obeyed. He had to behave. Those chains would hold him back for years.

The sanctions to be imposed against Shaddam had been hotly debated behind closed doors. For a full decade, severe restrictions and controls would be placed on his activities, as prescribed by Imperial Law. During that time, the Landsraad, the Spacing Guild, and CHOAM would all have far greater influence in Imperial politics and business.

Spitefully, he wished he could afford to exile Fenring again, to punish him for the amal debacle. But after all of the Emperor's own mistakes—which, as the Count reminded him, he never would have made had he obtained Fenring's advice—Shaddam knew that if he had any chance of restoring his power base, he would need the devious intelligence of his longtime friend. Still, he would leave the Count on Arrakis for a while, to let him know his place. . . .

At last the priests finished their droning, and a curtain of silence fell over the assemblage. Rugi cried again, and a nursemaid tried to hush her.

Court Chamberlain Ridondo and the High Priest waited until Shaddam realized that it was his turn to speak. He had drafted a brief statement, which had been read and approved beforehand by Landsraad magistrates, the President of CHOAM, and the Guild's Primary Legate. Though the words were innocuous, they still caught in his throat, an insult to his Imperial Majesty.

He spoke with all the gloom he could summon in his voice. "My beloved wife Anirul has been stolen from me.

Her untimely death will forever leave a scar on my heart, and I can only hope that I will rule the Imperium with compassion and grace hereafter, even without my Lady's wise counsel and generous love."

Shaddam raised his chin, and his tired green eyes flared with the Imperial wrath he had demonstrated so many times. "My investigation teams will continue to study the evidence surrounding her violent death. We will not rest until the perpetrator is caught and this plot is unraveled." He glared out at the sea of upturned faces, as if he might spot the murderer among them with a mere glance.

Truthfully, he intended to do little to investigate the crime. The kidnapper-assassin had vanished, and if he posed no threat to the crown, Shaddam didn't particularly care who had done it. Most of all he was relieved that the troublesome, meddling witch would no longer interfere with his daily decisions. He would leave her empty throne in place for a few months out of feigned respect, and then would have it removed and destroyed.

The Guild and the Landsraad would be pleased that he had followed the approved speech. He finished quickly, in an effort to remove the distaste from his mouth: "For now, alas, we have no choice but to endure our grief and carry on—to make the Imperium a better place for all."

Beside him, Truthsayer Gaius Helen Mohiam stood with her head bowed. Mohiam seemed to know far more about Anirul's murder than anyone had been able to determine, but she refused to divulge her secrets. He didn't press her too closely.

Letting his printed copy of the speech flutter to the ground, the Emperor nodded to the green-robed High Priest of Dur, who in better times had performed Shaddam's coronation. Two Acolytes pointed their laser staffs, similar to the one his bastard half brother Tyros Reffa had used to shoot at him during the play.

Energy beams lanced out and struck the prismatic emerald crystal shards, heating the controlled ionization fires within them. A column of flame rose in an incandescent blaze. Perfumed smoke spilled through grates around the pyre, finally melting the calm, waxy features of the dead woman. The blazing heat made everyone shield their eyes.

The crystal blaze continued to build until the lasers went dim and the pulsing lights faded, leaving only crackling, hissing crystals and a fine film of white ash in the shape of a body.

PAYING LITTLE ATTENTION to the Emperor, Mohiam watched the cremation of Lady Anirul, who had secretly guided the long-term breeding program through its final stages. The unfortunate death of the Kwisatz Mother in this, the final generation of the Sisterhood's extended plan, left Mohiam to safeguard Jessica and her new child.

The Reverend Mother was troubled by her daughter's defiance and betrayal . . . and by the kidnapping of the baby and the murder of Anirul. Too many things were going wrong at a critical time in the breeding program.

Still, the baby was safe, and genetics was not a precise science. There was a chance. Maybe this son of Duke Leto Atreides would be the Kwisatz Haderach after all.

Or something else entirely.

Human comfort is relative. Some would consider a particular environment austere and hellish, while others are pleased to call it home.

— PLANETOLOGIST PARDOT KYNES,
An Arrakis Primer

Count Hasimir Fenring stood on an outside deck of his Residency at Arrakeen, grasping the rail and gazing out at the weathered buildings of the city. *Exiled again.* Though he retained his official title as Imperial Spice Minister, he wanted to be anyplace but here.

On the other hand, it was good to be away from the turmoil on Kaitain.

In the dirty streets, the day's last few water-sellers strode past open doorways, dressed in colorful traditional garb. Their pans and dippers clanged, bells at their waists jingled, and their high voices rose in the familiar, haunting cry of "Soo-soo sooook!" In the heat of late afternoon, merchants closed their shops and sealed the doors, so they could drink spice coffee in the cool shadows, surrounded by colorful interior hangings.

Fenring watched a cloud of dust kicked up by a groundtruck that rolled into the city, filled with labeled spice containers for transfer to off-world Guild ships. All of the records would pass through the Spice Minister's offices, but he had no intention of scrutinizing them. For the foreseeable future, the Baron Harkonnen would be so unsettled by his near brush with disaster that he would not dare tamper with the official accounting.

The Count's willowy wife Margot approached, giving him a comforting smile. She wore a cool, diaphanous gown that wrapped around her skin like an amorous ghost. "It is quite a change from Kaitain." Margot stroked his hair, and he shivered with desire for her. "But this is still a palace of our own. I do not resent being here with you, my love."

He ran his fingers along the spiderweb sleeve of her gown. "Hmmm, indeed. In fact, I believe it is safer for us to separate ourselves from the Emperor at this time."

"Perhaps. For all of the mistakes he has made, I doubt one scapegoat will be sufficient."

"Hmmm, Shaddam does not grovel well."

She took Fenring by the arm and led him back inside and down the vaulted hallway. Diligent Fremen housekeepers, silent as usual, went about their duties circumspectly, averting their blue-within-blue eyes. The Count sniffed as he watched them move from task to task, like mobile secrets.

The Count and Lady Fenring paused at a statuette purchased in a town market, a robed faceless figure. The artist had been Fremen. Thoughtfully, Fenring lifted the piece from its stand and studied the creased, smothering garments of a desert man, captured so well by the sculptor.

She gave him a calculating look. "House Corrino still needs your help."

"But will Shaddam listen, hmmm-ah?" Fenring replaced the statuette on the table.

They walked to the door of the wet-plant conservatory he had built for her. Reaching forward, she activated the palm-lock and stepped back as it glowed, unsealing the door. The humid smell of mulch and vegetation wafted out, filling Fenring's nostrils. It was an odor he rather liked, since it was so different from the arid desolation of this world.

He sighed. Things could be a lot worse for him. And for

the Emperor. "Shaddam, our Corrino lion, needs to lick his wounds for a while, and reflect on the mistakes he has made. One day, hmmm, he will learn to value me."

They stepped in among the tall, broad-leafed plants and drooping vines, under diffused light from glowglobes hovering near the ceiling. At that moment, mist nozzles turned on like hissing serpents; they floated on suspensors from plant to plant. Moisture sprayed Fenring's face, but he didn't mind. He inhaled a long, deep breath.

Count Fenring found a crimson hibiscus blossom, a bright stain of bloodred petals clinging to a vine, and on impulse plucked it for her. Lady Margot sniffed the perfume.

"We will make a paradise wherever we are," she said. "Even here on Arrakis."

The cultural borrowings and interminglings which have brought us to this moment cover vast distances and an enormous span of time. Presented with such an awesome panoply, we can only derive a sense of great movement and powerful currents.

—PRINCESS IRULAN CORRINO, In My Father's House

The return of the Atreides heroes to their homeworld marked the start of a joyous, weeklong festival. In the courtyard of Castle Caladan and along the docks and narrow streets of the old town, vendors served the finest seafoods and pundi rice delights. On the beaches at the base of the sea cliffs, bonfires burned night and day, surrounded by drinking, dancing, and merry-making. Tavern owners brought out the most expensive local wines from their private cellars and served enough spice beer to float a fleet of coracles.

It was a time of new legends in the making, with stories of Leto the Red Duke, the cyborg Prince Rhombur, the troubadour-warrior Gurney Halleck, the Swordmaster Duncan Idaho, and the Mentat Thufir Hawat. Thufir's key deception against the unmarked ships that had approached Caladan got so many cheers that the stern old Mentat seemed quite embarrassed.

Fresh from battle and a victory well earned, the embellishments to Leto's biography grew, with Gurney as the catalyst. On his first evening back home, filled with alcohol and good cheer, the scarred man took a place beside the largest bonfire with his baliset and broke into song, in the tradition of a Jongleur.

> Who can forget the stirring tale
> Of Duke Leto the Just and his gal-lant men!
> Broke the blockade of Beakkal and the Sardaukar there,
> Led his forces to Ix and righted a wrong.
> Now I say to you and listen well,
> Let no one doubt his words or his vow:
> Free-dom . . . and jus-tice . . . for all!

As Gurney continued to drink his wine, he added verses to the song, paying more attention to the music than to the facts.

ON THE DAY of his son's naming ceremony, a throng of well-wishers gathered in the Castle gardens adjacent to an arbor draped with aromatic silver wisteria and pink calaroses. On a stage inside the enclosure, Leto wore simple clothing to show his people that he was one of them: dungarees and a blue-and-white striped shirt with a navy blue fisherman's cap.

Beside him, Lady Jessica cradled their son in her arms. The infant was dressed in a tiny Atreides uniform, while Jessica had donned the clothes of a common village woman—a brown-and-green linen skirt and simple white blouse, with short, gathered sleeves. Her bronze hair was secured with a clasp made of driftwood and shells.

Taking his son in his strong hands, Duke Leto lifted the baby high. "Citizens of Caladan, meet your next ruler— *Paul Orestes Atreides!*" The name had been chosen to honor Leto's father Paulus, while the middle name, Orestes, commemorated the son of Agamemnon in the House of Atreus, thought to be the forerunner of House Atreides. Jessica looked at him with love and acceptance, smiling at her son and glad he was safe.

To the sound of the cheering crowd, Leto and Jessica crossed the stage and stepped down into the gardens, where they mingled with the gathered well-wishers.

Visiting only briefly from Ix, Rhombur stood on a grassy mound with his wife Tessia. Slamming his cyborg hands together, he applauded louder than anyone else. He had left Ambassador Pilru in the underground city to oversee the restoration and reconstruction work, so that the new Ixian Earl and his Bene Gesserit Lady could attend this special event.

Listening to Duke Leto describe his hopes for his newborn son, Rhombur remembered something his father Dominic had once told him. "No great victory is won without cost."

Tessia nuzzled against him. He put his arm around her, but felt very little of her body warmth. It was one of the deficiencies of his cyborg body. He was still growing accustomed to his new hand.

On the surface, he was cheerful and upbeat, with his old optimistic personality returning. But in his heart he grieved for everything his family had lost. Now, even though he had cleared the name of his ancestors and reoccupied the Grand Palais, Rhombur knew he would be the last in the Vernius line. He was resigned to the fact, but this naming ceremony was especially difficult for him.

He looked at Tessia, and a gentle smile formed on her mouth, though her sepia eyes revealed uncertainty, and faint lines of concern etched her face. He waited, and finally she said, "I don't know how to broach a certain subject with you, my husband. I hope you will consider it good news."

Rhombur gave her a game smile. "Well, I certainly can't stand any more bad news."

She squeezed his new artificial hand. "Think back to when Ambassador Pilru brought news of your half brother, Tyros Reffa. He performed every sort of genetic test to prove his case, and he took great care with the evidence."

Rhombur looked at her blankly.

"I . . . preserved the cellular samples, my love. The sperm is genetically viable."

Caught off-balance, he said, "You are saying that we could use it, that it would be possible to—"

"Out of my love for you I am willing to bear the child of your half brother. Your mother's blood would run through the baby's veins. A distaff surrogate child. Perhaps not a true Vernius, but—"

"Vermilion hells, close enough, by the gods! I could formally adopt him and designate him my official heir. No man in the Landsraad would dare challenge me." With his powerful arms, he swept her into a firm, loving embrace.

Tessia gave him a coy smile. "I am available for whatever you wish, my Prince."

He chuckled. "I am no longer merely a Prince, my love—I am the Earl of House Vernius. And House Vernius is not going to become extinct! You will bear many children. The Grand Palais will be filled with their laughter."

There is no doubt that the desert has mystical quali-
ties. Deserts, traditionally, are the wombs of religion.

—Missionaria Protectiva Report to the Mother School

Though grand events could take place in the politics of the Imperium, this sea of sand never changed.

With the hoods of their jubba cloaks thrown back and stillsuit masks hanging loose, two rugged men stood on a rocky ledge, gazing across the moonlit dunes of Habbanya Erg. Sharp-eyed Fremen manned the desert-watch station on False Wall West, watching for spice blows.

Since early morning, Liet-Kynes and his companion spotters had smelled the aromatic gases of an enormous pre-spice mass carried on breezes across the erg. Down on the open sand, listeners had heard rumbling sounds from the belly of the desert, deep disturbances. Something was happening beneath the ocean of dunes . . . but a spice blow usually came swiftly, with little warning and much destruction. Even the trained Planetologist was curious.

The night was quiet, a bated breath. Overhead, an ominous new comet blazed across the skies, trailing a river of mist behind it. The spectacle was an important, but undeciphered, omen. Comets often signified the birth of a new king, or the death of an old one. Portents abounded, but not even the Naibs or the Sayyadinas could agree as to whether the omen was good or ill.

High on the cliffs, able men and boys watched for a signal from the spotters, prepared to rush across the sands with tools and sacks to harvest the fresh spice before a worm could come. The Fremen had gathered melange in this manner since the time of the Zensunni Wanderers, when refugees had first fled to this desert planet.

Gathering spice by cometlight . . . As the ivory blue Second Moon rose into the sky, Liet looked at the shadow on its bright face that resembled a desert mouse. "Muad'Dib comes to watch over us."

Beside him, Stilgar watched with eyes as sharp as a bird of prey's. Suddenly, even before the spice blow, he called out a wormsign. A mound of sand in rapid motion ran parallel with the rocks that sheltered Red Wall Sietch. Liet squinted, trying to discern details. Other spotters noticed the movement as well, and excited shouts rang out.

"Worms do not come this close to our sietch," Liet muttered, "unless there is some reason."

"Who are we to know Shai-Hulud's reasons, Liet?"

With a slow-motion roar, the great beast heaved itself out of the sand below the high rock barrier. In the still of the night, Liet heard his Fremen companions draw quick gasps of breath. The enormous sandworm was so ancient that it seemed to be made from the creaking bones of the world.

Then, high on a cliff above, another spotter called out a second wormsign, then another and another—leviathans swimming beneath the dunes, converging here. The abrasive flow of sand made an undertone of whispering thunder.

One by one, more monsters emerged and formed a great circle with sparks of fire in their gullets. Except for the grating of sand, the worms were eerily quiet. Liet counted more than a dozen of them, stretching themselves as if to reach the comet in the sky.

But sandworms were violently territorial. Never were more than two seen together, and those two would be battling. But here they had . . . congregated.

Beneath his boots, Liet felt a vibration through the stone of the mountain. A sharp, flinty odor rose to mingle with the scent of melange leaking from the sand. "Summon everyone from the sietch. Bring my wife and children to me."

Runners vanished into the tunnels.

The huge, sinuous worms moved in synchronization, rising around the first behemoth, as if worshipping it.

Watching the spectacle, the Fremen made signs to Shai-Hulud. Liet could only stare. This would be something to speak of for generations to come.

In concert, the worms turned their rounded, eyeless heads to the sky. At the center of the circle, the ancient colossus towered like a monolith over the others. Overhead, the shimmering comet cast as much illumination as the First Moon, spotlighting the desert monsters.

"Shai-Hulud!" the Fremen whispered from all around.

"We must get word to Sayyadina Ramallo," Stilgar said to Liet. "We must tell her what we have seen. Only she can interpret this."

With a rustle of her robe, Liet's wife Faroula appeared at his side with their children. She handed their eighteen-month-old daughter Chani to him, and he held the child high so that she could see over the adults in front of her. His stepson Liet-chih stood in front of them to watch.

Out on the moonlit sand, the circle of worms writhed in an eerie dance, making a rushing friction noise. They moved counterclockwise, as if intending to create a whirlpool in the desert. At the center, the most ancient of all worms began to slump, its skin peeling, its rings sloughing off. Bit by bit, the old one dissolved into tiny living pieces—a silver river of embryonic sandtrout, like amoebas, that struck the sand and tunneled beneath the dunes.

The awestruck Fremen muttered. Several children hauled outside by parents and warders chattered with excitement and asked questions that no one could answer.

"Is it a dream, husband?" Faroula inquired. Chani stared wide-eyed, her irises and pupils not yet totally blue from exposure to the spice melange. She would remember this night.

"Not a dream . . . but I don't know what it is." Cradling their daughter in one arm, Liet took Faroula's hand. Liet-chih's eyes flickered, watching the moving worms.

The circling creatures churned about as the ancient one fissioned into thousands of embryos. The huge hulk broke apart, leaving only a cartilaginous husk of support ribs and rings. The shining downpour of sandtrout burrowed into the disturbed dunes and disappeared from view.

Moments later, the remaining worms dived beneath the sand, their mysterious ritual concluded. They surged away in many directions, as if knowing their brief truce would last no longer.

Shivering, Liet pulled Faroula close and felt her rapid heartbeat against his side. The little boy, waist-high to his mother, remained speechless.

Gradually the sands folded over in the wake of the immense creatures, leaving the stirred silica much as it had been at the beginning of the night, an endless sequence of dunes like the waves of an ocean.

"Bless the Maker and His water," Stilgar murmured, his voice joined by his Fremen companions. "Bless the coming and going of Him. May His passage cleanse the world. May He keep the world for His people."

A *significant passing*, Liet thought. *Something tremendous has changed in the universe.*

Shai-Hulud, king of the sandworms, had returned to the sand, opening the way for a new ruler. In the greater scheme of things, birth and death were intertwined with the remarkable processes of nature. As Pardot Kynes had taught the Fremen, "Life—all life—is in the service of Life. The entire landscape comes alive, filled with relationships and relationships within relationships."

The Fremen had just witnessed a remarkable omen, that somewhere in the universe an important birth had occurred, one that would be hailed across millennia to come. In his daughter's ear Planetologist Liet-Kynes began to whisper the thoughts that he could translate into words . . . and then fell silent as he sensed that she understood.

A process cannot be understood by stopping it. Understanding must move with the flow of the process, must join it and flow with it.

—First Law of Mentat

On the soft expanse of a carefully manicured moss garden under a mist of nutrient-rich fountains, Mother Superior Harishka performed her daily exercises, engrossed in the tiniest workings of her aged body. She wore a black leotard, while ten Acolytes in white garments did their own calisthenics nearby. They watched the sinewy old woman in silence, striving to be half as limber.

Closing her almond eyes, the Mother Superior focused her energies inward, calling upon her deepest mental resources. As a Breeding Mistress in her younger years, she had given birth to more than thirty children, each one containing the bloodline of a leading Landsraad family.

All part of her unquestioning service to the Sisterhood.

Wallach IX's morning air was cool with a slight breeze; distant hills still bore the patchwork cloak of melting snow. The small blue-white sun, the weak heart of the solar system, tried unsuccessfully to shoulder its way through a gray cloud cover.

Behind her, a Reverend Mother approached from the whitewashed buildings of the Mother School complex. Carrying a small, jeweled box, Gaius Helen Mohiam walked softly on the chessboard of dark and light green moss, barely leaving footprints. She paused a few meters away, waiting while Harishka continued her exercise routine.

With her eyes still closed, Harishka whirled and performed a *jeté* in Mohiam's direction, then feinted to the right. The Mother Superior's left foot shot out in a toe-pointing kick that stopped a fraction of a centimeter from the Truthsayer's face.

"You are sharper than ever, Mother Superior," Mohiam said, unruffled.

"Do not patronize an old woman." Harishka's dark eyes opened, and focused on the box in Mohiam's hand. "What have you brought for me?"

The Reverend Mother lifted the lid and withdrew a pale blue soostone ring. She slipped it onto one of Harishka's wrinkled fingers. Touching a pressure pad on the side of the ring, Mohiam summoned a virtual book in the air. "The journal of the Kwisatz Mother, discovered in her royal apartment after her death."

"And the text?"

"I saw only the first page, Mother Superior, in order to identify the work. I did not consider it proper to read further." She bowed her head.

Harishka worked the pressure pad on the side of the ring, slowly flipping the virtual pages in front of her eyes. As she did so, she spoke to Mohiam in a conversational tone. "Some people say it is cold here. Do you agree?"

"A person is only as cold as her mind tells her she is."

"Give me more than the textbook answer."

Mohiam raised her eyes. "To me, it is cold here."

"And to me, it is quite pleasant. Mohiam, do you think you could teach *me* anything?"

"I have never thought about it, Mother Superior."

"Think about it, then." The old woman continued to glance through the writings Anirul had poured into her journal.

Watching and trying to comprehend, Mohiam knew

that Harishka could never stop being an instructor, regardless of her lofty position in the Sisterhood. "We teach those who need teaching," she said, finally.

"Another textbook answer."

Mohiam sighed. "Yes, I suppose I could teach you something. Each of us knows things the other does not. The birth of a boy-child proves that none of us always knows what to expect."

"That is correct." Harishka nodded, but made an expression of distaste. "The words I speak at this very moment and the thoughts I have are not quite the same as any others I have experienced in the past, or which I will ever create again. Each moment is a jewel unto itself, like this soostone ring, unique in the entire universe. So it is with each human life, which is unlike any other. We learn from one another and teach one another. That is what life is all about, for as we learn we advance as a species."

Mohiam nodded. "We learn until we die."

ALONE IN HER workroom that afternoon, the Mother Superior sat at her highly polished desk and reopened the sensory-conceptual journal. On her right, an incense chalice burned, scenting the air with a faint aroma of mint.

She read Anirul's day-by-day account of her life as Kwisatz Mother, of the entirely different role she fulfilled for the Corrino family, and of her hopes for her daughter Irulan. Harishka reread one section, which she found chillingly prophetic:

"I am not alone. Other Memory is my constant companion, in all places and all times. With such a repository of collective wisdom, some Reverend Mothers feel it is unnecessary to maintain a journal. We assume that our thoughts will be passed on to a Sister at death. But what if I die alone, where no other Reverend Mother can access my ebbing memories and preserve them?"

Harishka hung her head, unable to suppress the sadness

she felt. Because Anirul had been killed before Mohiam could reach her, everything the woman had known or experienced had vanished. Except for fragments, such as this one.

She continued reading: "I do not maintain these pages for personal reasons. As the Kwisatz Mother responsible for the culmination of our work, I keep this detailed chronicle to enlighten those who follow me. In the terrible eventuality—I pray it does not occur!—that the Kwisatz Haderach breeding program falters, my journal could be an invaluable resource for future leaders. Sometimes the tiniest, seemingly insignificant event can mean a great deal. Every Sister knows this."

Harishka looked away. She and Anirul Sadow-Tonkin Corrino had been close at one time.

Struggling to compose herself, the old woman read on. Unfortunately, the bulk of the writings degenerated into irrational, fragmented words and sentences, as if too many voices had fought for control of the virtual pen. Much of the information was troubling. Even Medical Sister Yohsa had not suspected the extent of Anirul's mental disintegration.

Turning the virtual pages, Harishka read faster and faster. The journal described Anirul's nightmares and suspicions, including an entire page on which she wrote out the Bene Gesserit Litany Against Fear, over and over.

To the Mother Superior, many of the entries looked like madness, incomprehensible scratchings. She cursed softly. *Puzzle pieces, and now Jessica has given birth to a boy instead of a girl!*

Anirul could not be blamed for that.

Harishka decided to show the virtual volume to Sister Thora, who had designed some of the most complex cryptocodes the order had ever used. Perhaps she could decipher the syllables and sentence fragments.

Jessica's son was perhaps the biggest mystery of all. Harishka wondered why Anirul had sacrificed her own life for him. Had she considered this . . . *genetic error* . . . significant, or had it been something else? A foolish display of human weakness?

Uttering a prayer that their millennium-spanning breeding program had not been lost forever, she closed the sensory-conceptual journal. It became a gray mist, and disappeared into the soostone ring.

But the words remained in her mind.

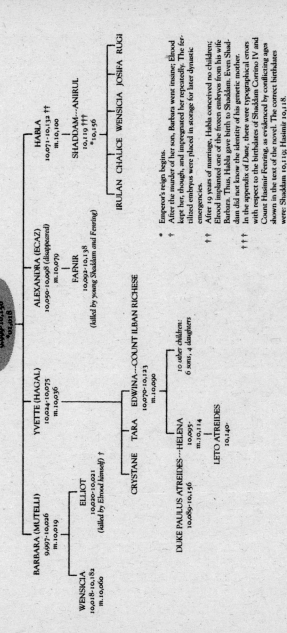

FONDIL III ("THE HUNTER")
9,997-10,156
*10,018

ELROOD IX
9,997-10,156
*10,018

BARBARA (MUTELLI)
9,997-10,026
m.10,019

YVETTE (HAGAL)
10,004-10,075
m.10,036

ALEXANDRA (ECAZ)
10,050-10,098 (disappeared)
m.10,079

HABLA
10,071-10,133 ††
m.10,100

ELLIOT
10,020-10,021
(killed by Elrood himself) †

FAFNIR
10,092-10,138
(killed by young Shaddam and Fenring)

SHADDAM~~ANIRUL
10,119 †††
*10,156

WENSICIA
10,018-10,182
m.10,060

CRYSTANE   TARA

EDWINA~~COUNT ILBAN RICHESE
10,070-10,123
m.10,090

IRULAN CHALICE WENSICIA JOSIFA RUGI

DUKE PAULUS ATREIDES~~HELENA
10,080-10,156
10,095-
m.10,114

10 other children:
6 sons, 4 daughters

LETO ATREIDES
10,140-

* Emperor's reign begins.

† After the murder of her son, Barbara went insane; Elrood kept her, though, and impregnated her repeatedly. The fertilized embryos were placed in storage for later dynastic emergencies.

†† After 19 years of marriage, Habla conceived no children; Elrood implanted one of the frozen embryos from his wife Barbara. Thus, Habla gave birth to Shaddam. Even Shaddam did not know the identity of his genetic mother.

††† In the appendix of Dune, there were typographical errors with respect to the birthdates of Shaddam Corrino IV and Count Hasimir Fenring, as evidenced by conflicting ages shown in the text of the novel. The correct birthdates were: Shaddam 10,119; Hasimir 10,118.